THE BOY SCOUTS
OF
BLOOMFIELD
AVENUE

ANTHONY ANGELO NARDONE

PAGE PUBLISHING, INC.
New York, NY

First originally published by Page Publishing, Inc. 2017

ISBN 978-1-68348-324-3 (Paperback)
ISBN 978-1-68348-315-1 (Digital)

Printed in the United States of America

PROLOGUE

The stately Orsini house was built under a dark shadow of old-world superstition. The evil eye, or Malocchio, as the old Sicilian stone mason put it. He witnessed firsthand the devil's work as three laborers died from diabolical accidents, so named, within the first month of construction. Be it as it may, the old Sicilian wasn't the only one who still believed. The manor house was built during the height of Newark, New Jersey's industrial boom—during the most prosperous of times for the risk-takers and capitalists from here and abroad who hadn't any fears, and all held unassailable interests in and around the city's skyline. It was a jagged skyline comprised of tall office buildings and factories and towering smokestacks made entirely of brick. It was a magnanimous era when bright orange glowing hand-lit gaslights sat atop tall, ornate cast-iron posts—their glowing flames glittered off the inlaid oblong granite and cobblestone that composed the bustling Bloomfield Avenue and its surrounding arteries. Their flaming illumination led horse-drawn carriages from the prestigious and genteel Montclairs through the conjecturing, scenic landscapes of the acreage and paths that lead through the Old Blue Jay Swamp and on up through the prominent Forest Hills.

The well-conceived and selected corner location for the home was a natural two-acre elevation at the intersections of Bloomfield and Watsessing Avenues. It boasted three rolling knolls of manicured green lawns that chased up from the granite sidewalks, past stately trees, cascading gardens of shrubbery, rose bushes, and brilliant flowering beds. The brilliant pearlescent white limestone exterior of the grandiose home served as a reflective, illuminated beacon for evening travelers as they neared—its own array of gilded Victorian era gaslights were arranged strategically about the property, both spaced around its circular cobblestoned driveway and its separate drive that led to the back stables. Huge outside ornate wall sconces adorned both sides of the ten-foot-high mahogany carved doors while smaller ones of exact styling graced the negative spaces between the tall french windows. The house was completed in 1877 and was an almost exact replica of a French manor house owned by a wealthy land baron and vintner just outside of Valbonne, France. The chateau was to be a romantic gesture with just—well much more than just—a hint of irony from a middle-aged Italian industrialist, Sergio Orsini himself, a well documented heir to the kingdom of Naples' wealth. The architectural masterpiece was intended solely for his soon-to-be bride whom he met one afternoon, on a visit, while strolling the French vintner's property. She was the youngest of three sisters, barely sixteen years of age, whose family was rumored to be of an unholy Gypsy bloodline. Her widower father and brothers tended the grapevines and orchids and landscape, and she herself, along with her sisters, maintained the title of "biddy" handmaidens and toiled alongside the rest of the servants. And of course they all lived in cramped quarters, under the straw roof of a tiny two-room cottage that sat tucked away from view behind the tallest grove of pubescent oak and olive trees. He was immediately captivated by her youthful beauty and, within days, convinced the girl to leave her impoverished life behind and run away to America with him. This outraged the father. He was relentless with his forbidding her to leave; however, his harsh words and threats could not stop her. And as she and Orsini drove away by carriage, her father wept some then violently cursed them both to hell in both his Gypsy tongue and Orsini's Italian.

The couple soon married and settled in comfortably within the grand Bloomfield Avenue residence. In the early morning hours, the wealthy Signore Sergio Orsini would be within the confines of his gothic conservatory. It was built high atop its own distinct tower rather than at ground level—a unique concept created intentionally. After dressing in the days' most fashionable business suit, before breakfast, Signore Orsini would sit comfortably amidst an array of fragrant flowers and plants. His roost was an adorned window seat that wrapped around three angled walls, custom made and expertly covered in luxurious, tufted burgundy leather that was made in his factories. The signore would peer intensely out his tall conservatory windows—this view, other than the tiled rooftops themselves, is the highest point of the property. His first selected field of vision was the rising gray ash from his leather tanning factory's tall smokestacks that sat far off in the distance, on the coal oil soaked banks of the Passaic River, in the industrial section of the obscure area known as East Newark. During the clearest of blue sky or the dark-clouded rainy days, the streaming smoke was visible. Even as the dark of night would befall, moonlight and stars would illuminate phantasms of shapes as the smoke billowed and rose high into the air until it was seen no more. This simple and indulging sight instilled a self-regarded pride of accomplishment, of even a nobler and greater joy than the splendor of his home itself; his second field of enamored vision was his beautiful young bride, Signora Donatella. She would already be up and dressed, impromptu, and in full gaiety, her flaxen hair gathered and tied casually in colorful ribbon, and was ever so eager to instruct her uniformed domestic staff. She was quite courteous and soft-spoken with the young maids, always with a warm demeanor in her voice as she instructed the methods and direction of the Orsini household. And the signora was most appreciative that they all—well, mostly all—spoke fluent Italian, French, and the hardest of languages, and the burden of her new recitation, English.

During the evening hours, while his wife would prepare for her bath, Sergio would be again on the same conservatory window seat, waving off cloud-burst-sized cigar smoke as he sipped French brandy from a bulbous snifter. He would sit, with a closed book in hand—absorbed with thoughts of which he suspected all well satisfied and successful businessmen, and older men with young, sumptuous wives, ponder. When the weather permitted, he would open the huge windows. And as he sat he would meditate and be soothed by the echoing, rhythmic percussion of horse hooves on the cobblestone. He would tap his fingers on the sill in time with the rolling clatter made by oversized wheels of richly detailed handsome carriages, the family Surrey and doctors' buggies as they passed by his prestigious property, he himself the proud owner of a barouche carriage along with fine steeds and driver. The drivers sat proudly erect and tall in their seats with whip and reins in hand—some wearing garish hats, others just a simple cap. They regulated the horse's gaits at their choosing up until a point of interjection of command by the mostly blue-blooded passengers inside—some demanded slow and steady while others more rapid, at a magnificent canter or hasty trot, either way their commands heeded. Orsini's sense of proficient pride again would glow brighter in his heart than all the gaslights below, this from knowing that it was his stately leather that lined the interiors of just about all the carriages. And his leather formed the very shoes and boots worn by the occupants and the drivers, even the horse's saddles and bridles—his distribution not limited to just the East Coast, not only on Bloomfield Avenue but also now throughout the entire country. He would sometimes act the shy child, being almost clandestine, and peer through the tiniest of slits in the drawn velvet drapery as sometimes the clatter would come to a standstill, and formidable shapes of inquisitive and fancier faces would mystically illuminate from the gaslights as they nosed up to the opened carriage windows and tilted their heads way, way back—to absorb the complete beauty of the mansion. Its only flaw, as many passersby thought and could be overheard in the practiced perfection of the English language, was, "How garish, how excessive—why on earth would one build such a palace among common merchants and marketplaces?" Needless to say, Orsini was proud of his Bloomfield Avenue beaconed land-mark—a white elephant, as it was soon becoming known as. This gossip was the whispered insults and mockery among the wealthy families—the very well-to-do and the prominent businessmen that would, themselves, soon seek residence in the same neighborhood.

So on and on went the blissful and prosperous lives of the extraordinary and celebrated Orsinis until one day, tragedy struck. Horrific tragedy presenting itself as awful and as ghastly as it could have ever before been conceived or written—even of the macabre mind of the era's late Edgar Allen Poe. The chores and duties of scheduled spring cleaning were all being doled out and assisted by Signora Orsini—she always insisted on supervising the staff of the prerequisites of every tiny detail pertaining to the upstairs master bedroom and her husband's cherished conservatory. These cultured lessons learned during her early apprenticeship as chambermaid. A new maid, a young, sassy French girl, was orally obstinate and ada-mant with her denial, in all three languages, of how Signora Orsini was instructing and insisting her on how to clean the paired tall sets of french windows that sat above his favorite perch, his tufted win-dow seat. The task required the maiden to swing open both framed panels and sit atop the thick windowsill and wash, from the outside, all panes of glass. Again the young maiden refused, then again and again until, finally, she stormed off. As the maiden walked away, the signora chastised her in a choppy English dialect, "You are relieved of your duties as of now. Pack up and leave this house. I will finish the chore myself." And just as the signora's last words were spoken, she vanished; only a seemingly distant shrill of a scream was heard. The young maiden turned and walked back into the room. She slowly stepped toward the window. She stood in dumbstruck amazement, and had an almost disbelieving smirk on her face, as if assuming the signora was playing some sort of devilish or practical joke on her—that is, until she looked down from the great height of the opened conservatory window. Her hand rose swiftly to her gasping mouth, but it could not hold back the terrifying scream as she stood frozen, eyes forced open wider than imaginable, staring at the con-torted figure below, the Signora Orsini lying hauntingly still on the cobblestoned drive—their polished sparkling grayish hue now slowly turning a dark crimson of flowing blood.

The dark and bleak months that followed the tragic and chilling death of his young bride saw Signore Orsini withdraw from the out-side world, completely. His body and soul slipped into a sorrowful lament, an almost macabre state of constant mourning. He let go the domestics, entirely—even the kitchen help and outside gardeners. Just about every room in the mansion was sealed including his mas-ter bedroom and cherished conservatory. He resorted to sleeping in whatever stained, dust-covered chair or chaise or floor rug that would accept his now drugged and brandy-laden body until he awoke, much to his dismay, and then walked aimlessly amidst cobwebs and broken and disheveled remnants of what was once fine Italian and French Provencal furniture, now reduced to mere firewood. Gone now was the ever-lingering smell of fresh flowers, replaced by the rank odor of filth.

Orsini's one true heartfelt regret was never putting the image of his true love on full-scale canvas, in brilliant oil paint—her flaxen hair and deep blue eyes; her perfectly proportioned ruby lips and petite body; and her skin, her soft, radiant olive-toned skin that only a commissioned talented artist, the very best money could buy, could miraculously bring to life. Only a few photos of her existed, kept in gilded frames. Her life-sized portrait was desperately missed and often thought about so he might find a form of solace as he could sit and sulk under her beauty rather than the tall, obnoxious "sailing ship" scene that hung above the fireplace—the only used fireplace in the great room of the house. The picture hung in a macabre, crooked sort of way; its ornate dust-and-ash-covered frame bore the wrath of flame and handheld objects that were violently thrown at it as did the canvas itself. And he thought, *When it finally did come crashing down, it too would burn…as firewood.* Signore Orsini cared no more for life as he once knew it or as it was now in its present state, but he had not the courage to pull the revolver's trigger that was always in sight and sometimes held up to his temple by his own hand.

The Orsini mansion was destined to ruin and it seemed no one could stop it. The sturdy padlock and chains wrapped around the front ornate iron gates were rusted to the point of complete inoperability, but they served their purpose well. Passersby on foot would not so much as glance at the eerie, abandoned castle—especially children, and especially at night. Whispers of the gypsy curse would abound as they'd increase their pace for fear of bad omens or ghost sightings. The glass atop the conservatory seemed to reflect light in an evil way. However, there would always be a caring person, someone anonymous who would bring food to the ailing, grieving Orsini—and with a degree of regularity—was left always at the rear door. Orsini never let the couriers into the house. He forbade it. Nor did he care to know their identity. He never opened a door in their presence. These considerate acts of sheer kindness were all but ignored—Orsini rarely ate; only through a fundamental inner requirement did he take a bite of a stale piece of bread or sip cold soup. He'd rather drink, heavily, the narcotic-laden tonics and glassfuls of brandy supplied to him by the doctors and the nefarious alike. He would open the door for them—and they would spread the horrific details of the shell of a forsaken man—the filthy, unshaven, and unkempt ogre that lived within those walls. Though quite thankful was Orsini, and to all, as his sober-stated letters would read, his imperative and dark request was to never be disturbed and not a visitor was to call—ever. The letters he received but never opened were just tossed and scattered in piles and long forgotten. And every so often, as kindling would be thought of and used, they were ripped to shreds and thrown into the flaming hearth.

It was on a very cold January night, 1882, during his darkest semi-consciousness of self-pity, pain, and lament, and violent innuendos, the already drunk and delusional Orsini took a long, hard swallow of a powerful opiate—a freshly uncorked morphine-based tonic—and then another and another until the bottle drained. His impaired and weakened state had not even the bit of strength needed to throw it at the decrepit sailing ship; he let it slip from his fingertips and drop to the floor—as did he. In time his hallucinating mind awoke—his drugged thoughts and visualization chased a teasingly seductive and beautiful Signora Orsini up the flights of the marbled balustrade staircases that led upstairs and the conservatory. He thrust the weight of his feeble body against his shuttered bedroom doors in a steady concession until, finally, the center locks gave way and he burst through into a darkened, cobwebbed, and dust-infested room. He stood frozen, eerily still. His heavy-lidded and delusional eyes were immediately drawn to the outside orange glow glinting from the tall french windows of the conservatory, and a familiar bliss entered his heart. A dust-covered bottle of brandy and glass still sat on a tarnished tray atop his beloved window seat. The musty, stale smell of decayed plants and overall neglect and derision of the room shattered his soul. The short-lived feeling of joy left just as fast as it entered. He began to sob. Then he chillingly screamed her name over and over, "Donatella, Donatella…" Without reservation he ran then leaped willfully and strongly, with a determined fury, into and the locked french windows, bursting them wide open. His limbs made not a flailing movement of any kind, almost as if his deranged mind knew the futility of such an act as he plummeted, body and soul, to the cobblestoned drive far below. A comet's trail of shattered glass and splintered wood followed as he came to rest—on almost the same exact crimsoned, bloodstained section as did his wife prior. His lidded eyes were amazingly still alive, staring wide open from their darkened sockets. Reflecting within them was a flame of a gaslight and his beloved Donatella, turning her head in a wisp—glancing over her shoulders, as she ran off in the far distance.

Over time as if destiny or the fates willed it, the mansion became an unholy place that even the Orsini heirs from Naples shunned. It was now just a withered eyesore. Potential buyers wanted no part of the anticipated high cost of repair, and once told of the tragedy that occurred, they ran. Superstitions and ghost sightings pertaining to the property ran rampant over the years and well past the turn of the century. Only a few brazen neighborhood kids dared to venture up the now weeded knolls and throw stones, testing their arm strength and accuracy on the tall french windows.

Then came a new burst of industrial growth and wealth. A new era of architects and builders brought more well-conceived colonial-style estates and prestigious country homes and manors that were built all around and including the area now officially known as the Forest Hills section of Newark and in very close proximity to what became Branch Brook Park. And so as the surrounding commercial areas of Bloomfield Avenue gave birth to industries, office complexes, storefronts, and shopping centers throughout, the large corner property sat, still high on a hill, its perimeter encompassed by a twelve-foot-high galvanized cyclone fence that bore, what seemed to be in place for decades, a simple sign that read, now a very faded, "For Sale."

On a comfortably warm and breezy Sunday afternoon, in the early spring of 1946, three well-dressed men of true distinction climbed out of a chauffeur-driven limousine and walked about a certain corner property on Bloomfield Avenue—an old, neglected, and weather-beaten mansion. The two younger men wore stylish fedoras wrapped with wide silk bands, brown in color as were their suits. They shared ambiguous looks and whispered words between them: "Why this is the Orsini mansion, or was in its day." "And why are we eying this eyesore, I wonder?" The older gentleman proudly wore a Kippah bearing a beautifully embroidered Jewish star. His stride was deliberate as he marched the length of the property with ridged hands clasped firmly behind his back, his diligent eyes in constant motion, scanning every square foot. His name was Levi Horowitz, a wealthy and successful real estate developer who managed to escaped Nazi Germany years prior with his immediate family—along with a vast portion of his wealth. His words were nonchalant to say the least, and in well-spoken English, he stated, "I just bought this property. It completes the package of the entire block." The two younger well-dressed men that flanked his sides, his dutiful sons, listened with distracted ears. A proud smile contorted the father's thin pale lips as he then looked directly into each son's eyes, consecutively, back and forth, and said, "Tomorrow morning we go to the attorney's office to sign the papers. The title will be solely in both your names. The taxes are paid well into the New Year. It's my gift—and my challenge to you—a test and trial, one might say, to see and judge how you'll both live up to the task of improving this shambles of…of this once-magnificent corner property. And turn a profit! Then we'll discuss the possibilities of joining my firm or going out on your own. Understood?"

Both young men stared aimlessly at the haunted house that sat atop clops of dried dirt and straw-textured grass, overgrown brambles, and hideous vines. They then looked each other in the eye and smiled, exactly and purposely at the same time. Their tiny hands extended out one by one, in the direction of their father's already extended hand, and one by one the elder shook their hands gingerly.

Ideas flew about the rear of the limousine from the young sons as they drove off. Their Ivy League worsted wool suits wrinkled with enthusiasm as they spoke on the way back to their father's office. They envisioned countless possibilities for the property. First, it was decided the disheveled place and the neglected property must be attended to and somewhat renovated—and of course as cost-effective as could possibly be. "Granted, it is large enough to subdivide. And believe it or not, it needs very little work to bring it back to its glory. But we must think of the property for its commercial value," said the father. The brothers jested between themselves then reminded their father of the Orsini curse, the Malocchio, as the superstitious Italians fear. "So then we will turn it into a boarding house—a morbid rooming house—for ghosts." "Or a funeral parlor—yes, that's it, a very morbid funeral parlor." Their father offered no more opinions or comments on the newly purchased property except for, "I wouldn't worry about superstitions or hogwash curses, and they cannot harm you. Only time and money, when not on your side, can harm you, nothing else."

T wo imposing men designated as sentries were anchored on both sides of the grand Italian Social Club's rear doorway. Both of the burly doormen were stoutly dressed in stiff black suits, their necks bursting at the collars bounded by uncomfortable ties. Their slumping and lax postures camouflaged their speculative duties, and both were barely visible as they leaned up against the wrought iron pillars that held up the burgundy canvassed canopy that covered the walkway. Their spiritless faces reflected the burdensome task at hand. They hid in the shadows, chain-smoking cigarettes, and hoping for a breeze to bring relief from the heat and humidity that gripped both on this miserable August evening in 1959. Suddenly the sentries' haughty postures changed to spry and alert as they watched a long black Cadillac slowly round the driveway at the top of the hill. The Cadillac's headlights cut a path through the night's darkness as the red bullet taillights followed. The driver's face became illuminated by a lamppost. His eyes became affixed in a pensive stare with both sentries as his car rolled past the entrance that they were guarding. The two men gave a reluctant nod to one another as the Cadillac eased into a parking space, its red bullet taillights glowing brightly in the night.

Joey Lotta was the larger, more primitive of the two. He spoke first, then spat on the ground, "Big Anthony and his brand-new fuckin' Cadillac." "Yeah…that's him all right," replied his associate; then he continued with a bumbling, "Ya can't miss that meat hook of an arm hangin' out the window." The brute Lotta scoffed, "Since when he comes around?" His words had a degree of loathsomeness in them. "Rico said he was gonna' stop by?" "What—for the game?" snapped Lotta as he pulled a tightly folded piece of paper from his lapel pocket and held it between his thick fingers. "He ain't on the list…" His partner offered a mute frown and a shrug. "What do I know, Joey. That's all I know—Rico said he was comin' down."

The hulking man approached the rear of the club, the Pope's mansion, as it was now so befittingly nicknamed, slowly, moving between the shadows, his facial features peering through cigarette smoke. He kept his head down for most of the way until he knew exactly when it became close enough to look up. The immense angled shadow his body cast climbed the white stone wall of the building as his face became partially illuminated by the lamplight at the end of the driveway. He squared his shoulders and let his arms just hang loosely to his side. His cigarette dangled gingerly from his purplish lip. The rising smoke forced his puffy eyelids into sinister slits. He now found himself directly in front of the two sentries. Tension filled the air as he stared intensely at the guy on the right. Then he turned and snarled at the other brute, "Well, whadda 'ya say Lotta?" His words and presence were intimidating. He looked again coldly into the eyes of the bodyguards then read to himself the words of the bronzed wall plaque above the majestic doorway: "BENVENUTI UOMINI D' ONORE" (Welcome Men of Honor). He scoffed aloud as he mulled those words then continued with a disparaging, "Since when they got yous' working as doormen Lotta—don't you got some heads to bust?" His statement drew not a laugh from either goon. Instead, Lotta partially blocked the entrance and said spitefully, "Since when the Pope lets you walk in here?" Big Anthony let out a sarcastic huff of a laugh and drove his shoulder into the chest of the thug. "I go where I want." He shot an evil look at the other guy then shook his head toward the door. "Rico inside?" "Yeah, he's inside," the goon replied. "Who else inside the place?" growled Anthony. "Batista, a few of the other guys, and the players is all," he said. Anthony's face became inquisitive. "No Albie?" The goon shook his head no to the question. Anthony smirked then turned toward the brute Lotta and asked glibly, "What size shoe you wear?" Before the thug had a chance to answer, Anthony flicked his cigarette butt on the ground. "Why don't 'ya put those big feet to use—and step on that." The crude remark and disrespectful antic left the thug staring at the ground, fuming. Big Anthony's instinct was to throw a looping left hook at the goon; he was at such a disadvantage. Instead he held his temper and just stormed past the sentries then through the doors. The leather soles of his shoes echoed on the terrazzo floor of the long hallway. And as he walked, he gently caressed the carrara marble that adorned the wall with his fingertips and thought such magnificent beauty to be wasted on such bums inside.

It was a quiet evening at the posh and private club, as weekdays usually were. Frank Batista and Rico Caprio were standing casually behind a large rolling banquet bar sipping whiskey, smoking, and making—on occasion—usual wise guy remarks. Flanking their side was a small buffet with the scattered remnants of fresh cold cuts, breads, and salads. The two men kept close watch on the strongbox full of hundred dollar bills that sat under the bar as the price of admission—the minimum buy in was five thousand dollars. Both men were somewhat startled as the tall oak doors flew open. Rico's face bore a look of relief then anger. *It's about time this guy showed up with my money*, he thought. Big Anthony's gambling debts were amassing. The burden of collection, the vouched word, was on the head of one of the Pope's capos in charge of such activities, Rico Caprio. Big Anthony gave his solemn word a week ago last Tuesday—assuring Caprio that payment would be made starting with a ten-thousand-dollar installment that he would have in a week's time, Tuesday—and that was yesterday and yesterday came and went, leaving all empty-handed. The big shot was nowhere to be found. Rico fumed as he thought the balls on this man to walk into the Pope's Social Club with such a bold strut.

Batista was the first to speak. He adjusted his black horn-rimmed glasses and with a sincere and welcoming voice said, "Good ta' see ya', Cheese—been a long time no—*Chefai...* "This warmed the big guy's heart just a touch as he reached out to shake the mobster's hand. But his blood ran cold as ice water at the sight of the greasy-looking Rico Caprio. Caprio returned the compliment with a look of disgust and sharp words, "You're a day late, my friend." Anthony barked back, "And a fuckin' dollar short too—like you, ya' runt." Anthony winked at the now laughing Batista. He too agreed in silence that Caprio was a small-time weasel and had absolutely no business with this "thing of theirs." Big Anthony reached behind then pulled a sealed envelope from his back pocket. He held on to it for a brief second, and then laid it flat on the bar, his mitt-sized hand all but completely covering it. His eyes perked and he took a long, vigilant glance over his shoulder. He was distracted by the familiar and tempting sounds of a poker game especially of chips being raked and gathered. The faint contentions of men laughing and cursing amongst one another that drifted from the far corner of the room made his mind race and his eyes bug. Batista knew what was to happen next—he read the big guy like a book—so he intentionally began to walk away. "I'm gonna' check on our guys in the other room, be right back." His intentions were twofold: a reason to leave the room and also to give warning to Big Anthony of the room full of muscle that was always on hand at the Pope's Palace.

Big Anthony reclaimed the cache of cash. He stared fiercely at the poker table then back at Rico. "I see an empty chair over there... Gimme ten large worth of chips." His voice was clear as a bell as he pushed the wad of cash toward the hesitating Rico. "I said gimme' ten large. Now." "C'mon, Anthony." Rico implored as he cupped his hands into a pleading prayer-like position and winced at the wicked stare of Cheese Marino who snarled, "Gimme the chips or you're gonna' think this place was still a funeral parlor—and you, the guest of honor." Rico reluctantly obliged. Anthony offered a compromising smile and said jeeringly, "Whatta ya' worried about, didn't Albie tell ya', there's plenty more where this's came from?" His reference was of the respected capo Albert Marrone. It was a manufactured lie, a dupe to sweep Caprio off his feet. "Go ahead and call him" was the dare. Anthony spoke his words over squinted eyes. He knew that would never happen.

The cardplayers were sitting under the subtleness of a hanging Tiffany light and an ominous cloud of cigar and cigarette smoke, betting and raising and bluffing and cursing all very gentlemanly–like, as they do each week for what has come to be known as the executive poker game. And while they played, and played hard they did, they kept watch over themselves and the designated dealer. The notoriously popular game played weekly was an extraordinarily high-stake, no-limit poker extravaganza, frequented by nothing less than the obstinately rich and famous. And usually the same players sat in week after week, undauntedly. It was a game commonplace with professionals and politicians as well and had an open invitation for an occasional well-known athlete or some Hollywood star, all eager for the action of winning or losing obnoxious sums of money among themselves as they sat alongside the likes of well-known underworld figures—and of course the Pope himself, who rarely attended but always lets his presence be known by the rake and his ominous bodyguards who ensured the safety and anonymity of the players. It was not a game for the weak at heart or the deeply indebted.

Anthony bolted toward the game, his chips in tow held neatly in a wooden rack. "Evening gents." Not a familiar face among the crowd, with the exception of the seasoned dealer who spoke, "Well hello there, Cheese, I mean Anthony, Big Anthony." His spoken words served as a form of announcement to the rest of the table. All of the cardplayers peered at the mobster with doubting eyes. His dark wavy hair was unkempt and long overdue for a trim. The cloths he wore, although neatly pressed, seemed just a little too small for him. His lumbering body and huge forearms came to rest heavily at the table and caused everyone's chips to rattle. The players' arms and hands impulsively hovered over their own stacks as a way of protecting them. Their facial expressions announced the arrival of a thief! One whispered to another, "Do you know this man?" The fellow cupped his mouth and spoke covertly, "By reputation *only*." The dealer winked at Cheese and welcomed him to take his seat. He knew that if the big guy was getting in the game, it was a sanctioned act. Formal introductions were quickly doled out and cards were dealt.

Batista returned surreptitiously, with one of the goons in tow, Gaetano Altieri. He sensed not an ounce of trouble and remarked at how all at the table were well receiving the big guy—and instinctively, he was compelled to ask—or rather "bust balls" as he thought, *So who 'da call to okay the buy in?* It was Rico's game tonight, he was solely in charge. Batista was there for moral support only. Rico was a big boy. A call to anyone would be considered an uncompromised act of weakness in the boss's eyes. And Rico recognized the connotation. He expanded his chest and shot back, "I gotta' call somebody—since when I gotta' call somebody." Enough was said to the capo Batista.

Big Anthony's acquisitive hope of cleaning up at the card table proved disastrous and further aggrandized the hopeless losing streak he was on. He attacked the pots and the players with large aggressive bets and frivolous bluff raises with the intention of using brute strength and a tired reputation—trying his malfeasance best to intimidate and chase the wealthy away, leaving their money behind. That ploy did nothing more than show how desperate a man and how poor a cardplayer he actually was. Big Anthony surely underestimated the quality of the gamblers he sat with. One by one each gritty cardplayer that sat at the exclusive table called and reraised, outplaying and beating him with slightly better hands and, in some cases, bragged bluffs. Ira Silverstein, a prominent attorney, found himself going head-to-head with Big Anthony all night long and always emerging the victor in each and every hand. Ira would soon find himself in the line of fire with the defeated gangster's evil eyes after out drawing Big Anthony's three aces with a lowly straight.

As more hands were played, Big Anthony's lack of poker skill was further exploited. The sizable bets built enormous pots for the winners; however, for the big losers such as he, well, he could only watch dejectedly as his pile of chips dwindled. Hours passed and Big Anthony lost yet another head-to-head contest with the brazen attorney from Livingston. Then a seemingly harmless and mediocre wisecrack from the gloating Silverstein sent Cheese over the edge. He was not at all shy in announcing his displeasure. The vile language and slurs that ensued rolled off a repugnant tongue and were enunciated by a meaty and pointed finger. The lawyer offered a sincere smile and a very unpretentious handshake while the dealer gave a reassuring look toward the rest of the players but it was to no avail. Suddenly Anthony attacked the lawyer, fiercely grabbing him by his throat and literally dragging him off the table then tossing him across the room like a rag doll, sending the executive game into complete shambles. Big Anthony had a way of using the descriptive innuendo of a "wall" when he threatened violence: "I'll put you through a wall" or "I'll nail you to the wall." Tonight it was the simple but austere, "I'll put you against the wall…" And that he did. He hard slapped the attorney's face with every word he spit and snarled, "You open assed mother fucker…you had no business in that miserable hand." The game was now in chaos. Scared men panicked and scattered as chairs flew back. Batista sensed the unwise impending calamity just seconds before it happened and wisely scooted to the men's room. What he did not see could harm no one—no testimony could be offered. It would take three more henchmen to pull Big Anthony off the bloodied and humiliated Ira. With the a few wailing shrugs Anthony was freed from their grasps. Then he smartly began to exit the club with a disconcerted strut but not without first hard shoving Joey Lotta on his ass. As all the men regained their composure and acknowledged the game had just broken up, it was the wise guys who huddled tightly and whispered worriment between themselves, and Rico Caprio, knowing his days would be numbered, woefully sighed. "The Pope is not gonna' like this at all."

2

The plunderers of organized crime, the gangsters, the mobsters, the wise guys, and all of their colorful cronies loom heavily in New Jersey. And throughout the years, organized crime, by definition, fell under the rule of the mighty New York crime families. And so it may be true as of today, in the 1950s, the New Jersey syndicate does share a strong and venerable bond with the ever so prominent and sanctioned *Luchese* and *Genovese* families of New York and Brooklyn. It is thoroughly, and without dispute, owned and operated by Angelo Ruggeri, the undisputed reigning boss of New Jersey. Angelo Ruggeri, the most feared of mobsters—the infamous bootlegger of that bygone era. Angelo Ruggeri with his short, wiry stature and ferocious reputation who earned the dubious nickname of "the Pope," and his prominent crew of made men, throughout the state, at his beck and call—his capos—men like Frank Batista and Albert Marrone, just two of many who did his malevolent bidding and fully obey the rules concerning his personal pride and joy of this part of the Brick City, the infamous North Newark's First Ward, and Ruggeri's pious Bloomfield Avenue.

In the early open book years, Franco "Tick Tock" Batista and his cousin Roberto "Bobby Breeze" Batista both got their start with the Pope while in New York City and under the rule of the mighty *Genovese* family. Bobby Batista was recruited and became a soldier of the prominent Profaci family of Brooklyn while Frank Batista ventured to New Jersey where he united with and, over the years, has proven himself to be a well-respected and trustworthy capo and enforcer for Don Angelo Ruggeri. Batista is tall in stature, a ruggedly built man with a distinct Roman nose and whose once jet black hair matched his ebony horn-rimmed eyeglasses. He was tagged with the moniker Tick Tock early in his career for his uncanny ability to build highly effective incendiary bombs and exploding devices using a simple wiring technique hooked up to old-fashioned wind-up alarm clocks—a well-honed craft and a service that is still requested at times. It's an art he claimed to have learned during the war, and when the refrain echoed among the crew he hadn't served his country, another safe and secure draft dodger as they so vociferously put it, he then claimed instruction from a munitions factory he once worked. That also proved a falsehood, so he chanted, "The Boy Scouts—I learned when I was a Boy Scout."

As the years passed, Angelo Ruggeri amassed an army of street soldiers, the likes of which organized crime and other criminal factions had never imagined. And along with his mighty political connections, law enforcement ties, corrupt leaders of industry and Union affiliates, all on his proscribed payroll, he was a hard force to reckon with. Other leaders like Albert Marrone and a select and significant few soon came onboard—they from Pennsylvania. As another alliance with the Pittsburgh mob was established, Ruggeri's protection and mighty power was now between two rivers. Then cunningly, strategically, with brute force and grim violence, he made his way ultimately to the top of the heap. And as for Angelo "Pope" Ruggeri himself, he's the living, breathing epitome of what a mobster should be—he set the bar.

His influence reached deep into Newark's city hall from early on and had, and still does have, strong support from all the politicians from Newark's wards, especially the heavily Jewish Third. Ruggeri mastered the art of negotiation and the power of persuasion by the corrupt politicians themselves. They were the ones he allied with on the streets of New York City and Brooklyn in the early days of Prohibition and organized crime. They were the old Tammany Hall political machine. When in New Jersey, he would dine and feast during the Great Depression with the late Meyer "Doc" Ellenstein, the then mayor of Newark—to discuss ways on how to rid the streets of the so-called Jewish, Irish, and German gangsters that were giving everyone a bad name. His sardonically witty opine had all convinced that they were ones to blame each and every time a dead body was found. Police and prosecutors alike would all be off chasing fabricated or spurious leads manufactured by Ruggeri's people. And by the early and mid-1950s, he had the entire Essex County Prosecutors Office, the entire Newark City Commission, even Mayor Carlin, and the police commissioner firmly convinced it was still now and always had been other ethnic gangs, *not* the Italians, responsible for all the crime in America, and not just in the city of Newark.

Ruggeri has always been recognized by all as a cold and calculated criminal and unquestionably feared by all for his decisiveness to make quick disposal of any type enemy, in his secret society or the outside world. He is an indigenous sociopath with a cunning mind, trusting only himself. He is able to commit murder at the drop of a hat. Everyone feared him for that reason. He had no mortal enemies that could outfight his street soldiers or match his wits, although one or two did foolishly try. Some of the reasoning and rationale that make up his motivations and prompt his actions astounded even the fine-tuned criminal investigative mind of law enforcement themselves.

Ruggeri's Bloomfield Avenue emerges from the bowels of Newark's urban inner city Central Ward sector, with a starting point that maneuvers its narrow artery northwest from the municipality of Harrison and East Newark across from a murky, obscure section of the Passaic River. It continues through a labyrinth-like grid of narrow old asphalt-covered cobblestone streets and roadways as it crosses McCarter Highway and intersects Broad Street, Riverside Avenue, and Broadway. The roadway doglegs left slightly as it crosses over Summer Avenue and Crittenden Street then junctions with Park Avenue as it leads you to the more affluent areas of the North Ward and Forest Hills sections. The neighboring town of Belleville will lend its influence as it intersects the avenue at certain boundaries. This part of the avenue takes on a completely different look than that below Summer Avenue. It's a thriving part of the city, predominately Italian American, sons and daughters of the old-school pioneers who first set up shop. The avenue transformed into a wide four-lane boulevard with newer, more modern professional buildings, commercial strip malls, restaurants, and an expanse of dime stores, retail stores, and variety shops. Miles of decorative eighteenth century street lamps illuminated the roadways and paved sidewalks at night—cherished remnants of the past.

Mixed in with the newer architect of the commercial buildings and all so prevalent on the avenue plus the adjacent side streets are stretches of older freestanding "district" like buildings and storefronts. They consist of mom-and-pop-style business, mostly eateries, sidewalk cafes, and markets. All started by Italian immigrants years ago and passed from generation to generation, just as they stood years ago. Dedicated, well-established little shoestring operations all privately owned by hardworking immigrants and their families. The savory aroma of fresh-baked bread and other Italian cucina delicacies entice all that walk in front of the culinary establishments, this done by design. And also done by design, mixed in and well camouflaged, is the ever so prevalent panache of mobster influence the neighborhood welcomes with open arms as they also do Ruggeri's own garish and archetype Southern Italian eatery, the Sicilian Café.

This clandestine secret society of mobster dug in years ago and planted their corruption and extended their vices so openly to the good citizens of every neighborhood. The unabashed civilians, as they are known as, possess a subtle but obscene desire, and are ever so eager to participate. The illegal gambling that runs rampant up and down both sides of the avenue and the side streets takes shape in small back room bookie operations located within dozens of inconspicuous business fronts like barbershops, candy and newspaper stores, small coffee/espresso, shops, and luncheonettes and is considered, for the most part, harmless.

Store owners, merchants, and customers vigorously study the Daily Racing Forms and various other taut sheets faithfully each morning, arguing amongst themselves over breakfast as they carefully select their horse bets, exactas, daily doubles, and trifectas. Others will throw a few dollars away betting the "numbers" or buy a neighborhood lottery ticket. Many more of the successful and savvy business owners will lay down sizable chunks of cash betting on their favorite professional sports team with the foolhardy notion that they, come the end of the season, may actually be ahead. With all things in common, the merchants knowingly participate, without apology as a way of paying tribute to the Pope and the men who keep their city streets and markets protected from the dregs of society. And as for the daring or the higher society crowd, they'll find a completely different type of entertainment supplied by this secret society and under the guise of the Social Club.

The ever so prominent and prosperous Italian Social Clubs, the ones containing the more formidable and illicit betting parlors, operate on both sides of the Hudson River. They all have a distinct and diacritical air about them, all borne from the desire to preserve one's

Italian/Sicilian heritage and customs of the old country and mostly all borne from the Prohibition era. And just as the speakeasy was created for the love of whiskey, corruption, and sinful needs, so were the Social Clubs. Soon after the end of World War II, during that postwar era of new wealth and opportunity, they began to flourish ever so boldly—all injected with the cash the Prohibition enabled mobsters to accumulate, and all are under the rule and watchful eyes of the New Jersey and the New York mob bosses.

They were, at first, innocently inspired by the early VFW Halls—just slightly altered to accommodate the welcomed seedy and wanton vices, preeminently gambling and prostitution. Then along came the better-established Social Clubs, especially in and around Essex County, where the moneyed lived. They come in a sweeping variety of shapes and sizes, each one having its own personalized character or peculiarities and each one gratifying their patrons to a degree—some much more profound than others, but all with some form of, shall we say, a profuse satisfaction to scratch one's itch. Some are recognizably notorious and others innocent enough to hold Sunday Mass at, and all, for the most part, are an enormous cash cow for the organization. Most of the sanctioned clubs have very visible street-level entrances, accessed from the main avenues or second floor berths above very legitimate business. Some are located down long leery alleyways and some are isolated around the backs of buildings—all catering to the citizen who could pay the price of admission, citizens lured by the temptations of the seemingly harmless vices of organized crime.

The "Members Only" type of license granted to operate the clubs was relatively easy to obtain by just about anyone who filled out the city application and paid the fee. They were sanctioned with the right to sell alcohol in moderation to the members and their guests, and felt very little, if any at all, interference from the state's Alcoholic Beverages Control Board. The more clandestine Social

Clubs, the ones with the infamous hush-hush type back room gambling, the ones that cater to the more well-known hard-core vices were all licensed to people outside of the organization.

The paper was inked by carefully selected, unpretentious citizens. They would mostly be very old and quotidian-type citizens, mostly antecedents of organized crime with sneaking suspicions but no true knowledge of the vice within. And for the right price, all could care less about what went on behind the closed doors. They and their families where well taken care. No matter whose name was on the license, the one common thing all the clubs had with one another is that they fell under the rule and jurisdiction of the organization, the bosses so to speak, who guaranteed their safety and their existence. They all paid a designated monthly tribute to the capos of the neighborhood for protection, and all were obligated to purchase needed supplies from the organization, at whatever the going price was. The clubs were filled with mob-owned vending machines—cigarettes, pool tables, pinball, and jukeboxes were all part of the mix. The jukeboxes were considered sacred by all the club owners and outfit guys, by far the best cash cow in any joint. Everyone loved music and all were encouraged to drop nickels, dimes, and quarters into the slots to keep the atmosphere jovial.

The jukeboxes contained ample recordings of only mostly Italian artists: Dean Martin, Frank Sinatra, Tony Bennett, Perry Como, and Jerry Vale, to name a few. An occasional Mario Lanza or Louie Prima were thrown into the mix as was a record or two from some unknown Italian artist discovered at the Festival della cazone Italiano.

A story resounded throughout the neighborhood about a young colored kid who once worked for one vending machine companies that serviced the jukeboxes. He caught a little bit of a beating because he took it upon himself to insert Nat King Cole's "Christmas Song" into the mix of some of the clubs' jukeboxes without permission. The beating he suffered was child's play compared to the one some lowly patron received one night, doled out by the hands of a wise guy for reasons unknown other than his ranting about how he "hated that black bastard." The citizen's demise was ignoring the wishes of the mobster, whom he thought was just busting balls and playing the subtle song over and over after he was warned.

To any layman entering a sanctioned club, the activities about the place would seem surprisingly harmless and almost family like. The atmosphere would be jovial. Old and young men alike, sitting at neatly arranged tables all playing cards drinking, laughing, and cursing, some in their native tongues. It was in the infamous back room where all the illicit action took place: blackjack games, craps, slot machines, and poker. Anyone who ventured there had to have a crystal clear understanding of the word *Omerta*.

This high level of organized gambling was reserved for only a select and invited few, and they were all expected and bound by their solemn oath to understand and respect the rules. The standing rule would require a fellow wise guy to vouch for any newcomer venturing into a high-stakes games. In other words, he would take full responsibility for the player's integrity, honor, and ability to repay any gambling debts and in many cases enforce and monitor their payments. This initiation of a newcomer was always accepted by the local loan sharks that inhabited the clubs for the sole purpose of getting someone in over their head. They sat like vultures eagerly waiting to swoop down on the financially wounded prey. Their job was to hand out markers and cash advances to the unsuspecting suckers or *sfruttatores* for the obvious reason of keeping them in the game and continue them on their losing streak.

There are only a handful of exclusive posh clubs in and around Essex, Passaic, and Bergen Counties or throughout the five boroughs of New York that have the ability to attract a high level of professional gambler. Those type players who will only frequent the clubs they can only construe with their own personas, all in a class above the conventional fraternal hangouts, all upscale and possessing a degree of high-society and notoriety class, and all very well protected. And then there is Angelo Ruggeri's place. His uniquely distinct and discriminating private Neapolitan Social Club sits high above most buildings on Bloomfield Avenue—that by an inherent reason, and certainly not conforming with his usual "keep a low profile" scheme of things. While it is no true secret the famed mansion belongs to the Pope, its documents of public record will tell a different story, and if asked by certain individuals, Ruggeri will admit to being just a patron. However, and befittingly, he gloats as he comments strictly to his own inner circle that its size and grandeur does add an even more imposing aura to his *umo d'onore*—for men of honor as the sign reads in gold leaf print at the front and rear doors. But it is for that exact same intentional reason of secrecy—the outside of the French château styled home is kept in the recondite shadows of only a scant amount of incandescent lighting fixtures. Living and breathing souls of seasoned tree-stump-necked bodyguards and sentries occupy the negative spaces of where a lighting fixture once was. Their presence and watchful eyes replaced the once brilliant and gaudy converted gaslights, lanterns, and wall sconces that made the white house seem like a bright Christmas card scene. On many a night, the clientele present was so posh and well known, normal players—even well-to-do sanctioned patrons—were denied access to his Bloomfield Avenue palace. They were diverted to his other still privy and private club.

His first sanctioned club was on Roseville Avenue, a place so entertainingly illegal and so well politically protected and guarded, was considered way back when, and still is by all, a top-shelf operation. It offers house-backed, casino-style gambling and executive-type high-stakes card games and avails itself to those with the obnoxious sums of money and a strong heart to play. And since it answers to no one, it was the first club to stay open until four in the morning—then, until and if needed or requested, breakfast was served. This ensured the action continues way past last call at ABC-regulated establishments. But when the impromptu and sudden golden opportunity arose to acquire his second club, this palatial mansion on the avenue just two short years ago, he did so with very sly boots and adroit and baneful efforts—as the story has been told—to only a select few.

* * *

Years earlier, Domenico Zarrillo, along with his brother Humberto and their widowed mother in tow, fled to New Jersey from their home in New Orleans, Louisiana, and their jobs as undertakers. Like so many other Italian and Sicilian immigrants during that era and in that area, they fled to escape the indiscriminate persecution that was being imposed by the city and the local *Medigans* of law enforcement, their own father having died in prison for a crime he did not commit. Both brothers were masterfully trained morticians and found immediate work at a funeral parlor in Belleville, New Jersey. They honed their skills and learned every aspect of the business of death and decided to venture out on their own in April of 1947.

The two somewhat naive and unsuspecting brothers found a reputable pair of realtors and signed what they thought to be a ninety-nine-year lease with "the option to buy" a prestigious private residence on a corner lot of Bloomfield Avenue. The obscure history of the property was told vaguely to the two Sicilian brothers, and they interpreted it merely as a storybook fable. They stood proud when told by the realtor, "It was once owned by the heirs of the wealthy Italian nobleman who designed and built the place for his personal residence. Please, gentlemen, have a look around." The rejoicing brothers agreed the place, though rather large, was perfectly suited for their plans to convert into an elegant funeral parlor. They both agreed that the newly renovated and freshly painted property and floor plan lend itself ideally for an undertaking establishment. They beamed as they walked about exchanging encouraging words of approval spoken to each other in their native Italian.

The exterior's ornate wooden trim was painted a heavenly white—to stay in contrast with the original stone. Its majestic front limestone and marbled entrance had a wide concrete and stone landing that rose two steps up and led to a pair of handsome mahogany doors that stood ten feet tall. Both hand carved with leaved vines and grapes and angelic cherubs. A well-applied deep stain accented the natural grain of the wood and was well protected by heavy layers of varnish. Both sides of the entrance doors were adorned by two Victorian Era wall sconces that were over three feet in height and cast dancing shadows well past the marbled Corinthian columns that held up a huge balustrade portico. And the french windows— such elegance and architecture the two Sicilians had seen but only in books. There was a wide doorway on the side of the manor; the brothers envisioned that area with a canopied walkway, and a rear granite porch entrance with custom french doors. It would be perfect for escorting families of mourners and their guests in and out somberly with unobstructed ease. Around the back of the manor was a wide stairway that led to the basement. It would be ideal for a more modern-style Bilco double door and gurney ramp, they thought. Adjacent was a separate four-car garage that first served as a stable years ago. The two car-length driveway, originally inlaid cobblestone as was the front circular drive, was now paved with over four inches of asphalt. The Bloomfield Avenue entrance drive ran adjacent to the property's length then doglegged left to Watsessing Avenue. A picture-perfect layout! So anxious were the Zarrillos to take occupancy they turned a blind eye to legalities and left all the details and particulars to the shrewd realtors and owners, Harold Horowitz and his

brother and business partner, Barry, both the principals of the established real estate management /holdings firm H Horowitz and Sons
Incorporated. They both were extremely anxious to rid themselves of
the place for the time being.

The Zarrillo brothers had an excellent reputation with the citizens in the area regarding and applying their trade as the Horowitzs
soon found out. The realtors graciously offered and insisted that
their firm lend the money needed for the setup of the venture and
hold the deeds. "We'll handle the entire boring, tedious details, gentlemen, trust us" were the solemn words of Harold Horowitz. And of
course the Zarrillos did. They eagerly pooled every cent they could
amass along with the capital lent by the Horowitz's firm, and thusly,
within just a short time, the gaudy house was transformed into a fully
functional and exquisitely furnished funeral parlor. The huge basement area was converted into a sanctified morgue with a mosaic-tiled
floor and with two standard marble and stainless steel dissecting-au-
topsy tables, rows of shelving and cabinets stocked with supplies.
One flight up either by stairway or via Otis freight elevator was a
beautifully created showroom where sample caskets of various woods
and polished metals were displayed while the remaining sectioned
rooms were converted to simple but ceremonious viewing areas. The
Zarrillo brothers, together with their mother, resided above the parlor, in the huge converted second- and third-story living quarters.
Their business took off as word of mouth quickly spread throughout
the neighborhood's mainstream of the brothers' compassion and generosity. They provided mourners an apprized service at a very modest
price, accepting the rich and poor alike.

The immigrant brothers were honest, trusting men and thought
all businessmen were alike. Neither brother was savvy with the
American way of conducting business. Neither brother could read
or for that matter understand the English language that well. Their
prepared paperwork associated with their business, death certificates

and things of that nature, were prepared in longhand Italian—or on the preprinted forms bearing recognized words in English. Nevertheless, both brothers were men of their word: honest, forthright, and diligent. Each month two checks were made payable to the Horowitz brothers then hand carried to their office in the nearby town of Verona.

One check would be for the monthly lease of the property and another was payment on the loans. A third check, according to their understanding, was to be placed in an escrow account and one day used as the down payment to finalize their original agreement to buy the land and property. On rare occasion, receipts were given to the undertakers, but for the most part, as they agreed, a handshake would suffice.

Over the years just about every family from Newark and the surrounding area attended a wake offered by Zarrillos in one of the garish visitation rooms. Angelo Ruggeri would ultimately attend a funeral service held at the establishment in the early days of its operation. He commented to the brothers in their native tongues, "This place is magnificent, and would you believe in all the years in this neighborhood, I've never once set foot inside this old mansion. I was always afraid of the curse." His kind words were acknowledged by laughter and the bowing heads of the Zarrillos. Ruggeri continued as he walked the interior in awe of its spender. "Had I known, I would have bought it myself." And immediately, a fraternal bond was formed between Ruggeri and the two short, cherub-faced Sicilian undertakers. He recognized both of them as truly men of honor. They both recognized the stature and hushed notoriety of Ruggeri and most of the attending hulks of men accompanying, and without saying a word, vowed to him their anticipated loyalty. Their eyes bugged as some men were overheard whispering to one another about the Don's orders and referring to him as the Pope. And as the years passed, their friendship with the benevolent Ruggeri grew to one of true friendship, and it was not long before the Zarrillo brothers were offered invitation by Ruggeri himself. "You must come to my restaurant, with your mother, and if you wish, drop my Social Club. I'm sure you will like the atmosphere." He gave a nefarious look and said, "But I don't think it wise to bring Mama there, *hai gabide?*"

And soon the brothers would dine at the Sicilian Café and visit Ruggeri at his Roseville Avenue club on somewhat of a regular basis. In addition to indulging the wanton vices offered, the brothers would sit and talk at hours' length with the Don about their relatives still living in the old country and the true history of the Sicilian mafia. The brothers were well aware of the level of Mafiosa he was and would drink to his health and good fortune each and every time they met. They would offer their favor or service with no qualms or repentance. To them he was just another businessman, a very dapper man. Always well dressed in fashionable Italian designed suits that he had custom made from a Jewish tailor he was a close associate of. Because of his shorter height, only five feet nine inches, he insisted on more broad, padded shoulders. He was always clean-shaven and was seemingly proud of the two noticeable scars over his right brow, souvenirs of his hooligan youth. He had the nose of a prizefighter, and a full head of curly, dense hair, of a steel wool color and texture. He carefully parted it on his left side, dead center of his good eyebrow, and pomaded the curls like ocean waves toward the opposite shore. He was so proud of his hair that he seldom wore a hat. Domenico once told the Don in all sincerity that he reminded him of a *Dotore* he remembered from his home in New Orleans. He too an innocent Sicilian that was tortured by the medigans. They all would share intimate stories of life and family, and on many occasions Ruggeri would dine on homemade raviolis prepared in the Zarrillo kitchen by their mother. The level of respect and honor that the two brothers held for Ruggeri had been immeasurable and one day would be sealed in blood.

The Zarrillo brothers were just three short months shy of their ten-year anniversary and were planning a celebration. Their festive mood was interrupted when a "Certified Letter" marked URGENT arrived in Monday's mail from the office of H. Horowitz and Sons. Somewhat confused and uncertain of the legal dialogue and cluttered text they sought out the help of local store merchant they befriended to act as an interpreter.

The shopkeeper dropped what he was doing and obliged. He carefully read the letter over and over again to the bewildered brothers. He paid special attention to the closing statements that clearly defined the orders to vacate within the next three months explaining the lease will not be renewed based on some pre-agreed clause written and stating the property is *sold*. Perhaps it was only a mistake, the Zarrillo brothers thought, and a misinterpretation? The empathetic shopkeeper apologized for their misfortune as they were discernibly upset in his presence and in front of his customers eagerly trying to pay for merchandise. The shopkeeper took a timeout from the calamity and handed the brothers a card with a local attorney's name on it. They uniformly gave each other a wide-eyed stare as they noticed the name *Ferrigno* next to the *Esq.* A *paisano*, they both relevantly thought.

Be it as it may, the next day resulted in utter disappointment. Domenico, who spoke the better English of the two, tried to explain his situation over the phone to the receptionist at Robert M. Ferrigno's Law Office. Frustration set in even more when the callback came from the esquire Robert himself who wanted more details of the mishap, and since he possessed only a limited understanding of the Sicilian dialect, the communication factor turned into a calamity. The brothers frantically tossed the phone back and forth to each other as if it were a hot potato, taking turns shouting into the receiver what Ferrigno thought to be Italian gibberish. Domenico's face went blank as he soon realized he was holding a receiver with a dead line attached.

It was agreed, Umberto would handle the afternoon visitation wake for the recently departed Michael Zimmerman, and Domenico would go himself to Horowitz's office and straighten it all out. Within a half an hour Domenico was in the reception area, indignant and demanding to see one or both of the brothers. His request fell on deaf and discourteous ears. The secretary of the firm (who also happened to be Barry's wife) grabbed the letter the undertaker was waiving frantically in her face. She shouted, "It's written in simple English. You are to VACATE the property by this date." Then she gave her final NO, denying entry and telling him that he will not be able to see either of the Horowitzs at this time, and threatened to call the police if he persisted. He left with his tail between his legs and with a feeling of hopelessness in his heart. He drove back home sobbing and muttering words of contempt toward the conniving Horowitzs in loud and well-spoken Italian. Suddenly a fulgent thought shot about his brain. As he drove his feelings of despair turned to anger. He carefully, and with determination, deciphered the true meaning of the letter and realized he and his brother had been duped—intentionally cheated. Domenico was a proud man. His befuddlement became more defined; his thoughts were now crystal clear. Even proud Sicilians need help from an ally now and then, especially with matters of vengeance. It was getting late, and he felt he had no time to waste. He pushed down hard on the gas pedal of the hearse and sped down the avenue then turning right on Roseville Avenue. He eased the hearse over the curb and parked in the back of club that his *potente amico* owned.

Don Ruggeri welcomed the undertaker with outstretched arms. He noticed immediately his friend was not his usual convivial self, almost reluctant to return the admiration of an honorable hug.

Ruggeri sensed deep sorrow as he stared into his tear-filled eyes and felt fear in his trembling handshake. "What is it, my dear friend?" Ruggeri asked in their native Italian. His voice had a genuine concern. "Chefai bicuridu—aunda ciunca?" Domenico stood uneasy in the crowded front room of the private club. His eyes were nervously darting as he muttered in his native Sicilian tongue, "It's a private matter—may I talk to you, in private?" "Walk with me," Ruggeri said, also speaking Italian and with an accommodating arm around the undertaker's shoulder. They walked together to the far back of the club and sat at corner booth. Ruggeri summoned a waiter to bring a bottle of anisette and two glasses.

Both men toasted one another, and after sharing a couple of shots of the fiery licorice-flavored cordial, the bald undertaker spoke impatiently and in Italian, "Mannagia dial—la miseria…" And for the next few minutes he explained remorsefully the pickle he was in. The Pope listened carefully to everything the undertaker was saying with compassion for the man. He first calmed him as if he were a child. Next, he instructed the visibly upset man to compose himself, go home, and tend to the grieving families that are waiting for his services.

Ruggeri spoke firmly to the undertaker, telling him he must do nothing rash, and also instructed him to tell no one of their meeting. "This will be between you and me and no one else…gabide?" Plans were made between Domenico and Don as he escorted the undertaker to a rear exit door. He would meet him the next morning at his funeral parlor, and the two would drive to his lawyer friend and resolve this, what he referred to as a tiny matter. Ruggeri put his arm around his friend's shoulder, once again telling him over and over "not to worry," he would do all he could to aid the brothers as a way of thanking them for their friendship and respect they've showed him for all the raviolis over the years.

The next morning found Domenico in a black suit and tie and a crisp white shirt, anxiously waiting in front of the funeral parlor. He stood near the street, sentry-like, holding tightly to his breast all the documents regarding the lease he and his brother had signed years ago along with boxes of cancelled checks. The driveway by the side door had mourners gathering for a funeral that was in progress—all waiting and lighting up cigarettes as the pallbearers began loading the bronze casket into a shiny black hearse.

A black Buick sedan pulled into the driveway and almost became part of Mrs. Zimmerman's procession. Domenico realizing that they were here for him scurried to the car. He was greeted by a hulk of a man with a forced smile and darting eyes, dressed in a full-length gray wool coat and very well polished shoes. The enforcer opened the rear door with determination then directed him with a mimed shake of his head and a gruff voice: "Climb in, friend."

Domenico felt the weight of the goon shake the automobile as he lumbered back inside the vehicle and hard slamming the car door shut, further startling the already nervous undertaker. The car was heavily scented with aftershave and cigarettes. Domenico noticed the absence of Ruggeri. He questioned the two hulking men up front who crudely but politely explained that the Pope would be waiting at the lawyer's office and not to worry. A few scandalous and nonchalant words were exchanged between the mobsters that Domenico assumed pertained to his situation. A befuddled look stretched his jowls. "Don't look so scared, my friend," said the passenger. The driver chimed in with a snide laugh, "I guess he thinks he's goin' for a ride." Domenico sat back deep into the upholstery of the sedan and wondered just how serious this situation was going to get.

The ride to the township of Nutley was a brief one, and not another word was exchanged between the three. The two men up front dwarfed the chubby undertaker, and it was reminiscent of parents driving a child to school. The driver pulled up in front of

William Caruso's Law Office and double-parked. He told the undertaker they would be waiting for him and the Pope around back, and then indicating with an ominous nod of his head it was time to get out of the car. Noticing a puzzled look on undertaker's face, the driver asked, "You know where you're goin'?" Domenico exhibited just a little apprehension as his eyes looked around then acknowledged to the thugs that he would find his way inside the building. "Grazie, and thank you for the ride," he said proudly.

A polite, smartly dressed young secretary announced his arrival over the office intercom then escorted Domenico through the double dark stained oak doors. Ruggeri was sitting with his legs crossed smoking a cigarette making small talk with Caruso as Domenico appeared in the doorway hat in hand and respectfully waited for permission to enter.

"Didn't I tell you he was a gentleman?" Ruggeri said to the lawyer with a proud smile as he addressed Domenico in their native Italian. "Come in, my friend, and sit next to me." Ruggeri beckoned to the man but did not rise to greet him. Introductions were brief and Ruggeri explained to Domenico slowly that Caruso already knows the gist of the problem and to hand over whatever paperwork he had.

Willie Caruso is a fast-talking fidgety lawyer and was one of many the Pope used for semi-shady real estate and land sale transactions involving third parties or straw buyers, of which the Pope did numerous ones around the city. He is a savvy man in his mid-sixties who'll be the first to tell you he has been around the block a few times. He stands out in court corridors, dapper with his slicked-back silver hair and his pencil-thin mustache and bushy eyebrows that both danced constantly around his writhing facial expressions. He is well versed with real estate law and mingled well with mobsters and shysters who made up a huge part of his client base and like the Pope was very politically connected. Domenico sat unnerved with an uncomfortable queasiness in his paunchy belly as Ruggeri calmly sat studying the memorabilia and clutter on the walls and shelves while he blew smoke rings in paced succession.

It took Caruso all of about two minutes to scan through the simple lease and loan agreements and canceled checks. He mumbled to himself as he did so then rendered a simple verdict. He shook his head a bit, grimaced, and mournfully said, "Okay. If this is all you have in the way of legal documentation, we are in trouble, gentlemen." He made a shrugging movement with his drooping shoulders and stretched out his face. "This is a basic-read lease, and shrewdly worded. There is nothing violating or unconstitutional about it. It is very much like a preprinted document one can obtain at any legal supply or printers office with a few delusive addendums attached. It contains a lot of rhetoric and a slew of redundancies that grant everything for the lessor and nothing for the lessee. Like I said...unless we can prove criminal intent from the get-go, and if this is all we have, we're fucked." The sad news was translated to the Sicilian undertaker who made a determined inquiry regarding the checks. Ruggeri offered raised eyebrows. "This is worthless evidence!" Caruso said. He waved the documents over his head in frustration. "They tell us nothing. They prove only rent paid to Horowitz. These other checks could be for anything. However, in this case, they are clearly indicative of repayment for monies borrowed and for some cockamamie maintenance fee, insurance, whatever." The lawyer's frustration was evident. "The text and language in these papers confuse the hell out of me." *How could this man in front of me have been so naive?* was his emerging question he thought to himself. *And he signed this without counsel?* Domenico began to question the evidence. Domenico began to question Ruggeri. He wanted an explanation regarding the lawyer's rashness. Willie Caruso sighed. He gave the men a hesitant request for silence with a raised hand as he picked up the desk phone and dialed. And as the phone was ringing, he cupped his palm over the receiver and said acutely, "I'm curious myself?"

The lawyer announced himself to the party that answered the phone on the other end and after a brief dissertation found he himself talking with Barry Horowitz who acted as both legal advisor and accountant for the firm. The conversation was fast paced, direct, and controlled mostly by Caruso, who cited contractual law and case histories off the top of his head while using inference and making innuendos regarding past and present politicians, spewing legal folderol that neither of the two men sitting across from him could understand. Caruso fell silent and bore a withered look of contempt on his face. And for a brief moment, one would sense a verbal scolding was presented him from the party on the other end of the phone. Seemingly chastised, he picked up the lease and began to read it at the request of Horowitz. His voice was subdued. His arms whimsically flailed about as he boringly tossing out a few "I see that, sir" and "correct—yes—I read the terms of the monies borrowed—correct—yes, you are correct" into the receiver. After a while he became the compliant listener of a drag one-sided conversation until he said "Thank you for your time, my friend" then disturbingly hung up the phone. His facial expression was one of utter frustration as he tapped his fingers together then intertwined them and said, "Like I said before, we are fucked. Let me rephrase that—he's fucked."

The lawyer's discovery and the grim news was translated into Italian by Ruggeri and conveyed to the undertaker. "The lease was not for ninety-nine years but only ten as clearly stated and agreed. And the extra money you were giving Horowitz was paying for insurance and maintenance on the building 'as agreed' and outlined in the lease. Horowitz is not gonna' back down or reconsider at any cost." Caruso spoke again, remorsefully, "At best, gentlemen, my opinion of this is sheer and utter bamboozlement. The lease expires on midnight, period! We can ask a judge for an extension and file suit, but in all sincerity, he has not a chance in hell of winning." Ruggeri listened with a sorrowful, impassioned look on his face. The lawyer may feel the argument with the realtor lost but Ruggeri will not.

The ride back to the funeral parlor could have been for Domenico's own service. He was a grieving, heartbroken man in deep lament, mourning over the loss of his life's work. Ruggeri spoke words hoping to soothe the pain but to no avail. The undertaker thrust his head against Ruggeri's chest and sobbed uncontrollably. He spoke in a rapid Italian dialect as he asked forgiveness for being so careless and naive and believing the Jew realtor, swearing to God and Ruggeri on his mother's *life* that he honestly and wholeheartedly believed he was to own the parlor one day. He asked God why he was cheated. Ruggeri coddled him in his arms and assured him things would work out. He would see to it personally.

Ruggeri did not waste an ounce of time with what in his heart he knew he must do. He felt the undertaker's pain and anguish and was consumed by it as if it were his own. His first order of business was to find out just who Harold and Barry Horowitz really are. Could they be phantom property owners for others, and how are they moving around the city in their capacity without paying tribute? Ruggeri's political connections reach deep into city hall. He has powerful people in all levels of government: the city planners office, the building department, and city councils. He knows mostly all the inspectors and the hotshots in licensing and permits and they all know him. Nothing moves, construction-wise, in or around the city without his knowledge. Angelo Ruggeri indirectly owns hundreds of properties throughout the city and suburbs as well, all in phantom corporations and discrete shell companies—without any direct incrimination or connection to him. He orchestrated hundreds of inside-trader types of real estate transactions for all of his associates and politicians whom he considered allies, making millionaires of most while literally disposing of the opposition. For these bold tactics alone, men—all men—feared him. His voice was emphatic as he spoke, "I want to know everything about these two, this H. Horowitz and Sons Realty group, or whatever they call themselves."

Ruggeri was hell-bent on stopping these bantamweight real-tors, these so-called developers whom he had never heard of, from screwing one of his own *Paisan*. The thought of that alone, the gross disrespect, outraged him to the point of—? Within a day he had a list of every property holding H. Horowitz Inc. had. He learned H. Horowitz, the realty group, got its start in the Bronx when the father was still alive. It then expanded when the family moved to New Jersey. Upon further inquiry, an ugly story emerged. It seems the elder Horowitz, the recently departed father, swindled hundreds of his fellow Jews out of their sole possessions, abandoning them with the empty hopes of ever fleeing the Nazis. They were all left behind. Such evil treachery on Horowitz's part. *What type people are these?* thought Ruggeri. And it was determined that the elder Horowitz was equally responsible. Ruggeri now wished he was still alive to answer for his sins. "So they're a bunch of despicable slumlords rambling about and now buying property on my turf right under my nose." Ruggeri's words were malignant. He came to find out that there was not a buyer for the Zarrillo property. Not a contract in place. The Horowitz firm owns a nice tract of land next to the funeral parlor that was acquired a few years before the old mansion was leased to the Zarrillos. The Horowitz's had plans all along to level everything and construct a modern strip mall/office building complex on the property—a venture that would turn all concerned into very wealthy men.

The following morning brought distressing news. The Pope's original plan was to sabotage the entire project through his connections in the department without getting his hands dirty. "I'll just buy them out, case closed," he shouted into the phone's receiver. They all came back with the same guff: "If we had only known sooner?" The wheels are too far into motion to stop now. Plans have been approved and permits are already issued.

More inquiries were made by Ruggeri to further understand the level of enemy he was dealing with. Everyone who knew the Horowitzs commented on how shrewd they were when it came to the business of outright cheating people, a clever act of expediency taught by their also conniving father. The Pope realized they were not going to be at all cooperative. The thought of it all made the Pope's blood run a bit colder and diminished his hopes of a reasonable solution. One of his close collaborators inside the building department asked Ruggeri just how far he wanted to take this stoppage attempt, while another assured the help and cooperation of the local Union to run interference throughout the project. Ruggeri agreed that the timing was not right. He politely declined the offers for reasons he was not willing to discuss. Everyone understood the implication.

The next day, Ruggeri summoned his most reliable *capos* to discuss a more immediate plan of action. Time was not of the essence, with the lease termination date more than three months away. He could wait it out and see if there was a chance his connections with the City of Newark could quite possibly come through with a plan to halt the Horowitzs' project. However, Ruggeri was an impatient man and wanted it put to bed now to avoid any additional unforeseen problems.

Ruggeri sat in silence within the confines of his private office. Frank Batista sat opposite, also silent. The office was designed like a military bunker, a "castle keep." A separate concrete and steel constructed room built inside another room with a reinforced steel door with a locking dead bolt on the outside and two more commercial dead bolts on the inside. His contractor friend that designed and built it said nothing more than a bazooka could penetrate its shell. It was an impregnable fortress providing a safe haven in the event of a raid. The room had the simplest of basic furniture: a desk and a couple of chairs and a small bookshelf and safe bolted to the carpeted concrete slab floor. An efficient and separate ventilation system kept the contained air cool and fresh. A black rotary telephone sat in the center of the table and separated the two men. It was connected to an untraceable *pirated* line secretly installed by another cohort from Western Electric. It could dial out to any number and was reached by someone who knew the four-digit code that could be changed every so often.

Ruggeri's mind was consumed with preoccupied thought. His confidence level soared in regard of the soon-to-be revealed plan. Frank Batista was a trusted and proven capo. He sat in anticipation, looking directly into Ruggeri's eyes through black horn-rimmed glasses, and awaiting his orders. He puffed incessantly on his Lucky Strike cigarette, ever so anxious for the details and instructions he was about to receive. Ruggeri slid a piece of notepaper toward Batista. On it were written words and he said, "This is what you say—no more, no less. They'll listen." Batista adjusted his thick-framed black glasses, a color and style chosen to match his neatly kept jet black hair. His thought also was the frames made his nose look smaller. Frank looked away with skeptical eyes then spoke ever so reluctantly, "Mannaggia la Miseria…I hate talkin' on these goddamn phones." Ruggeri replied confidently, "This one you needn't worry about…" Frank responded, "It ain't this one I'm worried about, Pope… what about the—the *stunads* on the other end? Their line could be bugged." The Pope smiled ever so lightly and rolled his eyes as he said, "We ain't gonna' worry about that—now make the call." Ruggeri's eyes narrowed to just evil slits. Batista had butterflies in his stomach over such an easy task at hand—stage fright, he thought. He made another adjustment of his glasses before clearing his throat while lifting the receiver from its cradle and dialing the number to H. Horowitz. Acting under the guise of an interested client, he introduced himself to the voice at the other end as "Gianni Rullo, owner of the Sicilian Café." Harold Horowitz came to the phone, introducing himself, and acknowledged his familiarity of the establishment. Suddenly Batista's words flowed with ease, almost second nature.

An invitation was extended to Horowitz. It was an invitation for a business luncheon, a very private meeting, so to speak, so that they might discuss a very worthwhile proposition. "I'm going to put a very lucrative deal on the table," Frank said in earnest. He also guaranteed that the food prepared would be the best Italian fare in the city. Horowitz listened to more then asked for details. Batista lit another cigarette, looked down at the written script, and said coyly, and most businesslike, "I'm very much interested with the possibility of renting some space in your up-and-coming mall venture." This took Horowitz by complete surprise as his worried face expressed. He had thought he, up until this assumed point, had done his very best keeping the project a complete secret from the outside world. "I'm curious, Mr. Rullo?" he said with raised brows. "How did you hear of the mall?" "Let's just say we share the same mutual friends down at city hall," Batista answered matter-of-factly. "I would be willing to pay you top dollar for the space…you name the terms." After a few more exchange of words, the meeting was set for noon the very next day. The very brilliant business minds of men will converge at the Sicilian Café.

The next day, Harold Horowitz left his office with plenty of time to spare. The conversation about the meeting was kept vague and obscure with his brother; he himself wanted the gratification of sealing such a lucrative deal. It would be worth a cash bonus for him personally—this written provision between the partners was their father's idea, to encourage healthy rivalry and competition. The gloating realtor arrived promptly at the Sicilian Café dressed in his best Brooks Brothers wrinkled brown tweed suit that hung shapelessly on his puny frame. And while not a devotee of Italian food—he considered it to be old-world and peasant-like—he was looking forward to the gracious, free lunch promised.

Harold Horowitz was a shrewd businessman as was his brother and late father. The brothers were graduates of Harvard Law and both very knowledgeable men. Undoubtedly, Harold was savvy about his business and the laws pertaining, but his well-sheltered life made him naive of the ways of organized crime and their rules, codes, and methods. Perhaps to him they were mere storybook characters. Only on rare occasion did he ever hear his late father speak of a Jewish mobster he had dealings with. The thought of ever crossing paths with these so-called mobsters in his business world, in his mind, was inconceivable. Those type courses were not taught at Harvard Law. He thought nothing out of the ordinary as he walked from his parked car toward the restaurant, passing rows and rows of shiny and new Cadillacs and Lincolns. He had not paid one bit of attention nor thought anything suspicious about the four street soldiers who stood sentry, guarding the Pope's visit.

Although Frank Batista had never met the realtor, his intuition prompted him to action as soon as he laid eyes on the tiny balding man who was entering the restaurant. His guess was that he could only be a man of no more than thirty years of age, but looked much older. He rose up from the small table he shared with Joey Lotta. "Mr. Horowitz?" he said with a querying look on his face, eyes squinting but a beaming smile attached. "Yes…I'm Harold Horowitz." Frank Batista was, as expected of him, impeccably dressed in a dark blue suit and a coordinated tie. Horowitz eyed him up and down. Batista towered almost a good foot over the puny Ivy Leaguer. He grabbed hold of the back of Harold's arm gently and gave a congenial tug. "Please…follow me, the boss's been expectin' ya'," he said with a most convincing wise guy voice—his hopes were the little man did not recognize his voice from their phone conversation. On cue, the huge brute of a thug rose from the table and followed both men as Batista led them through the packed and bustling restaurant toward the kitchen.

Once inside the garish restaurant, Horowitz displayed more naivety. He never once, just out of sheer curiosity, looked over his shoulder and wondered as to why the brute of a man was following them just a step or two behind. Nor did he acknowledge the dozen other known mobsters scattered around the eatery, various tables, and booths, sitting guard, their shady eyes fixated and following him as he took his tiny feeble steps. Their each and individual hoodlum persona exceedingly stood out among the actual patrons who were dinning. His eyes not once glanced out to catch sight of the mobland memorabilia or the hundreds of thin framed black-and-white photos of the many celebrities and politicians that uniformly filled the walls, all in warm embracing poses with the Pope Ruggeri himself. His ears paid no attention to the colloquial slang spoken by the seated mobsters or the Italian mandolin music that eased over the speaker system and filled the room. And then finally he was led into the boisterous kitchen area and caught sight of Angelo Ruggeri, impeccably dressed, sitting alone at a neatly set table at the far back corner. And as his senses reacted favorably to the aromas, he still had not a clue he was in the den of a vicious, amoral mafia chieftain who, in fact, was the true proprietor of the elegant Sicilian Café 'Ristorante.

Ruggeri had a deep, utmost respect for his Jewish peers and business associates. They were, in his heart and mind, tough, honorable soldiers. Many came from the same impoverished neighborhood he had emerged from. They all fought side by side in the underworld trenches and had all, for the most part, been victorious. He put his head down with a pique, resentment, that burned deep into his soul as he watched the party approach. He felt immediate contempt as soon as his cold eyes fell on the realtor who was now standing in front of him. He envisioned his hands around the throat of the little

Jew, choking the life out of him. The voice behind a forced smile beckoned the words, "Mr. Horowitz...please...have a seat." Ruggeri made an inviting gesture with his open palm. "Mr. Rullo?" the eager and enthused Horowitz began. "It's nice to meet you." His words were followed by a genial attempt at a handshake. Ruggeri ignored the introduction and sat with his hands folded in a controlled anger then replied gravely, "Well, not exactly, Mr. Horowitz?" Ruggeri's face was impassive, but Horowitz could read the contempt in the Pope's eyes. He took his seat with a fearful reluctance.

Ruggeri did not waste any time, nor did he mince words as he got to the real underlying reason he wanted to meet with Horowitz. Each word spoken was accompanied with a meaningful shoulder shrug or a gesture that portrayed compassion rather than rage. All for the sole purpose of convincing the realtor to reasonably reconsider and sell the chateau to the undertakers. An offer of far more than the true market value was put on the table with the hopes of enticing Horowitz. Every reasonable angle was presented to the realtor but to no avail. He firmly rejected them all. He made it clear to Ruggeri he was not going to sell at any price. Ruggeri was exasperated. With all hopes lost for a satisfactory settlement, he changed his stance and came at the little man with threatening innuendoes. He would use his powerful political connections to "make life miserable" for Harold and his partners. "I'll turn your track of land into a parking lot." Ruggeri raged. Harold's ignorance to the foreboding threat was apparent. He stood his ground against the clandestine mobster. In his heart he felt he was the better negotiator when it came to this type of business dealings. "Mr. Rullo. My plans will not be waived or influenced." Horowitz said curtly, "Legally...there is nothing you or your associates at city hall can do to enforce a stoppage of my project. I'm protected...legally!" Ruggeri stared coldly at the realtor. "Yes, you are...legally...Mr. Horowitz?" Ruggeri said with a doleful frown that turned into a sinister grin then continued. "I want you to think about the lives you are potentially ruining, the Zarrillo brothers in particular. They were led to believe that, one day, the property would be theirs alone." Horowitz quickly defended his stance. "They knew quite well of our long-term plans, and shame on them if they didn't thoroughly understand the terms and agreements set forth and shame on them for not preparing for the future." Ruggeri felt sick to his stomach. He broke eye contact with Horowitz and turned his head away. The smile left his face. His eyes looked directly into the eyes of Batista who was standing only a few feet away; then they solemnly shut as his head bowed slightly, an indication the meeting was coming to an end.

Ruggeri looked begrudgingly at the realtor who obviously was celebrating some sort of victory in his own mind. His face bore a seemingly satisfied look. It was a look that Ruggeri took as a vexed insult. "Suddenly I am not hungry," he said dismissively. "However, you're welcome to stay and have yourself lunch...on me." Ruggeri stood and called for a waiter who was standing by the stainless steel chef's line. "Show this man to a table. Give him anything he wants." Horowitz offered a parting handshake and said with a forced smile, "It was nice meeting you, Mr. Rullo." Ruggeri once again ignored the gesture of friendship. He kept his hands at his side and said coldly, "No, sorry to say...but it wasn't."

Over the next few weeks all specialized capos and enforcers were called for. Albert Marrone, the most seasoned and probably the most respected of Ruggeri's capos, was given the task of assembling a crew to keep a constant surveillance of the Horowitzs during the day—from the time they left their houses in the morning until the time they leave the office at night and all stops in between and to pay close attention to times and patterns. Frank Batista was assigned the evening watch. Both capos knew their trade well.

The Pope had one of his connections at the phone company pull all the records from the Horowitzs' business and home listings, all the addresses to their private residences and what seemed to be a summer home at the shore community of Lakewood. Each address was written down in code for his people to monitor. Barry had a home in Roseland, right under Ruggeri's nose, and Harold lived in Verona, just five short blocks away from the office. The surveillance work was going well as the reports came in to the Pope.

The unsuspecting Horowitz brothers ran through their day with a routine you could set your watch by. Albert said the office they occupy was a perfect layout for what they needed to do. And as he spoke he sketched some on a brown paper grocery bag. The small office building was tucked away off the Main Avenue on an adjacent artery. It sat between two side streets that led to a residential area and had lots of trees bordering its L-shaped blacktop-paved parking lot. Albert continued with a blow-by-blow description of the Horowitzs' habits.

Gail and Barry Horowitz arrive each morning promptly at eight. They arrive in separate cars and head directly to the back lot that has six designated parking spaces, all parallel with one another. Harold pulls in between eight-thirty and eight-forty-five depending on whether or not he stops for bagels. He parks his Chrysler next to Gail's car religiously, for some odd reason, and never next to Barry's. They all use the rear entrance to come and go throughout the day. Visitors, on the other hand, always use the main front entrance.

Each day Gail leaves for lunch and returns in less than thirty minutes' time, lunch bag in tow. Harold will sometimes leave around 10:00 a.m. but always returns no later than 3:30 p.m. The few clients or vendors that happen by during the business day routinely use the side lot that has angled parking, and all enter through the front door reception area. Frank Batista chimed in with Albert and commented on what "sitting ducks these assholes are" as they ran down the evening news report for the Pope. Again like clockwork.

Gail is the first on to leave at precisely four. Harold follows exactly one hour later, locking the door behind him. The dedicated Barry is left alone toiling over the books until six. The intensity and determination in Ruggeri's eyes grew with every word spoken by his *capos*, and Batista made an annotation concerning the Pope's deep interest, basically asking what's in it for them—meaning the organization. "Maybe a couple of free funerals?" was Albert's laughing reply only to be cut short by the Pope as he said, "I take this all very personal," with a loathing in his voice. "And so will you," he added sternly. A paroxysm of hatred ran through his wiry-framed body as he continued to rant over the gall of these two men.

In his eyes they were nothing more than slumlords who inherited a small empire of seedy apartment buildings—*ghettos*, to use a better colloquial word—from their late father. And all centered in the most decrepit areas of the Third Ward. The two Horowitz brothers now wanted to expand their wealth to a better part of the city using deceit and bamboozlement under the guise of the law. The two brothers were young and eager. Both were well dressed and well educated; however, they should have chosen another profession.

Ruggeri outlined the exact details of a simple plan based on the information his captains brought forth. There was no need for him to physically see the layout. The word of his experienced crew was enough. He wanted to snatch one of the brothers and coax them into leaving Zarrillos' funeral parlor alone. The old-fashioned way, the Bloomfield Avenue way. He left the table and entered his private office at the rear of the club. His conversation with Domenico was brief and spoken in Italian over the phone. They agreed to meet at the funeral parlor, Wednesday, at precisely 4:00 p.m. There would be only one corpse in the front viewing room, the recently departed Carmine Guida, and another on a gurney downstairs in the preparation room.

Albert Marrone, all 250 pounds of him, drove the dark gray Chevy sedan throughout the side streets that surrounded the office encampment with peeled eyes. His cocked fedora sat snugly on top of his silver-gray head of short-cropped hair. Joe Russo, the smallest of the trio, sat next to him, fiddling with a black wool *gupaleen*, and John "Dee Dee" DeAngelis, weighing in at about 240 pounds, sat inconspicuously in the back, his *gupaleen* already on his head. Albert glanced at the time on his watch as Gail Horowitz drove her car out of the parking lot and made a left on Derwent Avenue. It was 4:06 p.m. Operating under the cover of the cold, dark January night, Albert switched off the headlights and eased the sedan into a parking space far away from Harold's Chrysler and out of the vision of the office. He shut the engine and looked at his watch. It was 4:51 p.m.

Harold Horowitz put his arms through the sleeves of his drab wool coat and neatly wrapped it around his puny body as he looked up at the round clock on the wall that read 4:59 p.m. He slipped his small hands into a pair of gloves, placed his Russian fur hat on his head, and said in his naturally feminine voice "Good night" to his brother as he grabbed his briefcase, and left for the evening. He cut through the damp, biting air toward his car with his head down and coat collar wrapped around his pale cheeks. He never noticed the dark sedan parked or the two sinister men that emerged from it until it was too late. Within seconds, with the swiftness and stealth of a commando unit, the two gorillas snatched Harold off his feet and whisked him away like a bad child, knocking his hat off his head during the brief ruckus. DeAngelis wrapped his mitt-sized hand over Harold's mouth and smothered his futile attempt to scream while Russo held him by his squirming legs. They threw him head first into the outstretched arms of Albert, who pulled him forcefully into the backseat of the sedan, he himself cursing over his arthritic pain as he tightly held down the realtor. Harold was stunned by a close-fisted heavy blow to the back of the head and a numbing shot to his kidneys delivered by Russo who climbed into the backseat as well. In a matter of seconds the puny realtor was bound, gagged, and lying on the floor under the weight of his briefcase and Russo's feet who assured him if he made any movement at all he was gonna kick his *fuckin'* brains in. Albert slid behind the steering wheel and they calmly drove away. It was exactly 5:06 p.m. All three mobsters lit cigarettes while Harold Horowitz pissed his pants.

Albert Marrone made no eye contact with the approaching sedan driven by Frank Batista, his fedora cocked to shadow his face in true wise guy fashion. With him were two passengers, Joey "Two Ton" Lotta and Angelo "Al" Alteri, both fierce, evil, and brute ugly men. All were en route to seal the other brother's fate. Batista tossed his Lucky Strike cigarette butt on to Claremont Avenue as they slowly passed Horowitzs' office and turned up the street that led to the driveway. The black sedan backed into the same parking spot as did the other crew. The three sat motionless and waited until the upstairs office lights went dark.

It was 6:10 p.m. Barry Horowitz had his back turned to the parking lot with the key in the rear door lock as the two hulking men wearing longshoreman's garb briskly approached, their black wool *gupaleens* pulled tightly over their brows and ears and guns drawn, their vaporized breath steaming like charging bulls. Sensing the looming approach by their mirrored reflection in the glass door, Barry spun around and stood frozen against the brick wall of the office, his eyes hypnotized by the sight of the two massive men that appeared out of the shadows and now completely blocked the vision of his parked car and his escape.

Lotta, the evilest, was the first to shoot—without remorse or hesitation. He put three fast rounds of the silencer-equipped .45 caliber automatic into the chest cavity of the doomed accountant. The force slammed him back into the closed door, sending his body into a seizure. Within seconds, Alteri sent more bullets into his midsection and groin area, causing the man's feeble legs to buckle behind him as he fell to the ground in an unnatural position.

The two gunmen simultaneously emptied the remaining rounds into the lifeless corpse, sending bone fragments from his skull and pieces of pink brain tissue flying, leaving him unrecognizable. An eerie red mist of blood mixed with the smoke from the guns hovered over the dead man's body like a cloud. Alteri pried the briefcase from the dead man's grip and stripped him of his personal belongings. They calmly got in the awaiting car that had pulled forward. The trio drove out of the parking lot, making a right-hand turn into the residential area. They all lit up cigarettes and commented on how easy of a hit it was. The car full of mobsters laughed and wondered when the body would be found, giving reference to all the sealed and shut windows of the nosy neighbors that probably hadn't heard a thing. They were right. The body would lie there for hours, but once found, the gruesome underworld elimination of Barry Horowitz would send a chilling message.

The men drove to a very precise and specific address deep in the heart of the city's poverty-stricken Third Ward. They picked their time, wiping everything clean, then tossed a brown grocery bag that contained the handguns, the dead man's wallet, and his Presidential Rolex watch in an alley where it was sure to be found. "Mannaggia la Mort…" Batista cursed to himself over the act. He wanted to keep the Rolex.

Prior instructions had been given to Albert to drive back to the funeral parlor and wait in the car entertaining their little friend until Batista arrived, which should be around six or six-thirty. The shaking realtor was facedown into the floorboards of the car being tormented by verbal descriptions of what the gangsters were going to do with him, telling tales of torture and unthinkable punishment, all of which were recalled from the memories of actual past hits. Harold felt another flow of urine leak from his uncontrollable bladder. He forced himself to fight off the panic from his mind. He could not think of absolutely any reason why this was happening to him. Surely, he thought, this band of thugs meant business, but they must realize that they have the wrong fellow. *What enemies do I have?* he said to himself. He lay motionless and talked himself into a more poised state of mind confident that when he got untied he would be able to convince these people that this must be a terrible misunderstanding.

Harold heard the sound of the fine-tuned engine of the approaching Chevy then the opening and closing of car doors as his kidnappers all exited the vehicles, including his watchdog. The men huddled and exchanged a series of inaudible utterances; then all became quiet to Harold's ears as they all merged to the rear cellar doors. Batista left the group and started to walk into the parlor's side entrance when he turned to the thugs and said, "Who's watchin' our friend over there?" The goons laughed and lit cigarettes and exchanged glances among themselves then at the parked car. Two Ton replied with a dumfounded look, "Where the fuck is he goin'?" He did have a point.

Angelo Ruggeri spent the hours prior to the Horowitz's kidnapping and sanctioned hit together with Domenico and his mother in their upstairs apartment feasting on fine imported Italian cheeses and meats, talking about the former archaic Sicilian *mafia* and the more modern *La Cosa Nostra*, the meaning of honor amongst men and the long-standing tradition of *vendetta* and *Omerta*. He was trying to extricate the undertaker's soul and conscience into acknowledging and accepting the methods of his extortion through the use of third parties' stories. Ruggeri was actually giving instruction and forewarning to Domenico and suggested he, and his family, "close the funeral parlor for a while and take a nice vacation somewhere." Domenico raised a brow and said, "But, Don Ruggeri, our business?" Ruggeri answered curtly, "Continue your immediate business then close, after all, gentlemen, it's not like people have reservations for the near future to come here as a hotel, and just as soon as my business is finished with these men, you'll return." The hypothesized metaphors were recognized by Domenico who gave a nod of approval and let Ruggeri know he was "most appreciative," but he did not need to lessen the blow about what was going to happen. He gave his oath on his mother's life that whatever he heard or saw would go to the grave with him. He wanted the realtors to be punished, and rightfully so. His now brazen anger flared. "We must have vindication," stressed Domenico, "for the anguish and torment they put us through, and still they were at it." Humberto entered the apartment and humbly apologized for the intrusion. He informed Ruggeri of a man downstairs waiting for him. Ruggeri sensed a weakness in Humberto's character a long time ago, and it was agreed, along with Domenico, to keep his brother in the dark about the hideous plot to save the funeral parlor. Ruggeri followed the two men down the banister stairway where Batista was standing and received a commendable nod from the neatly dressed gangster. Humberto was given instructions by his brother to stay upstairs and mingle with the friends and family paying their respects to the departed one and made him swear on their mother he would not come down to the morgue. It was agreed. Ruggeri followed the short, bald man down an almost secret passageway far from the mourners who were smoking and crying in the downstairs waiting room and away from the smell of flowers.

The gangsters standing outside were all dressed in blacks and gray overcoats with their collars pulled high around their necks. They blended well with the dark shadows of the funeral parlor. A metallic-like squeak caused them to cast a look at the cellar door that slowly crept open, giving way to the basement embalming room and the moonlit bald head of the undertaker. He gave a nod then let the door close. Frank Batista returned to the group. He signaled to Marrone, and without a word spoken, almost as if their actions were rehearsed, all went into action. Batista walked briskly back to the sedan, carefully climbed in, and began backing up until it was parallel with the cellar doors. He had his arm swung over the seat back, looking through the rear window as he offered some words of encouragement to the fellow hogtied and gagged on the floor. "How ya' doin' back there, my friend? Don't worry, it will all be over soon." He glanced at his image in the rearview mirror then back at the realtor. "Do you think I look like Cary Grant…" Only a murmured moan was returned. Russo and DeAngelis walked to the edge of the driveway and acted as sentries, smoking cigarettes and keeping an artful eye open for any passersby. Al Alteri grabbed the outside handle of the cellar door then waited for Frank Batista's lead.

The little man on the floorboards felt the powerful arm strength of Joe Lotta as the mobster reached in and lifted him off the floor then dragged him out of the car. Lotta then literally threw him down the gurney ramp that sat under the Bilco cellar doors and into the arms of Alteri. The puny realtor was dragged some, his knees and shins bruised on the concrete floor, then roughly dropped flush on his chest and chin by Alteri. The calmness he forced on himself in the car was now replaced with a daunted state of convulsive shock as he lay in darkness, hands and legs bound, and writhing in pain. The entire crew scurried down the ramp into the dark chamber that was illuminated slightly by a fluorescent lighting fixture on the other side of a partitioned wall. Horowitz heard the metal door gently close and a faint squeak of the well-oiled hinges and throw bolt as it locked into place.

Lotta and Alteri lifted Horowitz up like a piece of cargo and clumsily tossed him on his back atop the cold bed of the morgue dissecting table. The porcelain chimed from the force of the drop. Harold was hurting. He was also petrified and confused about all the cloak and dagger type of mysteriousness happening. He prayed someone would remove this awful gag so he might have an opportunity to speak. Harold's wide-opened eyes became blinded as the bright overhead fluorescent light of the lamp was turned on. He tried to focus on the laboratory-like surroundings and the nauseating smell of embalming fluid and death. He turned his head side to side and rotated his eyes, but his field of vision was limited. He could not at all conceptualize where he was.

The men stood scattered about the room out of Horowitz's sight and in complete silence. Ruggeri motioned to the two shooters and pointed to the partitioned room then said softly, "Go change." The men hustled behind the partition and stripped their blood-splattered clothing off, piling them neatly on top of the sheet-covered corpse lying on a gurney. They slipped into fresh clothes that were folded and waiting then walked out and took their position alongside Batista. Tomorrow, Mr. Virgilio will be prepared for viewing, neatly dressed in a fine blue suit and laid out inside a silk-lined coffin resting comfortably on a cushion of bloodied evidence.

The somewhat slow and deliberate scuffing of shoe leather on a cold tile floor was the only sound heard as Ruggeri casually walked around the table. He stopped at the right side of Harold. "Nice to see you again, Mr. Horowitz." His voice was soft and downbeat. "Do you know who I am?" All Harold could do was motion with his head as he uttered a muted no to the outlined features of the man that stood in front of him. The lighting fixture above was blinding. Horowitz was forced to close his eyes as Ruggeri walked to the other side. Ruggeri bent his torso slightly toward the realtor. He was in a position that made the fluorescent light and cigarette smoke eclipse his features. Harold reopened his eyes slightly and saw the outline of the devil himself. Ruggeri silently motioned to the undertaker to act. Harold felt the undertaker's cold hands as he somewhat gently began to remove the gag from his mouth. Harold summoned up a bit of courage and tried to speak. Ruggeri forcefully put his hand over Harold's mouth to mute him. "Listen carefully to what I am going to say to you and answer my questions truthfully, and you may walk out of here alive." His voice was deliberate, and every word was spoken with perfect enunciation and just a hint of a slight Italian accent. Ruggeri never raised his voice in anger. "I'll ask you again… do you know who I am?" He leaned closely into Harold, and as his features became crystal clear, Harold immediately recognized him from the restaurant. He spoke with a tremble in his voice as he barely uttered, "Rullo." "I'm afraid, Mr. Horowitz, that you've made a mistake about that. My name is Ruggeri…Angelo Ruggeri. I'm not at all afraid of telling you that because chances are, you will never live to tell this story?"

Suddenly Harold put two and two together. He'd heard of this man before. He'd even seen some published photos in the newspapers. He closed his eyes and acknowledged the awful truth and surmised identity of the man standing over him—Angelo Ruggeri, the notorious mobster. His words were faint. "I-I have a suspicion." Harold continued in a dreadful way. "But surely, sir, there must be some kind of mista—" His words were cut short by the cold hand of Ruggeri placed over Harold's mouth. Ruggeri leaned toward the frightened man and gave a pensive stare directly into Harold's tearing eyes then said with a vile tone in his voice, "Shut your mouth. I don't make mistakes." Harold lost all control of his emotions and began sobbing under the weight of the mobster's palm.

Ruggeri reached for a towel then motioned for the undertaker to come into Harold's sight. As he wiped his hands, he asked Horowitz with a nefarious grin, "Do you know this man?" Harold answered in a disbelieving tone of voice, "Mr. Zarrillo?" It suddenly came to light. Harold's eyes bugged. He was in the morgue of the funeral parlor, recalled to his memory from a chattel inspection he had done on the place not too long ago. He began sobbing again. "I still don't understand. Why are you doing this to me?" Ruggeri motioned for Zarrillo to step away, and for the first time since this nightmare began, Domenico felt some trepidation and broke out in a cold sweat. His fear was Ruggeri was going to ask for his abiding hand in murder, but as Ruggeri began to speak, his inclinations changed. Ruggeri began castigating the little man in a very chastising way, denouncing his behavior he had displayed, not only to his friend the undertaker, but also to all the poor people he had abused and exploited over the years, calling his crimes far more heinous than any offense he himself has ever committed. "I may travel with a dangerous crowd, Mr. Horowitz, take a look around, and make no mistake about it, these men are dangerous, but you, you're a virus that must be destroyed, the way you tried to destroy the Zarrillo family."

The scolding turned loathsome as Ruggeri's tone turned into the devil, with threats and promises of death. "You see, Mr. Horowitz, we do not have to hide behind the letter of the law. We have our own rules. If it were up to me, your blood would be draining on this table right now." His words turned to rage as he demanded apologies for the double-cross of his good friend and a full admission of his guilt. Harold sobbed and wholeheartedly confessed to everything and more. He was in mortal fear of his life, now sweating profusely under the weight of his overcoat and the menacing threat and anticipation of death.

Ruggeri felt there was no need for everyone to be in the room. He gave a simple order to the two shooters. They were to leave and go stay with Albert who was outside waiting. Then Ruggeri said in a baneful tone, "Mr. Horowitz. I am going to give you one month to get your affairs in order." Horowitz felt faint as the last words spoken made him shiver. "Take a good inventory of your assets and search for your life insurance policies." Ruggeri paused and lit a cigarette. He hovered over the man and gave him a sour look and said, "You are going to be allowed the luxury of doing that." Silence filled the room briefly as he exhaled smoke into the rays of the fluorescent light then bent over and whispered in his ear, "Your brother is not as fortunate as you are." Ruggeri walked around the foot of table and came up on his other side. Horowitz's eyes followed. Ruggeri shot a stare at the undertaker as if to prepare him for what he was about to hear next. "He lies in a pool of his own blood as we speak," he said with grave resolution. Harold's eyes were red and swollen, and his mind was drifting in and out of a dream state. He knew the tone of Ruggeri's voice and the menacing words he was hearing from the dapper man talking truly indicated that he was not kidding. Harold was terrified of what was going to happen to him next. Ruggeri whispered instructions to the undertaker who immediately left the room. He began opening draws and cabinets looking for a knife or blade to cut the ropes that were binding Harold. After a brief search he produced a long scalpel-like tool from one of the drawers then walked back to the table.

Harold lay trembling on the dissecting table with his eyes closed, fighting back his culminating tears. He did not open them until he felt the rough hands tugging at his bound arm. Ruggeri ordered him not to speak as he began cutting through the rope that held him. He said in short, steady breaths, "In a short while, within a few days, men will come to visit with you. They will be businessmen I know and will make you an offer to buy out what you think is your little empire you're trying to build in my city…your little ghetto as I see it. And you will sell them everything that you own, every piece of property, every piece of dirt…with the exception of your home. I have no interest in that although I should put you in the street as you have so many. These men will present you with an offer and you're to accept it, no questions asked." With those words spoken, Domenico came back in the room and unlatched the dead bolt of the outside door then the Bilco doors. The two men lumbering who came down the ramp were recognized by Harold. His eyes bugged. More evil men from the Italian restaurant, he thought, as Ruggeri continued. "And I assure you, Mr. Horowitz." His words were cruel and sarcastic. "If you resist them in any way…you will be back on this table and I *will* drain the blood from your veins personally. Do you understand, Mr. Horowitz?" A despairing "Yes" was answered back. "Good," Ruggeri said. His tone became more benign as he spoke, "We're going to let you go now…with the hope for your sake…you understand my wishes. If I hear of any inquires made…if I hear one thing, from anybody, about our little meeting tonight, and believe me…I will, your life is over. Do you understand that?" Harold's head rolled onto his right cheek away from the threatening voice as he acknowledged the heed. He did not want to look at Ruggeri anymore and hoped his memory would be erased from his mind as he heard the brutal man speak again. "I know you live in Verona and that's fine. If you wish to stay there, that's fine also…but I never want to see or hear of you again." He finished and gave a silent order for his goons to take him away and then began rummaging through the realtor's grip-style briefcase that contained a mélange of contracts and other real estate–related papers. Harold's disheveled body was hoisted to its feet and held in place by the firm grip of John DeAngelis as he waited for further instructions. The feeble legs of the little man gave way under the pain of his bruised knees and he almost dropped to the floor. He made an inquiry about his briefcase and was answered by the Pope in a vile tone, "You won't need this anymore tonight. Tell the police it was stolen by the niggers that mugged you as was your watch and wallet." Ruggeri motioned his head toward the exit doorway and said "Get him outta' here" as he handed the briefcase to Batista with instructions as for what to do with it.

Angelo Ruggeri's work was finished. He watched all leave then walked over to the sink and feverishly scrubbed his hands as if to wash away his sins. He and the undertaker rode the elevator up the one flight and parted company. Ruggeri found his way back through the hallways that led him to where the body of Carmine Guida lay in state. He signed the guest registrar and picked up a small offering card off the podium then proceeded inside to pay his respects to the grieving widow along with her family and to firmly establish an alibi, just in case.

Harold Horowitz strained to get his sore, listless body out of the backseat of the sedan and did so before the goons made good with their threatening gestures and offering a helping hand as they did earlier. He winced and moaned and hobbled the short distance to the small all-night diner on the corner. His distorted image reflected in the bright stainless steel shell of the building. The patrons inside paid little to no attention to what seemed to be just another derelict drunk as he entered. Their eyes quickly shot front with a foreboding shun in anticipation of an attempted handout. That was not the case. A feeling of dread and apprehensiveness caused his hand to shake as he dropped a coin into the slot of the pay phone and dialed the number. The voice on the other end belonged to Gail who sounded uneasy and concerned. Barry had not come home as of yet, nor was he answering the office phone, and she was getting worried. He assured her he was okay and said he would be home soon.

Harold became lethargic as he dropped the black receiver back in its cradle and replayed in his mind the horror of the tale told him by Ruggeri. Was it true? Would this evil mobster actually commit murder to get his way? The unequivocal answer his conscience replied was yes. He dropped another coin in and dialed up the Bloomfield Taxi Service then took a seat at the counter. He began to feel nauseated from the reeking smell of fried onions and burnt hamburger meat as he waited for the cup of coffee ordered. Not a soul paid attention as he sipped black coffee with his trembling hands.

The cabbie let Harold out in front of his office then sped off. Harold limped up the driveway toward his parked car then froze in a cold fear. His brother's car was still parked in its space. He forced himself not to look at it for fear he'd spot his brother slumped over the steering wheel. He groaned as he bent over to retrieve his misplaced hat lying on the ground; then he woefully hobbled to his car.

As Harold swung the Chrysler from its space, the headlights caught glimpse of the twisted mass of a lifeless body lying in the shadows. Could this be his brother? he thought. Harold closed his eyes in disbelief, ignoring the situation as if it weren't true, then quickly headed home. A miscellany of morbid, fearful thoughts interfered with his driving. And to make matters worse, he was greeted suspiciously at the door by his all-so-worried wife.

She first began to scold the little man as one would a child, a child who broke curfew, but suddenly just stopped and stared in a quandary at his visible afflictions along with the agony he was in. He concocted up a remarkably believable story of how he was accosted by two young black youths while visiting one of his tenement projects. Harold received a short reprimand and a look of disgust from his wife as to why he would even go to such a despicable place at night. Another well-told lie ensued. He firmly rejected her request to involve the police and told her to make no mention to anyone about what he had just told her for fear of his life. She timidly obeyed his wishes.

Harold downed a couple of sleeping pills with hopes that the sedative would ease the anguish he was in and put him quickly into a deep sleep trance. He laid his head on the pillow anxiously awaiting the narcotic to kick in, praying it would prohibit his subconscious mind from reliving yet another nightmare of what he had just experienced. The phone rang at two-thirty in the morning waking him. It sent convulsive shivers throughout Harold's drug-induced body. Forced by a few startling shakes from his wife to answer, he fumbled with the receiver some as he leaned over to do so. At first his mumbled words were incoherent. Finally, he slurred "Hello…hello—who is it" as he cradled the receiver between his ear and pillow. The hysterical and spasmodic voice on the other end was Gail; her frenzied words were hampered amidst a bevy of shrilling screams and incoherent stammering. The police detectives had just left her house informing her that her husband was found *murdered* outside their office in what they believed was a robbery gone astray.

A quick investigation ensued as just a matter of protocol. The case was pretty much an open and shut one, and proved relatively easy for the investigative detectives and the state prosecutors. The evidence was overwhelming. An unsuspecting black youth, a known gang member with an extensive criminal and drug record, was apprehended with both handguns used in the murder and the victim's wallet in his possession, his wrist adorned with an exquisite Rolex. The information was provided anonymously. Although Harold could not positively pick him out of a lineup as the one who actually mugged him, he quickly recognized his brother's possessions as they were entered into state evidence. He also squeamishly perjured himself, as he was instructed to do, during the inquest and the brief trial stating that the defendant was indeed the one who beat and robbed him on that cold January night. The inexperienced hand-selected public defender was no match for the justice-seeking prosecutors and could not produce one witness to back up his client's alibi. It would take years before the truth that could have exonerated his client is known. Reginald White was sentenced to death for the manufactured crime and the grisly murder of Bernard Horowitz in what was the shortest murder trial in Essex County's history. The atrocious assault charge involving Harold was dropped.

After Harold buried his brother, and within a very short time, he inked the documents relinquishing all of his real estate holdings in New Jersey to three separate real estate management holding firms. All of his deeded assets were sold for far below their appraised value—under the guise of "wanting a quick liquidation" of the properties so he could forget his horrific ordeal. The Horowitzs' empire consisted of thousands of units of bricked tenement and apartment houses, some prominent, others pure slums; all of his retail and commercial holdings and thousands of acres of undeveloped land; all gone and now belonging to Ruggeri and his "shell" real estate machines. Harold sold his Tudor-style home in Verona and relocated in Southern Florida. His widowed sister-in-law retreated to Lakewood, New Jersey, and became a Hebrew schoolteacher—and all were never to be heard from again. The anticipated money that was to be made on this shanghai of a transaction was going to be astronomical according to Ruggeri's people who immediately began slicing up the healthy portions of the pie amongst the favor-granting and future corrupting politicians that made up some of the matriarchal figures in the Pope's world.

The quizzical Zarrillo brothers along with their mother returned to Newark after a monthlong stay in Italy. They continued to operate their business from the Bloomfield Avenue funeral parlor until the completion of their new establishment that was currently under construction. It would be an almost exact replica of the French chateau that they once almost had, and now would be all theirs, proudly standing on a prime corner piece of property located on Pompton Avenue in the secluded, upscale suburb of Verona, New Jersey—the charitable compliments of Angelo Ruggeri.

3

Hinsdale Place is tucked away at the far end of an old, addled neighborhood of North Newark. It's one of the last residential streets located in the far northeastern part of the city—beyond it the factories, railroad yards, highways, and the nefarious waterfront, and as of late, a calamitous construction site. The short, twisting street doglegs from Broadway and ends at Chester Avenue with a cemetery in the middle. It's a curious type of residential street lined with large, matured maple and oak trees, their insubstantial roots breaking through the concrete sidewalks at will, and their irregular husky branches would, under sunlight and moonlight, cast peculiar shadows everywhere. The thick bark of some of the old, tattered trees had been chipped away. The sturdy tree trunks were riddled with deep-cut knife wounds, target practice by teenage street gangs showing off their skills; others bore cupid's hearts and arrows of the young couples who, over the years, skillfully carved the promise of love everlasting.

On any given hot summer day, the softened asphalt street would be overrun with impish children with dirt-smudged faces and threadbare clothes dodging and chasing each other playing their street games of *ringalereo* or hide-and-seek. In some instances the children would be running from an irascible mother who was with a wooden spoon in hand, a threatening gesture that a good beating was to follow.

The meager homes that ran up and down the narrow street were all mostly multiple dwellings, two- or three- or four-family units built just before the Great Depression, and with an array of materials, anything on hand that builders could find. They were occupied by the families of immigrants migrating to Newark hoping to find work in the area's factories, railroads, or waterfronts. Some of the homes were conveniently built on low-level ground while others were elevated following the natural grade of the land; this method cut down on the amount of excavation that would have been called for to arrange them neatly, in a tidy row after row. Most of the small, raised front yards sat behind painted cinder block retaining wall, walls that doubled as balance beams, circus tightropes or baseball backstops for the children who imagined. The centered aging concrete steps and stoops that ran from the sidewalks bared their coarse poured aggregate and were now beginning to show their settled age in the form of distinct cracks that ran helter-skelter.

This Friday, morning will arrive in a huff on Hinsdale Place. Daybreak will come in the form of an enormous *kaboom* from the demolition crew's heavy steel wrecking ball. The burly crane operators along with the rest of the heavy equipment operators of Union Local 825 begin their shift at precisely 5:30 a.m. and have little to no regard for the still half-asleep neighborhood. These ragtag groups of iron men who work for the Lyndhurst Construction Corporation form their work gangs with the rising sun in their eyes and billowing diesel soot in their lungs. Each crew member will break away from the morning "roach coach," swallowing the last bit of a soggy bacon and egg sandwich or a buttered hard roll, slurping down the rest of the bitter coffee served, and grumbling amongst themselves. "I thought it was supposed to rain today?" was the common refrain heard between the men as they all mount and systematically fire up and ready the machinery they are to run, much to the dismay of the irascible and provoked residents whose lives and daily routines are affected by the highway construction project. "Fuck 'em," "Fuck 'em all" were the exact words used by the belligerent crew foreman directed genuinely to the complaining residents of the city of Newark, New Jersey. He continued barking orders to his crew. "Don't listen to them. It's way too hot this time of year to begin any later in the day, and we bust our asses today, we finish early, and no work tomorrow."

Hate letters were sent and sullen phone calls were made to Mayor Leo Carlin's office, his hands tied tighter than a kidnap victim. He had bigger fish to fry. Just before the concrete was to be poured for a foundation of one of the overpass viaducts, workers noticed what seemed to be human body parts entangled among the reinforcement rods. The investigating police detectives confirmed as they examined the hoisted bodies and the crime scene together, "Out-of-towners." The pencil-thin mustache slithered atop the snarled lip of Detective Accardi as he stated to his partner covertly, "Our boys wouldn't do this type of work without a permit." Then he wiped the sweat that rolled from his slickened dark brown hair with his handkerchief. His partner winked and answered snidely and gave a short nod, "Yeah, you're right. They're mobsters from Brooklyn. There is something about holes dug and concrete that attracts this type activity." Duly noted and agreed by both, the New Jersey wise guys are not that concerned over their dirty laundry. They'll leave it in the streets, in the rivers or at more classier places like the men's room of the Palace Chop House or the Robert Treat Hotel.

Later that morning, Mayor Carlin bum-rushed the press out of his office and did his best to pacify the remaining demonstrators that set up camp outside his office door. He reminded them of their vote. They all read, supported, and approved the city's memorandum. "They knew of the up-and-coming project, after all, it is their tax dollars paying for the much needed roadway improvements," stressed the mayor. But still they all objected to the project's early start time and the increasing amount of gross disrespect that the gruff and rude laborers show the good citizens of the neighborhood.

As the early morning progressed, groups of annoyed citizens would mulishly gather along the site amidst the rubble and airborne debris. Threats of physical harm and wishful death directed at the foulmouthed passersby could be heard from the men wearing the grime- and dust-covered overalls and yellow hard hats. The good citizens would pugnaciously return the compliments via obscene hand gestures and a steady refrain of bawdy curse words. They would not be intimidated by the loads of concrete and stone dumped from bulldozer buckets and aimed at their feet as they gawked and spat at the crew from behind the perimeter barricades of cyclone fencing. And when the dust and smoke cleared, they would all chime in again. Passing mothers would frantically cover with the palms of their hands the innocent ears of the children to protect them from the thunderous crashes and the crew's vile vulgarities that also echoed. One really disturbed and provoked resident turned sniper and fired a few rounds from an M1 carbine into a crane's long steel boom from the rear window of his Hinsdale Place house with the high hopes of putting it out of commission. The operator thought his life was threatened, but it was determined by Newark's finest, the shots fired were indeed just warning shots and not aimed or intended for any one individual. The Union upheld the denial of hazard pay that was subsequently requested.

The undisputed fact remained—the thundering sound of the demolition was unrelenting. It echoed loudly off the rear of the row houses that lined the northeastern section of the city in rhythmic succession. And all day long it would persist. Each and every precise impact of the chained ball that repeatedly swung from the crane's screeching cable hurled thousands of pounds of concrete, brick, and steel to the bottom floor of what once was the Federer's Meat Packing Plant with explosive roars. Each crashing roar was accompanied by large plumes of dust and debris that lifted high in the air and a deliberate snarling "Yeah" from the operator's gritting teeth.

Despite the fact that most of the working citizens had already begun their day, grimacing as they heard, and watched as their coffee cups rattled in their saucers and cupboards, there were still a few neighborhood night owls who still wanted a little more shut-eye and tried like hell to ignore the construction din.

There was one teenage boy in particular, still comfortably asleep in spite of the incessant racket, kept trancelike in a deep unconsciousness by the gentle, almost metallic whir of the running window fan. But before long his semiconscious body would begin to react to the clamor with restless, involuntary tossing and turning as if it were in anticipation. Suddenly one huge tremor shook the house violently. It rousted the sleeping teenager from his dream state, causing him to sit up at attention in his four-poster bed. His face bore a stunned expression of "What the hell was that?" The boy's previous night's escapades kept him out until almost two in the morning, and he prayed the forecasted rainstorm would put a damper on the construction, allowing him a little more sleep, but no such luck. The storm would not come until later on in the day. And with his eyelids now wide open, the teenager was slowly becoming fully conscious and aware of the noise and fracas closing in around him.

The kid stretched out his arms and yawned in relief as his awakening soul slowly and grudgingly accepted the irritating racket. He folded his hands behind a head of rumpled black hair and laid back in his bed unmoving, with the exception of his eyes that were darting back and forth toward the direction of each detonated sound. His facial expression bore a look of curiosity as he turned his head to and fro, trying to identify each and every sound he was listening to. Explosive sounds of demolition mixed with boisterous human voices all continually grew louder and louder as they persistently seeped in through the seams and cracks of his bedroom door.

And along with the deep vibrations, he heard the turbulent roar of the Caterpillar diesel engines that powered the mammoth yellow bulldozers, front-end loaders, and road graders all working in unison—leveling and paving a new stretch of highway not more than one hundred yards from the back of his house—all creating gnarling sounds of grinding gears and clangs from heavy machinery and a salvo of roaring pistons from powerful truck engines. The rat-a-tat of the bursting jackhammers and the thunderous bangs of the concrete and debris being scooped up and slammed into the steel beds of the ten-wheeled Kenworth dump trucks added to the commotion. An occasional cannonade of loud laughter and cursing fanfare could be heard between the burly crew supervisors and their laborers as they chomped on cigars shouting and lamenting at one another, condemning their work duties, the city of Newark, New Jersey, and the miserable August heat.

The trumpeting of automobile and commercial truck horns resounded from the bumper-to-bumper morning traffic. The doleful motorists were painstakingly annoyed for the detour that snaked them around the site until finally becoming a crawl's pace on Riverside Avenue and the adjacent roadways. To further exacerbate the situation, a fool-hearted commuter completely ignored the flagman's barrier and his command to stop. His Buick sedan nosed out just far enough to be met and crushed by the Caterpillar's steel tracks as the operator sped blindly in reverse. The operator's mordant response was a cynical "Ahhh fuck it" as he continued wildly on his way without missing a beat.

The boy's attention turned to his closed bedroom door. He heard the escalating sounds of a raised temper and the raging voice of an obviously infuriated woman. The voice the boy listened to was distinct and repellant, one he recognized immediately: *his mother*.

He tiptoed to his door and cracked it open ever so gently. He listened with opened ears and peered into the kitchen with wide eyes. He was able to just see his father's profile and every so often a flash glimpse of his mother. Her ponytail swayed hotly as she moved about. She began slamming cabinet doors and drawers as she cursed, having what seemingly was a one-sided argument with the man who sat calmly at the kitchen table. Her drumfire was accompanied by the soft voice of Frank Sinatra playing on the radio that sat on the counter. The censurable man sitting squarely at the kitchen table showed little emotion. He was doing his very best to ignore her rants and raves as he hid behind his morning newspaper, slurping his coffee and chain-smoking his Lucky Strike cigarettes. But on occasion, he would duck his head down and flinch some. The boy cowered some and bore a devilish smile as he thought, *I wonder what the old man did now.*

The kid left the door ajar and leaped back into bed. He glanced at the old alarm clock and the time it read. He wondered hard and was suspicious as to why his old man was even up at such an early hour. Something important caused his mom to raze the old man. This type argument, this almost daily common occurrence, was usually reserved for dinnertime. He listened intently to the razor-sharp tongue of his mother as she unloaded a barrage of verbal scorn as only she knew how. She was not at all afraid of the hulking man or his feared reputation. "You son of a bitch…how could you?" Her voice broached emotions of rage and anger coupled with heartrending sobs. "What are we supposed to do now?" There was a brief silence then bedlam returned. "You're no fucking good, Anthony, you never were." Her soprano-like voice made an almost metallic sound as it reverberated off the hanging pots and pans and the stainless steel baker's racks that filled her huge kitchen. As she began to realize her exasperations were falling on deaf ears, each new outburst became louder, more black and vile, until the man finally surrendered.

The deep, husky voice that finally succumbed to her wrath did so with a calm and serene tone of voice. What could he say? He was guilty. He could only beg her for forgiveness. "Everything's gonna be all right, dear," he said with attrition. "You're gonna' get the money back in no time. I swear to ya'. Now ya' just gotta' trust me on this one, okay, hun, gimme a little time." The few carefully chosen words he continued to speak were of an apologetic nature. Sincere words and phrases said with the hopes of settling her down, which they eventually did.

And after a long silence the only sounds the boy heard from the kitchen was the sausage meat sizzling in a cast-iron skillet and the swooshing and pinging the fork was making as his mother whisked and beat eggs feverishly in a glass bowl.

The last time she had counted, there was over five thousand dollars neatly wrapped, placed inside a wooden cigar box, and carefully hid deep in the back of the darkest corner of her closet, and it was discovered by her, just this morning, the box was empty. The woman's piercing voice escalated as she began another bombastic attack of verbal anger and mimicry. "Everything will be all right, dear—everything will be all right—gimme some time—trust me. BULLSHIT. That's all you know how to say." She was beyond frantic. His serene basso voice answered, "C'mon, hun, settle down now." "Goddammit, Anthony," she replied. "That money was supposed to go toward the house, our house." The glass bowl echoed loudly as she slammed it on the countertop. "The house you been promising us for...how long now?" She caught her breath and her anger. Her tirade eased as she began to pour the scrambled eggs into the skillet.

The kid managed to hear enough to understand the gist of the argument and why his old man was taking such a beating: money! It was always about either money or respect. In this case, it was the lack of both, from his mother's standpoint, and the frustration of a middle-aged scorned housewife faced with the burden of trying to make ends meet with the paltry allowance given to her by her husband each week. The onus of her husband's nonchalant attitude when it came to him pissing away thousands of dollars gambling and staying out all night long gallivanting with his hoodlum friends was just more than she could bear. And to add insult to the already injured spirit of the woman was the brand-new 1959 Cadillac Coupe de Ville parked in the driveway. The boy sighed a bit and laid his head back on the crumpled pillow. He slowly drifted back to sleep for only what was to be only a short while.

The boy was noticeably startled as his bedroom door abruptly flew open and immediately found himself the recipient of his mother's wrath. "Whaddya' gonna' sleep all goddamn day?" she snarled. Her pencil-thin brows were raised and her eyes wide and pensive. "You're another one, a real *scorchamend*. Breakfast is almost ready. Now get the hell out of bed before I get angry," she yelled as she slammed the door shut behind her. He dared not say a word. Her chilling voice could still be heard beyond the closed door loud and clear as she continued. "I wish I could sleep all goddamn day like everyone else around here."

The kid yawned wide and rubbed the gritty sleep from his eyes. He grudgingly crawled out of his bed and let go with an audible moan that accompanied a good stretch of his cramped back and leg muscles. With a couple of steps he was in front of an old wooden dual-framed window of which one section was halfway opened. A small rattling window fan was wedged between the other; it was turned off instinctively by the boy with a flick of a switch. He pulled the cord on the venetian blinds to fully raise them and squinted at the bright morning sunlight they let in. His first attempt to raise the window completely was in vain. With his open palms and a grunting "Jesus Christ," he gave the structure a second forceful heave upward to further lift up on the heavy shell and engage the counter weights.

The old wood and glass shuddered and the rope pulleys creaked as the framework rose up in stammering intervals, then soon was fully open to let in the early morning August heat in all of its glory. The air was thick, humid, and just about as loathsome as the sooty black smoke billowing from the diesel exhaust pipes of the machinery below. He leaned out of the open window almost up to his waist, balancing his weight on the sill. The boy was very tall for his age, standing almost a solid six feet, and his weight was close to 180 lbs of naturally lean muscle mass—a well defined specimen with broad shoulders and chest and thick arms, a physique that made him seem older than he actually was to all he met. The gold chain he wore, a medal of St. Francis, and a gold Italian horn attached, shot out bright glints from the sunlight as it dangled from his neck as he observed the view in all directions. To his left he saw a barrel of a man dressed in dirty denim pants and a stained raggedy Guinea T-shirt with a crusty old painter's hat atop his bald head. In the corner of the yard attached to a chain and running circles around a tall rusted pole was the old man's German shepherd, barking feverishly at everything and anything. The old man's sweat was dripping down his face and off thick patches of silver hair that protruded from under his T-shirt. The burly coarseness practically covered every square inch of his arms and back. He too was making a racket banging away with a hammer driving nails into what looked like a wooden something or other.

The kid watched the old man for a couple of seconds. Then with a slightly bewildered look on his face, he waved and shouted out, "Hey...Mr. Tremarco, what are you building?" It was supposed to be a backyard greenhouse, according to the blueprint. The old wiseacre shouted back, his voice competing with the construction din, "It's a coffin...for my old lady, who wants to know?" The kid retorted with a frown, "Oh yeah...while you're at it, why don't you build one for that dog of yours." The old man grimaced and laughed, coughed a few times, then spat a nice hocker on to the ground.

The kid shifted his weight a bit then pulled himself back into the house. He stood hunched over, silent, with his elbows and forearms resting on the windowsill. His sight drifted and became focused on the barbed top edge of the rusted chain-link cyclone fence that ran along the backyard property line. He was somewhat hypnotized as his eyes followed the jagged brim of the formed cut and twisted wire until the fence itself disappeared behind an old withered, white-washed garage. The boy hadn't really noticed just how much that old structure was leaning to the left until now, and it seemed ready to topple over. An old rusted, tattered wheelbarrow with splintered handles was resting up against a piece of weathered plywood that was nailed to the side of the garage. It covered the opening that was once a window. Next to the wheelbarrow, sitting on top of a pile of crumbled concrete block and brick, was his old Tonka Toy bulldozer he enjoyed playing with as a kid, and that seemed not so long ago. Its bright yellow paint all but gone now replaced with dents and dull patches of rusted metal. Gone also were the tomato plants and vegetables that used to grow in his father's now forgotten and abandoned victory garden. The small patch now just a barren section of dried dirt and weeds surrounded by a mass of rusted twisted chicken wire nailed to half-standing poles. The kid rolled his eyes and let out a rueful laugh. The only thing detectable in the backyard that wasn't covered in a dirty red oxide or severely weather-beaten, tattered, or in complete ruin was the brilliant black ebony paint and gleaming chrome of his old man's Cadillac parked below, nosing out a couple of feet past the rear of the house's corner edge.

The boy gave the backyard a last look with a deliberate regard. His eyes squinted as he looked beyond the fence and the construction site, past the railroad yard and factories that sat in the industrial wasteland, up over the elevated highway viaducts, and slowly focused in on the distinct skyscrapers of the New York skyline rising above all the dust and smog and glistening in the sunlight. An intense desire lay heavy on his heart. One day when he was older, wiser, when the timing was right and he had enough money, he would move far away from this absolute slum of a neighborhood that he lived. The kid gradually awoke from his daydream and lost all interest in the goings-on behind his house. Breakfast sounded like a great idea. He slipped into a pair of gray athletic sweatpants and a Guinea T-shirt that were both draped over a chair then readily took inventory of his tiny domain.

The twelve-by-twelve-foot bedroom that he slept in was atypical and for a teenager. The furniture that was scattered about was old and scuffed, and calling it used would be an understatement. A high-back mahogany armchair that doubled as an end table and clothing valet sat next to the tarnished four-poster brass bed. On it sat personal things and a very old-fashioned wind-up alarm clock that no one in the household had ever heard ring. One truly interesting fact was, if a stranger poked his head in for a peek, the sparse room hadn't a scant of any visible evidence that would give indication that this was indeed a teenager's room. It was more reminiscent of a room occupied by a secluded tenant seemingly all alone in the world. However, the closet told a different story. One pull of the lightbulb chain illuminated an array of freshly pressed pants, mostly black, and matching Italian knit and cotton blend dress shirts hung, perfectly spaced, from a sagging round pole that stretched wall to wall as did the shelf above; its contents were some neatly folded sweaters and an assortment of shoe boxes. A couple of exquisite imported Italian suits sat to the far right, still covered with the "martinizing" paper from the cleaners. Lying on the floor were four pairs of shoes, shined to a mirrorlike finish. Needless to say, it was his room and it suited him perfectly fine, lending itself to what was considered his pleasures and hobbies: fine clothes, reading *True Crime Magazine,* and creating secret hiding places for his ill-gotten cash.

The kid slipped out of his room and followed the *faux* Persian carpet runner down the hallway on tiptoes. He paused at the spot in the wood floor that creaked to eavesdrop a bit and noticed the ruckus between his mother and father had subsided and was now amazingly a light and peaceful conversation. He shook his head in disbelief. How did the old man talk his way out of that one? He was accompanied down the hall by the soft crooning voice of Perry Como. It drifted from the speaker of the old box radio that had its own sanctified place on the counter and was hardly ever turned off. The aroma from the breakfast fare was enticing and made him anxious to sit down and eat. His mother's rule was that he was to wash his face and hands and brush his teeth as soon as he woke up before he entered the kitchen. A simple request he had no problem abiding by. As he passed his mother and father's bedroom, he glanced over and studied with regard their framed wedding picture sitting atop the dresser. His parents did once make a handsome couple.

The boy rinsed the octagon soap from his face with a couple of palmfuls of cold water then gingerly, and with a degree of care, used his wet fingertips and the palms of his hands to style his unruly hair. He looked at himself in the mirror admiringly, pompously. He knew it and he certainly heard it enough—he was a handsome kid, and now, having reached puberty, was ever so giddy proud of the crops of dark hair forming on his body. His father was right when he said "Eat the hot peppers, kid, they'll put hair on your chest." The boy's mother along with relatives and strangers alike would always say, "You look just like your father when he was young," and it was true, he thought, as he studied his facial features so altruistically in the mirror. He had all of his old man's recognizable traits—black wavy hair, shadowed sad eyes, a chiseled chin, a defined roman nose, and just slightly oversized ears with fat lobes.

He exited the bathroom with only the day's felonious wrongdoings on his mind. He began to sort out his agenda knowing that his father would ask and would expect a detailed list of events. He must be prepared with the lies he would tell him. He thought and gloated, today shouldn't be any different than any other day since exiting Barringer High's classrooms and starting his summer vacation two months ago. While other classmates he knew were assembling at the Arlington Avenue Elementary School playground, choosing up sides for a baseball or basketball game, or congregating for a day of swimming at the community pool, he'd be doing what he liked best, running chores for his father and his circle of thieves, or better yet, for one of the other wise guys from the neighborhood. No bagging groceries for this young man—no, sir. There'd be no toiling with a lawn mower or a rake, and he was not to lift so much as a hammer or push a wheelbarrow for his uncle Lefty's boss for fifty cents an hour. "Chump change" as his old man would so colloquially put it. And as was pointed out by avenue wise guys, he wasn't about to take two busses to Hillside to pump gas at his uncle Joe's gas station either. "And what—smell a' grease n' oil like all grease monkeys do—whatsa' matter with you?"

Instead the kid chose a more prosperous vocation. He would be making his scheduled rounds on and off Bloomfield Avenue, from what was considered one end to the other of their claimed and sanctioned territory, running his exploited deeds for a select group of wise guys who rely on the prowess of this slick, young street urchin. Yes, today was going to be just like any other day in his life, so he thought. Perhaps had he known the true events that were about to unfold on the eve of his sixteenth birthday, he would have stayed in bed.

The name on the boy's birth certificate read Anthony Joseph Marino. He was the only child born to Celia and Anthony Salvatore Marino and was considered by both beholding and ever-so-grateful parents a miracle baby since twice before Celia's attempts at motherhood resulted in the deaths of each fetus before her third month of pregnancy. She always blamed her husband for the prior mis-carriages—perhaps it was the stress and torment that he put her through. Her semi-religious husband always blamed God. Either way, she finally gave birth to a perfectly healthy eleven-and-a-half-pound baby boy on August 20, 1943. Her husband, having a very dark sense of humor, joked after his son's birth and, counting all toes and fingers, would tell everyone, to the point of almost bragging, that his kid's size made up for the first two his wife had lost.

And as the boy grew he was introduced by his mother and came to be known as Tony. Some of his father's crew and other neighbor-hood cronies tagged the boy with their own sobriquets derived from and according to the rules of respect and humor. He was known as Little T, Tony Boy, kiddo, and Sonny—that last being the moniker his father liked that soon evolved to simply "son." And he thought how funny that his father never called him by his birth name, as his mother always had. He would only use the name Tony in third-per-son conversation. To the boy's face, it was always an informal: "Hey, son, I want ya' to do this, or son, do that…" And God forbid someone should use any form of a bitter or hateful nickname on his son—God forbid, although this type of trademark was very common around the Praetorian mob-controlled city and throughout the neighbor-hoods within. Practically everyone on the avenue had some kind of pseudonym, a well-earned nickname attached or tied on to their names. The motivation for some of the monograms would be obvi-ous—derived from certain traits or characteristics or sprung from an obvious physical disability that one might have either been born with or acquired. Perhaps this act of labeling was considered a sin and cruel by some, but no one could stop it, nor did they at all want to. And it would always be an everlasting form of laughter. And now the young Tony Marino would take offense to anyone besides his own father who ever dared call him Sonny Boy.

The patriarch of the Marino family, Anthony Sr., Big Anthony, is in every sense of the word, a mobster, and a rogue mobster at that. His cardinal business has been and still is crime. His partners and associates were now just a small handful of the local wise guys and a few career criminals that run rampant, their hands in a variety of everything considered to be unconditionally illegal and immoral. He was quick tempered and quick fisted. An imperious sort of man who never had a kind word for anyone, and it seemed the older he got, the worse he got. He was known in his younger days as Cheese, a nickname given to him years ago by one of his cronies and a duly noted name that carried every bit the reverent and underlying meaning of a Big Cheese—an old-fashioned acclaimed honor that only a few could actually back up with action. A few of the older Outfit guys and capos still referred to him as Cheese Marino while the younger and newer crew members renamed him Big Anthony, a nickname that size-wise suited him to a T.

Cheese has never been an indulgent man who doted on or liked to conjure up old heartfelt memories, but he did like reminiscing some and relish his life in the past, privately, and in his own way. In his opinion the past was a much better lived time for him. He was happier and so much richer then. In his younger days his persona was gregarious, that of a *persona importante*—a big shot with a pocket full of cash and no boundaries or limits on spending. He had the charisma and magnetism of a Hollywood movie star, or so he was told by many. He was well respected and somewhat feared by his peers, the men who made up his inner circle of bootleggers, loan sharks, bookmakers, thieves, and murderers. Physically he was a big man, standing six feet tall and weighing around 225—that of course in his prime. He boasted broad shoulders, beefy arms, and a thick neck that held up a large stubborn Calabrese head. His muscularity and his hardened facial features came from a rugged childhood of toiling labor and brute strength fist fighting in the coal mines and steel mills of southern Pennsylvania where he grew up.

Now the big man was lugging around an extra fifty pounds of fat that wrapped around his once defined muscular chest and torso like padding on a NFL linebacker; pushing his waist close to a size 44. His once full head of wavy black hair was now thinning and receding some and showing a lot more salt than pepper. The deep-cut age lines and battle scars he bore about his forehead and around his eyes, perhaps induced by years of worries and challenges of mob life, were more prominent than ever. With all that past glory days now gone by the wayside, he was just about eking out a living being forced to carry out menial tasks and chores for the various factions of crime families that ran the New Jersey mob and the city of Newark. He was flat broke now and deeply in debt to all the wrong people.

And now he sat, peacefully, with lit cigarette in hand. The steamed morning argument had subsided. He blew smoke rings in succession and watched from, afar, his wife doing what she did best: cook. Ceil was a short well-built woman, curvaceous with shapely thighs, buttocks, and large breasts. Her skin and complexion were almost a golden tone. Her face was virtually free from wrinkles, even around her large hazel-colored eyes. This was something she often thought of as a fluke considering her age, her worriment, and her strife. Her small bowed nose was attractively askew, broken slightly along with a pinkie finger, both the result of a tomboyish altercation with a neighborhood bully when she was a child. She was a tough, feisty woman who came from good Italian stock and, since a young age, has spent most of her time in a kitchen. Her dyed dark brunette hair was pulled back tightly in a ponytail that fell just below the nape of her neck and rested on the back of the light blue house dress she was wearing. She was graceful in her movements, her side-to-side sashay about the kitchen, from stove to sink to the refrigerator almost dancelike, keeping time with the beat of the music playing from the radio. Her voice could be heard humming or copying a lyric or two. Her prior madness and rage was now in check. How did he let her become so full of rage? Big Anthony thought as his face wrinkled into a boyish smirk. He glanced over her shoulder and peered out the rear kitchen picture window. The blue sky he viewed was being choked by clouds of dust and debris and huge puffs of dirty exhaust, and still the clamor of heavy-duty construction. Big Anthony's eyes were fixated, staring into blind space. He pulled a cigarette from the pack, almost second nature, without ever once focusing on his action, then placed it between his tired lips and lit it up. The smoke he exhaled slowly vanished along with his wife's hopes and dreams of ever moving out of this house.

The Marinos lived at 62 Hinsdale Place and occupied the second floor apartment of a very old converted three-family house. The white clapboard siding that extended below the shingled mansard roof covering the house was starting to weather as now also the once forest-green trim. A dull gray painted concrete stoop with a galvanized pipe railing took you to the brand spanking new solid wood entrance doorway that seemed so out of place. A small handwritten sign was tacked next to what used to be a doorbell. Its faded print read "Please use side door."

The old house was owned by Big Anthony's mother-in-law, also named Celia, who bought and paid for the property with the proceeds from her late husband's life insurance policy and herself residing on the first floor. The third floor was nothing more than converted attic space apartment rented out to whoever wanted to climb the stairs, now presently occupied by a young Japanese couple. Anthony Marino and his new bride accepted a gracious invitation and moved into the Hinsdale Place residence right after they got married in the early spring of 1939. It was to only be for a short time until they were able to buy their own home, which in itself was an uncompromised idea and promise that had been lingering for years.

The entire decor of the Marino flat was indicative of their son's room—a mishmash of drab furniture cramped into the tiny living room space. However, their bedroom set was of fine highly polished dark wood of the Italian Renaissance style, and actually purchased at a fine furniture store on Abington Avenue. This was Ceil's restoration in the faith of her husband's word and bond. But it seemed that, as of late, Big Anthony's refrain of "We'll get new stuff when we move" was so redolently beginning to fade as the wallpaper. As a quick fix and a cunning way of appeasing his wife, Anthony concocted a wild scheme to remodel their apartment, one requiring the original floor plan to be completely forsaken. The original wall separating the dining room from the kitchen was torn down to create a huge combined cooking and eating area for family gatherings.

A long wooden table with thick carved ball and claw legs was the centerpiece of the *Cucina*. It was a handcrafted piece comprised of fine wood and was meticulously finished and just about filled the entire room. Ironically, this masterpiece of a table was surrounded by an odd assortment of wooden chairs—all but two being unrelated to one another. Over the years many a *pezzonovante* sat side by side at that table, and all feasted on impressive Italian and other ethnic dishes prepared solely by Ceil. Her cooking was so renowned throughout the neighborhood that top chefs and owners of some of the finest restaurants in Newark would ask the big man for an invitation to dine and steal a recipe or two. The savory aroma rising from a commercial oven and stove filled the air, and was the first thing one noticed, and was evenly distributed throughout the house and neighborhood by a large ornate ceiling fan that spun silently. The second thing, besides the table, was the gigantic oversized atria window that practically took up the whole exterior kitchen wall. Not part of the original architecture by no means but meticulously fitted into place. The old original double-framed window was removed to bring in the material needed to build the entire kitchen project.

Big Anthony was proud of the job his wife's brother Lefty did on the remodeling project. And he has a standing invitation to sit down at any Marino Sunday dinner. Joseph "Lefty" Carollo was a carpenter by trade and managed to pilfer and steal every piece of wood, every nail, every door, every cabinet and countertop, the linoleum, and the exquisite atria window from all the new home construction he worked on. His labor and supplies was tribute used to pay down a gambling debt owed to Big Anthony and the rest of his cohorts.

The teenager bolted into the kitchen with a ravenous appetite. He went directly toward his mother. She was standing at her usual and desired perch, the stove, with her back to the room. The kid offered a casual "Mornin', Ma" without at all mentioning the morning ruckus that had just taken place. His thick skin was well tanned with respect to family squabbles or wars in this case. He watched his mother put the finishing touches on the prepared breakfast of sausage, eggs, fried peppers and potatoes, and a loaf of toasted Italian bread. He poured himself a cup of freshly brewed coffee from the percolator atop the stove and headed for the table. He spoke to his father inquisitively, "Mornin', Pop. You're up early." His father returned the greeting in his gruff style without looking up from the morning paper's sports page. Tony took his seat and wondered why his father was up this early—and dressed? He was either dressed for success or court, thought the boy, in his best wise guy fashion: black and white Italian knit short-sleeve shirt, black dress slacks, see-through silk socks, and black alligator shoes. The clothes and shoes, in spite of being somewhat worn, were still quite debonair and befitting of the aging thug. The strong smell of sandalwood from his Zizanie cologne was competing with the savory smell of the just-fried sausage and potatoes and eggs that were on their way to the breakfast table.

Both men were silent now, bouncing legs and drumming fingers, waiting impatiently for breakfast. Another detonation of construction din made both father and son flinch. They looked at each other then at the kitchen window, grimacing at the racket. "Whaddya gonna do?" his old man commented nonchalantly. Tony said with a grin, "I heard old man Schwartz took a couple of shots at the crew the other day." His father replied tongue-in-cheek, "Crazy bastard, too bad he missed, or did he?" Anthony growled and complained out loud as he caught another newspaper headline: MOB VIOLENCE CONTINUES. The article contained the sketchy details of someone he knew that was gunned down in the streets of Brooklyn. "Jesus Christ…another one bites the dust," he said with a grimaced frown. "He was a bum anyway." He gave the daily obituary page a glance; this was a morning ritual many saw as morbid, but Anthony assured all that there was a method to this kind of madness.

The clicking sound the gas jets gave as they were turned off and the customary slam of skillets being piled into the sink gave notice that food was on its way. Ceil Marino gave her prepared breakfast a final taste test for seasoning then began to pile up the plates as she asked, "You boys ready to eat?" "I'm starvin', bring it over," Big Anthony shouted back at her with the tenacity of a bear. The old man sat with a boyish grin on his face as he shuffled the newspaper aside, extinguished his cigarette, and squared his huge forearms and elbows on the table, assuming his favorite "ready to dig in" posture. His position was at the head of the renaissance table at the far end of the room where he could sit and observe the entire goings-on in the kitchen and enjoy the view from his picture window, a view now compromised, but this duly noted seating arrangement would never be compromised.

Ceil's loosely fitting house slippers spanked the floor with every step she took as she carried two enormous plates of food from the stove to the table where her two men sat with their mouths watering. This large-scale meal prepared this morning was not for any special occasion; this was the way she cooked and they ate on a daily basis, and one should ask why father and son were so big.

Big Anthony gave his son a congenial backhand slap on his arm, raised his eyebrow, and said, "Watch me get your mother goin'." "Pop...you already got her going this morning. *No*," the kid said with a bemused smirk on his face. Big Anthony shot him a cocksure grin then winked as he turned toward his wife and said, "Hun...how many times I gotta' tell ya' about carrying those heavy plates, next time you make two trips." He finished the glib remark with a hearty laugh. Tony Boy let out a congenial laugh himself out of respect for his old man's sense of humor; he was simply acknowledging the joke his old man stole from an aired episode of *The Honeymooners*." It was a joke he heard numerous times before in other types of similar situations. Big Anthony belted out a somewhat harmonious "Ti voglo ben'assai" in as best a tenor's voice that he could muster as Ceil turned her back in a huff and shook her head in a mocking semi-disgusted way. But by the time she reached the stove, she bore a whimsical grin. The loud, loose-slapping heels of the house shoes she constantly wore around the house was the object of another standing joke between the father and son, and he said aloud, "She'll never be able to sneak up on us, kid."

Both father and son dueled as they plunged their forks into piles of food and began filling their plates and mouths, not necessarily in that order, with the savory breakfast sausage, peppers, potatoes, and eggs. They truly seemed to be hungry men. "How is everything?" Ceil asked humbly as she stood by the stove. She already knew the answer by the voracious chomping sounds. "Maronna mia...delicious...come sit down...have something to eat before your son devours it all," Big Anthony said amusingly as he gently slapped the back of the kid's head. "No, no, you two eat. I'll eat later," she said with a soft voice. Then she elevated her tone. "Just save me a little, and eat slower. It's not a race you're having," Ceil said as she began to clear off her kitchen counter and fill up the sink. For some strange fixed reason perhaps only known to her, she would never sit down at the table and join all for meals whether it was breakfast, lunch, or dinner. She was old-school about such things, very subservient and catering even with the invited Sunday dinner crowd who always were family or close friends. She would always wait patiently until everyone was seated and the family-style dishes served were on the table. Then, and only then, when all guests were well into the meal, would she take her reserved seat and join in. It was just the peculiar way she was. Perhaps it was an inherent oddity, or she sincerely got great enjoyment watching people eat and enjoy her cooking, as her husband and son were doing now.

Big Anthony gazed at his son and pondered moody thoughts as he shoveled the food in his mouth. He sighed and then with a baneful tone in his voice asked his son, "So…whaddya got goin' on today?" "Not too much of anything, Pop," Tony replied reluctantly also with a mouthful of food and a contrived smile. He suddenly knew this conversation was not going to go well at all just by the change of attitude written all over his old man's face. He watched with his peripheral vision his father's weak smirk turn evil, upside down evil. He sensed anger in his father's eyes as his second question forced the boy to look into them. "I gotta' run a couple of errands for Tick Tock, that's about it." The boy's tone became intentionally casual and confident. "Then he's gonna bring me to the club and see if I could work the card game tonight. The small game—he's been promising me a shot at it." This he said very nonchalant, almost amusingly. Big Anthony hid his displeasure of the words his son was speaking behind the *Star Ledger* until he could stand no more. The paper folded shut in a violent way. Then it was tossed across the table in a disheveled heap. The boy's innocent grin was erased by his father's hard hand slap to the table. It shook the room and echoed off the walls. Tony did his best to ignore the rage by slowly grabbing for another forkful of food, but the devil made him look up. He watched in fear as his father's demeanor immediately turned ice-cold. It was as if the devil himself suddenly put an obscene mask atop his father's face. His old man snapped back at him, his voice ringing like Satan himself, echoing louder than the bulldozers working outside.

"Yeah…well, I think I'm gonna need ya' at my place tonight," he said sourly as he jabbed his fork in the general direction of his son's head. This forced his son to instinctively jump from his seat. "The place needs to be straightened out a little. I want to run a game tonight too…and what's up wit you hangin around Pope's joint so much anyhow?" His anger was building. His face again became more distorted with hatred as he ranted, "And I told ya…stay the fuck away from dat guy's joint for a while, goddammit!" He finished his tirade with a nefarious stare into the boy's flinching eyes.

The boy's voice became insolent as he tried to return the stare. "Whaddya talkin' about…I never hang at the Pope's place. And whaddya' worried about that for anyway. I'll stop by your place first if you want, all right!" Tony Boy said flippantly. Big Anthony's face was a grotesque beet red. He flew off the handle and went into a wild and impetuous rage. "Worried…who's worried? I look worried to you. Thadda be the day I worry 'bout you or the fuckin Pope. And you know what, fuck that Batista too and the rest of those Bloomfield Avenue bums." Big Anthony was spitting food from his mouth as he surmounted a tantrum. At this boiling point, violence was sure to follow. His puffy eyes became slits as he screamed, "Fuck em'all." Big Anthony gulped down the last bit of food he had on his plate. He swallowed his coffee and slammed the cup on the bare wood table with a tumultuous bang. Then he sprang his feet like an animal ready to attack. He was visibly infuriated and breathing fire. Ceil turned around and took a step toward her husband with both arms raised as if to place herself in harm's way, between her and the boy. Big Anthony pointed a vile finger and snapped at her, "You stay outta' this…you."

His large menacing bull-like body first moved left behind his son's seat then back to the right. His criminal psyche almost made him reach out in a more physical rage with the intent of harming his son. He had all to do not to. His hand was raised and ready to hard slap the boy's face. Then he restrained himself and took a deep breath. He began circling the table without ever once taking his eyes off his son until he felt his biting anger subside. He bore true meaning and genuine verity to the undisputable "Don't get Big Anthony mad." Thank God, both mother and son thought, as the phone rang. It sounded detached from the group and ever so loud. Ceil answered it immediately, her voice somewhat shivering, "Hello—oh hi, Albie…yeah, yeah—he's right here…" Her brow wrinkled and her eyes squinted and divulged every bit of hatred she could muster. "It's Albie." Anthony rolled his eyes reluctantly then took a deep breath. It took a few seconds for him to calmly rise from the table, his voice now coercively jovial as he said, "Albert—long time no see— *ma che quest?* For you, my friend, anything—but let me call you back in a few—*gabide?*" Big Anthony did not let on that anything was wrong in his secret society, and with mustered strength in his voice he barked at his son with a half-cocked arm and pointed finger, "I gotta' run. Call me later, and don't let me find out you were anywhere near the Pope's place—I'll put you against the wall." With continued anger, he stormed over to the bay window and leaned out. He waved his clenched fist at the construction crew and barked another loud tirade of profanities, all directed solely at the crew, along with threats of a violent and agonizing death. This made both mother and son flinch. The crew, in return, casually and jointly gave Big Anthony the finger.

Within seconds, as if nothing at all had happened, Anthony's face turned charmingly innocent, and he woefully sighed as he went to caress his wife and offer his usual routine goodbye kiss. Ceil snapped her head back and shunned him in disgust. Her actions created more Marino anger, renewed anger. His arm flew up in what was a mock display of a backhand slap as he growled through clinched teeth, "Yeah…*lasordida*…you too!" He stormed away red-faced. The strong scent of his cologne followed him out of the room and lingered in the air long after the door was slammed shut.

The wooden staircase creaked loudly under the weight of the lumbering Anthony as he began his descent down the two flights at a double-time trot that suddenly slowed to a crawl. He broke out in a shivering cold sweat. He braced himself against the stairwell wall and waited for what he thought was next to come. He hoped a massive heart attack would rid his life of the struggles, the burdens, the debts. But it did not come—instead came the inherent guilt of his vile outbursts toward his son and wife. In the deepest part of his soul he knew his ranting was nothing more than a fallacious cover-up of his own fear and worry. He knew what the phone call from Albert Marrone was all about even before he hung up the receiver. It was a subtle reminder of the surmounting debt owed to the Ruggeri Organization that now is a grim topic of daily conversation among the Bloomfield Avenue mobsters. Big Anthony wants desperately to keep his son away from the potentially dangerous knowledge that could and would be a threat to his own life if he persists with the mobsters. Perhaps this reason is why he vehemently scolded the boy only this morning and forbade him from Ruggeri's club. He knows the impending repercussion of his recent past actions at the sacred club and his now larger debt was going to be addressed harshly by Ruggeri. He just did not know when. Surely Albert knew this, the reason for the distressing midmorning call.

The argument presented by Ceil this morning was only the tip of the massive iceberg, one so large it was capable of sinking a fleet of Titanics, and he laughed to himself over that fact. If she knew just how much her husband actually owed to the boss of the New Jersey crime family, her bombastic rant would have carried far more fury than it did. She would have plunged that kitchen knife of hers that she so expertly wields deep into his chest. Ceil only knows of the money that was in the shoe box. She was not aware of the ten thousand dollars her husband borrowed from his ever-so-generous brother, money that was to be used to pay back gambling debts incurred over the last few months, debts that continually mounted as the luckless Anthony threw good money after bad, betting haphazardly on long shot horses and losing not with extreme worriment but with blatant stupidity. Then he would make even more ludicrous bets on sports matches, always opting for the long shot odds. And finally what could be considered the biggest mistake of his heedless life, the poker game, and he honestly thought and willed his fate with the strained rash hopes of recouping his losses that miserable night, that night at the Pope's white mansion that further indebted him. And yes, the man does have balls for he still gloats over the fact it took three of Ruggeri's men to subdue his rage and send him on his way, with a sense of hapless pride in his gait. It would be the same type hapless self-pitied gait he now was hobbling as he approached the bottom of the stairwell. He glanced back up the dark stairway and thought for a split second about bounding back to his home to offer an apology for all the morning fireworks and ask Ceil for forgiveness. That penitent gesture of goodwill was briefly lived. His face became contorted as he let out a rueful sigh and then said a wrenching "Ahhh *fanabola*" as he slammed open the doorway that led to the hot blacktop.

Ceil Marino gave a furtive stare in the direction of the intentional slam her husband gave the back door. She listened as the mighty V-8 engine roared and then disappeared down the driveway. Her wide-open eyes focused on the slovenly stretch of landscape that grew from outside of her kitchen window. Her body stood frozen. Her blank hypnotic stare was fixated on the shantytown beyond her backyard. Her innermost thoughts silenced the ongoing clamor of the construction. The clothes hanging on the line that ran from her window made her reminisce about the time her pet parakeet Peety got out of his cage and flew out of the open kitchen window. Each day afterward, she would hang his birdcage on the clothesline with the hopes he'd see it and return. The bird never came back. The sadness was reflected in her face as she turned away from the window.

Ceil was an uneducated woman, solecistic and unread, but being in possession of enough street smarts and common sense to survive in hers and her husband and son's world. She stood quietly and began to reflect on her troubled mundane life with the feeling of self-pity reigning strong. A doldrums life of menial chores: cooking, cleaning, doing laundry, and catering to a husband who hadn't any redeeming qualities. Well, perhaps just one that she could think of. Not once, throughout all of his fits of rage and anger, the bitter arguments between them, had he raised a hand to her or his son. And for that she was thankful. But this last burst of fury he displayed sent a bevy of mixed emotions through her mind. And the mere fact that he had no respect or disregard for her by stealing the cash she had managed to put away pushed her to the brink. First, sadness, then deeply rooted fear and worry for her and her son's future, and lastly vehement hatred and scorn for this ugly man who had just stormed out of the house. Tears of self-pity soon filled her eyes but were caught and replaced with hateful thoughts. She hoped he would never return.

Tony reached over for the disheveled morning paper that lay on the table and made a futile attempt to read some of the headlines and articles. The current events held his interest for all of three or four seconds before his mind wandered. Even the comics proved a bore. His puffy eyes gazed straight ahead in a daydream stare. His father's outburst had struck a nerve and made him wonder about the real reason for his anger. He had not an inkling of the trouble his father was in with the Bloomfield Avenue boys. And he nodded to himself in agreement that it certainly wasn't anything he had said or had done lately, so he thought. Tony gave the paper a toss into a heap and sipped his coffee. His mother joined him at the table with her own cup of coffee and the remaining pot. "Want some more coffee?" she asked. "Sure, Ma, yeah," he said. She poured the hot black brew in his cup and plopped down where her husband sat. She grabbed a fork and started picking on the remains of breakfast that the two men had left behind. There were a few moments of silence that surrounded the breakfast table. Then Ceil blurted, "You feeling okay, son?" "Yeah, Ma, I'm fine," he answered in a short manner. As most young teenagers, he was reluctant to hold an honest conversation with his mother and found it hard to look her in the eye. Most would call that guilt as he did also. And he certainly wasn't about to confess any sins to her.

"What was all that about with your father? Why did he get so mad? What's going on with you two?" Ceil asked concernedly. "I don't know, Ma...you know him," the boy said. "He goes nuts sometimes...like I heard you goin' nuts on him this morning. Same difference." The two sat in silence for a while. Then Ceil reached out and gently toyed with her son's head of wavy hair. Her face searched for the innocence of the moment as she made an attempt to change the subject and the atmosphere at the kitchen table. "Your birthday is tomorrow, huh. How old you going to be?" Ceil asked as she ruffled her son's hair a bit. "Sixteen, Ma...you know that," Tony said with a shy skittish grin. "But I think you want me to be six again?" Ceil spoke from her heart, "I'll make a nice party for you Sunday. Nice dinner, chocolate cake, we'll have some people over," those words said in a way that only a mother knew how to. Her son replied humbly, "That's all right, Ma. You don't have to. It's no big deal." Tony knew that no matter what he said, nothing, but nothing, was going to stop his mother from preparing a birthday feast for him Sunday. His eyes widened. "Well, if you're gonna, make some gnocchi...okay. We haven't had them in a long time." He finished his words with an ardent smile on his face. It was his favorite pasta dish. Bar none. Homemade morsels of delicate dough made from a simple mixture of cooked potatoes and flour swimming in red sauce, the gravy. So it was bequeathed and sealed with a wink of her eye. Homemade gnocchi it will be, along with platters filled with meatballs, sausage, braciole, and salads. Another feast!

Ceil Marino watched as her son's face grew resplendent, as did hers, with the anticipation of Sunday. Then slowly her face saddened and took more of a melancholy expression. Her eyes were fixated on her son. He was getting older, more mature. She was losing her baby boy to imminent adulthood. Sadness turned to fear. Perhaps her son was following all too closely his father's malevolent lifestyle? A ruthless, savage lifestyle and reputation she was well aware of before they married. She knew the type of roughish man he was and is, the business, his associates, with how he earned his living. She knew and she accepted it.

Her resonant concern now was that she no longer possessed the power, either physically or otherwise, to dissuade her son from the obvious poor choices he was making in his young life. He was too big to hit anymore as when he was just a child—and yes, it was Ceil who had the heavy hand and not his father. She alone dished out the punishment, sometimes harshly in the form of physical beatings that he received over the years. Perhaps she was too severe with her son? Then again, physical punishment was all she knew. A good spanking, with her shoe, her hand, a wooden spoon. What she thought to be a mother's tough love that may have now tempered the boy to the point of being impervious to pain and discipline. She could only hope that one day her boy will realize the importance of an education, on his own, and unlike her and his father, be inspired to go to school, continue an education past the basic high school curriculum, hopefully college or trade school. His current education was being taught to him on the avenue, Bloomfield Avenue. His campus was the stretch of neighborhood that ran from Summer Avenue to the Garden State Parkway right in the heart of wise guy territory. His classroom were the saloons, social clubs, and street corners that were in such abundance; his teachers and professors were the street soldiers, Angelo Ruggeri's capos and *Soldatos*. They come in droves teaching their version of psychology, the psychology of crime. The capos and street soldiers, the loan sharks and the bookmakers, the murderers and thieves that line the avenue and back alleys, all providing a hands-on crash course offered at University of Organized Crime. The boy was studying hard and rising quickly to the head of his class, but he had so much more to learn.

Ceil's overwrought feelings were dissipating. She shrugged them off like the true trooper her character proved her to be. She's already survived hundreds of heartbreaks. She was thinking more clearly now, more lucent, and was glad that the vociferous morning events had finally passed. Her simple mind was conjuring up a more carefree day ahead.

Tony instinctively grabbed the sports page of the *Ledger* up and buried his face in a story about Mickey Mantle and his father's beloved New York Yankees. "You want anything else?" she asked. "No, Ma…I'm okay," he said with a shake of his head. "So what did you tell your father you plan on doing today?" she asked suspiciously as she gathered the breakfast dishes.

He rolled his eyes then answered in a short, borderline nasty tone of voice, "Nothin', Ma." There was a second of silence. Then he said, "Hang out, I guess." Then he ranted sarcastically, "And what's with all the questions—you, Daddy. What gives—whaddya' want me to do, join the Boy Scouts…" "And what's wrong with that idea?" she asked with a quivering voice. "Maybe you'll learn how to grow up and be decent and not be like that father of yours, or his cronies." Tony tossed the sports section down on the table and let out a mocking "Ha…you married him…" Then his words became cheeky. "Oh, for chrissakes—join the Boy Scouts…get lost."

"*Statagitt*…you're just like your father with that smart mouth of yours." A violent look took over her face, and with a cocked and raised arm she snarled, "One day I'm gonna slap it for you." Tony flinched at the likely act; up till now, his mouth would be the only thing she hasn't already slapped. Tony lifted his head until his cold eyes met hers then spoke with a direct and inconsiderate undertone, "I'm gonna go to the avenue, Ma." The tone of his voice truly angered Ceil. *He's sounding too much like his father*, she thought. Ceil sat and fumed. The simple truth was, the boy's speech was full of slang just like his father's. His thick street accent was raw and sometimes vulgar to a point. He would become very loud and animated when he spoke, describing words and actions with just about every part of his gesticulating anatomy. His arms would flutter and recoil with motions and hand signs and pointed fingers. His *persona* was a mimicking combination of various characteristics and peculiarities he obtained from the all so many older, more mature wise guys he hung around with—a little bit from this guy, a little bit from that guy. The words and phrases he used were carefully chosen one-liner or clichés he stole from old movies he watched, which made him sound older than he actually was.

His father did show concern with the boy's pronunciation and made an attempt to correct it during his son's earlier, formative years so to speak. His theory on teaching him proper English was to sit him in front of the television or radio and tuning into a British broadcast or airing movie and grumble in his own slang, "Listen to how these people talk. That's how you're spose' ta' sound." The lesson did not work but he did pick up a few classic lines that he would incorporate in his repertoire, and if he indeed wanted, he was quite capable of speaking like Laurence Olivier; however, he preferred James Cagney.

Ceil shot him back a look of dismay and hurried off with a pile of dishes rattling in her hands. The crash they made as they hit the porcelain sink startled him a bit but not enough to distract him from his sports story he was slowly reading, but the loud, fast-paced clacking of her house slippers did. She was over him in a flash with the look of the devil on her face, this time her fists clenched in hatred. "What are you going to do, hang around with your father and the rest of those bums he hangs around with?" she said with gritting teeth. "I got a bad feeling today, Maronna mia. You're gonna' get in trouble…you're going to end up a bum yourself, mister, you know that?" He refrained himself a bit. "Ma, please, you worry too much." His words offered for the sake of peace. Then a brief pause before he spoke with a more forthright tone, "Right now I just want to make a little money for myself. It's innocent stuff, and I'm having a little fun. That's what summer vacation is for, now I want to earn a little money, save up for a car I'll be driving in another year." Ceil barked, "A car, like your father saved up, he can't rub two nickels together but he can buy a new car." She calmed a bit then began to speak again with a compelling voice, "And I'm not worrying. I'm just saying." His words grew louder and more intense as he abruptly interrupted her. "Ma, I know what you're sayin'. You're always sayin', and naggin', that's your problem. You're always—" Ceil's eyes became watery and she began to sob, her voice so remorseful now, "Okay, that's enough now. I guess I do just worry. I don't want you to end up like—" Tony read between the wrong lines. He jumped to his feet and became overly animated, wailing and waving his arms as he exclaimed, "End up like what? Like this? Livin' in a friggin' dump? Don't worry, I won't."

Her hand slammed the table forcefully, startling the boy. "That's *enough, goddamit*—how much I have to hear from you and your goddamn father." Ceil stared at her son with a contemptuous rage in her eyes and tried desperately to fight off the impending breakdown, but her emotions were overbearing. Once again her eyes filled with tears. She broke out in deep, sorrowful sobs. Tony's soul surrendered and suddenly he was overwrought, downhearted and remorseful, almost to the point of shedding tears himself, which he did, and both cried. He gently sat back down and wiped his swollen eyes then said remorsefully, "I'm sorry, Ma. I didn't mean—all that stuff." Ceil held a kitchen towel to her face. "You could be a real *Scocciament*, you know that?" Her voice became subdued as she dried her eyes some and let a quiet take over the room for a moment or two. Ceil glanced at her son with half a smirk and said, "Just like you're father!" All will be calm after the storm. Tony returned a sincere smile and nodded up toward a decaled plaque that was hanging on the wall. It read "I don't want to be a MILLIONAIRE. I just want to live like one." "Yeah, I know, Ma, but ya' know what?" His eyes firmly fixed on the tiny plaque. "Like I said before, you married him." They both laughed at the one bit of truth that rang out in the Marino household. Then Tony chimed in with another, "But we eat real good, don't we, Ma?"

Tony dashed from the table. He zapped into his bedroom and returned in a flash, and as he sat back down he smirked and gently slid a crisp fifty-dollar bill toward her clasped hands. She became startled. Her eyes opened widely as she backed away from the table slightly and asked, "What's this?" Tony grinned. "Why don't you go to the church tonight, Ma. Go play bingo...with the girls. Ya-know, have some fun...on me," he said proudly.

A fifty-dollar bill coming from a soon-to-be sixteen year old was a lot of money in 1959. His mother recognized that fact; however, just like the ill-gotten money received from her husband, there were no questions asked. No judgment rendered. She took the bill and stashed it deep in to her bosom and said "Thank you, son" as he scurried off back into his bedroom.

Ceil sat quietly in a sorrowful state as her meditating soul came to terms with the morning's embittered events. Her eyes scanned the newspaper's bold printed headlines of which she had absolutely no interest in trying to read or understand. To her the paper's only usefulness was to act as a receptacle for what was left of the breakfast, just something to scrape the orts from the plates into and throw away. She felt tattered. The arguments between both husband and son had left her exasperated. She had only the energy to let out a rueful sigh. Ceil lives a simple but methodical life; however, this morning's brawl did play a little heavy on her heart and soul. And now she is second-guessing her true existence. Perhaps she's grown accustomed to the workaday chores and humdrum social life? She does what is expected of her around the house. She cooks, cleans, cares for her only child, and gives herself sexually to her husband as frequently and as often as he desires though as of late his amorous advances have been few and far between. This sudden lack of interest is leading her to believe he has a *goomatta*, another woman on the side. This is an accusation that he flat out denies. He blames his high blood pressure and his excessive weight for his faltering libido.

A catchy Tommy Dorsey tune began to blare from the radio. The upbeat tempo gave Ceil the simple salvation needed to tackle the job at hand: the breakfast dishes that were piled in the sink. Her ponytail bounced in a rhythmic form about her shoulders. Suddenly her doldrums mood dissipated. The severity of the argument was almost forgotten already. Her husband, for as rude and callous as he is, will always take the time to call no matter where he is or what he is doing to see if she needs anything before he comes home. He'll bring home mostly all the meats and groceries for her to prepare. What more could Ceil ask for? Another feeling of glee entered her soul. Tonight dinner does not have to be prepared for anyone. There will be no chores to worry over and no Anthony. This Friday night will be all hers to do with exactly what she wants to do. She will not answer to a soul but her own. Chances are her son will eat at one of the local pizzerias or Italian delis, and her husband, well, he'll be out all night gambling. She's not planning on seeing his hulking body till morning when he'll come strolling in with a bag full of fresh-baked bagels or Italian pastries.

Tony entered the kitchen showered, ready, and anxious to get into the streets, his hair combed in a pompadour and held neatly in place by an application of fragrant pomade. His agenda would be full, at least up until mid-afternoon. His time would be well occupied with the chores and duties that his mentor Frank Batista had in store for him. He would visit his father's place out of respect, as he was asked. His evening would be capped off with the thrill of working at the Pope's notoriously posh club. This he would do in spite of his old man's warning rage and resentment.

He quickly hugged and kissed his mother who was at the sink with both her hands submerged in soapy water. In a huff, he uttered a brief "Later, Ma" and just about heard her say "Don't get into any trouble. What time are *you*..." before he rounded the hallway and bounded down the wooden spiral stairs in double time, leaving behind a trail of cologne that lingered a bit, just like his father's had done. Ceil finished the last of the morning dishes. She began to mumble aloud to herself. It would be a communicative attempt of self-defense on her part against the men in her life. "Boy Scout...that would be the day he became a Boy Scout...the little shit that he is..."

Her mood was more jovial than ever. She was pleasingly all alone now, rid of both hooligans. Suddenly a burst of newfound vitality erased her burdensome state of mind, making her feel so alive, so like a real woman as she sang along to an upbeat song by Dinah Shore that filled the kitchen. Ceil dried her hands. Then she eagerly grabbed for the old black rotary telephone and dialed. Ceil hoped that Margie would like to join her for a casual unconstrained night of bingo at St. Michaels Church followed by some *anisette*-laced espresso and pastries at Roberto's Café. They would both sit and flirt with the waiters or any passersby for that matter. It would be her treat.

4

Miss Joan Jankowski was sitting noticeably pert on the painted gray front stoop of her parents' handsome duplex. Joanie, as she preferred to be called, was just as strikingly pretty and presumptuous a young woman of sixteen could ever possibly hope to be. Her mature and curvaceous body, the perfect roundness of the cheeks of her firm buttocks, were accented by a pair of skintight white short shorts and rested on a colorful beach towel. Joanie's long, dark brunette hair was pulled back into a French braided ponytail that swept just below her shoulders. A classic red and white polka dot midriff sleeveless blouse boasted perfect coordination to a pair of white sneakers with red laces covering her just pedicured feet.

She had on a slight trace of rouge along with a primrose red lipstick that enhanced her natural facial beauty and made her seem to look a little older than she actually had been. This was a look that would surely have gotten a vote of disapproval from both her mother and father had they been there. Their absence was the unsullied perk a teenager gladly accepted from working parents. The girl's light olive skin tone was glimmering, manifested by her ethnic blend of a Sicilian/Polish heritage. Joanie's mother would liken her daughter's appearance to the Hollywood starlet Jennifer Jones. This adulation would go right to the young girl's head.

Joanie sat with her knees pulled tightly up against her noticeably developed breasts. Her bare arms were wrapped around a pair of healthy well-defined legs. Her large oval-shaped eyes shut and her head tilted some, resting on her bare kneecaps in a semi-sensual, semi-chaste pose. Next to her sat a tightly packed suitcase containing all the accoutrements a young teenager needed for a weekend down at the Jersey Shore. A tiny transistor radio was set to its highest volume and tuned to Music Radio 77 WABC, New York's premier rock and roll channel. The young girl's entire body was pulsating and both feet tapping in perfect rhythmic timing to the song blaring from the tiny radio, "Lipstick on My Collar" being sung by Connie Francis.

Joanie was impatiently awaiting the arrival of her cousin Barbara. Both Barbara and her friend Vickie were on their way over so the three girls could begin a weekend adventure at the shore town of Seaside Heights. This would mark her first time ever away without her parents. The planned unchaperoned weekend was the rage topic of mutual conversation between the girls for some weeks now. She was whispering aloud to herself and gingerly biting her bottom lip as she squeezed her thighs together. "Hurry up please…God…it's almost ten o'clock. Where are they?" The radio voice of Herb Oscar Anderson announced, "Coming up next, the morning news and traffic report." The broadcast of snarled weekend traffic and delays on the Garden State Parkway made her antsier than she already was.

Tony rounded the corner of Lincoln Avenue and immediately noticed her poised up on the stoop. His heart raced as he stopped suddenly and began to nervously formulate a plan as to what to do and say. The boy harbors an immeasurable crush on this girl and always had since as far back as he could remember. And as of late, as adulthood approaches, his thoughts of her are much more sensual. Be it as it may, his heart continued to beat out of his chest as he continued down her street. Joanie lived on a very narrow one-way street that had barely enough room for cars to park on both sides against the curb while allowing the traffic to drive down the middle of the travel lane. Although only a few short blocks away from Hindsdale Place, the newer more uniformed brownstone homes that line both sides of her street, gives the block more of a ritzier look than the rest of the neighborhood.

He was nearing her stoop. Tony openly changed his boyish persona to "cool" as he jammed his left hand in his pocket and swung his right arm, in synchronization with the slight dip in his step. His hipster-style gait slowed from its fast-paced stride to almost a standstill in what was hopefully a chance meeting with the girl of his dreams. He hoped she would spot him first and call out his name. He'd been walking on her street an average of three times a week hoping for the opportunity to present itself, and here it was and there she is, in all of her teenage physical splendor. He sighed to himself, *What a doll*, and as his heart skipped another beat, he sang just above a whisper, "To be here on the street where you live."

The now teenagers had not been strangers. Both knew each other since Mrs. Kirkland's kindergarten class and all through Arlington Avenue Elementary, each having a childhood crush on one another from time to time and his lasting right up to and including this very moment but with its limitations. Tony's father, with his own looming reputation, and the son's now up-and-coming "guilty by association" reputation was making itself known around the neighborhood. And the rumored narration heard was enough for Joanie's parents, especially her father, Henri, to encourage and insist that she stay far away. His rough and tumble "juvenile delinquent" style attitude really hadn't frightened her—nor has it ever, but for the sake of peace and parental respect, as of late she kept her distance and just observed him in awe from the sidelines. It was needless to say, he did have the mannerism and appearance of a young hoodlum portrayed so magnanimously in the cinema. He ran with a wild bunch of street thugs who called themselves the Golden Guineas. The members of the gang were all related to or had connections with someone of the local *Mafiosi*, and all had a vision of becoming mobsters themselves.

Joanie caught sight of the boy walking down her street seconds after he turned the corner. At first she had not an inkling of who he was and never on her block had she remembered ever seeing this character before. He was swank dressed in a black-and-white short-sleeve Italian knit shirt unbuttoned, and completely exposing a silk Guinea T-shirt that was tightly tucked into a pair of black dress slacks, perfectly tailored to just the right length over silk ribbed black socks and a pair of black featherweight shoes—every bit the young wise guy.

And as she wondered just where exactly he came from, as he neared, she caught glimpse of the familiar black pompadour combed high and wavy, and she answered herself just above a whisper, "He looks like—Tony." Suddenly her eyes lit up. She felt an instigated excitement build, a real stirring as he neared. She jostled herself a bit. Her arms went to rest at her side with taut elbows, her breasts naturally thrust out, and her glistening outstretched legs crossed at the ankle. This quick imitation of a modeled vogue pose was done with the hopes of getting his attention that unsuspecting to her already had done so.

Tony remained coy. He continued down the street on the opposite side to the point of almost passing her by completely; then suddenly he stopped dead in his tracks. He mimed a double-take in her direction, dramatically, and for her to see, with wide eyes and a raised inquisitive brow. He broke into a huge smile as Joanie waved excitedly and shouted, "Hey, mister." Her voice brought out his true boyish character and erased any mobster persona he harbored underneath. He just bolted in between two parked cars and dashed across the street, almost getting run over by an old Ford that came barreling along. He showed a demonstration of his bravado by signaling the driver with an Italian salute. Then with a lively dance-like jog, he was on the sidewalk directly in front of her stoop.

"Hey…Joanie…how have ya' been?" he asked in his best wise guy manner and with his heart racing. Joanie leaped to her feet and vaulted down the gray concrete stairs. She was taken aback by his smile and the handsome lines of his face. Her widespread arms quickly wrapped around the boy's upper torso and she gave him a loving, welcoming hug. She felt his arms fold around her in an embrace that seemed to last for a lot longer than the few brief seconds it actually did. "Tony. I haven't seen you for such a long time. What have you been up to?" Joanie took half of a step back and let her hands follow the contour of the boy's outer arms down until they reached his hands. Her fingers intertwined with his, and she gave them a frolicsome twist side to side and back and forth. "You look so nice," she said admiringly. Tony kept hold of her fingertips then gingerly yanked her toward him until their bodies met with a delicate slam. He brought her arms to her side and held on to her hands with a firm grip. Then with a semicircular motion he pushed her away some then gently reeled her in almost as if it were a choreographed dance step. His jubilant smile never left his face.

"So do you, Joanie…Maronna' Mia…you look more than nice, kiddo. You look gorgeous!" he said as he ogled her a bit. He broke away from their playful hold suddenly then nervously looked around the perimeter and boundaries of her house. His anticipated fear was real. He took a step back and he motioned with his head toward the front door. "Whoa. Where's 'yer father? He sees me out here he'll want to kill me…the crazy Polack that he is," he said tongue-in-cheek as he led her by the hand and nervously guided her to the stoop. His eyes were glued to the front door with apprehension. "Stop…he's not that mean…he's just…well, you know…my father," Joanie said as she twirled and plopped herself down on the bottom stair. "Not that mean! What about—the time—when was it, two years ago. He chased me around your backyard with a pipe. What was that? I had to jump over your fence to get away." His words ended with a swivel of his hips and head and arm pointing to the south. Joanie brought her hand to her mouth to cover a grin. Her eyes got wide. "Oh…I remember that. You were waiting for me…for what? I can't remember now. Oh well…you know how fathers are with their little girls," she said with eyes glittering.

Tony stood next to her, closely. He raised his right leg up then let it come to rest on the second stair. He folded his arms and propped them up on his knee. "You don't remember, huh? I was gonna take you to the Abington Avenue school fair that afternoon," he said sincerely. "But we never made it." He sighed in jest. Suddenly his eyes were drawn like magnets to her V-neck blouse and the soft mounds of her breasts. The fresh scent of jasmine and bergamot rose from her ever-so-noticeable cleavage. "Where did ya' get those?" he said as he motioned his head directly at her breasts. "I don't remember seein' those last year." "What…these?" Joanie said proudly as she pretentiously put her chin down and squeezed her arms and shoulders together, accentuating her cleavage even more. "I don't know…I woke up one day and there they were. Where did you get that hair on your chest?" she said laughingly. She slapped the concrete stoop with the palm of her hand softly and said, "C'mon. Sit down next to me." Tony smirked. "That's all right. I don't wanna get my pants dirty." "Oh, stop." Joanie blurted. She dusted off the stoop with her hand. "There—is that better, Mr. Vanity Fair?" Next she yanked him by his arm until he plopped down next to her, up close, with their shoulders touching. The two kids faced each other and started to ask the same question at the same time. "So what have you been—" They spluttered and stammered; then both broke out laughing. "Go ahead. You first," Tony said. Joanie said sincerely, "I was asking…what you have been doing this summer. I haven't seen you around anywhere." Tony's brow wrinkled. "I guess you haven't been lookin' real hard. I come down this street at least once a week." Joanie remarked with honest astonishment, "Really! I've never seen you. What time about...this time?"

"No. Usually it's a little later in the day." He glanced at his black strapped art deco–style *Longines* watch. "Closer to noon." "Well, that's why! I'm at the pool by then. And I was at summer camp for two weeks. Just got back," she said, amused. "Whoa...the pool... summer camp...tough life. Me, I've just been workin' like a dog, and you know...just hangin' on the avenue," Tony said in full animation. "The avenue...my father won't let me near Bloomfield Avenue," she said with a frown. Suddenly, Tony was drawn by her fragrance. He leaned closer and gently toyed with her ponytail as he whispered, "Now look here, little girl, anytime you want to take a walk on the avenue or go shopping or just hang out, you let me know. I'll be waitin' on every corner just to escort you across." Her lips parted slightly as if expecting a kiss. It never happened. She smirked and sassed, "So what do I tell my father, that I'll be in the safe, respectful arms of a-a Boy Scout?" Those words sent a tingling shiver down the boy's spine.

"Speakin' of your father? Are you sure he's not around?" Tony asked nervously as he looked over his shoulder wide-eyed. "No, he's working. So is my mom." He raised his left brow until it formed a sinister almost devilish arc over his lidded eye. Then he smirked and said, "Ah haaaa...maybe we should go inside...fool around a little." He nudged her gently with his shoulder and said, "Whaddya say, little girl? I'll show ya' my Boy Scout's honor—" "I don't think so," Joanie said suspiciously, and then she gave him a coquettish bump back with her shoulder. "Maybe next time, big boy."

Tony quickly changed the touchy subject of which he was childishly nervous about. "Ohhh...I like this song. Go ahead...turn it up," he said as soon as "Dream Lover" started to play on the radio. Then he jumped off the stoop and began mimicking the singing style of Bobby Darin. Tony snapped his fingers and moved to the beat of the music then took a long, hard look at the travel case sitting on the top landing. His merriment stopped dead in its tracks. Joanie noticed the sudden change and started to worry as to what was wrong. Was her father home? She turned abruptly and looked at her front door then back at him. He brushed off his rear end with a couple of brisk swipes of the palms of his hands and neatened his opened shirt. A somewhat disheartened look was on his face, an expression of his true feelings. But he quickly assumed an actor's role and hid his disappointment. He motioned his head a couple of times and then pointed toward the direction of the little suitcase. And shaking his head in dismay, with a snarled half smile, he spoke with a reserved tone of voice, "Just my luck...I finally run into you after all this time and whaddya' you do...you pack up and run away from me...jeez." One would think that tears were about to fall. Then he gave her a teasing wink and laughed a bit. She laughed aloud and said, "You had me worried there for a second. I'm going down the shore for the weekend with my cousin Barbara and her girlfriend Vickie. They're on their way over to get me right now. I can't wait. I'm surprised my parents are letting me go...well, my aunt will be with us. I guess that's why. Anyway...can't wait!" Joanie said fervently, bouncing on tips of her toes. "Sorry, you'll just have to wait till I come home before you ask me to go steady." She winked at him and they both laughed as only teenagers knew how to. "For the weekend? The whole weekend? Nice...real nice," he said with a wink and a few complementing nods of his head. Tony Boy reached down and softly grabbed her hands and then gently pulled her toward him. She let the momentum of her body come to rest tightly against his. He held her by her fingers and, with arms outstretched, gave her a slight twirl as he released one arm and took the other over her head in a semicircular pivot, first in one direction then the other until the movement stop and they were stationary again facing one another. The scented diffusion of Ivory soap and cologne brought on by her motion hit Tony Boy like a thunderbolt. "Joanie, I gotta' say one thing. You…look…great. I feel sorry for everybody down the shore this weekend," he said remorsefully while shaking his head.

Joanie's brow wrinkled a bit, and her face bore on a wry and bewildered look. But before she had the chance he jostled some and laughed the words "Because the lifeguards on the beach ain't gonna be able to take their eyes off you. They're gonna let everybody drown, and the ones that don't drown, well, they're gonna die from a broken heart, like I am now." His movements ended with both of his clasped hands up against his bulky chest next to his heart. They both shared a laugh; hers was credulous and almost childlike while his was much more sinister, almost like the true villain he was trying to imitate.

"You are so bad, Tony," she said. "And what about you? Running around the avenue—how many little girls' hearts are you breaking?" she said with her arms akimbo. He didn't answer. He just stood there with a skittish look on his face. She should only know. His experience with girls is, to say the least, minimal. Most schoolgirls in the neighborhood feared him, anticipating what his handsome features will dictate and demand. "He thinks he's a teenage Casanova." Someone who could have virtually any sweetheart of a girlfriend he chooses. So their first instinct was to avoid him at all costs. "He'll just use you" was their blight. This certainly wasn't the case with this supposed to be Romeo. Yes, he had a few girlfriends throughout his young years, little Joanie Jankowski being one of them. "Puppy love," as his father would always put it. The extent of his romantic liaisons consisted of holding hands and awkwardly necking in the back row while on a movie date. Just once or twice maybe a brazen adventure of feeling up the local bimbo in Branch Brook Park with a little "is this how you do it?" wonderment. There were, however, some hot and heavy make-out sessions with a few older, more poignant girls of other neighborhoods, out-of-town parties thrown for just that reason, complete with the only allowed act of dry humping.

To date, the only explicit sexual encounters he had under his belt were just a few backseat sessions with a couple of the older prostitutes that frequented the avenue and worked in the mob-controlled whorehouses. They consensually would give him a blowjob or hand job because they thought he was cute. Only once could he remember actually having intercourse, and that was with a strung-out young black junkie who did all the work. The true fact of the matter, Tony was extremely nervous being so up close and now so personal with this very beautiful teenager who just completely captured his fancy.

"Hey...listen. They're having the feast at Saint Michael's next week. It's for Saint San Gennaro. It's almost as good as the one in New York. Let me take you there. Saturday night. Whaddya say... it'll be fun...I promise. Then I'll ask you to go steady. Maybe even ask 'ya to marry me?" he said with a nervous stammer. Joanie blushed and said, "Marry you...well, we're going to have to wait until we're out of high school first." Tony had no real comeback, just a fetching smile. Joanie wrinkled her nose and asked, "Didn't they just have a feast?" "That was the May feast. Different saint, same food, different saint," Tony said intently. "Well, I guess you can never have too many saints around this neighborhood," Joanie said with a snicker in her voice. "Should we invite 'em to the wedding?" Tony asked. Joanie absorbed the words Tony had just spoken. His voice and mannerism seemed so innocently charming yet sexy. It triggered a sensation way down inside, something almost intriguingly obscene that she was not able to identify. She felt her heart grow increasingly excited. If it had hands and feet, it would be doing pendulant cartwheel inside her semi-voluptuous chest. Tiny beads of sweat formed on her forehead and neck, and she felt a warm dampness under her arms and between her thighs. Suddenly the longing for the Jersey Shore gave way to a new excitement. She felt herself drift off into a magical and rather sensual state of mind. The absolute thrill and excitement of going on a real date with the kid she still had an inextinguishable crush on. Joanie was tickled pink.

"I would love to," Joanie said as if just out of a daydream. She had a brief apprehension enter her mind, but she coolly shooed it away. *My father doesn't have to know. And who cares anyway* was her silent thought. She offered a handshake to affirm the deal. Tony gave her a perplexed and almost confused look. "Love to what?" he asked. "Go to the feast with you, silly…what did you think I meant?" Tony smirked. "Then it's a date?"

"Yes, it's a date," she said as she threw her arms up and around his neck and gave him an amorous hug. Her eyes closed and she waited for his kiss once again. The boy's temptations were ever so strong as he pulled her close to his body.

The ambience of the embrace was interrupted by the leaky exhaust roar of a 1955 dull-looking blue and white Chevrolet Nomad station wagon. Gray smoke billowed from its tailpipe as it rounded the corner and came barreling up the street. The bubbly female driver maneuvered the vehicle to the left and accidentally banged up and over the curb with the front tire as she tried to park. The dashboard radio was blaring, and the animated girls were teenybopping and singing along with the music.

The two girls were young. Tony guessed them to be around seventeen or eighteen years old, and he was right. They were just a couple of years older than he and Joanie. Both were casually dressed in proper beach attire, shorts, bikini bra tops, and mesh cover-ups. The driver turned down the volume of the radio and shouted to Joanie, "Ready, cuz, let's go." She twisted her upper torso and leaned out of the open car window, crossed her arms, and rested them on the top of the car door. Her eyes fixated on the boy standing next to Joanie. "Who's your friend?" she asked. "Is he coming with us?" she said flirtatiously. "No, he's not coming with us," Joanie said discontentedly as she looked at him. "He's just a friend from school." Tony gave her a mock frown and mimed her words back to her then said coyly, "Heah...I got nowhere to go today. Make some room. I'll join ya's."

Introductions were quickly doled out amongst all the kids. Joanie leaped up the front stairs, clutched her belongings, then turned toward the street. Tony followed her up the stairs. "Let me get that for 'ya," he said as he grabbed for her valise then offered his arm and escorted her down the front stoop. The gentlemanly act he displayed got an affectionate "Thank you" from Joanie who was unmistakably impressed. Tony graciously opened the car door for her and stepped aside to let her climb in. He scored more points as his hands gently guided her into the rear seat. His eyes were immediately drawn to the sensual curves and crevices of the young girl's perfectly shaped ass and the tiny waistline and dimpled back above it. He sighed to himself and gently bit his lip. He tossed the suitcase over the seat back into the rear storage compartment of the station wagon, trying carefully not to hit Joanie in the head and clumsily almost did.

"Hey, girls," Tony blurted and paused, then said with some charm in his voice, "how 'bout a ride to the avenue?" Before anyone could answer, he quickly hopped into the backseat of the Chevy and nestled up to Joanie. The two girls up front simultaneously turned their heads to the backseat and looked at the boy who assumed the ride. "It's on the way...*no?*" he said with a shrug of his shoulders. All the girls agreed and off they went. The driver turned up the volume on the radio and blasted Frankie Ford's "Sea Cruise" for all to hear.

Tony felt a pulsating throb in his groin area and a fluttering in his stomach as his body nudged and pressed against the soft bare skin of Joanie's arm and thigh. His excitement and his manhood grew as he inhaled her sweet scent. He shifted his weight a bit and wrapped his right arm over the rear seat back behind her. Then he coyly let his hand slowly drift down until it rested in a cupped position on her shoulder. The moisture on her skin further aroused him. He leaned forward and, with his other free hand, tenderly started to play with the gold chain and cross she wore around her neck. He lifted the delicate chain away from her neck with his index and middle finger and slowly slid them down the chain length gently, rubbing the tops of his fingers on her skin. He stopped his movement before he reached the top of her breasts then looked into her eyes. With a couple of teasing little tugs, he lifted the crucifix from between her cleavage. "Pretty… and delicate," he said warmly. "Like you." Joanie blushed some as she said, "My parents gave it to me last Christmas. It came from Italy." "They must want you to be protected," Tony said with a raised brow. Joanie took it gently from his fingers and said, "It's blessed by the pope." Tony added a devilish grin and said, "Real protected." She looked up at Tony with large innocent eyes. A mischievous smile came upon her face as she said laughingly, "Maybe they do?"

The car rounded a turn and jostled their bodies into one another, forcing them closer than ever. The young blushing couple turned and faced each other, both letting their eyes meet with an alluring and provocative stare. Tony studied her oval face and became smitten by her beauty. He had never looked at her before and felt such passion. And now he was, and very strongly, perhaps because he was older with more mature hormones acting up? She had large symmetrical brown eyes, a small slightly bowed Italian nose, and full lush lips. Tiny glistening beads of moisture were forming atop her upper lip and at the corners of her mouth. At that exact moment, Tony felt a strong urge to kiss her lips. He pictured the sensual act in his mind as he tried to muster up the courage to do so. *Should he* was his first thought. Would the act be too much bravado on his part? Would he be moving too fast? After all, he thought, he was just getting reacquainted with her after all this time passed. Would the act be too brazen or borderline crude? Would it scare her away? What was she thinking?

Joanie sensed his urge. She wished he would kiss her. She wanted to be kissed by him and for her to kiss him back as passionately as her young mind and body knew how to. Her adolescent hormones were racing through her torso and up into her already semi-hard nipples. She started to make the first move. The car bounced again. A voice in his head screamed: *What are you waiting for? Kiss the girl, you fool! Kiss her! Kiss her!* The ardent feeling he had was turning into butterflies and shyness; then suddenly there was a burst from the front seat. He was saved by the bell so to speak. "Hey…what's going on back there, you two?" her cousin asked concerning as she caught sight of the action through the rearview mirror. "They look like they're a lot more than just friends to me," said the passenger skeptically. Her cousin spoke again snidely; her eyes chastised both through the mirror. "Break it up back there, Romeo and Juliette. Joanie, if your parents find out you two were making out in the backseat of my car, while I'm driving, it'll be *my* ass," her cousin snapped.

The two kids separated, readjusted themselves, and both leaned back heavily into the rear seat cushion. Tony pondered his decision to back off. He acknowledged internally the fact of being a little shy but inhaling deeply with the thought that he wasn't afraid. He kissed girls before, competently and adeptly—so other girls had told him. He faithfully watched enough of the old nostalgic movies on the television and attended the cinemas consistently to know exactly what to do. And he had a peek or two at a few stag movies while listening to lucid and explicit commentary from his wise guy friends. He studied the ways his many movie heroes always wooed and romanced the girls, and no matter how tough a role they played, they always got the girl—before they died. He could do that, just the way they could—he was Tony Curtis in his own mind. But now he thought, *I did earn her respect, hopefully, if nothing else but that*, and that he could live with.

Tony glanced out of the window and recognized the familiar miscreant surroundings of Bloomfield Avenue. *I should get out here*, he thought to himself with the dismay of leaving Joanie, and as the car approached Garside Street he said politely, "You could pull over anywhere here, girls, this is good, and thanks a lot for the ride." The driver slowed the car and veered to the side of the road and stopped, this time smashing into the curb with the right wheel and tire. Tony frowned, looked, and asked her straight-faced, with a pointing finger, "What's your name again? Barbara, right…where'd you get your driver's license from?" He let out a short mocking laugh and continued. "You better take it easy with this car. You got my little girl with ya'." He winked and smiled at Joanie. Then he looked at the other girl. "And you, Vickie, you better keep an eye on both of them, they could be trouble together." He spoke softly with just a hint of sarcasm in his voice, "Well, girls, have fun, and don't break too many hearts down there this weekend." He offered an impressionistic look of complete sadness to Joanie as he said in a jested whimper, "And you, look and remember me. I'll be all alone, waiting and walking Bloomfield Avenue until we meet again."

Tony lifted up on the door handle until it released. He threw his legs up and over the door sill and climbed out in an acrobatic style. He was standing in the street, bending at the waist with his left hand gripping the edge of the open door and his right hand on the roof of the car, fingers tapping out a rhythmic drumbeat. Finding it extremely hard to let go, he poked his head into the vehicle and said softly to Joanie, "I'll see ya', kid." Then he spontaneously climbed back into the car and knelt on the seat next to Joanie. He pulled her gently into his body and wrapped her amorously in his arms. He gave her soft kisses, first on her forehead, then her eyelids and her cheek, and finally a long, lingering kiss on her lips. Joan Jankowski melted as she felt his tongue sensually enter her mouth and massage hers. This brought another verbal assault from her cousin of which both completely ignored. He backed away and said with authority, "Hey. Don't forget. We got a date next week, *right?*" Joanie was oblivious to the question she had just nodded yes to—she was swooning as she replied in bewilderment, "Where did you learn to kiss like that?" Tony smirked then winked at her. "The Girl Scouts." Joanie was a bundle of teenage nerves and excited hormones. She had never been kissed like that before. "Are you going to call me?" she asked with trembling anxiety. "Do you even have my number? How will I get ahold of?" She continued to ramble with wide eyes but was cut short by Tony. "Call you…now what would your old man say if I called you?" Tony Boy said with a smirk. "Meet me there next Saturday night. Around seven o'clock. I'll be by the last row of stands in the back of Saint Michael's parking lot."

The driver of the car was growing impatient and let the car lunge forward a tad, almost knocking Tony over. He frowned at the driver and said, "Hey, you, Speedy Gonzales, wait a minute." He was annoyed but spoke calmly to Joanie, "Like I was saying, Joanie, you'll see my cousin's Zeppole stand. I'll be under the tent right next to it. Okay." He said, now beaming, "It'll be the tent with the *'talian* flag colors, not Polish." "It's a date. And you better be there," Joanie said enthusiastically. "Oh, don't you worry 'bout it," Tony said with a nefarious grin as he pointed his finger at her. "Scout's honor!" He thanked the girls very politely again and reluctantly slammed the door shut with both hands. He blew handfuls of kisses to the waving Joan Jankowski as the light blue Chevy wagon disappeared up the long Avenue.

Tony Marino started his jaunt up Bloomfield Avenue briskly, with his entire grandstand aura on display. He was on the sunny side of the street and whistling the gleeful melody of that song with the sweet scent of Joanie still fresh in his mind, and his mirthful actions seemed choreographed and intentional as he envisioned her, herself watching from afar. He was proudly expanding his chest with each and every spirited breath he took, and his stride was broad and fast-paced, almost buoyant, like a feeling of walking on air. He would leap off his feet every so often to playfully slap the bottoms of the No Parking signs along the curb and also the fringes on the storefront canopies. His entire body was alive with an exuberance never felt before.

The excitement of meeting Joanie was racing in his heart, propelling his mind with wild, vivid thoughts of next Saturday night when he would see her again. Of course he would not or could he not wait until then. Starting Monday of next week, he'll again walk her street each and every hour of each and every day until another chance meeting prevails. He will, if necessary, camp out in front of her house, with or without the permission of her father. He was truly an engrossed teenager in ebullient love. *Today is going to be remembered as the best day of my life*, he thought to himself.

As he crossed Mt. Prospect Avenue he quickly put his gaiety aside and became the hooligan he was supposed to be. He stopped for a second to button up his Italian knit shirt using a dress shop storefront window as a reflecting mirror. A comb was lifted from his rear pants pocket and carefully used to neaten the pompadour of black hair, and his more mature wise guy face was practiced, all to the enjoyment and delight of the young teenage store clerk, who sat smiling from behind the counter. He gave the girl a wink then headed up the part of the avenue that quickly turns into the heart of Mafia territory. It's this Runyonesque part of the city, this wicked domain, he loves so much. It is here he would take orders and carry out duties delegated to him by the street soldiers under Batista's reign, and as of late, solely from Batista himself. This little parcel of real estate that ran from where he was standing and continue north until it reached the overpass of the Garden State Parkway. The neighborhood he was so familiar with. He stood frozen for a bit and glanced over his shoulder. He stargazed down at the avenue as it twisted some then became a hill that slide to a very evil place, and this stirred up evil memories. Just below Summer Avenue, just about right where he is standing now, is a dark dangerous ghetto-like area comprised mostly of seedy old brick and mortar *Christopher Columbus* styled tenements, antiquated building and warehouses, abandoned semi-decrepit factories, and rows of decaying wooden storage garages tucked up and down side streets and alleyways.

In the heart of this beginning grid, hidden away on narrow obscure back streets, are slews of illegal gypsy auto body chop shops that welcome stolen automobiles with open arms. The shops are all set back from the main roads, well hid on their property, and not easily accessible by the general public. Dubious mechanics and body men, all mostly illegal aliens, quickly dispose of the iron literally in minutes, with the deftness and skill of a surgeon. It's a skill they've honed to perfection over the years in their own countries. The larger and more brazen of these shops are enclosed by a fortress of galvanized cyclone fencing with a top row of concertina wire riding the perimeter and thick chains with military-type Yale locks sealing the swinging gates. Inside this citadel of car thieves roam seriously mean and mistreated junkyard dogs to further deter an overzealous insurance adjuster, a homeless person, or a desperate junkie looking to boost a car radio and redeem it for a nickel bag of heroin. Camouflaged within this area are the many nondescript garages and small storage warehouses filled with the stolen merchandise carted away from hijacked trucks, all being inventoried and expedited by the local mobsters. And if a uniformed cop is present, it is for sure to pocket some protection money or choose a piece of swag for himself.

It is an area inhabited by mostly poor black and Hispanic families all crowding into decrepit multi-story *Le Corbusier* style tenements. The dingy dwellings sit above the rows of the neighborhood businesses: taverns/liquor stores, bodegas, and other ethnic shops that provide goods and services to the handful of the poor, righteous, and honest working class of people that blend in with the felonious through no choice of their own. The area's empty tenements and abandoned garages are the shooting galleries for heroin addicts and a stomping ground filled with a hodgepodge of degenerate drug pushers, thieves, and muggers. The lights of the Brick City will cast tall shadows against the factory walls and the concrete viaducts of the completely immoral and sometimes cold-blooded cheap prostitutes, all applying their immodest trade to any takers for a five- or ten-dollar bill or a rakish taste of cocaine or smack. This little bit of real estate, these few square blocks, had an immoral and sinful lure about it that the young Tony could not resist. He roamed the streets freely among the thieves and whores and junkies and winos carrying out his mob duties, unafraid, through the dark tenement stairwells and alleyways that reeked of the smell of stale beer and urine. And he would emerge unscathed—all referred to him as a connected guy. This gave a developing boost to his developing ego.

The tentacles of organized crime reached deep into this derelict honeycombed neighborhood, relying heavily on the income generated by gambling, vending machines, and the illegal sale of liquor. But the heroin drug trafficking on this turf that feeds heavily on human souls is a deep dark secret known to only a few mobsters and unlike the South and Central Wards that have a predominantly black population and well-known black gangs that govern and rule their world of drug pushers. However, the trafficking in this racy slum territory and extending well into the Iron Bound section was Frank and Bobby Batista's exclusively—a huge money maker. Only difference is that Bobby has to kick up to his Brooklyn crime family—so it was agreed; he gets the larger piece of the pie. Frank, on the other hand, very secretly pockets all the income generated from the sale of nickel and dime bags of heroin; this for him is somewhat profitable but also a very dangerous life-ending venture if ever found out by Ruggeri.

The clandestine drug business so encouraged and promoted over the years by Bobby Batista and his Brooklyn-based family was being secretively sold as the future of all family business. It has always been considered bad business by the old-school Dons that head the organization, although most turned a blind eye to it as they shared in the profits. It was a federal crime that ran the risk of long, hard prison sentences, which many had already done or currently still doing. Just recently someone of the New York family was facing a lengthy prison term for possession of a large quantity of heroin if convicted. While out on bail and awaiting trial, he was murdered. That alone the reason for the fear by most—for all knew the next one caught will choose informing over death any day. This now oversized and ridiculously profitable business was supposed to be Frank's cousin Bobby Breeze's action solely. He was to oversee the weekly, monthly drops and transactions, but as fate would have it, along came cousin Frank with a creation of the foolproof smoke screen plan he devised, foolproof plan both cousins are confident with.

Kilos of heroin were smuggled into the states via Port Newark or Port Elizabeth by the various factions of the Naples-based Cosa Nostra that controlled the manufacturing end of the business. The booty was well concealed between parcels of Italian provisions. The cash generated from this highly lucrative empire. was almost impossible to say no to, and Frank Batista, though he only received a small percentage, a finder's fee so to speak, was lured into the operation by his first cousin Bobby "the Breeze" Batista, himself a notorious Brooklyn-based *capo* with the Profaci family and very well versed with the narcotics trade.

The two devised a honeycomb of diversionary routes from Naples to Brooklyn to a small nondescript Italian deli then back to Brooklyn, sending any would-be undercover agent on a wild goose chase. The market was ideal for such a contrivance, small and inconspicuous. The slightest trace of the white substance was camouflaged with sawdust and grated cheese buried deep between the cracks of the oak-planked floor. The market's books were altered to reflect hundreds of pounds/kilos of imported provisions; in reality only a small amount of the monies sent was for gross weight shown on bills of lading of actual food stuff. The rest was for a high-grade narcotic shipped in by the *Famiglia* overseas. The cash showing on the books was payable to fictitious suppliers in Sicily and Italy then rerouted back into the Cosa Nostra's operation. This ploy of throwing curve-balls at the authorities would go on for years and never was detected. And as far as distribution goes, in their part of the city, along came Jake "the Snake" Trebbiano.

Jake was a typical sociopath, a vicious hoodlum by-product of the streets, growing up tough in the Iron Bound East Ward of the city, the Down Neck part of Newark. A high school dropout dedicated to a life of crime who, by the time he reached the ripe old age of thirty-one, had served a total of nine years behind bars for felonious assaults and armed robbery. He was tough as tough could possibly be.

Jake was tall and had a lean, muscular frame. He wore his dark brown hair long and slicked back. His dark drugged eyes, bulging and evil, matched his drab olive-colored skin—his chest, back, arms, and neck covered with bad jailhouse tattoos and an array of scars and burn marks. Dried and crusted needle tracks ran up and down his forearms. His mouth contained a mishmash of bad teeth. And when he spoke, he had a high-pitched nasally voice that hit you a constant barrage of "na'mean," "na'mean" after every curse-filled sentence. An ex-heroin addict himself, he jumped at the opportunity of becoming a part of the multilevel marking triangle of drug distribution.

Jake was an expendable but vital middleman whose territory started in the *Barrio* and reached all the way to the Iron Bound section of the city. He would receive a large package of the white powder from an unknown courier, cut it up, and repackage it into smaller bags, then hand it over to his street pushers who, along with him, sold it to the inconsolable users. Both of the Batistas knew that Trebbiano would swallow some downers on occasion or a bottle of Codeine-laced cough medicine—these considered harmless vices by many, himself included, and this reason forced them to keep very close tabs on him. However, he did his job well and was considered reliable. He followed orders to a T for his fear and loathing was not death but to bid farewell to the free world and again return to prison. His light gray Cadillac could always be seen cruising in and out of the streets or parked as he made his rounds secretly dealing the white powder.

On occasion Jake would reluctantly accept the aid of a young and enterprising Tony Marino—this done at the dubious request of Frank Batista, sort of a trial run—for his own selfish and mercenary reasons. Frank never knew when he would have to replace the Snake. The kid's job was to act as a designated lookout and observe anything suspicious. Jake seized this opportunity to turn the chore into his personal pleasure. Now he could inject his own veins once again with the euphoric blood-warming liquid narcotic as he made his baneful rounds with the kid at the wheel of the Cadillac. Tony was amazed at how well this man knew every twist and turn of the narrow streets of the unfamiliar territory to the kid, of this so-called Down Neck area, as Jake verbally navigated with his eyes closed and nodded in a drug-induced stupor. And of course the kid was to keep his mouth shut about any of this, especially to the Batistas. It was agreed.

This was one of the kid's favorite chores. He got to drive a Cadillac around all night and be home before midnight, the often neglected school night curfew set by his mother, with a crisp hundred dollar bill in his pocket. Money paid for his service well done. And as if Frank Batista was clairvoyant or just cursed by a *maliocch* within a month of the kid's first venture, Jake vanished with quite a bit of unpaid for product. It would be almost two weeks before the badly decomposed body of Jake "the Snake" Trebbiano was found in a vacant rat-infested apartment, lying in a pool of dried blood with his throat slashed and seventeen savage stab wounds about his upper torso. It was immediately filed as a crime of opportunity by a Puerto Rican street gang and went unsolved and soon forgotten by the Newark police and the commissioner.

A name was brought up for questioning in a very crafty way. Someone identified the young Tony Marino as one of the last persons to be seen with the late Jake, perhaps as early as only a few hours prior. When found out, the kid's whereabouts during that time was harshly questioned by Tick Tock and by a tough, penetrating, seasoned Newark police detective, Eddie Accardi. Both grilled Tony Marino for information. Batista accepted the kid's wily but accurate explanation of his activity with Jake prior in thirty seconds, and was never told the entire truth, especially about witnessing Jake's own drug use. The detective hammered away behind important, closed, and locked detectives' interrogation room doors for two hours but was told nothing. His last words to the youth were spoken impetuously, "Make up some bullshit story to your old man about where ya' been—and about that bruise on your face."

Tony's Omerta had gained the respect both of the Newark Police Department and Frank Batista for withstanding the intense questioning that was doled out by the vicious detective Eddie Accardi who admittedly said "I may have leaned on the kid a little too hard," this act of contrition meant for the ears of the boy's father. The boy kept his mouth shut, took his knocks and hard slaps well, and denied any involvement with the expired known drug kingpin. Such was life in that part of the city. Either of the Batistas made no inquiries, nor did he seek retribution. Frank was adamant about that. He could not afford any publicity in this type of misdeed, especially with his covert operation kept so secretly from the man that forbids drug dealings by any of his crew, namely the Pope. But in due time, the cagey Tick

Tock Batista and his cousin Breeze would recruit another to take over Jake's position. At first they thought to hand the reins to the young Marino boy; however, that decision was vetoed for the obvious: the kid was too young and thought by both to be openly innocent for such an undertaking—and both hated to face Cheese Marino if anything happened. His wrath would be equally catastrophic as would be the Pope's. The young Marino showed a far better talent for the more elaborate chores that would soon befit his persona. And Batista wanted to personally groom him for the bigger and better opportunities organized crime had to offer on his side of the street.

Now, today, in the real world of Frank Batista, he is agreeable with the Pope—narcotics had no place in the realm of his kingdom; he really wanted out. And he pleaded for Bobby Battista to be extremely careful, but from his end of the block, the operation was somewhat sanctioned by the New York people. There were only one or two very trusted soldiers under Bobby's rule that had any inclination as to what was going on. On the other hand, Frank Batista was not sanctioned by the Pope. He utilized out-of-towners and strangers to do his bidding. And as extremely cunning and cagey was his plan, that would cause the dominoes to fall all over Bobby and New York if ever a bust; Frank still worried about prison, about getting whacked. He feared the about surveillance techniques, so he had a careful network of messengers relaying orders back and forth. They communicated mostly person to person or through encrypted written letters, hardly ever over the phone. Frank Batista quickly complimented his decision to silently recruit the son of Big Anthony Marino to be his young protégé and to do his private bidding with the hopes one day he would be able to take a comfortable backseat to the grueling mob life and reap the benefits as so many others have.

5

Tony Marino walked in Corrado's Italian Meat Market with a bold strut and headed straight to the back of the store. The initial savory smell of the place immediately made his mouth water. His shoes slipped some on the worn and sawdust-and-grated-cheese-covered wooden floor, and as he passed the meat and deli case, he couldn't help laughing at his distorted reflection in the slanted glass of him trying to regain his balance. The two chubby men at the end of the counter fought back their laughter, to a point. They were dressed in just about pure white butcher's garb and stood vigilant, side by side, next to a pair of sparkling meat slicers behind the service area. "Whaddya say guys," he said as he waved to both of the clerks with a military type of salute. "You want a sandwich, kid?" one of the men asked in broken English. "Yeah. You choose. Surprise me. Make it a small one okay," he replied as he disappeared behind a partitioned corner wall.

The small Italian deli and specialty store is leased and licensed furtively to Giuseppe Cundari, a very old Italian citizen who is currently living very comfortably somewhere in Naples, Italy. The everyday operation of the store is carried out by Dominic Corrado and his two brothers, Vito and Mario. All three are from a small village just south of Naples and are living and working in the United States illegally. They are first cousins to Frank Batista. Tick Tock, as Batista was sometimes called by his closer friends and associates, fronted most of the cash needed to set up and open the place that for argument's sake looked and operated like a legitimate *mercato*.

Imported Italian cheeses, slabs of Prosciutto di Parma, salami, mortadella, and other Italian cured meats hung overhead, uniformly, from large hooks. And a crystal clear deli case chock-full of cold cuts and Insalatas stood next to bins of fresh Italian bread and rolls for sandwiches. Sparkling stainless steel racks and shelving ran the length of the store, jam-packed and stocked with canned and boxed imported Italian provisions. Two small tables sat neatly up against the front wall providing a window view for patrons to sit and eat. The place did make a great sandwich, and all the imported provisions were pure quality. Frank Batista took a thin slice of the market, usually in the form of prosciutto and other meats as did Cousin Bobby. The legitimate amount of money generated by the business, what they actually paid tax on, was impressionable, and the till was paying the staff and old man Cundari back in Naples somewhere. However, no one lost sight of the truth of Corrado's—why the place existed was solely to launder cash and act as a front for Batista's drug-smuggling operation.

Tony gave the steel back office door a couple of rhythmic taps and waited for an answer. A husky voice was heard in Italian, "Chi e…Chi sta bussando?" "It's me, Tony," he said back to the Italian voice behind the door. There was a moment of silence. Then the heavy dead bolt opened with a clank. A balding moon-faced man peered through the three-inch space he made with the partially cracked door. He spoke both Italian and English to the boy, both poorly. "*Chefai wayo*…whaddya say, kid. Ammonini," he said with a wink of his bulging bloodshot eyes as he opened it wider while motioning the boy inside. The man sat back down at a small desk and picked up the black receiver of the telephone he was talking on. The conversation he was having was completely in Italian and not at all understood by the boy who just stood and waited.

Dominic Corrado was short and thick with a "no neck" appearance and a huge head that grew out of gorilla-like hair from his rounded shoulders. His hairy balloon-like arms seem to be busting out of his white T-shirt that rose up over his waist, exposing a large rotund belly. He more resembled a villainous cartoon character that leaped from the artist's cell and took on a human form—and always with a shadowed, cynical look on his face exaggerated by dense, unshaven whiskers. Tony laughed to himself at the thought of how his father would refer to him as "a fifty-five-gallon drum with feet." And he thought he was a *finocchio*. Dominic Corrado was not at all connected with the outfit, just an essential front man for Tick Tock. "Heah, kid," the fat man said as he pointed to a stool with his hand cupped over the receiver mouthpiece. "Sedede....Senta fame'?" The boy understood the slang dialect and replied, "I'm okay, the boys will make me somethin' to go." He watched as Dominic gave him another wink and resumed his conversation of choppy Sicilian into the receiver as he scribbled notes on a piece of paper.

Tony rested his rear end on the edge of a tall wooden stool, folded his arms, and waited for the fat man to finish. He made an attempt to decipher the Italian words Corrado spoke, some he did recognize, but for the most part it would be futile to even try. His eyes scanned the ten-by-ten-foot rear office then became fixated on an old large black iron standing safe with gold decals and a large Yale tumbler. He became lost in thought about its contents and wondered who I. A. Goodman, the name printed in elegant gold leaf on the front of the safe, was. The heavy slam of the phone back onto the cradle startled him a little as he refocused his attention on Dominic.

"Here... *Wayo*," the fat man said as he handed Tony a freshly sealed airmail-type envelope, crisp and white with bright blue and red borders. It looked so important, patriotic, and Tony thought it to be a remnant of the Fourth of July. "You gonna needa'…ahhh… *comesegiam*…a haircut in aboutta' hour," he said with a sinister type of laugh as he tapped out a rhythmic *rat-tat-tat* on his wristwatch with his fat finger. His eyebrows raised some as he waited for the boy to speak. This being a frivolous game he played with the young hipster as he himself acted almost childlike—so anxious to fool the kid. If the boy was not sure of the intended meaning, it would ultimately cost him a dollar. And if he was correct, as he was 99 percent of the time, it would be a congratulatory slap on the back, an old-fashioned "atta boy" from his mentor, and also a buck. This is how the kid got most of his instruction relayed to and from Batista. Some messages were written, others verbal only and left up to the power of memory. The kid hadn't any inclination of the drug supply hidden amongst the imported prosciutto and capicola stashed deep in the Corrado deli walk-in fridge.

Tony took a quick glance at his wristwatch to verify the time then gave the bald man a settling nod of his head. No further conversation or instructions were needed, just a barely audible "Haicabid?" by Dominic. It was a simple euphemism that meant go meet Tick Tock at the barbershop at eleven o'clock. He took the envelope from Dominic's chubby hands, brought it up to his brow, and with a "tip of his hat" gesture said, "Salute…I gabide…Ciao" to the barrel-like fellow then stashed it down the front of his trousers. On the way out, a man behind the counter handed him a brown paper bag that had a wrapped sandwich sticking out from the top.

According to his Longines, he had a little time to kill. Manzo's barbershop was only about a five-minute walk up Bloomfield Avenue, so he headed for the next available shaded bus stop bench and plopped down. Tony pulled the sandwich from the bag and ripped open the wrapper. "Ahhh…*Cabagool*…*Moozadel*," he said to himself as he peeked between the bread halves. Still stuffed from the breakfast he ate, Tony only managed to get a couple of bites of the sandwich down before he got disgusted with it and chucked it in waste receptacle next to the bench—"a true sin," his mother would say.

He sat there semi-prone with his legs extended straight out beyond the curb and crossed at the ankles. His back angled and his shoulders firmly resting against the wooden slats of the bench, hands clasped firmly behind his head, fingers intertwined, and his eyes shut. It was a hot, humid summer day, and the kid could feel beads of sweat running down his back and sides as he began daydreaming and thinking about Joanie. He squinted and began talking silently to himself, "I betcha they're goin' through the Union toll booths right now. Maybe past 'em." He became anxious. "I wish I was with her. What if she meets another guy?" Jealous notions were building in his head. "Nah…she's with her cousins…and aunt. She'll be okay." He slowly convinced himself to calm down.

Tony sat up and felt the envelope wrinkle against his skin, and his thoughts drifted as to its contents. *Wonder what's in there, something important?* he thought to himself. *Can't be no cash…too light and thin for that. Probably just some papers, a letter maybe? I wonder just how important.* The bottom line was what's the difference? He had the envelope and he'll deliver it, no questions asked. His second intuition was the accurate one. It was a letter containing encrypted codes spelling out in Italian the details of when the next shipment of smack was to arrive—the day, the time, the location along with a few other related incidentals, where it was to be shipped and who was to retrieve it.

Could this kid be trusted with such high-level correspondence? Frank Batista believed so. He had all the confidence in the world in him, more than his own nephew who had the job prior. Tony was put to the test on many occasions. He was given many subtle cross-examinations and mock shakedowns just to see how reliable he was.

He passed them all with flying colors. Then he laughed aloud at the sheer stupidity of the spy game fat Dominic loved to play: "Go get a haircut in about an hour."

6

For as long as anyone could remember, Manzo's barbershop shared occupancy in an old, nondescript commercial brick and glass storefront building on Bloomfield Avenue set between Clifton Avenue and Mt. Prospect Street. Its neighbor was a small hardware store flanking its one side. Past it and on the far corner was a small combination luncheonette, newspaper, and magazine store. On the opposite corner, next to the barbershop itself, sat a threadbare tavern called Tory's. The shops outside mounted gleaming red, white, and blue barbers' pole. The inviting individual symbol was old man Manzo's pride and joy, surely now a worthy antique. He kept it in meticulous condition and could be seen each morning with rag and polish in hand, admiring proudly, and he had not a concern that a lot of his trade was dying off or moving to the more modern salons.

The shop itself was a long narrow three-station tonsorial with battle-worn leather Theo A. Koch chairs that sat on a dated black-and-white mosaic tiled floor. The swiveled chairs faced large framed mirrors and rows of shelves that held hair products by Clubman and Pinaud, carefully arranged by size. An array of fine-toothed long combs sat bathing in large sterile vats of alcohol and witch hazel. The reflection of the half-dozen mismatched wooden waiting room chairs would be seen by the patrons who sit tense under the pinstriped barber's cape. Their eyes met by the occupants who peered ever so stealthily over newspapers and magazines held high and firm awaiting their inevitable turn as patiently as can be. That section of rickety seating was on the right side of the establishment, war-torn chairs arranged in sets of three along a half-paneled wall that ran three feet from the floor and was capped by some lengths of well-chipped chair rail. A magazine cluttered knee-high table separated the chairs in the middle and another capped the far end. Old man Manzo managed to keep his shop a neutral territory, far from the grasps of organized crime. It was probably the only place on the avenue that did not harbor some sort of vice within its four walls. It's a shop that catered to mostly the old-timers who come in for a seventy-five-cent haircut, shave, or both.

The barbershop was a common gathering place for men to shoot the shit with friends, neighbors, and on occasion local wise guys while they patiently await their turn and all were forced to listen as Mr. Manzo told the infamous war stories as to who has sat in his chair over the last forty years. His reputation was impeccable. And if the wait seemed too long for some patrons or the conversation inside was too blasé, a trip next door for a short beer was always an option. His tonsorial legacy was proudly displayed and celebrated by the autographed portrait shots that were hanging on the walls of movie stars and dignitaries from the area. The place reeked of talcum powder, Old Spice cologne, and stale farts. Two large ceiling fans kept the thick cigarette and DiNobili cigar smoke circulating around bright fluorescent lights as it supplied a gentle semi-refreshing breeze.

As the kid approached the shop, the hatred of the barber's chair rang fresh in his mind. When he was younger, his old man would plop him in the chair and command Manzo to "give him a trim." But the trim was always the same, a crew cut. The kid despised that type of haircut because it would accent his already large ears, a trait he was so self-conscious about. When he was about ten or eleven, he went once with his mother to her salon, and that's where he has been going for his haircuts ever since.

The kid cupped the palms of his hands to the side of his face and glanced through the glaring glass of the shop window. He noticed that the Ingraham deco-style wall clock read ten fifty-five, ten minutes later than his expensive Longines wristwatch. "Whaddya say, Mr. Manzo?" Tony said as he breezed through the front door. He clandestinely greeted Frank Batista with a sly smile and an assured nod before he took his seat in the waiting area. He grabbed an old issue of *Sports Illustrated* featuring Rocky Marciano on the cover and buried his face in the text. It was a story he read a thousand times over.

Mr. Manzo solely occupied the first station. It was his and *his* alone. He was applying warm lather to the nape of the customer, readying him for a finishing shave. At the far station, a large portly Argentinean barber known as Tino was talking one of Ruggeri's goons into getting a razor-cut instead of his normal trim with barber's shears. His accent was thick, and the pronunciation of anything English seemed strained. The Argentinean barber was just barely insulting, and it was only old man Manzo who picked up on the connotations, all spoken partially in Italian as Tino mumbled in not so many words, "You have nice hair, mister, for such a *facciabrute*." This was said with a bold smile on his face.

The middle station barber's chair was in far better condition than the others and was always reserved for guest speakers and celebrities—in this case, Frank Batista. He had a rolled-up copy of *Ring Magazine* in his hand that he waved like a baton as he sat comfortably and swiveled side to side. It seemed like he was carrying on a one-sided conversation with an old man with bushy gray hair and a thick mustache, a *scumbari* citizen in off the street who was just peacefully waiting his turn. The conversation was more of a declamation or a lecture Batista was giving himself, and the old man seemed to eaves-drop and sometimes would close his eyes if he thought he should not have heard that. Still Frank ranted about how he should have invested in more diverse legal business as so many of his mobster friends have. He should have opted for far more real estate instead of just a shabby meat market or the half ownership of dive bar in Belleville. He cursed his loan shark book of business, claiming he is just too easy on the late payers. "It's not worth the fuckin' aggrava-tion chasin' these cocksuckers around for my money." Frank cast his eyes in the direction of the large goon on the barber's seat. "I gotta' pay him more than I collect to break a few heads so that I can collect more… *mannaggia la miseria*…now does that make sense to you?" The old man now slouched down and completely hid behind the *Star Ledger*. "Christ, if this shit doesn't get any better, I'm gonna' have to go sell cars!" Tic bellyached.

Tony sat and fidgeted and bit his lip as if he was fighting off an urge. The one annoying habit the kid had was staring at other people, intensely at times. It's been analyzed as an involuntary unconscious annoyance that all scolded him for. Harmless as it was to him—as he explained, it was his simple attraction to the obvious perfections or imperfections of other people. And he would compare their traits to himself and his circle of family and friends. So now the kid prac-tices the art of observing as he was taught the difference between the two—by, of all people, Frank Batista himself.

Tony peered obscurely over the top edge of the magazine, and as he sat, he furtively watched Frank Batista. He inconspicuously stud-ied and observed his mentor. He overheard the dialogue and clouded explanations over his nickname Tick Tock on many occasion and still gave careful thought on what exactly it was that they meant. He watched Frank's gestures and listened intensely and coupled them as the man spoke. Batista was indeed a teller of funny stories, and many said he missed his calling. His natural flare and wit for comedy even in the darkest hour ranked along with any professional stand-up comic who performed in the Catskills.

Tony had not a recollection of Frank Batista during his younger years although the gangster admitted bouncing him on his knee once or twice as a toddler. Frank reminded the kid in a peculiar sort of way somewhat of his own father—almost as both souls intertwined as if they had the same teacher in life—but in that sense only and not in any true physical sense of the word. Frank was almost as tall as his old man but weighed about fifty pounds less. Still, with a powerful built. Like his uncle Joe, so he thought. He had a full head of shortly cropped salt-and-pepper hair that he neatly parted on his right side. Tic would look in the mirror and smirk then ask, "So do I really look like Cary Grant?" Some people would answer yes, but most no, not with those sinister eyes and the large sinuous, self-proclaiming Roman nose that held up a pair of black horn-rimmed eyeglasses. He was about the same age as his Big Anthony, both in their early fifties, and Tony felt he shared his father's philosophies plus a lot of his mannerisms. Frank wore the same cologne as did his father, and both had a fondness for Jack Daniels whisky and Sinatra songs. Tony read the jealousy in his father. And by self-admission, the kid treats Batista with the same level of respect and admiration as he does his own father, maybe even a little more at times, and this metaphor on the kid's part is so very evident and at times tears at his father's insides.

A light classical aria began to play from the radio. The fat, jolly Tino brought his arms and hands over the head of the brute in the chair and with razor and comb began to emulate the famed conductor Arturo Toscano. His jubilance was spilling over onto the shoulders of the customer in his chair who was not at all amused. He sat tense and glared the most evil hate from his eyes, reflected and observable in the mirror. The fat barber feared this look that instinctively forced him to turn away from the ugly black eyes of the patron. He glanced over at the kid sitting quietly in the waiting area and forced a chuckle. "Heah, kid, whena' you gonna' leta' me cuta' you hair? I givea' you a nicea' razor cut…huh," Tino said with his thick Italian accent. The guy in Tino's chair got expressively annoyed. As the barber turned away to say something again he shot daggers at him, once again via the reflections in the mirror. "Heah you!" he exclaimed as he grabbed his smock and yanked him practically off his feet. "You're gonna' pay attention to what yer' doing and bullshit later, or I'm gonna break this fuckin' arm off." Tino turned white as a ghost and said humbly, "Yes, sir." "I don't think the kid trusts your razor, Tino," Old man Manzo said as he wielded his own razor over the stubbly hairs on the back of the customer in his chair. The jolly barber boasted. "Whaddya mean… he no trusta' my razor. I am an artist with this," Tino spoke with confidence as he waved the stainless blade over the head of the large man he was working on. "Ainna' thatta' right, mister?" he asked the man as their eyes made contact in the mirror.

Tino bore a long face as the evil patron shot him a sinister look. "Why don't ya' just shut the fuck up and finish. We'll see how good 'ya are when I get up. You better not make a mess with my hair, buddy. I'm warnin' 'ya," the burly man snapped back. Tino acknowledged the threatening stare and humbly smiled into the mirror. He nonchalantly made an adjustment on the barber's chair and turned it around to face the opposite wall as he continued. "He gets his haircut at some fancy salon, right, kid? What's it cost you, 'bout five bucks, huh?" Tic chimed in as he winked at the kid. "Ohhh, you like the girls to cutta' you hair. You likea' the way they rub againsta'you, huh, kid?" Tino said, joshing. His thick Italian accent was accompanied by a folly of gyrating motions made with his large belly and hips. The oops type of facial expression Tino made was apparent to Batista. Tino made a slip with the razor, shaving a little too much hair, creating a shiny spot of reflecting fluorescent light with the man's scalp. And as he tried to correct his mistake it just became worse. Soon the patch expanded and then he drew blood. Perhaps it was the fact that Tino's razor was honed to a scalpel-like edge or that Lotta had such a thick skull, but the mobster did not even flinch; he had not felt the slice. Joey Lotta's dark wiry hair was indeed difficult to cut with a razor as Tino was regretfully finding out. He quickly tried to cover up the mishap by immediately switching to a pair of shears and a swift combing motion. Thank God he had the chair facing away from the mirror and he decided that the only thing to do was simply shave a similar patch on his other side of his head, so at least both would be symmetrical.

Joey "Two Ton" Lotta is indeed a ruthless, evil button man and the Pope's number one enforcer. Everyone on the avenue knows and fears his reputation. He is known in the underworld as a true *malendrina*, and uglier they do not come. He is a very sinister tough guy, a braggart at that with absolutely no human conscience whatsoever and a hair-trigger temper. He has well over a dozen murders under his belt. Lotta is a brute of a man who bares permanent scar tissue around his eyes and over his brow that were peppered in from his earlier days as a professional heavyweight boxer. The Pope bought out his contract from an indebted manager and put him to better use. Tic was well aware of the explosive rage he was capable of, witnessing his punishing work firsthand on many occasions, and could only hope the barber's mistake will go unnoticed and, even possibly, draw a laugh from Joey Lotta. He sat back down and continued his conversation with the old man waiting his turn.

Tino cursed to himself over the incident, in a chiding way and in his native tongue, words just barely audible. This immediately got a reaction from the thug sitting in his chair. He yelled, "Whad-ya do? You fucked somethin' up, didn't ya? I'm warning you…I'll fuckin' slice off one of your ears," as his face grew red with anger. The entire barbershop sat up at attention.

"C'mon, boys…take it easy now," Tic said as he lit a Lucky Strike cigarette. His covered worry was he knew the man in the chair wasn't making idle threats.

Lotta fired back, "C'mon nothin', Tic. I didn't want this fuckin' 'Gagootz' touchin' my hair in the first place. I think he's half a fag." '

Tic stood up and walked to Lotta. He bent forward and clenched his teeth. He whispered in his ear, "Lascialui…sfacimm…he's a poor soul of a barber…leave him alone." He quickly reassured the goon that his haircut was just fine and instructed the barber to finish. He rolled his eyes at the chunk of hair the barber sliced away and said under his breath, "Uarda la ciunca!" Tino respected the warning and was about to say something in return. Tic cut him short. He put his forefinger to his lips. "Shut up and don't get him started," he snapped.

Mr. Manzo took the dollar bill from his customer he had just finished with and thanked him for the twenty-five-cent tip. He whistled to the aria playing on the radio as he promptly began sweeping the cut hair on the floor into a neat pile. His gaiety soon stopped and apprehension set in as the little barber glanced down and observed the ugliest display of anger developing right in front of his eyes. He stood frozen with the broom in his grasp and watched as Tino swung the swiveled chair around so the patron could see himself in the mirror. Joey Lotta gave Tino a shove then leaped out of the chair. His eyes bugged out of their dark sockets and his jaw and mouth tightened to an ugly snarl. He stared intensely into the mirror turning his head side to side. "What's dis?" he said with his fat finger poking at the bald spots and the slight bloody slice created by Tino. His tone of voice was an angered crescendo.

"I knew I shoudda' never let you touch me wit' dat' fuckin' razor. You made me look like a fuckin' clown."

"Please…sit back down…I can fix…" Tino emphatically urged. He really set Joey off when he dabbed some astringent on the open cut with a cotton ball.

Joey Lotta's infuriated anger exploded in what was worse than a rage. "Yeah, well, why don't ya' fix this… ya' fat fuck." With that said Two Ton snatched a pair of long barber's shears out of an alcohol-filled container. He swung his lumbering body around with astounding speed and plunged one of the opened blades deep down into the meaty part of the fat barber's upper chest. "I warned you, motha-fucka," the mobster snarled as he reached for the stunned barber to inflict more pain.

Suddenly pandemonium broke out. The ghastly cries from Tino were borderline hysterical and made heads turn from the sidewalk traffic out front. All the barbershop came together in a pileup almost slap-stick-like as the wounded barber let out another horrendous scream. Tino fell backward as a compilation of Italian curse words spewed from his lips: "Miserabile figlio di una cagna non va bene bastardo!" Tic jumped out of his chair and grabbed the hulking arm of the wobbling barber and tried to break his fall. Tony leaped to his feet and shadowed Tic. Tino instinctively grabbed hold of both their arms. Old man Manzo screamed, "Ue goombah," and charged Two Ton with a broom held horizontally across his chest in a futile attempt to restrain his still menacing threat. And just before Lotta tripped and fell over old man Manzo, the mobster's forward motion sent the tiny barber reeling into Batista who, in turn, sent flying the agonizing Tino directly into the little *scumbari* with the bushy mustache. In a split second, the entire melee of men collapsed on the wooden waiting room chairs completely shattering one and sending the rest into complete disarray.

Batista quickly and calmly rose to his feet and assumed the role of referee. He separated everyone and held Lotta at bay then assured the panic-stricken barber his wound was not as serious as was the grotesque image of the scissors sticking out of his chest led on to be then got the panting Tino off his feet and propped him up in his barber's chair. He summoned Joey Lotta to a private huddle. "Get outta here, you big fuckin' gaguzz, and get a message to Accardi right now. Tell him to tell the boys in blue to disregard any citizen complaints or concerns about this. Better yet tell him to meet me here soon as he can…Gabide." The goon gave a simple acknowledging nod and disappeared through the rear of the shop. Manzo came to the aid of the barber with a glass of water and then shot a disquieted look at Batista. Frank draped his arm over old man Manzo and stuffed two one hundred dollar bills in the barber's smock with a reassuring "This should take care of the damages" connotation. Then he said with conviction, "And I'll take care of the medical bills for this guy." He placed his hand under Tino's trembling arm and gave a tug. "C'mon, big guy, you're comin' with us." An encouraging nod of his head instructed the kid to help him walk the grazed Tino to his car. "Do me a favor," Batista addressed the kid. "Grab a coupla' towels, in case he starts bleeding out all over my seats." And as they walked he consoled and guaranteed the sobbing barber that he'll be fine once they get him to the hospital. Batista had to keep reminding the feeble barber of the tragic accident that had just befallen him with an indirect reference and subtle innuendos until Tino finally understood the gist and said, "Yeah…what an accident…*oh il dolore miserabile!*"

As Tino climbed into the front seat of the car, Frank Batista turned to the kid and asked, "You got something for me?" The kid responded with a wink then silently reached under his shirt. "No, not here," Tic replied with a cautious look over his shoulder. "Meet me on the corner of Ridge Street in about an hour." Tony said nothing. He gave a mock military salute and darted up an alley. Within what seemed to be seconds, an unmarked police cruiser blocked Batista's escape. Out stepped Detective Accardi. His contorted and intrusive face peered into Batista's driver's side window. "What gives?" Then he looked at the barber and gave Batista a wide-eyed stare. Batista in turn nudged the wounded barber who looked at the detective and moaned. "I—hadda—an accident." Frank Batista asked with all sincerity as he pointed to the shears protruding from the burly chest. The detective calmly shook his head with a look and the thoughts of the merriment never ceasing around there. Batista asked casually, "You wanna drive him to Clara Mass?" Detective Accardi squinted and snarled, "You fuckin' nuts, you take him, best I do is escort ya' to the Park."

Old man Manzo caught his breath and settled his nerves. He smiled at the lone mustached patron sitting patiently and excused himself as he straightened up the chairs and restacked the magazines. He was piling pieces of the broken chair in the front of the shop when another customer innocently wandered in. Manzo gave a short apologetic look and said, "Just a little accident. Not to worry, please have a seat," and the man did as he was told. Old man Manzo walked over to his station and stood proud with a clean blue and white barber's towel draped over his shoulder. With a swift and clean movement he whipped the towel from its perch and gave his trustworthy barber chair a couple of brisk snaps and swipes, and then spun it around and confidently shouted, "Next."

7

Big Anthony Marino was commandeering his Cadillac up and down Lake Street with the skill and prowess as would a vintage sea captain navigating an ocean liner toward a port of call. He swung a wide and illegal U-turn when he reached the end at Park Avenue then proceeded back up the street toward Bloomfield Avenue then repeated the entire voyage. He paid absolutely no visual attention to the motorcycle cop parked, kickstand in place, and he himself leaning in full uniform, wrapped up in a sensual conversation with a dark-haired beauty casually waiting for the downtown bus. Big Anthony carefully maneuvered the long black body of the Caddy into what he considered the perfect parking space—one that was shaded by the stately trees that grew tall overhead from the adjacent Branch Brook Park and acceptably close enough to his final destination. If in fact it was a legal space was of little to no concern. Even though the air-conditioning unit in the Coupe de Ville was set on full blast, the big guy was still sweating profusely by the time the car was officially parked. This much argued, but mute point, was due to the fact that he rode around all day with his driver's side window down. He liked to rest his huge arm on the door sill and get what is commonly known as a trucker driver's tan. The open window also let out all the dense blue smog from the Lucky Strikes that he chain-smoked along with the freon-chilled air.

He swung the Cadillac's long door open and threw his heavy framed body into motion with an audible grunt as he exited the vehicle. His heavy feet made the soles of his shoes crunch the dry dead leaves and twigs that were strewn around the blacktop and sidewalks. He adjusted his shirt as he headed up the street for a prearranged meeting with his closest and dearest friend and ally of many years, Albert "Albie" Marrone.

The two had met as kids, growing up together, fighting and playing on a cloistered farm commune where they lived with their own and a handful of other Italian immigrant families in the old coal mining community of Greensburg, Pennsylvania. Both were the sons of recently recruited *Calabrian* men who were brought over from the old country to work and toil in the black anthracite mines that ran throughout the valley's mountain ranges.

By the time they were teenagers, the boys inherited a reputation for being rough and tough street brawlers and notorious thieves afraid of absolutely nothing and respecting no one. And in time, for adventurous reason, Big Anthony's older brother Joe, who just had graduated high school, chimed in. The three roamed the tiny run-down streets of the neighboring shantytowns creating havoc wherever and whenever they could and stealing just about anything that was not nailed down.

Growing tired of working, sweating, and slaving fifteen hours a day side by side with so many of the ailing and faint miners, all breathing in the noxious coal dust, they decided to get involved with the many new bootlegging opportunities Prohibition had brought about to their area. The three started running alcohol and beer for the local gangsters and good old boys, driving old and cumbersome World War I army trucks from the small backwoods towns to the more prominent cities like Pittsburgh and even as far as Akron,

Ohio. Their unafraid brashness for this type of grueling work combined with the submissiveness of cracking heads and even murdering anyone who stood in their way soon became legend. Their adventures caught the attention of the more powerful East Coast mobsters who quickly recruited them to their *Famiglia,* utilizing their talents and savagery for handling or hijacking the many loads of whiskey that were moving up and down the dangerous routes and highways out of Canada.

The Marino brothers took up residence in a small reminiscent farm community and suburb of Newark, New Jersey, called Hillside where Big Anthony lived until he got married. The brothers sided with, and were under the guidance and rule, of a cunning Jewish mobster named Abner Zwillman, who was considered by many the *Al Capone* of the east. Zwillman had nominated the sleepy township of Hillside to be the home base of his bootlegging, vending, and black market operations.

Albert Marrone had a gifted insight when it came to choosing sides, and his allegiance went to the New York-based *Luchese* crime family. He was taken under the wing of an up-and-coming mobster by the name of Angelo Ruggeri, a natural born enemy of Zwillman. Albert made his bones as so many others had with a petitioned act of murder during those illicit of times. He took the sacred *La Cosa Nostra* oath in 1939 and is still an active member, considered as close a *consigliore* to Don Ruggeri as anyone could possibly be.

Big Anthony made no qualms or contrition when it came time to display his loyalty and allegiance to Zwillman, and it was Zwillman to first offer help when he was arrested for murder in 1937. Big Anthony was accused of beating a man to death, a reluctant non-payer of a debt in actuality. Zwillman got the charges reduced to a simple manslaughter charge for which he served four months of a one-to-five-year sentence. Perhaps his accepting the Jew's help and not the up-and-coming Ruggeri was something the mobster considered a lack of respect that would eventually bite Big Anthony in the ass. He would always semi-mock Ruggeri's crew, especially the boasting Sicilians, and he was tough enough to get away with it. He would mockingly tell them that the only true Sicilians were originally *Calabrians* with boats enabling them to cross the narrow inlet from the tip of Italy to the island of Sicily. The rest of their bloodline came from the surrounding area, especially the tip of Africa, insinuating that the old-timers had black blood running through their veins that could only be cleansed by mixing their blood with that of a pure-bred *Calabrian* such as he was. This form of braggadocio against his crew, though only hearsay in the Pope's eyes, he himself a Neapolitan, he never heard the disrespectful words firsthand—but agreed in his heart with the big guy.

The oversized ego of Big Anthony denied him the recommendations needed when it came time to open the books and vote in new members. And he was accused by many of his connected peers over the years of not having a sincere bona fide level of honor, the vital trait necessary for indoctrination into the *Cosa Nostra*. By the late forties to the early fifties the newly formed McClellan Senate Commission was hot on the tails of the Appalachian named mobsters, forcing them to close their books for a while to new members and stay out of the limelight. This further reducing Big Anthony's chances of ever getting made.

Anthony's brother Joe took a backseat to mob life and opened a gas station with his son but occasionally helps out his brother with his affairs. The recent untimely death-suicide of Zwillman now has forced Big Anthony to seek out work from the Pope. It was Ruggeri who shunted him aside with a menial bookmaking operation and continues to keep him toward the bottom of the list while he and his cohorts reaped the profits from the hard work and blood of Zwillman as they took over all the dead mobster's operations.

A loud but muffled series of vibrant chimes was heard from inside the brownstone as Big Anthony pushed on the doorbell. At that moment Anthony tried desperately to recall the last time he had actually visited his old friend and confidant. His memory served up the answer. It was over two years ago when he paid his condolences upon the death of Albie's wife. For this he felt ashamed. It took a few minutes and another push of the doorbell until a velvet window curtain moved slightly from inside the house. The thick dark-stained oak door opened silently on perfectly balanced, well-oiled hinges. The burst of chilling ice-cold air from inside the house was ominous to the visiting chum as were the tightly drawn velvet draperies on all the windows. An unshaven brute of a man with short-cropped gray hair and perfect dentures appeared. The natural scowl that spanned his huge squared jaw slowly broke into a broad smile. "Cheese. *Chefai*, it's good to see you, *ammonini*, c'mon in." Big Anthony returned the compliment and displayed his gratitude to the man for granting him the visit with a gregarious hug and an adulated kiss on the cheek, the signature greeting among such men of honor. The two spoke almost in code to one another, in a broken slang interpretation of the Italian language. Albie grabbed hold of his friend's meaty arms and squeezed tightly with admiration. "Still the *gaguzz*." Big Anthony squeezed back. "You ain't no lightweight yourself, Gaguzzalonga" (Big muscles). Though the two men have been friends for years, this was only the second time Big Anthony had visited Albert since he bought the three-story vintage brownstone eleven years ago. For that he felt more ashamed.

Big Anthony could easily measure his friend's level of success as he entered the home. "Ma Che Bell,'" he exclaimed. Albert's furniture was luxurious, made of the finest of wood and silken fabric adorned with solid gold or silver accents. Obviously hand selected by his late wife, thought Anthony. He admired his friend but thought that he never had real taste in anything. Nevertheless, his eyes scanned the thick cherrywood crown molding that followed every foot of the ceiling corners. The same baroque molding ran along the base boards and door trim and blended rakishly with a large beautifully carved wooden staircase that led to the lofty rooms above. Every inch of wood well polished and rendering a scent of lemon oil that permeated the entire house. Plush imported area rugs carried throughout the first floor rooms and created a pathway to a large traditional and freshly remodeled kitchen equipped with all the latest new-fashioned appliances money could buy.

Albert Marrone lived and obeyed all the rules set forth by his peers. From the outside, his home had a modest unadorned look that blended well with the neighborhood, including a three-year-old Buick parked in the driveway. The inside held the grandeur of a nobleman's mansion, and everything was paid for in cash.

Big Anthony followed the slightly hunched hulk of the man through the darkened rooms as he led him inside and toward the faint fluorescent-lit kitchen at the rear of the house. He found himself refraining from his usually long, lumbering strides as so he wouldn't step on the hobbling man in front of him. Albert was dressed in a velvet floor-length robe that hung over his huge drooping shoulders. It covered a white Guinea T-shirt, a pair of striped boxer shorts, and shin-high black dress socks. The sleeves of the robe were pulled up tightly above mitt-sized hands with twisted fingers, thick wrists, and brawny forearms. His short gimpy steps were accompanied by sharp, stinging pains in his hips and joints brought on by a degenerative bone disease and severe arthritis.

Albert strained to turn his head around. "*Chefei*, so for what do I owe the honor of this visit, Mr. Marino, Cheese Marino?" Albert said, half smiling and with a sarcastic overtone.

"C'mon…don't rub it in," Anthony said with a disappointed voice. "I know I've been a real *scustumad* about comin' to see ya' lately." Anthony immediately recognized the amount of discomfort his old friend was in. "So how are ya' feelin' these days, Albie?"

Albert grunted. "Fuckin' arthritis is killing me. I can just about move some days. Get yourself some coffee and have a seat...*sedeti*," Albert said as he motioned around the kitchen with his hands before easing himself into a chair at the head of the table.

"*Minch* Albie...*facciu fridda,* dis' cold air you got blowin' around here can't be good for your bones," Anthony said as he rubbed his hands together then waved one overhead in a circular motion referring to the noticeably icy breeze flowing out of two round ceiling vents. He poured a cup of black coffee and sat down at the table on Albert's right side with his back against the wall, carefully inching himself into position.

Albert pointed his finger upward and said proudly, "Central air condition. I just had it installed. The units came from a friend of mine down in Florida. You gotta' have it these days," as he reached into his robe for his cigarettes. He pulled a Camel from the crumpled pack with his gnarled fingers, placed it between his lips, and lit it.

"Yeah, I guess you do. It sure is hot out there," Anthony said. He paused some then continued with a raised brow and a descriptive *brrrr*. "You could hang meat in here, Albie."

Albert swirled his hand as if describing a spiral staircase. "Take my word for it. Arthritis or not, it's a blessing. Have a *shfooyadell*," Albert said as he pushed a plate of the crusty Neapolitan cheese-filled delicacies toward his old friend.

Anthony reached for one at the very top of the pile and sunk his teeth into the flaky pastry with a loud *crunch*, sending crumbs flying all over the table where he sat.

"Lemme' get ya' a plate." Albert grimaced as he made a feeble attempt to rise off his chair.

"Sit down, Albie. I'll get one. Where are they?" Anthony said, lifting himself up. His size and clumsiness forced the table to eke forward, sliding the wooden legs across the tiled floor with a loud screech.

"Up there in the cabinet. Over there," Albert said as he blew cigarette smoke in the direction of the cabinets where the dishes were stored.

"I hear I'm in big trouble, big, Albie… *mannaggia la miseria!*" Anthony said curtly as he sat back down and swept the loose crumbs into his plate with his hand.

Albert sighed. "Yeah…I heard that myself."

"Good news travels fast, I guess," Anthony said grimly and with a mouthful of pastry. He dusted off his hands and grabbed another.

Albert's tone of voice became serious. "I hear you're into the *bookies* and *shys* to the tune of about fifty large. Not to mention who the fuck else 'ya robbed…that true?" Big Anthony silently nodded his head in agreement, his mouth again completely filled with *shfooyadell.* Albert's eyes widened. "I also hear you got a little crazy at his executive game the other night…what 'er you *umbriag…oobatz?* You choked and smacked around a prominent *civilian* at the table. You put him against the wall," Albert said, long-faced. "That's not good, Anthony."

Big Anthony lit up a Lucky Strike and took a deep drag then sat silent with his hands folded and head down reminiscent of a child being scolded.

Albert spoke with a deliberate tone, "Look, I know you've been down on your luck a long time now. Everyone knows. You're on a losin' streak. It happens, but what the fuck were you even doin' sitting down in a game like that in the first place? I'm surprised Pope even let you in the door."

Big Anthony frowned at his old friend. "He wasn't there. And who the fuck was gonna keep me out? Edi-conosc...Sfaccimm. I had ten Gs in my pocket, thought I could bust the game open. There's nothin' but a bunch of rich assholes from Livingston in that game,"

Anthony said, red faced as his agitation mounted. "None of them knew what they were doing."

Albert let out a loud roaring laugh. "Those assholes took you for ten large—but none of 'em knew what they're doin'…" His voice was a scoffing mimicry. "Plus, another ten grand you strong-armed from Caprio. What's the matter with you? When are you gonna' learn…for chrissakes. Cheese, you of all people should know when your snake bit. Stay the fuck away."

Albert started to speak again when a loud smack on the table from Anthony's hand echoed the room. "Albie, with all due respect, I didn't come here for a fuckin' lecture… *numu fai schumbari!*"

Albert looked at him steadily then asked with suspicions, "Where did you get the ten Gs?"

"I got it from my brother," Anthony replied grimly. "I was gonna use that cash to pay down some of my debt."

Albert shook his head back and forth almost in a mocking sort of way. "Your brother always was a generous man but Cheese…fifty grand. At two points. That's a G-note a week in *vig*. Anthony, you're brother can't be that generous, no one is, and when's the last time you kicked anything up?" Albert said with beckoning hands.

Anthony was gently gnawing on the inside of his mouth with his teeth. "It's going on a month…four weeks today, as a matter of fact. Now I owe fifty-four grand…plus the juice. But who's countin' *che coz?*" Anthony said, forcing himself to smile and look Albert in the eyes. "I had the money in my hands, at the club, and…" Anthony became silent. His face was imprinted with fear and imminent danger. His head bowed.

Albert started going off again with more determination than ever. "So whaddya going to do now? I mean, c'mon, we all know that you've got brass balls. You're still trying to flash. You're still trying to get some action around town. You're driving a new fuckin' Caddy and you haven't made a single attempt to pay the man back," Albert said somberly. "That's not good, Anthony…that's not good at all… *uarda la ciunca!*" The words and warning were spoken with a pointed finger.

Anthony's face took on the look of an impish child being scolded. He snapped back in his defense, "The Caddy was paid for last year…when I ordered the thing. What do I do? Sell it… What the fuck am I gonna get for it?"

Albert's eyes bugged. "It's something—it's a sign of…well…saving face…kind of." Albert was stumbling over his words. "Something you've been doing ever since I knew ya'. You're always saving face, always in the shit. You know, before you called for this meet, Pope asked me to intervene. You know, get in the middle and work things out for you. He was sincere with me. He wanted me to talk to you… before this thing got outta' hand…you know…remind you of the rules. He wanted me to talk to you because of friendship and outta' respect. Your respect…our respect. How many guys you know go this long without a visit from someone, a harsh visit? You still think it's the old days."

Albert's words were stern but genuinely from the heart, so Anthony thought. Albert had made his point. There was a degree of respect extended from the committee to Anthony regarding this matter and all realized it. And just maybe Big Anthony does now?

Albert put his personal differences aside and asked humbly, "Now…Cheese, what can I do for you?" Albert paused some. Then he cocked his head slightly and held up his hand. His huge fist clenched tightly; his index finger was pointing straight up in the air as he spoke fervently, "But before you ask, I ain't got fifty large to lay out on your behalf. This is on your shoulders."

Big Anthony extinguished his butt in the crystal ashtray with a couple of taps and said, "I didn't come here to ask for any money, Albie." He swept the cake dish and coffee cup to the side and squared his burly arms on the table resting one atop the other. "I came to ask you to try to make things right between us." His words were straight-forward and sincere. "Between me and the Pope…that's all I'm lookin' for." He inhaled deeply and expanded his chest. "I'm willin' to work off my debt with him, anything he wants. But the prick won't let me earn." Anthony became loud and animated. "No one shows up at my games anymore, none of the Pope's crew anyhow. It's like they're told to stay away, and you know that's true." Albert gave a nod of agreement. Big Anthony continued his complaint. "My book of business is down to a couple of players that can't get action nowhere else. I got no money left to *shy*. The guys don't even use my cars anymore. I mean where do I go from here?" Anthony finished. His chest was heaving in and out as he lit another cigarette. Albert followed suit and thick smoke soon filled the air.

Albert's eyes became thin slits, and his voice took on a scolding overtone. "Ya know, Cheese, that whole Zwillman thing never sat right with any of the outfit guys, especially the Pope. They all expected you to…you know…be with us… when we came out here."

Anthony said with a half-cocked smile, "Yeah, I know. I shudda' followed your advice, but I thought they were all together…all tight with one another. I thought it was Zwillman callin' the shots. He made it clear he wanted me with him."

Albert said sarcastically, "Why wouldn't he…you were the CHEESE in those days."

They both laughed until they coughed on the cigarette smoke that filled their lungs. Big Anthony's face bent into an inquisitive grin; his facial muscles were pushing his podgy cheeks around his dark circled eyes, illuminated by the hospital-white glow of the fluorescent ceiling light, almost making him look ghostlike. "Albie, you got sons, how did ya' keep them away from all this?" Anthony continued using hand gestures. "I worry about my kid. He's getting to close…too close to Batista. I swear…he gives that guy more respect than he gives me." He finished his words with a grimacing look upon his face and shaking his head in a mournful way.

Albert sensed the pain in his old friend's heart. "It hasn't been easy, Cheese. We didn't set such good examples for our kids, did we?" He drew on a cigarette, raised his eyebrows, and continued. "I forced them to study. Made them get good grades in school. Little Al cried for a week 'cause I took him away from his neighborhood friends and sent him to Newark Academy. So did Louis. But I say 'Too bad.' Now they're both in college." Albert's crooked finger pecked hard on the table. "They want no part of this shit or this city for that matter. Besides, Cheese, you think our kids coulda' been' as tough as we was in the day? They ain't got the stomach for it like we did."

Anthony did listen some but paid little attention to his friend's sermon. A semblance of thoughts whirled in his head trying to justify and vindicate his soul. *I did the best I knew how with my boy. He's old enough to know right from wrong. His mom did teach him that* was his silent answer to Albie's soapbox dissertation?

"Albert, you ever wonder why some guy's horses always finish in the money while others never get out of the gate? You know what I mean? Like me…the bullshit luck I got."

Albert sensed the feeling of self-pity his friend displayed in his voice and quickly retorted, *"Ma che quest fratu.* We create our own destiny, Anthony. It's true, but it's God's *will* that leads us down the paths. We have no choice in that decision." Albert's finger was raised and the words he spoke were pious. "Look, before I can even try to speak on your behalf, you must go to the Pope with some form of tribute. And you must go now. Give him your Cadillac 'fer Christ sakes. You have a lot full of old Chevys you can drive. You must make amends. Offer an apology. You must make a first move of concession. You would want the same courtesy extended yourself now, wouldn't you?"

Big Anthony barked, "Whaddya mean? Beg? Is that what you're askin' me to do, Albert...Baffangul?"

Anthony's words ended with a long frown. Albert became visibly annoyed with his friend's bravado. He said with gritted teeth, "No...I don't mean beg. That's completely out of character for you, you *scocciament*. We all know that—just try and pay him the money you owe. That's all he wants, and that's the right thing to do—nothing more. Then, humbly walk away." Albert used all of his strength to lift himself off the chair and said, "Just walk away from it all. Jesus Christ...don't ya' think that after a while we would all love to walk away from the life?" The entire kitchen shook some as the aging mobster slammed his open-palmed hand into the door frame as he turned and disappeared through a narrow doorway that led to his basement. His words following him down the stairs.

Anthony sat in silence, briskly rubbing the cold off his huge forearms with his hands. His eyes stared at nothing in particular; everything now was a blur. The electronic whir the fluorescent kitchen light was making was eminent and began to soothe his nerves. And for a few seconds, remnant daydreams of gloried days past danced around his mind until the sound of scuffling of slippers on wooden steps brought him back to reality. He lit another Lucky Strike and blew gentle smoke rings toward the ceiling. Then he nonchalantly stared straight ahead and watched Albie out of the corner of his eyes as he hobbled back to the table.

"Take this," Albie said as he laid a tightly wrapped brown envelope on the table in front of his friend. "There's five Gs there," he said proudly. "Don't worry 'bout payin' me back right away. But 'ya gotta' pay me back...*haicapid?* Take this straight to Pope. Make your peace offering." Albert finished his words with a prayerlike motion of his hands. Anthony let out a sigh. "Ma che cozz'u fai?" He acted all so surprised but really had expected a lot more. He stood up and stuffed the package into his back pants pocket and said with a tearful eye, "Grazie caro amico, grazie mi frato." The two men exchanged farewell embraces, and Albert, not wanting to take the long walk to the front door, guided his friend to the rear exit and said, "Be careful, don't do anything stupid." And as the door shut Albert whispered, "U'arda la ciunca." It was a warning in slang Italian that fell on deaf ears.

The loud whizzing of the commercial-sized air-conditioning unit that piped the icy vapor into Albert's house caused Anthony to turn his head and stare with bulging eyes. It sat butted up against the house on a concrete slab a few feet away from the rear door. The thing was huge, he thought. It should be on the roof of a factory or a hotel, was his first impression as he said to himself out loud, "*Stanna mabaych!* No wonder the fuckin' house was 'freezin.'"

The hot August wind was starting to stir and began to rustle the tall treetops throughout the neighborhood. The scudding clouds were casting long shadows along Lake Street and the adjacent park as they played hide-and-seek with the sun. The dense and oppressive humidity was making everything sweat including the black ebony paint on Anthony's Cadillac giving all indications of an imminent rainstorm. Big Anthony sat in his idling car waiting for the AC unit to spew out its cold air from the vents. He listened intently to a might burst of wind, almost as if it were speaking to him. He lit a cigarette, cracked the driver's side windows halfway down, and exhaled a large puff of blue-gray smoke. He cursed some and frantically swatted his pant leg as a rogue ash singed a hole and gave his thigh a little burn. "Another fuckin' burn hole," he said aloud, grimacing, of which his clothes had many. His mind was racing furiously, repeating the words his friend spoke over and over in his mind. A feeling of desolation mixed with fear and apprehension came over him with an overwhelming conviction of *What do I do now?* That thought repeated in his mind as he stared at his image in the rearview mirror.

All at once the melancholy feeling inside the big man left as he exhaled cigarette smoke, and before he was able to take another drag his spirits were lifted by his thoughts. Judging from the conversation he had with Albert, his problems with Ruggeri no longer seemed that dire. *What's to worry?* Albert was right. If the Pope was that upset or worried about his debt, surely someone would have reached out and leaned a little on him a bit. Other men have been killed for less. Albert was told to talk to him "out of respect." That meant something in Anthony's mind. It also might have meant that he became too expensive to whack. The underworld motto is "owing is better than forgetting." His fifty-thousand-dollar debt could escalate three times that amount with the added juice. Perhaps Albert was also correct with saying that Anthony owed the Pope nothing more than money. No further indebtedness or outstanding obligations, it would be easy to severe his ties with the organization. That's what he would do. Like Albert said. Walk away. Now with the feeling of being a man at the crossroads of his life, Albert's words rang even louder in his ears, "We create our own destinies." All of a sudden his distrusting, cynical half chimed in. Why only the five thousand dollars? Why not ten Gs or twenty Gs for that matter? The prick could afford it, and rightfully so. He should have offered the whole amount. Was this Albert's way of blowing him off?

Perhaps it was Albert's intention of taking the easy way out? Knowing that if he blew this small amount money Albert gave him, Big Anthony would also blow any further opportunity for Albert to help; he could never ask him for a favor again, or from anyone in Albert's crew. Big Anthony was pondering his options. His criminal mind told him to go back inside and snuff the life out of the old, crippled man then ransack his basement. There was probably a small fortune hidden down there. That would be the answer to all his money woes. No. Wait. The Pope knew of this meeting. He was sure of that. Albert surely reported their pending get-together days ago.

He would be the first they would suspect if the capo turned up missing. Not a good idea by any means, and besides, he couldn't bring himself to whack one of his oldest and dearest friends.

Big Anthony put the Cadillac in motion, and as he drove, he frantically thought out a plan for the path of righteousness he knew he must take. His erratic driving was consistent with the vivid thoughts that rattled his brain. He was *not* a *made* guy. He swore no oath of allegiance to anyone. It would be an easy transition. First, he would go visit the Pope and give him the package containing the five thousand and the pink slip to his Cadillac. Albert was right again. He did have a car lot full of sedans he could drive. After that he would ask to be put on some sort of payment plan for the outstanding debt. The Pope would grant him that out of respect! Then he would call his brother Joe. His brother was always preaching to him about getting out of the rackets. Go legit! Become his partner with another gas station or turn his seedy car lot into a real retail auto establishment. His brother Joe had the money and would never say no to an honest business proposition. He would get his son Tony Boy involved also. It could be a chance to get him off the mean streets and away from Frank Batista.

They would all work together—him, his son, and his brother Joe. It was his brother Joe who years ago had the insight to walk away from this life of crime. And it was his brother Joe who, after burying his own wife from cancer, a few short years ago, begged Big Anthony to do the same. He offered to take him in, as a partner in the gas station that he and his son operated, letting Anthony know that there was plenty of room for all.

Joe Marino did make a lot of money with Anthony and his gang, and he socked it all away, investing it wisely in a nice brick Tudor home in the Westminster section of Hillside and a comfortable four-room summer rental cottage in the remote shore community of Ortley Beach. He owned the corner property on Central

Avenue in Hillside that was just up the street from where Zwillman once had his headquarters and where his Flying A gas station now sits plus another two, still vacant, commercial lots that are up the block, investment property he bought a couple of years ago from the late Zwillman. He lived a semi-law-abiding life, not completely fearful of a little criminality or malfeasance, but for the most part was an all right civilian who never forgot his roots. Joe would be hot for this venture. Why it would be the first completely honest thing his brother ever asked him to be in on! Big Anthony couldn't wait to drive another five minutes up the avenue to call him from his office. He pulled to the closest pay phone, dialed up his brother Joe, and excitedly outlined his plan, to which his brother said, "I'll catch up with ya' later." Big Anthony had a broad almost childlike grin on his face as he slammed the black phone receiver back in its cradle. He anxiously lumbered back into his flagship and, without any disregard whatsoever, sped out in front of all the oncoming traffic.

Frank Batista sped his Cadillac up the wrong side of the roadway en route to the Clara Mass Hospital emergency room with the injured Tino at his side. "Take it easy, big guy, we're almost there," he said to Tino in a reassuring voice. He reached with his right hand and rearranged the towels that lie on the car seat where Tino was and said with conviction, "Keep that towel tight on the wound…help keep the bleedin' contained, and don't let that scissor pop out—it'll be like a gusher in here." Tic obviously was more concerned with not getting *any* bloodstains on his leather upholstery. The Argentine just moaned in an Italian dialect as he had been doing for the entire trip. Frank remarked on how little bleeding there was almost, commending the large barber for his efforts on not staining his seats.

The hospital emergency room was not at all busy as the two men entered. This brought a sigh of relief from Batista's lips. He loathed hospitals almost as much as courthouses or police stations. Tino had his arm wrapped around Frank's shoulder, and Frank was struggling with his size and weight, trying to keep them both balanced.

There were only a handful of "common ailment" type sufferers sitting in the rows of pale green vinyl chairs and patiently awaiting their turn as Frank plopped Tino down in a section away from the others. A woman sitting gasped at the grotesque sight of the shears protruding from the blood-soaked smock of Tino. Frank blew past the Triage station and headed without hesitation toward the double doors marked PRIVATE. He grabbed the first nurse he could find. "There's a guy out there had a nasty accident." The nurse was clearly unmoved by his words. She just nodded her head, continued on her way. Frank shouted in dismay, "Okay then, I'll just go sit with him." The nurse gave her seal of approval by raising her arm and waving.

Frank returned with hypothetical words of encouragement for Tino and spoke to him as if he was a child, "Your doin' real good, big guy. Nurse says there's nothing to worry about. The doc will have you outta here in a jiffy. Now whaddya gonna tell the Doc if he asks?" Tino replied as his heavy breathing made his chest tremble, "I slipped and fell down." "Good…good boy." Frank said then reached into his hip pocket and pulled out a wad of cash. He gave his thumb a lick then peeled off three one-hundred-dollar bills and stuffed them into the barber's folded hands. "Here take this. It should be more than enough to cover the bill. If not, I'll pay the rest myself. Okay," Frank said audaciously then gave him an honorable slap on the back. "Look, big guy, I really gotta' run. When you're done here, grab a cab ride back to the shop, and I'll see ya' later, all right?" Frank said, giving Tino a thumbs-up hand sign and a delicate pinch on the cheek. As he exited, Frank said in his poorly spoken Sicilian dialect, "Be brave, my friend. Be strong, and don't forget, keep your mouth shut." As he began to drive out of hospital parking lot, coincidently, Detective Accardi was once again blocking his escape. The two drivers maneuvered their autos until they were side by side, close enough to converse. The detective asked, "Everything all right in there?" his words spoken in his usual unconcerned monotone voice. Batista replied with a wink and a nod, "What could be wrong—it's a fuckin' hospital." Both sped off in different directions, and both watched each other disappear in their rearview mirrors. Frank sneered and thought about how much he distrusted that crooked cop.

It seemed so very long ago, years ago, that a driven and decisive Newark patrolman named Eddie Accardi was just another rookie cop, fresh out of the academy. And so it was, such a very long time ago, that he went on his first tour of duty. And indeed it felt like ages ago before he first was considered for any type accommodation, then promoted and allowed to brandish the distinctive scalloped-shell-shaped shield that read "Newark Police Detective." And now, today, as he drives his unmarked police cruiser up and down Bloomfield Avenue, he often thinks and says aloud the truism "It has been a long time."

By the end of his rookie year, Officer Edward Accardi of Newark's Second Precinct already had an extensive and outstanding arrest record accompanied with numerous citations from his captains, police commissioners, the DA's office, and even Mayor Carlin himself. His service record was impeccable. Star studded and commendable since his graduation from the police academy September of 1935. He was usually the accredited arresting officer or an attributing factor involved with hundreds of area burglaries, drug-related felonies, illegal gambling, and crimes of murder. A worthy record that made him rise quickly to the top and receive a "duck soup" promotion to detective by the police commissioner in what many thought was record time. And soon a rank of lieutenant, his last promotion by choice, was to follow. A native of the North Ward, and raised in the opulent Forest Hill section, and still living, along with his wife and two children, in the same home he and his father conjointly own.

His father, an Italian immigrant who entered the country illegally in 1921, fleeing criminal charges from his homeland, found safe haven and security in the city of Newark, New Jersey, and he, his wife, and their five-year-old son were immediately granted citizenship in the United States thanks to his first cousin, mob boss and politically connected Angelo Ruggeri. Ruggeri was able to pull all the necessary strings to harbor his cousin and find him easy work in a large well-established bookbinding factory.

The voiced concern that the son of one of the Ruggeri's cousins was joining the police force brought a stir throughout the underworld. Surely a young man of his physical size could be more suited for their activity, on their side of the law. Accardi was short and so intriguingly resembled a bulldog—slicked-back brown hair, a natural scornful look, and a pencil-thin mustache. This being his egotistical joy knowing that none of the mob was allowed to wear one. At first all of Ruggeri's capos had dire worriment, but soon, after a reasonable explanation was offered, the tides slowly turned toward the other direction. Refrains of admonitions rang like church bells. It soon became considered a secluded victory for everyone connected with Ruggeri's family. What he proposed, created, was ingenious. Could you imagine the concept, the subtleness of it all, Ruggeri's own internal *spy* so to speak, consorting and fraternizing with both sides for the *good* of just one? Ruggeri would groom him to his standards, to be a model cop and criminal alike, working hand in hand and keeping the streets of his city and its citizens protected from low-level thugs and punks that generally harm the innocent and take away from their cash cow. Eddie Accardi would be a man of honor; A *made*

Man with allegiance first to his *Famiglia* and sworn in blood, and then the citizens and the police department of Newark.

Lieutenant Detective Eduardo Accardi services the diverse neighborhoods of the Second Precinct that comprised the Northward Community of Seventh Avenue, Upper and Lower Roseville Avenue, North and Lower Broadway, Mt. Pleasant and the Forest Hills section, and swore to uphold the oath he took…for both sides. And if he must do so, now as in the past, extend his long arm of the law or the lawless as far as he sees fit. His policies are harsh and austere in some cases and compassionate in others. If a lower avenue dreg or an undesirable from another part of the city wandered in with illegal ideas, they were beaten to pulp first then dealt with legally afterward if he saw fit. If a local neighborhood adolescent was caught out of line, he would hand carry the youth home to his parents, give them a stern warning, and tell the kids and the parents there would not be a second chance. If a respectable parent was caught out of line, the cop would escort him to Ruggeri.

Nothing illicit or illegal, especially stolen goods or any variety of swag, moved in or out of the city without the mob's knowing about or having their hooks on. If a truck was hijacked or a burglary or armed robbery was committed by some renegade outside of the outfit, the *capos* would immediately summon their network of street spies and stoolies to bring forth a name of the felon, or else. They considered that act to be downright disrespectful—first, condemning the freelancing thief for daring to come on their sacred soil and without going through the proper protocol, take food from their mouths, and second, bring unnecessary heat from the authorities onto their turf.

It may be all so easy for an enterprising thief to drive off with a load of fine Italian suits or a truck full of cigarettes, even abscond with a cache of jewelry, but what does he do with it then? It is almost impossible to fence such a boodle of hot items without involving organized crime. And God forbid the felon should pick the pockets or cash registers or the safes of someone connected; it would be all over for the lost soul. Once they find out it was a low-level renegade thief or a desperate drug addict that committed the crime, what would happen next would be considered a paradox of justice. The rogue crook would be sought out and lured to one of the many warehouses or other safe mob-occupied locations under the guise of fast "cash on the barrel head" money, usually much more than the going rate for such swag. He would then be severely beaten and tortured to give up any other accomplices or any other known jobs that were to go down. The merchandise would be distributed among the outfit and the authorities, and the felon would be handed over in a neatly wrapped package to the arresting officer for swift and stringent justice.

The name on record of all these types of haughty "busts" was always Edward "Eddie" Accardi. Eddie was hand-fed "collars" that were carefully selected by his underworld partners. Sacred information was leaked his way. It led to busts that would benefit all involved, boosting his arrest record and opening up more opportunity for the mob that preyed on human weakness. Every once in a while, though, they would be forced to give up one of their own as a sacrificial lamb to the gods of justice. It would be a prearranged bust, usually a gambling charge or another vice-related offense where the perpetrator would be guaranteed short and easy jail time at a "country club" state facility. His family would be well taken care while he was away, his iniquitous job waiting for him along with a sizable envelope of tribute when he returned.

A dirty cop has the same fear and foreboding as any common criminal on the street; the odds are just much more in his favor of not ever getting caught in a dubious act of crime. Throughout history, law enforcement and district attorneys laugh about how the stereotyped "sloppy" criminals, the mostly black or other minority races, always get caught, if not red-handed, in the actual act, than it will be through some easy and apparent undercover investigation of some sort. Maybe a slip of the tongue of a jealous and anonymous rat or bona fide informant would be their demise. And when caught, they would bear the brunt for all the others who skate free.

When Edward Accardi first joined the Newark Police Department, rumors where flying throughout the academy about the young man's possible affiliation and family blood ties to one of the biggest mobsters in the city. When his appointment/assignment came to work out of the Second Precinct, the innuendos became more profound, more of a disesteem, a reference of being born with a silver spoon in his mouth. "Not to worry" was Ruggeri's impervious retort to the plaint and ordered the young officer to dare anyone to tie their names together by blood or marriage.

The rookie patrolman Accardi seemed a little addled by the demand but mulishly did exactly that. He denounced the accusations loud and clear, inviting anyone who wanted to waste their time and "dig through archives" or "climb family trees" that they were more than welcome to make inquiry. To further enforce his resolution, he put up a month's salary as a bet. The ploy worked. Eddie had been on the force less than six months when an eager beaver in the Internal Affairs Department took the bait, utilizing all of his resources and some of the FBI's as well. It was, in fact, someone from the Federal Bureau of Investigation that suggested the search. After a two-month investigation it was confirmed; there is no connection anywhere on record, just as Angelo Ruggeri had known there wouldn't be.

A carefully laid plan was devised and executed many years ago, long before the young Edward had plans of ever becoming a cop. Angelo Ruggeri came from the tiny Neapolitan village of Casoria just north of Naples, Italy. His family was small—a mother and father and sister, an uncle and aunt and two cousins; Massimo and Renata Ruggeri and their child, a boy named Eduardo. They were in fact the only living relatives Ruggeri actually had still living on the other side.

Massimo was involved with the old Sicilian mafia, smuggling guns from the mainland to the island. Soon he became a wanted man by the Sicilian government and was being searched for in and around Naples. He turned to one of his family members from the United States whose reputation had spread across the ocean. This man he was referring was a man of great power and respect. He was known as a *degli uomini*—a leader of men. The man was Massimo's very own cousin, Angelo Ruggeri. Ruggeri was compelled to help since it was his uncle, Massimo's father, who helped his family make the journey years prior and agreed to smuggle Massimo and his family out of Italy.

A dirt-poor sailor from Sicily was found "quarantined" to a small bedraggled sanitarium, stricken with tuberculosis and unable to travel back to his homeland. His name was Emilio Accardi. Well aware of his failing health and forlorn situation the bedridden sailor graciously agreed to the intricate scheme that was outlined and presented to him. An Italian war bond for the amount of one million lire would become payable to the dying sailor's wife. The proper documents would be produced, birth certificates and passports for Emilio Accardi, his wife, and their four-year-old son. Passage was booked on an Italian freighter sailing from Naples to New York July 1921, and the ailing sailor was transported to another remote sanitarium in the village of Casoria under the name of Massimo Ruggeri and left to die.

The new-born Accardi family welcomed the sight of the New York harbor and the tiny island of Ellis. When the investigation came to light, Eddie demanded a written letter from IE exonerating his name and any association with known mobsters plus the young detective's salary for the month. It wouldn't be for almost another fifteen years before the Accardi name came up for investigation this time by the federal government and the McClellan Senate Committee agents, again finding nothing incriminating and the filed sealed and stamped CLOSED.

Angelo Ruggeri ignored the rules completely when he allowed Eduardo to enter the secret sacred world of the Cosa Nostra. Traditionally, only full-blooded Italians or Sicilians were to become made men, of which Eduardo certainly was. Men with only partial Italian blood were excluded as where any member of law enforcement, active or retired, as also Eduardo was. This long-standing tradition kept a lot of well-groomed gangsters from taking the oath of Omerta; however, they all still functioned well within the realm of the underworld but were without a sworn allegiance. Historically, all the mob turncoats where not made guys. Ruggeri wanted Eduardo to completely understand and swear his allegiance.

Ruggeri held a semi-private initiation in the basement of his estate, the first time ever. Attending were Eduardo and his father, Emilio. Ruggeri's most sacred capo, Albert Marrone, was also there in sworn secrecy along with an expendable capo by the name of Jimmy Algretti. After the short ritual of accepting Eduardo into the brotherhood, drinks and a light lunch of Italian sandwiches were enjoyed by the men. The elder Emilio Accardi stayed behind and watched as the other three men left the confines of the apartment-like basement of Ruggeri's home. They all entered an awaiting car, but before the driver stepped on the gas pedal, two shots from a revolver rang out. The bullets aimed at the back of the head of the doomed Algretti. Eduardo was the triggerman, acting from the backseat with Marrone at his side giving him a solemn nod of acceptance over the smoking gun. Algretti was suspect of soon becoming a rat; for that crime he was executed. The truth was Ruggeri, in addition to the alleged accusations about the man, wanted no witnesses other than Marrone to the initiation as to avoid any future controversy with the rest of the commission.

When Eddie Accardi took his oath of allegiance with the Pope, the first thing he was taught was how to hide assets as secretly as his father hid his real identity, under the guidance and supervision of Ruggeri himself. Eddie sought out and married a blue-blood Italian, Phyllis (née Palumbo) whose family are heirs to a wealthy olive oil importer/exporter and herself a graduate from NYU, now working as an executive secretary to the president of the Ronson Corporation. Their combined salaries more than justify the modest but comfortable lifestyle they live. They co-own, with Edwards's parents, a large brick home that sits on a fortressed lot on the corners of Highland and Montclair Avenue, and at one time had Angelo Ruggeri as a neighbor.

The lake house, dock, and the fifteen-foot sport fishing boat at Budd Lake shows a 25 percent ownership in their names, the rest divided up with his in-laws. Phyllis drives a modest car and he an old pickup truck plus his police cruiser. They have just enough debt to show they are living the American dream. Their checking and savings accounts are well within reason, no large sums of money moving in or out suspiciously.

The couple has a modest portfolio of blue chip stocks and bonds, and they also receive a small annuity from her family's olive oil business. Every legal amount of cash that one could be gifted has already been done so by both sets of their parents. The Accardi family takes a modest vacation, sometimes twice a year, and they pay their taxes. Edwards's spending habits will lead even a master sleuth down a dead end trail with absolutely no hopes of finding the over two hundred thousand cash he has buried in a well-secured wall safe in the basement of his mother-in-law's Upper Montclair home or the acre of property awaiting his retirement in South Florida. Detective Accardi follows closely the advice set forth by the Pope and always checks his rearview mirror.

On any given day or evening, Eddie could be seen cruising the serpentine streets and the invariable avenues of the Second Precinct in his unmarked Ford sedan sometimes with his old partner Pasquale "Patsy" Covella, who is now retired, but on occasion, either to reminisce or as a favor, would joyride some. For the most part, Patsy was an honest cop who did not mix in with or interfere with any of Eddie's extracurricular activities but saw nothing wrong with a little clean graft once in a while to subsidize his modest detective's salary and better his children's future. High-level mob chores were carried out solely by Eddie. Today Detective Accardi was traveling sans his underling with a list of duties and special surveillances ordered up by the Pope and noticing that one of the items on the list was just coming into view. The afternoon skies were now completely overcast, creating a thick grayish haze over the entire North Ward as far as the eyes could see. The high noon sun was completely cloud covered, revealing just an apperception of a dull orange ball. The unlit sky was comforting on the pupils, but there was no relief for the relentless heat and humidity. Only an approaching storm bringing cool wind and rain could ease the choke hold.

Tony Marino walked out of Menotti's Corner Market and stopped briefly to gulp down a few swigs of ice-cold milk from a glass pint container. He started up the avenue toward the spot Batista had designated with the thoughts of Joanie again fomenting in his brain. He turned his head in the direction of the visibly darker, almost black skies that were to the south and immediately thought of the ruined weekend the girls would be having if it was raining down the Jersey Shore. His first instinct was to laugh to himself thinking, *Good. Serves her right. She should be here with me. Why should she be enjoying the sand and surf without me? She's probably stuck in her motel room bored, and I hope she is.* He said this to himself gloatingly. He hoped that it would storm the entire weekend.

He prayed that it was pouring rain in Seaside Heights, confining her to inside the motel room, keeping her prisoner and pining for him as he was pining for her. An exalting feeling again gave in to the Jekyll/Hyde psyche that suddenly leaped out of his chest. Perhaps it would rain, and rain hard at that. And she would seek the shelter of the boardwalk and its many hangouts, and it would probably be filled with guys his own age or maybe older, all drooling over her bikini-clad body, touching her, admiring her breasts, her shapely thighs, and plump ass as most men would. How would she be acting? Would she be there flaunting herself at them? Flirting with every good-looking guy who happened by, all of them trying ever so hard to get in her pants.

His teenage rage was eating at his insides, making his anger apparent in his eyes as the thought of her with another was more than his macho Guinea character could handle. He tried desperately to block them out. A sudden rhythmic honking of a car horn that seemed right on top of him brought him back to his senses. He caught a glimpse of the slow-approaching unmarked police cruiser as it veered toward the curb. Tony kept his eyes glued to the blacktop then nonchalantly looked up. He grimaced as he immediately recognized the slicked brown hair and the pencil-thin mustache of Detective Eddie Accardi.

The detective leaned over from the driver's seat and hand cranked the window down on the passenger side. Just the physical sight of him intimidated the kid. The cop's biceps were bulging out of the cheap blue short-sleeve shirt he was wearing. A cheap tie seemed to choke the thick neck of the detective and turn his face an unsightly reddish hue, the color of mad. His polished brown shoulder holster held a snub-nose .38 special with a modified wooden grip and stood out like a sore thumb. It bore a warning notice of "shoot first and ask questions later."

Accardi stared the boy down some, almost frisking him visibly; then he said with a stern voice, "Jump in. I need to talk to you about something." His cold cruel fix was intense. Tony froze in place and just studied the man. He was ever so leery to obey his order. The detective unlatched the car door and swung it open as he said intently, "Don't worry, kid, if this was a bust, you would have already been handcuffed and lying face down in the gutter. Now get the fuck in the car." Tony had no choice but to obey the detective. Running would be futile. His only thought was this must be another gambit or ploy of some kind ordered by Batista? There couldn't be any real danger here was his next assumption, so why not get in? Tony's cunning mind was already in motion as he said to himself, *Just act cool and play the game.* He laid his container of milk down next to the curb and climbed inside the car.

As the detective prepared to drive off he eyed his side and rearview mirrors, then ordered the kid to roll up the window. Tony reluctantly obeyed; the cruiser had a repulsive smell of stale tobacco and sweaty feet. He thought it needed a good airing out. The boy felt a little uneasy but soon realized the truth of the cop's words. He sat still and silent, with his eyes front. He began to study the man from the corner of his eyes, his peripheral vision, a subtle trick he learned and was becoming quite proficient at. He had good antenna and was able to read people in an uncanny sort of way. Eddie's facial profile was almost angular with a flattened nose that was a consummation of years of organized boxing with the Police Academy League and street fights. His mouth had a permanent scowl that pulled his thin mustache down, giving him a sort of half-man half-lion look and paired well with his deep, guttural, and angry voice. He was tall in the saddle and seemingly fit. He rode with the seat back as far as it could go as he held the wheel with long outstretched arms, which gave him agility and freedom of motion to enter or exit the vehicle without obstruction.

The two rode silent for a while until the detective broke the ice. "Ain't that your old man ahead of us? It is…isn't it?" The kid noticed the pensive stare of the detective then recognized the distinctive sharklike fins and red bullet taillights of the Caddy as it cruised two car lengths up from them. "Yeah, that's him," the kid remarked then laughed and said, "He always got his arm hangin' outta the window." The detective said amusingly as he noticed Big Anthony flick a cigarette butt out of the car, "You can't miss those meat hooks. Hey…I should cite him for littering." The boy let out a forced laugh then turned his head away from the cop in disgust. He began to daydream as he looked out of the passenger window.

Tony praised the air-conditioned car, to himself, and in spite of its rank odor, its coolness was a relief from the summer's heat and humidity. He suddenly seemed glad that he was picked up by the intrusive detective. His sweat was dissipating. As they drove and passed all the familiar sights of the Bloomfield Avenue, Tony thought just how many people are wondering why he is riding shotgun with a cop.

Eddie took another quick right hand turn off Lake Street and slowly began weaving in and out of the adjacent side streets for what seemed to be an eternity, but according to the kid's Longines, it was only six minutes. The kid noticed the detective's eyes were glued to the rearview mirror with intensity, almost unmoving as he navigated the cruiser through the narrow streets, driving on what was pure instinct and guided by some sort of internal radar. The cop had great peripheral vision also, and though his eyes were staring straight ahead, he was able to observe any type of nervousness or an unconscious "tell" the boy might have that would enable him to pressure point an offense of interrogation when the time came. The boy sensed a feeling of anxiety on the cop's part, and he tried to anticipate what would be his next move, the nagging question of why the hell he was in the car still fomenting in his mind. Whatever the reason or whatever Eddie had in store for him would surface soon enough.

The cruiser picked up speed as it rounded a turn and headed up Heller Parkway. The detective's eyes were ignoring the mirror and now were steadfast on the road they were driving on. He took a sharp left turn into the Park, heaving the vehicle on its shock absorbers. The inertia of the turn forced the kid to awkwardly brace himself. His hands and feet searched for something solid to steady his shifting weight on the slippery vinyl seat covers. The aggressive driver made another hard sharp turn and brought the cruiser to an abrupt stop in an empty parking area. The boy had no time to brace or prepare himself for what was to happen next. The strong right arm of the detective slammed the gear shift lever into park and in a split second movement had the kid by the back of his hair twisting his head upward while his other hand came under his jaw and slid into a viselike grip around his throat. He placed his square scowling face to an inch away from the boy and snarled, "I know you're dirty, kid… you're dirty with drugs." The boy felt the heat of the cop's pungent cigar breath as he continued. "You think we don't know what you're up to? You're probably holding right now, huh, kid?" The boy felt his windpipe closing. He gave a breathless shake of his head *no*, fighting the gorilla grip of the detective. "We've been watching you for a long time now…ever since that Trebbiano incident. Who ya' workin' for? I want a name or I'll break your fuckin' neck," he said, still showing his teeth. The detective caught himself and turned down his temper. He eased off the choke hold then let go of the boy's hair. There was a moment of dead silence; then he truculently ordered the kid with a "Let's go, you…open the door and get out," himself making the first move to exit as the boy reluctantly followed suit. This shakedown was forceful and dire on the belligerent detective's part, Tony Boy thought. Nothing at all like the other rousts he had been put through by his mentor. *This felt all too real.* His inner voice was asking, *Does this guy really think I push drugs? What was he really digging for?* He thought as his hand grabbed the door handle.

Eddie was already next to the passenger side of the door, waiting, before the kid's feet touched the blacktop. He snatched the kid by his shirt, forcefully lifting him out of the cruiser. Tony naturally resisted and thought for just a brief moment of challenging the detective but wisely decided not to. It took the rogue cop all of his strength to spin the kid around and throw him face first into the side of the cruiser. The cop then methodically guided both of the boy's hands behind his head while he applied pressure to the nape of his neck with an open palm. "Don't fight me, kid...now step back." He commanded. The boy felt himself slip into an awkward and vulnerable position, anticipating more physical punishment. It came in the form of a well-placed kidney shot that sent a sharp, numbing feeling to his legs. The words "Spread em" were followed by a couple of riveting kicks to the insides of his ankles by the detective who proceeded to frisk him.

The cop's hands probed and patted him from head to toe. He lifted a wallet out of the kid's pocket and tossed it on the roof of the car. Using both hands, he swung the kid around, slamming him hard into the cruiser. Trepidation and fear was in the boy's eyes as the detective continued the now frontal body search. "Word on the street, kid, is you're pushin' smack," he said with staggered breaths. "That true?" He gave him no time to answer before he turned sideways and said, "Empty your pockets." First came out a small wad of cash. The cop snatched the folded bills from the boy, thumbed through the cash, then shoved it in his top shirt pocket. Next came some small change and a single door key that the he clanged on the roof of the cruiser.

The approaching summer squall sent a hard gust of wind across the gray skies above Branch Brook Park, rustling the tall tree branches and scattering hundreds of birds to seek shelter elsewhere. The detective took a step back, approving the nearing storm by turning his head into the forcible breeze. He inhaled deeply, expanding his burly chest almost as to demonstrate an act of bravado. Tony followed his motion and faced him eye to eye. The cop moved into him closely. His rough demeanor became much more passive and kind as he said, "Tell me the truth. Are you pushin' drugs?" He continued soothingly. "I can help before you get in over your head." His words seemed sincere but cunning. "No, sir," he said curtly but with conviction. "I don't know where you're gettin' you're information from, but it's not true." "Shut up," the detective said sharply before the kid could get another formed word out of his mouth. "What else you hiding?" Those words made the kid freeze in fear. Should he volunteer the letter he has stuffed in his waistband that is now practically down to his crotch. Is this what it is all about? Perhaps just another test to find out if he is "stand up." But why such a roughhousing. At that moment Tony realized that there could be an ulterior motive for the sham raid. He really knew nothing about drugs. He may have had a slight inclination about Tic and his brief association with Trebbiano, who was a known drug dealer. Or perhaps he heard something here or there but nothing substantial and nothing that could be corroborated?

He knew of no evidence or no one that could point a finger at anyone, especially Frank Batista. The kid knew the drug business was taboo, and that's all he knew. But let's say Batista was involved. Tic would never leak that out and tip his hand. He would never involve or trust a cop with such a guarded secret, especially one so close to the Pope. An act of that nature on Batista's part would be like signing his own death warrant.

Eddie Accardi is considered Ruggeri's eyes and ears in the deep dark city on both sides of the street. Eddie Accardi is also a smart and savvy detective well versed with the street hoodlum ways. Over the course of his career he probably frisked thousands of young punks and drug dealers. It came to no surprise for the kid when Eddie's hands reached under his clothing and down his pants discovering the airmail envelope stashed there. He gave the boy a cold stare followed by stinging slap across his face. "What the fuck is this?" he said inquisitively, holding the envelope over his head. He again asked the kid, "What do we have here I wonder?" His face took the look of a wise old owl. And his eyes squinted and became calculated as he produced a small pocket knife and gingerly sliced open the sealed envelope and removed its contents.

The cop studied the Sicilian gibberish with a bewildered look on his face, trying to decipher some meaning of the scribble. He couldn't make out a word. The almost stupid look on his face was sincere, reinforcing the fact that Tick Tock did not authorize this. Again he asked the boy what it was, only this time more unpretentiously. Tony looked at the black ink and said humbly, "I dunno'. It's something my mother gave me for my father to look at." He looked at the cop with the eyes of a puppy. "I think it's a shopping list of some sort…I really don't know…I can't read it." His words drifted. Once a cop always a cop as Eddie's suspicious nature made him ask with raised eyebrows, "Then why was it down your pants?" Tony Boy was confident his fish story convinced the detective and said simply, "I didn't want to lose it. My mother would kill me."

The tension in the air was beginning to subside. Detective Accardi let out a woeful sigh and said sympathetically, "Sorry things gotta' little rough, kid. No hard feelings…okay." His face actually tried to smile as he continued. "You're a good kid. Everybody likes you. And you're old man too. I'm just doing my job." The truth of the matter was Accardi had deep hatred for Big Anthony, and now he let it fester and build up against the kid. He hoped one day he would either arrest or gun down one of them. He handed the boy back his envelope and finished. "Grab that shit off the car. C'mon, I'll give you a lift back to the avenue." Detective Accardi let the boy off in front of Branchbrook Hobby Shop. And as he lifted up on the door handle, he said, "Thanks for the ride." Then he asked with a cocksure grin, "Can I get my money back too?" Accardi held out the kid's cash and said sarcastically, "Here, go buy 'yerself a toy." Tony watched cautiously as the cop swung an illegal U-turn and sped away in the opposite direction. He held his breath until the cruiser was out of sight.

As he drove, Detective Accardi glanced at the address to one of the locations that were written down on a small notepad: M and M Motors. This one would be saved for later. The Pope had given him a list of a few Social Clubs, bookie joints, and taverns with the standard instructions of what to do. He would observe the street traffic of patrons in and out of the establishments, take names, monitor anything his judgment deemed nefarious, jot down some license plate numbers for a DMV check, and any other type of noticeable covert activity he wanted to make mention of when he reported to his other boss.

Ruggeri would routinely make certain that the PSEG truck randomly parked on a side street or any other type of utility vehicle was truly on the job and wasn't filled with infiltrating government agents. His intense probing of the utilities created an innate stir with the phone company after a Bell Telephone supervisor found out about a lowly installer who was being monitored and was noticed to be in an unauthorized part of the North Ward several times a week. It was later learned that the guy had an insatiable appetite for the lowlife prostitutes who worked the sleazy neighborhood streets and was just exchanging company favors for blow jobs. When Ruggeri found out the poor lost soul was fired, he immediately got him back in Ma Bell with the new job title of supervisor and reminded him who was it that helped him. He should never forget his friends.

Angelo Ruggeri kept a close eye on everything and everyone around him. His network of spies reached far into the corridors of the justice department. The phone company and the public utility departments was also at his complete disposal; just about anywhere a record could be kept he had someone feeding him information. He had only to pick up a phone and reach out to one of his secured contacts and have an accurate and detailed account of every activity going on around his prided kingdom. Eddie Accardi was just one of many cogs in the Pope's wheel of organized crime.

Eddie sat and calculated the rest of his day while parked behind a Social Club operated by a small-time bookie named Jelly Gianelli. He was suspected of laying choice bets off to a gypsy Jew bookmaker in Hillside for a bigger percentage of the losses than he was receiving from the Ruggeri organization. Action like this that would get a woeful cackling from the crew, "Why the fuck they even try?" With now only one more stop to make after this task at hand, Accardi figured he would be able to get back to his office by three-thirty, do some paperwork until his shift ended at 4:00 p.m. He would get his recorded information to Ruggeri, gather up his wife and two kids, and be off to his four-bedroom custom-built lake house in the secluded community of Budd Lake, New Jersey, where he hoped to be grilling thick rib-eye steaks and drinking ice-cold beer by seven tonight.

C eil Marino awoke from a horrific dream with an audible shriek. "Maronna mia" were the only words she could form and say with her parched lips. She jumped again in fear as she heard the neighbor's dog bark a few times. She sat in a cold sweat with her heart racing feverishly and her eyes wide open trying to recall the details of what was just envisioned in her mind. At first she saw wild dogs, huge vicious dogs. They were in the dreary distance. Their dull squalled black coats of fur blended with the eerie darkness. Their glowing red eyes only visible as were their frothing fangs. Bloodcurdling screams from humans could be heard along with bellowing snarls and growls.

Suddenly the wild dogs were up close, directly in front of her, biting and savagely tearing the flesh and limbs from faceless people. People who she recognized at first then watched their identities disappear, erased from her memory. The wild animals turned on her. She ran and hid next to her husband. The wild dogs began chewing through her bedroom door that she had just slammed shut. Her husband laughed at her from the background; then he too was viciously attacked by the animals. That's all she could remember before everything became just a vague thought and within a split second disappeared completely from her memory.

Ceil glanced at the tiny watch fastened around her wrist and uttered a disconcerting "Oh shit" out loud. She gave her napping mother a gentle rub of the hand. "Ma...wake up." It was already after one o'clock. "I'm running late, Momma...I have to go." Ceil spoke until her mother opened her eyes. Apparently the two dozed off watching their afternoon soap operas. Ceil said again, "Momma, I have to go now," then mumbled something nasty to the television exemplifying her contempt for the game show "Queen for a Day" that was airing. Her mother opened her eyes fully as the applause meter on the television was selecting the afternoon contestants. "What are you going to do tonight?" her mother asked in broken English. "I'm going to bingo with Margie. I'll see you before I go," Ceil answered as she left the room. Her house shoes echoed *tat-a-tat-a-tat* down the hardwood floor in the hallway.

Ceil noticed the dark almost sinister color of the sky and the increased wind rustling the trees from her mother's kitchen window as she placed her empty coffee cup in the sink. She bound up the spiral staircase and ran into the kitchen then immediately began reeling in the heavily starched white T-shirts and boxer shorts that were snapping crisply on the clothes line. She began scolding them like little children as each piece was flung into a brown weaved wicker basket. "The hell with you. You'll get folded and put away later." Ceil hurried the laundry chore and prepared herself for a shower with the hopes of getting on with her evening before it rained.

Tony felt the first raindrop hit his shoulder as he crossed over First Avenue. A few larger beads of rain splattered him and the ground in rapid pulsing bursts. The sky quickly turned a ghastly black while the gusty wind forced every form of life to run and seek shelter. Brilliant bolts of lightning and rapid ear-shattering thunderclaps echoed directly overhead. By the time his foot hit the curb on the opposite side of the street, it began to rain cats and dogs. The dark sky opened up with pellets of large globules of water that sent him in a full jog toward shelter. The fresh pouring rain made brisk pinging sounds as it hit the tin roofs and overhangs of the building and a drumlike din as it ricocheted off the hoods and roofs of the cars parked along the avenue.

He wedged himself tightly into a shallow door-framed entrance of an old 1900s art deco–styled building at first; then he stepped it up a couple of doorways more and stopped under the small, slightly twisted aluminum awning of Philly's Social Club. Tony Boy stood flat against the structure, jammed tightly in the entranceway with his forehead butted up against the tattered wooden door. He gave the tarnished brass door buzzer two long steady pushes with his thumb and hoped someone would answer. Rumor had it that old man Philly had died some years back. Tony thought perhaps a new owner would continue with the club, and he did spot a faint light inside through the dusty glass of the storefront window. It took whoever was inside a few minutes to come to the door, and by that time the barrage of rain diminished to a slight trickle falling from a dull sun peering sky. The boy's fear of being struck by lightning subsided as he swung his body around and faced outwardly toward the street. Steam was actually rising off the hot pavement below. His eyes were drawn to the heavens as the one last volley of thunder was heard far off in the distance. Then the rain seemed to have stopped altogether.

The door opened on creaking hinges, and a bald-headed dwarf of a wrinkled old man chewing on a cheap unlit cigar looked up at Tony. The old man recognized him from the neighborhood and on occasion saw him running his mob errands. "Whaddya say, kid?" the old man said with a raspy voice; then he pushed the boy aside and poked his creased bald head through the doorway, turning his crusted eyes up to the sky. His pale, pasty skin almost became transparent as it blended with the dull gray misty atmosphere outside. "It ain't over yet," he said assuredly, talking through the side of his mouth. His observation of the sullied clouds blocking out the sunlight and a gust of damp wind prompted him to continue. "It's quiet now…but we're gonna get a nasty one later. I can feel it in my bones." The old man complained some in a language the boy had never heard before then turned and walked inside the dim indistinct room. He grumbled, "C'mon' in," then turned and took a long look at the boy. "I'm Philly. I know who 'ya are, so…what are 'ya up to…what can I do for ya? I know you're not out on the avenue helping old ladies cross the street…like a good Boy Scout…or are you…let me guess? You're the Boy Scout of Bloomfield Avenue tryin' to earn a merit badge?" The old man laughed hysterically until a congestive cough and wheeze almost stopped his natural breathing.

Philly's joint was typical of all the Social Clubs dotted in and around the shops and business along the avenue, just a lot older. And in its prime, it was a popular hangout for the area's locals. The owner on record was Peter "Little Philly" Cerulli. He got his nickname after a brand of dime store cigars that he chain-smoked, and he was not at all connected—other than buying supplies or the use of their vending machines to anyone in organized crime. The only gambling done was among the steadies that frequented the club, neighborhood old-timers who would sit at round tables smoking cigars, drinking *grappa* and cold beer, cursing each other as they played the fast and furious Italian card game *Ziginette*. Perhaps an occasional gin rummy game would surface? And perhaps Philly, on occasion, would take a modest cut of the pot, but that was the extent of the organized crime that went on in his place.

The place was dimly lit and barren of any color whatsoever. It was crypt-like and silent with the exception of two rust-covered Hunter overhead fans that dangled from a dirty gray old English-style block-patterned ceiling. They made a continuous, dull gnarr with every strenuous rotation. The decor of the place was cobwebs and dust, thick-layered dust that covered the entire room. A twelve-foot-long saloon-type bar counter and a row of rickety stools ran down the left side of the narrow room with shelves behind it holding a comparatively small amount of obscure liqueur bottles, Italian cordials, and wines, some so old the labels were barely legible. At the end of the bar sat an old, dated espresso maker and a few grimy demitasse coffee cups. And what once could have been called a kitchen was peering from a doorway in the back.

The boy's eyes were adjusting some to the darkness of the place. Visible now were a couple of small card tables. A few tattered tables and chairs ran along the opposite wall, separated by a jukebox. An etched glass-front cigarette vending machine, scantly filled with Lucky Strikes, Camels, and Chesterfield Kings sat by the front door. The place did not have a back room since it was not privy to the casino-like gambling that was prevalent in mostly all the other mob-run Social Clubs. It was an old-fashioned traditional gentlemen's club where men could escape the nagging clutches of their wives for a few hours and regain their masculinity.

Tony climbed up on a high-back stool at the beginning of the bar and sat down. The place had a very peculiar and almost rancid smell of old men and stale tobacco smoke, and he couldn't remember the last time he had ever walked through the door. His jogged memory suddenly shouted *Never*. The rain had stopped, and he should have quickly said goodbye, but out of respect, he decided to visit with the old-timer since he was gracious enough to open the door and give him shelter. Tony rubbed his eyes some, and as he sat he suddenly felt a chill. The club suddenly felt strange. Oddly, it began to take on an eerie persona, and it seemed as if a third person was present but unseen. Lights burned brightly then went dim; furniture appeared to be rearranged every time the kid's suspicions would force him to take another gander about the room. The dust was vanishing from some of the liqueur bottles, and then suddenly they seemed new and full. It was a phantasmal feeling, an almost haunted feeling that the old man paid not a bit of attention to.

Tony nervously spoke the very first words that shot into his head, "Heah Philly, my uncle Lefty ever stopped around here for a drink?" "Who?" the old man grumbled as he began to straighten up some bottles on the shelves. Tony forced a smile and said, "My uncle Joe, they call him Lefty, he only lives up the street. I figured he hangs out here now and then." "He don't play here anymore, kid. No one does," Phil said with a subdued snarl. The old man peered at the boy and asked, "You're Big Anthony's kid, ain't ya?" The old man continued. "Cheese Marino—I mean your father, right?" "Yeah, that's me. You know my father?" Tony said, his voice now more sincere and warm. "Of course. Who don't know Cheese *Marino?* He's got the car lot up the street…that sells no cars," Phil said cynically. The old man reached down behind the bar and pulled a little green sparkling bottle of *Coca-Cola* from the ice box underneath. Tony noticed that the bottle seemed to glow and was quite luminescent against the background of the darkened room. The old man snapped the cap off on a wall-mounted opener and placed it in front of the kid. "Here. Have a drink, kid. I'd offer you a beer but I know yer too young," the old guy said amusingly as he puffed his cigar. "You're old man still run those crap games? He used to have the best game in town in the back of that garage of his. People came from all over." The old man seemed to have come alive. His words were spoken from the heart and sounded gnarly from between his closed teeth that held on for dear life to his crusty cigar. He continued. "He used to have everybody there. People from Hollywood…in tuxedos—Sinatra and all of his cronies, dames in evening gowns, New York mobsters, politicians, you name it. They were all there," the old man said with lidded eyes and a cocked smile. "Ohhh…the good old days," he exclaimed as he reached around and grabbed a bottle of *Strega* and a shot glass then looked up at the big round clock on the wall that read two forty-five and said, "I guess it's late enough." He poured himself a shot of a bright amber liquid then raised his glass and said, "Salute." His demeanor became mysterious and he said dolefully, "Tell yer' old man to be careful." Tony Boy winced at that remark. He thanked him for the Coke and touched the bottle neck to Phil's shot glass, completing the toast. The old man squeezed gently the short unlit cigar with his fingers and held it as he downed the brandy. The cigar was back in his mouth before his glass was down. "I gotta' have rocks in my head thinkin' anyone will show up tonight. These old-timers don't come out in the rain," the old man said in a huff. "Ya never know, Phil…maybe it won't rain," Tony Boy said optimistically as he turned his head and glanced over the top of half curtain at the front window.

The old man lifted his short body up on his toes and he leaned over the bar. He peered out of the storefront window with a deliberate stare. The sky that seeped in through the panes of glass was dull and gray and almost became coalesce with the threadbare curtains and the drab painted wall. The old man looked at the kid through contrite eyes and warned, "We're gonna be in for a storm, kid…*a bad one.*" He gave the kid a dark, chilling look, and after a few seconds of silence he said, "Go home, kid…go home and stay out of this—you don't want to get caught in the storm." His words seemed to linger some, held about the room in or by a sort of a reverberating echo mimicking "the storm—the storm—the storm." The room fell dead silent for a brief few second or two, until a loud, clamorous ringing came from a black desk phone that sat on a cobweb-covered shelf in the center of the back bar. It startled Tony and caused him to jump up out of his seat. "Who the fuck could 'dat be? Nobody calls here anymore," growled Phil. The old man answered the phone then looked at the kid with concern. He frowned a bit, shrugged his shoulders, and said woefully, "It's for you." His faced twisted to an almost obscene mask. "It's the devil." The voice on the other end of the receiver was Batista's. He was calling from a pay phone inside a tavern just up the street and seemed annoyed as he asked coldly, "What the fuck are you doin' hanging out in that joint? And who answered the phone?" Frank said with a sour look. Then he said, "I thought that dump was closed. How the fuck did ya' get in?" The kid had a puzzled look on his face as his eyes combed the room gawking and thinking the voice on the other end was actually in the room with him. "How did ya' know I was even in here—and how did 'ya get the number?" Tony said with his eyes firmly fixed on the front door. Batista said sternly, "I saw you walk in. I just took a shot with the phone book, and the phone—I'm amazed it worked. Didn't you see me parked across the street—or hear me beeping? I'm waitin' twenty minutes already." He adjusted his sunglasses and waited for a response. Tony Boy snapped back with a raw tongue, "No, I didn't see you across the street. What's everybody followin' me around today?" Tony was being ambiguous, referring to the cop incident that happened earlier. Tic fired back a fury of his own. "What the fuck is that supposed to mean?" Then with a clueless look on his face and continued. "Start walkin' and I'll pick you up in a couple of seconds." "Where do you want me to go?" the kid asked. "Just walk. I'll find 'ya," Batista snapped as the phone went dead. Tic was untrusting of any telephone, especially the ones that were on the avenue. Even though Ruggeri had the more commonly used equipment monitored for wiretaps on a regular basis, he still felt uncomfortable talking over the wire. His conversations were always short, no more than a minute or two, lacking specifics and full of euphemisms.

Tony saluted the old-timer in sort of a Boy Scout manner, three fingers held to his brow, and headed through the front door that, alarmingly, slammed extremely hard behind him. He reached around and grabbed hold of the doorknob and tried to turn it. It held fast in a locked position. He fell backward off the small stoop then took a step up to the storefront window and peered in. To his amazement the windows were boarded up from the inside. How strange? He gave the property and the faded words that read along the front of the awning one last look; then he thought hard of the old man's words. He let out an audible "Jeez" and said to himself aloud, "Yeah, Phil… really…who the fuck would ever come into your place?"

10

The red bullet taillights of the Cadillac Coupe de Ville seemed alive and individual, almost as if they had their own playful souls and buoyant agendas. Their luminescent glow bounced over the curb and sliced the dark, dreary haze of the day, giving chase to the long black body of the Cadillac as it rode up the fifty or so yards of the paved driveway that leads to M&M Motors. Big Anthony sped the Cadillac past a couple of rows of unevenly parked Fords and Chevy sedans that sat lifeless in pools of dirty rainwater. He grimaced as he jammed on his brakes in front of the locked cyclone fenced gate. He would have to dodge around puddles on foot to gain entry. He felt more at ease once behind the fence and quickly closed the gate behind him then reattached the chain and padlock. He would leave in place the two-foot-square metal sign with the red block letters CLOSED, attached on sturdy S-hooks facing the street. This would be the first indication to any passersby. No game tonight. This would command any and all not to enter the driveway and just continue up the avenue. Anthony felt disgruntled at first, but all in all his feelings lightened as he climbed back into the car and headed for the back lot. He realized he was a happy man, in good humor with the thoughts of soon packing in the mob life. He guided his flagship into a parking space next to two overhead garage doors in the rear of the building and bound up the stairs leading inside.

One would think that the red letters spelling out M&M Motors on the attached painted sign on the front facade of the building would indicate that this business gave way to something associated with automobiles. From the street it had all the markings of a functional used car lot, auto repair, open to the public. The true fact of the matter is that the place was nothing more than a dubious front for all sorts of criminal activities and had been since day one.

The business license and the ninety-nine-year lease were in the name of an old crony of the late Zwillman as was the property deed. When Zwillman had the operation, it was once a legal enterprise selling used cars to the public. Anthony and his friend Albert took it over years ago for the sole purpose of the illegal gambling, fencing stolen merchandise, and laundering mob money through the books. The Jew objected at first but soon came around when his tribute was increased because of the money-making efforts of his old friend Cheese.

A large blackboard was set up in partitioned back room and was used to post odds of games and horse races for the woeful betters who filled the place on a daily basis. And in his heyday Anthony ran a lucrative dice game that was held every Friday and Saturday night and attracted all types of high rollers and diehard back alley crapshooters. The entire concern was under the protection of Newark's finest and the notorious Ruggeri who both presented a bill for their services. As for the automobiles parked out front, well, most of them were stolen, branded with untraceable, erroneous titles, and were mostly just used by crew members as getaway cars and mob hits. If a poor lost soul wandered on the lot, he was quickly shooed away or discouraged to buy a car by a wise guy posing as a salesman. They'd always ask for a ridiculous amount of money for the car and hand the customer a take-it-or-leave attitude. Only once could Anthony ever remember a well-to-do out-of-towner actually agreeing to the price gouge. His spoiled son wanted the car, this resulting in an actual sale. The entire crew roared with laughter, and Anthony found himself in a frenzy trying to produce a legitimate title for sedan. The local citizens of the neighborhood knew better and just stayed away.

One of Zwillman's favorite memories of all the scheming was how Anthony would hire the homeless drunkards that inhabited the area. He'd give them light, menial chores to do like wash the cars or pick up around the property, things of that nature. Each one was paid a few bucks, and each one had an accident/life insurance policy provided by one of the Jew's connections listing someone in the crew as *beneficiary*. Every once in a while an unforeseen mortal accident would befall one of the lost souls. Perhaps while in a drunken stupor, one would freeze to death sleeping in the backseat of a sedan parked on the lot, or one would be found crushed to death on the railroad tracks. On occasion a body would wash up along with the debris in the Passaic River, all unfortunate accidental deaths that resulted in a nice cash death benefit settlement that was readily collected and split amongst the boys. This scam lasted only a short while due to the suspicions of the insurance companies and the emerging shortage of bums in the neighborhood.

Big Anthony's pace was brisk and airy as he entered the dimly lit building and zigzagged around piles of scrap iron, rusted car parts, and old tires. He entered the makeshift casino and let out a rejoicing "Baffangul" directed to the long handmade craps table and the imaginary high-society crowd gathered around it as he passed by.

Word was put out on the street about resuming the renowned crap game, and it was to be the highlight of tonight's activity as it once had been each Friday night prior, but now the plans were changing. He augmented his decision to shit can the idea of a dice game with a robust "Fuck the game, it's a loser anyway." It hasn't been the cash cow it once was for a long time now and is currently just a dull burden. His mind was still racing with ideas and arrangements of the legitimate game plan he wanted to discuss with his brother.

Anthony entered the front office and cleared off a bunch of scattered papers and debris from his desk and plopped his large frame heavily into a high-back wooden swiveling chair. It creaked as old weathered lumber would in a windstorm as the mobster strained its limits. He was antsy and full of pizzazz finding hard to sit still. He nervously rolled his fingers in a drumlike tap on the top of the desk while his left leg spasmodically bounce up and down. He swirled around in the chair and was amused by the strange sounds of *squeak* that sang out, left to right and back again, then jumped up and grabbed a cold beer from the office refrigerator, the refreshing cold swig forced a mandatory burp as he leant over and squinted in search of the on/off switch of the office television set. The metallic sound of television tubes and circuitry warming up clashed with the crackle Anthony's rough hands made as he spread open the slats of the aluminum venetian blinds with anticipation of his brother's arrival. He paced in front of the window furtively; then finally his energy came to rest, and he again clumped heavily back in his chair. He was at ease now and indulged a long swig of the cold Rolling Rock beer. He thought to himself that the older he got, the simple things that make him now say "Ahhh" have changed.

The television screen burst into a snowy picture of *Gunga Din*, the feature film that was airing in the afternoon slot of the Million Dollar Movie. The bulging envelope of cash gave Big Anthony an annoying nudge against the seat back, cueing him to remove it before it got lost. His first instinct was just leave it on the desk since he was going to get it to Pope as soon as his brother left, but his gut feeling told him to hide it. Just in case! He rose up and went to a little storage room that sat outside of the office. He slammed open the door and fumbled for the cord to the overhead light. His eyes scanned the tiny closetlike room for a place to stash the package. His choice was the second drawer of the metal filling cabinet, laying it next to a Colt .45 Combat Special.

Big Anthony's emotions were winding down some, and his breathing became eased and refreshed. He plopped himself back in his chair and laughed to himself as he mulled over a silent thought. How many people could feel this blissful knowing that they owe over fifty thousand dollars to one of the most ruthless mobsters in New Jersey and not have hardly a penny to their name. It was just another annoyance to say "Fuck it" to. His anticipation of his brother's visit was starting to make him antsy as was the worry of his brother's interest with his plan. He must sell this idea. Big Anthony stood up and cracked the slats of the venetian blinds open and peered out onto the avenue and its flowing traffic. A sudden burst of lightning gave him a startle, and his reflexes caused him to jump in his skin. Now he wondered heavily just where his son was.

Frank "Tick Tock" Batista was not bullshitting at all when he told the kid he would meet him in a couple of seconds. Tony had not taken more than one or two steps from Philly's doorstep before he was razed by the signature *beeeeep-be-beep-beep-beep* sound of the trumpet-style horns from Batista's Cadillac. The blare gave him a startle. There he was—double-parked in the travel lane, causing the increasing afternoon traffic on the avenue to swerve around him with a flurry of cursing road rage. Frank sat calmly, hiding behind a pair of thick-framed Ray-Ban sunglasses, paying no mind at all to the irate motorists piling up behind him honking their horns in disgust. He sat gloating with a wry smirk on his face and his inner thought of *Yes, I do own the fucking road.*

"Ya smell like mothballs comin' out of that dump," Frank barked as the kid climbed into the front seat. His brow wrinkled as he asked, "Who let you in that joint? Who answered the phone? I thought it was closed." The boy answered curtly, "It was rainin'. I had no choice." Frank said almost coach-like, "There's always choices, my boy, ya' gotta' think about 'em." He gave the boy a cocked look and a pointed finger. "Always think before you act. That's the best advice I'll give ya' today." "Old man Philly let me in. He opened the door. You're right. The place is a dump," Tony said and finished with raised eyebrows and a short laugh. Frank gave him a strange look and paused briefly, and then said, "Kid…Philly died about five years ago, couldn't have been him you were talkin' to…ah fuck it, it don't matter." Both dropped the subject.

Frank had a sincere fondness for the kid. "His boy" was the way he would refer to him among his peers. Batista was a devout bachelor with no known children of his own. He realized he was in competition with Big Anthony vying for the boy's affection and loyalty. He had taken him under his wing with a bona fide devout interest. He trusted the boy wholeheartedly and knew he would make a fine soldier one day. He was plenty tough and displayed a natural mark for silence and respect. Frank pulled into the lane of oncoming traffic with complete disregard and sped up the avenue.

Tony observantly noticed Batista had the same driving habits as Accardi, driving with his eyes fixated in the rearview mirror then darting left and right to the other outside mirrors. He drove slowly past Ruggeri's Social Club and eyeballed everything and everyone around the general vicinity then swung a U-turn and sped in the other direction. The boy laughed to himself as he noticed it was again the same thing the cop did earlier. They must have attended the same driving school. They drove in dead silence for a while with no set pattern that the boy could see. Ruggeri's club was in the other direction. Frank broke the silence and asked, "Ya got that thing for me?" Tony's eyes widened and he returned an affirmed nod. Frank became enthusiastic. "I got it all arranged for you. You're gonna work the front room tonight at the Pope's club. The tables will be filled with players. You'll be helpin' out Fat Vito. It's good action. Your tips alone should be a couple o' hundred not to mention the night's pay." The boy suddenly felt mixed emotions, cold feet so to speak. He was excited about the opportunity work high-level card game, but he felt dismayed and almost ashamed about disobeying his father who had given him strict instruction to stay away. A minor botheration he would deal with later. He would finally get the opportunity to get some more recognition from some other crew members. The thought of tonight's chores and Frank's words energized his mood. Frank continued with a nod of confidence and a wink. "And don't worry, Fat Vito's a good kid—young, like you—yous' guys will hit it off right from the get-go."

Fat Vito Tutolo also known as Junior was the son of Donald "the Cyclone" Tutolo. Donald Tutolo, himself a made guy whose specialty was fencing all the stolen merchandise hence the nickname Swag for the outfit. His territory was vast, but his concentration was mostly hijacked shipments from the New York and New Jersey waterfronts and the terminals surrounding them. But the seasoned mobster would never turn down an opportunity to convert a premeditated stolen load of anything from anybody into cash on the barrel head. Batista laughed until he cried as he told the kid Tutolo's most outlandish escapade ever. It was the time he diverted a military shipment of close to four hundred Colt .45 Combat Special sidearms en route to the newly opened Earle Naval Weapons base in Colts Neck, New Jersey, under the shadows of World War II. The automatic weapons were handed out throughout mob land much as Christmas presents were handed to anxious children. Everyone had one. However, the heat generated over the theft was intense. The government and the military were literally up in arms. Tutolo struck a deal to return two hundred handguns, swearing that's all he mysteriously found while monitoring the docks for any type of espionage.

He felt it was his patriotic duty since he was unable to serve his country because of a medical deferment—every soldier in the Pope's army had some type of deferment during the war. Tutolo insisted that no government reward was necessary. The blame was placed on a suspect GI supply sergeant who was, in fact, dealing black market weapons and other forms of military contraband—such a traitor. His cries of innocence concerning that particular theft went unheard, and he promptly faced a court martial that ultimately sent the dishonorable soldier to Leavenworth Penitentiary.

Tony sat unmoving as they drove in silence. All of a sudden a cold, grieving feeling rushed over him as they passed the familiar logo of the Coca-Cola bottling plant. His cheerfulness sank into a doleful sensation of guilt as he uncontrollably envisioned the face of old man Philly and the bottle of Coke he offered. His words echoed in his head, "Go home, kid…go home, kid…go home, kid." This uncanny thought burned deep down in his subconscious mind.

He closed his eyes briefly, and a morbid phantasm of his father and Phil unfolded in his thoughts. Both were sitting in that rundown club languishing over their hard lives and their despairs. Then he imagined them both dead, lying side by side. He thought to himself, why do we conjure up such nightmarish notions? Who makes us think of such horrible things?

Frank swung a hard left at Grove Street. The swerve of the car immediately shook the kid out of his trance. He entered the employee parking lot of the Charms Candy Factory and nestled his car in between two others in a space facing the street. Tick Tock's voice was all business as he said, "Gimme' the envelope." The boy felt hesitant as he rustled through his undershirt and gingerly pulled the red-and-blue-bordered crumpled mass from his waist. He prepared himself for the worst. Tic's first review upon seeing the wrinkled paper was that it was "stashed down there too long." It was an innocent thought at first until he noticed it had been torn open. A rage flamed up in his eyes as if he had seen the devil himself. He gave the boy a look of contempt. Perhaps the kid was putting the mentor to some sort of a test? Batista's eyes were dead cold. "Did you do this? You open this up?" he said with a scornful voice; then he looked again at the crumpled envelope with scrutinizing eyes, examining it from every angle. He carefully pulled the letter out and gave it a pensive stare then placed it back in the opened envelope. Frank was cunning and always thought out his words and actions before he spoke. He began to contrive possible scenarios with his calculating brain as to why the sealed envelope was tampered with and by whom before he spoke again. "I know this wasn't opened when you got it, and I hope to God you tell me the truth about why it is." The boy had no reason to lie and Tic knew it. He had accepted in his mind what he had anticipated. Something went awry. He knew the fact that the boy would never do such a disrespectful thing. He also knew that the words the boy would speak would be the Gospel truth. He just wanted to hear his statement. The boy's words became chaste-like, and he answered with no apprehension, "It was your friend...he took it from me and he opened it." Frank was dumbfounded. His face became twisted with consternation and confusion as he asked, "Who? What fuckin' friend are you talking about?" The boy's instinct of not squealing on anyone forced his mouth shut until he realized that the mob world is filled with so-called snitches that feed information to one another for ulterior motives, motives based on principle and honor for the goal of protection or warning.

Principles and convictions travel up a ladder of allegiance, and his allegiance is to Frank Batista, not the cop. "Your detective friend, Eddie...Eddie Accardi. He's the one who roughed me up and took it from me—he opened it up." His words were unshaken and he spoke from his heart. Batista's blood ran ice-cold through his veins to the point of causing him to shiver. His criminal mind immediately thought, could the Pope or Accardi *suspect* anything about his dealings? Tony Boy proceeded to tell Frank the entire story of the frightful ordeal he went through, every detail from beginning to end.

How the cop became physical and accused him of dealing drugs. He told Frank how at first he thought it was him who put the cop up to it as yet another test of loyalty but then had a change of heart. Frank asked him if he thought it might have been his own father who conjured up the sham raid, but that idea was quickly dismissed by both of them.

The looming bemuse was the reference made to drugs. Why drugs? That was Frank's unspoken grim thought. Frank listened attentively, watching the boy's eyes, studying his body language, observing every movement his face made as his mouth formed the words. As he listened he thought and he analyzed and he pondered the same thing over and over again judiciously in his corrupt and criminal mind, searching for the answer or the reasons. Why the rouse of the kid without his knowledge or consent. His final analysis was just one of association and chain of command. Who would give such an order? The thought of a police investigation suspecting his boy was involved with drugs was preposterous. Even if it were true, he would have heard something on the street level at the minimum. There was no clear evidence at all to suspect the kid was actually a drug dealer; everyone knew that was outrageously untrue. Detective Eddie Accardi takes orders directly from the Pope. No one else! Period! End of story! The tension dismounted, and the two actually had a laugh about how the boy said the letter was a list from his mother.

Frank praised the boy for his bravery and honor with the situation, saying how some grown men would have cracked under Accardi's intimidation. And he further congratulated him on being the first ever to con the great Accardi and insisted that he forget about the incident in its entirety. All was agreed to then Frank casually passed a comment, "So tell me, kid…when you were telling the cop about it bein' your mother's letter and all, did you read it… did he show it to you?" The kid picked up on the underlining ploy immediately and said "Frank, number one, I don't understand a word on that paper, and number two, I don't give a fuck. It ain't any of my business." Batista knew he had an ally with the boy. He also realized it was time to faultlessly watch his back.

The conversation between Batista and the kid during the trip back to Ruggeri's club was congenial and upbeat. It was made up of instructional dialogue on the do's and don'ts of working the big room of semi-high rollers and wise guys. "Remember, kid, you're gonna be like a waiter, not a slave," Frank Batista said emphatically. "And don't talk to no one, only if you're asked a question, and then say 'I dunno.' And never look anyone directly in their eyes. Never! They don't like that. That only works if you're selling insurance, and you ain't selling insurance. But in the same respect, you don't take any shit from them, the citizens I mean. From wise guys, well, that's different. Act tough if you feel the need, you ain't training to be no Boy Scout, but always show a level of respect." Frank explained theory and techniques that would make him stand out and shine above the rest of the apprentices that got a bump up into the organization by being savvy while under discerning eyes, namely the Pope, although if he were there, his attention would be focused on the activity of the celebrated players in the back room. "Chances are, kid, he won't even notice 'ya, not that it's such a bad thing, but that's just how he is with the hired help. Chrissakes, he don't even notice me half the time."

11

This would only be the second time the young Marino kid ever entered Ruggeri's exclusive Bloomfield Avenue mansion, and it would be the first time *ever* he ventured down the marbled hallway that led to the main barroom and the rest of the notorious establishment. His prior visit was restricted to just helping the crew lug cases of whisky from the garage then slide them down grocery rollers into the basement. His only other involvement with Ruggeri was at the mobster's Roseville Avenue place just two months earlier. He was on clean-up duty for a gala held there celebrating a recent release of a local wise guy from federal prison.

His eyes opened wide as he followed Tic through the mansion's rear entrance of what was once an elegant funeral parlor. He held his head high and expanded his broad chest as they blew past Ruggeri's bodyguard that stood sentry. He paused momentarily just to gather his senses and take in the awe of the tall arched ceiling that ran the length of a huge marbled hallway. Batista was already at least ten steps ahead, his fast-paced gait and shoe soles echoing a rhythmic beat. He turned and chimed, "Well, 'ya comin' in or what?" Tony was in complete awe of the stylish vogue sophistication of the club that still carried the luxuriant scent of fresh-cut flowers throughout.

Classical Renaissance artwork hung, spaced in perfect proportion. Tall vases and urns along with statues depicting Ancient Rome were discernible in all the areas one would expect them to be. They passed the exquisite marbled balustrade banisters that wrapped around a stairway leading down a small flight of steps to what used to be the parlor's embalming room, morgue area, and visitors lounge. Now the area was transformed into another fortress room for the Pope. Another matching balustrade banister sent you another two flights up to a secluded living space that was once occupied by the undertakers themselves, this now a luxury suite used as the Pope's headquarters and acted as his home away from home. Only two aspects of the original mansion were compromised and removed completely; the towering conservatory and the huge downstairs kitchen; however, both could still be recognized in the few framed and vintage photos of the labeled Orsini mansion that hung inconspicuously around the barroom. Ruggeri felt not a need for a workable kitchen on the first floor. If food was requested, it would be catered in from his restaurant. Of course close associates of Ruggeri would dine upstairs, with the Pope himself. A collage of Ruggeri's personal framed artwork were carefully spaced on the walls and escorted you up the stairs, of course by invitation only as the ruby-red velvet rope and brass divider blocking the stairway indicated.

Continuing down the hallway, on the left, was a pair of tall solid oak, handcrafted french doors, very important looking doors that sealed off the infamous back room card game action from the rest of the chambers. Another similar setup was on the right just a few yards up the hallway. One of the garish back rooms had an entire Las Vegas–themed casino atmosphere behind the locked doors. It was complete with fully functional gaming tables trimmed in fine felt along with a variety of slot machines, all of which were registered as the sole property of a legal Nevada gaming outfit. Ruggeri was listed as a consultant to cover up the illegal possession of the equipment just in case of a rare and highly unlikely raid. The stored casino equipment was just that as far as anyone was concerned and used only for charitable events. And one last highly secluded and guarded back room was used strictly for executive-type high-stakes poker games.

The two entered through yet another set of french doors, both held invitingly open by miniature brass castings of male lions sitting on their laurels. This rear entrance of the great ballroom that at one time held the divided and separate viewing rooms that were once occupied with coffins of the dead—and always a rumored ghost story abounded. Once inside Tic, as he was commonly referred to inside the place, instructed the boy with a thumbed gesture and a true wise guy smirk. "Go over there, sit at the bar and wait for me. Go meet Vito. He's expecting you." Batista gave him a congenial smack on the back as he headed for a table tucked deep in a corner niche where three other men were already seated.

Tony, acting ever so discreetly, slid the bar stool away from the brass-plated foot rail and took a seat. He was still and silent, acting incognito as he let his eyes size up the grandeur that was all around him. The club's decor was designed to give the occupants a feeling of being in an old-fashioned Prohibition era speakeasy. Highly polished and richly stained crown molding ran the lengths of the ceiling. Felt-lined poker tables mounted on ball and clawed mahogany legs sat on thick plush burgundy carpet and were strategically arranged throughout the room. Rows of beautifully hand-carved high-back booths with tufted red leather seat backs and cushions ran uniformly along the walls all under the ambiance of imported lighting fixtures. It was truly a magnificent sight.

Vito Tutolo was behind the bar restocking the mahogany ice boxes with clanging bottles of beer. He gave his head a half turn to look at who just sat down. "Whaddya say?" Vito said with a nod of his head. He stood and outstretched his arm in a gentlemanly offer of a handshake. Tony grasped his chilled hand as Vito continued. "You gonna be workin, with me tonight, right?" "Yeah, that's what I was told," Tony said with a half-cocked smile and a responsive nod.

Tony Marino was usually reserved and somewhat closemouthed around strangers. He had noticed Vito around just about all the neighborhood haunts—restaurants, pizzerias, and even at Pope's other club on Roseville Avenue numerous times—and even said hello to him once or twice. He felt he had earned the right to speak openly to Vito. After all the ritual introductions of "Who do you know?" And "I know this guy, do you know that guy?" And after a few tales of bravado had been shared between them both, an immediate bond of friendship was formed. Vito was only a couple of years older than the kid. Tony guessed his age to be around twenty or twenty-one. He remembered that Vito quit Barringer High during his senior year, the same time Tony entered as a freshman. Vito's hulking but solid 275- pound physique gave indication there was a good deal of muscle underneath his stretched skin. One could also tell by his appearance and persona that he possessed gargantuan strength and an inbred mean streak that stretched a mile long. Both of the young men had a propensity for fighting plus a sweet tooth for violence and soon found themselves engaged in a lengthy conversation about boxing in general while they sized each other up, unsuspecting, just in case they ever met in opposition in a gladiators' arena. They had both known well a local middleweight by the name of Charlie Fusari, whose oil-painted picture of himself, donned in boxing shorts and gloves, striking a lifelike defensive pose, was hanging on the wall.

The kid's antenna was up. He listened with one ear as Vito gave him instructions on what his job detail would be. He tried doggedly to be completely cognizant of his staring problem, and his head rang with the instruction from Frank. But as fate would have it, he sensed and saw through the corners of his eye that the men sitting in the antique high-backed booth at the end of the row were tossing an occasional glance up in his direction. Although the conversation was muted by the Dean Martin music playing, he sensed they were talking about him. All of a sudden he felt an uneasy knot in his stomach form. An uncontrollable force made him turn his eyes left, directly into the black, merciless stare of Ruggeri himself. Not wanting to send the wrong message with a meddlesome stare, he quickly turned his attentions to Vito and continued his unconcerned clamor with the brawny kid about the absolute nervousness of nothing at all. Vito put a swift halt to their conversation just soon as he got a beckoning wave from Batista. Tony sensed something else was wrong and immediately tried to read into the situation—but he mustn't look over. His contemplative mind was unable to decipher any type of logical answer to appease his gut feeling of worriment. His suspicion of the sudden disappearance of Vito was all for naught; Vito was just ordered to go pick up a crew member who was stranded on the road with a flat tire and no spare as the replacement wise guy bartender relayed to the kid.

The vision of Ruggeri flashed through Tony's mind and he could not help again casting his eye in the notorious mobster's direction—but only what was a designed casual glance. He wondered why this tiny old man of maybe five feet ten inches tall that weighed no more than a hundred and fifty pounds was so feared throughout the underworld. He also gave deep thought as to why the man chose this profession. Ruggeri was born to immigrant parents like so many other children in his neighborhood of Brooklyn, New York. He started going to the same schools as did the others his age who themselves went on to became doctors, lawyers, or legitimate business people that, in all due respect, he would look like when you dressed him up in a suit and tie. Perhaps the world was out of silver spoons when he entered it?

Angelo Ruggeri was in control of the narrative with his trusted capo Albert Marrone and an out-of-town mobster by the name of

Vincent Tortorello. Tort, as he was known as, was summoned to the Pope's headquarters to explain, as mobsters often do, of the details behind the recent execution of a friend of theirs from Brooklyn by the name of Frank Abbatemarco. And before the night ended Tort was to take back to Brooklyn a stern warning—there was to be no more dumping of bodies in Newark. Tortorello was with two thugs, his driver and his bodyguard. "We can't be too careful these days," he said to the table in general. Ruggeri summoned a member of the crew over to go and show Tort's people the club. "Give them a nice tour of the place then go outside and check for flat tires before yous belly up to the bar, gabide."

The old-school Don Tortorello was quick to tell a story and loved to listen to a good one himself. He was a typical storybook mobster: thick neck, balding with a left eye that seemed permanently closed from years of thick hot cigar smoke drifting into it. Tort "washed" his illegal income through the books of a fleet of green top ice cream trucks that were ever so popular with the neighborhood kids of Brooklyn. He was Ruggeri's age, about sixty, overweight, and talked with a slight lisp. He was too vain to wear glasses, so his drivers and bodyguards became his seeing eye dogs. A few laughs were heard from the group and some heads turned. Ruggeri and his party were having mixed emotions with their exchanged tales about the old days. The faces got long and foreboding as they recalled the times they ran with the likes of Al Capone and Salvatore Lucania through the shoot-em-up streets of New York. Such memories were recollected from Prohibition; many millionaires were born from that era, and so many died. This was Tort's first visit to Ruggeri's lavish club and was highly impressed. He commended the Pope on his latest venture. "I hear there's an interesting story to tell about this place, Pope, am I right?" he asked with a hush-hush tone of voice. The Pope shot him a furtive look and winked. "There's always a story, my friend. Maybe one day I'll tell it to ya'." Both men laughed out loud in a venerating way. A few "remember when" tales were kicked around between them, and Tort commented on how lucky Ruggeri was to be able to go off on his own to New Jersey. The talk of luck got a glib reaction from the Pope. He openly bellyached about the "pain in the ass" Kefauver Committee and the McClellan Senate Committee, the Appalachian raid, and the rest of the unbribable pricks from the federal government and the justice department. They were drawing out good men and turning them into government witnesses, the lowest form of rat. The conversation drew a pensive "What the fuck are they trying to prove" catechism from him.

The subject next turned somewhat political. They offered their opinions regarding the overthrow of the Cuban government by Castro's rebels. They frowned and fretted and cursed the ordeal—their lost gambling and hotel interests. Both shook their heads in utter disgust over the countless amounts of money and human lives lost as was the tropical-themed home Ruggeri once owned on the isle. Suddenly the bellyaching Ruggeri seemed distracted by something. Obviously already annoyed, he said with a scornful voice, "Tic, what is that punk kid doing here?" Batista turned his head and peered around the edge of the booth and said, "Who him? That's my boy. That's Cheese Marino's kid." Before he could get another word out Ruggeri shot back, "I know who the fuck he is, that's not what I asked you." Ruggeri's demeanor had become no-nonsense, and Batista felt coldness between him. He sat calm and carefully chose his words. He let his eyeglasses slide down on the bridge of his nose, and his eyes peered over the edge as he said, "Pope. We talked about this kid. I wanted to give him a chance to work with Vito…here… at the club." His words came laboriously. "Is there a problem?" he asked gently. Ruggeri said unsmiling, "There's no problem, unless you want one? I just don't want him here. Maybe you have a use for him, but I don't. Get rid of him," he said gravely. Batista spoke with a hushed voice, "C'mon…he's a good kid. He's got a lotta' heart for

Chrissakes, does whatever I ask of him…no questions asked." His voice became absolved. "He's passed every test I put him through… with flyin' colors—" Ruggeri cut him off abruptly. "Does he have the fifty-grand his father owes me? Is he here to work off the debt?" Then he hit Batista below the belt. "Are you willing to pay the debt or vouch for his old man?" Frank had to bite his tongue and curb his displeasure. He could never show anger to the Pope no matter how much his blood boiled. Any display of distemper now toward Ruggeri could result in death in this situation. That's how ruthless a man he is, and he would never give a second chance or a pass to anyone who shows disrespect. The best Frank could do was to adjust his thick-framed glasses and continue to plead his case. "Pope …with all due respect…please listen to me." Batista's words were borderline indignant. "He's a good kid. You've seen him around the Roseville Avenue club a million times. He's got some good qualities." His words fell on deaf ears. "Let me be the judge of quality. I'm better at it than you. If he is anything like his father, if his father's blood runs through his veins, he has no quality, or respect. Now I'm going to say it for the last time. Get him the fuck outta' here and let him know he is not welcome unless he does have the fifty grand. What you do with him on the outside is your business, but remember, it could also fall on your shoulders." The conversation was over.

Frank Batista crumpled his Lucky Strike in the ashtray in a way that did not display any type of anger or chagrin and calmly eased out of the booth. He walked over to the unsuspecting Tony who now was in a deep conversation with the just returning Vito. Without a word said, Tic slipped his hand under the boy's armpit and gave him a forceful tug off the stool. With a fast pace, he escorted the boy toward the men seated at the booth and headed for the back door. Batista gritted his teeth and growled in the boy's ear, "Don't look at 'em." As soon as they exited the club the kid broke loose from the grip with a strong backward throw of his arm. He had a baffled and flustered look on his face. He barked with a malevolent voice, "Frank…what the fuck is this all about?" Batista stood silent for a moment then sighed. He pulled no punches with the boy as he explained the conversation that had just taken place regarding his father and his unpaid debt. Batista clenched his teeth and said, "Nothing more, or nothing less!" Batista scowled again. "That's the way it is in our world. The way it's supposed to be, and that's that, kid." He turned away from the boy and reentered the club.

If anyone were to take a head count of all the made men and their crews of mobsters, goons, bookmakers, and loan sharks that jacked around the Pope's clubs on a daily basis, the numbers would be astounding. Ruggeri always believed that there was strength in numbers. They would all be in their chosen groups of three or four taking care of their secluded and secret societal business—some waiting for orders or instructions to filter down from the boss himself. Such was their sole existence for being in the club.

Ruggeri was eagle-eyed on the top of the marbled staircase that led to his concrete fortress as he waited for Frank Batista to walk back inside. During that brief interlude, Ruggeri formulated an immediate decision. He dismissed Batista and gave Albert Marrone an order to follow him downstairs. Batista read between the definitive lines. Marrone was quick ordered by the Pope as they walked to find and his two top enforcers, Joey "Two Ton" Lotta and Gaetano "Aldo" Altieri, to get ready to pay a visit to Big Anthony. The tone of Ruggeri's voice was dire, and Marrone had a distressed premonition for the request as he watched the little tyrant walk away, unlock the steel door of his chamber, and disappear inside. Within moments, as he sat and pondered, his private line rang. It was Accardi checking in.

Angelo Ruggeri kept his engine of crime and corruption hitting on all eight cylinders for a simple reason—he was the boss; he acted the boss. Unlike his compatriots who relied heavily on the word of

one, a consigliere, to advise and comment and reinforce their conniving plots and schemes, Ruggeri never trusted the word of just one
man, nor needed any man to sit alongside and advise or compete
with his sound decision making. This left him able to give himself
a cocksure pat on the back with little to no regrets as to past perfor-
mances of choosing his destiny his way.

However, Ruggeri did rely heavily on precise information he
gathered from his captains, soldiers, and spies so he could formulate
his own agenda and battle plan. These were his trusted and trained
men, his men of honor who religiously obeyed while showing the
utmost of respect, and they themselves knew a mistake on their part
could be their last.

The last and final task Eddie Accardi had to do before he was
able to finish his shift and clock out for the day was to observe the
address that was last on his list then report his findings to the Pope.
Although his much anticipated weekend getaway at the lake house
was well on its way to becoming rained out, he still was anxious to
put his caseloads aside and head for home, which could attest to why
the information phoned into Ruggeri was sketchy at best and out of
harmony from the detective's usually perfect work.

Eddie parked his unmarked cruiser on Berkeley Place in a position that gave him a perfect view of the parking lot and entrances of
M&M Motors. He had been at this spot earlier, before the rain had
started, and noticed the only car parked anywhere, other than the
inventoried handful of jalopies, was Big Anthony's Cadillac, and now
as the hour approached 4:00 p.m., it was still the sole vehicle in the
back lot. This led him to believe the man was all alone in his office.
And that was a fact. As Eddie drove off, he had no idea or any way
of knowing that Tony will be shortly jumping off the city bus that
stops on the avenue directly in front of the place, nor did he anticipate the late arrival of Big Anthony's brother Joe. This would be the

vital prognostic information that would *not* get reported to the Pope when Accardi called and said, "He's all alone."

Young Tony Marino thought hard as to why he was dragged from back of Ruggeri's club and tossed directly into the back parking lot, along with his aching pride, as if he were an insignificant piece of broken furniture. Nothing but nothing as of yet in his short life had hurt as bad as being chastised and expelled from the Pope's place, and by his *hero* of all people, his mentor Batista, who was powerless to come to his aid, and he knew all too well his father will also fail at the task. He flailed his arms wildly and slammed his clenched right hand fist repeatedly into his open palm with brute force.

He was fighting mad as he rounded the corner of Columbus Street and headed back down the avenue toward his father's car lot. The animosity he immediately felt toward his father was matched only by the contempt and hatred that he brooded over the Pope. He could accept the fact that business is business, but why was he to be persecuted for the gambling sins of his father? What strange under-world rule was this? Or perhaps it was his father's wish come true. He was warned to stay away from the Pope's place just this morning. Now could it be his father was behind and the root reason of his expulsion from the club? Whatever the case may be, Tony knew he was out, but for the reasons explained by Batista and not as the favored request of his father. His embitterment turned into a displeasing pique as the cold feeling of dejection and humiliation swarmed his soul, and no matter how hard he tried, he could not hold back the tears that flowed from the thin slits of his shadowed eyelids.

Just at that moment and too close for comfort, a crack and brilliant flash of lighting gave way to an echoing rolling thunder that cleared his mind and made him pick up his pace. His jogging-like gait turned full throttle as he raced to meet the avenue bus that was approaching the curb at its designated stop. The driver straightened his cocked cap and gave the kid a wink, letting him know that he just made it. The hum of the rear engine and the acquainted musty smell of the bus soothed him as he slowly caught his breath and sat back in the worn vinyl-covered bench seat. He would relish this short ride he still had to travel.

His thoughts drifted back to an easier time in his life as he reminisced. As a young boy, he and his mother would ride the bus that took them under the Garden State Parkway viaduct and into the more affluent suburbs and towns that rose above the boundaries of his domain. She would take him by the hand and walk through the upscale neighborhoods of Essex County; Upper Montclair, Glen Ridge, and Bloomfield, where the moneyed lived. They would jut in and out of nimble cobblestone streets and window-shop the more opulent stores and boutiques than the ones they frequented in their neck of the woods. They would walk past the impressive homes, all with their neatly manicured lawns and blooming flowers, all owned by the ones that ventured past the inner sanctum of his turf. All owned by families with mothers and fathers who worked at seemingly normal jobs with meaningful careers. She held her boy's hand tightly and hoped a guiding message would travel into his tiny body and mind that "If you work hard enough, this is what you will have...this life, my son." These are all the aspirations of parents who wanted just a little bit more of an opportunity for their children, to attend the more prominent school systems of the communities, and of course, rise above the things his old-school father never paid attention to or cared about. The more desirable suburbs have also welcomed many a mobster who recognized the more suitable cover these neighbor-hoods provide from the unwelcomed notoriety that comes with the territory as did Angelo Ruggeri, who went past the viaduct and hid in the hills of Roseland, New Jersey, leaving the enterprises of the neigh-borhood in the capable hands of his *caporegime* and their solders.

There was another brilliant crack of lighting and a roll of thun-der as the sky suddenly turned black as nightfall. An angled fusillade of blinding rain pounded the windshield of the bus. Tony signaled for his stop. He hesitated a second before he attempted the mad dash exit through the just-opened bus door and up the puddle-soaked blacktop that led to his father's office. He snatched the newly purchased and unread *Newark Evening Newspaper* from behind the cursing bus driver's seat. He creased it over his head and bolted up the twenty-five yards of driveway with long gazelle-like strides. The gusting wind and stinging downpour challenged the boy's athletic ability to stay balanced. Big Anthony laughed aloud as he watched through the open slats of the venetian blinds. His son's legs that were moving faster and kicking higher than a New York Giant runningback during football practice. The old man cracked the door a bit and waited with a childlike grin on his face. His son entered in a huff and gave his old man a disgruntled "Hey" along with a cold shoulder as he stormed directly into the office bathroom. Tony Boy lifted his wet Italian knit shirt away from his body using his fingertips and gave the fabric a gentle shake, cursing the rain and hoping his fifty-dollar shirt hadn't been ruined. He began combing his pompadour when he heard his father shout, "I thought you were gonna' call me before you came by. What if I needed something?" His son answered with a curt tongue, "I didn't have time. It started to rain. Or weren't you watching?" The tone of voice annoyed his father, but he wrote it off as just the kid's anger being caught in the rain. He spoke sincerely, "You hungry? Your uncle Joe's on his way from Casa Di Pizza." Quiet filled the room. Big Anthony stared at the television set for a few seconds, mesmerized. "Hurry up out here. I got somethin' to tell ya'." His son took his time as he exited the small bathroom. He shunned his father and kept his eyes fixed on the television as he walked about the office. The kid purposely avoided the forced eye contact that his father was trying to establish. "Whatsa' matter with you?" his father asked with righteous concern as his eyes followed his son pacing about the office. He sensed something wrong with the boy.

Tony skittishly paced the office, only to stop and take good long hard looks at the array of black-and-white framed photographs his old man had nailed up on the walls. The nostalgia of seeing his father as a younger man, a handsome man in various poses with other big shots of the day, calmed him. The pictures compelled him to see his father in a more proud and dignified light. He always doubted the validity of the one his father boasted the most: six men lined up at a bar somewhere in Bayway, Elizabeth, all dressed in dark suits with wide lapels. His father, the tallest, stood dead center, cigarette in hand and a wide grin on his face, flanked on both sides by brutish-looking thugs including Albie Marrone and his brother Joe, and all on their way to the New York Opera House. "The opera house or a hit?" was always his question.

He ignored his father's words and just gazed through the window, letting himself become hypnotized by the falling rain. He didn't answer his father until he heard him once again: "What's the matter with you I said?" Suddenly Tony snapped out of the self-induced trance he was in and shrugged off the self-pity. The second time his father asked the question he was much louder and direct and the hard-pressed poke in the middle of his back commanded he give an immediate answer. Tony turned, hesitated, and then began to blurt out the events that unfolded at the Pope's place. He could not look his father in his eyes. The boy became very animated and descriptive as he spoke candidly to his father of the hurtful events that had just transpired only fifteen minutes prior.

The kid's eyes began to tear up as he continued his convulsive tirade. "They said you got no respect for them, and now they want to take it out me." He resolved. He held nothing back.

His father just sat back in a heap in his swivel chair and sadly listened to the punishing words of his son, his young son whose birthday was tomorrow. His dire stare was one of a labored man, a brokenhearted man. The disparaging remarks coming from his son's lips hit him harder than anything ever in his life. The more he heard, the redder and the more embarrassed he became until he heard enough.

Big Anthony let the weight of his upper body carry the chair forward under squeaking springs until it stopped dead with a loud metallic crunch. His chest expanded with a deep inhale of air through his flared nostrils, and he held it there for a noticeable amount of time; then he said humbly as he exhaled, "It's all right, son. It's over. We ain't gonna worry about the likes of the Pope no more." And with steady pride he became Big Anthony again—suddenly Cheese Marino leaped out of his heart. He folded his bulky arms over his midsection, cocked his head at his boy, and said most decisively, "I'm gonna' pack it all in—all of this rackets bullshit. It ain't payin' no more. At least not for me anyway." His voice had a crescendo building. "Me and your uncle got a plan to bail us all out. We got it all figured out, son. I'll be able to pay off that miserable prick Ruggeri and walk away. Like your uncle Joe did years ago." He stood up and came around from behind the desk and continued his defined speech, he himself becoming very animated and excited as he paced and talked. "We're gonna turn this place back into what it used to be. A fucking used car lot…a legitimate place. We'll all be partners. You, me, your uncle Joe. Who knows? We get big enough, we can open another place." Tony was calm now, believing and now listening with more attentiveness. He actually became enthused with the idea and hoped, for his father's sake, that this was a legitimate plan and not just another scheme his old man was concocting.

The headlights of the Buick bouncing over the entrance curb announced the arrival of Joe and three large pizza pies, two plain and one with anchovies. His father lifted another chair from the corner of the room and slid it next to the desk then cleared some more clutter. "Get the door for your uncle." He commanded anxiously to his son. The aroma of the fresh-baked pizza pie was acknowledged before Joe was. It aroused the starving giant and impelled him to start groping for the unopened top box still in the grips of his brother. "Whaddya got here?" Anthony asked impishly. "I got *ah beetz*... geez, Anth...wait until I get through the door for chrissakes," his brother said, turning away from the big man. Then he directed his attention toward the kid. "Whaddya say, Tony...Jesus Christ...you get bigger every time I see ya'," Joe said as he gently laid the boxes down on the desk. He gave his nephew a jovial hug and began yelling at his brother who had already folded a wedge of the *ah beetz* and began chomping away. "Anthony, there's paper plates and napkins in the bag." He looked at the kid and said, shaking his head, "Geez.... your old man never changes, does he?" A barely recognizable "I'll be changin' today" came from the pizza-stuffed mouth of Big Anthony as he peeked under the other closed cardboard box. "Whaddya get all plain...how come no sausage or pepperoni?" Anthony asked. "The one on the bottom has anchovies." Joe exhorted then continued to preach. "Its Friday. You're not supposed to eat meat?" Anthony shot a guilty look to his son and said, "Too fuckin' late for that. We already ate about five pounds of sausage this mornin', right, son?" He finished his words with a playful slap on his son's back. "What's the difference?" Anthony added, "We're all goin' to hell anyway." No one laughed at that comment. The next few minutes of conversation was muffled by heavy breathing from pizza-stuffed mouths. There were a few grunts and groans mixed with some short words accompanied by nods and shakes from everyone's head as the three gulped down pizza and soda and kicked around Big Anthony's plan.

Tony sat back and took the time to really study the two brothers as they sat side by side with the same quandary he had about the Pope earlier. What makes men take the paths they choose in life? The two brothers had a remarkable resemblance to one another, yet their mannerisms were so opposite of each other. Joe was almost a year older than his brother almost to the day, and the two could, in all actuality, pass for twins. Joe had more gray hair, straight short hair that was parted on the side, while his brother's longer, wavier hair was combed straight back. All of their facial features were eerily similar. Joe had a little bit more of a darker complexion, but that could be attributed to the fact he worked mostly outdoors, under the sun, while his brother was more nocturnal. They both stood at six feet, but Joe was about fifty pounds lighter and appeared to have more defined muscle tone than Anthony. Joe, unlike his brother, very rarely dressed up though his dark blue monogrammed work uniform was always pressed and only had a slight odor of oil and grease. The hairline cracks on his hands and fingertips and under his nails, in spite of hours of soaking them in stinging bleach, were permanently tattooed with the black color of grease.

Almost an hour had passed by, and the boys were still devouring slices of pizza and sharing huge energetic grins between themselves. Suddenly the sound of an approaching car made Big Anthony's demeanor change to alarm and prompted him to stand. His faced turned inquisitive as he noticed another set of headlights slowly creeping up the driveway. He dropped his half-eaten piece of pizza, walked to the window, and flicked the switch for the outside flood-lights. He peered through the venetian blinds as the dark-colored sedan came to a complete stop. At first he thought it was just a cou-ple of players looking for the Friday night game until parts of their burly faces became distinctly illuminated by the glow of the flood-lights that show through the windshield. The blinds made a metallic crackle as he spread them open and gave a penetrating stare at the two men in the car who parked head on in front of the office. He let the slats ricochet back and said out loud, "What the fuck do these two guys want?" He turned to Joe with an incensed look on his face then looked at his son. Joe sensed the uneasiness in his brother and asked, "Who is it? You expecting anyone else?" Anthony shot his brother a fretful stare and said, "It's Joey Lotta...and that other goon Altieri." His faced turned red and flushed with a worrisome look. Joe stood up and made his presence known and visible at the window. "Why do you think they're here?" he asked. "They ain't here for no social call…I'll tell you that," Big Anthony said as he locked the front door. He then turned to his son with a display of anxiety and ordered him to the back room and stay completely out of sight. He gestured to his brother to sit down and stay calm. He scooped up the boy's uneaten pizza and tossed it in the garbage can next to the desk then yelled to his son who was already in motion, "Tony…wait." He ran up and put his arm around his son's shoulder and whispered in his ear, "There's an envelope in the file cabinet." There was a compelling silence; then Anthony said, "I want you to take it, and as soon as you can…sneak out the back door, climb the back fence, and go home. Right now—you got that? Go right home, no matter what, and …be careful." His words were dire.

Tony tiptoed into the small storage room, pulled the cord for the light, then gently closed and locked the door. His anxiety mounted inside of him as he relived the story Tic told him earlier about the pending trouble his father was in. He sensed his father was in danger, and the arrival of Ruggeri's goons was slowly turning him into a bundle of nerves, a feeling he knew he must fight off. It then suddenly dawned on him. This was the first time he had ever heard his father call him by just his first name and not son. He fidgeted through the first drawer briefly then found the bundle of cash in the second lower drawer. His eyes became wide, and he froze some as he stuffed the package securely in his waistband. He held his breath and stared boldly at the gun metal gray Colt Combat Special .45 automatic also lying in the drawer. With just a slight gentle push the drawer closed in silence; then he shut out the light.

Two of Ruggeri's top enforcers were sent to pay a visit to the welshing Anthony with instructions to "teach him a lesson" of respect, something that the Pope felt has always been lacking in the unpolished mobster's life ever since the day he could remember, the days that date back and were tied in with the Pope's archnemesis, the recently departed Zwillman. He had let Big Anthony go a little too far and could not afford to show any signs of weakness when it came to disciplining the delinquent gambler. The Pope cursed himself for the mistake of not addressing this situation months ago, and the recent act of Anthony's slapping around a prominent attorney from Livingston at his executive game caused too much of a stir and was the ultimate insult in the Pope's eyes. Men have died for far less of an infraction; however, dead men tell no tales, nor do they pay back owed money. A message had to be sent, and it had to be delivered in the handwriting of the evil Joey Lotta.

Another massive streak of lightning discharged, and a simultaneous rolling percussion of thunder let all on Bloomfield Avenue know the storm was directly overhead. Al Altieri made a thumbing gesture toward Joe's parked car; then he took notice of the multiple shadows moving about inside and commented to Lotta, "I thought you said he was gonna' be alone?" Lotta ignored the statement. The two goons gave each other bemused stares as they sat inside the car, silent, their eyes fixed on the windshield wipers that were trying to keep up with the tempo of the drumming rain. They were apprehensive at first because of the surprise visit from a stranger, his presence known but not his identity. "Hey, I thought they said he was alone?" griped Altieri for the second time. Lotta just grunted and squeezed the steering wheel with white knuckles. They exchanged bewildered glances at one another as they pondered the task at hand but quickly rescinded any thoughts of not finishing the job ordered by the Pope himself for fear of what might happen to them. To change horses in midstream would prove disastrous; however, the two were not prepared for the chain of events that were about to take place. The bleak thought had never entered their criminal minds. Joey Lotta looked at Al with an upside down frown-like smile and said, "Fuck it, Al… let's do this thing."

The heavy hand of Two Ton Lotta made the framework and jambs shake as he pounded on the locked door with aggression. Joe gave another look of bewilderment to his brother and shrugged his shoulders with an inquisitive gesture. "What gives, Ant…?" Anthony just stared wildly at his brother. "I owe, brother…big-time, they're here to collect." Big Anthony turned his perplexed expression into a forced smile. He waited just a brief second and said coyly, "Yeah… who is it?" Joe was beside himself as he asked, "The ten Gs—that wasn't enough?" Big Anthony shrugged a bit then nodded his burly head *no*. A guttural voice was heard in unison with another boom of thunder. "It's me, Lotta. Open the fuckin' door. I'm gettin' soaked out here." Anthony clenched his teeth. He strategically stood to the left of the door, away from its natural path, and gingerly opened it with his right hand then took a cautious step back. The small L-shaped room soon was filled with gargantuan mobsters. Altieri barged right in and watched as Anthony and Joe made room for both mobsters to fully enter. Lotta followed and started to shake rain from his large frame while he shot daggers at Anthony's brother. "I didn't expect to see ya' here, Joe," he said then looked coldly at Big Anthony. "Whatsa' matter, you didn't see us in the car out there? You both were lookin' through the window a minute ago," Lotta said with an agitated voice. "Yeah…but to tell ya' the truth…I didn't recognize you, Joey…or the car?" Anthony said sarcastically. That in itself was a true giveaway of impending trouble. They were driving a customary getaway car, an easily disposed of Chevy sedan, and not Lotta's Cadillac. Big Anthony took a sidestep to his right with his eyes glued to Lotta and said, "What brings you guys out in such shitty weather. Ain't yous' afraid of catchin' a cold?" His acrimonious comment was just a sincere example of the wiseass personage that naturally reigned in his heart. His eyes showed absolutely no fear whatsoever.

Anthony made the innocent mistake of turning away while he nonchalantly asked, "You guys want some *ah-beetz?*" Both his fists were clenched hard, and his hope was to now beat Lotta to the punch. Lotta blurted, "We ain't here for no pizza. Ruggeri wants his money…you got?" "All I got today is *stugatz*, boys—and some pizza," Anthony said sarcastically as he began to prepare for battle. Brother Joe sat back in his chair and careened his untrusting vision from one thug to the other then back again, and for a split second the atmosphere in the room seemed reposeful; then Joe suspiciously felt the bad vibes. Suddenly his eyes bugged at what he saw. It was too late. He had zero time to react or to warn his brother. The heavy leather-wrapped blackjack slid down from under the sleeve and into the firm grasp of Lotta. With lightning speed and form of a trained prizefighter, Lotta swung his arm in an arc and brought the blackjack crashing down on the crown of Big Anthony's head. Anthony's vision went dark under a deadened thud. His massive frame dropped to one knee with an audible groan. Blood spurted from the one-inch split, and the pain shot down into his neck muscles as the severely stunned Anthony fought to keep his balance. He instinctively turned his weight into Lotta and reached out. His brother Joe spontaneously jumped to his aid but was immediately blindsided by two forceful blows of a revolver wielded by Altieri. The momentum of the blow sent Joe reeling into the television, crashing it to the floor with him on top of it. The brow over his left eye cracked open and began spewing blood down the side of his face. His clouded brain heard the barbarous voice of Lotta: "Stay outta' this, Joe. It's got nothin' to do with you."

Lotta did not know Joe personally. He only knew of him through his storied reputation of years ago when he himself was a brutal enforcer for his brother Anthony and the Zwillman gang, but he felt, if deemed necessary, he would punish him along with his brother without a second thought. Anthony's blurred vision and benumbed reflexes could not prevent Lotta's second vicious blow. His raised arm did little to block the shot that caught just above the bridge of his nose almost dead center between his eyes. Blood gushed immediately from another deep wound. It forced his right eye to swell up and turn into a purplish bubble. The blood flowed down the side of his face as he felt the throbbing pain from his skull worsen. Big Anthony was fighting desperately to stay conscious and tried to defend himself with outstretched arms. Lotta took a deep breath in and held it as he swung the club down yet again, this time down on his forehead right below his hairline. Gushing blood turned his salt-and-pepper hair the color of crimson, and the force of the blow sent the ailing hulk to his hands and knees. His head wounds were spewing blood. Big Anthony desperately tried to find some strength and coordination to rise to his feet. Lotta was amazed at the boldness of this wounded bear. He was half unconscious and wildly gasping for air trying desperately to lift his girth off the floor and try to mount a comeback. Lotta raised his arm to levy another blow. Finally, Big Anthony's brain signaled "enough pain felt" and shut him down with a groaning exhaling of breath as he collapsed on the floor.

Altieri had his revolver aimed at Joe, who was now fully cognizant and sitting up, his hand held to the tender knot and gash over his brow. "Don't make a move, Joe. Don't you make me shoot you," Altieri said. His worry was the chance of the brother lunging at him. The idea was actively racing through Joe's mind as he keep his eyes glued to the every movement of the mobster who held him at bay, knowing that one false move would result with a bullet from the gun of the seasoned killer. Another boom of thunder caused Altieri to flinch, but he still managed to keep his steadfast posture. Lotta held the blackjack up, half cocked so to speak, as he reached down and grabbed the big man with the intentions of just rolling him over on his back. Big Anthony slowly began to regain his senses as he felt the mobster ease his body around. He watched through blurred vision as Lotta raised the weapon. He did not want to get hit again. With a sudden surge of second wind energy, Anthony found some balance then grabbed the looming goon by his wrist. With an awkward swing, he grazed Lotta's jaw with a closed fist. He heard his brother shout in anguish, "Stay down, Anthony...stay down." Lotta was galled by the act of persistence and became alarmed by the strength of the man's grip. He would have to use all of his power to break free from the iron grasp of Big Anthony who knew if he managed to get hold of him with his other hand, the tides would turn. Lotta saw the determination in the wounded mobster's face and read the play. Lotta's face became repugnant, and maniacally took on the look of a stone-cold killer, "You motherfucker...you don't know when you've had enough?" He redirected his power by shifting his weight and just barely escaping Anthony's grasp. Lotta drove a solid knee to the temple of the kneeling Anthony that sent him against the wall and almost unconscious once again, but amazingly, he still managed to hold tight on Lotta's wrist. "Now I'll fuckin' kill ya'," Lotta growled then clenched his teeth. He brought a powerful arm up ready to deliver what he wanted to be the last and final shots to the head of the still struggling Anthony. Brother Joe closed his eyes as he knew the death blow was soon to be levied. He whimpered the words once again, "For chrissakes, Anthony, stay down...stay down..."

Altieri was the first to notice the kid cautiously round the corner wall of the office who then suddenly and purposely let his presence be known to all. But it was a startled Joey Lotta who reacted immediately to the familiar clicking sound of the automatic slide as it loaded the first .45 caliber shell into the chamber. Lotta turned his body and only had seconds to react to the kid who was standing in a perfect shooter's stance no more than eight feet away and aiming dead center. The room fell silent as the question that ran through Two Ton's vile mind was *Does this punk kid even know how to shoot that gun?* Little did he know the kid was taught how to shoot to kill by his father and his uncle years ago as the three would roam the junkyards and piers down on Doremus Avenue hunting the rats and wild dogs that inhabited the waterfronts?

The sight of his severely beaten father obstructed the boy's conscience as to the seriousness of the anticipated act he was about to perform. His entire body tensed as he listened to the voice inside his head say "It's the same as shooting just another wild animal." The boy was beyond scared shitless as his trembling hands indicated. Altieri, always thinking as a criminal should, thought, *Who do I shoot first?* His immoral instinct compelled him to take aim at the boy, but his path was blocked by large frame of Lotta, so he quickly aimed the barrel of the gun back at Joe. And with wide eyes he growled again, "Don't make a fuckin' move, Joe."

Big Anthony let go of his grip from Lotta and eased into a contorted pile of freshly butchered meat on the floor, his twisted upper body weight being supported by his one elbow and arm. His other hand instinctively patted and pressed his head wounds with a degree of pressure. And steadily, all the muddlement from his clouded head was clearing his thoughts, and the pain did not matter anymore or interfere with his bent ability to think and act—he shot an evil look at his son, a look that so clearly screamed "Shoot the bastard."

Lotta slowly lowered the blackjack to his side and began to stare the boy down with cold eyes—the idea and inference that he too would lower the pointed gun as well. He watched as the kid trembled some. "Put the gun down, kid, and take it easy," he said coaxingly as he made a lowering gesture with his hand then took a careful and calculated step forward, his eyes announcing the exact spot. "There ain't no need for guns here, kid." The boy reacted spontaneously to Lotta's words and body motion by quickly reaffirming his already steadfast grip on the weapon while he also took a step closer. His fear and intimidation left his soul. This made everyone in the room restless, and eyes darted to and fro. It startled Lotta more than he would have liked to be. The wielded weapon was pointed dead center into the mobster's chest, and Lotta could well see the aim. At this close range he could not possibly miss, and the seasoned mobster was well aware of the stopping power of the gun. But still he doubted the kid's ability or willingness to ever pull that trigger. It was a ploy? Carefully, he inched his way closer with the hopes of disarming the kid. Blood pumped quickly through Tony's veins, pushing his adrenaline to a level never experienced before. He wanted to say "Drop it" to the thug who was silent and keeping his uncle at bay, but Lotta did not give him the chance. He watched as Lotta's face grew more grotesque than ever. Joey Lotta's eyes bugged, announcing his soon-to-follow rage. Suddenly he lunged forward with his hands raised, and the last question his subconscious mind would ever answer during those brief last few seconds of his life was "No way this kid got the balls to shoot."

The rapidly fired rounds of the .45 automatic exploded from the barrel and entered the massive chest cavity of the mobster in a perfect cluster. The impact forced his huge frame back a couple of steps. The bullets smashed his boned breastplate into fragments; the ricocheting slugs and shattered bone sliced through the vital arteries of Lotta's heart and lungs, forcing an explosion of blood from his nose and mouth, causing instantaneous death. His eyes turned into dark glasslike marbles, and his lifeless carcass dropped heavily to the floor almost on top of the ailing Anthony. The boy stood frozen in time. He instantly shut his eyes as his body became numb. The ringing in his ears made him oblivious to his surroundings.

The distracted and confused Altieri did not have an opportunity to take aim and shoot. He had not a second of retaliatory time. The hulking Joe leaped up and viciously grabbed the mobster around his thick throat with a powerful right hand. With a mighty shove and an audible warrior's cry he drove Altieri straight armed into the wall with a heavy thud. With his left, he wrestled the revolver from Altieri's grip until it dropped to the floor; his right hand continued a viselike grip around the gangster's throat causing his eyes to bulge from their sockets.

Anthony looked into his son's eyes fearfully, then at the dead mobster who was bleeding out on the floor. Instinctively, he leaped up and immediately went to his brother's aid. He formed a tight fist and drove a thunderous right-handed blow to the side of Altieri's face that sent him immediately to the office floor. Joe backed away and watched as his brother dropped his knee and all of his weight onto the midsection of Altieri. Five more heavy head shots were delivered by Anthony in a fit of savage rage, rendering the mobster unconscious with a broken jaw, broken cheekbone, and a shattered eye socket. His face was more bloodied than was his attacker.

Big Anthony exchanged dire looks of worriment and uncertainty with his brother and son as he stood up and gained some composure. He gawked at the battered face of Altieri then turned to his son who seemed to be suffering with his own emotional stress. Tony was dazed. His eyes wide open and his mouth agape. His father lumbered over to his side. He hovered over the bullet-ridden body of Lotta and whispered, "You okay, son?" Tony returned a traumatized "Yeah." The dire situation was apparent, and it showed in Big Anthony's facial expressions. It was not one where you would asseverate a congratulatory "Good job" or cheer for your "son, the quarterback" who just threw the winning touchdown at a high school football game, or exhibit anything else less than regret and repentance for involving the innocence of your only son, and worse yet, making a murderer out of him. Perhaps it could be justified, like father like son? The guilt and burden was on Big Anthony's shoulders only, and he had to find a way to extricate his brother and son from any involvement. No one could ever know the truth.

Anthony walked over and kicked the handgun away from the reach of the downed mobster, Altieri. He grimaced to his brother. "We're gettin' too old for this shit!" The comment got a slight nod of acceptance from the semi-dazed Joe who was walking out of the office bathroom with a wad of bloodied paper towel pressed tightly against his fresh wound. Anthony went into the bathroom and began to examine his wounds in the mirror as he splashed cold, refreshing water over his bloodied face. He dabbed the open cuts and winced with pain as he applied pressure to stop the bleeding that after a few moments began to clot then turned into raw gel-like mounds. He found it almost impossible to organize his thoughts as the replay of the shooting boggled his mind and kept him from clearly thinking of what he was to do next. The first order of business became vivid and clear as his confusion left him, and the blueprint of an idea forced a grimace on his reflection in the mirror.

With the dauntlessness of a battlefront general, Big Anthony walked decisively through the office; he carefully avoided the puddles of blood. He summoned his brother and son to huddle by his side. He gave a an unsettled look again at the lifeless body of Lotta as if he might overhear what was about to be said. "Nobody has to know you two were here and no one will ever find out." He turned to his brother and said, "I'll fade the heat for this." He gestured to his son and said to Joe, "You get him outta here. Now. And be careful you don't step in *no* blood." He walked to the window and continued. "Thank God it's rainin'…give us a little cover." He fired his orders rapidly as he looked at his son. "You go with your uncle. Go straight home. Don't say nothin' to yer mother, and gimme' that gun." He took the weapon from his son's hands and spoke to his brother, "Take him straight home. Nowhere else, got it? This never happened here, as far as you two guys are concerned. It never happened, gabide?" Joe gave a thumbed hand gesture in the direction of Altieri, who at that moment gave signs of coming to. Joe said, "What are you gonna' do with these two?" Anthony shot back a firm "Don't worry about them. Now beat it…botha' yous." His adrenaline was pumping as he hugged his son and said, "Don't worry, son…everything will work itself out. Remember. You can never say a word about what ya' diii…"—he caught his words and finished—"about what you saw here today." Big Anthony's eyes filled with tears as he said, "Now hurry up and get outta' here."

Joe took a step toward Tony and with a shake of his head said, "C'mon, let's go, kid." He froze in his tracks and turned abruptly. Facing his brother, he asked with deep concern, "Anthony…whaddya going to do now?" He flared his arms and said, "I can't leave you alone with this mess." "Joe, get the fuck outta here." Anthony fired back as he pointed to the front door. He walked over to the wall and shut off the outside floodlights. He peered out through a thin opening he made with the venetian blinds, making sure no passersby were around. "Hurry up. Go now," he said anxiously. "C'mon, get outta here." He rubbed his face with his hands feverishly. "I'll figure something out—don't yous' worry. I'll find a way outta' dis mess," he said as he hurried the two out of the office. Anthony slammed the door shut and threw the dead bolt. He leaned his shoulder heavily against the door and listened as the auto started and sped off. He peeked through the blinds once more and watched as the taillights rolled over the curb and vanished down the avenue. Big Anthony pondered some very dire thoughts then raised his eyebrows and said with an unsure smirk, "I'll call Albie?"

12

Not a single, solitary word was spoken between nephew and uncle as Joe zigzagged through the back streets, fighting the cutting rain and lake-sized puddles en route to Hinsdale Place. No thoughts, emotions, or opinions were uttered as they both kept their silence of the gruesome events buried deep in the back of their minds. Both prayed the horrific event would play easy on their conscience and vanish as if it were a bad dream. Tony truly hoped his father spoke the truth when he assured him everything would work out for the best although his apprehension of a simple solution gnawed at his insides with the dogma of the chilling facts. A murder would have to be covered up. The murder just committed by him on a highly ranked soldier of the Cosa Nostra was not something easily swept under the carpet.

Tony's tense fear was eased somewhat by his uncle's temperate words as he pulled into the driveway and stopped by the side entrance to let him out. "Tony, the important thing is that you say nothing… like your father said, especially to your mother." The kid reached for the door handle then paused. He turned his head toward his uncle with a look of bewilderment on his face. Almost instinctively, as if Joe knew exactly what his young nephew was thinking, he began to answer the boy's unspoken speculation. "Remember…no matter who asks…anybody…the cops…the wise guys…no matter how they try to trick fuck you, and they will, you gotta' stick to your story." Tony nodded in agreement. "You gotta' come up with a real good alibi as to where you were today, can you?" Joe asked seriously. "I was with Batista this afternoon," the boy answered. "He drove me over to the club, ya' know, Pope's place…" He hid the truth from his uncle about being expelled from the club. "Then I went by my father's place… that's it." Joe became inquisitive. "What time was that? I mean the last time Batista or anyone saw you?" He asked. "I dunno…around three, three-thirty…right before it started to rain real hard," the boy answered. "Did you tell anyone where you were going when you left the Pope's place?" Joe asked with raised brows. "No…I just left." Joe let out a deep breath and said, "Good. Keep it that way. As far as anyone is concerned, you went right home…to avoid the storm, got it? No one will ever find out." Uncle Joe gave the kid an open-handed slap on his knee and said, "Me and your old man been through this shit a million times, believe me, he'll find a way to make it right. He'd never let anything happen to you…or for us for that matter." Tony gave his uncle a reassuring smile as he jumped out of the car. His uncle gave him a heartening wink in return.

Joe pushed down hard on the gas pedal, spinning the tires on the drenched pavement as he sped off. He hoped and prayed that the normal fifteen-minute ride from North Newark to Hillside wouldn't have any unforeseen delays. He wanted to make the trip in ten. Joe glanced at the dashboard clock that read five forty-five. *I got plenty of time*, he thought to himself. His son would be closing the station in another twenty to thirty minutes. He also knew that his son Nicky would not close up before he heard from him. Joe had more than enough time to do what he needed to do, and that is to establish his own iron-clad alibi. That would be an easy task. Where the hell else would he be besides his own service station, next to his son, pumping gas and making repairs? He was also confident about his nephew's ability to provide his own alibi, one that would not place him at the scene of any crime scene—what crime? Joe was cocksure that his brother Anthony would be the last man standing. Alteri, although still alive when he left, was as good as dead. Joe was sure of it. Alteri would not have the opportunity to give his testimony to anyone except the devil himself. As for his undaunted brother, Joe knew Big Anthony would take this secret to the grave with him.

Big Anthony sat slumped in his office chair, head tilted back and arms folded gingerly on top of his belly. An eerie silence was about the room. Suddenly and with an evil malice, he hard shoved Lotta's dead leg away with his foot. He felt his facial muscles weaken as his jaw dropped open. He let his vision turn into a dazed blur, a daydream, and now was at peace as he thought about absolutely nothing. He instinctively and slowly shifted his weight and turned his head toward the rustling noise of Altieri. The battered thug was trying to push away from the wall and rolled over on his side. Big Anthony rolled his eyes in utter disgust as the dazed gangster moaned and tried to lift himself to a sitting position. Big Anthony groaned audibly as he reluctantly lifted himself out of the chair. He took a firm grip of the cocked and loaded .45 as he slowly walked over to the severely injured thug. With a mighty shove of Anthony's foot, the maimed gangster was flat on his back again and staring down the barrel of the shiny .45 automatic.

Altieri's swollen purplish face had doubled in size from the fractures. He desperately tried to utter words that could not be understood, verbally, but his bugging eyes told the story. He was begging to be spared. Anthony took aim at the mobster's chest and watched his lips contort as more garbled speech tried to leave his bloodied mouth. Anthony's face bore a sullen look as he stood over the maimed mobster and said, "You got yourself into some fuckin' mess here today, Al." Altieri could only hold his breath for the few seconds prior as Anthony fired the remaining bullets into his chest until the slide jammed open into the reload position. Another violent burst of lightning lit the office. The lights, both inside and out, went black. This lasted for just a few seconds, and during that brief time Big Anthony looked up to the heavens, hoping, praying for some sort of a divine guidance. He peered out between the taut blinds with deep thoughts, fearful thoughts.

Ceil was just about finished getting ready for her Friday night gala. She was completely dressed and standing in front of the bathroom mirror tapping her feet to a lively jazz tune playing on the radio. She was in the middle of a voiced argument with a piece of unruly hair when she heard the back door slam shut. "Who's there?" she said with a surprised voice as she poked her head into the hallway. Tony had already entered his bedroom. He turned quickly and poked his head into the hallway as well. "It's just me, Ma." Ceil gave up the fight with her hair with a conceding "The hell with you" and walked to her son's room. Tony was standing in front of his dresser mirror unbuttoning his wet shirt. Ceil stood in his doorway armed with a mother's intuition and inquisitively asked, "What's wrong?" She studied the boy with intense eyes then continued. "Why are you home so early?" She took a couple of steps closer to her son. Her voice became probing. "You're never home this early on a Friday night." He tossed his shirt into the closet and walked past her heading toward the kitchen, intentionally avoiding eye contact. He opened the refrigerator door and peered inside through stargazing eyes, this something all boys instinctively do when they do not want to talk to their parents.

Ceil walked into the kitchen and turned down the radio. Tony felt her prying eyes and turned around, forcing a smile. "What?" he exclaimed. Then he pointed to the picture window and the dreary rain that prevailed. "I got caught in the rain…decided to call it an early night," he said as he disappeared back into the refrigerator. "I didn't cook anything if that's what you're looking for," Ceil said contritely. Then mother's intuition forced her to ask again, "Are you sure you're not in any trouble?" Her voice was stern. "Ma, whaddya keep asking me for?" He was finding it easier to lie to her now. "No, I said." He shut the refrigerator door and walked past her again heading back into his room. This time he looked her in the eyes. Ceil shot him back a cold stare and said, "All I do is worry…you and your father." Ceil walked back into the bathroom talking aloud with a voice of discernible disgust. "I'm tired of worrying about you two." Tony gazed out of his bedroom window and into the gray stormy sky. He became hypnotized with the raindrops as they pelted the panes of glass. He could empathize with his mother's worry, and now as his worry turned steadily to fear, he shivered.

Big Anthony perked up and sat at attention. He began a series of inventive conversations with the two corpses that flanked him. His facial features became maniacal as he cursed his now dead adversaries' souls to hell. It was an eerie sight—both bodies lying in heaps, casting irregular shadows of their former selves on the walls that eerily seemed to stir about. The only bit of illumination inside the place was coming from the dull lightbulb that sat uncovered and just simply screwed into a ceiling fixture in the washroom, and on occasion, a glint of lightning from the now distant storm. Anthony's pain and bleeding from his wounds had subsided. He tossed another damp and bloodied paper towel onto the already accumulating heap on the floor. He sat back in his chair and took a deep breath while dismally pondering the ominous situation he was in. He lit a cigarette then asked Joey Lotta, quite sincerely, for his opinion of the four inescapable choices he was mulling over in his head. The first was a simple one—could go on the lam. However, with his finances in complete ruin and he flat broke, he would not be able to run and hide far enough away from the vengeful Ruggeri who, all knew, would never let this act go unpunished. And of course the certainty of endangering his family would be imminent. Perhaps he could simply surrender to Ruggeri? He could try to give a logical explanation as to why he killed two of his top people—made men—rather than just take the deserved punishment and the endeavored message to heart as were the intentions. That proposal was applauded by the revenant ghostlike image of Lotta who rose up from the corpse and agreed. "Now you're talkin'," the apparition said, "go take it like a man." Before the ghost vanished it made a solemn promise not to squeal on his son, complimenting him on "having the balls to shoot." Then the fading apparition echoed the also fading words, multiple times, "No one was spous' a' die here today—no one." The third hard choice was to surrender to the police and face the courts and the legal system. Again his dwindled finances would come into play as his defense would be costly, but he was reminded by the visible spirit of Altieri that rose from the dead, "Even a smuck lawyer would be able to plea this fiasco down to a simple case of self-defense." Anthony thought that one through. Add get the prosecutors to allow a manslaughter verdict to be rendered down? He answered the ghost back, "Yeah… what could I be facing—at best, a few years in the joint?" With that said, Joey Lotta appeared again and interjected with the fact that Ruggeri would "never let it get that far" before he had him *whacked.* All three shook their heads no to the fourth choice, which was to simply blow his brains out with Altieri's revolver that lay next to him on the desk.

Big Anthony opted for his third choice as the one that posed the best odds for his survival. His surrender must be done very carefully and discreetly with only a handful of police around who would whisk him away to the confines of the Second Precinct jail. He must contact someone he could trust within the organization to make the necessary arrangements to ensure his safety. He picked up the phone and dialed the Pope's club with the hopes of reaching out to his friend Albert Marrone.

Angelo Ruggeri left his secured basement bunker and took his position back at the booth. Albert Marrone was sitting all alone, caring about nothing and sipping on a fresh Jack Daniels that Vito had just delivered. Frank Batista was making the rounds throughout the club with the visiting Tort mingling humorously with the crew and talking about the evening's proper and improper plans. Ruggeri glanced long and hard at his watch then asked Albert coolly, "You hear anything about our friend yet?" Albert shook his head no at first then shot back churlishly, "Nothin' yet." He too looked at his watch and said, "I'm sure they're on their way back by now. How long could it take?" Ruggeri was still fuming over the report of the meeting the two Paisan had earlier, which prompted him to act because Anthony did not take heed to Albert's warning. Why did he not come directly to the club with the five thousand dollars like he was supposed to have done? It was, in Ruggeri's eyes, a complete disregard for Albert's friendship and respect. And he adamantly let Albert know his feelings on breaking the rules. "Maybe your friend will not act so out of line anymore—the situation, his situation could have been a lot worse, Albie, and you know that," Ruggeri said sarcastically. Vito walked from behind the bar and walked to the table both men were at. He excused himself to Ruggeri as he turned to Albert and said with worriment, "You got a phone call." And with raised brows, Vito pointed to the black desk phone on the shelf behind the bar. Albert's eyes widened with a look of expectation indicating to Ruggeri that this must be Lotta checking in.

Albert immediately recognized the doddering voice of his old friend as he spoke. "Ya could have warned me, my friend," Anthony said unpretentiously. Albert shifted his stiff and rigid body into somewhat of a secretive stance behind the bar and whispered, "It was too late to call off the dogs…*Che Cozz*. I tried to warn you this afternoon." Albert turned and looked up at Ruggeri who was all ears at the booth trying to get a gut feeling for the conversation. Albert's eyes became alert with the words he heard. "That didn't sound like a warning to me, especially 'bout those two dogs—well, anyway, now you can forget about those dogs—I-malano-miau—they ain't barkin' no more," Anthony snapped back. Albert picked up on the connotation and turned his back to Ruggeri then spoke in whispers into the receiver, "Whaddya mean by that?" His voice was filled with concernment as he continued. "Are you okay…*Ma che cozz'u fai*?" Anthony's face turned red and twisted as he listened to Albert's words. His gut feeling told him his old friend had a hand in the plotted attack and suddenly felt he had made a blind mistake calling him. "Things got a little outta' hand over here, Albie…I'm gonna' need some help," Anthony said. "Help with what?" Albert tried to keep his words riddled. "You need help with what? Those two dogs…where are they now?" There was a long pause of silence. "They're lying on the floor right next to me—asleep." Anthony sassed back. "They're never gonna hunt again, Albert." Albert was aghast. "Aduzipach?" Anthony broke off the charade with the conversation and said coldly that he had just shot both of them dead. "I had no fuckin' choice, Albie. It was self-defense…you hear me—duyavatch?" Then he laid out his precise intentions to Albert about the idea of surrendering to the police. "I'm here all alone, my friend…all alone—and whoever you send, tell 'em to bring lottsa' biangolin—gabide." Albert shook his head consistently as he spoke, and after a while he reluctantly concurred and agreed with his old friend it was probably the only option he had left. He agreed to meet him at his office in fifteen minutes, alone, to finalize a plan.

Albert hung the phone up in utter disbelief and stared aimlessly into space as he walked slowly back to his seat. He moaned from the

sharp arthritic pain in his joints as he slid his aching body back into
the booth he shared with Ruggeri and grimaced as he began describing
the bleak details of what was just told to him. "*Mannaggia la mort'*.
He killed them, both of them, *jamokes. Chepreca—Chepreca*," Albert
said with shrugged shoulders and a confused frown. For about just a
minute or so there was silence at the table. Ruggeri's face bore a blank
stare, and it took a while longer for him to ask the only haunting
question that came to mind. "Was he alone?" Ruggeri asked apprehensively.
Albert nodded slightly. "So he says, Pope. *Che Cozz*. So he
says." Other than his eyes bugging slightly, Ruggeri made no sign of
emotion as he listened. He was stupefied by the fact that his most
skillful professionals were waylaid by the aging mobster and found it
hard to believe he acted alone. He aired his opinion to Albert who,
in return, just shrugged his drooping shoulders and said, "Whodda'
figure that big *gaguzzalonga* still had it in him?"

Ruggeri's focus was now on the countermeasures to cut short
Anthony's notion of involving the police. It would be an act that
could only spell utter disaster in the Pope's eyes with the foreshadowing
thought of the big man cooperating with the justice department
and turning against him. After all he was not a made man and had
no code of honor to live by with nothing more to lose and all to gain.

Ruggeri's wheels began to turn inside his criminal mind as he
quickly formulated a plan and conceded to Anthony's request for a
confidential police escort out of his office. He told Albert to return
a call to his indiscernible friend and explain that to meet him personally
would not be a good idea. "Tell him less involvement of our
people would be for the better, and tell him you can't come but you'll
send a reliable cop to get him, and tell Anthony he's not to say a word
till we send a lawyer, and tell him absolutely no more phone calls."

Big Anthony was all out of options now. He hung up the phone
with a hollow feeling deep down inside his gut. He was suspiciously

leery about the conversation with Albert and even more so with his decision to give himself up to the police, but what could he do about it now? His hand had already been tipped, and there was no turning back. He stood up in a huff and lumbered to the storage room and grabbed the partially empty box of .45 caliber ammunition from the file cabinet. He returned to the front of the office and peered through the window then began talking to the dead Lotta once again. He felt his adrenaline rise. "Just in case anyone else but the cops comes walkin' through the door, my friend." He sat down at the desk and released the clip from the Colt .45 and began jamming the cartridges into position then slammed it back into the gun and snapped back the slide. Then he began to feverously wipe it clean with a hand-kerchief. "They'll think they're walkin' into the fuckin' Alamo. Remember the Alamo, Joey?" He leaped up again with the .45 in his grip and lumbered over to the office window. The feeble aluminum blinds were no match for his clumsy force and bent audibly under it. The heavy rain had subsided and was now just a light steady stream with an occasional lightning flash and a distant rumble of summer thunder. Big Anthony calmly sat back in his swivel chair and threw a heavy leg up on the edge of the desk. He lit a Lucky Strike cigarette and positioned the Colt .45 at arm's reach. And as he waited to be handcuffed and escorted to jail he calmly blew smoke rings up over his head.

Eddie Accardi entered his house through the rear door that led into a small foyer then a step up and into his kitchen. He was greeted by a handwritten note sitting on the counter in the exact spot his wife knew he would lay down his keys. The note read "Went to pick up the boys. See you soon. Love, Phyl." Their two sons had been stranded at the ball field where they were playing all afternoon until the rain came.

The detective relished the fact that the house was empty. It was something that he rarely experienced although he did have some well-appreciated quiet time when he worked the early shift. His wife's job kept her occupied until five-thirty or sometimes six; then the Garden State Parkway held her captive for another twenty or thirty minutes as she drove north from her office at the Ronson Corp. This allowed the stressed detective the pleasure of pouring himself some aged Scotch whisky over ice and enjoying a cocktail or two as he either prepared dinner or ordered take-out for his wife to pick up on her way home. The tasks were evenly divided over the two-week period of his shift until he occasionally rotated back to nights. Phyllis left her work earlier this afternoon with the intention of a weekend retreat at the lake house that, in spite of the rain, was still the game plan judging by the packed suitcase she left by the front door.

Eddie was settled in his leather recliner that sat in his den and had just taken his first swig of the fiery amber liquid when the phone rang. *Obviously it was Phyllis* was, his initial thought, *who else would be calling at such a wrong time.* The voice on the other end was a familiar one, and the instructions were cut-and-dried. He had exactly fifteen minutes to rendezvous with the black Plymouth Fury in the parking lot of the Sicilian Café. The message and the order could not be ignored.

13

Big Anthony stared intensely at the patterned reflection of the headlights as they cut through the venetian blinds and climbed up and across the office wall and ceiling. His anticipation grew. He acknowledged to himself only one car had turned in from the avenue. This gave him a feeling of relief knowing there was no posse in tow. He prayed to God it was Albie. He was up on his feet now and peering out the window at what he recognized as an approaching unmarked police cruiser. Only the outline of a driver was visible. Where's Albie? He held his breath and stood silent and still, almost statuesque, and watched as the car crawled up the driveway, past the locked cyclone fenced gate, and then parked alongside the now dead mobsters' car. The driver's features were hidden. Where's his hat? he thought. Most cops wear hats, especially in the rain. Big Anthony quickly reaffirmed his seat at the desk and kept his vision on the illuminated headlights still reflecting into the room, and in time they turned off.

It would be almost two minutes before he exited the vehicle. A single car door opened and shut, and only one set of footsteps could be heard on the loose graveled approach to the concrete steps. The gentle rapping of knuckles on the front door was a relatively light and benign announcement compared to the sirens and guns-a-blazing raid Big Anthony had envisioned. He sat in his chair with his hands interlocked behind his head and calmly shouted out, "It's open, come on in." His well-rehearsed and memorized testimony was in place, and Anthony was prepared to tell his side of the story to anyone from the Second Precinct. After all, it would be his version that would hold all the weight in a court of law. *There are no other witnesses*, he gloated silently to himself, *so whoever you are, I am ready to surrender*. He shifted his weight ever so slow and sat uncomfortably on the edge of the chair as soon as his wide-open and bloodied eyes caught a glimpse of the pencil-thin moustache and evil jowl of Detective Accardi. The detective nonchalantly made his way over the threshold then shut and locked the door behind him. Big Anthony let the burden of his sore body and weight carefully rest on his elbows, and he sat perfectly still as the cold detective entered the room. Anthony's eyes were glued to the slick Accardi, watching him nervously as the cunning detective assiduously walked the room and assessed the crime scene. His worriment now was the fact Accardi was alone.

Anthony noticed the .38 snub-nosed Special fastened in its shoulder holster but paid no attention to the throwaway revolver that was strapped to his ankle. The detective fiddled with a few wall-mounted switches until he came upon the right one that shed more light on his subjects. "There, that's better. Now I can see just what the hell is going on here," Eddie said as he shot furtive glances back and forth at the dead men's faces. He looked Anthony directly in his eyes and said, "Or what went on here?" Eddie had his hands folded behind his back as he nudged the dead Lotta with his foot and said, "My compliments." He looked at Anthony with a grim smile and nodded his head. "You still got what it takes." The detective grimaced at the battered head and face of Anthony, and with a waving hand gesture to his own he said sourly, "It came with a price, huh, amigo? I won't bore you at all with that old 'does it hurt' joke. I know this is no laughing matter." Then he walked over and glanced out of the office window through a bent slat. He let the knuckle of his closed finger glide the length of the closed venetian blind as he turned back to Anthony and said, "You know I gotta' take you in… but before I call for backup"—he made a customary look with his face and shrugged his shoulders—"just routine." Accardi focused his attention to the .45 automatic lying on the desk within arm's reach of Anthony. Then he roughly counted the spent shells lying about. "Is that gun loaded…or should I say reloaded? That is the murder weapon, right?" Anthony just nodded and said, "Yeah…to both yer' questions, but don't worry, I'm not gonna' make a grab for it. That would be suicide, huh?" Accardi gave a smug grin and said, "I'm not worried about that, Anthony…but why don't you tell me what the hell happened here, from beginning to end, for my report. It will help with your defense if I have your explanations in *my* report." Those spoken words from Accardi put Anthony at ease for the moment.

Eddie focused on one section of the room at a time and tried to visualize as he listened to Anthony's version. Walking in slow, measured steps and making mental notes as he tried to reenact the entire fracas and match up Anthony's description of the events to the actual crime scene. He made a predetermined analysis based on the positions of the bodies as to basically how they were standing at the moment the shots were fired. He observed the cluster of bullet holes in each of the victims and the pools of blood as Anthony told him of the alleged assault that prompted the shooting.

Detective Accardi, as did Ruggeri, found it hard to believe that one man could successfully defend himself against the likes of these two bruisers let alone bring them both down in a hail of bullets that were fired with such careful aim and accuracy. The three boxes of pizza along with the two place settings still on the desk and a third in the trash can together with the contradictions of Anthony's story just confirmed in Eddie's mind that the big guy was lying through his teeth. He could not have acted alone; no single man is that tough, but for all intensive purpose, this meant absolutely nothing to the detective; he was just trying to get an accurate report for Ruggeri who would want answers for his own self-satisfaction.

Eddie started asking a line of direct questioning using a different approach with the hopes of piercing the thick, stubborn skull of Anthony. At first, his demeanor was calm and collected, like a good cop. Now it was time to be the bad cop. "So tell me again," he asked concerning as he began recreating the crime and acting out Anthony's movements. "You were standing here when they broke through the door?" "No, I let them in," Anthony said, obscuring. Eddie continued with a raised voice. "Then Lotta started to beat you with what...the blackjack...right?" His arm raised and his finger pointed. "The one over there?" Both sets of eyes focused on the weapon lying next to Lotta in a pool of his own congealing blood. Eddie paused then stared at Anthony with a puzzled look on his face. "Then you shot him...correct? Where did you have the gun?" Anthony did not reply or react in any way. "Then you shot Altieri... or did you beat him first...or did you shoot Altieri first and then Lotta...I'm confused here, Anthony?" Eddie slowly reached down and picked up the revolver that was Altieri's. He examined the fully loaded weapon and tucked it in his waistband and just stood with his arms folded. He glanced around at the many spent cartridges on the floor and tried for a count. They all seemed to have been fired from a .45 automatic all right. But their positions on the floor did not jive with Anthony's story. "I think you're full of shit, Anthony." Anthony remained cool. He took a deep breath then lit a cigarette. He rolled his eyes as he turned his head toward Accardi. He let out a puff of smoke in the direction of the cop and said, "Yeah...you believe what you want...I'm tellin' ya'...that's how it happened...the best as I can remember." His voice indicated that was growing tired of the bullshit.

Eddie changed the tone of his voice and asked casually, "Anthony, come on now…tell me the truth. Was there anyone else with you here that could bear witness for your defense? It is not going to be an open-and-shut case of self-defense if that's what you're thinking. Ruggeri will see to that. This is his personal property you trashed." The underlying connotation gave the big guy something to fret about. Albert must have said something to the Pope, but that was to be expected. Eddie reconnoitered the crime scene once again and said, "It looks like you had what, two or three guys here with you? Come on, big guy, there's no need to cover for anyone." Anthony immediately recognized the ploy being used as Eddie continued. "I mean… really." As Eddie changed back into his bad cop role, he became very animated as he waved his arms wildly and pointed his finger at the table and the pizza boxes then said, "It looks like you were having a party here today, was this before or after you killed these two goons?"

Anthony tried to remain calm but felt he was slowly losing it and wondered if that was the intentions of Accardi. Was he trying to get him to the point of insanity and lunge for the handgun on the desk? It would be a justified shooting in the department's eyes. Anthony was not going to give him that opportunity. "I told ya… that pizza was from yesterday." Eddie shot back. "They look pretty fresh to me, maybe I should ask the pizzeria when these were delivered? Where are they from, Casa di Pizza?" A long silence fell on the room; then Accardi started to pressure. "So, Anthony, then tell me who else was here—yesterday?" He knew how to apply his trade. Anthony tried desperately to think of a name that could not be traced by the detective, this, the reason he always read the obituaries, to memorize and have a name that could not be verified, but none came to mind. Anthony took a long deep breath and said, "Eddie…

with all due respect…what the fuck difference does it make now. I'll let my lawyer worry 'bout my defense." Anthony's antagonism was growing inside under the preclusive questioning. Eddie walked over and stood in front of Altieri's body and continued the probing. His eyebrows raised as he spoke, "Did your boy tell you I picked him up today?" Anthony's face grew long when he heard that. He honestly could not remember if his son had mentioned that to him or not, but he was not going to fall for still yet another trick question. He held his composure and said with caution, "I haven't seen my son since this morning…back at the house." The detective leered suspiciously into Big Anthony's eyes and asked sharply, "What about the note he had? He said he was dropping off a note from your wife?" Eddie paused with a long-faced stare and waited for an answer. Big Anthony looked straight ahead. He stared directly into the eyes of the detective as he averred, "I don't know nothin' about a note." Then he scowled at the detective and asked rudely, "Are we done here? 'Cause if we ain't, I was gonna' order another pizza." Eddie took inventory of the room one last time. He realized the big guy was not going to surrender or confess anything more, at least not to him anyway. How he would act when the government agents and the DA's office get ahold of him would surely be another story. This was the worrisome conversation he held with the Pope just a short while ago. The cop wore a look of frustration then made a fast gesture for Big Anthony to stand up on his feet and said, "Yeah, we're done here. Let's go." As the words ended, he reached for the revolver that was tucked in his waistband. His move was as swift as a gunfighter of the Old West.

Some people imagine, no matter whatever delusional state of mind they're in, or how evil a person they were in life, their parting death bed vision will be one of trumpeting angels, heavenly angels surrounded by luminescent clouds of white, or a bright flashing light that will lead the way. Perhaps for others who know better it will be the devil rising from the burning flames of hell. Some are convinced that their entire life will flash before their eyes and extend those last seconds to the end of their mortal existence. For Cheese Marino it was a collage of visions of the woes and regrets of a life of failure, his rueful wishes undone, his most regretful mistakes.

His body went numb. His mind was lucid, and he lost the courage needed to mount a defense. His arms felt held at bay by some unseen force as he watched Eddie take precise aim with the pointed revolver. There were no visions of a glowing heaven's gate or godly images. He did not see hell or purgatory, but at that exact moment of truth, he heard an old man laugh then a baby cry. A saintly voice inside his head whispered "Let it go." Was it Ceil's voice? Suddenly everything fell silent and time stood still. Anthony felt all three slugs burn through his chest in rapid succession as they pierced his heart's blood vessels and lungs—and as he gasped he instinctively placed both of his hands to his chest as a desperate measure to hold in his life's blood and soul that now bubbled out in pulsating bursts. He dropped to the floor on his once sturdy knees. He thought, *Where are my angels?* He silently begged for forgiveness as he felt his life diminish. The last few moments of his mortality were again visions of dismay and how so close he was to getting out. So close was he to breaking free and starting a new life—so goddamn close. His eyes focused on the shining Colt .45 lying on the desk, but he had not the mortal strength to reach and grab for it. The old man's laughter returned; then the angelic voice echoed again, "No more Anthony... no more," and with one last and final gasp, Big Anthony Marino slumped to his death.

Eddie walked up and pondered over the lifeless body of the big guy and the situation briefly. There would be no need to check the pulse for it was surely gone. Eddie Accardi stood over many a dead body and recognized its patent look. Then he moved back. He adjusted the limp body of Altieri and making carefully sure he himself did not step in any pools of blood. He took his handkerchief and wiped the murder weapon clean of prints then intricately and decisively placed the revolver he had just fired into the dead man's hand. He curled Altieri's fingers around the weapon and fired another shot into the corpse of Anthony. He did the same with Anthony's body and placed the .45 automatic in his hand. Accardi had investigated hundreds of murder scenes and knew exactly what the arriving patrolmen and detective's report would contain. And the chances were he himself would be the investigating detective.

He knew precisely what the coroner's office would list as the cause of death and how they would sum up their report for the courts, and if it weren't written the way the crime scene played out in his mind, he would simply have documents changed and no one would be the wiser. Eddie took one more look at the dead players and dialed the four-digit number from the rotary phone on the desk. The voice that answered was Ruggeri, and it was a detached "Hello." Eddie spoke in a whisper and said, "It's over. Now in about twenty minutes, we'll need someone to make an anonymous call in to the precinct about the gunfire they just heard. I'll see you later."

The ever-so-popular neighborhood Friday night bingo game held at Saint Michael's Church starts promptly at eight o'clock. Both Fathers Tykes and San Fillippo will be at the front door assisting the men and women and the nuns who volunteer handing out the bingo cards and supplies and collected the admission fees and selling the nightly specials. Both priests will be greeting their parishioners, wishing them all luck, and reminding them of mass on Sunday. Dominic Bongiovi will be on the PA system reading the letters and numbers off the bouncing ping-pong balls as they shoot out of the machine.

Ceil would always arrive early and rummage through the hard composite pressed bingo boards in search of the newer ones, cleaner boards with her lucky numbers, and to find herself a choice seat away from the jinxed players. She was hoping that her phone ringing was

Margie saying that she was on her way. "Ceil, it's Albie." The voice on the other end of the phone sounded alien to her ears. Her forehead wrinkled as she stared out in complete bewilderment for a moment. Then it registered. "Albert?" she replied. The seriousness of his voice hypnotized her as he spoke. "Ceil...I got some bad news. It's better you hear it from me rather than the cops."

Ceil let out a terrifying scream in reaction to the grim news that was told to her by Albert. She instinctively dropped the receiver out of fear. Her hands clutched her face as her gaping eyes stared at the phone in absolute horror as she let out another shrieking "Noooo." Tony came running into the kitchen from the living room and saw his mother's torso sprawled on the kitchen table, her face white as a ghost. He picked up the receiver that was lying on the floor and uttered a couple of "hellos" into the dead line before he hung it up. He spoke not a word. His instinct told him the call was nothing but bad news. But about what? "Pops in jail" was his first silent thought. Ceil looked up at him, her eyes already red and swollen, and said trembling, "It's your father." His eyes filled with tears, and he became terrified about what he was going to hear next. "He's dead." She could just about get the words out between her gasping sobs. "Tony... he's dead...they found him just now...he was shot." Her tears were uncontrollable now as she tried to speak. "He was murdered by his mobster friends." Then she threw her head and her folded arms flat on the table and cried hysterically.

Tony stood over her but could offer no consoling words or embraces. He was numb. He was in total shock and disbelief. Her words echoed in his mind. Her sobbing frightened him as he did the only thing his pounding brain allowed him to do. He slowly turned and walked into his bedroom and sat down on the edge of the brass bed, his eyes wide open, staring trancelike straight ahead. His jaw was agape. It was a mistake, he thought to himself. Surely it was a mistake? They were talking about the others in the room? Not his father. He prayed to God it was the others. He saw them both, on the floor. His father was so much alive just a short while ago that murdered was the last thing he could associate him with. If it were true, life on Hinsdale Place would never be the same. He shook his head to quell the tears and the thoughts of murder and again reassured himself it must be a mistake. It has to be a mistake. Tony looked back at his sobbing mother with sorrowful eyes. A few solemn words of prayer, barely audible, came from her trembling lips. He knew he could not offer any words to soothe her. He would just have to bite his tongue until the story broke.

Eddie Accardi was as slick a mobster as he was a detective. He was in the kitchen of his widowed mother-in-law's Upper Montclair home talking to her regarding her health. He joked and told her to stay away from the boxful of Italian pastries her daughter sent over. "Not good for your sugar mom." She shooed him away with an indiscriminating laugh. He picked up the phone and dialed his wife apologizing for his sudden call to duty and said he will be home shortly. She was in complete understanding of this ever-so-common occurrence and agreed that the weekend trip to the lake was best put off until better weather shined. When asked, he lied about the real reason for being at her mother's house, the unexpected dire meeting summoned by the Pope.

Accardi and his wife were basically the sole caretakers and were the executors to the estate of the recluse old lady that never left her prestigious brick colonial house, other than an occasional trip to the doctor. The prestigious home sat nestled down in a deep wooded lot on Upper Mountain Avenue, mixed in with the snobbish blue-blooded neighbors who always minded their own business. It provided an excellent cover for the detective's own shady business. He converted her basement into a private office for himself, reminiscent of Ruggeri's bunker room, only much more lavish. It was fully furnished with rich leather couches and chairs, a hand-carved sixteenth-century French desk, custom-built oak bookshelves, and plush wall-to-wall carpet all surrounded by waterproofed and sound-proofed concrete walls. No one knew of the place with the exception of his immediate family and the Pope, and even the Pope knew nothing about the location of the concealed wall safe that contained his personal records and his cache of cash that would be smuggled in stashed at the bottom of brown paper grocery bags. Eddie Accardi kept nothing incriminating at his Forest Hills home, nothing at all that could possibly tie him to organized crime, and nothing could tie him legally to this place. Very rarely did he ever meet the Pope in public or at his clubs or restaurants. On occasion he would venture in to the Sicilian Café to enjoy a good meal. Any face-to-face business with Don Ruggeri was done here or at the Pope's fortress in Roseland, which was the reason, as the Pope put it, for this emergency meet at the Upper Montclair house. The chimed doorbell announced the arrival of the Pope with his capo in tow, Frank Batista. Both Ruggeri's driver and bodyguard accepted the instructions to remain in the car and stand sentry.

Eddie greeted the men at the door with a somber nod of his head. He was not at all comfortable with Ruggeri's decision to bring Battista along, but that discomfort was erased by a disregarding, secretive whispered comment "Don't worry about him" made by the Pope. He quickly led the way in silence through the stately foyer and down the stairs that led to his sanctimonious den. The men acknowledged the old lady with an "Evening, ma'am" as they passed the living room. She sat unstirred. Her eyes glued to the television set.

Ruggeri had felt it necessary he discuss the many concerns that were on his mind about the shootings and wanted Batista present because of his personal involvement with the son of the murdered Marino. And to try and determine who else might have been there, Ruggeri had a biting premonition about others being present and felt strongly of their, whoever they might be, involvement. He had to sew up any loose ends about this and to put to rest any fear he might have about a future vendetta the kid or the brother might carry. Vendettas were a way of life with the mob, and Ruggeri had just ended his own personal vendetta he held for over twenty years with Zwillman by taking out the last soldier in the old Jew's gang. It was over twenty years ago during the Prohibition era that Zwillman almost succeeded with the attempted assassination of Ruggeri.

Eddie placed a select reel of recorded jazz music and fed the one end of the magnetic tape through the head of the intricate and latest piece of high-fidelity stereo equipment. He adjusted the volume to a loud but not a deafening setting. Eddie walked to the bar and poured three glasses of bourbon neat. The men clanged their glasses with a customary salute and drank ironically to each other's health. The austere feeling among the men was apparent, and no one bore a smile. Ruggeri and Accardi took a delicate sip from their glass and watched as Batista downed his drink in one lasting swig. Batista grieved and said, "How the fuck did we let things get so outta' hand?" Ruggeri shot him a cold intense stare. "That's not important now," Ruggeri snapped. "What's done is done, it's history, and I don't want to hear no more about it." The mobster directed his audience to sit down as he continued. "Do you honestly think he acted alone?" he asked Eddie the question with raised eyebrows. Eddie replied with squinting eyes, "Yes and no. I mean he certainly could have. After all he was a pretty tough guy, you know…I wouldn't want to tangle ass with him myself." Batista chimed in nonchalantly, "The boys did walk in the front door…right. It's not like they ambushed him." Batista poured himself another shot of whisky and threw it down his throat. His face acknowledged the burn as he continued. "And what did yous' think…that Cheese was gonna' sit there and take a beatin'…c'mon now, we all know that wasn't gonna' happen…and besides, who the fuck else coulda' been there? Eddie here said he cased the place all day…*no?*" Batista gave a sharp look at the cop as did Ruggeri. Eddie took a sip of his drink and gave a reassuring "Right. I saw nobody come in or out." "My concern is revenge?" Ruggeri said wisely. "Just how crazy or vengeful is his brother or son?" He threw that question out in general almost as if he were talking to himself, but the others offered sane and logical answers. "Anthony's family knew the risks— live by the sword, die by the sword." As explained and characterized by Batista. Ruggeri was satisfied and agreed. Neither brother nor son was a threat. However, Ruggeri still sensed something not right. A vendetta against him was not the only reason for his concern.

There were other suspicions to be dealt with such as the fact that two of his best soldiers were dead and not by his order. This act of defiance could not go unchecked in his world to be adjudged by his peers. He would not rest until he was absolutely sure no one else was involved. If in fact there were more than just one shooter, then that person or persons must be brought forward. An act of this magnitude could never be allowed to go unanswered or not avenged. Justice must be doled out by the Pope. "I got my guys going through the neighborhood on both sides of the street trying to find anyone who may have heard or seen something," Accardi said imperatively. "Let's face it, Pope. It was a perfect night for a crime. The pouring rain kept everyone's head down and doors and windows shut. It washed away any evidence." Eddie pulled the order slip from Casa Di Pizza from his top pocket that he found at the crime scene and held it up in the air. "I know those pizzas were fresh," he said with conviction. "I went here just before and talked to the owner Nino and his brothers. They all know Big Anthony personally, and his brother Joe and his son. They all swear that none of them were in the pizzeria at all today, and none of his guys made a delivery to his joint. The place was too busy for them to remember who placed the order, and no one remembers anybody who came in that fits the description of his brother."

The three talked for close to an hour in the basement office rehashing the day's activities, leaving no stone unturned, acting out every scenario that could have possibly been. Frank Batista sat through the meeting with a strong sense of suspicion embedded in his mind. Neither the Pope nor Accardi mentioned the fact that the boy was picked up and questioned that afternoon by Accardi. He only mentioned that he did see the kid walking on the avenue. That was a piece of information that surely should have been talked about. The omission of it clearly indicates collusion between the two as they intentionally hid that fact from Batista. *Maybe they were waiting for me to say something?* was Batista's inner thought. His other silent thought was *Fuck em…I ain't sayin' a thing.*

The meeting broke with the Pope covertly handing Accardi a wrinkled brown paper lunch bag, its hidden contents a ten-thousand-dollar payment for the arranged hit on Anthony. Eddie nonchalantly laid it on the bar then escorted the men to the front door.

Batista made it halfway to the parked car when he turned to Ruggeri and said, "Shit…I forgot my cigarettes and lighter. I'll be right back." Ruggeri grimaced. Things of this nature really irked him. "Yeah, go ahead. I'll wait in the car, but make it snappy." His bodyguard promptly opened the rear door. He also watched carefully as Frank bolted back up the drive. Batista gently rapped on the glass pane trying to get the attention of the old lady who was visible through the bay window of the living room. She attentively jumped to her feet and opened the door. Frank smiled and then whispered, "Sorry, ma'am…I gotta' go back downstairs. I forgot something." He put his finger to his lip in a "be quiet" gesture as he flew past her. "I'll be right back." The old lady nodded her consent.

Frank was about to knock but tried the doorknob first. It was unlocked. He made not a sound as he opened the cellar door and tiptoed down the flight of stairs. The jazz music was still playing, only now at a higher volume, and at first glance, Accardi was nowhere in sight. Just as Batista was about to make his presence known some movement of a sort made him take a quick look to his left. He noticed that a large bookshelf unit was swung into an open position away from the wall and partially concealing Eddie. Batista's eyebrows raised high above the tops of his glasses. He could not see much of anything except Eddie's back. He stood silent and statuesque as he secretly tried to observe what Eddie was doing. Batista realized that he did not want to be caught in this compromising and delicate situation. He slowly slid his pack of Lucky Strikes and lighter off the desk and scurried quietly back up the stairs.

Eddie had not a clue the mobster had reentered his sanctimonious den. He was completely oblivious and hard at work arranging bundles of cash that were already stacked inside the wall safe, making room for some more. When he finished, he returned a diary and ledger book containing his personal records of dates, times, and names back on top of the piles. He then carefully placed a docile file containing some handwritten notes and a photograph of Frank Batista back in the safe. Lastly, he slid a small door open that concealed an expensive piece of recording equipment and, with a flick of his finger, turned the switch to its off position. He took a chronic and routine look over his shoulder then swung the door shut. He had an impious look on his face as he spun the combination tumbler repeatedly until he was satisfied of its security.

The news of the underworld massacre that happened on Bloomfield Avenue traveled through the neighborhood like wildfire. Phones rang off the hook amongst all confirming the pending rumors to be the truth that Cheese Marino and some members of the Ruggeri clan were all dead. A few short hours had passed since the dispiriting news that somberly swallowed up the Marino household and left an eerie quiescence throughout the Hindsdale Place flat. Ceil had already spoken with her brother-in-law Joe who volunteered to make the necessary calls and arrangements and let the small remaining family Anthony had left know of his passing. She called her brother Lefty and asked him to relay the saddened news to their side. Ceil sat alone in the living room with just the accompaniment of her black-and-white television displaying the image and comedy of Milton Berle, he acting the clown, and that would get an occasional laugh from her. During commercial breaks she would curse her god for all of her unanswered prayers, when what she so wantonly asked for were never granted her, and why the cruel request she prayed for this morning was avowed. Her words still rang out in her head as she remembered wishing that her husband would never return home.

Tony entered the room where his mother sat with his head hung low. Without a bit of hesitation he handed her an envelope. He watched her eyes grow wide as she thumbed through the cache of hundred dollar bills. "It's twenty-five hundred, Ma. Daddy wanted you to have it," he said coyly. She stared at him in bewilderment and said, "When did he give this to you?" The boy answered back, "A couple of days ago. He wanted me to hold it for him." Tony managed a straight face as he told the bold-faced lie. His mother still had a look of astonishment on her face as she spoke, "How do you know he wanted me to have this?" holding the envelope up in the air. Tony scolded her. "Ma…who else should have it?"

Tony turned and entered the unlit kitchen. He stood in front of the sink, the spot usually occupied by his mother, and thought of the bitter brawl that had taken place just this morning. And as he peered out through the picture window and into the empty black of night, the baleful words again of old man Philly from that decrepit club rang loud in his ears. Had he obeyed, would his father still be alive? The darkness hid the mercenary construction site and the shantytown view from sight. The distant lightning bolts behind the clouds illuminated different views of the jagged industrial skyline, randomly casting spectral shadows and defined outlines of the factories with their tall smoking chimneys and the silhouette of the familiar New York City skyline. The gentle drum roll thunder was almost rhythmic and soothing to the ears. The thousands and thousands of flickering lights from the distant factories and the bridges were magnified by the rain. They glinted through the panes of glass, creating a starlike quality, rendering the scene almost picturesque and holy. Perhaps this was the view his father saw, the hidden and obscure beauty of the night?

Tony's eyes filled with tears. His body went limp as he tightened his grip on the edge of the sink he stood in front of. Then he began sobbing uncontrollably. Ceil eased herself next to him and offered her son a consoling shoulder to cry on. They held tightly to one another and cried. "He's gone, Ma…" Tony sobbed. "Daddy's gone." Ceil could only comfort him with the words his father used so often. "I know, son. It'll be all right. It'll be all right."

S aturday morning arrived with more dark clouds and heavy rain as mother and son sat quietly at the kitchen table drinking cups of black coffee and munching on slices of burnt Italian toasted bread smeared with butter and grape jelly. Both sat in silence as they paid homage in their own minds to the fallen patriarch of the household. Ceil's mother and sisters joined them around eleven o'clock, bringing fresh rolls and sliced cold cuts from Manganero's market. Her girlfriend Margie showed up at noon with a fresh tray of homemade manicotti, and her brother Lefty arrived soon after with his wife and two sons carrying a large casserole pan of veal and peppers.

The entire day was spent greeting the many friends and relatives that dropped by to pay their respects. This ran well into the evening. Mostly all brought home-cooked or catered offerings that soon filled the counters and stove top. Tony split his time between watching television and picking on the abundance of food that lay around, and he did his damndest to stay out of sight. He avoided any conversation or mingling of any kind with the guests, even his cousins who he was so close with were ignored. The few conversations he did overhear were short and curtailed as people carefully avoided asking about any discernible facts regarding Anthony's murder. Every so often, someone would offer a reverent word about the big guy, innocently spoken words that would hit a nerve and cause tears to fall.

Brother Joe made an early morning visit to his late brother's home and wept incessantly in Ceil's arms. Next he hurried to Elizabeth General Hospital for some needed emergency medical attention to repair the gash he had over his eye. He wrote down in detail, for the record, on the forms presented to him that it was indeed a work-related injury. He was quite emphatic over that for he knew inquiries would be made. Right after the hospital visit he made an obligatory trip to the city morgue to identify his brother also for the record, something he insisted Ceil or Tony not be a part of. He called Ceil concernedly throughout the day from his gas station and told her he was expecting Anthony's half brother to arrive soon from the almost seven-hour drive from Greensburg. It was agreed he would see her tomorrow and take her to the funeral parlor to make the necessary arrangements. He spoke briefly to his nephew to make sure he was okay. The rain continued throughout the day as the guests dwindled, leaving mother and son alone, the same way that they began their day.

The last caller to arrive brought neither gifts nor condolences. Detective Eddie Accardi got his way with the department and was assigned the mob massacre as it was now unofficially known as. He had never been to the Marino home and only knew Ceil from the neighborhood. He was met at the front door by Ceil's mother, who then guided him to the front entrance of the upstairs apartment. He quickly entered, introduced himself, and offered his sympathy to both Ceil and her son. Tony kept a suspicious eye on the detective and listened with caution as the cop spoke and asked his mother just the basic of questions about her husband, his known associates who may have been with him at the time of death. He silently objected to the savvy demeanor of the woman but acknowledged to himself that she really had nothing to add to what he had already known. He then said cunningly, "Tell me about the letter, Ceil…the one you gave your son to deliver to your late husband?" Eddie's eyes furtively went back and forth staring at both of them. Ceil looked first at the detective then her son with a bewildered gape. She began to fumble with the words she tried to speak, and at that moment, Tony rudely chimed in, "I lied to ya' about the letter," with a sharp tongue. Tony had hatred in his eyes. His words rolled off an evil tongue as he continued with the attitude of nothing to lose now. "She knows nothin' about it." Eddie stared at him with the look of the devil waiting for the explanation the kid offered. "The letter was for Tic. It was from one of his girlfriends—she gave it to me and said not to let anyone see it." Eddie wanted desperately to grab hold of the kid and punish him for the dupe but knew he couldn't, not now anyway. "Why should I believe you, kid?" He scowled. "Ya know, Eddie…I don't give a FUCK if you believe me or not. Go ask Batista himself if ya' don't believe me." The boy's eyes filled with tears as he stormed away from the table and shouted to his mother, "Ma, you don't have to talk to this guy anymore." He gave the detective a pensive stare, "Anything else…sir?" Eddie stared the kid down with a look of the devil, a look that spelled trouble for the kid just as soon as he surfaced again on Bloomfield Avenue. Then he calmly thanked Ceil for her time and offered one more condolence before he said, "Good night."

Brother Joe arrived early Sunday morning as did more rain. He brought with him a box of fresh Italian pastries from Ferraro's Bakery and Big Anthony's half brother, Tomasino Cupido. Ceil had not seen her distant brother-in-law for years, not since the last time Anthony drove her out for his own stepfather's funeral, and Tomasino had never met his young nephew.

Tony was already showered and dressed and introduced himself to the uncle who in turn offered a jubilant smile, handshake, bear hug, and complimenting homage; the entire greeting seemed to go on forever. Tony was red as a beet from the exuberance his uncle had bestowed and quickly asked his uncle Joe how his freshly stitched and neatly bandaged eye was, just to change the subject. As things quieted down all took a seat at the table. Tomasino regretfully explained the absence of his sister Josephina. She stayed home to tend to their ailing mother who was stricken with diabetes and had what was diagnosed as the beginning stages of dementia.

They all sat around the table. Their reunion so to speak conjured up grand memories of the past. When Anthony and Joe were just two and three years old, their true father Salvatore was stricken with the Spanish influenza and quickly died, a young man leaving his widow Rosa behind penniless, and with the task of raising their two small sons all alone. Rosa, out of sheer desperation, married the first kind man that happened along, not a handsome man by any means, and considerably older than her, but he did have the capability of supporting a family and showed a true love interest. He was a kindhearted soul and took an instant affection to his new stepsons and never once raised his hands in anger to either. The next three years brought two more children into the household, and for the most part, they became a closely knit family. Neither Tomasino nor Josephina ever married and still live in the same farmhouse they all were raised in the predominantly all Italian Eighth Ward section of Greensburg, Pennsylvania.

Tomasino was an odd-looking sort with hardly any resemblance to either of his two stepbrothers. He had short legs with bulky thighs, a barrel-shaped upper torso with extremely long, thick arms, and a head of unruly thin curly black hair. His cherub-round face was covered with dark moles and birthmarks as was the rest of his body. He was almost troll-like but spoke softly and well defined and came across as a humorous storyteller who knew many and always had one on hand that would fit the occasion. He wrapped his bulky arms around his nephew and held on tightly as he whispered in the kid's ear, "*Che malanova mi hai*...I can't believe it." Tony liked him immediately. Ceil excused herself so that she could get dressed and ready. Her motherly instinct compelled her to tell the men to eat and enjoy the food that was still left over. And as she showered and primped herself, more sadness took hold of her heart. During all the past few days' happenings she had completely forgotten it was her son's birthday.

All three men were left alone at the table, and this would be the first time, since the shooting, Tony was able to speak with his uncle. Joe opened the conversation by telling his nephew that the police impounded the old man's Cadillac and that he would have to pull some strings to get it back. Tony felt apprehensive about talking in front of a stranger and made an indication to his uncle Joe who waved his hand in disregard and said, "Don't worry about him. He's well aware of the work me and your old man was involved with." Joe gave Tomasino a playful slap in the cheek and said, "Ain't ya', Tomas?" Tomasino nodded at both of them with a mouthful pastry. He chewed, smiled, and swallowed then uttered a woeful "Too well" followed by jovial laugh. "I don't get it, Uncle Joe." Tony was at ease now and began with shrugged shoulders. "When we left yesterday...he was alive. There was no threat by those two guys. There was no way that, that one guy...the one lying on the floor could have overpowered him...not in the shape he was in. Somebody else must have come by?" Joe nodded his head in a concurring way and said, "Of course someone else showed up. Someone your old man trusted, or he would have never let them in through the front door." His face turned grim. "I think that someone was Albie." He paused then raised his hand with his finger pointed. "But we're never gonna find out...are we now? What is important and necessary is that we forget about it. Put it away and understand it's the way it is. It's the code that they live and die by. There's nothing we can do to change it now…we can't bring him back." Joe's voice became staid as he continued. "Now what we do is give your father a decent burial—then move on. We know he sacrificed his life for us." Joe looked first at Tomasino then back into Tony's eyes, and with deep concern he said, "Now the plan is getting you outta sight for a while." Joe looked back at Tomasino, and they both nodded their heads. Joe had previously discussed the situation with his half brother that was also in complete compliance. Tony became all ears and knew what they were going to say next would disappoint him. "We all agree that the streets here could be dangerous for you now…even for me, for that matter. So Tomas has agreed to take you back with him, let you live there until this thing blows over. You never know about this Ruggeri. He's a dangerous man, and don't think that a vendetta isn't on his mind… or vengeance. Your father did leave a big bill behind…unpaid…due the Pope." Tony listened to the words of his uncle and, out of respect, did not demonstrate his true feelings. Vendetta was also on his mind as he swore silently with clenched teeth to himself, at the table, he would one day seek his revenge on the men that betrayed and killed his father. At that exact moment his uncle Tomasino reached out and gave him a reassuring grasp on his hand, almost as if he could read his mind. His uncle Joe spoke almost joshing as he said, "Even your mother agrees. It'll do 'ya good to get away from here for a while, and who knows, you may like it out there enough to stay…maybe it'll make an honest man outta' you." For the moment Tony just accepted the final words of his uncles without any sign of emotion except for a few select moments of hatred that bled from his eyes.

Ceil reentered the kitchen dressed in the traditional black garb of a mourning widow and announced to all in a calm but painful voice, "I'm ready to go now. We have a funeral to plan." She then turned to her son, and with a somber hug she found the words that followed taxing. "I almost forgot, Tony, happy birthday. This one we will never forget."

15

Joanie Jankowski arrived home late Sunday evening exhausted and disappointed, cursing under her breath over her dismal rained-out weekend just spent at the Jersey Shore. She wearily climbed the front steps, suitcase in tow, and paid no attention to the tiny realtor's SOLD sign that was on a hinged frame staked into her parent's small front lawn. Neither Joanie nor her parents had any idea of the tragic event that happened Friday night past. She climbed the stairway that led to her bedroom and thought to herself how good it was going to feel to sleep in her own bed.

Joanie's uneventful weekend for the most part was spent almost entirely in the tiny motel room she shared with her cousin Barbara and Barbara's girlfriend. Joanie stayed amused playing cards and board games then staying up all night long taking shots from a pilfered bottle of rye whisky and receiving an explicit sex education from the girls as they talked of their libidinous exploits with the boys. The sensual conversation coincided with all three as they eavesdropped on Aunt Terry. She was guilefully shacked up in an adjoining room with a man who was soon-to-be husband number three. The constant downpour kept them off the beaches, and the stale disinterest of listening to any more carnal knowledge from their chaperone forced them to the boardwalk arcades where they managed to show off their bikinis and indulge on sumptuous sausage and peppers sandwiches and pizza. They watched *Some Like It Hot* four times in two days at the Strand movie house and played rounds and rounds of indoor miniature golf. During one nighttime escapade, they sat giggling in the backseat of a Cadillac and were given a tour of the area by men three times their own age. The confused and cozen men vied hard for the affections of the young beauties and grew excited at the dalliance of sexual innuendos the girls promised in jest as they broke up in uncontrollable laughter.

Her mother was waiting up and greeted her with an inquiring "Well, how was your trip?" Mom was coy as she inspected her daughter for any noticeable hickies or bruises. Joanie yawned as she spoke, "It was okay, I guess. It rained all weekend but we still had fun. I just wish I could have gotten a suntan. Anyway…I'm tired. I'll tell you about it in the morning." "All right then. Good night now, sweetie," her mother said as she kissed her on the cheek. "Nite, Ma."

Joanie awoke early the next morning and joined her parents in the kitchen for coffee and their usually light breakfast. "Good morning, Mom…morning, Daddy," she said with a still half-asleep voice. She plopped herself down next to her father. He peered over his newspaper and returned the greeting as did her mother. The morning ritual was ever so calculated. Her father sat quietly at the breakfast table dressed in his heavily starched blue shop uniform. Mom would prepare breakfast for all then package up a couple of sandwiches for her and her husband's lunches. She would tidy up the kitchen then hurry along her husband as they prepared for their drives to work at the Western Electric Corp. He would always leave at least thirty minutes before she did.

Henri sat at the table with his daughter at his side leafing through the morning paper. His eyes widened and he became engrossed with the article tucked away in the local section that read MOBSTERS DIE IN

A HAIL OF GUNFIRE. As he read through the print he became charged and said aloud, "Don't we know these people?" then turned to his daughter and said, "Joanie, isn't he the boy you go to school with? I mean his father, isn't this the father of that boy?" Joanie glanced over at the newspaper as did her mother, and her mother said, "Oh my god…yes…that's the family that lives around the block on Hinsdale Place. The Marinos." Joanie's heart began to pound inside her chest and became nervous with fear. "That's Tony's father!" she exclaimed as she pulled the paper from her father's grasp and read the article over and over. She then franticly turned the pages until she found the tiny obituary that read "Beloved husband to Cecelia (née Carollo) and devoted father to Anthony Jr." Her eyes filled up with tears as she said, "I don't believe it—I just saw him the other day." "Who did you see, dear? Mr. Marino?" her mother asked frowningly." "No. I met Tony just the other morning, out in front of our house," Joanie said incandescently. Her father looked at her sternly and said, "When was he here? Joan…what did I tell you about that kid…trouble… nothing but trouble." Her father growled. "Ohhh, Daddy!" Joanie said in disgust as she bolted to her room in tears.

The following morning, Joanie had a strong urge to call Tony, and she would do so just as soon as her parents left the house. She rummaged through her little address book and then her mother's but was unable to find a connecting phone number. The one she had from elementary school had been disconnected. She dialed the high school with the hopes of retrieving a home phone number, but the janitor who answered was of no help. Joanie showered, dressed, then walked the few blocks to Hindsdale Place, umbrella held high. There she stood on the opposite side of the street, facing the Marino house with the hopes Tony would look out of a window and come running down. The arriving cars of strangers that pulled up in front of the house made her feel uneasy and uninvited as she peered from behind the sopping umbrella. It was soon felt she had waited long enough.

Her love was nowhere in sight. She turned and headed home. She would just have to wait until Saturday when their planned date was set, but Saturday was such a long way away, and the anticipation began to disquiet her already. *Maybe he'll visit me sooner.* She hoped and thought.

Dinner was over and done with at the Jankowski house, just the dirty dishes scattered about along with the portentous quiet. The tragic murder hitting so very close to home kept everyone's mouth mute of conversation. Joanie's mother, finally tired of the silence, blurted, "I'm so glad we're moving away from this neighborhood." Joanie's jaw dropped. She looked at both her parents in astonishment. Her body quivered as she spoke. "Moving…when are we moving?" she asked. Her father began to speak and outlined the coming events that were unfolding. He told her of the promotion to tool room supervisor he was to get at the Green brook plant along with a substantial raise in pay and how they already have a deposit on a home in Warren Township and already a buyer for the old place. Joanie listened with an acrimonious stare and commented on how it was all planned out without either one of them letting on or asking her opinion. "What about my school, my friends here?" Joanie asked. "You'll be able to transfer to Saint Mary's Academy. I've already checked," Her mother said a matter-of-factly. Her father interjected, "You'll make new friends and visit the few you have here." Joanie's eyes began to fill with tears. "Are there any other surprises I should know about?" Joanie shouted as she stormed out of the kitchen in a flux.

Joanie was intelligent enough to recognize that her feelings were more hurt than upset or angry about moving away from the place that she grew up. She also recognized that her attempt of a childish hissy-fit was exactly why she was unenlightened about the plans. After a minute or two of deliberate thought, she agreed with her inner self that moving away from this neighborhood was the best thing that could happen to them as a family. She often wondered why they hadn't moved years ago. Her parents had already separated her from the few elementary school friends she had known by sending her to a private parochial high school and forbidding her to hang around the local teenage spots.

Her sadness fomented not from soon leaving behind her childhood memories but knowing she will be leaving behind the teenage boy who recently stole her heart. She wished now that they were closer in a relationship so she could comfort him in this obvious grieving time but was confident that when they met again she would be able to do just that. In all actuality, the thought of moving away actually excited her in a way, and she hoped Tony would feel the same since the two would be driving soon. It would do him a world of good to get away from this neighborhood as well, she thought. And as well she thought that the Warren Township isn't that far a distance to keep them apart. He would just have to accept the fact that he shall be dating an out-of-town girl now.

The Thursday morning gravesite service for Anthony Marino was blessed with sunny skies and gentle breezes. Family members and mourners bid their final farewell then, and all lumbered over the moist, grassy terrain toward their automobiles. Joe was the last to enter the chauffeured car waiting to take them back to the funeral parlor, and as they rode men sat in silence Ceil wept at her image in the glass of the limousine. It jostled her gently as it weaved through the paved and narrow driveway of the cemetery, under the mature trees with their tall green canopy of leaves and shadows, past the array of headstones and monuments. "All the souls," she whispered softly. The silence ended just as soon as the limo turned onto Broadway. Joe gave his nephew and stepbrother a deliberate look then said almost in a snarled whisper, "It was Albie, that son-of-a-bitch." Tony opened his eyes as wide as did Tomasino and both listened to more. Ceil shut hers tightly. "It was our old pal Albert Marrone. You wanted to know who the traitor was." Joe pounded his closed fist into his chest and said, "I can feel it…right here. I knew it all along. And that no good cop…he's as guilty as sin. He's covering something up. And he had the gall to show up today." "He was talking with you, Joe. What did he say about that bandage over your eye?" asked Tomasino. Tony's eyes opened wide with a pensive stare directed at the floorboards. Joe replied in confidence, "I told him the truth—I banged myself in the head with a wrench—what I got to lie about?" Ceil remained silent, in a daze, just staring at absolutely nothing at all.

The farewell luncheon went well as all ate and drank and toasted the big guy posthumously. Tony felt a sigh of relief as he listened to the comforting words of his uncle Tomasino. He spoke solemnly and told Tony not to think of his father as dead but rather as just away on some sort of a business trip or a vacation knowing that one day they should meet again. He told the boy that the memory of his father will stay fresh in his mind forever and, "don't be surprised if every so often you actually hear his voice or feel his presence." Tomasino explained how that little juxtaposition worked so well for him when his own father passed away two years ago. There was a short discussion about Tony's trip to Greensburg. It was suggested that the two should get on the road just as soon as possible, and it was agreed tomorrow morning they'll be on their way.

Tony spent very little care packing his clothes and the few other belongings he decided to take as he quickly filled the tan-colored vinyl suitcase. He had already gathered his valuables and stash of money, close to five thousand dollars, some addresses and phone numbers, and wrapped it all up in aluminum foil and stuffed it snugly in a pair of shoes then wedged it inside the suitcase. His heart felt saddened with the thought of not being able to see or say goodbye to Joanie before he left but quickly erased the notion with the conviction of what good would that do—would just add to his misery. It's best he just forgot her for now and hoped that maybe he would meet her again one day if the fates would permit it. He too, like his mother, was feeling the woeful regret and the haunting by the warning of being careful for what you wish for as he remembered that morning of Friday last he pledged to get away from his neighborhood someday. He hugged his mother and promised to fulfill her request of calling her every week and promised to "stay out of trouble." There were biting tears between them as he hurriedly said sobbingly "See ya', Ma" and assured her he would be back home in "just a little while." Ceil watched the back door close and cried and savored the tiny bit of fragrant cologne that lingered in the air. She took a seat at the table in her familiar position of alone, only now with no one to fight with or to cook for.

By the time Friday had rolled around, Joanie's anticipation and excitement was overwhelming; the occasional doldrums thought of her moving away were quickly shrugged off. Be it as it may, she had no way of knowing that Tony was already gone. Had she, and the merriment would not be. She gleefully danced around her room with a couple of rakish summer dresses that were to be narrowed down to the one she would ultimately wear to the feast tomorrow night. She chose a white linen dress with a red rose pattern that came to the knee with a flared hem. It was a dress of her design and created in her home economics class. The empire cut gathered under her breasts and the squared neckline was revealing but still virtuous. She looked adorable.

Joanie did tell her parents truthfully where she was going to but lied about why she was going to the Italian feast. "Oh, Dad…I'm meeting my girlfriends there." She snarled. Her father grumbled something as she left the house, but she paid him absolutely no mind. He insisted on driving her to the fair, which she agreed to and assured him she would find her way home by the negotiated curfew time of eleven-thirty.

The Saint Michael's Church parking lot was transformed into a mélange of small carnival rides strategically placed around a grand Ferris wheel. Souvenir booths, games of chance, and eatery stands that offered every conceivable type of Italian foodstuff known to man lined the perimeters of the large parking lot with just inches of space to spare between them. Italian songs and music filled the air and rose above the chatter of the jovial crowd and screaming parents and children. The scene was reminiscent of the Seaside Heights Boardwalk she had just been to. The aromas were ever so tempting, but Joanie would not dare disturb her fresh minted breath until she first kissed her sweetheart. She would allow him to choose the selections and envisioned being hand-fed by her Romeo and nibbling tiny bites of delicacies from his fingertips. Joanie purchased a tall paper cup of freshly squeezed lemonade and stood unmoving with her back to the crowded fairgrounds. She silently hoped that Tony would see her then come from behind and wrap his arms around her. That moment of thrill passed. She walked fast-paced toward the hand-painted signs that read in big red letters, FRESH ZEPPOLES. And as she circled the area of the zeppole stand, she honed in on every boy that had black hair with the hopes one would be Tony.

Joanie was certain that this was the location of the meeting place Tony had described. It had to be? *Tony, where are you, why are you hiding?* she wondered. Patrons sat in rows of tables under the colorful banners of the Italian flags. Two young and very attractive girls dressed in loosely fitting peasants uniforms tended to the crowd of people gathered at the counter. The two young men dressed in white chef's garb were frantically plopping fresh dough into vats of hot oil and carefully removing the cooked zeppoles to drying trays that sat on a large table. Their tall rumpled chef's hats flapped to and fro with every movement they made and gave them the appearance of two bemused clowns hard at work. Powdered sugar streamed from tin containers shaken by the girls and gently settled like falling snow on the fresh-cooked pastries. Joanie studied the features of the young zeppoles chefs; they both resembled Tony in a way and gave indication to her they were the cousins he was talking about. A few nonchalant peeks around the stand were made, and then a huffy look of "where the hell is he" fell over her face.

She made her way back toward the entrance, fighting through the crowd of families and the groups of teenage boys and girls that lined the main colonnade of the fair, and then back to the zeppole stand. Her eyes scanned every face in the crowd, but there was not a glimpse of her date. Once back at the stand, she politely excused herself as she nudged the customers in line until she was in position to ask one of the young cousins standing behind the makeshift counter if he had seen Tony. He replied no with a simple shake of his head; then he turned to his brother and asked him. Joey walked to her and said he hadn't seen his cousin since the funeral. He gave her a condoling "Sorry… but I tell him you were lookin' for him the next time I see him." Joanie said it wouldn't be necessary and walked away with an empty feeling and a mixed emotion of anger and despair. The hour was approaching ten when Joanie regretfully realized he was not going to show. She tired of retelling the many storied lies to her friends she met at the fair as to why she was really there, so she decided to leave the fairgrounds heartsick and anguished. As she walked away and although so conclusively heartbroken, she refused to allow her mind to be cluttered with the miscellany of the possible reasons as to why Tony did not show up. It did not matter anymore.

Over the next few weeks Joanie's stubbornness resisted any further inquiry about Tony's whereabouts or why in fact he had stood her up and, as of yet, his sudden disappearance and why he has not made one single effort to see her. And if in fact it was a mourning process over his departed father, surely he must know that she would be there for him. He must realize that? Regardless, he was out of sight, and she refused to pursue it any longer. But be it as it may and as most oddly as it sounds, some compelling force would always make her get off the school bus blocks before her scheduled stop. She walked the avenue with the thought of him on her mind hoping, just hoping, for another chance meeting. Once she even walked in front of his house. And faithfully, every day after school she would diligently sit on her front stoop and gaze up the street daydreaming as she relived that special summer morning when the two had last met and she fervidly remembering their last kiss.

Joanie occupied her time and last days on Lincoln Avenue preparing for the moving day and the upcoming semester at her new school. She grimaced at the list of required reading she was already to have finished. She had drawers and closets to go through and boxes to pack. She spent two days sorting clothing and childhood souvenirs into categories of what to keep and what was to be given away to charity or simply tossed out. As the days passed the final morning came to be. The chilling September morning was a clear indication of the soon-to-arrive fall season. It would be the first one spent by the Jankowskis in their new Victorian-style home in Warren Township. Both mother and daughter took their last tribute walk through the old house, dutifully double-checking for anything they might have been left behind. An empty spool of thread was lightly kicked by Joanie; it bounced and spun wildly across the bare wooden floor. Its meek sound was amplified and echoed within the furniture bare room. Oddly, the spool took a portending turn and rolled to the exact spot it just was, at Joanie's feet. Perhaps she knew why.

Both women stood on the sidewalk now, arm in arm, joyless and melancholy. They watched with an unspoken air of regret as Henri and his friends loaded the last box of belongings into the rented truck then sealed the rear door shut with an audible clang. A very despondent and sad Joanie Jankowski sat alongside her mother in the family sedan and could not hold back the sentimental tears of her childhood past. She nudged up against her mom and wept sorrowfully. The caravan of movers rode single file up Lincoln Avenue, and all waved goodbye to their old neighborhood then to the corrupt and wicked Bloomfield Avenue and its entire moral wrongdoings. Joanie wept again as she held on to her gold cross and prayed for her lost love as she wondered what in God's name had happened to him.

16

Tony Marino's eyes had been shut for most of the initial journey to Greensburg. He was faking sleep, a forced act that he decided was forthright and brought upon him for fear of the mundane questions and issues that he was sure his uncle was itching to blab about. And although he tried seriously at times to drift off, he was not at all able to sleep a wink. A strong sense of remorse and abnormal thoughts had settled in his gut and preoccupied his simple mind. Almost immediately as the trip began and now more than ever, he was bitterly feeling homesick as he second-guessed his decision to leave Newark. His fear was he would be labeled a coward who ran away from it all. Finally, he opened his eyes and gazed perplexingly at his own distorted reflection in the window glass. Every so often he would catch a peripheral view of his uncle's odd profile, and he would, on occasion, turn his head and look at him.

The setting August sun was beginning doing its job of creating long casted shadows and a crimson sunset. Tony paid little to no attention as to just exactly how long he and his uncle had been traveling US Route 22 west in the Ford Fairlane—and judging by the ever-changing landscape and the unrecognizable, odd lot names of towns that branched off the exit ramps of the highway, he realized that he was traveling far away from his element. He tried to phoneti-cally pronounce in his mind the Township names etched on the metal highway signs, surreal names, unheard of names: Lebanon, Oldwick, Gladstone, Peapack, Tewksbury, and Califon. His eyes blinked some as he wondered if Ruggeri lived in such rural country as they are now passing through. And his anger once again surmounted know-ing that Ruggeri did live in a mansion fortress somewhere up in the distant hills. An eerie chill ran through his veins as they passed a sign that read Jamesburg. It was the storied place where so many of his mobster friends and gang members talked about serving out their sentences when they were younger, at the state reformatory and juve-nile penitentiary that sat deep in the farmlands of that sequestered community.

Even the air had a distinct smell—sweet fragrant pine, freshly harvested grain, and plowed earth and horse manure—a strangely tolerable and healthy aroma. The familiarity of the city's congested highways that weave their way under and over a network of bridges and viaducts coalesced to a long corridor of smoothly paved road-ways that snaked through never-ending fields and farm acreage and close-cropped evergreens and other pine trees that climbed up ele-vated mountains as far as the eye could see.

The industrial parks and factory smokestacks, the city skyline, and tall illustrious high-rise buildings, brownstones, and lowly ten-ement row houses were sublimely transformed into a vista of rolling hills and mounded parcels dotted with colorful foliage the likes of which the kid had never seen before—except in oil paintings and books. Rural storefronts with wooden signs were randomly arranged along the roadside; fenced corrals and old barns and distinct silos emerged in the faint distances. Sometimes the fences would follow the lay of the land all the way down to the highway's shoulder as would the herds of Jersey cattle, sheep, and horses.

At long last his uncle and he finally made eye contact that was so long overdue. "Hey, wayo…guaglion…como se tala? capish?" Tony laughed at his uncle and said, "I don't speak too much Italian, Unk, just a few words and…" His uncle laughed back, "Neither do I. Your aunt speaks it well…proper-like, 'cause of Grandma Rosa. She speaks or understands very little English. Your father and me and your uncle Joe, we can show you just how to butcher such a beautiful language." And that is all it took for the eager and ambitious Tomasino to strike up a conversation that would last the entire rest of the trip. And before long Tony found himself completely engrossed and captivated by the stories his uncle Tomasino began to tell, humoring and sincere stories and tales about his own early childhood. Family folklore and the ever-so-grand memories of growing up with his sister and two shielding stepbrothers, Anthony and Joe, and their then childhood pal, Albie Marrone.

Tomasino began as far back as he could remember and told his tale as if he were reading from a storybook. He spoke candidly of what terrors the three boys had been since their first meeting in grade school and how none of them made it past either the sixth or seventh grade. "Thank God they're gone," their teachers all said when they eventually quit coming to class. Tomasino laughed until he cried.

He explained how they ardently took to the rough-and-tumble streets at an early age and ran with the other delinquent gangs that truly were the forerunners of the "dead end kids." The three fought their way to the top of the garbage heap and became the recognized kings of Westmoreland County. They hustled at the pool parlors, rolled the drunks, and stuck up the rich poker players in the wee hours of the morning as they stumbled to their cars or hotel rooms. They loved to steal everything and anything they could get their hands on. The loot would be handed over to the neighborhood fence by the name of Tiny Mazzarino who was a first cousin of the notorious Pittsburgh mobster Stefano Monastero who would one day further their careers.

Tomasino continued with an almost animated demeanor. The words spoken were with wide eyes and jovial laughter. He bragged about how protective and vigilant his older half brothers were of him and his sister Josephina, they themselves young innocent children, being a constant object of hateful ridicule by neighborhood bullies. The older Marino brothers would physically punish the cruel kids who poked fun or razed their siblings because of their somewhat anomalous and truly immigrant looks and the fact that their father was a Guinea ragman, a junkman who rummaged through the garbage of others, so they thought. Not only did they go after the punk tormentors of the small rural towns, but also they would beat severely the redneck coal mining fathers and their older clan members for not teaching their children better manners. And as time passed and Tomasino and his sister grew, the Marino brothers had instilled so much fear in the townspeople that no one dare crack wise to brother and sister or their father, Carmine Cupido. Everyone would willingly go out of their way to help the family with some sort of voluntary act of kindness.

Tomasino's voice was soothing, and his words were spoken with a degree of intelligence, unlike the crude locution of his brother Anthony. Tomasino was the only child of the clan who actually received a formal education. He graduated high school with honors and went on to attend Seton Hall University in Pennsylvania. He finished two complete semesters, locally, at the Greensburg campus before going to work with his ailing father, and began tending to the daily chores of a junkman. It was a meager living of dealing with scrap metal. Iron, used auto parts, and rags, anything that could be turned over for a few pennies a pound and is the same business that Tomasino does today.

Tomasino lit a cigarette, pointed and chuckled at the road sign that read LATROBE 250 miles, and said, "Best beer in the world, son, Rolling Rock." Then he laughed. "But I'm sure you already know that." Tony immediately caught his intent and thought of the tiny green bottles of nips his father had at the house and the car lot that everyone knew he would sneak on occasion, obviously. He inhaled the cigarette smoke that drifted about the interior. The idea of smoking had never appealed to Tony; he always shunned it, but suddenly an urge came over him to light up a Camel. He politely asked his uncle if he could have one of his. "Well, I guess you're old enough. Go ahead and help yourself," Tomasino said. Tony lit the short tobacco stick and let his mouth fill with smoke then blew most of it out through the side of his closed lips before inhaling the rest. His uncle observed the act and turned to him and said, "That's the exact way your father used to smoke those things, God rest his soul." They both became silent. Tomasino said in all honesty, "It's gonna' be hard to talk about him, but you must…you can never forget." The kid nodded his head in agreement and took another drag, only this time the smoke caught him the wrong way causing him to choke a bit. He still could not see the attraction to cigarette smoking, but he enjoyed the tobacco taste.

The two drove a little while longer then stopped for gasoline and coffee at a Circle 76 truck stop outside of Allentown. They had decided not to eat any of this traditional truck driver's fare. They would wait until they were closer to home. His uncle said that Josephina would probably have plenty of food left over, or they could stop at an Italian eatery he knew of in Latrobe. The boy left it up to the uncle since he was the one driving and said, "You make the call." The boy wanted to hear more stories from the garrulous uncle Tomasino, but before he gave him a chance to speak, he asked if Uncle Joe had told him any of the gruesome details of the shooting. Tomasino's face became long as he replied, "No. Not in any great detail. He did say what we already know, that you might be in some sort of danger as a result of the feud going on." Tony laughed and said, "I never heard it called that before." "Well, that's exactly what it is, and it's been going on for years with those guys," Tomasino said in a droll manner of speaking then continued. "Your uncle and father were caught up in the middle of the whole thing." The boy listened with all ears and asked, "How do you know so much about what's been goin' out here?" His uncle took a deep breath and answered, "I've been really close with your uncle Joe over the years. You could say that I've acted as his consigliore, as they would call it." He gave the boy a poker-faced stare then said, "I'm the one who advised him years ago to get away from those gangsters, and he listened. Something your father should have done but it was too late for him. He was too weak for such a change." The boy swung around in his seat and looked at his uncle with wide eyes. His uncle adjusted his vision from the road to the kid's eyes then back again. "So you know what went on back there. Uncle Joe must have told you the story," the boy said with a presumptive voice. "I know enough," his uncle said in a brusque manner. "Let's just leave it at that. But don't worry, your secret is safe with me. We're family, never forget that." His words were guileless and had a "no fooling around" connotation to them as he finished. "We all have secrets that we are to take to the grave." Tomasino's statement was consequential at best and hung in the air for a few minutes but was brushed off by his nephew who knew not to intrude on someone's private thoughts or feelings. If they were to be discussed or made public, in time they will. Tony drifted with his own thoughts for a moment then began coaxing his uncle for more stories about the younger days of their lives.

Tomasino began another pique but somewhat dark tale of how Tony's father and Uncle Joe tired of the drudgery of the steel mills and the Coking factories that both tried to work in as young men. Tony became all ears as his uncle explained how they slowly turned to a life of "opportunistic crime," as he described it, in the depressed neighborhoods of East Greensburg and the surrounding areas. They soon earned a pugnacious reputation, a violent reputation that was growing on a daily basis. Their lawless escapades were becoming larger than life in Westmorland County and spreading all the way up to Pittsburgh. They became known as vicious brawlers and amateur racketeers. Together with their friend Albie, the trio could and would literally fight an entire barroom full of hick miners and transients that littered the railroad towns around Greensburg and hung around the downtown section, the area that was abundant with nightclubs and gambling joints. During that reckless era around Prohibition, they traveled a circuit of the honky-tonks and bars, cheating and fighting their way through the crowds. "This was right around the time Albie began calling your father Cheese," Tomasino said then finished with the rest of the story.

Their favorite ploy was busting out the area's crap games or the poker games. They would partner up inside a place and cheat the cards or the rolling dice to favor them until they had won all the money or were caught manipulating, at which time they would turn the place upside down, dodging bullets and the law and cracking as many heads as they could while they swooped the cash off the tables and floor in the process. It was almost like a staged armed robbery without any weapons although later on in their adventures at least one of them would be packing a gun as an added precaution. They began another career as burglars and truck hijackers when the action around the gaming joints became too risky for them.

Their efforts did not go on unnoticed, and they were recruited by a Pittsburgh mafia boss by the name of Stefano Monastero who put the trio to work in his rising crime empire as collectors and strong-arm men. The three musketeers soon began running alcohol and hijacking shipments that were traveling around the Lake Erie areas of Steubenville, Ohio, and down into Pittsburgh. The news spread quickly about how this gang out of Greensburg mistakenly hijacked a shipment that was destined to Ruggeri on the East Coast. Monastero's new crew incapacitated eight of Ruggeri's best bootleggers, killing three of them. Monastero was disconcerted by the error of his people and assured Ruggeri it was not an act of a backstabber. He offered immediate restitution out of fear. When asked what Ruggeri wanted to make things right between them, he said, "Keep the alcohol, but I want your shooters to come work for me." It was agreed, and that's how the trio ended up in New Jersey.

Tomasino pulled the Ford into the parking lot of Denunzio's Chophouse. The eatery had been on his mind and his grumbling stomach for the last hour. He called his sister from a pay phone and told her of their plans. "Don't bother Joe…we'll eat out." The boys would soon be dining on fine rib-eye steaks covered with roasted hot cherry peppers and fried potatoes and onions. He told the boy that they were not too far away from their final destination and laughed as he forewarned Tony about the strangeness of his aunt Josephina. "Picture a woman who looks like me with the disposition of…lets' say your father," Tomasino said as he took a swig of Rolling Rock. "And she can drink us both under the table." Both men laughed as they continued eating and sipping on ice-cold beer. Tomasino finished his beer and asked the kid if he would like another one before he ordered, to which the kid said "Sure." Then he complimented the kid for being a very good listener because he always nodded and agreed at just the right times during conversation; he showed a plausible attentiveness but kept his mouth shut, a trait well liked by Tomas. Tomasino continued to talk as he ate and told his nephew that a good listener could hold a conversation with the most intelligent of men and walk away leaving the speaker with the idea that he just spoke with someone as intelligent as he. It was considered by Tomasino to be a masterful art of deception on the kid's part and meant it solely as a sincere compliment.

The surrounding rural countryside that rose up on both sides of old Route 30, the traveled road that led to the farmhouse, was ominously dark and unlit by any form of a streetlamp. This frightened the boy some. He was not used to such black of night. Tomas followed the high-beam headlights of the car instinctively, and every once in a while they would illuminate the surrounding rural real estate. Broken bits of white fence and reflections of painted tree trunks would jump out like ghosts in the roadway. A standing bevy of deer would catch Tony's attention, and they would stare at him with red glowing eyes then scamper out of sight before he could comment.

Just about all the circa 1800s-style homes had rustic wooden fences around the perimeters of their rolling property, all painted a whitewash and all holding back dense green foliage and trees; some had large front acreage for livestock grazing. Others were a virtual junkyard of old rusted John Deere equipment along with equally rusted old sedans and pickup trucks. They all had old-fashioned metal mailboxes that sat on crooked or leaning posts planted just a few feet in from the main road. They too were painted as white as could be. The headlights of the Ford illuminated the post-mounted mailbox that had the name Cupido painted on the side in block letters as Tomasino turned up the rutted gravel driveway that led to the house. The night was pitch-black and bursting loud with crickets. There was an almost biting chill in the air as the sounds of Mother Nature greeted the weary travelers.

He could not see but the tiny shadowed outline of a woman. He heard the stretching spring-like sound the screen door made as it opened then suddenly slammed hard under the recoil of its hinge; its loud snap caused a neighbor's dog to bark. Tony had to bite his tongue from laughing at the sight of his so-called eccentric aunt who bolted through the front door and rested under the centered ceiling porch light, swatting at a few pesky moths. She stood waiting on the foot of the stairway of the Victorian-style porch with an enormous grin on her face and nervously wiping her hands on the apron that draped down from her thin waist. She held her hands together tightly in front of her and wedged them deeply inside of her inner thighs as she bowed her wee torso up and down fervently, as if she was trying to control her bladder. She most certainly was, as Tomasino had described her, a spitting image of him only much thinner, almost skeletal. She gave Tony a warm hug and a slobbering kiss from her alcohol-and-tobacco-tainted breath. Her prevalent smile reached from ear to ear. This was the first she had ever seen him in the flesh. She immediately commented on how much he resembled his father, an assimilation he was growing tired of hearing but accepted it from her as a compliment out of respect. Her voice sounded like a man who was trying to impersonate a female, deep and husky with a trace of feminism. Tony laughed to himself as he noticed the calico housedress she wore seemed to be two sizes too large on her tiny frame. It bore the stains of a true Italian kitchen.

Once inside the front door, Tomasino instructed the boy to leave his suitcase at the bottom of the landing that led upstairs and then asked him to "Shhhh…be quiet…don't wake her up" when they passed his grandmother who was sound asleep and snoring gloriously in a makeshift convalescent area that once was the dining room. That got a grin from the kid and he thought to himself everything that he walked on so far from the outside stairs up to the spot he now stood in the kitchen creaked as loud as could be and could surely wake up the dead.

Tony was immediately grabbed as he entered the kitchen because it resembled so much the kitchen from his home on Hinsdale Place. It was large and airy with a huge wooden table in the center of the floor. The kitchen had an old-world look; an assortment of pots and pans and utensils of all sorts hung down from a ceiling fixture above the stove along with garlic bulbs and an array of peppers and dried herbs. And a cluttered counter boasted a farm-style sink with a large picture window behind it.

Aunt Josephina displayed affection toward the boy as she patted and tugged at his arm requesting him to sit at the dinner table. She placed a cold bottle of root beer soda in front of him, and then she poured herself some vodka into an already used glass that contained half-melted ice cubes. She sat next to the boy and again expressed her sympathy over the loss of his father, her beloved stepbrother, and mentioned to the boy that she had spent more than an hour on the phone with Ceil just before they arrived. The fluorescent light from the ceiling fixture accented her short-cropped frizzy dark hair and made the discoloration of her pink-and-flesh-toned scars from a burn accident more pronounced and of which she was very self-conscious of. She would almost offer an apologetic explanation to any onlooker for the slight disfigurement. Josephina's eyesight was poor, judging from the thick lenses of the spectacles she wore, and her speech just a little impeded. One evening while she was preparing a meal she got a little too close to the gas flame that blazed under a skillet. The flame quick set fire to her hair then engulfed her head in flames. Josephina's words were spit out in short rapid sentences as she retold the story. She rolled her *R*s over a set of extremely crooked teeth and had a sizable gap between her two front ones.

Tomasino poured some brandy into a plain glass tumbler and sat at the table. He offered little in the way of conversation and said to his sister that he was just "all talked out and thoroughly exhausted from the entire ordeal." The two men sat there and yawned noticeably over the drinks they were sipping from and, after a little more brief conversation, were encouraged to "hit the sack," as Aunt Josephina put it. The dining room had been converted to a sleeping area as a convenience when Carmine had his stroke, and now mother and daughter both slept side by side on a pair of twin beds. Just off the kitchen and next to the laundry room, a full bathroom was added, including a shower. It proved a valuable asset to both women who found it difficult to climb stairs anymore.

Josephina bid everyone a good night and retired while Tomasino escorted his nephew upstairs to his room, pointing out the bathroom that they will be sharing from now on. He hugged the boy and told him he probably would not see him in the morning since he began his day at around five or five-thirty and gave him a fervent reminder that he is family and very welcomed to stay as long as he wished and to treat this home as if it were his own. It was a gracious and cordial communiqué that helped him to sleep like a baby.

Tony awoke early the following morning with the hopes he would be able to see his uncle off, but had just missed him. He freshened up a bit—his normal morning ritual before any thought of heading down. His shyness convinced him to wait until he heard some noise downstairs before making his presence known. The gruffness of his aunt's voice that rose from the kitchen and a familiar aroma cued him to gingerly make his way down the creaking stairs. He had never before felt such nervousness or ill disposed about entering a room in all of his life as he had now, but once inside, his reluctance flew out of the window as he laid eyes on the old woman who was his grandmother.

Grandma Rosa had such a glow in her eyes, constantly, despite having led an exhausting life during some of the worst of times. The old woman was up and sitting at the kitchen table with a finished bowl of farina and had a look of "more" written on her face. On the placemat in front of her were some remnants of the breakfast fare. Josephina just wiped off some solid farina clinging to the sides of her mouth. This was only the second time Tony had met the old woman and only the first of his recollection. He was taken aback by how much she resembled his father and could not help staring. She was a large-breasted woman with a full head of thick, coarse gray hair that was pulled tightly back into a clump behind her head and held together with a rubber band. Her solid chin had a few hirsute whiskers poking from spots, and Tony noticed how remarkably smooth her skin was, hardly any wrinkles at all; perhaps she had never worried. He smiled at both woman and gave both a good morning kiss on the cheek.

The old woman's eyes gazed widely at the sight of the boy, and her elderly marked face broke into a jubilant grin, one of a much younger woman as she began a harangue of Italian words and phrases that almost sounded bitter, and soon her face bore the look of ire as she continued and waved the boy to her side until he was close within her grasp. Tony was amazed at the power the woman had as she grabbed his arm and held on tightly. Tony looked at Josephina with half a smile as she promptly joined in on the conversation. She spoke perfect Italian and quickly translated for the astonished nephew. "She thinks you're her son Anthony coming home after all these years away." Tony figured out the gist of what Josephina was telling the old lady who just rattled on. "Tony, come sit down by her…maybe she'll shut up," Josephina said beseechingly then began to speak to her mother in English, "Ma, this is your grandson… he's not Anthony. This is your son's son…Cheese's kid." She coyly switched to Italian as she continued to speak to Grandma Rosa. Josephine became frustrated with the chore of trying to explain the family tree. "Ah…she doesn't understand." She moaned to all.

It was best decided that the old woman be spared the truth about her son's passing. Josephina commented on how she wouldn't understand anyway, so they left it alone. Tony let his grandmother continue speaking and made a few patronizing "Yes, I understand Italian" nods with his head. Josephina put a plate of what looked like six eggs and about a pound of bacon in front of him and said with a wrinkled brow, "Your mother said you're a big eater…so EAT."

17

As time began to slowly heal all of his wounds, Tony began to enjoy, thoroughly, his newfound family, especially the royal treatment he was receiving, this obviously inspired by the fact that he was the returning son of their prodigal son. He was accepted wholeheartedly by both aunt and uncle. And his presence did conjure up many a story by both at the dinner table. There was not a scarcity of conversation there, or food—just like back home. Now he understood his mother's wish for him to stay here for a while, to learn new traits and break old habits? There was neither a Bloomfield Avenue here nor a Frank Batista, not a trace of criminology in the air, but he knew that would change. As for now, he would spend the days helping around the house, fulfilling the menial chores that his aunt found for him to do. They were simple tasks, fun tasks that were more befitting a youngster. He especially enjoyed helping her tend the garden and of course helping around in the kitchen, while receiving valued cooking lessons. And he would help his uncle with anything he asked. The majority of his spare time was spent rummaging through the ancient history of the farmhouse, with its surrounding old barn and garage and shed and deep cellar all filled with chests upon chests of nostalgic treasure—old rusted tools, clothes, and gadgets, even a child's toy or two. He would pretend to be a child growing up in the past era of his father as he just let his imagination run wild.

In due time, Tomasino expressed to the boy Ceil's wishes, along with his own, for him to finish high school, and said, "We're gonna' leave that decision entirely up to you, kid. September is right around the corner." His one demand was if he opted not to go to school, it would be mandatory that he find a job and pay a weekly fee of twenty dollars for room and board. This he hoped would encourage the kid to rethink completing his education, at least up until and graduating high school. The very next day, he handed his uncle a hundred dollar bill and respectfully said, "This will cover my first month, Unk, in advance, and I'll look for a job right away."

Tomasino felt a slight disappointment with the luckless decision but accepted it and said he will aid the boy's search for a suitable job and assist him with getting his driver's license, much to the kid's surprise and delight as he found out that Pennsylvania will allow you to drive at sixteen years of age. Within a couple of weeks the boy was working for a friend of his uncle at the nearby Coking facility of Clairton Works and tooling around the rural country roads in a 1949 Mercury coupé. Tomasino said, "It looks like a piece of shit but runs like a top. And it has a practically brand-new backseat." He finished his statement with a wink. And no sooner did the kid fill the tank up with gas, he began to ask and entice just about every young, unsuspecting country girl he met to climb in that backseat, and of course they would most reverently and religiously jump in and out of. These seemingly innocent girls were no match for the sly and wicked Boy Scout from Bloomfield Avenue, and neither were the hayseed, hick young men that also tried to compete for the local girls' affections. The boys of the neighborhood, of which a few had befriended the stranger from the big East Coast City, quickly ceded their ties that bind them to the farmland innocence and fell under the naturally occurring criminal spell of Tony. He quickly became their decisive leader by making very short work of the reigning tough guys and taught all the true meaning of street smarts along with organized shoplifting and other dutiful crimes. Tomasino heard the stories told from the townspeople and just laughed. "Truly like father like son, just so long as he doesn't get hurt or hurt someone else."

In keeping with his delinquent but charming demeanor, Tony would always call his mother religiously, every Friday, right after work, sometimes from a pay phone and other times the farmhouse, and would fill her in on the week's innocent episodes and events. He felt a peacefulness knowing she was adjusting well to the loss of his father and the decision to send him away. He commented on how wonderfully his aunt and uncle have treated him so far and remarked on what a good cook she was, especially her gravy that he said "was almost as good as yours, Ma." She laughed at that comment, and then the two laughed at what oddballs Tomasino and Josephina were, but both had the hearts of saints.

The sacred dinnertime at the farmhouse was spent as family. Together the men feasted on whatever Josephina concocted from the freshest of ingredients of meats and vegetables and homemade pasta. During the nice weather months the family would always dine, alfresco, either under a handmade grape arbor or on the back veranda. After dinner, if no other plans were pending, the three would sit around the table or the front porch and listen to Tomasino tell his amusing stories about the past and some current events that made up his plebeian existence. He would advise his nephew as to what young girls are available and tell of their virtues, a bipartisan point of view he would strictly declare as "just hearsay." Tony would smirk some and say amusingly, "I'm way ahead of you, Unk." And they all would roar with laughter as Uncle Tomasino slowly became soused on homemade wine, moonshine, and apple brandy from his neighbor's stills and vineyards.

On some nights the boys would play gin for hours while indulging in heart-to-heart conversation as Aunt Josephina, herself with half a load on, would routinely tend to Grandma Rosa then retire to bed usually at 9:00 p.m. A rare favorite movie airing on the "Late Show" just might keep her nestled in her chair in the living room past eleven o'clock. And just as his young nephew would, at least once or twice a week Tomasino would primp and spiff himself up for a night of cabareting at one of his favorite watering holes in the downtown area of the East Side around East Pittsburgh Street and East Otterman Avenues, spots that would soon attract the growing interest of the young Tony.

A year had passed almost to the day on one particular and exceptionally warm August night, after his uncle had consumed about half a bottle of a neighbor's moonshine, Tony learned a deep, dark secret about the lost soul of the man that changed the way he thought of him forever. Tomasino brought up the subject of love and marriage and why he remained a bachelor all these years. He began telling his nephew that he himself lacked the handsome prepossessing looks or the money needed to support or to justify his wants and needs for beautiful women. He had not the attributes of Anthony and Joe Marino, the brothers recognized that fault at a young age, and to cheer up their kid brother they would compare him to the matinee idols of the day Rudolph Valentino.

His tale was told not in the jocular or raillery tone of his normal fashion but with a sullen resonance that matched his tearful eyes. Over the years the beautiful women he desired flatly denied his advances each and every time he would pursue. He could never bring himself to settle for a mediocre companion more suitable for the class of man he was because of the aphorism "That's all that would have him."

Tomasino would seek out the younger attractive prostitutes who worked the streets and clubs of downtown Greensburg. They would give him solace and satisfaction in their arms for the price of admission, and he found great comfort with their company and still does to this day. There was one girl, years ago, who became very special to him, almost as an obsession, and he succumbed to her beauty and, in his eyes, her unadorned innocence. She was a Russian immigrant who found herself stranded in the slovenly world of prostitution but swore to one day give it up if she could find a man who would accept her abused body and soul. Her name was Naida. She took an instant prodigious liking to Tomasino and listened to his promises and plans of marriage and his wish to make an honest woman out of her.

Naida began foregoing her evenings at the brothel to be with Tomasino as they truly entered into a relationship with one another. That idea was strongly opposed by the pimp manager of the brothel, himself a Russian who tried desperately to discourage her behavior, and began severely beating the young girl and claiming possession for him. She would sob to Tomasino who was appalled at the sight of her bruises and became overly concerned as their time spent together began to dwindle. Tomasino cursed himself for not acting sooner. He found out from another prostitute that Naida was beaten to death one night by the seedy pimp who paid the authorities to have the crime swept under the carpet and vanish from the police records.

Tomasino shot the last generous swig from his glass and reacted to the fervid burn as it slid down his throat. He stood up and asked Tony to follow him as he left the veranda and led the boy past the almost depleted tomato vines that were in the garden. The drunken Tomas stumbled a bit as they approached a large grouping of mature white birch trees that sat alone in the far corner of the yard. They seemed to have had no real rhyme or reason for being there, or did they? He gave the boy an outstretched arm that forced him to stop. Tomasino began to speak with a rancorous voice, "These trees were planted over twenty years ago, son." Then he continued. "Do you know how I remember that?" Tony had an ominous expectation about what he was about to hear next. Tomasino took a few hurried steps ahead and turned slightly away from the boy. He wobbled some then unzipped his fly and began to urinate on one of the tree trunks. Just then a wicked summer gust of wind brought the tall, thick branches alive, almost as if they wanted to silence the tale. "Vieni qua…" He motioned for the boy to come closer. "It was over twenty years ago when your father, Albie, and me went to pay that Russian pimp a visit to avenge the death of Naida," Tomasino said grimly. He finished his business and turned back around to face the boy. His face was evil and threatening as he spoke, and he became animated with his hands. "We caught the miserable *schifozz* in an alley behind the brothel as he walked to his car. He had a hooker on each arm. Your father and Albie shooed the whores away and began to beat him to a pulp. Never have I seen a human take such punishment." He acted out the movements with every word he spoke. "They held up his slumping body by under his arms, one on each side of him. His head drooped to one side. His eyes were swollen shut. His face was bloodied and unrecognizable. I called his name with the hopes he would see me then I sliced him open like the pig that he was." His words were accompanied by a thrusting and twisting of his hands, and his face bore a sinister smirk. And the more animated he became, so again did the sudden wind in the trees. "We let him bleed until he was no more. The stench from his *stendinz* is still fresh in my nostrils." Tomasino took a step backward and waved his arm in an arclike motion. "He's buried right here…under these trees…along with the bloodstained clothes and shoes we were all wearing. The next day, my father saw the freshly dug earth and shook his head in disbelief. He knew what it was used for but made no inquiries." That night he showed up with a load of seedling trees that stood about this high." Tomasino raised his arm in the air and finished. "He made your father and your uncle Joe dig some more holes and plant them. Albie was nowhere to be found. Of course I helped and my father often gave me a queer look as to why." Tomasino began to smile and took a deep breath and said, "For the last twenty years or so I have been pissing on the grave of that son-of-a-bitch." He began to laugh heartily and threw both arms up in the air. "He did make for good fertilizer…along with the limestone and lye. Look how big they've grown."

Tomasino's drunken laughter subsided and gave way to a couple of grievous sighs. He turned to his young nephew and said with a droll direct voice, "I still hate that fuckin' Russian for what he did." The wind flared up again, this time accompanied by a loud whistling sound that tore through the treetops. He stared directly into his nephew's eyes and continued. "And I have no qualms or regret for what I did to him. God knows that your father had no problem with it either." Tony stood frozen and listened intensely to his uncle. "Mannaggia la miseria…he deserved to die," Tomasino said with the resonance of a priest. "And I have not lost a minute's sleep over it…not once in all these years has my conscience ever bothered me about…about the murder of that *sfacimm* piece of shit. And I'm a religious, God-fearing man."

Tomasino's face looked ogre-like in the shadows of the pale moonlit evening light. He rested some and bowed his head then said nonchalantly, "As time went on only a few diabolical words were ever mentioned about the incident until it was washed from our minds the way we would erase a nightmare. The protective holy spirits of our family see to that. And I've never confessed this mortal sin, not to any priest, not ever—although I know one day I must." With a quick and sudden movement he reached out and firmly clasped Tony's head between the palms of his sweaty hands. The boy was noticeably startled as Tomasino pulled their faces toward each other within inches apart. Tomasino's grip was strong but with a degree of affection. His cigarette-and-brandy-laced breath was rank and caused his nephew to flinch as he began to speak. "It's okay what you did," he said as tears filled his eyes. He eased his grip of the boy's face to almost a caress. "And it will be okay to avenge your father's death one day…if you want." The wind settled as the two walked back to the house.

That same night, Tony lied in his bed wide awake, restless eyes opened and darting about with his uncle's lecturing words and conversation fresh in his mind. The slight buzz from the alcohol he had was all but gone, leaving just the beginnings of an agonizing headache. He glanced over at the round-faced alarm clock that read 2:35 a.m. and was not at all concerned with the 6:00 a.m. wakeup call that was soon approaching. He folded his hands and let them lie on his chest as he prayed to God for the courage and wherewithal to one day return to his home and carry out the inevitable vendetta against the men who had taken his father from him. It surely would be his ordained destiny.

The Indian summer was far behind all at the farmhouse now. Another winter was quickly moving in, draining all the variety of green life from the tall canopy of leaves and the colorful perennials. The stately elms, maples, and oaks gave one last bit of gasconade as their leaves proudly displayed the brilliant colors of autumn before succumbing to old man winter. The mighty green spruce and fir trees beefed up their limbs to ready the heavy snow they would support. Wintertime, as Uncle Tomasino reminded the kid, was "Casso di freddo!"

And it was at this time in mid-December that Tony learned the sad news. His longtime childhood sweetheart that he so lately pined for moved away, "far away," as his mother described. Up until now Joanie was kept silent in his heart. He never imagined the thought nor had any inclination that she would ever move away from the old neighborhood, and he truly believed that one day he would return to her awaiting arms. "But where, Ma…where did Joanie go?" Tony asked incessantly. Biting down hard on his lip to restrain the tears, he exclaimed dolefully, "Where, Ma? She must have said something to you…no? She wouldn't just leave with…without tryin' to get word to me…as where I could find here…huh, Ma…nothin', Ma…nothin,' not even a phone number…?" "No, son…I'm sorry she didn't say a word. I found out only last week that they were gone," Ceil remorsefully replied. And that was the end of it. He could only manage to get a short "Bye, Ma" out of his mouth before his eyes swelled with tears, sorrowful tears born from such a bitter melancholy that change men or boys forever. He felt rage and a sudden urge to slam the phone receiver down—to smash it into fragmenting pieces as his heart now was. But he respectfully thought that it was his mother on the other end, not a demon. He gently placed it back in its cradle. And the tears that he wept that day he carried to bed with him. They continued far into the night as his simple mind fought to recall and keep fresh the memory of the last time he had seen Joanie. He envisioned himself kissing her deeply, lovingly, their bodies pressing hard into each other. This was a burning mortal desire he had for her. His eyes grew heavy and tired as he felt sleep coming on. Then suddenly he grew fearful of the forthcoming sleep for some reason and felt his heart beat wildly. To awaken from a nightmare and then fall back asleep only to drift back in the same bad dream would be hell. This he feared, as it had happened before. His only simple salvation now would be to wish a wisp of a dream with her in it, and that would truly be heaven. It did not come.

Instead he dreamt of winter, the icy-cold chill of winter, and of his late father and himself together under the snow drift that amassed high atop the awning over the side door of his old house on Hindsdale Place. In his dream he was a young boy—maybe all of five years old, dressed in bulky snowsuit and a silly commando-style hat with furry earflaps. He was wedged between his father's legs, almost to the point of being restrained from joining the neighborhood kids that were hard at work shoveling the snow from the long driveway;

his father shouting commands at them as he laughed. The boy felt so secure, clinging to his father's sturdy legs. Then suddenly summer came to his dream and he sat and played while his father shoveled and hoed the manure in the garden. The tomato plants grew as tall as trees and their leaves a pale green and the abundant fruit a bright red. His father's voice echoed as he gave the neighborhood kids instruction to protect the garden and the crops it would bear. "And don't let any harm come to this garden and all will get a basket of vegetables for your family." His father's laughter became resonant and loud in his dream, loud enough to awaken him from it. Suddenly his father's voice was ever so crystal clear about the room. Tony lay with his eyes wide open in the black of night. He heard it again, and it echoed from overhead. "Tony…son…everything's okay—everything will be all right." Just as his uncle had foretold, his father spoke to him for the first time since his death.

It was very soon after the last dispirited conversation Tony had with his mother that his heart turned bitter cold—evil, for a better choice of words. The once burning desire to return home, to Newark—to his beloved Bloomfield Avenue, was completely gone now, as was his father and Joanie. In the months that followed, he lost all interest in life back home as he once remembered it and vowed to himself to adapt this newfound life in the quiet rustic hills of Westmorland County and the town of Greensburg.

He eventually fought off the hurt, anguish, and heartache of Joanie until they were a mere mnemonic thought—but an ever-so-irritating thought, and nevertheless, with each day he began to notice and feel an obscene hatred steadily consume his conscious mind. It was a malignant spirit, persuading him, longing for the vile criminality to spring from his soul. And as he neared manhood, the bitterness he held was apparent to just about all who would meet him.

He frightened most, usually the strangers that would innocently brush his shoulder while walking the street or the supermarket aisle.

And God help those that resented his hostility and shoved back, and there were a few that quickly felt the power and fury of his angered fists. His aunt and uncle read the antagonism as well, and a confirming conversation Tomasino had with Tony's mother was held in strict confidence. They agreed to just let him be, and for good reason. Perhaps the good son would reappear? Be it as it may, Tony was always on his best behavior at the farmhouse, completing the chores doled out without question or aversion, and he showed his congenial guardians the utmost respect. He was kind and courteous always, at the farmhouse—for that Tomasino would be a true protector and think of Tony as his son or younger brother. And Tomasino also realized that if push did come to shove, it would now have to be him to come to the boy's rescue.

The weekly phone calls to his mother were dwindling, as was the benevolence in their short conversations. However, he did send a monthly package containing cash mostly, and sometimes trinkets and souvenirs he picked up from around the area with an enclosed card or little note of some kind, reassuring her he was okay and to quote his late father, "Everything's gonna' be all right, Ma…and say hello to everyone for me." Every so often, Uncle Joe would call the farmhouse and keep the kid abreast with the latest scuttlebutt from Mobville, USA. This topic perked him up and seemed to spark some long lost interest, especially about Frank Batista, but nonetheless, it was a short-lived conversation.

18

Celia Marino's words rang out loud and bitterly and with deep resentment as they echoed chillingly off the surrounding tombstones, the small family crypts, and the statuesque saints of Mt. Pleasant Cemetery. "Goddammit, Anthony, goddammit," Ceil repeated over and over as she stood in front of her late husband's grave quivering in grim disgust. She tightened the knot under her chin that held her scarf taut and continued to curse while she closed her eyes and shook her head, gently in denial, "Goddammit, Anthony, how could you have been such a scustumad?" Her breath vaporized in the frozen January air and blended with the bleak gray sky that surrounded the cemetery. The biting cold gnawed at her tear-filled eyes as she continued to curse her fate and that of her deceased husband. She pulled a tattered tissue from the pocket of her gray wool coat and dried the moisture from her eyes and squeezed her runny nose until it dried some. "Why did you let them do this? How could you let this happen? Oh, Anthony, Anthony, you *stuppiad*. How could you?" A question shouted loud enough and intended for both her husband and God in heaven.

Ceil repositioned her scarf over her mouth and exhaled then took in a deep shuddering breath of the chilled air through her nostrils. Her fingers lightly touched the inscription of her husband's name that was carved into the marble headstone, Marino. It was ice-cold to the touch even through her wool gloves. A silent prayer was said with a bowed head and streaming tears. Then she turned and walked away. A few winter black birds seemed to wish her a goodbye as they sat among the bare and twisted branches of their winter perches, making almost human sounds. Their wings fluttered and heads bobbed to and fro as they continually scoured the ground searching for a morsel of food.

The frozen crusted ground layer of snow crumbled beneath her feet as Ceil nimbly made her toward the cleared path that weaved through the eerie cemetery and led to the front gate. She completely ignored the other names and inscriptions on the many headstones she passed. None of them were important to her. A gust of icy-cold wind ripped through the bare oak and snow-covered evergreen trees and hit Ceil full force at her back, causing her to stumble on the frozen earth and colorless grass of the cemetery. She almost went to the ground. "Son-of-a-bitch," she mumbled harshly aloud as she barely caught her balance. She grabbed the lapels of her coat and held them tightly to her breasts.

Ceil came around the bend on Hindsdale Place with the forceful, biting wind still at her back. The propelling gusts covered her with the white mist of snow from the high piles amassed along the curbs and the tree limbs as if it still was falling from above. The arctic blasts were making her walk on the frozen sidewalk in awkward steps, causing her to move faster than she had wanted to. The section of Hindsdale Place she was walking began to straighten out and gave Ceil a clear view of the row of houses up ahead including hers. It was her home stretch; just a few more steps, she kept repeating in her head. Suddenly she froze in her tracks, defying the arrogant wind. She let out a frightening "Oh my god." She watched in astonishment as her late husband's glistening black Cadillac rounded the opposite corner of her street then turned left into her driveway—the red bullet taillights bright as can be vanished past the front of the house.

Her heart began to pound in suspense from inside her chest, and she could feel perspiration begin to drip from her underarms as she began an almost jog-like gait the rest of the way home. This was the first time since the death of her husband that she laid eyes on the shiny black Coupe de Ville. The bane of heated arguments during his life disappeared with the remnant exhaust smoke. The car was now a sight for sore eyes. Her curiosity ate at her as she wondered who was behind the wheel. Her inner prayers were for it to be her husband. Let him be there in all his grandeur carrying sacks of groceries and meats for her to prepare was her questionable wish.

Ceil turned up in the partially snow-cleared driveway and noticed the familiar features of the man already at the side door entrance. He stepped up on the six-inch concrete landing and stomped the snow from his work shoes then pulled the leather and fur ear-lined cap from his head as he waited to greet her. "Why it's Joe," Ceil said aloud as she hurried up the driveway. She hugged her brother-in-law under the overhang and said, "What are you doing here with this car?" "Bet you never thought you'd see this ever again," he said, beaming. His face bore the look of a devilish child as he dangled the car keys in front of Ceil's face. Then he pointed to the Cadillac that he just plowed through the snow up to what was considered its usual parking space. Its front end raised some, perched atop a snowbank. "Oh my god…you're right…I never thought about it. I thought it was gone forever," Ceil said in amazement as she reached into her coat pocket and produced a set of house keys. She stood in astonishment as she stared at the bullet taillights then at the rakish angle of the sleek and shining body then back again. "I don't believe you got his car," Ceil said. Joe let out a sigh and said, "Yeah, well, it wasn't easy." He gave Ceil a gentle nudge with his forearm and said, "C'mon…open the door…it's freezing. I'll tell you about it inside."

Their footsteps echoed off the bare plastered walls as they climbed the wooden steps. Joe peeled off his winter coat and hung it along with his hat on one of the wooden pegs attached to the coat rack fastened to the wall outside the apartment. It has been awhile since his last visit. Ceil followed suit and did the same. "I tried to call you but…no answer," Joe said as he took his designated seat at the table to the right of where his brother sat, the one he always sat at. Ceil rummaged around the kitchen a bit, checking to see if everything was in its proper place, and no apparent mess was visible. "I was at the cemetery," she said. Joe nodded with a doleful look. "I'll make coffee…you got time?" she asked. Joe said without hesitation, "Yeah, sure."

Joe was finally able, after over a year and a half of legal embattlement, to pry his late brother's Cadillac free from the restraining talons of the evildoers within the justice department. He began to give Ceil all the details of his victory.

It had been stored away in a government compound with hundreds of other vehicles that were either stolen or seized in various raids and considered case evidence vis-à-vis State's evidence. That included the dozen or so odd lot autos recovered from M&M auto. A now dull yellow placard was glued to the windshield of the Cadillac that read boldly STATE PROPERTY. Its dust-covered body had been embellished, frequently with the words "Wash Me" in a finger painted type of print by passersby. All of the vehicles were awaiting a similar fate of the junkyard or were to be auctioned off to the public and a few private prearranged buyers eager to assume ownership. Someone's brother-in-law from the department had his eyes on the ebony beauty with the bullet taillights. After months and months of diligent writs and documents presented to the courts as to who should be the rightful owner, Joe finally drove it away, legally.

Joe watched as Ceil prepared the coffee. His anxiety was building as he blurted, "I got some more good news for you," with a smart grin on his face as Ceil poured the coffee. "You're gonna collect the life insurance money…every cent of it," Joe said sublimely. "That's wonderful, Joe…thank God," Ceil responded with a sigh full of relief. The small amount of life insurance she carried on her late husband was at last to be paid. The ten-thousand-dollar death benefit would finally be hers and paid in full from the John Hancock Life Insurance Company. The debit life-accident policy she so diligently paid for each week was at first denied, citing a clause that prohibited the benefit paid if the death was a direct result of a criminal act or possibly a suicide. Again after months of correspondence and arguments on Joe's part, and the help of Willie Caruso Esq., the underwriting department agreed to accept that Big Anthony's demise was in fact an "act of murder" carried out by a "highway man" as defined and written in the policy and forcing the double indemnity clause to be enforced.

Big Anthony Marino left this world unexpectedly and, like most mobsters before him, left his financial and legal affairs in complete disarray. Ceil searched frantically for the various documents and records requested by the government agencies and the probate court. None could be found. Not a single record. Even his brother Joe had not a clue where the big man kept anything important in his material world. Ceil was ultimately denied any type of Social Security benefit since there was no record of him ever paying into the government fund. As a matter of fact, no one actually knew what his real social security number even was. He never filed a tax return and, like other mobsters, lived his life under various aliases, none recorded with the government.

The entire character, what seemed to be a facade, of Big Anthony's life was not entirely his own fault. He was born during the same year that his mother Rosa gave birth to Joe, only eleven months later. She was somewhat embarrassed by what was known as an Irish pregnancy and never recorded Anthony's birth. Rosa found a willing midwife to assist with the delivery, and both kept it their little secret, hidden from friends and family alike. He lived his entire life using forged and falsified documents; even his own Social Security number was bogus. When it was absolutely necessary to use one, he would jot down his own father's or his stepfather's number, or a combination of both. Technically, to some government agencies, the 250-pound man did not exist. Both Joe and Ceil drank their coffee black with just a little bit of sugar or *anisette* added.

They were both on their second cup and continued the conversation. "So what do you hear from your son?" Joe asked. Ceil's response was upbeat and positive. "He's really enjoying himself out there, Joe. He's adjusting well, so I'm told. I talk to him almost every week." Her demeanor became a little downtrodden as she continued. "But I still worry. He's too much like his father, and I hate when people shrug a casual shoulder and say like father, like son." Joe listened intensely and recognized her anguish. "He could be a devil at times, so Josephine tells me." She paused a bit then continued. "I don't know...trouble finds him or he finds trouble." She finished shaking her head slightly. Joe's face turned into a blank stare. The jovial mood he was in when he entered the apartment was quickly replaced with an icy fear. He tried hard not to let his sister-in-law interpret his chill as his mind played back the horrors of that fateful afternoon as it so often did. His life was transformed to one of a man on the run, constantly looking over his shoulder, wondering when the truth would be found out, wondering when they would come after him for reprisal.

The empiricism of the strength he had in the old days recaptured his weakened thoughts, and he snapped out of his worrisome daydream. "Don't worry about that kid of yours. He's plenty tough," Joe said with an assuring smile and nod of his head. "The boy will find himself." He continued. "Like we all did." Ceil wanted to believe him, but her eyes told a different story. "I heard that Tomasino got him a job…and a car. I think he even has a few girlfriends out there. Ohhh, I hope he's happy. This is what he needed," Ceil said with a buoyant voice and clasped hands. "You just gotta' hope he makes the right choices for himself," Joe said with raised eyebrows. He felt his soul slip away once again as the fear factor began to take over, making him relive the image of his nephew firing the deadly rounds into the mobster. "The kid's been through a lot," Joe said with a degree of seriousness. "Most kids his age would have snapped." Ceil's intuition told her there was more to Joe's connotations than he was leading her to believe. She found the courage to ask the question that rested heavy on her heart. "Joe…I never asked about what really happened to my Anthony?" Joe completely ignored her and let the question just linger in the air. Her voice began to strain. "Was my son involved in any way?" she asked directly. Joe hesitated before he spoke. He gave Ceil a look of bewilderment. "Involved? No… how could he have been involved?" Joe said with an evasive tongue then inhaled deeply. "Ceil…c'mon…we gotta' try to forget all of this and move forward with our lives," he said encouragingly. "Your son will be fine. We gotta' get you going now," he said with a smile. "You still got a life to live." Joe gulped down the last of the coffee in his cup then stood. "I gotta' get back to the shop." He jingled the car keys in front of Ceil and said, "I'll park the car at the shop for safekeeping. Who knows, one day maybe your son will want it. Or maybe one day you'll get a driver's license." Both laughed at that thought and comment. His mind wandered once again to a dismal thought as he gazed out of the kitchen bay window into the dull, overcast gray sky. "You need anything? You must need some money maybe?" he asked with raised eyebrows as he plunged his hand into his front pants pocket. Ceil quickly stood up and raised her hand to stop Joe. "No…no…no…Joe. I'm fine…really…I'm fine. I have a little money that my son gave me." She was referring to the cache of cash handed to her the day her husband was killed. She kept that a well-hidden secret from everyone and kept the cash buried deep in her closet. She smiled and continued. "He just sent me a letter along with a couple of hundred dollars. He's a good son." She sighed. "But thanks so much, Joe. You've already done so much for me. I could never repay you." Her words and actions were sincere. "But really, Joe…I'll be okay…now with the life insurance money coming. We don't need too much around here." Ceil let her arms raise and held her palms open graciously. "There's only me and Mamma, and my brother helps us out a little." Joe listened as Ceil's eyes widened. "And Albie, God bless him, he stops by every month or so with a little something. Sometimes it's money, or sometimes it's food. And other times it's both." Ceil finished with a smile.

Joe's eyes squinted upon hearing Albie's name mentioned. He turned away from Ceil for a moment then gave her a derisive stare. "Albie, huh…what's he been up to these days? Does he say much of anything? He's never once as much as give me a call the *mezzamort*," Joe spoke under his breath. "No, Joe…he's a nice man…" He was oblivious to the words Ceil spoke to him. His mind froze. Perhaps it was because he knew deep within his heart and soul that it was Albert who set his brother up. The vile thought of "He visits out of guilt" burned through his mind; however, now was not the time to rehash such biting thoughts. "Heah…girl…you're doin' better than I am," Joe said with a forced smile. Joe had a thought then bit his lip. He hadn't the nerve to dare bring up or ask Ceil for the cash he gave his brother just before he died. That act he felt surely would bring bad karma. "Well, if you need anything, just call okay." "I will, Joe, I will."

19

Willie Caruso's writhing facial tics were working overtime as he shuffled the legal papers and land sale documents quickly between all parties concerned. It was William Caruso Esq. as the plaque read, and the law office of the same, to act as the chosen counsel to handle and quickly expedite the real estate deal that was on the table. The brokering of the deal was indeed a triumph for the slick lawyer who always thought he had it in him to be representative of a completely legal deal. "Here you go, big guy, last signature, right here," Caruso said. Joseph Marino's huge hands were beginning to cramp up a little. He stretched out his fingers a bit then signed his name and dated July 1, 1962, on what was an endless pile of transfer documents that made him the sole owner of the building and property at 7713 Bloomfield Avenue, Newark, New Jersey, DBA, M&M Motors.

"And here's your check, Mr. Levine," the smiling Caruso said. "I hope my services were worth it?" His furry eyebrows rose at least a foot. They all laughed. Caruso continued. "I am sorry about the inventory though." He was referring to the fifteen or so cars that remained on the property. The City of Newark gobbled up the mostly stolen vehicles, and what they did not keep for themselves personally, they sold at auction.

"Well, it was great meeting you, Bruce, and your attorney... what was your name?" Joe said. Bruce Zwillman was the only grandson of the late Abner Zwillman and legal heir/owner of the property. His silent attorney was really not that important but he nodded just the same.

"Same here," Bruce returned the compliment with a "tip of his hat" remark.

Caruso motioned for Joe to remain seated as he cordially escorted Bruce and his attorney out of his office. He reentered his office and sat back in his chair, lit a cigar, and began feverishly scratching his ear and neck. "Joe, I don't mean to pry, but...it looks like you paid a lot of money for this land...what do you know that I do not?" Joe gave a grinning stare and said, "I don't know? Not much of anything really. I guess I want it for my baby brother's legacy. Ya know...he had it all those years. Guess I want to keep his memory alive. Kinda' like in posterity, I guess you can say." There was a few seconds of silence; then Joe spoke gravely, "It was the last place he was at...maybe I'll turn it into a mausoleum." "Well, anyway...I wish you luck, Joe," Caruso said with sincerity. "And keep me in mind if you want to do something else with the place." They shook hands and said their goodbyes.

As time passed, Joe moved around the city much more decidedly and with far less apprehension as he once had. He worried less and less about the Pope, his once foreseeable retaliation or any form of revenge. And he slept better. His concentration on business was much more focused than it had been for some time. Profits increased hugely as did the workload, thusly enabling Joe to give his son a substantial pay raise and bonus—this gesture done to assist and oblige his son's wishes to move out of the house and get on his own. Joe Marino was flat out convinced there wasn't a single shred of evidence that could possible tie him to the murder and mayhem that happened at his brother's place three years ago. If there had been, he would have surely been approached already.

He enjoyed driving his late brother's Caddie around once in a while and was tagged by some who remembered the flagship bounding about the neighborhood now with the nickname of Big Joe. He kept the ebony black cruiser in tip-top shape with the hopes of one day presenting it to his nephew Tony, the true heir to the car, and in conversation with the boy would joke about only using the car when he had a lady friend, an occasional date, in his company. "Tony, I promise to keep the backseat virgin…for you only." And to further ensure its well-being, he kept it garaged at his Hillside home rather than the busy service station.

Joe left the service station at precisely 4:00 p.m. and made his way to the Garden State Parkway North. Although the traffic heading north was usually light on a Friday at this time, Joe wanted to make sure he would not be late. He was on his way to meet some potential tenants for his Bloomfield Avenue property. Billy and Jerry Damato were longtime customers and friends of Joe. They were both auto wholesalers and expressed an honest and sincere desire to rent M&M Motors for both a legitimate wholesale/retail operation. They were all to meet at 5:00 p.m. at the property. Joe volunteered to bring some fresh pizza from his favorite old neighborhood haunt: Casa Di Pizza.

Joe's mouth was watering from the aroma of the always busy pizzeria. He bolted through the front door and politely nudged his way through a crowd of about three deep at the counter. With a wink he got a waitress's attention and asked if the order he called in was ready. She in turn relayed the message to the boys at the ovens. The to-go pizza orders were stacked high atop of the 700-degree oven with the customer ticket wedged between. "Lemme' see now… for Joe? I got one plain, one with sausage 'n' peppers, and one with anchovies," the pizza chef shouted as he looked up. "Hey, Joe…long time no see." He continued as he recognized an old customer. "Yeah, it's been a while, Jimmy…so how ya' been?" Joe shrugged. And he thought to himself that this was probably only the second time he's been in the store since the night his brother died.

Jimmy Palermo was a seasoned pizza maker and a degenerate horse bettor all at the same time. You might say that this was his entire life and has been for the last twenty-some years, working seven days a week, fifteen hours a day. He was sorrowfully in his mid-forties, overweight, bald, and lonely. He made a great pie, but he was a natural loser at the track. The local bookmakers loved him and his nonstop action. His employment was secure at Casa Di Pizza so long as his brothers Nino and Johnny owned the place. "Joe, I think you're da' only guy that still orders anchovies…old-school–like," chimed Jimmy. Joe then said, "Yeah. I guess…whaddya these young kids know today?" "Ya, got dat right," Jimmy said as he spun a pizza round in his hands. "So whaddya' doin' in these parts, Joe?" Jimmy asked as he ladled the bright red tomato sauce on the fresh pie dough.

Joe paid for his order, shuffled the three boxes on the counter some, and said, "Gonna meet some maybe tenants at my brother's old place…maybe open it back up." "Really…dice games?" asked Jimmy coyly. There was a long silence as Joe first slid his arms under the pizza box then said, "No! No! No! None of that stuff anymore. It's gonna' be a real car lot…maybe." Another patron of the pizzeria held the door for Joe as he left. Jimmy Palermo opened the hot oven door and skillfully slid the unbaked pie into a perfect position then glanced at the departing Joe. He shut the oven door and had an eerie feeling of déjà vu.

The night wore on, and around 7:00 p.m. things slowed at Casa Di Pizza. Johnnie kibitzed with the young, shapely waitress that adorned his place and reminded her of the duties they expected from her while Jimmy studied tomorrow's racing form. He daydreamed some then shuffled through a desk drawer until he found the business card of Detective Accardi. At first he just mulled over the card, flipping it between his fingers from side to side and front to back. He paused some then rigorously dialed the number titled Personal Desk Number and waited for the soon-to-follow gruff voice, "Hello...who's this?" Jimmy straightened up and said, "Hello, sir. It's me Jimmy from the pizzeria...you know...Casa Di Pizza."

Accardi grunted from a relaxed position in his easy chair. "I didn't order any pie, my friend, so what's up?" "Heah remember that shootin a while ago, at Big Anthony's place?" Accardi perked up and strained his memory back to the day he interrogated all at Casa di Pizza. "What about it, Jimmy? Didn't we talk already?" he asked firmly.

"Yeah, yeah, yeah...but is it still open? The case, I mean?" the squirming Jimmy said. "I think I got something for you. The guy you were askin' about. The guy that bought the pizza...I tink' I know who it is...but I'm wonderin' if there's something in it for me."

Accardi spoke calmly, "That all depends. When can we meet privately?"

20

The obscure, threatening tentacles of the black rain clouds that seeped down on Westmoreland County, Pennsylvania, were beginning to pulsate over the low-lying mountains, fir trees, and valleys almost portend like, as if they had something evil to say. And they did—a fierce storm approaching, and it would come fast and without much disregard for residents or commuters alike. Tony was on his way to work when he first caught glimpse of the menacing storm clouds out of the corner of his left eye as he cruised east on the rural Lincoln Highway. He guided his Mercury coupé onto the shoulder of the road and quickly rolled up the windows. *Just in time*, he thought to himself for as soon as he pulled back into the travel lane, the sky opened and spewed blinding sheets of rain. He was sharing the road with mostly semi-tractor-trailers that stirred up a thick, dirty mist from their spinning wheels further hampering his vision through the windshield. Annoying as they were, he was thankful of the glow of the trucks running lights that outlined the rear containers, guiding his route along the roadway.

It was exactly 6:00 a.m. when Tony exited the Mansfield Bridge. Patsy Kline's "I Fall to Pieces" finished and the radio announcer warned of an impending summer storm that's "heading our way this

Saturday morning—here and the following counties of—" Tony blurted sarcastically, "Oh yeah! No shit," as his car bounced over the railroad tracks that ran parallel with the murky river. The endless sight of the black coal cars unmoving on the railroad tracks was a cruel reminder to him of the 1,500 tons of coke the plant turned out each and every day. Coke that came from tons of coal he and the work gang shoveled. He entered the parking area realizing he was running late and there would not be a chance in hell of finding a parking place within any reasonable distance to the entrance, so "fuck it,' he said as he created his own.

The dense black smoke billowing from the tall brick stacks was suppressed by the rain and mixed with the steam that rose from the angled roof of the factory. It created a sinister mist about the entire property. He wedged his lunch bag against his chest. His gait was flat out furious as he dashed toward the big, open rusted iron doors of the oven houses and the dull crimson red glow that beaconed from within as well as through the skylights and windows and reflected off the oil-laden puddles scattered about the grounds.

Once inside the Gothic building, he loosened up some by stomping his feet and giving his rain-soaked body a shake. He reached for his time card and eased it into the slot. The surmounting dins of the already running machinery, metal against metal, clanging, banging, deafened the time clock ring as he punched the card. The noise suddenly became muffled and an eerie quiet came to be. And he heard, for now the second time, his father's voice echoing crystal clear, "Tony…son…son…" First, it seemed to come from his left. Then it was an echo behind him, "Tony…son…" He gave his head a faltering shake and went to place the time card back in the rack. The date leaped out at him. 19 August 1962. Today was the anniversary of his father's death. Tomorrow would be his nineteenth birthday. Would his mother call? She hasn't so far, and no one understood the reason why better than him. No one wanted to dredge up the memory of that dreadful day. She would call a day or two past the date with a belated birthday wish, always apologizing and he always forgiving. Then a card would arrive by mail, offering once again a belated birthday wish.

The kid pushed on to the locker room and hurriedly stripped down to his skivvies. He donned his crusted denim overalls and his charred and stained steel-tip boots. He slid his tattered railroad gloves into his rear pocket, affixed his gray striped and coal-smudged locomotives hat on his head, and stormed into hell.

The intense rain to some is considered a burden, an annoyance. To others, like the crew that manned the blistering oven houses at the Clairton Coke Works, men who work in *hell*, hard droplets of cool rain and wind was a blessed relief. For as long as it lasted, the twenty or so coal crew gang at oven house 2 would be finding each and every open steel-framed window or doorway during the course of their twelve-hour shift, and let Mother Nature shower away the black soot off their denim overalls and soothe their heat-singed skin. They would let their railroad-style hats fill with water then douse their welcoming heads, like children playing. Ah, the rain, the blessed rain, it couldn't be more welcome than on this hot August day.

The steady, dense rain would also quell the nasty aroma of rotten eggs that reeked throughout the twenty-acre complex of Gothic-style brick and iron coal houses and oven rooms that created the sulfur mist during the process that creates "last furnace" coke. Steam from the rusted surface of the huge hot exposed maze of piping conduit that ran from building to building hissed a serenade to the oversized brightly painted valve mechanisms that sat spaced between the conduit. And the heavier the rain, the better, the men thought. It would certainly keep the steel bosses from venturing out of their dry, secure office sheds and completing their rounds of bihourly inspection for the day's production chart. This spared the men the demeaning feeling of being a slave to the job. The flow and heavily dripping of water supplied rhythm as it ricocheted and sloshed. It became the conductor for the workforce inside oven house 2. The rain and occasional thunder would set tempo for the brumal tsar-inspired composition of the "Szara piechota" that the mostly Polish crew would sing cadence to all day long in amusing and dire dialect, and ironically, the gang would get more work done than if the bosses were around.

Working in the oven house was a labor-intensive, dangerous, and dirty job. Hard goddamn work only for the strong, both physically and mentally. It would wear you out, and only the strong could survive, and strong they were. And just about surviving? The twenty or so men that made up the factory's daily work gang were mostly of second-generation Polish and were all related to one or another at Clairton. Their bodies bruised and scarred from toil. Their black stained overalls crusted in soot and tar. The hair on their mighty arms singed away. They were brute, ugly men, bearing broken teeth, missing teeth from acts of silly bravado—opening bottle caps, chewing iron. Their image and personas were ones of industry, steel, US Steel, all given birth names, ironically derived from Slavic saints, as if their mother's knew their sons would need all the help they could get to protect and shield and to keep from their fateful destinies. Today they would be relieved of the hellish heat of oven house 2 by the cool rain sent from the almighty heavens above. Tony took his place at the end of the ten-man line—next to his already soot-and-sweat-covered peers. The laborers gave each other about three foot of breathing room between them all—just out of arm's reach. His designated spot was next to Stanislaw Gadzinka, a six foot three brute of a man with horrible teeth that matched his stale smell, and directly across from Stanislaw's younger brother, Kazimer. He also was a brute, but not in the same category as Stan.

The kid has been feeding coal alongside the rest of the work gang in oven house 2 since he was sixteen and is becoming quite evident in his calloused hands and hulking muscles that glisten from coal-dusted sweat. His face grimaces as it bears down with each heavy shovelful of the black carbon tossed onto the huge conveyors that feed the 3,000-degree ovens. The merciless heat was unrelenting and gave the kid good reason to wear his hair a little shorter these days. Stan turned and hissed at the kid, "Yer late…Steel boss gonna' dock ohwr." "Yeah…whatta' you care?" Tony snapped. "And do me a favor when you talk…look dat way 'cause your breath is like death." Stanislaw became angry. His pace reflected it. Stanislaw growled in a thick, hard-to-understand broken English, "Shovel faster—*Kurwa Matka*. You are making me fall out of rhythm." He drove a hard elbow into the left arm of Tony and growled again, "Shovel faster, you piece of shit Guinea." Tony raged. "Go 'head, keep it up, you Pollack mutt, and I'm gonna' give ya' a mouthful a' coal. I'm in no mood for your bullshit, so shut the fuck up, or I'll knock out the last couple of rotten teeth you got…motherfucker…and don't think I don't understand what you or your stupid fuckin' brother is saying." The two exchanged vile insults until Stanislaw threw another elbow. Tony's oppressed anger broke loose its chains. He raised his shovel and threatened. "Touch me again. I'll hit ya' with this shovel—right across that ugly fuckin' mug of yours." The rest of the gang further up the line thought this was staged amusement, and all would throw a few of their own digs in, laughing along the way. And while this type of bitterness between Tony and the Gadzinkas has been going on forever, this episode was leading up to a little more than the usual ten minutes of cursing each other mixed with some harmless shoving.

The absence of the steel boss led to a morning full of squalid bickering between the two and was slowly turning evil. Had the steel boss been present, he would have put an end to this nonsense long ago before it got this far out of hand. If you were to size up both Tony and Stanislaw, the slight edge would have to go to the big Pollack, and Tony always was leery of him in the past. The Pole was bigger and slightly stronger, at least with arm strength, judging from prior arm wrestling bouts and shoving matches the two had. He also had a good three inches in height over the kid's six-foot frame. Stanislaw was older as well. The Pole had at least ten or twelve years on the kid, and this created hesitation for a brawl on the kid's part, not for fear but out of respect for age. On the other hand, the kid was certainly no slouch by any means, and his physical sight did intimidate most in oven house 2 and around Greensburg. And on and on the tension surmounted between the two, side by side slinging coal, exchanging vicious threats, shoving each other, and as fate would have it, even soothing rain could not cool off the tempers.

The obnoxiously loud buzzer announced the ten o'clock break, and within seconds the conveyor belt came to a halt as did all the machinery. Only the oven's whirr of blasting heat could be heard. The men broke from their spots and started to walk toward the break room. Stanislaw spoke first to his brother loud and for all to hear, "I shood teech this 'Wloski Szumowiny' goowd lesson Kaz."

Kaz was in front of his brother. He turned and spoke through his teeth to Tony, egging him on more and more. "Did yooh know what hiy' said dis' ti'yme?" Both the brothers laughed as did a few more of the Polish workers. "He cawwaled you Italian scum." Tony shot daggers into Stan's eyes. Stanislaw slowly turned and said, "Pieprzy Matke. Hey Guinea peashh'of shyt…" He continued to butcher the English language with his poor pronunciation, but Tony understood well what he meant as he heard "That means go fuck your mother." That was it—good night, Irene—the kid finally had enough and wailed at the top of his lungs, "Heah scumbag, you Pollack piece of shit. You want some of me—come and try?"

Stanislaw stopped dead in his tracks, turned, and faced Tony. The kid steadied his body and squared off against the big Pole. He was by no means afraid of a brawl. He certainly had his share of them and knew how to handle himself well. He was tutored by some of the toughest men in New Jersey and extended those lessons to the toughest of men in Greensburg. "You wanna' teach me a lesson, motherfucker—well, bring it on!" Tony snarled.

Stanislaw moved in with a slow and deliberate crouch, raising his bearlike arms as a wrestler would. Tony made short work of the Pole's attempt at a lunging grab. The kid threw a hard quick left upper cut before the Pole could overpower him. Stanislaw's head snapped back and down he went onto a pile of raw coal, in his grasp, the gold chain the kid wore around his neck. Stanislaw looked at it in disgust before tossing it away.

Tony adapted a defensive stance and awaited retaliation. The stunned and embarrassed Stanislaw leaped up and lumbered clumsily toward the kid. As he neared he threw a wild roundhouse right hand that Tony slipped easily under. The kid's assumption was 100 percent correct—the big Pollack did not know how to fight. The kid attacked from a favorite crouch position, one he mastered by watching fight clips of Rocky Marciano. Tony brought a right hand clenched fist from the floor and, with a perfect upper cut form, smashed the Pole solidly on the left side of his jaw—his fist followed through with a perfect arc. The big Pole's head snapped crisply as he flew backward then dropped hard to the ground again. This time he was severely dazed, his jaw already swollen and purplish in color—he spat blood on the factory floor. The price of the kid's boxing stock just climbed a little higher on the NYSE. And Stanislaw suddenly realized he himself was not in the same class of street fighter as his much younger adversary. Before Stanislaw could get set and counter, the kid lunged in, staying low to the ground, and rained a heavy left-right-left combination to the face of Stanislaw, carefully aiming and sizing the area around his eyes. One more solid right hand delivered with the momentum of a discus thrower crashed squarely on the Pole's nose. In less than thirty seconds, Stanislaw was beaten to a bloodied pulp and unconscious. The dripping rain that fell from the rafters could not revive him.

Feeling much bravado now, the kid went to the gathered and silent crowd to settle all oven house scores. Without a moment's hesitation, he dropped Kaz with a vicious right that he brought from his childhood; then he exclaimed through gritting teeth, "Who else gotta' fuckin' problem with me?" That remark was timed with the arrival of the steel boss who walked unknowingly into the mayhem. Magnar Bartek was quickly informed by the work gang, and in Polish, how the Italian boy beat the shit out of the mighty Gadzinkas. Bartek listened with keen interest. He made the mistake of trying to manhandle the kid as he ordered Tony to accompany him to the general offices of the Clairton Coke Facility. As the buzzer blew announcing the end of the coffee break, Kaz was sitting on a coal pile holding a bloodied rag to his fractured eye socket, Stanslaw was still out cold, and lying in a heap, slumped against the corridor wall that led to the break room, was the freshly battered Magnar Bartek. Upon notification, a few more plant supervisors made their way over from the office. Tony flung his arms up in a surrender stance as he walked past, "Yeah, I know, I know. I'm fired, right?"

The boy was spared the legal entanglement and threat of any atrocious assault charges with the intervention of his uncle Tomasino. He set up a private meeting with the Pollock brothers, the supervisor Bartek, along with Thomas Rossiter—the owner himself, and Tony. They gathered in Rossiter's office. Tomasino conclusively reminded Mr. Rossiter of the boy's age and the age when hired, howbeit a favor granted—what judge would forgive Rossiter for putting a youth "in harm's way—an environment of hardened steel workers?" as Tomasino put it. Case adjourned.

Not much was said between the two on the ride back to the farmhouse, very reminiscent of the kid's original trip out here. Perhaps his uncle was angry? He gave no indication at all. Tomasino pulled his truck up to the front porch of the farmhouse and gave the kid a wink and a grand smile. "Go ahead inside. Your aunt wants you to call yer mother…let her know every thing's okay. Now I gotta' run a coupla' errands then we'll figure something out for you—later."

Tony jumped out and said without a quiver, "All right. Thanks, Unk…see ya' later."

Tomasino watched the kid bound up the walkway then disappear inside the farmhouse. He tried to empathize with the kid. He most certainly understood the boy's anger, which he knew, for sure, was enormous and unbarring. He felt the anguishing sorrow that must be buried deep in the boy's heart over the loss of his father and of course his own actions. Tomasino could not find it in his heart to any way try to discipline the kid. He would let the boy sort it out for himself as he and his brothers all had to—like all young boys must. It's all part of growing up, he thought. In time the kid will come to terms as to what path he would follow. Tomasino smiled a crooked smile at himself in the rearview mirror and said with determination, "What boy, big brother of mine—you're son is a man now."

That evening at the farmhouse, as they feasted on bowlfuls of *shcarole* and beans and country pork spare ribs, Tony confessed a desire or a need to return home to Newark, to his mob life still waiting him on Bloomfield Avenue. "I know I caused you some trouble, Uncle Tomas, with your friends at the factory…and chances are I'll cause you a lot more," he spoke sincerely, "and you're not gonna live that down, so maybe it's best I leave." Tomasino felt the guilt of failing the boy and failing his mother. She had hoped the stay in Greensburg would break his bond with mobsters, but Tomasino sensed the cardinal desire of the life even stronger now deep within the kid's soul. He could read him like a book. Tomasino's face was distraught as he asked, "Are you sure you're ready to go back?" It was a simple question. The harder questions, the ones about vendetta and revenge, were not brought into the conversation. Tomasino's wish was to let the boy seek out his destiny, here in Greensburg, amongst the old-school regime of the Montesero family, then decide for himself if, in fact, this will be the chosen path.

Tomasino suggested to Tony that after dinner they get cleaned up and take a ride downtown to East Pittsburgh Street. The boy was all for the idea; having been there a few times on his own, he was excited and eager to go. While it was not Bloomfield Avenue, downtown Greensburg had its share of dive bars, nightclubs, and jazz joints along with the back room gambling clubs and of course whorehouses, and one seeking that sort of action could definitely have a good time down there.

Much like anywhere else in Mobville, USA, all the noted vice and corruption in Greensburg, Pennsylvania, especially on East Pittsburg Street was operated, offered, and controlled by the wise guys. They may act and talk a little differently than their constituents in New Jersey and New York, but make no mistake about it, they were just as lethal. In this part of the country, all the wise guys worked under, and paid tribute, to the powerful Pittsburg boss, Stefano Monestero, the still reigning *Don*. His captains and their crew did the roadwork from a few different locations in and around the Pennsylvania/ Ohio borders, one of the places being Rozzell's on Tremont Avenue, downtown Greensburg.

It was a well-known mob hangout, frequented only by the wise guys themselves, or a select group connected with. But a few citizens, as they were referred to, were allowed and did manage to find a warm seat and good conversation here in this place. It's a saloon where you could openly hear conversation about stolen merchandise, "swag" as it was more commonly referred to, truck hijackings, and high-profile burglaries from just about every crooked dockworker, truck driver, or conniving patron sitting laggardly in the booths or at the bar. Cases of clothing and racks of apparel of all sorts littered the floors of the executive office as well as utility closets and storage units. Along with the clothes were cases and cases of just about every oddball assortment of general merchandise one could think of. And just about all day and night, those boxes would either come in or go out; the infamous backdoor mob business of every kind was conducted openly here. And Rozzell's had a high-level poker game every weekend to further entice its patrons, or anyone sanctioned to enter the game.

Tomasino pumped his brakes of his Ford Fairlane as he bounced into the parking space on East Pittsburg Street. He fumbled with his cigarettes and lighter and slid his car keys under the front seat. Tony watched the act that he had witnessed before. Tomasino always left his keys in the car as to not lose them and never cared about locking his car. "What's to steal?" was his pardonable answer. Immediately, out of the glittering neon of the nightclub marquees came a young prostitute named Candy. She recognized Tomasino and slithered into a sensual pose. She approached the two with a sultry gait but was politely shooed away by Tomasino. He shot the kid a humbled look and said to the young hooker, "Not tonight, my dear." Tony said as they rounded the corner onto Tremont Avenue, "Hey, Unk...don't let me stop you." Slightly embarrassed Tomasino said, "No, not tonight. Tonight we drink a toast. I'll save up a little more cash for her." An indication she was a little out of his league.

"You're gonna' toast what?" Tony asked. "The birthday we all forgot about—again." "That was two days ago. As far as I'm concerned, leave it forgotten." "Yeah you're probably right." There was a short silence; then Tomasino spoke again, "Not a good idea here to celebrate birthdays. You're too young to drink. But don't worry. Don't say anything but don't worry. These guys are all friends of me, your father, and your uncle. So we'll drink to them." "I got it, Unk," Tony said as he held open the door for Tomasino. He gave his uncle an assertive grin and held up his wallet that he had removed from his pants pocket. "If they do ask, I have my other ID with me." It was easy to obtain an illegal driver's license for the purpose of sneaking into the neighborhood taverns and bars frequented by college kids as Tony found out weeks after moving into Westmoreland County.

Tomasino was fresh-shaven and dressed like a businessman in a neat two-button blue suit. Tony had on a dark blue Italian knit, opened at the chest, and a pair of crisp creased, pleated pants. Both looked like they truly belonged at Rozzell's. The two Dapper Dans first bellied up to the bar, but then Tomasino changed his mind and opted for a table that caught his eye in the far back corner of the house. An older cocktail waitress, in her fifties but still very attractive, was standing at the drink station at the far side of the bar. Her name was Carla and was not only a fixture in Rozzell's, but a lifelong resident of Greensburg. She was never married and shared her bed in her younger years with Stefano Monestero. She was his *Goomata*. That was in the old days if you were to ask her. And she would also say she shared herself with Big Anthony and his brother and his friend Albert. She took a slow drag from her cigarette and came over with a round bar tray in her hand. "Tomas, it's nice to see you, honey," she said with a genuine smile. "What can I get for you and your?" Her question paused as her eyes focused on Tony. Tomasino extended an open palm and said, "My nephew! Carla, say hello to Tony. Tony, say hello to a good friend of mine, and your father. Carla. Carla. Please, sit down for a second." Tomasino gestured to the waitress as he slid a spare chair under her bottom. "You know who this is?" Tomasino's face bore a broad smile as he said, "This is my brother Anthony's kid." Carla's eyes became wide. "Oh—my—god," Carla exclaimed. "He looks just like Cheese." The boy sat up at the table and rested his weight on his forearms that bulged from his shirt. His left eyebrow rose slightly and rested under a natural curl of his "black as coal" hair. He always looked older than he actually was. "It is so very nice to meet you," she said as she leaned in and offered him a dainty hand-shake. He stood up and obligingly took her hand in his then leaned in and placed a tender kiss on her cheek. "Same here, ma'am." This made the seasoned Carla blush three shades brighter than her already red rouge.

Carla gave a seal of approval look to Tomas and said, "And polite too. I like that." "Polite? I don't know about that." Tomas continued. "He's a lot like his old man." They all laughed. "Bring us a coupla Rollin' Rocks, sweetheart, okay," Tomasino said. "And a coupla' shots of Wild Turkey also," Tony added. "Seems like old times around here," Carla said as she scampered away. Tony sat up and took a mental inventory of the nightclub, sizing up the place so to speak. His basic instincts Batista taught him. Be aware of your surroundings—any potential dangers. Locate the nearest exits, the men's room—watch who comes and goes and how frequently? But this was a place, he thought, that even Batista himself would approve of. A place his father once hung out in—he thought that admirable.

Rozzell's was not a busy place, but then again it was a Tuesday night, and it catered to a noticeably conspicuous crowd only. The place had the hush-hush aura of the private clubs back home. A mostly all-male clientele and all well dressed, even the obvious working-class patrons wore nice clean clothes with their hats removed, and all speaking with hands to their mouths or in impressionable code. A few scantily clad women, obviously the working girls, pranced around and drifted in and out of another room that was at the far right of the main cabaret room. Tony wondered as to why his uncle had never made mention of this type of place. Maybe to keep his opinion of him innocent and pure, he thought, or to keep this place away from him, thinking he would like it too much to stay away. He was right. Rozzell's had a large tattered oakwood horseshoe-shaped bar that dead ended into a brick wall. On the far side was where the bar separated on a long hinge and flipped up, allowing access to the inside arena. Next to the opening was two big grab rails with a rubber serving mat in the center. This was Carla's station. The boys at the table watched as Carla assembled their order and a few others while she talked to two men, neatly dressed in suits and ties, flanking her left side. They couldn't hear the conversation, but they knew it was of good things. Both the Marino and Cupido name was respected in this area.

Eyes went side to side among each other at the bar, and faces bore smiles as they gave acknowledgement to Tomasino and Tony. South Side Sal Ianuzzi was the acting manager of the joint and also a captain in the Monestero crew, and sitting next to him, the acting bouncer of Rozzell's and enforcer for the crew, Patsy Vizzoni. "Tell 'em I'll be right over," Ianuzzi said to Carla as he held up his glass toasting the men at the small table. Ianuzzi came to the table and was met by Tomasino. He stood and gave the man a hearty embrace. Then he offered the mobster a seat across from them. "It's good to see you again, Tomas. And we were all wonderin' when you were gonna' bring the kid around," said Ianuzzi with a sly laugh attached. Carla brought over a tray of Italian sandwiches, which were the extent of the food served in the place. And after a few scant but formal intro-ductions and a revealing chain of command in these parts, the con-versation was all about the big Cheese as he was *known*.

The group toasted away almost a full bottle of Wild Turkey that was now at their table, and Carla squeezed in between the partygo-ers to clean up and remove some empty beer bottles. A few more well-wishers who knew Cheese came over to say hello to Tony. Some were hearing of the death of Anthony for the first time, and they offered their deepest respects. Ianuzzi told his tales from the old bootlegging days and began each story the same way: "I shouldn't tell you this but what the fuck." They all laughed and Tony, though he heard most of them already, gave his undivided attention as Ianuzzi spoke, "Your old man had lottsa' juice in these parts, kid. Christ. I remember the time him and your uncle Joe busted up this place one night, over a crap game or something. Cheese went to put on his cashmere coat and saw that someone had tossed a lit cigarette butt on it. It was still smoldering' He went nuts…wrecked the place. We couldn't control him." Ianuzzi was in tears from laughter. "We were all sorry to see him go," Ianuzzi said, and bit his lip. "Sorry. That came out wrong." He ended. "Not as sorry as we are," Tony said, and his uncle nodded.

When the talk shifted to the gangland murder of Greenburg's old friend, all the gaiety left the table and voices became somber. And when they were asked innocently what happened, Tomasino and Tony volunteered very little information. "We don't know what happened. Nobody knows. Even my brother Joe knows nothing." Tomasino preached. But even if the truth were told, the Pittsburg crew, who shared allegiance with the New York factions, would probably let Tomasino harbor and protect the kid. Ianuzzi wore a long face. "Well, if it makes 'ya feel any better bout' it, very little was said to us as well."

Tony excused himself to go to the bathroom, and while he was gone, Tomasino found it the perfect opportunity to get in Ianuzzi's ear. He told the gangster the reason the kid was here was for safe-keeping, away from the evil and unhealthy memories and away from any vendetta that might be languishing by the Pope. Even though his innocence or involvement was not in question, why take a chance? "We want to let things blow over back east," Tomasino said. There was a long pause; then Ianuzzi said, "I understand. So how can I help?"

Tomasino thought of the members of the Montesero family as his own and spoke candidly to Ianuzzi. He explained the problem the kid had at the coke works. He asked Ianuzzi to think about taking him under his wing. "Give him safe haven here. Find him some interesting work with your family. It's his destiny—for now anyway. I just think he'd be safer here than Jersey. I know the kid won't let you down, and I will be in your debt," Tomasino said.

Ianuzzi brushed some cigarette ash from the lapel of his double-breasted suit and answered, "I like your nephew, he's respectful, and that's good. Tell him to come see me tomorrow. But not too early, anytime after two o'clock is fine."

They both watched as Tony emerged from the men's room. As a matter of fact, just about the entire room had their eyes on him. He was huge in stature as he walked toward the table in full confidence of his surroundings. Already, rumors abound the barroom spoken from the hand-concealed and covered lips of the patrons, and all spoken in covert whispers. A burly truck driver sitting at the bar spoke to his buddy through the side of his mouth as Tony passed them by, "I hear they brought him here from New Jersey to be a leg breaker."

21

During the early years of young Tony Marino's apprenticeship, under the reins of Philly Ianuzzi and the rest of the crew that called Greenburg home base, he became a good friend and a running accomplice of Frankie Furio. Frankie grew up in Greensburg and was the son of a Teamster "over the road" truck driver. His father, Frank Senior, is himself no stranger to, nor is opposed to a well-versed staged hijacking and on occasion will still surrender his rig, or a fellow Teamsters rig, into the ever so ready clutches of the Monestero crew. And ironically, he ran some with Cheese Marino back in the day. You could say that it was in his blood, or all their blood, both fathers and sons. The younger Furio, Railroad Frankie as he was known around the inner circle of thieves, is another well-rounded member of the Pittsburgh family whose sole purpose in life is stealing.

One of his favorite illegalities was breaking into railroad boxcars and piggyback freight cars that move steadily on miles of cold forged serpentine track, flat-bedded containers that hold desirable merchandise within their locked and sealed cargo doors. The mob term was "swag" for such merchandise. Cases of untax stamped cigarettes and liquor or high-priced electronic equipment, fresh off the boat from

Asia, would flow freely within the core of Mobville. Neighborhood fences and outlets as far as New York reap the profits from the sale of hot cases of valuable canned tuna fish or prepackaged razor blades and sometimes a load of expensive French perfume. Precious metals like copper or nickel, sometimes even silver and gold, are well sought after and almost always carried in their raw, refined state hidden in boxcars. Frankie has an uncanny talent of smelling and identifying the cargo in the closed containers, and his nose was on the money about the contents just about all the time.

Frankie, like Tony and a few of the other active crew members, was not a made guy but followed the code of honor diligently and was a true earner. His physique was lean and wiry, which lent itself to the rigorous demands of burglary and breaking and entering. His short-cropped hair and fair skin gave him the appearance of a Boy Scout rather than an up-and-coming mobster. The two scalawags singlehandedly robbed and hijacked more freight from the surrounding area's railroads and trucking companies than any single forwarding company was legitimately contracted to deliver. Their backyard playground was the never-ending stretch of railways, interstates, and docks and the thousands and thousands of square feet of storage and warehouse space that spread from Ohio to Greensburg. They would hop freight trains, spring board off pallets, and sail through jimmied windows and doors of warehouses like acrobats. There wasn't a lock they couldn't pick or an alarm they couldn't bypass or a guard dog they didn't like. They truly enjoyed their chosen profession of crime.

Their newfound cash cow was in its humble beginnings. Frankie couldn't wait to tell Tony that his cousin just got a job for the Merchants Delivery Service. MDS, as it is more commonly referred to, just opened a huge terminal a mile up the road from the Lackland warehouse and between himself, Frankie, and Frankie's cousin, don't stand a chance in staying in business for any length of time.

Tony Marino was well received and well liked by all the Monestero crime family, especially since they had already known the celebrity of his bloodline. As Stefano well put it, "The apple doesn't fall far from the tree." In a very short time, he had established a code of honor and a sense of belonging among his new mafia peers, and it would be a bond of obligation and friendship that was going to be hard to break. Perhaps it was the honorable and gladly received embrace he had hoped to get from Angelo Ruggeri? He kicked up more than his fair share of tribute to the bosses, and the act was dually noted. Both captains in Greensburg and Don Stefano Montesero himself were happy with his work and earning potential he brought to the clan.

They admired his tenacity. He was indeed a bull, like his father, but with a polite grace that would always get him a pass if he did make a few mistakes. He did have a temper but would only direct it at a true enemy and never at a friend or another member of the crew, and he showed the bosses the utmost respect. He always had a kind heart for the underdog, like his father, and that made his job of collecting difficult at times. A strong-arm collector was expected to lean hard on everyone they came in contact with and lean even harder on a delinquent gambler or someone too deep into a shy. He considered himself fearless but did show a slight sense of weakness when it came to teaching someone a lesson. This eventually came to pass.

The Lackland Forwarding Company had been a cash cow for the Monestero crime family for years and years. It was a safe haven for truckloads of whiskey and beer being transported between New York, New Jersey, and Pittsburgh and Ohio during Prohibition. After the Eighteenth Amendment collapsed, the prime real estate was quickly converted to what it is today, a three-hundred-thousand-square-foot forwarding station owned and operated by one of Stefano Monestero's old bootlegging crony, Tommie Rafferty.

Tommie Rafferty bore the scars of Prohibition and bootlegging across his ebbing hairline of curly reddish gray hair and his bushy eyebrows. A large man, well over six feet tall with a prominent and pronounced beer belly. He usually wore Brooks Brother's suits, the ones usually preferred by politicians and always with a pair of colorful suspenders

The property sat alongside a major spur rail of the Pennsylvania railroad and in between the Lincoln Highway and Route 66, making it ideal logistically. The warehouse space was leased out to three separate trucking companies, a large livestock feed company, and a produce middleman, all having ties and owing tribute to the Monestero crime family. The way tribute was paid was through an elaborate scheme of misplaced cargo and manifests along with a carefully laid agenda of hijackers being tipped off as to where and when the good stuff comes in and leaves the warehouse.

As seasoned gangsters realize, know, and understand, they are not the only ones with the hands in the cookie jars. Freedom of dishonest enterprise is for all those who wish to take the risk. And many did at the Lackland Forwarding Company. The temptation was just too much for anyone that had just the least bit of larceny in their soul. The human nature of the sociopath would prevail. This was good to an extent. Most of the stolen goods were traveling by railcar first then on to trucks, making it a federal crime of interstate proportions.

The Monestero crew would applaud each and every time an enterprising thief was caught by a federal agent stealing cargo from *their* warehouse. As a result of good police work, the heat would naturally come off them. And ironically, most of the inside information given to the Feds about illegal activity came from one of the crew's own who were carefully placed in a key position within the Lackland employ or the employ of the trucking companies. These workers usually held menial jobs within the warehouse or inside the office, inside dockworkers or paper pushers. The hard-nosed and tough worker bees came from the Monestero family. And the family members would sometimes give praise or commend the crook for devising such an elaborate foolproof scam.

Mostly all private citizens who were caught stealing went unpunished by Monestero for he knew the federal prison time was a hell's sentence on its own. Their fear and concern would of course be one of their own insiders—part of the organization who had an inclination to go into business for themselves, hence the enterprising thief who could possibly put the Monestero family in harm's way if ever apprehended. This is why if one of their own was stepping out of line, punishment had to come hard, and it had to come swiftly.

The evidence the Monestero crew had was undeniably accurate—the double-crossing thief was marked. The orders came directly without any hesitation at all from the boss. "I want the kid to get his feet real wet on this one. Tell how important it is for me that he does a good job." Patsy Vizzoni gave the boss a cocksure wink and nod and bolted through the office door.

Bill Green worked directly for the Lackland Forwarding Co. He answered to only his immediate supervisor, John Longo; Longo answered to Otto directly to Rafferty. And eventually, they all answered to Stefano Monestero. Bill Green was a twenty-eight-year-old Korean War vet, and his was titled expeditor of incoming and outgoing freight for Lackland before it went into the private sanctions of the other companies within the warehouse walls. When orders come down for a certain load or some particular cargo to go south, it was Bill Green's expertise and his essential key role that enabled the wheel of crime to roll. There were a lot of key players in positions, and the way the corporate ladder was constructed, no one knew who the other was. They only had one face to worry about and take orders from. And that face was Patsy Vizzoni. You see, all the shit that would sometimes roll downhill would always end up on a wise guy's shoes.

It came to be known that Mr. Green had been an enterprising young man, and he and his cousin Carl were fencing the merchandise, Montesero's merchandise, out of a seedy pool hall in Arlington Heights called Dukes. That part of south Pittsburg was run by Anthony Fresolone. He had full control of all the slim pickings regarded as family interests in the predominately all-black neighborhood. It was Fresolone's keen eye that first noticed just about everyone in or around Dukes would walk in the joint in nondescript rags or leisure suits and walk out wearing a nice Valentino suit.

Dukes was owned by an ex-heavyweight fighter named Randal Bassey. He was thought of as somewhat punch drunk but still currently had a fearfully tough reputation and demonstrated his pugilistic talents on just about anyone who got out of line in his joint. He was rumored to have sparred with Rocky Marciano and had a down-home dislike for Italians.

He kept his place free from mob guys, and they were obligingly willing to stay clear and accept him as a renegade. Fresolone told Stefano in the early days of Dukes that this *Ditzune* just was too stubborn. "The only thing he would understand was if we beat him senseless and burned his joint to the ground." Let him have his own gambling book of business with his people was the consensus of the Monestero clan. "It doesn't add up to much anyway" was Fresolone's blight. "It's not worth the effort. We get the bigger action anyway. The smart niggers know not to bet large with Randal." This was not the case anymore. Montesero felt that Green and his cousin and Randal Bassey and Dukes had to go.

The information provided assured the boys that who they needed to see tonight would be inside the pool hall unsuspecting. And all were well versed as to the severity of the visit. Fresolone nodded to his driver and said, "We'll be right out." He was to wait outside with the car running, handgun ready to ward off any innocent bystanders or brave hearts. The local police would not be an issue, they seldom came down to this area anyway, and tonight a message was sent for them to not respond to any calls until they were told.

Fresolone and Vizzoni wore black top coats, their hands buried deep in the pockets with fingers wrapped around large revolvers, old revolvers that would be impossible to trace if left behind and would put large fatal, gaping holes in anything they were fired at. Tony was the standout as he followed the older crew into the dingy, smoke-filled pool hall. He stood a foot taller than the other two and seemed huge under his loosely fitting black sweatshirt, black chino jeans, and brown canvas construction boots, his hands covered with black police issue "bean bag" gloves.

The hour was approaching midnight, and only a handful of silly sloppy-drunk pool players lingered as did Bill Green and the boxer. Fresolone gave a forced smile and said, "Evening, gents. It's been a long time since I was in this shit hole." His rouse was to instigate as he said, "Still smells like cheap wine and piss in here." He made his way to pool table that Green and Bassey were leaning on. Carl Green was fiddling with a makeshift clothes rack that harbored about a dozen dark-colored suits. All eyes immediately focused on the suits then on one another. There was a long silence in the room that was filled with a lot more than tension. Anthony Fresolone broke the silence and said firmly, "I want to talk to you two." He pointed at Bill and Randal. His eyes gave a stare to another group of players and he said sternly, "Alone." Bill Green recognized a problem right away and laid his cigarette in an ashtray. He made motion for the three others shooting pool to leave. "Go ahead, boys. This here is a private thing." Bassey lived up to his reputation as being thick and stubborn. His words stuttered from between yellow stained teeth, "Hold up now…" He marched right up to the tight group of mobsters, and with all the evil he could muster he said, "What the fuck you messin' round here for. You know gat' damn well you ain't welcome here, and you ain't got no gat' damn business here." Vizzoni stepped to his right, giving Tony an alley to move up in before he spoke. He motioned his thumb much like a hitchhiker in the direction of the suits and said with instigation, "This place is looking more like Bamberger's Department Store than the piece of shit Moolie hangout that it is."

Randal Bassey took a step back, and Tony immediately recognized it as a defensive move. He realized it was his time to act. He visually sized up the muscular frame and the marred face of the ex-pug. He judged a safe distance between him and Bassey and spoke with a wiseacre tone. "Hey," he said with his right hand finger pointed. "You're the one that used to be a boxer, huh?" Bassey's bald head and brow wrinkled and let moist droplets of sweat run down the side of his cauliflower ear. "What the fuck that gotta' do with you?" Bassey barked. Tony readied himself, his left hand measuring its target. He snickered and whispered to the hulking ex-prizefighter as he looked down, "Your shoelace is untied." A convulsed silence fell on the group.

No. The kid really did not say that, thought Vizzoni as he laughed hard to himself. He fought hard the urge to burst out laughing as he wanted to do, but that would surely ruin the moment. Fresolone could only look in amazement as the baffled Bassey stupidly looked to the ground. He was hit by a fierce left uppercut thrown by Tony that should have put him down. It did stun and stagger the unsuspecting oaf and put him on wobbly legs. Bassey instinctively tried to put his hands up to block whatever was to come and stared out with foggy vision still unaware of the dupe. The two mobsters pulled the western-looking revolvers from their coats and the obvious took place.

Both Carl and Bill Green froze then followed the direction that the pointed guns told them to go stand. Tony emulated Rocky

Marciano and had mastered his boxing and punching style. He savagely went to work on Randal with precise and well-placed heavy punches, punches designed for a heavy bag hanging from a chain connected to an I-beam. He delivered a powerful left hook then another, then a right uppercut and a left all thrown from a coiled waist and shoulder, and all finding the defenseless target. The powdered lead that was sewn into the tops of the gloves opened Randal's face up like a can of ripe bright red tomatoes. How the man was standing was probably the reason he was a heavyweight contender at one time.

The three "brothers" at the other pool table did not look back as they bolted out the front door stumbling into one another and jamming up the doorway. One replied to an inquisitive passerby While he ran in stride with his hand tightly holding down his tattered fedora, "Don't you go in there, brother, dem' Italians in there… bustin' up the joint. I knew it wouldn't be long."

Tony took a shuffle step to his left of his opponent, cocked a mighty right hand, and delivered a straight punch that landed squarely on the jaw of Bassey. The force sent him straight over the pool table and then to the floor. Fresolone looked at the kid in awe and said, "You can hit, kid." Tony caught his breath and inhaled deeply through his nose.

He measured Bill Green from the corner of his eye and stepped in. He landed a strong right hand sucker punch to the side of Green's head and he dropped like a fly. By Vizzoni's orders, the kid savagely broke Green's jaw and cheekbone with three more huge thundering punches. Vizzoni tapped the kid on his shoulder and took a look at once at Green's face; "He's had enough" was his determination. He first looked at the unscathed Carl then nodded at Randal as he said, "The boss wants him to eat through a straw for a while. And he wants me to remind you not to say a word or we'll come back here and really fuck up this place." Vizzoni walked over to where Randal was lying and noticed him coming to and moving ever so slightly. With a couple of hard well-placed kicks to the Randal's side Vizzoni coaxed the ailing ex-fighter to roll over flat on his back. Blood spat freely from his nose and throat forcing Randal to cough profusely. Vizzoni snarled, "Here lemme' help ya' some." He picked up a cue stick and slammed it hard over the edge of the pool table. The force snapped it in two. The others in the room watched with abhorrence as Vizzoni dropped his knee heavily on Randal's midsection. He wedged the thick end of the cue into Randal's swollen and bruised mouth and twisted until a grotesque sound of broken bones could be heard by all. Carl Green was left unharmed and was dared to say a word to anyone. All that was injured was his pride as he was forced to remain in wet, pissed, stained pants. He was ordered to put the suits in the trunk of the car then instructed by Fresolone to "call an ambulance, or better yet, take them yourself to an emergency room. No one is coming to this shit hole."

Stefano Monestero was pleased with the work of Tony Marino as reported and placed a gold star next to his name, along with an envelope containing a one-thousand-dollar bonus. He turned the office and the everyday duties of the family back to his trusted capos and reminded them of the tribute needed weekly then hopped into his waiting Cadillac and sped off back to his home and family in Pittsburgh.

As time passed, Tony reverted back to his old ways when it came to the art of debt collecting. He'd rather take a soft approach with poor souls that got behind on their payments. It was not in his sinister nature to be that diabolical and inflict pain under those circumstances. "A moral dilemma," as his uncle Tomasino would equate. There had to be a more soulful and an almost personal reason for him to do harm, of which he was quite capable. Subsequently, he would voice his dislike for that type of violence openly to both capos, even as they allude to the books opening up for new members. Tony's disinterest with being made by the Pittsburgh crew was kept completely in the dark from them.

The fact was he had no interest. He only expressed his need and desire to earn money. And he showed a preference for the less violent challenges of mob life; he took an immediate liking to burglary and hijacking trucks. He'd rather do an armed robbery or a heist that required savvy and expert precision, capers that he could shed some ideas and theories he had concocted. The kid had a natural flair for such duties.

22

Weather-wise, it was a perfect mid-September night. Inviting clear skies, cool, not a trace of humidity or an antagonizing insect in the air. A perfect night to be at a ball game, Joe thought. In person, at Yankee Stadium, and not squinting to watch the tiny TV picture tube that was on. A satisfying breeze ventilated in and out of the opened overhead bay doors and circulated throughout the building, almost cleansing away the rank smell of motor oil, grease, and gasoline fumes. Joe sat comfortably in the tiny office of his North Broad Street gas station with the door propped open with a hunk of heavy iron. It was a three-bay structure that was appropriately named Joe's Full Service. The illuminated sign was proudly displayed under the winged logo of the Flying A Gas Company.

It was an ever thriving business with a perfect location, on a very busy and highly trafficked main thoroughfare, not far from the Hillside Avenue entrance/exit ramp of Highway Route 22. Joe's prices for service and fuel were, as he put it, "modest and honest.' This was the reason its customer base flourished. Joe was leaning back in the wooden swivel chair with his feet propped up on what seemed to be the only free corner of the battered, junk-cluttered desk. A huge black telephone sat perched atop a stack of phone books. There were spindles full of work orders and receipts, all with oil-smudged fingerprints and at least six or seven piles of other invoices all with heavy bolts or car parts holding them down as their edges fluttered by the wind force of the small table fan that was running. Joe's lit cigarette would flare each time the air current passed by, and each time he took a drag, the fan would blow the ash into thin air.

The double clang of the air hose disrupted his concentration of a Yankees-Tigers game that was being broadcasted on WPIX channel 11. With eyes still fixed on the tiny TV and the voice of Mel Allen announcing, he unconsciously rose out of his chair and looked to his right. His eyes only caught the rear end of the dark sedan as it drove past the gas pumps and rode over the other air hose with another double clang. The disgruntled Joe cursed under his breath, his favorite Yankee Joe Pepitone was at bat, facing a full count.

Joe stepped just outside the office door and watched as the car eased into a space on the far side of the building, next to the restrooms. He acknowledged the tail fins of the new 1964 Cadillac but not the car itself, or its owner. Joe's eyes darted over at the men's and ladies' room keys attached to a block of grimy wood both hanging from nails in the wall, anticipating the customer's needs. Then he looked over his shoulder at the office clock that read seven forty-five. Dusk was just setting. Joe instinctively opened an electrical box on the wall and flipped a switch turning on all the outside floodlights and sign.

It took about a half a minute, but it seemed a longer amount of time to the now anxious Joe, until he heard the door mechanism activate and the car door open and slam shut. *Only one person*, Joe thought to himself. For whatever reason, Joe was worried about this visitor, and his hunch was a mobster just climbed out of the car. Mobsters do bring worry and fear wherever they go, fear that is somehow announced, subconsciously, before they even arrive. Joe sensed danger, something he hasn't felt in a long, long time. He quickly stepped back inside and checked his bottom desk drawer. A sense of relief was felt as he glanced down at the .45 caliber automatic sitting under a shop rag. Then he positioned himself with a clear view from inside the office.

The driver of the car came into full view as he turned the corner and walked toward the office. His facial features became luminary by the floodlights that were turned on. It was Frank Batista. And he was alone. Joe said casually as their eyes met, "Frankie…what brings you around here?" A well-deserving question since Batista never comes to these parts. Frank Batista had a huge sincere smile on his face and said, "I was in the neighborhood, thought I'd stop by and say hello." Batista offered an obligatory embrace and Joe responded with respect. Both exchanged hearty pats on each other's backs. Joe became distracted to the point of fearful. He pictured another car of goons pulling up, guns ablaze. His daydream was interrupted by Frank's voice. "*Che Fai*, you stay open late now, Joe?" Frank adjusted his thick-framed eyeglasses then poked around the door that led to the unlit bay area. He let out a short laugh and asked, "What are you, all alone too? So are you just bored or greedy or what? 'Cause it sure don't look that busy here, Joey, to be opened this late." Frank had a silly smirk on his face that let Joe know his questions were innocently placed. *It is just a casual meet*, Joe thought. He laughed and said, "Yeah, it's really not that busy at night, but it's starting to pick up." Joe shook his thumb at the oil company logo and said, "Headquarters wants me to stay till ten. And they just want me to pump gas. They can care less about repairs. They're greedy pricks. So me and my son alternate nights. But now I gotta' think about putting on an attendant." "But you still work on cars?" Batista asked inquisitively. Joe smirked and said, "Fuckin' aye, I do."

Batista glanced over at a glass decanter half filled with coffee sitting atop the warmer of the Bunn Machine, its red on button glowing and inviting. "How's the coffee, Joe, any good?" Frank asked. "Yeah, I just made it not too long ago," Joe said. Frank walked over to the coffee station and inspected a couple of used paper cups that were lying around. Joe went to the small bathroom inside the office and came out with a heavy clean coffee mug. "Here, Frank. Don't use those cups, they're dirty. I got no milk though, just that powdered stuff, and there're some packages of sugar to your left, in that box," Joe said. Frank helped himself and said, "I drink it black, the way I like my women." This got a chuckle from Joe who said, "I think I'll join you. You want a little anisette in it?" "Sure," said Frank. Frank heard the crack of the bat as Joe Pepitone slammed a double up the right field line. "Yanks are havin' a good year, huh, Joe?" Frank said. Joe took his eyes away from the game and said, "Yeah, they are. It's a close race, but they got a good shot to go all the way."

The two fumbled a bit trying hard to create some genuine small talk between them until they stumbled upon common ground. They could not ever think of meeting without some reminiscing about the old days, which they ardently did for a while and with enthusiasm. Then shyly they talked candidly about their love lives, or lack of it, as Tic put it. Joe said amusingly, "Yeah, my late wife's sister is always trying to fix me up. I really don't want any part of a relationship." He made a promise to himself against the best wishes of his dying wife to never remarry. "Thank God we got the whores to turn to," Frank said. Joe listened attentively as Frank brought the subject of present-day gripes, and sincerely bitched about mob life and all of its trials and tribulations. "It's getting to be a real drag, Joe," Frank said.

"I don't miss it at all. I honestly don't see how you guys stand it anymore? What am I saying, honestly? I mean dishonestly. And I still don't sleep that good, Frankie. And I don't think I got anything to worry about anymore," Joe said. Frank laughed and said, "I know what you mean, buddy boy. I always say to myself, if I could only get out, like you and your..." Joe knew what Frank was going to say, and he made no comment or reference to it. He saw the sadness on Joe's face. Frank shook his head, and after a moment of silence between them he said, "So how's the kid? Goddammit, I miss that kid. He was like my own son, you know." "You mean you haven't heard from him?" Joe said with candor. "Not at all!" exclaimed Frank. "Not a word, and he knows how to reach me, in confidence, if he wanted to. I guess he don't want to?"

Joe bore a frown and said, "I think you're wrong, Frank. I mean over the years, each and every time I talked to him, he always asked about you, sincerely. You know, how are you doing, how's yer' health? And he asks me all the time if you ever tried to get in touch with him? 'Tell him to call me,' he always said, and I always say the same thing, that I never see you anymore. Besides, what difference does it make now?" Joe finished his sentence with a shrug. "Remind me when you leave, I'll give you the number," Joe said that without hesitation or worry. It was no secret that Tony was in Pennsylvania. Not hiding out but more or less trying to start a new life, away from gangs, crime, and violence. It was his mother's wish. No inference was ever made that he was on the lam, fearing for his life. "Anyhow, I hear he's doing real well, according to my brother Tomasino," Joe said emphatically and with an undertone of "Who the fuck needs you, Frank?"

Frank dawdled some as he poured more coffee then came right to the point. "Tell me, Joe. How come you never reached out about your brother?" Joe sensed the innocent but shrewd way Frank posed the question. "I don't mean it in the way your thinking." Batista could read his mind. He reached in his pocket and pulled out a pack of Luckys and shook a fresh butt out and grabbed it between his lips. "Not for revenge. Nothing like that but more of like…what happened? It's still a mystery at the camp you know—Ruggeri's club—to me anyway. I'm sure Ruggeri knows the truth." Joe gave him a bland look and said, "What's the point?" Joe still was up in the air about Frank's prying. Is it still enough of a mystery at the Pope's place that he sent an emissary to flush out more information and that Ruggeri does *not* know the entire truth? He hoped it was all put to bed by now. Joe raised his brow and said, "I knew my brother owed...and owed big. He told me. I even gave him ten large to help out. I knew he went to see Albie...for a pass, and to arrange terms."

They were both smoking cigarettes now, heavily. Frank became stern with his words. "I mean the shooting itself, Joe." Joe's eyes became wide as Frank continued. "You don't believe that bullshit theory about the gunfight at the 'ok corral,' now do ya?" "What else should I believe, Frank?" Joe sensed Frank's antennae up. "That's what the papers said...that's what Accardi said." Joe grimaced. Frank spoke openly and said, "You know I was at a meeting at Accardi's home away from home right after it happened. It was just him, me, and the Pope. Why me? 'Cause of the kid...they know how close he is to me, or was to me? They wanted my input about a vendetta... not about you so much but about Tony, your nephew, Cheese's son. They're the pricks with vendettas. And all the while they kept talkin' to me in riddles. I did find out that for some strange reason, Accardi had a tail on your brother all day." Joe's words became somber. "So why are you telling me this?" Joe felt the worst fear about Batista's visit was now over. He felt he was here somehow or someway asking for help, but not from Joe. It would be Tony's help he needed. "I know Accardi was the last one your brother saw," Frank said remorsefully. "Then it was Accardi that killed him—just as I thought. And I know it was my brother's dear friend Albie that set him up," Joe said wearily. "Well, no one knows that for certain, do they, Joe?" Joe was dumbfounded and tried to conceal his thoughts as Frank continued. "I was at the club when your brother called. Albie told me out of guilt, I guess...but he never really said anything. Just that the big guy was in trouble. And he wanted to set up some kind of meet. A surrender is the way Albert put it. In my opinion it was innocent on Albie's part, and I'm sure if he could turn back the hands of time, he would have straightened your brother's debt out with the Pope…that afternoon, if he had known what was gonna' happen." Joe just shrugged his shoulders and said, "It's what you guys do, Frank. And if you're here to goad me into some kind of retaliation against a cop, it's not gonna work. I've been out of the life too, too long." Frank smirked and said, "It ain't nothing like that, my friend." There was a silence; then Frank said with hostility in his voice, "He is no fucking cop… uh-uh. He comes at you over both sides of the fence." His voice was calm now. He lit another cigarette as he said, "I swear I think he's coming after me for something. I just have that feeling…a feeling of being tailed. And the Pope, I think he holds me personally responsible for the fifty Gs your brother owes." That comment got a rise from Joe as he said, "Is it on me, Frank?" He was referring to the debt. "No. No. No." Frank assured him. "Your name never comes up, Joe. They know you're just a citizen now and have been for the longest time." Frank's brow wrinkled as he continued. "Ya know, Joe…this thing of ours…it's not looking too promising lately. I'm getting bad vibes. And you know we feel that. I can feel it in my bones. There's a shit storm on the horizon." Frank might have exceeded his boundaries, so he thought, but he told Joe anyway about the secret wall safe Accardi has behind the movable bookcase. "Just like you see in the movies, Joe." Frank caught himself before his confession revealed too much true knowledge. "I'm still confused, Frank. What do you want from me?" Joe said.

Frank suddenly snapped out of the seemingly trance he was in. The resolute look on his face was gone, and he beamed. "So tell me, Joe, are you making any money with that car lot you opened up on the avenue? You never know. I may be in the market for a crash car or two." Joe said, "I just collect the rent from the Damato brothers. It's enough to cover the nut and put a few bucks in my pocket. But then again, Frank, I really don't need much anymore. I live a simple life." Frank became serious again and said, "Hey…we go back a long way.

I'm serious about that car thing…something reliable…but untraceable…like the stuff your brother sold." Joe extended a handshake and said, "You come see me, Tic, I'll take care of it." The two shook hands, hugged, and as Frank started to leave, he turned back around and said, "Oh…by the way, let me have that number for the kid, and let him know I'm gonna' reach out."

Frank Batista left the gas station slowly and purposely passed what have been the most logical route had he been headed home, the entrance to Route 22 east. His eyes were fixated on the rearview mirror of his Cadillac. The normal fifteen-minute ride back to North Newark would take him at least a half hour now as he made erratic turns up and down main avenues and back streets to detect or try to catch a pattern of a tail. He worried some about the outright lie he told to Joe. It was only last week Accardi applied a choke hold. He was speaking for the Ruggeri when he told Frank, "The Pope wants to know how you're gonna handle the Marino debt. He don't care where it comes from. The kid, the uncle, or you, so long as it comes…and fast…'cause you all should know, the juice is still running and it's adding up."

Frank Batista was acting overly paranoid, and whether or not it was justifiable was not up for debate. He knew his fear was warranted for obvious reason, and it engulfed his thoughts and kept him from falling asleep at night. He knew if not now, then someday it will come to fruition. His demise would eventually come if not by the hands of one of his peers then by the law. He had already secretly moved from his apartment on Park Avenue to a newly constructed, pricey high-rise on Mt. Prospect Street because the new complex boasted underground parking. He felt safe with the word association of anything *underground*. The apartment lease including the utilities and the phone was in the name of a second cousin on his mother's side, a gentleman of eighty-two years of age who was actually resting comfortably in a nursing home in Irvington, New Jersey, and also registered to the old boy was the 1958 Plymouth Belvedere parked in its assigned space.

Frank had come to realize that perhaps he had just too much on his plate. It was becoming increasingly harder to keep his fidelity with the Pope and the everyday business at hand with him and his covert operation and obligation with his cousin's drug business. It was becoming just too much of a juggle. Sooner or later the two were going to collide. His cousin was nonstop with the pressure for him to move more weight—the amount of heroin—just as the black dealers were doing in their wards of the city. The kilos of smack that Alonzo Coleman and Willie Johnson—extremely well-known, successful drug dealers were pushing—was astronomical and all secretly supplied by Breeze and his crew out of Brooklyn. And someone wanted to muscle in, Frank so ingeniously thought—this the reason for meeting his cousin Bobby had arranged Friday. "We're leavin' a lottsa' money on the table, cuz," exclaimed Breeze.

23

Josephina Cupido was getting ready to do exactly what every modern American homemaker was about to do—tune into the afternoon soaps. Women of all walks of life and in all parts of the country found hope and inspiration from the likes of the daily broadcast *Search for Tomorrow* and others like it. She even donned her very latest housedress for the occasion. The small-screen Admiral portable TV sat on the counter right next to the new GE refrigerator with the Coppertone finish and had been on since early this morning, and she wondered how she had gotten along all these years without one. It replaced the old Zenith box radio and was all part of the latest kitchen gadgetry lavished upon Aunt Josephina, compliments of her generous nephew, bribes as he put it to compensate for his ever so lazy but accepted lifestyle he was now accustomed to. And now Tony himself received the equivocal blame for instilling the newfound lifestyle of his aunt who was soon becoming in the words of Tomas "a materialistic monster." Both men agreed and considered her quite the hustler—whatever her cagey little heart wanted were coyly selected and circled in her copy of *Red Book Magazine*. What an act—so surprised when gifts arrived. All agreed Grandma Rosa benefitted the most. She was now receiving the very best doctor's care that money could buy. Her bedroom was equipped with an actual fully automatic hospital bed to ease with her mobilization. She sat comfortably in a much more modern wheelchair, and her bathroom was renovated to accommodate her handicap. Therapists and home-care nurses were brought to the farmhouse to aid and assist Josephina and give Grandma Rosa the managed and sanative care that she needed. Another of Tomasino's blights was, in addition, to Tony "way too much" for his room and board; the kid also kept his uncle with a constant supply of gifts as well. Nothing frivolous, mind you, but the things his uncle cherished most of all. Tony brought him up to date with the latest, most sophisticated hunting and fishing equipment money could buy; shotguns and rifles with ammo, bows and arrows, and all the incidental camouflaged clothing that fit every hunting season. Tony had a thirty-cubic-foot chest freezer installed in the basement for the game fowl and venison his uncle bagged, plus all the prime meats and lobster acquired from his job, line of work.

Tony bolted into the kitchen with a sort of lumbering grace of a prizefighter doing roadwork. He gave his aunt the ritual good morning kiss on the good side of her face accompanied by a gentle squeeze of her shoulders and said, "What do ya' say, Aunt Joe?" She was engulfed with the story line of her soap, and any little distraction broke her concentration. "Shhhh. Go get yourself some potatoes and eggs…on the stove. They're still hot," she barked. Tony lifted the cover off the cast-iron skillet and forked a piece of the frittata into his mouth. Then he piled a healthy serving on a dish and took a seat at the table.

The timing couldn't have been better. Tony gulped the last bit of frittata down when the phone rang. Aunt Joe cursed. "Who the hell is that calling this time of day…goddamn salesmen I betcha—you tell them we don't need anything." Tony cracked a huge smile and said, "I'll get it, Aunt. You just pay attention to that show of yours."

The voice on the other end of the phone was a familiar and a welcomed one. "Hey, kid…it's me," Frank said. Tony smirked into the receiver and said, "Well, I'll be…it's about time you called out here." Frank responded sharply, "Hey…the last time I checked this phone we're talkin' on works both ways." Frank could keep the charade of anger up for a second or two before he gave up a laugh. "Only kidding, it's good to hear your voice." "Same here, Frank. My uncle said you were gonna call. Oh, and for the record, I called you a couple of times, on the house line. It was disconnected." Frank let out a sigh and said, "Yeah. Yeah. Yeah. It's a long story. I moved from that place." The conversation between them went on for a good half hour. They both spoke to one another in a parable, almost secret code, as both feared the infamous wiretap. Frank voiced his concerns to the kid much like he did to Joe. He got the point across to Tony that the Pope expected restitution of the outstanding debt his father owed. How somebody had to pay. "You mean from me, Frank?" Tony asked. "You, me, your uncle, this prick is leaning on everyone. It's a matter of principle with this guy, and he will not let it go," Frank said.

But every once in a while the conversation would lighten up, and one could understand it was just a long overdue call of friendship. "So I'm hearing a lot of good things about you from the Pittsburgh pirates I know out there," Frank said. "They tell me you're becomin' a regular heavyweight contender…" The kid spoke with a say-so in his voice, "I gotta' say, Frank, things are going good…so far, knock on wood." There was a slight pause as Frank searched for some kind words to say. "So how old are you now?" Frank asked. "Twenty, but out here they all think I'm older," Tony said. "Jeez…where did the time go? Seems like just yesterday we were on the avenue together. So do they know who you are out there?" Frank asked. "They know. They all knew my old man. I guess that's why I fit in so well." Tony laughed and said, "They're like a bunch of hillbillies here, Frank.

They're not ready for the likes of us, I can tell you that." Frank said with a stern voice, "Don't take any chances. They're still ruthless and cunning. Don't let your guard down." Tony said in earnest, "You always got good advice, Frank." Frank hurried the conversation and said, "Look. I gotta' cut you short, but let's stay in touch and let me ask this, are you ever gonna' come back to these parts? I could use you." Tony fell silent for a second then said, "I been thinking about it. But I think I have to put a plan together, now especially after you told me of the fifty large." "I didn't mean to upset you, kid. I should have never told ya'," Frank said worriedly. "Don't be silly, Frank. You did the right thing. Now we just got to put our heads together," Tony said judiciously. Frank listened to every word from the kid's mouth and said, "Look, if it's about earning, I'll make sure you're gonna' be with me and me alone. There's still a lot of money to be made here. And I will square things with the Pope, I promise you."

Tony hung up the phone with his head spinning from the fretful conversation he just had with his old friend. His feelings were a combination of uncertainty and fear but quickly realized they were nothing more than a true mirrored reflection of Frank Batista's persona, a well-known worrywart. He glanced at the kitchen wall clock and said under his breath, "Shit…it's getting late." Then he bolted out of the kitchen and up the stairs.

As he showered, a thousand scenarios played out in his head about the one thing Frank did say that made a little sense. His father's abandoned debt. But what could the Pope possibly do to anyone over the now lost but not forgotten money? In the kid's mind his father had already paid his debt, with his life. And so did he, and the rest of his family. And they still are paying each and every day in the form of grief. Then he realized the Pope still needed someone to answer for the act of violence against the family. He sought more vengeance.

There was an unusual chill in the air, something rare this early in September. Tony looked up at the afternoon sky and saw nothing but blue. There was no need to worry about a storm. His short-sleeve Italian knit would be just fine for the task of the day at hand. His shoes crumbled the soft gravel on the driveway beneath his feet as he passed his uncle's parked Ford and his old sidelined Mercury. He swung open the barnyard doors of the garage that glided without effort or noise on the sturdy well-oiled hinges.

While most of his cronies and peers preferred the dynamics of their long Cadillacs, the kid opted to be true to the first brand and family of car he owned. He breezed past his new ebony-black Lincoln Mark II and admired her luster. His choice of Lincoln was one of aesthetics. He thought the Lincoln coupé to be the better-looking car, and as for the brand, he noticed that Lincoln was the choice of ride for the late President Kennedy and the rest of the Secret Service.

He headed to the back of the garage to where the workshop was located. He carefully dodged and walked around mounds of junk auto parts and barrels of metal scrap that lay in unkempt heaps on the right side of the shop. The garage had an almost savory smell of aged timber and motor oil. The left side of the workshop where the large workbench and well-organized wall of hand tools were was availed by a clean and neat pathway. Tony gingerly moved an old sealed paint can in a position next to a four-foot-high cast-iron safe that sat with its door wide open. He leaped up atop the safe and gently reached into an overhead rack that held an assortment of odd cut pieces of housing lumber and trim. He pulled out a neatly wrapped plastic package from the far back of the carefully arranged wood pile. Tony unwrapped the package, reached in, and removed a one-thousand-dollar stack of bills, took inventory of the seven other stacks, then carefully rewrapped it all and placed it back gingerly.

He folded the crisp money in half and placed it in his pocket. He walked over and stood by the sink next to the workbench and reached for the Ivory soap that sat next to the Boraxo on the shelf. At first he was startled by the crystal clear "Hahahahaha" that was evident of his father's echoing laughter and said, "I know, Pop… it's a far cry from the fifty Gs you owe….plus the vig! And when are we gonna' talk about revenge, or is that something you want to forget?" And as he began to back out his car a striking feeling of sorrow speared his heart. It came out of nowhere and was spawned by no conscious thought. He closed his eyes and a clear, crisp image of his brooding past appeared—his forgotten Joanie. It had been a long, long time since he thought of her in such a sudden and smitten way—as he now was with an agonizing, throbbing pain deep in his cold heart. It was Joanie he wished he was going to meet and not his cronies or his whores that surely are waiting. Destiny is not fair, he thought.

24

Tony Marino and Johnny LaRocca had just finished some scrambling collection calls of a few overdue customers. It was one of his least favorable tasks, the lost souls of gambling degenerates that fall prey to loan sharks and evil bookmakers and that were forever behind the eight ball. Much like his father was in his last days on earth. And by no means was he shy at all about the use of violence as a means of punishment on the enemies of his bosses, when ordered. But he would much rather let LaRocca dole out the punishment in this type of scenarios. The ambiguity of it all was Tony was capable of inflicting pain at will to those he thought deserved it but could not bring himself to harm a deer as his uncle so often did, nor could he hit a child or a woman.

The two found themselves on West Otterman Avenue and suddenly had the urge for some corned beef and cabbage served up as only the Irish knew how. A good meal then a visit to one of Monestero's whorehouses, which was, to young mobsters, a perfect Saturday night.

Lillie's was an old established true Irish pub that specialized in imported beer and ales, and of all other things, corned beef and cabbage. Its roots dated back to the turn of the century, and it survived the Prohibition era by becoming a solid mob-operated speakeasy. The owner of the well-received family establishment, Bill Flynn, was tending bar and recognized LaRocca as soon as he walked in. He too recognized the mid-fortyish Irishman who stood above all that were bellied up too his bar. LaRocca gave Tony a slap on the arm then pointed to the area Flynn was standing. Flynn was over six feet tall and had a full head of dark, almost black hair. He spoke with a touch of the brogue that was slightly hampered by a flattened nose that stopped one too many fists. "Now if it's a debt you're here to collect, boys, I think you got the wrong place." The joking Flynn let out a roar and said, "What keeps you away for such a long time?" LaRocca shook his hand and said, "I guess the same thing that keeps you away from our dice game." "Well, if its money you're talkin' about, you may be right."

A young, attractive barmaid came up behind the two men and stood impatiently with a drink tray filled with empty beer mugs. Tony was the tallest and the widest, but it was the shorter, more stocky LaRocca who, to her dismay, was blocking her pickup area. She made a couple of honest attempts to hold the tray sideways and gently ease her way in, and when that did not avail, her Irish leaped out, "Well, Flynn. Are you going to let these guys serve drinks tonight, since they're both standing at my station and in my way?" She lambasted. Tony spun around in the direction of the pert voice and froze. His eyes looked down into hers. He noticed her petite size and the soft round mounds of her prevalent cleavage that peered out of her uniform. He gave her a soft smile and said, "Are we in your way, princess?" He stepped aside and gently tugged her in between himself and LaRocca. LaRocca reached up and removed his felt fedora exposing his bald head. He made a sweeping jester with his arm. "There, is that better?" he said sarcastically.

The barmaid ignored the mobster and stepped in closer to Tony. She was mesmerized. She too looked into his dark eyes and searched for words. "Princess?" she said questioningly with a sultry tone in her voice. "What makes you think I'm a princess?" Tony reached out and softly caressed the side of her face with his fingers and directed her eyes straight into his. "Your mother never read you any fairy tales when you were a little girl?" He spoke even more tenderly and almost childlike as he gave the locks of her hair a playful twirl. "You look just like a fairy tale princess." His words were sincere and captivating. He spoke to her with his lips slightly pouty. "Hasn't anyone ever told you that before? All you need is one of those pointy hats with the silk tassels." There was a silence between them; clearly they were both smitten. "So do you have an order for me, lassie?" Flynn asked, which she ignored. Tony ignored the bartender as well and put his lips to her ear as he whispered, "So what's your name?" She pulled back but found herself in his grasp. He held the back of her arm and gently squeezed her bare skin. "Cathleen," she said then smirked. "Call me Cathy." Tony put on his best smile and said, "Cathy, me and my friend here are going to sit down at the end of the bar and have a bite to eat. Now I know you can't join us, but sometime before we leave, maybe you can write your phone number down. If you're willing, that is. I would love to get to know you. That is of course *if* you are available?"

She watched as the two men made their way to the far end of the bar and took the last two seats next to the kitchen door. This was a semi-dive Irish bar that has never seen the likes of these two guys, and he was the type of guy, although he sounded to her like he was full of shit, that girls like her only read about…in storybooks. She played coy and kept her eyes front as she waited for Flynn to finish his rounds and service her. "Just who are those guys, Flynn?" she asked. Flynn paused at first then said scornfully, "They're mobsters, Italian mobster. And do yerself a favor and steer clear of 'em."

Cathy watched from a distance as the two sat and ate. She noticed the conversation that the two were having seemed to be held from behind closed doors. They communicated to each other almost in a sign language, and when words were exchanged, they seemed to be in secretive whispers as each man would take turns talking into one another's ear with a cupped hand held to their mouths. Her intrigue was fired up as the words of Flynn repeated in her head: "They're mobsters."

Her eyes were fixated and fastened on the well-dressed young man with the dark wavy hair. She watched secretly as he ate: his mannerisms, the way he chewed his food and sipped his beer almost as if it were a crystal flute of champagne. Her initial thought was that he was indeed a gentleman. She guessed him to be around her age, twenty-five—maybe more. It was nice to see some new young blood in a tavern that catered to mostly older working-class Irishmen and their wives. And to date, no one has ever caught her fancy as this kid did.

The men gulped down the last swig of ale from the pint glass and ordered two cognacs. Flynn's face bore a perplexed look as he scanned the shelves hoping to find a suitable brand. Tony had been watching Cathleen all the while he sat, but not letting on a bit. He studied her every move as she sashayed, almost dance-like, from table to table, taking orders. She served all the alcohol while two other girls ran food orders from the kitchen, a wise decision on Flynn's part.

His eyes fixated on the flowing side-to-side motion of her pronounced hips and watched as she sometimes leaned over, showing off that great ass and the complementing cleavage that she had. Tony hoped her almost rehearsed actions were for his eyes only. And without warning or announcement a fresh bouquet of applied cologne drifted above the aromas of both beer and corned beef and entered his nostrils. Gingerly, a slightly freckled hand and tiny wrist slid under his arm and placed a neatly folded bar napkin into his cupped hand. "Now that is not to wipe the mustard off your mouth. So don't mess it up or lose it," Cathy jokingly said as she vanished into the kitchen. Tony glanced at the phone number written in ink and stuck it between the wads of cash he carried in his left hand pocket.

It would take three attempts for him to finally reach Cathy on the phone the next afternoon. "Finally. I thought you were ducking my calls. It was gonna' be three strikes and yer' out, kiddo," he said jokingly. That turned out to not be the case at all. She explained her schedule kept her away from home with the exception of the early morning hours and her days off, which were Tuesday and Sunday. "And Sunday is my day to sleep in," Cathy chimed. They spoke for about twenty minutes or so, and he related to her that although he could literally talk to her for hours, it should be in person and not on the phone. His dislike and distrust in good old Ma Bell carried throughout his life. They did, however, get a lot of the preliminaries out of the way.

His amusement lit up when he found out her last name. "Carluccio! Never would I have guessed it with that red hair of yours. Half Irish…well, that has to be better than being half Polish," he said. She blurted out the obvious "I knew it" when he told her he was from New Jersey. "Like your accent won't give you away!" she exclaimed. They both lied about their ages, her younger and him older of course—by way of force of habit. He listened with half an ear as she gave him the play by play of how she left college during her second semester and moved from Pittsburgh with her fiancé. "What did you expect from the Medigans?" Tony bellowed. That statement forced a bewildered and lost look to come over her.

Tony spoke only a little about his personal situation—how he lived for the time being on a farm with his aunt and uncle and for reasons he could not discuss at this point in time. He did forewarn her, however, that like her his work schedule was taxing and occupied most of his time, which is why he does not have a steady girlfriend. "And besides, I haven't been lookin' around here too much. Maybe when I go up near Pittsburgh," he said with a laugh. "So what do you do for work?" she asked. "I sell heavy farm equipment." He lied again. She smirked and said, "I heard you were a mobster." "Well, that's only in case the farmers I deal with get tough with me." Her smile leaped through the phone. "I don't care what you do." "So it's a date then." He confirmed. She yelled back, "A date? When did I say I was going to go out with you?" as she bit her lip with excitement. "Tuesday...I'll call you Tuesday, okay." "What's wrong with calling me Monday night to see if I'm going to be available Tuesday?" she said with sass and confidence. Tony was acting submissive, only because he was captivated. "I'll be working all day Monday, but I will make time to call you, sweetheart. Who knows, I may need an alibi," he said with a slight smirk in his voice. "Listen to you, an alibi...well, make sure it's after eleven," she snapped. "I don't get home until then." Tony surrendered and said, "All right. But remember the three-strike rule."

Cathy Carluccio's standing reputation in and around Greensburg was squeaky clean as Tony secretly found out through the best syndicate stoolies that money could buy. And as he had suspected from his own intuition and nosing around, there were no scandals. No skeletons in her scant closet. No jealous boyfriend or soon-to-be ex-husbands looming. Just as he hoped it would be. There was not a single soul or neighborhood busybody that could find anything bad to say about the girl. Perhaps no one wanted to speak out of turn? She had no prior police record, not even a traffic citation as far as anyone could tell.

But some risqué rumors were bound to pop up. Many thought her to be married to the young fellow that once lived with her in the small apartment on West Fourth Street. She kept to herself in such a way that a lot of her neighbors did not know that her beau had moved away. Her life consisted of some shopping in the local markets and driving her almost ten-year-old Ford Fairlane to and from work. She put in long hours at the pub, and there also had a reputation of being genial but at the same time a little standoffish. Many thought of her as a prude. Some exchanged whispers of her being a lesbian. She would not tolerate rude, drunk men that would want to sometimes get a little frisky under the guise of romanticism, and she would be applauded for the occasional drink tossed in someone's face.

There were only a handful of chosen friends both here and at home that knew of Cathy's hardly scandalous personal, dull, and honest lifestyle. When and if Cathy socialized, it was usually with the girls from work and their friends—now considered hers as well. She only recently tried dating just two carefully selected partners her friends had recommended but found them just not right. And as far as sex went, being a young, healthy woman of twenty-nine, well, she knew she was way overdue.

Cathy pranced around her apartment with the effervescence of a prima donna ballerina, trying on fashion flawed, bargain basement dresses until she found the one most suited—it actually complemented the natural curves of her womanly attributes' body class. It would not be for another six hours before her date with the young man she had met at the pub. but the anticipation made her antsy. Nancy was the only one told of the upcoming get-together and swore secrecy. "He called me last night, just as he promised," she exclaimed to Nancy. Cathy wanted to see just what type of gentleman, or mobster, as Flynn put it, this guy was going to turn out to be and did not want to hear the familiar and bane "I told you so." "Don't worry, Nancy. I have plenty of dimes in my purse, and I will be calling you if he's anything but a gentleman. I'm not that kind of girl, and I hope he knows it." Cathy allowed herself plenty of time to pick up around her apartment then go and relax in a nice, hot bubble bath. A three-year-old white and red polka dot dress that she hardly ever wore was laid out on her bed as was a soft button-up red sweater.

Cathy sat composed on her pale yellow Danish-style sofa with her sweater draped neatly over the arm. She had the TV set turned off and the radio volume softly set playing the "top twenty countdown" according to Clark Race and his KDKE radio station. Her heart sank just a little as the Marvelette's hit "Playboy" got announced and began playing. Cathy fought off the inquisitiveness of her female nature for a long while but now had no other choice but to mull over just what type of girl this young man was accustomed to. She wondered if he was ever married. No. Too young for that, but you never could know. She herself was months away from matrimony. Why worry about it, she said to herself. She would find out soon enough.

Keeping with wise guy traditions, Tony did not date as the young adult crowd would describe it. He soon found out that trying to date normal nine-to-five office girls, college girls, or girls working in factories did not mix with his nocturnal schedule or the type of nightlife he and his cronies were accustomed to. He mostly had affairs and liaisons and intimacies with showgirls, waitresses, and prostitutes, mostly prostitutes from his first arriving in Greensburg and under the supervision of his uncle Tomasino until now. This was the way of life in the underworld and was accepted by all men and even a few of their suspecting wives. The sex trade was a thriving empire in the entire mob-controlled cities, and Greensburg had its entitlements. The kid was immediately drawn to the seedy, forsaken souls of the young and sometimes older prostitutes and thoroughly enjoyed their company, as did they him. Tony soon had his favorites and steadies that would greet and welcome his sexual prowess with open arms and open legs. There were no questions asked or chastising from angry, disappointed girlfriends. This type of liaison would be touted and heralded a date by any and all just as he thought they were. And he held in high esteem the words of wisdom of Mr. Frank Sinatra: "Treat a lady like a whore and a whore like a lady." Both parties soon would concede and consider their sessions of actual raw uninhabited sex more of lovemaking rather than an arrangement, and over time the sessions would become sacred as each offered to one another a tender accord, a shared passion; an almost human dignity was bestowed upon his whores. And this was the brand of lovemaking he learned.

Tony Marino stood sideways, in her doorway, cocky and ever so sure of himself, waiting for her to answer his rhythmic knock. He was dressed meticulously in a dark blue Valentino cut suit that accentuated his broad shoulders. Under the suit was a light blue Italian knit long-sleeve shirt with the white piped collar folded over his lapel. His wavy black hair glistened from applied pomade. His head was cocked slightly to the right and a devilish smirk on his half-puckered lips. "Here…these are for you," he said as he extended his arm out with a bouquet of lilacs. "I always see the guys do this in the movies, you know, show up with flowers in their hands,so I thought I'd give it a try. Plus, I like the color." Cathy was taken but acted leery as she said, "So I'm the first?" "That I ever brought flowers to? You are the first, kiddo." He pouted his lips and blew her an airy kiss then said with a broad, sincere smile, "You gonna' let me in or what?" He immediately thought just how good she looked in her flared and figure-enhancing dress. She read it in his ogling eyes, and she intentionally struck a vogue pose for him. And as teasingly were her intentions, he winked and gave her a wolfish whistle. Cathy spoke with a frivolous tone, "I don't know if I ought?" Tony then gave her a little nudge as he stepped inside the flat. His eyes casually drifted over the somewhat contemporary style of furniture as he commented, "Nice place you have here, Cathy. Oh, and by the way, if my drooling mouth or fluttering heart hasn't indicated, you look simply gorgeous. " He moved farther into her place and said again, "Nice place." His tone was comfortably affectionate, but his eyes were still ogling—she blushed.

She picked up on his bestial connotation of "let's just stay here tonight." *I will give him no wrong ideas of that kind of behavior,* she thought to herself. And to change direction, she said unemotionally, "Let me have the flowers please, I'll put them in some water." She turned her back and lit into the kitchen. No one has ever given her flowers before, and she scrambled for a container or vase. A mason jar would have to do. Her eyes gleamed as she took in the aroma of the lilacs and was completely aware he was watching with prowess.

She fought off any thoughts of lust or romance that was indeed brewing in her own heart. And to further rid his mind of any more amorous thoughts she spoke from the kitchen as she walked directly to the front door and roosted, "So just what are your plans for tonight?" Cathy shied away from eye contact. She picked up her sweater that was on the couch and began to slip an arm through the sleeve. Suddenly as if on cue, she felt his hands take over and begin to mold her into the sweater then finished with a tender cuddle of her shoulders, her already quivery shoulders

"Well, for one thing," he said as he opened the front door of her apartment, "I hope you're hungry." Thank God, she thought. She was famished. She thought of the dimes in her purse and giggled to herself. *He's taking me out to dinner.* She was in a trance. She heard Tony's voice, but the words he spoke became addled in her mind as she inadvertently asked, "What?"

Cathleen was in awe of the shiny black Lincoln coupé she was climbing into and the gentlemanly act of him opening the door for her. "Nice car," she said with a slow, deliberate delivery. "You like it?" he replied with a slight bluster in his voice. "I just got it. I said to myself as soon as I earn a good payday, I'm gonna' treat myself, and I did." Tony slid behind the steering wheel and said almost impatiently, "I say let's go to the movies first. Then out to eat. I know the joint to eat, you pick a movie, fair enough?" She glinted. "Deal." And off they went. The only movie showing downtown was a corn ball escapade starring Doris Day and Rock Hudson. It had just a tad of wholesome family valued sexual innuendo that forced both he and Cathleen into a natural snuggle.

Beginning from the moment Tony had picked her up and throughout the entire evening, he studied her as if she was a painting, a work of art, and not once was he detected. He was looking for a flaw in her celestial beauty and could not find one. As they drove his natural intuitiveness placed his hand on hers. She turned and gave a subtle smile. In the darkness of the interior, her face had a sultry shadowing from the faint streetlights and oncoming traffic. 'You like Italian food?" he asked. She returned a frolicsome type of wide-eyed nod. "Then I'll take you to this place I know, Denunzio's, how's that sound—ever been there?" Again as if in a trance, she silently nodded no. Tony reached for Cathy's hand with confidence and gave it a longer, gentler caress. She lifted her hand off the seat cushion and accepted his offer, and with a steadfast and almost impulsive urge by both, their hands were divinely intertwined. "It's a real good Italian restaurant. You'll like the food." This guy knows how to treat a lady, she thought to herself. A movie and a real dinner, all in the same night, what more could a girl ask for? Her inner feelings turned quickly from intimidation to an almost natural and genuine reposeful calm, an almost euphoric feeling of delight. Had she been drugged? Her response, though only seconds from his asking, seemed to her hours late. "I've never been there." "You're gonna' love it. I promise you," he said. Cathy then spun her head in his direction and said, "I've never even heard of the place." She laughed silently about her purse full of nickels and dimes—how embarrassing if he knew. Cathy felt and acted as if she knew Tony all her life. He made her feel incredibly comfortable and safe—for now anyway.

The hour was approaching eleven o'clock by the time they pulled into the parking lot of Denunzio's Chop House, and this seemed oh so normal to her date, not a sense of urgency at all. She, on the other hand, was now completely famished. He handed his keys to an attendant along with a folded ten-dollar bill and whispered instructions. With swaying hips and a distinctive pout, her growing concern for dining so late was written all over her face as he quickly read and said with a wink of his eye, "Don't worry about it, kiddo, when 'yer hungry, your stomach has no idea what time it is."

Tony was well received by the owner and the rest of the staff as he walked in, all asking how he and his uncle and the rest of the crew have been. A female cocktail waitress gave special attention. Cathy felt spellbound by the character of the restaurant. She was captivated by the obvious aromas of the food as she watched it hustled out of the kitchen by the attentive wait staff. And she was amazed at just how hustle bustle the place was for a Tuesday night, especially at this hour. Introductions were doled out, and they the couple was escorted to what seemed to be his favorite table in the most secluded far end of the restaurant. "I guess you come here a lot," Cathy asked inquisitively. Tony gave her a smile and said amusingly, "About once a week." Then he bounced his head as if counting and said, "Me and my aunt, my uncle, my *mobster* friends." She laughed off his smart aleck words then quickly sized up the place. It was as atypical of the newly introduced "rat pack" late-night supper crowd, lots of men in suits with scantily clad woman, much younger woman, sitting at their side. And some of the patrons, in her estimation, not knowing for sure but safely assuming by the glamour and glitz of their clothing, shoes and cufflinks, were a mixed bevy of entertainers and show people from the surrounding cabarets. Tony recognized her enamor of the place. He felt his ego expand, and for the most part, with the exception of a few hookers, she was the first true girlfriend he has ever brought into the dining room. The effervescent glow in his eyes was ever so profound.

As the couple sat and ate a starter course of lobster and shrimp prepared scampi style and sipped some Pinot Grigio, a waiter appeared out of nowhere with an order of stuffed mushrooms covered with lump crabmeat. "Our compliments," he said to Tony as he laid them gently at the corner of the table. Soon to follow was a steaming plate of gnocchi in a light pomodoro sauce with a house specialty of veal prepared three ways, accompanied by a plate of sautéed spinach and roasted potatoes. Tony was adamant about the plates of food reaching the table at the same time and the waiters obliged.

Cathy was in awe of the attentive service they received. It was something never experienced by the customers who ordered in the rash and snappy pub she worked. She wondered perhaps if it was because of who or what he was, or did everyone there get such a royal reception? As she looked around at the dozen or so late-night diners, the answer was crystal clear.

The small four-piece combo was on a break when Tony and Cathy arrived, and for most of their dinner their music was non-existent, at least to them anyway. After their last break, when they returned and took the stage, the announcement was made, "This is going to be our last set, so if you haven't got on the floor…" He caught her trying to hold back a yawn and said, "Come on, little girl. It's time to dance." The group broke into their rendition of "More." She was literally swept off her feet and carried onto the dance floor. He showed no qualms of his intentions as he held her body firmly against his, and soon both became one as they found the rhythm of the music and of each other's movements. He led her gently and she followed precisely to the only sensual two-step slow dance he knew, one taught to him by the whores.

His hands followed the smooth contour of her arms and back then stopped and rested on her hips. He gave them a slight jostling then let his right hand drop just below her buttocks as he pulled her up closer. She wrapped her arms tightly around his neck and tried hard to pull his towering body to hers. The lingering aroma of the soft soap she bathed with along with the scent of her perfume was ever so prevalent.

Tony became immediately aroused and rubbed his erect penis purposely into her inner thighs. She tried to thrust herself into the hardness she felt, and as they danced, they kissed. First, just a slight nibble with the lips, then hard and deliberate moist kisses. She was intrigued as to why his breath did not reek of the mounds of garlic they ate as she suspected hers did. Both openly tasted the fruitiness of the wine they drank with dinner. And to the chagrin of all the dancers on the tiny dance floor, the music ended with the standard sign off of the house band, some rinky-dinky ending of a vaudevillian-type comedy.

Both agreed that no dessert would be necessary as their appetites were sated, but a couple of glasses of *anisette* were in order. The warm licorice taste soothed Cathy's throat as it went down. And for the first time of trying the much bragged about liqueur, she truly enjoyed it, so another was duly ordered.

The excellent wine, the liqueur, the entire evening, put Cathy in a wistful mood. The waiter left the black leather folder that held the check gently on the table then graciously bowed to both. 'Thank you." She in an unshy but jesting manner reached for it. Tony grabbed her hand with unabashed force and with a smirk and a disciplining voice said, "There's an old mobster custom that whoever reaches for the check had better have the money to pay the bill, and I don't think that small change jingling in your purse will cover it—and don't think I don't know what it's for either. A cab woudda' cost a lot more money." And as busted as she was on all counts, so embarrassed, and almost resenting his snide comment that began to erase the bliss of the night, she offered a chaste explanation, "I just wanted to get an idea of what I would have to save if I ever wanted to take you here for your birthday." Tony began another chastising. He expressed his unrelieved dislike of birthdays, especially his own, and asked her please "don't ask why." She took his words to heart and sympathized to the obvious hurt that must have come his way—she could also read eyes.

Tony stood and extended his hand to his lovely date and said, "Well, baby, I'd love another dance, but the band went home. Look, the waiters are yawning more than you are. It's time to hit the road." His hands found her petite waist and he eased her into a dance position. "Now we can hit another all-night afterhours joint, go for coffee, go home—your call." She pulled him close to her and turned their sans orchestra dance step toward the exit. In that instant, she pondered and thought hard of her self-analysis of the evening—their first date, it was more than nice, and the lustful almost needful inner voice egged her on. And she knew, in that split second as he took a firm hold of her, what happens next. "No...it's your call," she said seductively.

What the hell had gotten in to her? Am I delirious? Both upright questions, she asked of herself. It was such a natural feeling—he is such a natural feeling. She offered no contrivable explanation to her questioning self. She would let this young guy sitting next to her, somewhat of a stranger, just pull over and take whatever part of her he desired. She nestled her head into his chest and waited as he threw his arm over her shoulder and began caressing whatever his senses found.

It was close to 2:00 a.m. when Lincoln's mighty V8 engine shut off, and Tony wiggled the little girl fast asleep in his arms. "Time for bed, princess." It was a short walk from the car to her doorstep. Cathy slipped her key into the lock and gave it a twist. The door crept open under her weight and she turned to her date. "Thanks for a really nice time," she said with deeply lidded eyes, and as expected, Cathy felt a genuine warmth deep inside as he forcefully pulled her into his arms. He spoke soft and sincere as he said, "You ain't getting away that easy. What would this all be without a good night kiss?" Both melted into one another as they had found themselves on the dance floor earlier, mouths seductively joined in long lustful kisses. Suddenly the sleepiness flew from her mind. She acted first and pulled him inside her small apartment. Tony kicked the door shut as they embraced one another, a feat so often seen in motion pictures and one he so perfected.

He followed her lead toward the bedroom and then took control. He gently laid her down on her bed, his hands caressing the soft cloth of her dress in long salacious movements, then her naked skin as he slowly and bit by bit undressed her. She wholeheartedly submitted. His hands fondled and caressed her delicately until he was under her panties and his fingers penetrating as deeply as humanly possible, his mouth and tongue orally massaging the soft mounds of her milky-white breasts, then on her fleshy pink nipples, her freckled stomach until he found himself between her thighs.

Their passion for each other carried into the wee hours of the morning until they finally collapsed in each other's arms. Complete exhaustion hadn't given Cathleen any time at all in the aftermath to think or reflect upon what just had happened—and she would cross that "I never did this with anyone…ever" bridge in the morning as she slipped into a blissful deep sleep.

Morning had already passed and the hour was approaching noon as the two unraveled from another rascal-type lovefest. Tony gave a look of miscreant bravado to his image in her bathroom mirror then emptied his bladder. Cathy anticipated his need for coffee and was already partially dressed in a short-short type of PJ set and at the stove. She heard the toilet flush a few times and then running water, gargling, spitting. Tony exited the bathroom with his hair slicked back wearing just his boxer shorts. He walked into the tiny kitchen as if he owned the place and said jokingly, "If we're going to make a habit of this, I'm gonna' need my own toothbrush and you're gonna' need a lot more toilet paper." She gave him a bewildered look and said, "You used my toothbrush?" He looked back with a bold cocksure look on his face. "Sweetheart, I think it's a little late to be worrying about germs between us two, don't you?"

Cathy's face was at first contrite then beguilement forced a burst of nervous, almost apologetic laughter. Her head dropped as she spoke in pauses, "I don't know what—what got into me last night—I—Ohhh—never—" Tony cut her short with a boyish grin. Her face bore a look of complete innocence as she blushed and looked up into his eyes. His pointed finger gently touched her lips, and he almost purred a soft "Shhhh, you don't need to explain a thing. I got into you last night." His odious tone of voice and squinting eyes got a hellacious laugh from her. He pulled her into his arms in a fondling embrace. "And I plan on doin' it a lot more, that is if you'll have me."

As the budding love affair progressed, Tony found himself juggling clumsily all of his time and all of his lies between the farmhouse and the loving arms of Cathleen Carluccio. Cathy, as she was more commonly called, was his latest conquest and to date the one girl he was the most serious with. The two young lovers would eventually become a solid newsworthy couple. Never had the lovebug bitten a couple as impetuously and blindly as it did these two. He had not ever experienced such wanton passion as he did with this feisty strawberry blonde. Perhaps because she was half Italian, half Irish, but it was the Irish gene and trait that prevailed. It was the Irish heritage that gave her a fiery personality along with long naturally wavy reddish-blonde hair and an almost radiant red, slightly freckled skin tone. It was this *Irish* that turned him on sexually as soon as he would see her, along with her big blue eyes, pink pouty lips, and her perfectly rounded *Irish* ass and nipples so pink even the best bred Holland tulips would be jealous.

Over the course of a few short months Tony had set up another complete household at Cathy's apartment, and by Christmas, his pageant of generosity to her was evident in every room of her small and cramped flat. Her slightly worn Scandinavian-style couch was the first thing that Tony replaced when he more or less took over her apartment, and it wouldn't be the last. He chose to make vast improvements to her lifestyle and to the decor and conveniences about her tiny flat in a relatively short amount of time. He was never thrilled about her place or her choice of thrown-together furniture. Her contemplation, her sorrow, was, is he doing all of this to please her or to satisfy his own larger than life ego? And this she found annoying. He notched out a small section of the closet for his just essential clothing and laughed at the occupied amount of space she held. Her answer was a glib one. "Well, stop buying so much, I can only wear one thing at a time." In spite of it all, she did have her moments of selfishness as she gloated over the colorful trousseau of sportswear, pantsuit, frilly dresses, and evening wear, and about a dozen pairs of matching shoes and handbags all neatly arranged in her closet.

Be it as it my, over time, Cathy began a constant tug of war between herself and of her newfound love's gluttonous generosity and became openly dismayed as to the way he spent money limitlessly—like it was going out of style. And this jealousy or envy applied to all others he gave to as well. This narcissistic worry, this semi-jealous hatred for materialistic things, soon manifested in her voice and her innermost self; this character trait, unbeknownst to her at the time, would lead to their downfall.

She set parameters, or tried to at least. She refused his offer of a newer car for her to drive. And she would secretly bring gifts of jewelry and other superficial trinkets back to the stores for refunds. Her eyes would sometimes roll at the amounts of money he would tip just about everyone who did even the slightest favor. She always suggested that if he should put the money he threw away in a savings bank, he might have something one day. He explained somewhat the reasoning why he couldn't or wouldn't. "Well, at least I don't gamble" would be his profound defense, a direct reflection of dislike of what his late father would do with his own money. "You would really bitch then, wouldn't you?"

As much as the Cathleen tried so hard to stay spiritually connected, Tony realized it was his maliciousness that as of late was causing their fondness of each other to become frayed. She was growing increasingly intolerant of his life and position within the Monestero family, a life she was now so very well aware of. Her complaint was that she felt duped into believing Tony led an honest life and now to accept his ways was weighing heavy on her God-fearing Catholic soul. She caught offensive overtones and innuendoes of the importance of being a made guy. She cringed at the thought of what crimes they commit, their talk of whores and girlfriends on the side. She loathed his friends as she loathed the cheap ass grabbers in the pub—she was well warned of his behavior but could not resist the charm.

His answer to all of this was to keep her isolated and away from it the best he could. And that could only be accomplished by his staying away from her, her apartment, and her ever-growing intolerable demands for a normal life consistent with what she recognized as such. And the meditative thoughts they once had of moving into a larger, more luxurious-type apartment was now not even a mentioned afterthought.

Tony understood her feelings most of the time and in his own fashion. He was for the most part compassionate—that emotion he knew well, especially when it came to apologies, of which he offered many. He had the patience of a saint, but he refused to go faster than one day at a time with their relationship now for his silent reasons and that irked her. She was a woman in her mind, and she recognized that he was a little boy in a big, tough guy's body and thought that if this was going to work out between the two of them, he was going to have to change. In her mind she would nurture the fact that what man is he that could make love to her as passionately as he did without a sincere desire to be with her, in a true and eternal relationship, as read about in storybooks? And she being the princess he so often referred to as? Perhaps, as with all naive young girls, it was just wishful thinking? She was now sensing he had a different agenda.

Tony kept raw, physical passion and love, as he understood them to be, both separate entities in his life. Truthfully, love and sexual passion as he recognized the two are worlds apart but must play off one another to be successful. The love of his life, his father, was gone as was the domestic and imported street life of Newark and his Bloomfield Avenue that he cherished and missed so dearly. And for the most part his mother's love was also gone. And there was Joanie, who he truly still pined for with a sincere passion and burning desire, a lost love that never came to be. He could only use his imagination to create in his mind the fantasy of how that would have played out. There was not a single day gone by that he did not close his eyes and think strongly of her. Her soft scent and tender bronze skin that he so briefly encountered was still etched deeply in his heart and memory. When he envisioned Joanie, he thought of her with reverie. And with Cathy, on many a night as he cuddled next to her in bed with closed eyes; he would passionately imagine Joanie next to him. She was thought of in a completely different light than his Cathy. He could only picture her as she was then, on the last day he saw her, as she sat next to him in the backseat of her cousin's station wagon—and now he regrets not kissing her, completely, at that exact moment, that warm August afternoon that now seemed so long, long ago. And to date every girl, every woman, he'd ever been with—woman that could more than satisfy any man and that any man alive would be ever so grateful to have, and though he loved them all to a degree, they were not Joanie. And now, for his heart's sake, Joanie must become only a fragmented afterthought in his mind, of a dream, or a book read, or he'll surely go insane. But the chances of that, a sheer impossibility, and he knows that for the rest of his natural life, he will always pine for and summon and conceive in his mind different chimeras of a lost love that never came to be.

It was beginning to evolve into a picture-perfect evening in late May throughout this rural part of New Jersey. A gentle warm breeze and serene quietness brought comfort to all who welcomed it. The setting sun still lit pathways on the ground of the colorful hues of springtime. It was well past dinnertime as dusk was starting to settle in over the township of Warren and the Jankowski household. The family scattered about to their own private nooks throughout the Victorian-style home that they lived. Henri retreated to the cellar to piddle with his tools and sip a little homemade wine he recently acquired while his wife finished the dishes. And then she would comfortably curl up on her couch to watch television. Joanie would retreat to her absolute favorite spot of the entire house. Joanie chose to sit outside on the wicker rocking chair in the rear corner of the home's spacious porch. The painted flooring of the porch sat up above a full flight of steps then wrapped itself around the front and both sides of the house. It was adorned by six fluted columns that ran the perimeter and everything joined to a sturdy railing that seemed to give the family and friends sitting a safe and secluded barrier from the rest of the wilderness that was their front and backyards. It was a stately veranda, reminiscent of a grand southern plantation manor tucked away under a tall canopy of green trees. It was a place Joanie could just sit and read a book or simply idle away the hours as she was doing right now and laughing to herself about her conviction to do so through all types of weather. Even the dead of winter could not deter her from meditating outside. Nor the hot, humid summer days or nights that swarmed with mosquitoes and would send an occasional harsh and intense thunderstorm—or a brilliant and titillating electrical display of Mother Nature that she cherished so. Then patiently waiting for the perfect evening such as tonight was for reminiscing.

Joanie could remember vividly how she at first hated this part of the country when the family arrived. It was wintertime then or almost winter as she remembered it to be. Trees were bare of their once green colored canopy—huge trees with twisted and eerie branches that would, as the wind blew, try to reach out and grab for you in a ghostly way. Trees that seem dead, with only small sections of withered leaves, all a drab brownish color, the rest rained down with every gust of wind until they covered every inch of the ground then raked and piled high as mountains along the road sides and in front of the residential homes. Often the dead, dried leaves were burned in large in trash cans by the neighbors, and thick smoke would add to the already dark, dreary sky. The surroundings this time of year were so reminiscent to Joanie of the story about Ichabod Crane and of Halloween that was just around the corner.

When Joanie first learned to drive, she would dread the long, winding single or double roadways that cut through the rolling hills and forest. Confusing roads that seemed never ending and would always get her and her mother lost. She remembered how long it would take to just run down to a grocery store that seemed and was miles away. And having to memorize landmarks of open fields or country barns or other rural reminders, a row of mailboxes or a church steeple were always road markers as to where to turn. And the horror of driving up and over rolling hills of snow-covered asphalt along with the fear of running into a white-tailed deer—and that was always present, all year long. Girlfriends were not just up the street anymore. They were huge distances away. Even next-door neighbors were acres apart, but this was the attraction—the charm of the country. But now the richness of a glorious spring was abound with bright colors and brilliant greens and made all feel glad to be alive with a profound certainty, in Joanie's heart at least, for now she would never consider trading her Warren Township or her Jersey Shore for any other part of the country.

Joanie was in deep thought on her porch this night. Her solemn thoughts were vividly imagining how it would have been had she grown up in this house, as a younger child, playing for countless hours on end on this very porch. As Joanie grew closer to womanhood, her grand porch was becoming even more of a mystical place to her. She hoped to have children of her own that would one day enjoy her sanctuary as she did and still does. And she could picture little ones riding tricycles, playing tag, or even roller-skating around their grandparents' porch—no, no, no, it was still her porch, still her private world where she would still run and hide and meditate and pout sadly over the boy she left behind in her old neighborhood.

The rumbling sound of the gas guzzling V-8 engine could be heard from a block away and forced the most distasteful look from Joanie as she could manage to put on her pretty face. She shook her head and felt the curled ends of her short-styled bouffant hairdo brush the sides of her face. If she were a few years younger, she would use the term *yuck* for her now steady boyfriend Jimmie Breuer. She only had herself to blame for this teenage romance from hell. But it was so late into the season and so close to graduation and prom that she decided to entertain his rude boyish ways until the time she could run away to college and dump his ass for good.

When you attend an all-girl school and a parochial school to boot, and you dressed complete with a gray and burgundy "just to the knee" plaid skirt, cardigan shirts, and sweaters bearing gold insignias of Catholic saints and knee-high socks, you could not be choosy when a somewhat handsome jock asks you out to the movies. Her choices of young beaus were divided into groups here in her suburbia. A young girl from Saint Mary's Academy or anywhere in Union or Somerset Counties had her choice of the collegiate type or the "hard guy" type, like the one she left behind in Newark, or the jocks. The jocks were always the safest bet and the ones all the parents approved of. She met Jimmy about a year ago after school one afternoon as they caroused about the local indoors mall. She was shocked that he took such an immediate interest and asked her to the movies while she was still in her Saint Mary's uniform.

Jimmy Breuer was in his senior year at Watchung Regional High School and indeed a jock. Watchung Regional was a good school with a good scholastic program and an even better athletic one that Jimmy was all over as a result of his father's insisting and monetary pledging. Jimmy was a Watchung Warrior who managed to letter in football and wrestling but had no desire nor was ever considered to play college sports.

His athletic ability and motivation was mirrored by his academic record of being one to just get by, by the skin of his teeth. His only attribute to the football team was his size; he stood just over six feet tall and had a well-defined and muscular body. That came from years of working with his father's building supply and lumberyard. He was, however, a pretty good wrestler in the heavyweight division but just lacked the desire to be number one. He was at best a C student who could care less about college, but would go only if his father insisted and paid for completely. He was content in knowing that he was the only heir to the Breuer Building Supply and Lumber of Greenbrook, New Jersey.

Joanie enjoyed his company at first. She managed to discern his dimwitted jockstrap behavior and wrote it off to male hormones, and that reasoning indeed made his equally idiotic friends more tolerable, even laughable at times. However, time did wear on, and so did her attraction to Jimmie. She slowly and steadily managed to reduce the nights out with him to no more than two, a formable idea that her father indubitably approved of. And when the young hormone-driven jock came over to visit, his presence was limited to the kitchen, den, and outside on the grand porch. So it was ordered and ordained that, basically, her father and mother somewhat approved of the fairly handsome German-Irish-blooded kid with a crew cut; they still did not trust his teenage hormones.

Joanie knew her parents and made herself and her mother a cold, sober, and solemn promise she would not lose her virginity to Mr. Jimmy Breuer no matter how hard he tried, tempted, or begged. Her mother was a little prudish about the discussion of sex with her daughter, but the brazen Joanie just let it roll off her tongue. "Mom, we hear about it all day in school. What's the big deal any way, it doesn't look that much fun either." Her shocked mother asked, "You mean you've seen pictures of…of…" "Mom, get with it. This is the sixties, you know, and don't think I don't know when you and Daddy are at it, and God forbid if I did it and got pregnant. I couldn't bear the thought of it, and have you or Daddy force me to marry that oaf and have his child." Her mom said simply, "Thank God for that."

Tonight would be a challenge for her at the Union Drive-in Theater, but she made it clear to him that she really wanted to watch *West Side Story* without being groped or manhandled. Of course he gave it his best Ivy League try, but Joanie was adamant about the absolutely no sex rule and swatted every attempt he made at a quick feel. Mostly she just practiced the art of kissing and would harmlessly make out with him as teenagers so often do, more of a learning session than a love session. And soon after the senior prom was over and done with, so was Jim Breuer. Joanie remained a virgin and Mr. Breuer was dismissed of all of duties as a boyfriend. Nevertheless, they'd be moments she missed kissing Jimmy, and on occasion, when that hormonal, semi-chaste feeling that came over her, as it so very often did, she'd retreat back in time and think tenderly of the hard guy she almost had as her boyfriend, that good-looking boy from Hindsdale Place, and the one and only time they've really kissed, the boy that she now only thinks of as a brief and distant memory of her past and sometimes cries over, a feeling her parents would not let her lament over.

The endless river flow of college brochures, applications, and acceptance letters that arrived in the mail, daily, was overwhelming. They were of all different shapes and sizes and all addressed to either Joan E. Jankowski or Miss Joan Jankowski; some came for John Jankowski, but none for her chosen Joanie, as she preferred to be called—just plain and simple Joanie Jankowski. She was never completely fond of the name Joan and its religious connection, but she always liked the ring of Joanie. She never mentioned to anyone her middle name of Magda—God forbid!

Marie Jankowski was usually home from her work earlier than the rest of the household, and it was her job to sort out and file the colorful booklets by order of reality. No matter how attractive the photo of the very success-oriented picture of a couple dressed in a cap and gown, the process of selection had to be done with a clear and budget-conscious head. She would arrange all the leading contenders neatly in a stack on the kitchen table for her husband to read over after dinner, based on merit and not how successful the caps and gowns made the graduates appear. She would circle in red ink their cost participation of the tuition.

Schools that were in the running like the more popular and pricey ones that of course her mother liked so much were left in the area of the large kitchen that was designated as the home office. They were examined by Henri in good faith only. His input and dissuasion was influenced by the almighty dollar of which he always won that argument. "We have to stay within the budget we agreed on, Marie." And then there were the schools that had categorically not a chance in hell like the enormously wild and notoriously radical universities or the Ivy Leaguers. Those school brochures along with any school past the Pennsylvania border or further south than Delaware were just tossed in the trash.

Both of Joanie's parents were fair, but they did let her know up front that the college selection process was not going to be at all a democracy. And Joanie did manage to rescue a few pamphlets of schools she had hoped to attend, especially the few her girlfriends had selected only to lose the argument as to why she needed to attend such schools. The one she did favor over all of them and the one that suited her chosen vocation was tucked away in the second drawer of her nightstand. It was for the colorful brochure from the fashion institute just over the bridge in the chic Chelsea section of Manhattan, New York City. She argued a strong case to both parents and overcame all of their objections. Her mother commented about the not-so-good reviews the university received, but she retracted her statement when Joanie showed her the cost comparison of her second choice of the highly rated Kent University in Ohio.

The overall cost of an education at FIT would be far less than the schools her mother chose for her and even further reduced if she was a resident of New York. That idea got a scowl and evil eye look from her father, but he too saw it her way after a while perhaps from the financial point of view. Joanie agreed to work while attending college. "I can always waitress." Something she was very used to already to help pay for her rent.

She pointed out that her grade average throughout her years at Saint Mary's was well above average, exceedingly, in spite of her waitressing four nights a week at Lombardo's Italian Restaurant. And she patted herself on the back for the exceptional grade she received in home economics, an extra electoral class she juggled with the rest of her college prep regiment. The deal clincher was when she promised, "Mom, Dad, I'll only be across the river. I'll get a car. I'll come home every weekend. It's what I want to do. At least let me try it for a semester, what can that hurt?" And so it was decided that night at dinner that Henri and Marie Jankowski could proudly say to the neighbors that their reasonably sensible daughter is going to attend the Fashion Institute in Manhattan.

Marie conceded to herself and realized that as far back as she could remember her daughter just loved to cut out the paper doll figures in the fashion magazines. She spent hours upon hours arranging them in scrapbooks. Throughout her years in elementary school she received accolades from teachers commenting on her natural flair for drawing images of women dressed in elegant gowns or in ballerina and fairy tale costumes. Her notepapers and book covers throughout high school were doodled on with chic-looking sketches of models in poses, the obvious and most boring classes having the most detailed artwork. The fashion industry was truly her destiny.

26

The reserved and hushed feeling that gripped some during that tranquil week after Christmas Day was reflective in the reticent stare of Angelo Ruggeri as he sat in his plush easy chair and puffed incessantly on a DeNobili cigar. The merriment of the anticipated "Boun Natale" was all swept away and gone as were the bright and colorful gift-wrapped presents that sat adorned under the decorated Yuletide tree that still rose to the ceiling in his ornate living room. And a winged angelic figure still sat atop, with a bright bulb inside, lit and emitting a lucid amber glow. How ironic?

The endless flow of gift givers, friends, and relatives who brought welcomed cheer to even the most coldhearted at this special time of year would tidy up and make way for another celebration. Ruggeri had little to no use for New Year's Eve galas or celebrations. He would never attend or host what he considered to be a silly spectacle of drunken fools. It reminded him of his business of bootlegging during Prohibition, the business that propelled his empire but left deep-rooted scars. The eve of January 1, 1965, was to the Pope a bleak grim reaper reminder of another year older and closer to the grave.

It was a typically cold and gray January morning as the three gruff and hungover mobsters convened in the parking lot of the Sicilian Café and waited for whatever instructions that would come. A meeting had been requested and set for the morning after the well-received Eve; its whereabouts was still a mystery. Vito "Junior" Tutolo, Paulie "Fat Lip" Ippolito, and Anthony "Hoss" DeSanti stood huddled within arm's length of one another in sort of a designed triangle, all trying to block the icy wind. They smoked cigarettes and weaved back and forth on very cold feet covered only with thin silk socks and fine Italian dress shoes. All wore dark topcoats and had fur felt fedoras atop their heads, with the exception of DeSanti. His huge head made it impossible for any haberdasher to find something other than a wool *goopaleen* to fit it.

Anthony DeSanti was the latest addition to the crew, not a pedigree by any true meaning of the word, but still an able-bodied seaman. He was previously a longshoreman, as was his father and uncles and cousins, all with a steady book of betters and all working on the well-organized Port Newark/Elizabeth piers, funneling whatever gambling revenue and stolen swag merchandise that was to be had, in the direction of Donald Tutolo and his son. Anthony DeSanti was thought to be a little slow—stupid in layman's terms. Nevertheless, he was grandfathered in a few years ago for his promising and predicable love of the game and his Goliath size.

DeSanti worked under and took his orders from both of the Tutolos, father and son. He was their problem child. Ruggeri immediately gave the go-ahead once the preliminary background check was done by Accardi to "get him workin' right away." Ruggeri wanted him to be groomed to follow in the footsteps of his old enforcer Joe Lotta. Lord knows he was big and stupid enough to do so.

Anthony DeSanti stood just shy of six feet tall and was as large if not larger than the late Joey Lotta or his sponsor, Vito Tutolo, himself considered by all to be a colossus. The thirty-year-old soon-to-be button man boasted an extremely huge torso and what seemed to be a thick, unbreakable neck. And at a glance he did possess an odd, out-of-balance shape. Be it as it may, it was the size of his head that prompted one of the other guys in the outfit to tag DeSanti with the moniker Horse Head as the name so adequately fit. This jested moniker got laughs from everyone but DeSanti himself, who would go into a storming rage each and every time the reference was made. Sometimes the commotion within the crew over the connotation would be so ruckus Ruggeri himself had to intervene before the obvious would take place. It was common knowledge and a locution everyone openly spoke; the only way to stop the charging bull would be to shoot him. He forbade the use of the sobriquet Horse Head and fined any and all that slipped. Instead the ever-teasing henchmen gave the kid the title of Hoss after the rough-and-tumble character played on the newly popular western "Bonanza," a name well liked even by the recipient himself. So it came to be known that Anthony "Hoss" DeSanti was now part of a crew.

Tutolo looked at his wristwatch and said, "What time are they coming to pick us up at?" The question was just thrown out for any to answer. The "they" he was referring to was Eddie Accardi. It was his orders to meet at 9:00 a.m. Paulie took a drag of his Winston and felt his body shiver and said, "Who's picking who up? He just told me to meet him here." With that said a familiar Cadillac pulled into the lot and sped to where the group was standing.

The ever-so-jocular Tick Tock rolled the driver side window down and tossed his almost expired cigarette at the gang's feet and said, "If that was a hand grenade, yous' would all be gone and the Pope would be outta' business. What the fuck are you all standing in the cold for?" "The place is closed," Tutolo said. "This is where he said to be…outside…waitin'.'" Frank laughed and said, "You stand out there like assholes. I'll stay right here in the warm car. And as soon as that joint of his opens, I'm goin' in for espresso and anisette."

DeSanti was the first to take the cue and tugged on the handle of the rear door. Batista activated the power locks and let the big man in. Six seconds later they all piled into Frank's Cadillac testing the shock absorbers limits as the lumbering bodies fell hard on the seats.

The Cadillac quickly filled up with cigarette smoke even though the windows had been cracked open an inch or so. Paulie took the last drag of his Winston and rolled his window down completely and tossed the butt to the ground. He held his face toward the chilled air just long enough to catch a verbal attack from the others about letting in too much winter breeze.

The boys watched in silence as an unfamiliar pickup truck inched its way into the parking lot, the driver just as concerned about the company he had waiting for him. He pulled to a space by the rear door and lunged out of the driver's seat. They all spoke among themselves and acknowledged that it must be one of the chefs getting ready to prep for the afternoon dinner crowd. Paulie let out a droll remark: "The Pope even got this poor bastard working on New Year's Day." Frank Batista was quick to comment. "Are you kidding? He wouldn't miss the chance to rake in the dough today. I was here one New Year's Day and the place was mobbed." Frank was talking to the guys in the backseat via the rearview mirror, and before he could get another word out, Vito gave him a heads-up slap on the arm and pointed.

Eddie Accardi made his way over the curb of the driveway and eased his Chrysler next to Batista. Both men rolled down their windows simultaneously. Batista suddenly got a case of the heebie-jeebies as the presence of Accardi usually makes him feel that way. Accardi had a black look on his face. His eyes scanned the men one by one, and he said, "Meet me up at the castle." Frank nervously asked, "Now?" Accardi scowled back. "Yeah, now. You know the way up there, right?" he asked Frank. Batista just nodded yes and rolled up his window.

Very seldom does Ruggeri invite any of the crew to his home and hardly ever for a meeting. Usually it is only to dispose of a body. And perhaps this raised the suspicion level in Frank Batista's head to the limits. "Which way you gonna take?" asked Tutolo, he being the only other besides Frank to ever visit the Transylvanian Castle that sits up in the deep and isolated woods. Frank hesitated before he spoke. His mind was still evaluating situation. "Up Bloomfield Ave, then I'll cut through West Orange and Essex Fells." He let out forced laugh and said, "The scenic route."

Paulie leaned forward from his backseat perch and asked, "So why the meet and why up at the boss's place?" The question was thrown out for anyone to grab. Vito turned and spoke, "Maybe they're gonna open the books for Hoss over here." That got a laugh from everyone. "Yeah, well, maybe they're gonna close the books on someone," DeSanti glibly added. No one laughed at that.

Frank Batista had the most experience out of all the others in the car about the everyday operation and intricacies of the mob's activity; nothing documented or etched in stone—just pure, seasoned speculation. He had firsthand knowledge of how things were supposed to go down, and while how very cagy and shrewd Accardi thought he was, Batista was still able to predict his moves—his God-given gift in life. He had on many an occasion been to Ruggeri's castle either for a ceremony or a hit. This was not going to be anyone's last ride that sat in his car. This meeting was all about something else.

Angelo Ruggeri once had a large Victorian-style home on Ballantine Parkway that was previously owned by a wealthy textile manufacturing magnate. It suited his needs perfectly, secluded and being a large enough mansion to contain his two daughters, himself, and his wife comfortably.

During the early days of his accomplished career and all through Prohibition, Angelo Ruggeri spent a lot of time hobnobbing with political figures of all sorts to reinforce his book of allies, one of them being a wealthy member of the House of Representatives, New Jersey, District 13. Ruggeri attended a fund-raiser at his mansion in Livingston, New Jersey, and was impressed with the fact that its design was taken from one of the great castles from the Republican politician's homeland of Scotland. Ruggeri thought the idea of a personal castle so novel he decided to build his own. The top designers were summoned and given the task of recreating a villa from his homeland province of Tufino, Italy.

A more than ample piece of real estate found tucked away in the Orange Ridge mountain range community of Roseland, New Jersey. The irregular horse-neck shape of the once Lenape Indian reservation made it subdued in the Essex County section. Its heavily dense topography of hardwood trees and tall hemlocks proved too costly for developers to install large tracts of homes up and down its mountainous ranges of sedimentary shale and quartz. So residents were few and far between. This area chosen was very desirable for the Don of New Jersey.

Ruggeri found it much more convenient and, ironically, less costly to import all the building materials from Italy rather than ordering it through local standard lumber supply houses; also, it was more concealing. No snooping building inspectors that follow large truckloads of lumber to final destinations with the hopes of snagging a code violator either for a shakedown or a feather in their cap. He did not worry at all about such trivial things; his building materials came directly from the sea port of entry, and any building permits or zoning code approvals, if needed, would come after the fact.

The few neighbors that did live close by paid little to no attention to the trucks as they forged their way up a natural winding path of the quarter of a mile or so that led to over five acres of a partially cleared plateau. This would be the job site and final location of the compound. A settler couple that owned a squalled home only fifty feet from the mansions driveway was quickly bought out, as were others within a good square mile of Ruggeri's driveway. This access road would eventually be squared and paved to form the one and only entrance to the compound. Its private entrance from Passaic Avenue would be protected by two massive stone pillars separated by an ornamental wrought iron gate along with an army of private security. And as a bonus, to ensure no trespassers, was some well-placed barbed wire intertwined with the rugged lay of the land and a perimeter of high-stone retaining walls, all surrounding the property, making the fortress virtually impregnable. The barbed wire is registered and listed with the County Zoning Commission, as a deterrent for the prominent white-tailed deer that feed on the vegetation in his garden and the occasional black bears that wander down from the mountains.

A team of FBI agents were once assigned to "monitor and set up close surveillance of the primary residence" and of the reputed mobster's activities within the compound but reported "Negative, we cannot achieve an advantage point for surveillance." Reasons noted was the use of armed private security at the front gates and at several other positions. And barbed wire intertwined with heavy forest vegetation along with cackling hens and hooligan-type associates in what seemed to be within the recorded boundaries reminding us we were trespassing on private property. The cackling hens was questioned by the head of the bureau and reported back to him the caged birds were abundant about the property's borders and would create a frenzied racket if startled or annoyed. The report ended with the determination that the only surveillance that was to be successful would have to come from the air via helicopter.

Ruggeri built a six-thousand-square-foot mansion for himself using the finest Italian limestone, travertine, and marble that he could find, all peach in color. It was reminiscent of the pretentious farm villas sparsely scattered throughout the Italian foothills owned by the rich vintners and land barons. Arched and rusticated windows and doorways encompassed the perimeters and each story separated by dominant gables flanked by carved balustrades and strategically placed gargoyles and birdhouses. Secluded perches were noticeable on the four corners of the third floor that held armed guards during the many family wars that took place between Ruggeri and his post–Prohibition era enemies. Two-foot-thick walls and a ceramic stone roof kept the outside elements from entering the home. The timber used for the project was milled from Italian alder and oak, and the grand molding that traversed the walls, floors, and ceilings were carved from Italian olive wood as were the cabinetry. Ruggeri and his wife moved into the newly constructed castle in the spring of 1942 and reside solely on the second and third stories. He has his own sanctuary on the floor that is ground level. It is an entire and separate living quarter, apart from the rest of the house, complete with a commercial kitchen and a huge dining room reserved solely for Ruggeri's personal business and private entertaining. Angelo Ruggeri's castle climbs majestically, three stories high plus an attic, and sits under a Romanesque slate roof, much like his Ballantine Parkway home. The main and secondary entrances rise up from two grand balustrade marbled stairways in the front and the side of the mansion. A lush and well-manicured landscape of trees, bushes, and flower-bearing vines seem to flow as nature intended, from the dense forest and then almost engulfing the entire mansion.

Eventually, his daughters would marry, and they did. Both chose very meek and humble men on their father's orders and perhaps this for the better. The Don refused his daughters and their families' occupancy in his home but still wanted them close by—so each was given a gift of their own home, both built kitty-corner of his mansion. A huge courtyard adorned with flowing fountains and well-placed hedged landscape and flower gardens separated all the houses. Life-size statues of Italian saints along with hundreds of exquisite imported cypress trees that stand twenty feet tall line the graveled walkways and courtyards in an intricate pattern.

In time, a grand garden was installed, overflowing with vegetables and tomatoes of every variety, all bowing to welcome a perfect morning sun and then the late afternoon shade and tended by his *paison* whom he had brought over from the other side. They, along with other hand-selected guards and watchmen, had their own residences farther up the property. A spacious piece of the backyard was cleared of the tall hemlock and maple trees to let in the all-day summer sun and warm the Roman-style swimming pool.

He made certain all the houses on the compound were equipped with the most modern conveniences of the day, and that each had its own steam heat and hot water systems. In anticipation of the loss of electricity in case of an emergency, Ruggeri had two huge furnaces built to supply heat and also to power a large steam-operated generator. These fabled ovens were commonly referred to as his personal crematorium and that many a fallen mobster were allegedly reduced to ash inside of them. Allegations vehemently denied by the Pope but he does lay claim to firing up the furnaces on occasion—to burn off some cleared forest growth or to dispose of the carcasses of dead deer that sometimes get caught in the barbed wire and must be euthanized. This somewhat grizzly task got the attention of the surrounding town's senses, and people complained about the foul odor in the air caused by the chore. Ruggeri was within his rights to burn whatever he chose, but he agreed to use a fragrant apple and mesquite wood to stifle and camouflage the stench when he did so.

Frank Batista paid no attention as to when he lost sight of Accardi's Chrysler as he drove the carful of mobsters to Roseland and to the Pope's castle. He could have continued on Bloomfield Avenue until he reached the Caldwells then to Passaic Avenue, but he decided to make a last-minute change of direction and take a hard left turn onto Roseland Avenue. He did promise the crew the scenic route. The newly installed traffic light was in his favor. The crew voiced their displeasure for the radical maneuver and caught a "Take it easy, fellas, take it easy, I got it under control" from Frank.

The usually green, lush landscape surrendered itself to the January cold season, with the exception of the mighty pine and spruce trees that still carried some snow on their boughs. The low-lying juniper and hemlock grew in abundance and made a hearty landscape shrub for the homeowners throughout the surrounding area.

More banter ricocheted among the occupants until the gothic pillars of Ruggeri's estate came into view. The black wrought iron gates were opened, and two men in heavy winter garb stood sentry. Their weapons were well concealed. There was a car pulled along the side of the paved driveway, just past the entrance, allowing free passage up but on call to quickly block the entrance in a moment's notice. The trained security were all men from Ruggeri's crew and communicated with sophisticated walkie-talkie equipment back and forth from sentry points all around the complex.

Paulie Ippolito was the first to speak as his eyes got wide. "So this is the castle." Vito, who had been invited up here maybe twice in his life, began shouting instructions to DeSanti about how to act around the Pope and whoever might be here. For all they knew it could have been Lyndon B. Johnson rehearsing his state of the union address. Frank Batista interjected and put the kabosh on Tutolo's spiel. "Don't listen to him, big guy, you'll end up in the ovens." All the mobsters' eyes got wide, and DeSanti said, "I heard about them."

They were at the gate for only a split second before one of the guards beckoned them through. If you looked hard enough, the glint of the concertina wire from the morning sunlight sparkled in the dense underbrush. They gave the appearance of lightning bolts shooting up and around the property.

Frank drove with certainty as he anticipated the dips in the road. He took the sharp left at the top of the drive wide just in case anyone was coming from the other direction entering the blind spot then a sharp right. The retaining wall gradually rose on both sides of the drive until it was over ten feet high at the top of the landing; then it ended at the complex entrance itself. As the driveway's incline became level, it narrowed down to a single lane. At this point the paved road had eight-foot-tall hedges that flanked both sides and ran twenty feet in length. At the hedges' end were two small guardhouses, one on each side with gazebo-type roofs connected to another set of pillars, both containing large growling black German shepherd dogs collared to thick chains both with just enough slack to reach an extended arm or a car tire.

The paved road was met by an eight-foot edge of inlaid cobblestone; then gravel covered the rest of the courtyard beyond that point. As the others gawked and gave comment on the pretentious surroundings, Batista focused on the familiarity of other autos and license plates of which he did notice a big Buick with New York tags parked next to another older Buick that belonged to Albert Marrone. He became more nervous now as the weight of the Cadillac made a crushing sound as it traveled over the gravel and continually questioned himself as to why.

He edged his Cadillac past Accardi's car that was parked at the far end of the circular driveway. All got out and made their way toward the congregation of wise guys all huddled around an open doorway cut into a larger barnyard-style garage door. Someone gave the seasoned and stained wood a rap and commented with an accompanying look of approval, "Real oak?"

One by one the mobsters filtered through the garage door that led into another entrance to the Pope's personal quarters. Each man turned and offered welcoming handshakes as they greeted each other. Some offered hugs of gratitude, others just a hearty handshake or a gracious kiss on the cheeks. At the door was Accardi also with an extended hand and a welcoming invitation. When all the guests were present, Accardi bolted the door shut then disappeared down a hallway that led to the private bunker.

There wasn't any formal name tags placed for a specific seating arrangement about the twenty foot long and sturdy banquet table— the exactly one dozen of large bodies just started to fall into seats randomly, as they felt comfortable; however, all shied away from the head of the table, that was knowingly reserved. Around the table sat the bowls and serving platters of fresh apples and pears and Italian rolls and pastry along with fresh cold cuts and cheese.

Batista found a seat next to the familiar face of Albie and cared less where the others he chauffeured up to the castle were sitting. "Happy New Year, Albie," Frank said with sincerity, offering his handshake. Albie coughed some then answered, "You know, you're the first to wish me one." His eyes scanned the room at the others starting to congregate. "I don't know half these guys…I must be gettin' old." "Yeah, like me," Frank answered with a scowl. He took a silent head count, and including the Pope and Accardi that were in the other room he made himself out to be the unlucky number 13. He grimaced at that thought; then he spoke with a more heartfelt tone in his voice and knew the answer to his question asked would not be the truth, "Tell me, Albert, just what is this all about, and why are we here?" Albie did not lie as he said, "Beats the shit outta' me." Albie tossed some cigarette ash into a large glass ashtray and said, "It ain't no Appalachia, that's for sure." Frank lit a cigarette then took a swig of the strong black coffee from his mug. "What gives with the New York crowd?" He tossed his head toward the two men from the Genovese family sitting at the front of the table both flanked the empty head seat.

The Genovese family had strong ties to the New Jersey crew and had blood relatives that reached out to the Monestero family in

Pittsburgh. Angelo Ruggeri considered himself an equal to all the heads of the five New York families, and no one argued the point. Albie gave hardly any thought at all about New York. He could care less and it was reflective in his voice. "I don't know, but their boss has been with Ruggeri since they came in." Frank looked first at the two men then quickly back at Albie. "So that makes me number 14," he said with a huge grin. No more bad karma about the number 13. Albie gave him such a twisted look that clearly asked, "What the fuck are you talking about?"

Both men sat and picked on the treats in front of them, and they would notice a quiet fall upon the group as the Pope came from behind the finely constructed door of his private office. He was well dressed as usual in a charcoal suit with red and silver striped tie. He would give a Pope's blessing to the crowd with his right hand and then whisper to Accardi as to who he wanted in the room next. He would slowly disappear down the hall, the door would close, and the bullshit and banter would resume.

Frank's eyes scoured the room looking for any strangers that may be lurking among his usual suspect cronies. Not a one could be found. It was a room filled of familiar faces. Was he the only one with reservation and outright paranoia about this meet, and rightfully so? he thought. Who else in this room is involved in his drug operation?

Finally, it was his turn for an audience with the Pope, and as it played out, both he and Marrone were requested by Accardi. That seemed odd to Batista. What was the connection between him and Albie other than the years of service and blood they both contributed. Marrone gave it absolutely no thought at all. He just wanted to go home. They entered the private office of the Pope and were led to their respective seats by Accardi who sat next to Ruggeri at a private table. Frank found it odd that a stranger (to him) sat behind the Pope's oversized desk. It was the underboss of the New York family Jimmie "JD" Insabella. And he had earned that seat as Ruggeri extended his respect. Insabella ruled over the largest of the five families and was first cousin to Stefano Montesero of the Pittsburgh fraction. He bragged of the firepower his street soldiers and capos possessed and feared no war that could be brought his way. And it would be decided that he and the Pope of New Jersey wage their own war against drugs.

Insabella sat in and gave recommendation to policy and position changes the Pope had requested for both families to prosper more than ever. They spoke with other captains from both crews in secret sessions about the drug empires growing fast around them, and both agreed that they too must get involved or go the way the old Mustache Petes of long ago did. Ruggeri spoke of his alliance with a certain federal agent, a DEA agent who recognized his stance on drugs as a taboo. Ruggeri laughed to Insabella about how the young agent praised him for his efforts in feeding the agency information about drug trafficking that may be going on in Newark. "And of course he feeds me the information we will need as to who are friends or our enemies are." Ruggeri concluded.

Both men sanctioned some well-needed hits on both sides of the river to deter the vast number of turncoat, rat informers, that were being enticed by the federal government on a daily basis. Both bosses listened carefully at the answers given by their subordinates to the gimmicky and ambushing questions placed before them. And as the parties left the room they would talk amongst themselves as to the validity of the answers. So far they were happy.

Ruggeri was the first to speak after a few seconds of silence and the clearing of Frank's throat. He introduced Insabella, and both Batista and Marrone gave their respectful acknowledgment of the Don. "First of all, let me say thanks for coming, especially you, Albert. I know it must be hard getting around these days with your arthritis." Albie gave the Pope a nod and a thankful smile in return. Even though the air was thick from cigar and cigarette smoke, Batista made a motion with a pack of Lucky Strike cigarettes, asking permission to light one up. Accardi gave a nod and a wink of approval. The Pope stood and placed his left hand atop of Accardi's shoulder then looked in Albie's eyes. "And this is why you were asked here today, to give blessing. As you all well know, Eddie is blood to the Ruggeri family, and he has been a valuable member to this family over the years. He holds sacred the oath he took, more than I can say of some we associate with. But then again, they're all gone now, or soon to be." Frank drew hard from his cigarette and adjusted his thick black eyeglass frames and continued to listen to Ruggeri, trying hard not to show any emotion. "I never named a so-called consigliere as you all know, although Albert has acted the part on many an occasion. Today in front of witnesses, I name Edward Accardi officially as acting consigliere of the Ruggeri family. He has only a few more months of service with the police department then he can retire." Ruggeri gave Eduardo a look of appreciation as he spoke. "And at that time he will be more involved with certain aspects of the family and hopefully let me enjoy life a little more." Jim Insabella shouted an Italian saying that meant he seconded the motion. Batista being the complete wiseacre whispered to Marrone, "I wonder if they're gonna' let him keep his cop car?"

As the room cleared, Accardi gave Frank a slight tug on his arm and motioned him to come in close as so not to be heard by anyone, "The old man wants you to bring the kid back to Jersey if you can." First, a long silence, then Batista gave Accardi an austere shrug as he spoke through his best poker face, "Really, I don't know if he wants to come back. I hear he's doing okay for himself out there." Accardi gave him an evil smile and said, "That's why he wants him back. He figures he owes him." Batista looked around to find the men he came in with then found himself left all alone. He noticed Accardi came and grabbed DeSanti, Tutolo, and Paulie Ippolito and led them into the den. He watched intensely as Accardi reentered the room flanked by Insabella. He regained his position at the head of the table and nodded to the two dapper middle-aged men who stood up, both experienced hit men, and sanctioned them to follow Accardi back to meet Ruggeri. All five men were brought together and introduced by Accardi after Ruggeri left the room. And a carefully laid plan was presented to the crew. Joe Agnelli and Dante DeRosa were the button men imported from New York to aid with the hit and to represent the also allied Genovese family, but it was requested that Anthony DeSanti make his bones with this job. Don Ruggeri had high hopes for the man he selected to replace the late Joey Lotta, and now he would be put to the test. Months prior to the meet a message was sent to Ruggeri from New York in response to a favor the Pope had requested. The Pope had always suspected Frank Batista of either trying to defect, or worse yet, help build a drug empire on Ruggeri's watch.

As prelude to the soon-to-be formed partnership and as a test to assure his loyal and continued allegiance, Ruggeri asked Insabella to spy for him, a favor if you will—as a way of guaranteeing their success and well-being, and also to quell a rumor. A couple of hand-picked soldiers were selected and shown some covert photos of Batista. They were asked that in their travels, if they ever saw this guy, they were to notify Insabella, especially if Batista ever showed his face in a few locations selected by the Pope, known locations of the rival Profaci family. And wouldn't you know it, not only did Frank get made sitting at a bar in Bensonhurst, Brooklyn, with his cousin and a couple of Profaci people, but also inadvertently lied to Accardi when the casual question of "What were you doing in Brooklyn last week?" was presented. Ruggeri pulled one of the New York triggerman aside and asked with determination, "Did you recognize him?" He spoke of Frank Batista. The triggerman looked first at Accardi then back to the Pope. "You can't miss those glasses. It was him all right. He was with his cousin, I know the guy, Bobby Breeze. He's a good guy. The only reason I was there was to meet this broad—" His banter was cut short. "That's enough," Ruggeri said contently. He had to reach up a bit to put his arm around the fellow's shoulder in a convivial show of friendship then said predominantly, "Come on and meet the boys."

Angelo Ruggeri was gloating as he headed toward the door that led into his retreat. He looked around at the various elegantly framed paintings that hung with precision on the finished walls of the four-car garage, any piece worthy of any grand parlor. He chuckled to himself as he remembered the answer he gave Insabella as he shockingly commented as to why a Bronzino painting of a beautiful bare-breasted maiden hung in the garage. "I only put good works of art upstairs."

27

Anthony "Hoss" DeSanti sat at the green felt-covered card table inside the Pope's club with his huge arms folded over his belly. The active card game had ended, and if the Pope were to see the mess created on his prized table, heads would surely roll. Remnants of peppers and egg sandwiches, bagels and doughnuts, along with overflowing ashtrays, cluttered just about every square inch of the surface, mostly in front of him. He listened attentively as Joe Agnelli, Dante DeRosa, and Edward Accardi discussed the final details of the caper they were about to embark on. Phil Ippolito and Vito rehearsed over and over again in their heads the roll they were to perform, and all exchanged precautionary what-ifs until Accardi intervened. "Trust me, boys, we been planning this for a long time now. I have left no stone unturned. It will go down as smooth as shit through a tin horn." A phrase all heard by the detective on numerous occasions, but no one ever bothered to ask what the hell it meant.

Alonso Coleman and Willie Johnson moved more heroin in a month's time than all the Jake Trebbianos could possibly move in their lifetimes. They did it with a brazen ruthlessness that only true barbarians could relate to or understand, and all done under the cover and protection of the Profaci family. This was a well-known fact that every Italian mobster in the big Brick City surreptitiously knew. And as long as it was peddled in their own ghetto, slum neighborhoods that held millions-plus citizens, where everyone is ethnically evil, no one at Ruggeri's camp or city hall cared. But little anyone knew or did they want to know that the ever popular euphoric amber white powder was overflowing into the chalky white neighborhoods and veins of the county's blue bloods. The only difference was that when discovered there, a psychiatric board of examiners helped sweep it under their rich Persian carpets.

Ruggeri was unconcerned over the long-term ramifications of drug use by those that chose and openly praised his crew from shying away from it, but as pointed out by Insabella, he had to, at some point in time, get with the times. Millions of dollars were flowing in and out of Ruggeri's empire without him seeing one dollar, not even a tax from the other families, their heads buried deep in sand like nescient ostriches and all crying innocent. Ruggeri had enough. War was not a stranger to the Ruggeri family. They survived the evilest of bootleggers compiled with the hardest of times and came out victoriously. This would be a cake walk.

It was a notorious and eminent fact that just about all the black hoodlums, dating back to the plantation slave days, were born with, as the old-timers would put it, a stupid gene. No matter how hard an expert tried to school them in the art of crime, someone of their ethnic brood would commit a huge blunder. Willie Johnson was far from stupid. but perhaps he was a lazy nigger and over time became very complacent, another infamous character flaw of the black criminal. He trusted his flunkies more than he trusted himself and had a disregard for rules or the disciplining of a bungler in his outfit. Mistakes made often resulted in himself calling Breeze and squaring it with all concerned. He would not hold accountable, as the Italians did, anyone who put the outfit in harm's way. Just as long as the money was flowing, and it was by the carloads, everything to him was Jake. The last night he spent on earth, he and his entourage had a private room full of drugs and booze and hookers of every color scattered all over the floor and furniture of a favorite haunt of his called Dupes.

It was a mostly an all-black clientele that frequented the jazz and rhythm and blues nightclub that stayed open well past the blue law curfew of 2:00 a.m. A few white patrons, mostly ones connected with the music business or perhaps true jazz aficionados, would make an occasional showing. Police on the beat of the Central Avenue club were well greased by the owners. It was not classified information when Willie and the boys were in the club raising a ruckus, but it was easy information for Accardi to get from a few close informants on his payroll.

Willie Johnson traveled, in perpetuum, with three tough and intimidating bodyguards, and all would be packing pretty heavy at all times, but they could only count one or two times that anyone stood in front of and threatened or complained about Willie Johnson in public, and to say that they were as complacent as so their boss was an understatement. They would all be in the thick of things, and on some nights of partying, they had to be carried out by the boss himself.

It was agreed that on this night DeSanti sat behind the wheel. At precisely 3:30 a.m., an unmarked patrol car pulled in front of Dupes. A uniformed police officer got out and began to knock on the front door. He was greeted by a large-figured doorman who was having a hard time trying to keep his eyes open. Paulie Ippolito stepped into the establishment then adjusted his sleeves of the blue coat and politely asked to speak with the owner or manager and that he did, in just about thirty seconds. A short, thin dapper black man wearing a much-wrinkled tuxedo appeared. "Is there a problem, Officer? I'm the manager," the black man asked in a raspy voice and a broad grin. He looked the cop in the eye and said, "You must be new to these parts?" The man squinted and looked for a name badge. The absence of one indicated a shakedown was in progress. He settled for a peek at the officer's small wallet-held shield and pulled a wad of bills from his pants pocket. The cop waved off the bribe and said, "I am new here, and we're catching a lot of heat from city hall about the hours you keep at this place. It's time to shut 'er down for at least tonight in let's say a half hour, otherwise I got to make a scene." The manager retorted, "Officer, our doors are locked, we are closed." "Cut the shit! Everyone out, you got it?" snapped Ippolito. It was agreed by the manager that Dupes would promptly reclose. "Ohhh, fuck it" was the words from Willie's mouth. "I was getting tired of 'dis place anyways. Let's book."

The patrol car drove only a few yards or so up Central Avenue then quickly doubled back and crawled up a narrow alley that led to the rear of the building that housed Dupes. "That's his car there, the Fleetwood," Vito said in a whisper. "So we wait." "What if no one comes out?" asked DeSanti, his hands tightly gripping the steering wheel. "Then we go inside and get 'em," Agnoli said in a firmer voice. "We didn't come this far without getting the job done." He gave DeSanti a good slap to the back of his head. "And don't jinx us, you. Just drive the fuckin' car."

Anthony DeSanti positioned the cruiser at the end of the driveway blocking the exit and facing Willie's Cadillac. His nervousness prompted another stupid question. "What if someone tries to get in that car over there?" He pointed to a Buick that was parked about a car length down from the Fleetwood. DeRosa scolded him now. "You gotta' be kidding me. Somebody tell this guy to shut the fuck up before I fuckin' shoot him."

The back door slammed open as a group of drunken people stumbled out in ones and twos, their facial features lit up by the overhead stage door light. Some sparkle shot from the gold inlay in the mouth of a boisterous henchman. "That's him, right there."

Tutolo pointed. Willie stood tall wearing a full-length leather coat with a rich fur collar; he was in the middle of the crowd of four men and two half-naked women. DeSanti reached for the controls of the cruiser. Vito grabbed his arm and said intensely, "Wait, wait, wait. Let 'em get closer to their cars."

No one from the group of henchmen including Willie himself was paying any attention; none of them noticed the unmarked cruiser waiting in the shadows, another blundering mishap by the completely drunken and stoned bunch. As expected Willie and three of his bodyguards hovered around the Fleetwood while the other three hobbled to the Buick. One of the women was overheard saying, "Well, if we goin' that far, I better go pee now." She shimmied and shook her tail back to the now locked back door of the club. "Shit" was uttered as she let go her grip of the door handle and then quickly she disappeared around the front of the Buick.

The two short staccato bursts of the shrill siren forced the men to freeze in their tracks. They all raised their hands awkwardly to shield their eyes from the bright spotlight that lit them up as the advancing police cruiser pinned them in. The girl squatting just let her bladder empty in a steaming pool as she said, "Oh, shit."

All the men quickly and systematically climbed out of the cruiser—all holding Remington pump shotguns. They formed a precise arc surrounding the entourage, allowing clear shots on all sides of the cars. A banter of mock ethnic curse words spewed from every mouth in the crowd. The uniformed Ippolito shouted with authority, "All of you, keep quiet and get your fuckin' hands up." Willie became annoyed and took step away from the Fleetwood. He found it strange that one cop was in uniform and the others were in trench coats and longshoreman's garb. "Just what the fuck are you boys up to? I hope this ain't what I think it is?" He had not a chance to say any more.

Anthony DeSanti was the first to get the go-ahead nod. His weapon was aimed at Willie, and he fired it with complete accuracy. Within seconds of one another, all the shotguns sounded off first with their fearful pump action sound, and then the shooters' audible grunts and verbal reactions of ire as they began firing the 12 gauge military grade buck shot bursts into the crowd of people. Willie was the first to go, taking a direct blast to his head, which just disappeared in chunks and a ghastly red mist. The rest had arms and legs completely blown off in the barrage as they tried to retaliate, futilely reaching for their own weapons, their ultimate death coming in the form of huge gaping holes in their torsos. All in all the shooters emptied twenty-eight shotgun shells into the crowd as DeSanti watched in awe then putting a few insurance slugs into the listless bodies with extreme prejudice. The innocent prostitute, club manager, and bartender fell as collateral damage. There would only be one left to tell this grisly tale, but she knew better. She slithered completely under the chromed bumper and literally pissed herself again.

The drugland massacre was over in seconds, and the boys were safely on their way to their next stop. Paulie Ippolito was dropped off at his car. The cop uniform was making him nervous, and it began to itch. It was agreed that he go to the rendezvous spot ahead of time and get ready for the delivery, and besides, they needed the room in the car.

This part of the job was crucial. Coleman had to be exactly where Accardi said he would be or the timing would be off. And there could be a chance the shooters get caught up in the sure-to-follow dragnet that would swoop upon the city after the murders were discovered. If Coleman caught wind of the shootings at Dupes, he was sure to go underground.

The surveillance compiled by Accardi was painstakingly accurate. Dozens of photos were taken and studied, and most of the shots were of the exact location that the crew was headed. Al Coleman was forty-six years old and looked nothing like a notorious drug lord was supposed to look like. He was of average height and weight and sported a very unruly afro hairdo. His facial features seemed lifeless, never a smile or nothing more than an empty stare.

He had a wife and three children safely tucked away in a nice country home in Virginia, and he kept a small unadorned apartment in East Orange high-rise, but spent most of his free nights with his girlfriend at her second floor apartment on Grove Street in Irvington. His dealing now with the heroin trade was of such a minimal that he never concerned himself over heat. That's what he paid other people for. He supervised from afar as guys like Breeze and his cousin Frank did the hard work. As for tonight, Al Coleman was snug and fast asleep in his girlfriend's bed.

The boys had just enough room to back the sedan into the driveway without hitting Coleman's parked Cadillac or protrude onto the sidewalk. The alleyway was obscure and the night pitch-black. They exited the car using extreme care as to not make a sound, and as always all the moving parts of the door latches and hinges were heavily greased to swing silent. They quietly entered the shabby residence through the side door as Accardi had designated. It was the one used only by Coleman and his girl and had no common access to the downstairs apartment. Vito remained sentry in the entrance foyer as the other three climbed the short flight. Surely the crime that was just committed in the bordering town of Newark would send alarms and APBs all over, so the crew had to act fast, and if they timed it right, they would blend in with the Sunday morning worshipers in about half an hour.

Ippolito gave the door a few gentle raps; then a few more raps on the door got the girl's attention. She opened her swollen eyes and instinctively nudged Coleman until he woke up. It was still dark out as Coleman laboriously shuffled his feet on the cold floor and went to answer the door. His instinct was to just stand still with his ear to the door and listen. There seemed to be not anything disturbing outside the apartment although he did hear an alarm faintly in the distance; then another set of light knuckle taps sounded and startled Coleman. He backed away with a surprised look on his face. "Yeah... who is it?" he asked in a whisper, and a nasally whisper was returned, "It's me, Breeze." Coleman's face became inquisitive to the point of being distorted. His voice was louder now. "Breeze...what the fuck are you doin' here?" The dead bolt unlatched with a click and Al Coleman was overrun by mobsters.

Before he had a chance to think DeSanti put him back to sleep with hard fist to the side of the head. The still sleepy-eyed girl in the next room heard the scuffle and had no time to react as DeRosa barged in the bedroom and put two slugs in her naked chest from a silenced Colt automatic. A third went into her skull.

Coleman was bound with duct tape hands, feet, and mouth, and dragged down the stairway like a piece of old luggage. He was tossed in the open trunk of the Chevy sedan, and as the first morning mass church bells chimed he was whisked away to a shuttered old tavern on Doremus Avenue in the oil barged port section of Newark, New Jersey. That would be the last anyone would see of him until his rotting mutilated carcass was found a few days later. The crime had to look like a true drug bloodbath between rival inner city gangs, and it certainly did.

28

Frank Batista's surmounting paranoia forced him to covertly rent yet another apartment, this time in the adjoining luxury high-rise building he supposedly shared with Uncle. The latest erroneous identity was created by not one but two names pulled from the *Newark Evening News* obituaries. It was under the alias of George Nicholas. Another car was parked in the underground parkway supplied anonymously by Joe Marino, a 1960 Oldsmobile 88. It was another beater of a car that blended well and ran exceptionally, and also registered to Mr. Nicholas.

His reaction to a coded message relayed via his mother was dire, but he knew he must keep his head. His cousin gave him a number to call and said with a touch of fear in his voice, "Right now—and hurry." It was just about midnight as he stealthily entered the stairwell that led five floors down to the parking garage. The overtone of being set up played over and over in his culpable mind. He would stand still as each floor landing was reached, and instinct would warrant an inescapable feel of the gun tucked neatly in the small of his back. His hands would fumble to silence the jingle of the keys that bounced loosely in his trousers, and as he felt them, he hoped they were the right ones. And as best he thought he was disguised with a wide-brimmed fedora and a longshoreman's peacoat; he never once suspected his only identifying trait was those goddamn eyeglasses of his. The Olds fired up like a charm. *Joe was a good wrench*, thought Batista, and then he left the underground garage.

Bobby "Breeze" Battista lived in the nice neighborhood of Riverdale, Bronx, New York. His neighbors knew something was not kosher about this guy but did not care. He like most mobsters that take up residence in a community bring a sense of well-being and safety that inadvertently runs off to all in the families in the community. No one gets out of line in a neighborhood that houses known mafioso.

He was four years his cousin's junior and had a head full of curly ebony hair. He was a surprisingly fit and well-built man, partially because of his silent partnership with a franchised gym and because of all the drugs, especially cocaine, he ingested. He did think with a very clear head and had the support and blessing from the Profaci crew to take whatever steps necessary to keep the ball rolling when it came to drug operation.

The dire and disheartening news he received had to be relayed immediately to his cousin. Breeze sat tight next to an isolated pay phone on Nagle Avenue. The window of his Lincoln was cracked, and the cold February night air ripped past his ear that was in anticipation of a phone ring. The cousins would usually meet, casually and in the open, on the New York side, usually in Bobby's neighborhood or at one of his usual haunts, under the protection of the Profaci family. The inherent fact that the two were related by blood was not a secret, and often they would, as cousins do, socialize. Batista sensed a noose hanging over his head and did not want to take any unnecessary chances. "This is how guys get whacked" was his outspoken thought to himself. Tonight the meet would have to be changed, and at the last minute, the location selected by Frank. It was agreed that since Bobby was close enough to the GWB, he would pay the toll, and the two decided on an all-night diner in the nearby town of Fort Lee, New Jersey. And both would instinctively drive in crooked and cockeyed circles to avoid any trace of a tail.

Batista was the first to reach the diner and snuggled into a booth that gave a clear view of the street entrance and on the opposite side of the restrooms. He had a cup of coffee brought to him. He took a look at his wristwatch that read almost 1:30 a.m. His concern was the bar crowd that would usually pile in an all-night diner would make it hard to communicate with his cousin on the still unknown dire situation. He rethought it out and believed that the Monday after Saint Valentine's Day had to be a dead night. He was right. Hardly anyone other than his cousin walked through the door during the two hours they sat.

Breeze walked like he was on glass as he entered and slid into the booth occupied by his cousin. He sat opposite and was quickly greeted by a waitress offering coffee and a menu. Frank thought it was a good idea to eat, but Breeze frowned and shook his head. "You ain't gonna' want to eat when I tell you this, cuz." The waitress obligingly laid the menus down and scurried away only to return in a second with another cup and a fresh handheld urn of black coffee. Breeze leaned back in the seat cushion and folded his arms, stretching the leather out past its normal seams. His face became black with anger as fire shot from his squinting and bloodshot eyes. They bounced nervously all around the room then landed on Frank. Silence prevailed to the point of inspiring Frank to ask, "What the fuck is going on?" Then Breeze spat it out. "They wacked both of my guys, not one but both, within hours of each other." He became silent and watched the horror consume his cousin's face. "We're dead men, Bobby, they gotta' know." Breeze fired back. "You forget. My guys already know the score. This comes from your camp."

Frank shrugged and asked the only question that came across his mind. "When did it happen?" Bobby unzipped his coat and settled in with elbows square on the table. "Sometime yesterday, I got a call from a cop telling me my buddy Al Coleman was in the trunk of a car somewhere by the Gowanus Canal." Frank frowned and asked, "What cop?" "Not your cop," 'Breeze said in confidence. The reference by Bobby Breeze was about Accardi; then he said matter-of-factly, "I gotta' a guy at the third precinct in Newark." Frank looked alarmed. He figured as much but never asked about the cooperation from the police in the black neighborhoods that his cousin's heroin flowed. Breeze spoke painstakingly, "My guy at the Third Precinct got a call about a massacre in the back lot of a joint called Dupes on Central Avenue. My main man and a couple of his Moolie stooges got shot to pieces. They blew his fuckin' head off with a shotgun." Frank pressed Bobby for more information with candor. "The guy in the trunk, the one dumped in your own backyard—that was a message no?" "I'm sure it was." Breeze acknowlegded. "And I'll lay ya' dollars to donuts he was tortured to give up everybody else," Batista said with reserve. Bobby did not seem alarmed at all by that statement. "Who the fuck is he gonna' give up? Me. I'm sure they already know about me. And who cares, this is Profaci's nightmare now." Frank snapped back with an angry voice. "What about me? Do they know about me too, Bobby? And how about the market, what if they piece that puzzle together?" Bobby Breeze rubbed his tired eyes and said, "Coleman was a good guy. Tough, I knew him from the army, we were stationed in Korea together, that's where he got his start with the junk, ya' know. I trusted him with my life back then, and I gotta' say he went down silent. And besides, he has no idea who the fuck you are. You were just my guy in Jersey, that's all he knew. You know we don't talk names. And as far as the market goes, they will never figure that operation out. Now I gotta' hold up shipments until we can regroup."

The two men sat with a long silence between them as they both fiddled with the placemats and placed silverware. Bobby Breeze wriggled his nose oddly and said, "You know now that I think about it, something to eat ain't a bad idea." Both men surrendered to the aroma of the diner and ordered steak and eggs with sides of sausages and hash browns. It made no difference to either because the way Bobby Breeze read it, New York and New Jersey were going to start a war with the Brooklyn mob over this shit. As a matter of fact, they already have. The question the two cousins threw around was when and where and who were the next to get it. But this is the life they chose, a living, breathing chess match with the devil himself. Frank hung up his peacoat on a mounted hanger and watched as the waitress carefully unloaded the plates of food from her extended arm to the table.

Frank felt a little more at ease after hearing his cousin out. He spoke high-spiritedly as he said, "Fuck it, cuz…if this is our last meal, so be it." He spoke in short bursts in between mouthfuls of food. You could tell he was annoyed. "You know I gotta' say something. Just what the fuck is this thing of ours supposed to be? We're made men, part of a…a…a family, or better yet an army. We're soldiers, yet we cheat each other, we beat up each other, we murder each other, and in the name of what? Could you imagine what people think of us? Friends…we're supposed to be loyal comrades. What the hell do you think normal people think of us? I could hear them now. 'Just what kind of guys are these that go around killin' each other?' I just don't get it?"

Joe Marino left his gas station early every Wednesday and would almost always go visit his sister-in-law Ceil. Sometimes she would cook a light dinner for him or have at least a generous amount of leftovers on hand or sometimes he would take her out to eat; either way it was becoming sort of a tradition. With the completion of the Route 21 extension, the trip to her part of the Newark was much easier now, as was it more predicable timewise—fifteen minutes tops from his Central Avenue location. This night he would show up early and feast on leftover Manicott and homemade meatballs, made the way they were supposed to be made. He would bring over only what Ceil asked him to bring: a good appetite.

Wednesday was also the night that Ceil and Joe would call the farmhouse and talk with Tomasino and Josephina. It was very seldom that Tony would be there, this disenchanting to Ceil as was the fact her son did call but not as much as she wished he would. Joe and Tomasino kept the reality of her son's mob life far away from her ears and say, "You know he's not a kid anymore, he's over twenty-one," this said with the fervent hopes of putting her mind at rest. They would speak only of the good things that came the boy's way, and he would exemplify that with packages of gifts and letters containing soft words and cash, this a big reason she found it not a necessary burden to return to work although she would decide to after a while.

Joe posed no valid threat to Ceil as far as spitefully picking up the pieces of her late husband's life and tossing them in her face. It was quite the contrary. He offered as much help and money to help her forget the horrible past. He had not a love interest with her as the gossip would lead you to believe, nor did Albert Marrone who still came bearing gifts. Perhaps he knew she was still very much a younger middle-aged woman, and at her own pace or in her own time, if she was ready for it, maybe she would "find someone," as her girlfriends put it.

Joe enjoyed the new Ceil, and offered comment and self-assurance about how much more buoyant and relaxed she now felt—and her noticeable weight loss. This said and interpreted by her words spoken as the onus and worry of not one but two adult hoodlums was lifted off her shoulders. Gone were the days of slaving over a hot stove cooking for the masses, and gone were the days of worry.

She recognized the new body she had, one that was hers as a much younger woman and sexy all the same even for a woman her age. She flaunted it with pride, and would buy a new dress each month as a promise she made to herself. And she would pamper herself at the beauty parlor. She would keep her furtive beauty to herself for untold reasons.

She mentioned to Joe, in a shy sort of hush-hush voice, of a certain man, a handsome man who rode the bus to work each morning after he visited his late wife's gravesite just a short stone's throw away from her Anthony's. It was a convenient visit for him both before and after his work as his bus stop was directly in front of the cemetery gate. Joe sat with wide eager eyes and listened as Ceil continued the story on how she met him there about a year ago, coincidentally, as they shared the same path leading to the gates. It was late springtime when the cemetery seemed to be not the place it represented but a place we all think of heaven to be like. Lush greenery and shrubs, fragrant flowers abound. Even the cold granite headstones and saintly statues had a crimson glow from the sun. At first his flirtation was something Ceil fancied—it had been a long time any male paid a drop of attention to her. His name was Sidney Margolis. He worked downtown Newark as a diamond setter for some jeweler. Sidney was Jewish and commented on how ironic his Selma was to escape the Nazis only to be stricken with an evil cancer that quickly and unmercifully took her life. Ceil hesitated with any form or annotation over the also early passing of her husband but with a tender voice Sidney took hold of her hand and said, "I saw the name on the headstone. I read the papers. No explanation is necessary." Ceil just smiled.

As time passed and summer approached they'd meet again. Sidney always with the compliments—how exquisite she looked in her new dress or pantsuit, her new hairstyle, then a true confession of his heart. He braggingly stated of how he had been noticing her since that past winter. He explained how he would sometimes sit at the bus stop for days and days trying to get a sense of when she visits. She hasn't been chased or sought after by a man other than her husband in years. Then one day she picked up on his true innuendos. The ever-so-charming Sidney casually let his hand fall and wedge between the closed gap of her leg, just above her knee, and gave her a gentle squeeze. He mentioned to Ceil that his apartment was just around the corner and casually asked her over for coffee or tea or anything she wanted to drink. He openly discussed his feelings of what he had hoped to be the beginning of a monumental love affair. She was flattered to the point of being almost embarrassed, but in all actuality, she became frightened. She avidly stated, "I don't think so." Then in a shameful tone of voice she said to Joe, "Could you imagine the nerve of him, but those Jews, they are pushy that way, huh Joe?" And as she shook her head in dismay she said, "And that was the last I ever saw of him." Joe's head was spinning—he didn't know whether to laugh or cry, so he answered in a semi-sincere wise guy connotation, "So you want I should have a talk wit this guy?" Both broke out in harmonious laughter.

The next morning as Joe sat alone at his breakfast table eating a self-prepared meal of soft-boiled eggs and burnt Italian toast. While slurping down freshly made coffee he caught a headline that finally made the *Star Ledger*'s front page: MOB-LIKE MASSACRE DAYS AFTER SAINT VALENTINE'S DAY. He read but did not recognize any of the names in print, nor did he understand the gist or the meaning of the headline—mob? What mob were they referring? The article was vague at best and gave mention of a reputed drug lord slain by a rival gang impersonating the police that did the shooting—the massacre as they described. And of course there weren't any witnesses. He knew the neighborhoods well and put two and two together. These are colored men the paper's sensationalism is referring to, not the mob he knew. Now that was a change, gangland violence without mention of one Italian, and he immediately wondered if any of the Ruggeri Bloomfield Avenue crew were reading the same story—and laughing?

Ceil was up bright and early and having her usual flippant conversation with her image in the bathroom mirror over some trivial thing or another. But by the time she reached the kitchen, all was now calm. The radio was on and Sinatra was crooning away. She sat and sipped her piping hot coffee and took an intimate and an honest inventory of her life. She truly enjoyed not having the hindrance or workload she once had—the constant catering to a most demanding husband and a son of the same chip off the old block. Ceil Marino was, to some extent, forever content on being a widow, and that extent was up to and including only the monotonous and wearisome tasks of housework. Unappreciated laborious housework as she could remember the last few years of life with her late-husband as being. She now had only a few menial chores; then the rest of the time was hers to spend as freely and wantonly as she so desired. Lately she had a desire and wished for the companionship of a husband. The elemental sexual covet that she lacked in her life. When her Anthony was still alive and up until the last few months he was on earth, they did share a somewhat awkward coquetting between themselves. It was more of just a release for the two but enough to satisfy an itch, a carnal knowledge that they had gotten used to. She was dead certain he still entertained his whores, and as she aged she lived with that idea just so long he came home each and every night, or no later than the following morning. But as time heals all wounds she began to think less of her own late husband and more and more of that handsome man she had met at the cemetery.

And now her sexually healthy libido was tugging at her. She knew she has a fairly attractive and desirable body for a woman in her early fifties and it should not go to waste. And it was decided by her and her naked sensual image she spoke to in the bathroom mirror, she had mourned long enough, and the promise she made to her late husband was falling by the wayside. The nights out with the girls, although so appropriate and for the most part enjoyable, were beginning to leave her very much unsatisfied. Overtures of sexual adventures were commonplace amongst the women in her group; even the old-timers laughed and joked about intimacies once shared.

And Ceil would be home alone thinking of herself and her husband as newlyweds and throughout all of their younger years when her Anthony's sexual prowess was distinct. Her eyes would close and the thought of lovemaking would dance vividly in her head. She voraciously blamed the changing world; the movies today are much more open and explicit about sex than the movies of the forties or fifties. She could only imagine what thoughts would be flying if it had been Sidney with her watching the *Night of the Iguana* on a first date instead of her girlfriend Margie. Then she laughed to herself. This was the first time in almost two years the thought of the handsome and anxious man who had so invitingly introduced himself to her at the cemetery gates.

This day and evening would be spent alone. She would have her hair styled in the fashion of Elizabeth Taylor, the actress that, Ceil heard so much, in her younger years she remarkably resembled. It would be the way she wore it in her latest movie. She would be daring and put on a pair of tight-fitting yellow pedal pushers with a matching blouse. If the June wind kicked up, she would wear a colorful kerchief fitted loosely and tied under her chin and have on the latest fashionable sunglasses. Then at precisely three-thirty she would take a nice walk to the cemetery and wait for the four o'clock bus to arrive.

The certain and simple fact was, Frank Batista could not ever sleep past three or four o'clock a.m. anymore. He had a prescription for sleeping pills tucked away in his medicine cabinet but thought them unnecessary and dangerous. He did not want to get taken by surprise, especially under the influence of narcotics. Batista felt if he couldn't get to sleep and stay asleep with a little alcohol or counting sheep, then it just wasn't meant to be. Darker glasses would hide the sleeplessness that blackened the puffy circles under his eyes. It was 6:00 a.m. and he was on his second pot of demitasse crooning along to a Francis Albert tune blaring. It would be pointless to hit the streets anytime before noon. His crew would not be anywhere near the avenue haunts or the Pope's place until after three. But his routine as of late was being the first at the club when it opened at 2:00 p.m. He knew that neither the Pope nor the recently retired Accardi would be there. Marrone would be there though sitting at his usual booth with the morning papers spread out in front of him.

Albert was truly old-school and showed up usually just to show respect. He had no real crew left anymore nor any doled chores. His once privileged duty of running the waterfront bookmakers and loan sharks was sliced up and given to the more active capos of which Frank was one. He was being slowly put out to pasture as his friend Cheese was—but he thought God forbid that type exit. Frank would sit some with Marrone, with a definite agenda, to pick his brains for any gossip and leave him with the deliberate gossip he wanted to spread.

The headlines still read in bold print—Gandlang—pure sensationalism, with the newspaper's opinioned theories of the happenings in the drug underworld. The bleak but obvious editorials were even worse. Some saying this while others meant that, and not a reporter was entirely accurate or knew the truth—and neither did Batista. He could only make assumptions, and wait as all others were, for things to die down. The true players regretted the war and the fact that they were definitely out of business for a while. Batista became reliant on that dirty drug money. It picked up the slack of his lackadaisical mob duties around the neighborhood and no one the wiser—just so long as the Pope got his weekly tribute of stacks of cash. Now he had the burdensome duty of getting his crew back up to speed, up and running and earning the old-fashioned way—loan sharking, sports betting, shakedowns, extortion, and of course stealing freight. The highlight of their daily conversation was some guy named Dr. Zhivago.

The June air was moist and cool and gave Frank a chill as he sat out on his balcony wearing only his skivvies, T-shirt, and slippers—his hair still wet from his morning shower. As he smoked, he jotted notes on the borders and print of the newspaper, his agenda for the day. Some personal notes and phone numbers not etched in his memory were divided among a couple of pieces of newsprint, some letters underlined or circled and some in his handwriting—undecipherable gibberish to even the keenest of federal agent. He carefully tore out a classified ad for a paper boy wanted and hoped it would serve as a reminder to call Tony in Greensburg sometime today. All of the memo notepaper would all be carefully distributed on his person.

Two Sicilian greenhorn custodians were pushing vacuum cleaners and emptying trash cans, the only audible noise that was heard throughout the Pope's club. Batista entered from the rear door and found his way to the booth Albert was at. "So whaddya hear? Whaddya say, my old friend?" Albert just grunted back. He was silent for a bit as he rummaged through the *Star Ledger* until he found the article he was looking for and anxious to share with Batista. Marrone jabbed at the print rigorously with his fat index finger. "Go ahead, read. Now they're trying to blame your cousin's outfit for this bloodbath." Batista showed no emotion as he knew that the papers were partially correct.

Frank waved for one of the janitors to come over to the booth. He reached in his pant pocket and dumped all the change he had on the table, sorting out the nickels dimes and quarters. "Here, go play some music," he said as he pointed to the silent jukebox along the far wall. He would feel more at ease talking aloud with some background music to serve as interference just in case of a meddling bugging device.

Frank had already read the article but acted surprised to amuse Marrone. "So what do you make of all this?" he asked. Marrone frowned and said, "It's got mob hit written all over it. Looks like the work we would do." He paused some then looked Frank in the eye. "I hear they found the one nigger in pieces in that trunk." He was missing fingers, teeth, and toes." Frank winced and let out a cockeyed "What?" Marrone nodded his head in rapid succession. "Sounds to me like they chopped off pieces of his feet." Frank immediately recognized mob torture; the gruesome details would never be made known to the public. He pressed on to keep Marrone talking, sensing his firsthand knowledge of the incident. Frank took a wild swing. "Sounds like you had a ringside seat, my friend…did you?" Marrone looked back at him with a "you got to be kidding" look and said, "I saw the medical examiner's report. I read the autopsy results." That was enough said or written between the lines to convince Frank that it was someone in Pope's organization.

One could only imagine the brutality of the act knowing that with each question asked another piece of his body and flesh was torn from him. Small caliber bullets were in found in both of his knees and thighs as well as both shoulders. A total of seventeen gashes caused by what the examiner described as a sheet rock knife or utility blade razor riddled his upper torso and face; his left ear sliced completely off. His singed hair was burnt to the scalp and other parts of his body were charred by an obvious blowtorch, a seemingly crude attempt to cauterize the ghastly wounds. The report concluded as did the medical examiner himself that the cause of death was from a multitude of trauma.

It was ignored at first, but now both mobsters winced at the worst percussion and clamor spewed from the speakers connected to the jukebox. The greenhorn pushed the buttons to the very worst

Italian folksong imaginable within the inventory of recorded discs secured in the racks. An elderly barista brought over demitasse cups and a pot full of fresh espresso to the booth. Batista's eyebrows rose to his hairline as he waved the custodian over. "The music...it's a little too loud." "I donta' no how to mahyke quiet" was his response. Albert blurted in an annoyed tone of Italian dialect, "You know how to pull the fuckin' plug out of the wall?" "Haigabid," acknowledged the man with a sour frown.

The men were now into their second hour of what was just a bullshit session, and talking about life in general in Mobville. "I hear the Pope reached out to Monestero about your *guaglione* out there," Marrone said casually as he slurped down a cup of coffee. "Reached out for what?" Frank asked with a painstaking look. Marrone gave a small half laugh and said, "It's funny. Like years ago, when they sent for his father...it's like history repeatin' itself." Batista recognized the connotation. Marrone continued. "The Pope wants the kid back here to make restitution. He thinks him and his uncle should be taxed for the sins and debt of the old man." Frank spoke quickly, "Who... Cheese...c'mon, Albert, that's over and done, isn't it?" Batista knew the vindictive nature of Angelo Ruggeri; his ruthless nature and greed were incontestable.

Frank took another long shot at Albert. He spoke remorsefully, knowing fully he was considerably shy of the once cache of cash he once had. "Ya know, if I had the fifty Gs I would kick it up to the Pope myself" He was silent then looked straight at Albert. "If I had *half* the money I'd kick it up." Albert's reaction was as expected, not the forthright thought of he himself paying for his dear old and dead companion but the impudent "And what about the vig running all these years?" Albert shut his mouth and looked into thin air. "And tell the kid to stop bad-mouthin' us here in Jersey. Whaddya' think, we don't hear things?" Frank silently sided with Albert on that one. He always told Tony to keep to himself his opinions about the Pope and what actually happened to his father. The conversation was beginning to make Frank sick to his stomach as was the sight of Albert Marrone. Frank gave his wristwatch a glance and sprang to his feet. He gave Albert a baneful slap on his bulky shoulder and said, "Don't get up. I know you're in pain." He thought to himself, *You should die, you old cocksucker.*

The rest of the day played out as Frank had hoped and expected, peaceful. No headaches or misfortunes but with hustle. He met with one of his soldiers and instructed him to take Ralph on some collections and then to be at a certain phone booth at a certain time later in the day. He was at that phone booth now as he gave the go-ahead to Nick D'Aloia to hijack a load of Lord and Taylor merchandise coming from Secaucus, and "make sure you bring it to the Jersey City warehouse this time."

Batista fumbled through his news clippings and found the one of the newspaper boy and within a few seconds after dialing the phone. The gruff voice of Josephine answered, "Hold on...lemme' see." He heard the buoyant voice of his—in his mind—adopted son, Tony Marino. Not a young boy's voice anymore but a voice that seemed much more mature now, and Frank thought, well, he was approaching his mid-twenties—that age in itself was considered the halfway point in a mobster's life. The two hadn't spoken for some time now, of which Frank was most apologetic for. "Don't worry about it, Ti'. I'm just as guilty. You always said that these phones work both ways." It was once described to the kid by Batista, ironically over the phone, that true friends could stay away and not talk for years, and on the day they did, it would be like never ever missing a beat. Not a word would be wasted on excuses, justifications, or chastises.

Tony began by bringing Frank up to date about all things good and bad in his life with the Pittsburgh crew and his girlfriend. That prompted Frank to relay the message about the gossip Albert Marrone had told him earlier. Then he gave the blow by blow of the impending doom about the drug thing. This left a shallow hole and a baneful feeling in the pit of Tony's stomach, and he expressed his disdainful feeling about the whole matter. They both laughed about Accardi retiring and the crack about him keeping the cop car, but for the most part, the dubious thought of that prick angered both. He was regarded by both Frank and Tony as still a dangerous man and ever so guilty in the shooting death of his father.

Tony's anger grew some but he remained calm. "Ya know, Tic, I don't know how they do it, but all I said one time, in anger during a card game at Rozzell's, was what a prick the Pope was to me that day he threw me out of the club. That was it!" "Need I remind you, kid, the walls have big ears attached to little rats" was Frank's words of wisdom in return.

Frank went on and reminded him of his own wishes for him to come back to Jersey. "I don't know who my real friends are anymore. I don't recognize any of 'em, and that's not a good thing in this business." He became silent a bit then said, "It's like we all got targets on our backs…all of us." He became extremely emotional and spoke with the sincerity of a priest or a father, "We have to form an alliance together, me and you, kid…you know I been watching you since you're a little kid for Christ sakes. I remember when you were born… it's the cradle to the grave, kid, you and me." Tony listened and took every word to heart. Then Frank threw him a curveball. "Tell me, kid…I know you're getting close, and if you want, you could really dive in, but is the life really what it's cracked up to be? Is it what you want? And if you had the chance to walk away, would you?" Those few words hit hard, and made both think in a brief silence.

Suddenly he was just a small child sitting with his mother listening and wondering as she cried over the misery that his father had given her time and time again. And then he thought of the day that his father expressed such hope and happiness for them all as he almost did walk away. He answered Frank's question with a question of his own, "What about you, Tic, if you had the chance, would you?" "You mean now, right now, walk away no questions asked, you bet I would." Tony sensed sobs coming from his tough guy mentor. Was he right? He need not know, but if they were tears, he would reassure it to be only human and tell his friend not to be ashamed. But instead, he kept quiet. We do all cry now and then. And we ain't as tough as we like to think we are, were the kid's thoughts.

Frank chimed in on a high note, "So forgetting the bullshit, you got a big day comin' up, don't ya?" Tony broke into half a smile. "You know I'm not much on birthdays 'cause of...you know why, but if it were up to me, I would love to celebrate it with you and my mother...back there." Frank agreed and said profoundly, "We gotta' put our heads together, kid, we gotta' put our heads together. Listen...just get back here, you come stay with me. I got plenty of room. I got a whole furnished apartment sitting empty. You could stay there. I could use the help with the rent." Tony spoke genuinely and from the heart, "Tic...I'll call you when I get there."

29

Cathleen Carluccio was alone in her apartment sitting with her legs tightly wedged under her buttocks and her dainty feet buried deeply in the soft cushions of her new sofa. A begrudging type of nervousness made her wiggle and stretch her toes to the point of creating a charley horse. Her resentment grew as she looked over the amount of stuff accumulating—more frivolous jewelry and silly electronic trinkets provided by the generous bearer of never-ending gifts, Tony Marino. His generosity was now overbearing. She constantly expressed a sort of resentment to his lavishness and the snide way he would comment on her pauper beginnings. Her constant refrain was vile at times. "Who the fuck asked you to keep bringing me these things I have absolutely no need for?" Still, every day was like Christmas, filled with gifts galore, and just about all of them, unbeknownst to her, stolen and all given to her to serve as reprisal for his uncontested sins. But it was this action of giving he found to be less committal on his part rather than picking up and moving her to another place, a place that she could mistakenly call their own.

Cathleen was about to have a lot of free time on her hands, and that worried her. Tony finally convinced her to quit her job and just stay at home and be a good girlfriend. "Learn to cook" was the encouraging thought. There was no need for her to work according to him. She agreed with one stipulation that she be able to go back to school on a part-time basis and work toward getting her degree. And that he allow her to work at the pub a couple of nights only to cover the manageable tuition costs. Money she refused to have him shell out for although he was ever so willing. He agreed to the terms. She made it in time to enroll in the summer semester at Westmoreland Community College.

Now her time was spent productively, and in her spare time she took inventory of her perceptible life with a gangster she well knew by now the certainty about that part of his life. She took a pencil to her situation and realized that the few redeeming qualities her young man possessed was not nearly the provision of the life she expected.

She did enjoy his company but found herself wanting to be with him less and less. She respected the fact that he didn't smoke or use alcohol and drugs as so many of the hooligans he brought around, and she found it noble that while sometimes she tested his Guinea temper, he never laid a hand on her. His lovemaking was still passionate when they did have sex, but lately he's been staying away for longer periods of time, a lot more than usual.

She found it annoying that he would drag her to his aunt and uncle's place just about every week for the high and holy Sunday dinner without one single regard for her desire or wishes to do something else besides eat macaroni and meatballs. She vehemently expressed her open dislike for the red gravy as they so commonly called it. This, he forewarned her, would be her demise and would end the idea of her ever being his bride, a thought that dismayed her now as well.

The routine Tony had gotten his girl used to was by design. If he had to stay out late, until the wee hours of the morning he would call and forewarn; then he'd stay away from the apartment for a while, at least a day or two, and then would casually show with such a masterfully produced alibi or excuse. There were times his work would take him out of town, or sometimes he would be just so dog-tired he stayed in his own bed at the farmhouse. He tried as best he could to shelter Cathleen from the harsh reality and existence of organized crime, but that was just impossible at times. If they attended a gala or a funeral of a fellow wise guy, she could overhear the contaminated inference of their everyday crimes—gambling or stealing or girlfriends on the side; severe physical harm, even murder, would flow from the hoodlums' lips in a cipher all their own.

When Frankie would visit the apartment, the talk was nonstop gibberish of stealing something or how much this score was going to be worth and who was going to take what load to the point of her just getting up and either leaving the tiny flat or going to bed and tightly wrap the covers around her shoulders in a defiant way of saying "Do not touch me tonight."

Cathleen always thought she had seen it all, but in her mind the shenanigans ceased to amaze her. Frankie and his cousin Vito came over late one night carrying a brownish uniform complete with jacket and a logoed ball cap for Tony to try on for size. Both men laughed and joked about what could be accomplished by just having the uniform on. Vito threw his hands up like a tailor as Tony emerged from the bedroom. "So how do I look?" Vito looked at Frankie and said emphatically with arms wailing, "No one asks when you show up they, just wave and let you in…anywhere…you could walk in the White House with that get-up on…no one the wiser."

Without any warning, rhyme, or reason, as most women will do, Cathleen exploded. She could not hold it in any longer. She recognized the Pullman brown color that was exclusive to Merchants Delivery Service, and she snarled, "Don't even tell me you are going to pull some scam, some fucking heist wearing that uniform, you two are really nuts, do you know that?" Cathleen raged on and on and cursed herself for getting mixed up with such sociopaths and how "don't you think I know that everything in this fucking apartment is probably stolen" while the three bit their tongues to stop from laughing. Cathleen's choler and cursing rang out, "Get out…get the fuck out of my, my fucking apartment, all of you just get out." Her swollen eyes looked at her Tony directly, with daggers. "And you first, and take these fucking bums with you!" It was a bloodbath.

She stormed in the kitchen for a second then came back. "I mean it, Tony…get out…the sight of you all makes me sick." Tony gave a solemn look to Frankie and whispered in his ear, "Guess this wasn't such a good idea—wait outside." He turned to Cathleen and felt no emotion, not a hint of a retaliatory defense—instead he just took a step past her and headed for the bedroom. She grabbed the material of the uniform sleeve that covered his upper arm and tried to spin him around. She sobbed uncontrollably. "I said to leave… please—just—leave." This the first bit of anger he felt. He gave his arm a strong shake loose of her grip; the force sprained her finger and caused her to yell out in pain and fall to the floor. He once again spoke calmly, "You don't think I'm gonna' go out in this uniform now, do 'ya? I'm gonna' grab a few things while you should calm the fuck down."

She sat at the edge of the couch with a cold, impassive look on her face. Tony walked out of the bedroom carrying a grocery bag with the brown uniform inside and another small gym bag. Their eyes met and stayed trained on each other as he left. "I'll call you tomorrow." He left her expressionless, with no feeling at all. To her surprise, she felt no real hate or animosity or reprisal or requital and certainly not any love lost. She sat there alone and felt absolutely nothing. And after a few minutes she would feel warm and relieved that he was gone. She was finished with all her crying and dismissed all angst—she actually felt quite satisfied. She sat up straight and she profoundly announced to her inner soul, *Good fucking riddance, Tony Marino*. She wondered perhaps if it was because of her first failed relationship that made her heart so cold and callused now. Or did she learn this all from Tony?

It was business at hand for Tony and his crew. He and Frankie and Vito met at a roadside diner on Lincoln Highway just about a mile up from the Lackland Forwarding Company just as soon as they left Cathleen's. The place was starting to fill up with uniformed truckers of all sorts and the various dockworkers that operated the tow-motors and the heavy-duty freight dollies and hand trucks, some very recognizable from their visits to Rozzell's but none coming forth with jovial "how do you do's." And for good reason; if a formal meeting was not arranged, then everyone remains a stranger.

Frankie watched as Vito nodded to a young MDS driver getting an order to go. The driver left and Vito was inconspicuously on his tail. Frankie and Tony lost sight of them as they walked around the corner of the diner. Then after a few minutes Vito slipped back into his spot at the booth. He scrapped the last bit of ham and eggs off his plate then began writing on a napkin as he said, "It's all set. Tomorrow night we're gonna meet him up the road. He's gonna drive us past the gate and let us off right next to the truck. It's been there like clockwork every night this week, and he says it's always there at the same time. The drivers are all on a tight schedule. He says we got at least a half an hour before the night loaders pull it up to the dock, it's that simple. The keys will be in it, just sign the log as you leave the yard and bring it back empty. When you're done, just walk out the employees' gate and no one's the wiser."

The truck they were talking about was an MDS delivery van that will be brought back with at least two hundred unique gift boxes of JFK commemorative gold coins from a nearby mint plus who knows what else. That was always the thrill of hijacking a truck. You never knew what else you would find. The score should net the boys at least ten to twenty thousand depending on the price of gold and the weight.

The score went down without a hitch, and that night the boys met at Denuzio's to celebrate. Their anticipated take, after tribute to Ianuzzi, should be a clean five thousand apiece. Not a bad day's pay. "Salute! Salute!" was heard around the table of thieves as they toasted one another and dined on enormous slabs of beautifully cooked veal chops. This was a tradition in Mobville. Always eat a real good meal before and after a score just in case. "Who knows, boys," Frankie exalted. "Maybe this joint turns out to be our personal Lackland Empire."

Cathleen stormed out of her Saturday exercise class in a fluster. It has been almost a week and not a call from that bastard boyfriend of hers. She kept gritting her teeth as she muttered the infamous "Ohhh fuck him" over and over and over. And as Irish mad as she was, she'd call up Mr. Anthony Marino directly, just as soon as she got to the apartment and let him have a real peace of her mind. Her heart raced as she noticed his Lincoln was parked in front of her building—in her parking space.

She angrily jammed her key in the lock when suddenly the door pulled open. Tony was on the other side with a glass of bourbon in his hand. "See what you make me do…drink in the afternoon." She had both arms wrapped around fresh-cleaned laundry as she gave him a nudge with her shoulder to pass. "Here let me get that…I'll be a good boy, I promise." Cathleen sensed his apologetic nature to always be real—sincere and from the heart. She conceded the hateful lecture she was prepared to deliver over the phone, and now she conceded her passion as his Guinea charm just seduced the hell out of her, and they were enrapt in the sounds and smells of raw afternoon sweat, whisky, and sex.

Cathleen sat up in bed and tried to focus on the five o'clock news that was just about five minutes into the latest story. Tony took a quick shower and redressed. He looked at Cathy and asked, "You want anything to drink. I'm thinkin' we go out and get some good

Chinese food tonight, what do you think?" Cathleen let the question of dinner fade into the air. She was preoccupied with another abnormal feeling gnawing away at her. The words spew flippantly off of her tongue as she asked, "Do you ever cheat on me?" This question caused Tony to stop dead in his tracks.

He thought hard about the question and stalled for precious time—then spoke with candor, "You know what, I'm gonna tell you the truth." Her eyes closed with fear with the sounds. "In the beginning I had other women…they were no concern to you and in my opinion were none of your business back then. If you're asking me do I have another girlfriend or wife or *goomatta* stashed over on West Pittsburgh Street or back in Jersey, the answer is no."

Cathleen saw through the slick mobster's smoke screen and realized he is truly a sociopath and so used to lying. In his mind the stories they concoct, be it fact or fiction, are to them the Gospel truth, and all must understand and agree. She spoke with arrogance, "No… no…no…I want to know if you ever cheated on me with another girl—since we been dating, seeing each other—you do know the difference, don't you? Have you been fucking someone else?" He looked at her, expressionless, and did not even try to figure her out; he just lied. "No, the answer is no to that form of questioning." He gave her a boyish look and crossed his heart. "Boy Scout's honor."

He sipped his whisky and waited as she freshened up. They drove to a well-known Chinese restaurant on East Pittsburgh Street without a word between them. Tony ordered everything on the menu, and as usual when the check came, Cathy could not help but sneak a peek. Her comment was raw. "Jesus…Chinese food used to be the cheapest food you could buy, you spent how much?" Her sentence was cut short. "What did I tell ya', about grabbing the check… do you want to pay for it?" Tony snapped as he scooped up the bill. Cathleen struggled with a fortune cookie and said sternly, again reaching for the check in his hand, "Fuck your wise guy rules. You want me to pay, I can pay." He slammed his hand down and crushed her cookie along with his. "There's no good fortune to be read here tonight." Then he slapped the crumbs from the table and his hands.

There was complete silence between the two as they walked to the car. She opened her own door. Tony squared his body in the seat and gripped the wheel. He cleared his throat and spoke calmly with a slight grin, "Tomorrow is my birthday. My aunt and uncle want to have a party for me at the farmhouse this Sunday. I know you can care less about Sunday dinner, so if you don't want to be there, I understand." Cathy looked at him with a bewildered stare. "I thought you had no use for birthdays...what's so special about this one?" He proudly replied with a sly smirk, "Twenty-three...it's gonna be my twenty-third birthday." He stared flippantly at her with a broad grin on his face. She grew irritated a bit and said, "What if I wanted to do something for your birthday, and you're so right, I'm not in love with your Italian food or your Sunday dinners." Tony replied coyly, "So what did you plan, did you even get me a gift?" She looked into thin air and sat emotionless. Tony pointed an evil finger at her and said adamantly, "I read you like a book, kid, you got nothing planned for me 'cause of the blowout we had last week, and certainly not a gift in sight, am I right? So how fuckin' thoughtful are you. If there were plans or a gift, you'd have them ready, you would have thrown them at me by now...and ya' know what, I don't want you with my family tomorrow or ever." He was vile with the words that spewed from gritted teeth. Cathleen was trembling. His anger was well beyond rage—it was lethal. She made another attempt to speak. His hand went up to silence her once again. "Ya' know, Cath', I had a good run here...we had a good run here——I don't wanna' hear no more!" Not a word was said as they drove, not an apologetic glance offered by either. With cold eyes staring straight ahead he spoke quickly and directly, "I'm thinking about going back to Jersey." She ignored the statement at first then raised her brows and said, "Go ahead…stay as long as you need." Her voice was silent but only for a second before she sassed, "What are you going to do back there…rob another truck?" His face turned into a look of solace as he said with straightforwardness and candor, "I'm thinking about moving there…go back to live." She let out a self-assured "I'm not moving there." She maintained her gutsy stance. "My family is up in Pittsburgh. If I move anywhere, it's going to be there." His eyes bugged and his hands gripped the steering wheel with white knuckles. Tony spoke as the devil would speak, "And who the fuck is asking you to come along?"

Not a word was spoken between the two as he drove her to the apartment. He watched her with his peripheral vision as she sat unmoving and her eyes shut. He knew she wasn't sleeping. She knew the sharp and violent turns made were intentional and by design, a harboring suggestion of hatred on his part. Cathleen sensed he was pulling up in front of her building and she quickly prepared herself to get out of the car. She clutched her handbag and took hold of the door handle. The chivalrous act of him opening her door was flatly denied with her flippant "Don't bother." She slammed the door hard and as he watched her once irresistible ass walked the path up to her apartment.

She took slow and deliberate steps, and she talked to herself aloud, "What balls he has…he's not even making an attempt to apologize." She heard his Lincoln accelerate and speed away. She turned completely around and faced the spot where his car used to be. "Why that fucking jerk…just wait till I see him again."

A small but well-iced chocolate birthday cake was sitting in the corner of the kitchen, covered under a domed glass cake plate dish atop a white paper doily. Tony noticed it as soon as he walked in. Josephine smiled and said, "Chocolate, made just like your mother would." Tony gave her a smile and a huge hug. "Ohhh, Aunt Jo, do I see gnocchi in the fridge." His uncle Tomasino gave him a whimsical "Shhhh" and a look meaning "don't squeal on me." Tony said, "I saw them there this morning when I had coffee." "Liar, liar," his aunt shot back in obvious jest.

Tony took a conscious gander around the kitchen, as he knew it would be his last. The all-day Sunday gravy, the red *sugo*, was simmering away with the meatballs and sausage and country ribs, getting a gentle stir every so often. Josephina had Grandma Rosa secure at the table while she manned the sink washing the spinach and 'shcarole and broccoli rabe for the salad and the sautéed greens. Uncle Tomas was in front of the television sipping on a Rolling Rock nip cursing the Philadelphia Phillies as they kicked the tar out of his Pirates. Tony took the stairs at a brisk pace, two at a time, and then began to round up his belongings with very little repentance. He was taking only his clothing and just a few photos of his extended Pennsylvanian family and a few rare ones of his father and uncles and cronies taken in their younger days—these he would cherish. He was leaving behind anything to do with Cathleen and tried so very hard not to think of her at all as he put her mementos in a cardboard box to be laid to rest.

Dinner was announced by Aunt Jo in her best Sunday gruff, off tenor's voice, "Let's eat." The laborious preparation of the birthday gala did not go unnoticed by the hungry eaters who tore through plates of food. When dinner was finished and the table cleared, all three sat and feigned laughter and masked the sorrow that was building—all pretended nothing was out of the ordinary. They all ate cake and slurped on coffee and toasted the birthday boy with six different types of liqueurs. Tony made a host of whimsical and distorted faces as he one by one read the cards that came from friends and family back east—this was the only way to hold back the tears. His mother's card had the most wishes handwritten in it: "Hope you have a great birthday and wish we were there with you. This was the birthday I always hoped you to have when you were sixteen. Hope you come soon, can't wait—Love, your mother."

Tomasino waited for Josephina to put Grandma in her room and return to the kitchen, and then with gleaming eyes he proudly slid a small wrapped box toward his nephew. Tony gave him a frown and said, "Unk...you didn't have to get me anything—and Aunt Jo—" His uncle gave a look of awareness and said, "It's not much. Your aunt and me kicked this idea around. We noticed that you never replaced that gold chain with the Guinea horn, so..." Tony opened the box and exclaimed at the beauty of the gold medal. "It's all the way from Italy...from our village," Aunt Josephina said with a stutter as she fought back tears. "The best gold money can buy. It's a medal of our family saint, Saint Francis of Assisi, and his birthday was the day after yours. And it was blessed by the pope, the store over there does that." She made the sign of the cross. Tony held the chain between his fingers, winked, and gave them both a seal-of-approval look. "It's got some weight to it. I'll wear it always starting right now." Josephina jumped proudly up and gave him a hand with the clasp.

The evening wore down. The *Ed Sullivan Show* was signing off the air, and Tomasino and Josephina were both yawning and watched on the sly their young nephew—also on the QT—rushing a few boxes past the living room and past his aunt and uncle until little by little all his belongings were neatly packed away in his Lincoln and the useless remnants just dumped in the big trash barrel outside.

Tony made one last trip down the old staircase, caressing the wooden rail, and purposely made each and every stair moan under his weight. He poked his head into the cozy living room and broke the anticipated news. "Hey, yous two, let me say my good-good nights now." His uncle bounded from his lounger and walked Tony onto the front porch with a heavy heart and said, "I gotta' feeling, you drive off, we don't see you no more." Aunt Josephina ran past Tomas and stood at the exact same spot when she first welcomed her nephew years ago. She began to sob uncontrollably and threw her arms around his broad shoulders. "We're going to miss you so much." Tony tried like hell to hold back the tears but was too weak. He gently squeezed her tiny frame—his voice cracked and said, "I wanted to avoid this dramatic shit" then cried like a baby. Tomasino was wiping his eyes and began to talk tough. "What about the boys at Rozzell's…you get their blessing?" Tony gave his uncle a confident nod, "Yeah, the boys all wish me well, and ironically, I had to give them a nice going-away gift." His uncle let out a short laugh and said, "I guess history repeats itself with those guys…first your father, now you." He gave his nephew a "from the heart" hug and a handshake. "Now you be good, huh…and don't be such strangers like your uncle Joe. You make sure you come back and visit. What is it an eight-hour drive? Or take a plane, they land here in Pittsburgh you know." Tony gave him a hug and said, "Why don't you think about moving to Jersey…" Tomasino laughed and said, "What do I do with these two hens inside?" Tony replied, "Take 'em with ya'. Settle down by the beach on the Jersey Shore. Yous' would love it." Another laugh came from Tomasino, only this one was a little muffled. "And what do I do with my friend under the trees over there. I sell this place and someone gets nosy. Then what? You want to replant those crusted Russian bones?" Tony laughed. "Not tonight…I gotta' run." With that said he bolted down the steps and jumped behind the wheel and said goodbye the best he could to the old farmhouse.

Tony had a notion to make a quick detour for one last stop at Rozzell's but quickly abandoned that idea along with any notion of a goodbye to Cathleen—and he thought it useless to pursue in any way the belongings he had left at her apartment—the pictures? He was certain beyond any shadow of a doubt that she would destroy them. His heart raced as he approached the on ramp for Route 22 East that read Philadelphia 300 Miles. He took a firm grip of the steering wheel and pushed down hard on the accelerator.

Cathleen Carluccio hadn't ever—not once during all the time she lived and worked in Greensburg—set foot inside Rozzell's, and never while she was in Tony's company had he ever once even mentioned the place let alone bring her there. She understood the obvious reasons. It was primarily a stag joint and she never argued the case. She did her best to ignore the existence of the vile place and its entire goings-on inside. Cathleen pulled into an illegal parking zone adjacent from the notorious bar and frowned some at all the other cars that did exactly the same. She was brazen now and had no fear of what was inside the mobsters' den. The young woman felt utterly scorned and considered it her outright duty to just walk—barge in— and confront this young man she had given so much of herself to. It had been over a week and a half and not a word from him. "What balls he had," she thought aloud.

It was 8:00 p.m., and although his car was not in sight, if he were going to be inside with his cronies, this would be the time. She aggressively swung open the front door and marched through the smoke-filled room of men as if she actually belonged, their eyes all over the fiery redhead and all wondering what henpecked soul she was about to drag out by the ear. It took a while, but after a few trips around the bar, dodging a few of the coarse and impudent "Who are you looking for, honey…c'mon…have a seat" and shaking off some would-be ass grabbers, she finally laid eyes on some familiar faces huddled around a small table in the far back of the room. This she should have known.

She kept her temper high and boldly asked Railroad Frank and Philly Ianuzzi where Tony was hiding. Her second attempt was directed at John LaRocca who just looked at her with empty vacant eyes. Philly politely asked her to sit down in the empty fourth chair that was butted up against the table. He pointed and said solemnly, "If he was here, Cathleen, he'd be sitting right there, honey…that's his place at this table." She felt the need to sit and listen. She dragged the chair slowly away from the table with a creaking sound, one she was ever so familiar with, and took a seat. The three men looked at one another shrugging shoulders and shaking heads until Frankie said, "I guess I'll be the one to tell you, kiddo." He paused as the other two men at the table lowered their eyes. The noise level in the room was subdued and she heard every word. "He's gone, sweetheart." The almost somber words ripped into her heart, and she thought, *Gone as in dead?* The only word she was capable of forming and getting over her lips was a frightened "Gone…gone?" LaRocca got up silently and walked away, and Ianuzzi spoke, "He's not dead, honey, so take that scared look off yer' face…he just got called away…he's going back where he came from…you knew that, didn't you?" His voice was almost caring. Her voice cracked. "No—not really." She wanted to find out so much more. She had so many questions as to why, but she just let it be and walked away with a deep feeling of emptiness. It was not in the cards for Cathleen Carluccio.

30

The meeting was set, the time was to be 8:00 p.m., agreed, and a location was one selected that seemed to please all—the Belmont Tavern. Wise guys loved to be surrounded by other wise guys, beautiful women, or food, usually in that order of preference. Frank Batista was excited about the place as was Joe Marino. He hadn't been there for a while and was keen for a dish of balsamic roasted chicken. Tonight it would be food—oversized platters of chicken savoy, steak Sinatra, and bowls of cavatelli with pomodoro and ricotta would be brought from the kitchen and set in the center of the table along with a couple of bottles of a good Amarone, and let's not forget the insalata and antipasto, and just the three of them—with a few waiting in the wings.

Joe rushed home to shower and get ready. The meaning of dressed up to Joe was a clean fresh pair of navy blue work chinos and a pressed short-sleeve white shirt. His one and only blue suit was for weddings and funerals only—hopefully neither in the near future. He was the last to arrive. He swung his car down Hecklel Street and saw Batista's Cadillac parked in a semi-private parking lot next to an unmarked police cruiser—Accardi's.

Joe entered the fairly busy establishment and walked past the long bar packed with two fisted drinkers and storytellers. All eyes were on him as he made his way to the far back corner booth where Frank and Eddie Accardi were already sitting. A plate of half-eaten Italian bread along with some fresh cold cuts and cheese was being enjoyed mostly by Batista who spoke while chewing, "Good to see you, Joe—oh madonna mia—I almost said Cheese, God forgive me." Joe reached out his hand. "That's all right, Frank, no harm." Batista read the guilt on Accardi's face as the cop just nodded in Joe's direction and offered a gruff "Same here, Joe." Then he rose to allow Joe to slide on into the middle of the circular red vinyl booth. "Try the *prozhoot*, Joe, it;s delicious. They get from Corrado's up the street." Frank nonchalantly spoke the words with his eyes on the silent Accardi. He threw them out there intentionally to see if Accardi made any kind of a reaction to the name Corrado. *Bingo…* Batista thought to himself. He's holding something good in his hand.

Joe made up a small plate and commented, "I haven't been here in a long time." Batista nodded some and said, "Me either…not since the Pope opened up his joint. He expects us to just eat there every day, like he don't already have enough of the pie already." That got a laugh from Accardi who very seldom breaks a smile—he knew wholeheartedly it was the Gospel truth. And as fast his laugh, even faster came the stone-cold poker face. But that was to be expected from a cop of over twenty-five years.

Batista raised his glass and said, "First things first, let's toast Mr. Accardi here. He is officially retired from the cops and is now one of us…salute. And I am happy to see that instead of a gold watch of which we all know he has many they let him keep the cop car." Frank and Joe roared. Accardi was silent. Batista continued. "I parked right next to it tonight and—" His words were cut short by the gruff Accardi. "Okay, that's enough of that bullshit." Joe's eyes just bounced back and forth as the two exchanged barbs. "Heah…

like I said you're one of us now." Batista began. "I can bust your balls anytime I want…"

The food was brought out fast and professional, all at once, and the wait staff quickly retreated to the sanctuary of the kitchen or tended to other patrons all sitting far from earshot of the trio. "This place used to be wall-to-wall wise guys in the day…remember, Eddie?" Frank Batista spoke from the heart. "Yeah, I do" was the short reply from the acting *consigliere*. Joe chimed in, "I remember they had a little combo playing on the weekends." He pointed to a now empty riser and small stage. Frank's advice for the table was "Fuck the band and the business. I gotta' tell ya', the food still smells amazing, let's eat."

Dinner was finished and the waiters cleared the plates, leaving only a pot of demitasse, a pitcher of ice water, and a bottle of Anisette. Hot moist towels sat atop clean white plates on the side of each man. The boys opted out of ordering dessert, all just rubbing their stuffed bellies as they lit up cigarettes. Frank blew smoke from the corner of his mouth and gave Accardi his undivided attention.

"The old man is gonna sanction the kid coming back…to work under your supervision and in any capacity you see fit." Accardi took a drag on his cigarette. It would be his turn to read into Frank Batista's hand with his next statement. "But no drugs." His words were almost cautionary. "The old man wants no more of that shit." Accardi's mouth shut and turned into a malapert scowl. He stared into Batista's eyes and waited for him to give a nod of approval. He did. Batista thought it best to just keep his mouth shut. No talking about drugs. This was not the time or place to defend himself on that charge.

Accardi's eyes spanned the dining room and he said, "Second thing is the tax…he wants you and the kid to pay off the debt of Big Anthony." He finished with his finger pointed at a very dismayed Joe. Joe knew to keep quiet and just listen until he was asked a specific question. Batista saw a little steam building up, so he placed his hand atop of Joe's and asked, "How much…tax are we talking here…you know I'm gonna have to kick in as well, Eddie, some of it is gonna' come out of my pocket too!" Eddie remained ice-cold as he said, "With the vig runnin' all these years, and considering the kid's earning potential both from us and the legit enterprises…an even hundred large." That threw Joe into a bothersome fit, squirming between the two mobsters. Accardi looked Joe straight in the eyes and said with foreboding "It could be worse, Joe." Accardi suddenly became alive and animated, highly unusual for his character. This got a worried look from Tic, and both he and Joe were visibly taken back from what they heard next. "We know you were there that night, Joe…we know you either were a part of or a witness to the whole thing that went on at Big Anthony's joint… that you now own." Joe immediately thought this was a bluff. If it were true, he would have already been gone a long time ago. Joe held his ground, and the words directed at him gave the go-ahead to speak. "That's a crock of shit." Accardi jumped down his throat. "I got an eyewitness Joe. He just came forth a coupla' months ago…the degenerate from Casa di Pizza." Joe's face flushed as Accardi continued. "One with anchovies and the other two were what…and for whom?" Silence was all over the table for a long time. "This meet is not to stir up old shit," Accardi said assuredly. "The old man desires no vendetta, nor does he fear one…not for anything that happened years ago. His wishes are to bury everything from the past here tonight and make no more mention of it. He wants to move on, and this is his ruling…nothing more or nothing less." Frank Batista understood the ploy. Accardi became the bearer of the outstanding Big Anthony Marino bond, a gift from Ruggeri who wrote the debt off a long time ago. It was his strategy discussed with the Pope that he was putting into play, and they would split whatever tribute they could squeeze from both uncle and nephew. It took a while for Accardi's words to sink in, but all agreed and exchanged handshakes. Accardi took a swig of the last bit of anisette and just got up and left. Frank motioned for the check and gave a half frown at it when it came. Joe reached into his pocket, and that got a sharp reaction from Tic. "Don't be silly, Joe, you paid enough already."

Frank "Tick Tock" Batista drove off watching through his rearview mirror as Joe climbed into his car. He said to himself that Joe was the lucky man tonight if in fact Accardi's words were true. He would have to pay just a shakedown tax. It was only money. And if all else were true about tonight, then Batista considered himself to be a dead man.

Just as expected, it was a very quiet Friday night at the Pope's Bloomfield Avenue club, the reasons were discussed and surmised by himself and Eddie Accardi as they sat in their reserved booth. Perhaps summer vacations? July and August is the most requested time that everyone took off for the Jersey Shore or the nearby cold clear water lakes; whatever the case may be was of little or no interest to the Pope. He slid out of the booth and asked Accardi to follow him downstairs. They sat across from each other in the confines of the Pope's private office, his castle keep, and spoke candidly. "Let's face it, we're not dealing with a bunch of fuckin' *Moulinyans* here, we're dealin, with the mob," Accardi said with attentiveness and his firsthand experiences. "We tortured that nigger for days and what did we get…some bullshit about how he thinks the stuff is being smuggled in, and that is not a hundred percent. Believe me, he did not have a name to give other than Batista…Bobby Batista." Ruggeri acknowledged and said, "Even the Feds are baffled…and the big guy in New York can't put a finger on the true ringleader over there in Brooklyn. His guess is the Breeze and his cousin…so what do we do?" Accardi lit a cigarette and swung around in his chair. "I think we pick up our friend." Ruggeri pondered that idea real hard and said, "Then we would have to make him disappear. I still need him around for that other thing with the kid." Accardi threw his hands up in the air and said, "So what, we get two birds with one stone. The kid has got to go anyway." There was a brief silence as the Pope lit a Camel. "He owes me a lot of money…and I think he is worth a lot of money to the organization." Accardi frowned and said, "You know best. Me…I think the kid comes after us looking for revenge. We can always lean a little harder on Joe…he'll pay up especially if the kid disappears." The Pope made a cocksure grin and shook his head slowly from side to side and said, "Nahhh…he got no idea I ordered the clip on his old man. I found that out from Montesero a long time ago. And besides, it was an accident…sort of." Accardi rubbed his eyes with the palms of his hand and said, "So we're back to square one." Ruggeri extinguished his cigarette and said, "Batista got to disappear…Bobby Batista…we know he's a major player in this thing, so he goes and we sit and watch where everybody runs to. That will tell the story." Accardi was thinking now like a cop. "We got to get word to Tic in a sly way. He may just get spooked and go underground. A lot of people may go underground." Ruggeri shrugged his shoulders and said, "So then we find out where underground is. And besides, there is not going to be a lot of people involved in this. You know…only a few to worry about. My understanding is the Dons in New York only have a couple of capos involved. They stay ignorant by design to avoid being connected with this dirty business…" Ruggeri's voice became repelled. "Imagine we are going into a business that everyone keeps as a vile secret among each other. It's the only way to make it work." Angelo Ruggeri stood and made a gesture to Accardi to follow him to the door. "Go get DeRosa and DeSanti. We do this fast."

The two mobsters along with Paulie Ippolito drove the Chrysler sedan deep into the heart of Manhattan. They took the vehicle to a garage where it was retagged with New York plates and a New York inspection sticker. The trio wanted to be sure to drive the streets of

New York without Jersey plates. They took up temporary residence at a safe apartment on East Houston Street for the week or two it would take to do the job. That night the trio was treated by one of the New York bosses to feast at La Mela's Restaurant to establish just a hint of an alibi. Their work would begin the next day. They left the apartment early and drove over the Williamsburg Bridge and made their way down to an address on Hicks Street in Brooklyn Heights. Ippolito got out a short block away and walked up to the converted loft-style apartments and scanned down the list of names on the registry.

His finger stopped on the one he had listed on a matchbook cover. The name was Wilson. Her first name was Trina. Trina Wilson was a young light-skinned negress that Bobby Batista snatched up from the streets of Newark and away from the likes of Al Coleman before he got his hooks and drugs too deeply under her skin. She thought her ethnicity to be more Cajun than black. Either way Trina was Bobby's girl, his little black token lover girl that he keep secret from his crew for obvious reasons.

Black woman and wise guys did not mix that well in the public eye. Perhaps this the reason she was kept such a dark secret that even the likes of Ruggeri's spies had a hard time getting a line on. She was kept in a somewhat luxurious and secluded lifestyle for Bobby's eyes alone. It was a lifestyle she liked and had grown quite accustomed to. This fact of the shared secrecy was made clear to Trina who had strict orders to never discuss their relationship with anyone.

He came back to the car and gave them the thumbs-up. It was the right address. Bobby split his time between his Riverdale home and the Bensonhurst mob haunts and all points in between and staggered his two- or three-night stay with Trina in the Hicks Street loft.

It was agreed after casing out the rest of the addresses he bounced around to, Trina's place was the safest place to take him. "He always goes there alone" was the information the trio came up with and sent back home. The orders were to "take him whenever they could," preferably alive, and bring him back to Jersey. The take came on the third night of the stakeout.

The first night began the count of Bobby's usual three-day tryst with Trina. The boys watched closely as Bobby arrived at 8:00 p.m., disappeared inside the lobby, and then quickly exited the loft by a side door with the sexy Trina on his arm. The next day he stayed inside the loft apartment until 3:00 p.m. He went about his normal routine in and around Brooklyn and returned to the loft that evening carrying a bag full of groceries or takeout food and went into the building through that same side door. The third day the boys were back bright and early. The tail they had on Breeze took them for a rerun of the day before stops, obviously collecting from his sports books. The men raced back to the loft and pulled into the designated spot that belonged to Trina. Bobby's guard was completely down as he pulled up and cursed the older crusted Chrysler in his space. Like the hotheaded wise guy he was he jumped out of his car and began laying on the horn with the hopes of getting the parking violator's attention.

Anthony DeSanti appeared from nowhere in droopy clothes and said stumbling, "I'm sorry, mister, I'll move it right away," but before Bobby could get another bitter curse word from his mouth the other two made their run at him. Batista recognized the plot before it unfolded. He had his .45 out and in his hand in a split second and gave Ruggeri's muscle men no other option but to hit him quickly dead center of his chest with three silenced slugs from their own guns.

What separates true wise guys from other criminals is the amount of bravado or balls they demonstrate. They are most impressionable when it comes to the immortality of their line of work and the ability to commit murder at the drop of a hat. The selected ones were considered professionals though none ever attending a university or vocational school that taught their trade of criminology. There wasn't a bit of panic or hesitation amongst the three men who stood over a now dead body even as the chance of being recognized or captured loomed high over their heads.

Yes, they were in a secluded section of a private parking lot; some people began to peer out of their opened bedroom or kitchen windows while others who were already outside on a balcony looked down discursively and then went back inside their apartments. It was a clear summer night that saw passersby, of course with no knowledge that they might have just witnessed a mobland hit, and as they began to wander around the neighborhood streets, they accepted what they might have seen as surreal at best.

The scene was almost a well-rehearsed, choreographed piece of work. The trunk flew open, and two men in dark longshoreman's garb tossed what could have been a body inside of it. The trunk slammed shut. A motor started, and the Cadillac backed up some to let the driver of the Chrysler out of the space; then both cars drove to the corner, turned left, and within seconds, were completely out of sight. No license plate numbers were written down and no one got a good look at any of them. The police were notified of a disturbance, and what seemed like hours later two uniformed police began a brief investigation with maybe one or two at best who really could only assume, and for the record, nothing out of the ordinary was found. The numbered parking space was listed on a registry next to the name Trina Wilson, and when she was questioned, she offered not a clue. Yes, it's her assigned space, but since she doesn't drive, she had no idea as who could have been in her space that was always left empty.

It was well past 2:00 a.m. when Accardi got the news of the trio's arrival at the front gates. He sat alone in the downstairs den of Ruggeri's home. He hung up the phone from the front guardhouse then quickly summoned Ruggeri. The Pope descended the back spiral stairwell that led from the master kitchen and said, "Let them know that I am not that happy about the way this job was handled. You rushed it. I wanted him alive." Accardi apologized and said, "Are you coming out?" Ruggeri declined with a head shake no then said, "Just make sure they got the right guy. I have my doubts about this crew."

Accardi's silenced inner thoughts upon seeing the dead Bobby Batista in the trunk was *Ruggeri gave the order to take out this ranked capo with such ease of execution that no one is safe in this thing of ours.*

The next morning saw all mobsters leave the compound of the castle in Roseland, and as they drove back to the city, the pale gray smoke billowed from the chimney of the big furnace. They passed a middle-aged couple jogging along the rural Eagle Rock Avenue and having brief words with each other in between strained breaths. "I smell firewood burning…it smells like mesquite…who on earth burns firewood in July?" was the lady's concern. "It's probably our gangster neighbor…burning up the dead deer on his property."

A solid week passed, and the lonely and somewhat worried Trina had not heard one single word from Breeze. She found that odd. He would always call her if anything just to check up on her and make sure she was still in the apartment. She very seldom ventured out for anything, but now she was forced to go get the everyday staples needed to survive, namely food.

She dressed very casually in some wrinkled workout garb she picked up from the floor then took a quick run to a neighborhood market for a few items. While there she grabbed a newspaper and thumbed through the pages and print hoping to find an article indicating something might be wrong with her gangster lover. The store clerk knew her and her Bobby and answered no to her question of "Have you seen him around lately?"

Back at her apartment, she rummaged through a kitchen drawer until she found an address book. In it was a couple of reminders in case something like this ever happened, the first being "say nothing." Under the *B*s was a single phone number written below three others that had been crossed out. She knew it was his cousin. She recognized the name, and she also knew she was told to "break glass only in an emergency."

31

Tony Marino's exact and methodical plan was to drive through the night and by the break of dawn should find himself crossing the Delaware River and onto the New Jersey side of the great river. And he did, right on schedule. He was glad of the decision to drive east while the sun was down. It would be hell otherwise. As far as a good night's sleep before the trip, he knew that was not going to happen. The anxiety and thought of returning to his home kept him awake for the past few nights. As far as the fear of falling asleep at the wheel, he was confident that his mind would be racing a mile a minute, faster than his Lincoln could ever go with vivid thoughts of past and present. That would be enough of a stimulant. He would sleep when he got home. And as the sun began to rise in the east, and right on cue, so did the blistering August heat and the reputed East Coast humidity. *What a welcome*, he thought. He enjoyed summer in the city—in Newark, New Jersey. And although Tony was comfortably dressed in cotton slacks and a loose-fitting cotton open-buttoned shirt, he began to feel a little sticky cramped up in the leather seats of the Lincoln, even with its ample air-conditioning system. His only stop during the entire trip was just once, for gas, and noticed now deeply in New Jersey; it was almost time to stop again.

According to his careful calculation, he had enough fuel to get him to Hinsdale Place, but why take a chance. He would drive a few more miles and then stop, but a wild idea entered his head. He bore down again on the gas pedal and raced up the two-lane highway. Tony was oblivious to the large road sign that leaned slightly and welcomed all to Warren Township. It was a blur as he sped past it.

The sun was now a bright orangey-yellow ball staring him in the eyes as he saw the sign for Hillside Township up ahead. He slowed a bit as he drove under the Bloy Street overpass and pulled into a greasy spoon all-night diner that sat just past the bridge. He thought the time he made was pretty good. His Cartier clock in the Lincoln read 6:10 a.m.

The diner was packed with the usual fare, the bodies and the smells of truckers and longshoremen he was so used to being around in Greensburg. He took a corner booth and ordered a double of everything breakfast to which the waitress commented, "All righty then…" His eyes were drawn to the sight of a giant bowling pin identifying the establishment that sat across the highway then became mesmerized by the traffic zipping by. He sipped his coffee. He let the sounds and the sights of US Route 22 sink into his head. He was home. In the town his father also loved so much.

Tony paused for a second at the Lincoln's door and brought a closed fist to his chest. He belched and hopped back in the car. It would be only a short drive to the Central Avenue exit. The Lincoln almost drove itself over now very familiar territory. His original plan was to surprise his mother first then call his uncle Joe but since he needed gas anyway.

Joe took a stroll out of the office and asked the slouched driver, "What'll it be, mister?" "Filler up, high-test, and check the oil—" Joe never looked into the car and had no idea. He did not recognize the kid or the hoax as he went about his business. The young man in the car continued rattling on. "Then check the air in the tires and clean the dead bugs off the windshield, and while yer' at it, polish the chrome and—" "Whoa, buddy, slow down a bit." The driver's door of the Lincoln swung open, and to Joe's amazement, there stood his nephew. "Holy shit…I heard you were coming in, but I never expected this."

Both men gave each other gregarious hugs and slaps on the back. Tony laughed and said, "I just thought I would surprise you. The idea came to me half an hour ago." "Jesus…you did, Tony… you sure did. It's sure good to see you," Joe said with a huge, warm smile on his face. He backed up a step and placed both of his arms on Tony's shoulders and gave him a congratulatory shake. "And you still keep growing…you look bigger than ever…bigger than the last time I saw you before you left." Joe gave him another from head-to-toe inspection and said, "Your hair is shorter…" "Yeah, I started wearing it little shorter these days." "Well, at least you still got a full head. My Nicky is starting to lose his already." Joe took a look at Tony's feet and asked, "What the hell are those on your feet?" He was wearing a type of meshed loafer, the likes his uncle has never seen before. Tony gave him a wink and said, "Italian…imported…fresh off the boat. What size you wear?" Joe answered, "I'm a twelve." Tony said, "Me too," as he popped the trunk open with the remote. He reached around and pulled a matching pair out and said, "Here, I got a helluva' deal on 'em."

Joe stowed the fuel nozzle back in its cradle and said, "Go park your car and come on inside." "All right, but just for a second, I'm anxious to see Ma." Tony took a look into the open bays of the station that both had a car up on the lift. "By the way, where is Nicky Boy?" Tony asked curiously. Joe smiled and said, "He comes in a little later on. He does just about all the mechanic work around here now, and he's in school till about eleven—going for some kind of certification for all this new type electronics coming out. You know he's married with a six-month-old baby at home." Tony gave his uncle an obliging look and said, "Yeah, I heard. I remember when the invitation came to the farmhouse. We wanted to come, but you know how it is—he got our envelope, right?" Joe replied with an understanding, "I know what you mean, kid. I hate to think how long it's been since I been out there." Tony let out a whistle and said, "Christ—how time flies."

Tony laughed then asked about his old man's Cadillac. That gleaming ebony and chrome beauty that Tony thought was at the station, in his uncle's possession. It was as his uncle explained "under a wraps, literally, in my garage in Hillside." All of a sudden, as he was listening to his uncle Joe ramble on, the fatigue of the trip set in. He let out a tired yawn and told his uncle he would catch up with him later, to which his uncle readily acknowledged. Another car sounded the air hose and pulled to a pump. "Go ahead. I'll see you when-ever—and say hello to your mother for me. We don't get to see much of her anymore, and thanks for the shoes," Joe said with a shrug and a comical frown. Tony wondered what he meant by the comment that put a mysterious face on his uncle, but he had no interest in sticking around to hear the answer.

As he continued home, he drove onto the Route 21 spur and saw the completed section that was just a demolition zone a few short years ago. He was tempted to stay on the clean and smooth asphalt but made the last-minute left turn onto Broadway, and it was as if he never had left this impoverished neighborhood—not one iota of change. A cold fear ran through his veins as he parked his car in front of the cemetery—a more profound feeling of sadness forced tears to his eyes as he searched for his father's gravesite. Once found, he bowed his head in silent prayer then gave the headstone a kiss. He wiped his crying eyes and spread the moist of his tears on the etched letters of *MARINO* and the dates. This was the first time he saw the headstone, a thick, sturdy piece of highly polished granite purposely left rough around the edges. His father would approve of it.

Tony parked in a space on Hindsdale Avenue four houses down from the old house and walked slowly. The sidewalk slab in the front of the place was still cracked and raised up a good six inches more than when he remembered, a giant tree root to blame. He rounded the corner of the driveway with anticipation; then he stopped for a second. His soul begged to see the old man's Cadillac in its familiar place but did not. As he walked up the driveway, his imagination flashed visions of himself as a young boy running up and down, from one end to the other. Funny, now he thought, the driveway did not seem as long as it once was. He ran his hands along the clapboard siding and let his fingertips catch on the warped ends, and after just a few steps he was at the end of the house staring into the barren back-yard. He sheepishly poked his head farther into the yard and looked up at his old bedroom window, then over to the large atria window that still had crystal clear panels of glass.

From the rear, the distant quiet hum of motorists and an occa-sional rumble of a semi's Jake brake accented the new stretch of high-way, not the excavation fiasco he once remembered. Instinctively, he cast his eyes next door, into the neighbor's yard; the barking dog was gone now, as was the pole that restrained it, and he wondered if old man Tremarco and his wife were also. Nonetheless, now a defined structure and painted a forest green was that contraption old man Tremarco threw together some years ago. Maybe his wife and dog *were* buried inside of it.

The side entrance was locked. He reached high up to the over-hang and counted three rows of down. Tony knew exactly how far in his hand needed to go. He pried the top soft tar shingled up off the bottom tier and slid a house key out from between. It had been there since his father died; he was sure of that. The door opened with a slight squeak of the hinges as he stepped inside the tiny foyer.

They haven't been oiled for a while, so he thought. He placed a foot to the side of the first step of the old wooden staircase, this to quell the creaks that were sure to come if he walked dead center, then proceeded in swift strides and on the balls of his feet up the stairs, scaling them two at a time. He could hear his own young voice echo from the very top of the spiral staircase as well as his mother's voice. He stopped midway and watched himself as a five-year-old lose his footing and tumble down the first flight; that spill resulted in a broken wrist.

As he reached the top landing he recognized the deep oaken smell of the hallway woodwork and could almost sense his father's strong-scented cologne still lingering. His escalated joy almost forced him to gather in his arms some of his mother's garments that hung from the coat rack. Immediately he thought of his father's old trench coat that once hung. It was so bulky and constantly slipped off the sturdy peg, always in a contorted pile on the floor and always a nagging incident that would warrant a curse from both his mother and his father as they stooped to pick it up. His father believed the coat was haunted, perhaps to him a forewarning of his own future? He expected at any time to hear his father's loud voice as he had heard in the past, but it did not come.

He took a long look back down the stairway from the top floor and just thought of the grand memories for a brief second before he knocked a rhythmic rat-a-tat-tat on his mother' s door. Within a few seconds a familiar voice asked, "Who is it...Momma...is that you?" The door unlocked and flew open before Tony could say boo. He stood there, hands, arms akimbo, and said, "Ma, what if I was a robber, or worse yet, the Boston strangler." Ceil just screamed. And she screamed his name loud enough, over and over, until both his grandmother and the Saitma family on the third floor opened their doors in a panic. Ceil quickly pushed her son into her flat and yelled not to worry. "My son is home."

Ceil was ecstatic, thrilled beyond conviction. She embraced and kissed and hugged until he literally had to grab her arms and restrain her. She did not know where to begin or what to say or what to ask her returning son first. So she just fussed and fussed on and on and he let her. Men have returned home from wars and have not had such a welcoming.

And as an Italian mother would always ask a son, "So are you hungry…let me fix you something…you look a little skinny." "Ma…I'm 210 pounds. That's about thirty pounds more than when I left." She returned her words in a huff as she poked at him. "No way… You have no waist…no belly…" Tony laughed and beckoned his hands as he said, "Ma…that's a good thing!" He gave his mother the once-over, from head to toe. "I can see that you lost a few pounds yourself. You must be working out." Ceil blushed slightly and said, "No, no, no…I just don't eat that much anymore." She held back the real reason for her newfound shape.

The commotion eventually came to an end, and Ceil brought some fresh-brewed coffee to the table and at the place where they used to sit. "I know what it is," Ceil exclaimed. "It's your hair…it's shorter, not all in your face like when you were a teenager. It makes you look older." Tony just smiled. "Ma, I am older." He looked around to find the location of the odd whir he was hearing. Not a fan, he thought. He rose and followed the sound into the living room. "Ma," he exclaimed, "is that an air conditioner in the wall?" Ceil came in and laughed. "That was the first thing I bought with that money your father left. Your uncle Lefty installed it. It cools the whole house. And I have one in my bedroom but not the spare room, your old room. You will have to leave the door open to let the coolness in."

The reunion was truly a pleasure for both, and he thought how funny life works, after only about twenty minutes or so, it was as if he had never left home. "Wait till I tell your uncle Joe. He wanted me to call him as soon as you got in." Tony gave her a reassuring smile and said, "I already saw Uncle Joe, at the gas station." Then the conversation was about Joe. But something she said caused him to point a shameful finger at her. She slipped about the man friend she was actively seeing on a social level. "And there are the nights I stay at his house." And Tony put two and two together from the words his uncle spoke to earlier. He did not know whether to laugh or cry or take a protective stance. The idea of his mother with another man was too much to comprehend, and to think of her engaged in sexual activity with any but her husband, his father, was beyond reproach. So he thought to laugh is better than to cry. And on and on Ceil boastfully talked to her son about how they met and on and on about his dead wife in heaven with Daddy. "Even though she's Jewish…and I know your father is in heaven…"

That thought prompted him to ask, "So, Ma, if he's up in heaven as we all want him to be, and if he's watchin' us as we always say… whaddya' think he's sayin' about old Sid over here?" Ceil snapped back, "Ohhh, stop it. God protects him from that. He doesn't see us in bed." Tony put his palms up. "Ma, please…spare me the details… and I thought that when women got older, that stuff went out the window. And I'm gonna' guess that's why you lost weight, huh? " "Ohhh, bite your tongue. I'm not that old…forty-five or fifty isn't that old. And that's not the reason. I told you…I don't cook like I used to anymore," Ceil said. Tony gave her a foolhardy frown. He wanted this conversation to be over, and "Ma…you're older than that." "Well, not by much," she retorted. "And besides, Sidney thinks I act like and look like I'm thirty-five." Tony shook his head in dis-belief. "So whaddya' telling me, you lie to him about your age?" Ceil came right back. "You shut up, you lie about your age, you always did." "Ma, I made myself out to be older, not younger. And I guess this Sidney guy don't eat your cookin' either?" Ceil snapped again, "So what's the difference, a lie is a lie, and don't you say anything to him. And he loves my cooking. We just eat small noshes now." That was it. He wanted to hear no more.

Tony gave her a reassuring hug and said, "I'm a little tired. I think I'll take a nap." He tossed his head in the direction of his old room and said, "He don't sleep in there, I suppose?" Ceil shook her head no. "He never sleeps here. What would I say to your grand-mother? I stay at his place." She took him by his arm and ushered him into the room. His first reaction was to wince at the strong smell of mothballs that reeked from the closet when he opened the door. He had left a few shirts and some pants and just wondered if they were still here. The closet was stuffed with his mother's winter clothes. "I need the space" was her reason and the answer to the look on her son's face.

Tony kicked his Italian mesh loafers off and plopped on the bed, like he did as a kid. The old steel spring mattress and box spring moaned a little but held his weight. He jumped out of the bed and began tapping sections of the floor with his bare foot. His brow rose a bit when he found the spot. He unbuttoned his shirt and pulled at his T-shirt until it gave rise. Five tightly wrapped bundles of cash were spaced evenly around his waistband. One by one he gingerly lifted them and tossed them in a pile on the bed. Then he got down on his knees and painfully, with his fingertips, pried up the loose floorboard and then, one by one, stashed the money between the floor joists. A quick and forcible jolt sealed the floorboard. And again he acted the child and lunged onto the bed. He folded his hands behind his head and thought of what dreams or nightmares he was about to have. The one nightmare he did not want to have was fresh in his thoughts. How uncomfortable it would be if he wakes up and finds Sidney drinking coffee with his mother…or even worse.

The room was dark and unusually silent. It also had a cool-ness that was completely out of character of the house on Hindsdale Place, especially in the middle of summer. Tony opened his eyes and immediately felt some stiffness in his back. He had not been used to sleeping on such a horrible mattress, but young bones will heal fast. He got up and took a peek at his wristwatch that was on the bureau. It was just after 7:00 p.m.

His face bore a very surprised look as he counted on his fingers the hours he was asleep. And now a good shower. He muttered a distasteful "Ah shit" when he realized that all of his belongings were still in the trunk of his car along with a second boodle of cash. The thought of that gone put his sore back muscles on the back burner, and he fumbled through the dark hallway until he found a familiar light switch then bolted down the stairs.

He grabbed his valise and a garment bag then took a firm grip of the Sears gym bag stuffed deep in the trunk of the Lincoln. That bag would be stashed in the basement in another secret and well-devised spot. When finished, he carried the rest of his stuff back up the stairs. The hot shower he took was indeed a relief. He dusted on some talc and cologne and dressed fast as he was anxious to get ahold of his old friend. He took a few steps into the kitchen, it was an old habit he had, and just looked around, then opened the fridge. Tony noticed the kitchen had a clean lemony scent, not the aroma of olive oil and garlic that he was used to. It was lit by only the glow of a wall light that was plugged into a socket next to the refrigerator. There was a piece of notepaper on the counter under the picture window that his mother left in her style of gibberish writing with few words, a phone number, and an address. Tony dialed the number and let it ring for a good ten times. No answer. So he decided to just go to the address his mother had written down.

Frank Batista exited his apartment and walked on tippy-toes. His ear was to the ground, as he furtively made his way across the long connecting walkway that led from his building to the building next door. He pushed the up button of the elevator and waited. The Otis machinery was brand-new and operated smooth as silk, something he was pleased with. He had no qualms entering the elevator car alone, knowing it engaged precisely the way it was designed but always stood off to the front corner of the car, back against the wall, and held his breath when the doors sometimes reopened. He rode it up four floors and exited; then he took the stairs hastily down to the garage and made a beeline toward the Oldsmobile, the selected car he would drive today. He was certain no one was on his tail as he left the parking garage and drove away. Frank Batista drove with his eyes glued to the rearview mirror and talked to himself over the songs playing on the radio. For one thing he chastised himself for being so paranoid. The words Accardi spoke were the words of a businessman, not a henchman. Ruggeri wanted peace within the crew, that was evident, and Frank shouted to his image in the mirror, "You of all people should know…if they want ya' dead, you're dead. Stop worrying about this shit." He made a left onto Parker Street and parked the car halfway down the block. It was only a short walk to Corrado's market and his pace was fast. He was curious about what he was going to hear.

It was 2:00 p.m. And the place was empty. There were a couple of customers taking the last bites of some sandwiches at the small tables up front, and that was it. Frank was greeted in Italian by the two counter men, and he returned his compliments and greetings. He ordered a sandwich and grabbed a lemon soda from the ice box. He glanced to the rear and saw that Dominick's office door was shut. That was no surprise to him. He turned to the counter man and said, "Go tell Dominick I'll meet him up front."

Dominick took short troubled steps as he walked to the front of the store. He took his place at the table and gave Frank a look of depression. Frank put up his hands, his palms almost in Dominick's face. "Ohhh, don't tell…that look you got is bad news," Frank said. "I got a call from the other side. Nobody's heard from our cousin in over a week. I don't know what to do…" Dominick's eyes got wide, and he leaned into Batista. "I'm sitin' on two kilos. They're wrapped up in the fridge mixed in with a coupla' of prozhoot." Dominick forced a smile and said, "Ciao, and please come again," as the two customers got up and walked out. Frank swung his body around and got up close to Dominick. "I got a call from his girl, that cute Moolie he's been bangin'. He was supposed to have shown up last week and nothing, he vanished into thin air. The cops have been grilling her, they found his car, registered to some other Ditzune but with her address, all banged up, just a coupla' blocks from her house. She's playing dumb, but then again from what I heard from him, she is dumb, what the fuck can she know? I'm surprised she had the sense to call me." Dominick grunted. "Sounds to me he went on the lam, dumped his car, and bingo, you know…now you see him, now you don't." "I don't buy that, Dominick, he would have gotten word to us if that was the case. He would have gotten word to Naples," Frank said. Dominick shrugged his thick shoulders. "Sounds to me it was life-threatening, if he bailed out like that, somebody tried to ambush him. First, they whack his two main dealers then they come after him. Anyway whadda' we do with the two hams I got sittin' back there? I can't send them back, and they're lookin' for the *fazool.'"*

Frank's eyes bugged under his horn-rimmed frames and instinctively reached around to the spot his gun would normally be. "And this shit we don't need, plus I'm not 'packin." Dominick gave him a dumbfounded look at the same time the tiny door-mounted bell announced the arrival of Eddie Accardi and John LaRocca." Frank did his best to make light of the situation. "*Che Gazzo…*whaddya' followin' me around." Accardi whispered something to LaRocca and pulled up a chair. "The Pope wants some cold cuts." Frank hit him between the eyes. "Since when you errand boys? I mean with the small shit like this." Accardi gave him a smirk. "I was in the area, we had to put my mother-in-law in a nursing home. There's a good one on Mt. Prospect." There was a silence. Then Accardi spoke, "Don't you live over there now, Frank?" "Yeah, I do as a matter of fact. I moved my mother in a high-rise. I gotta' take care of her now. It's convenient. Her doctors are in the medical building just up the street."

LaRocca was back in as fast as the short conversation took, empty-handed. "So where's the *gabagool*?" Batista asked. "We ain't delivery boys," LaRocca barked. Then he gave Frank a smirk. "I'll send a kid down later for it. It's for a special card game going on right now…high rollers, something you don't know about, Tic." "Fuck you, John" was Frank's comeback. Accardi chimed in matter-of-factly, "Heah…speaking of the kid, when are you gonna bring him around? The Pope is ready to sit down with you and him." Frank gave him a wink and said, "I'll let you know. As soon as I hear from him we'll arrange it." Accardi took a look at the sandwich sitting on the table. It was already cut in half and still in the wrapper. "You gonna eat all of that?" he asked. Frank gave him a frown as Accardi scooped it up.

Dominick and Frank both knew that without Bobby their drug business was all washed up. He had the savvy and the connections on the street to peddle the stuff. Frank gave a serious look and said, "Let me see If I can find a buyer, who knows, maybe we stay in the game. I got a new player in town. But you better get word to the capos in Naples and tell them to ease up for a while. It wouldn't be a bad idea to close up shop for a while." Dominick shrugged his shoulders, causing the hair on his back to meet the hair on his head. "I just got word another four kilos comin'. Oh, and speakin' of Naples, the old man died." Frank gave him a twisted look and a frown. "Cundari, the guy this place is licensed to. Some lawyer over there wants to resolve the partnership or some shit. I don't know. I'll find out and let you know." Batista was silent for a while then said, "You know what, tell them we're goin' on vacation the end of August and we'll straighten everything out when we reopen."

Batista left Corrado's and spent the rest of his day making his baneful rounds, chasing a few deadbeat gamblers that owed him money and then lending others some more. He estimated his net worth on the street of over forty grand owed him. And at the rate his crew operated, well, he wouldn't have enough time to be a rich old man like Albert Marrone. Marrone openly griped about the lack of income he saw from the shy business and was quickly reminded by all that. "You cheap bastard, you have to spread some money on the street first," and not hoard. And as the day wore down, Frank's attempts to uncover any news about his cousin just led to more dead ends. He was hungry but opted for a good night's rest instead of dinner

The thought of another charade beneath the parking garage was eating at his insides, and so he decided to block from his mind his apprehensions and his fears of being whacked and take the short way home. He swung the Oldsmobile into his own parking garage and found a relatively close enough spot. He reached under the passenger seat and blindly found the Colt automatic pistol. Out of habit he kept the engine idling as he scanned the garage for any unfamiliar cars parked. Just as he reached for the key in the ignition tires squealed onto the concrete floor and sounded like they belonged to an impatient driver. He dropped down below the dashboard and tried to get a look at the car that from the sound of it was at the far end of the lot and now heading back. There was another tire squealing that echoed loudly, this time from the braking action of the auto.

Frank heard a car door open. He poked his head over the dash and just caught a glimpse of a figure climbing back into car that coincidently was parked adjacent from his own Cadillac. This alarmed Frank profoundly. The car sped away again, and Frank made a mad dash for the elevator, his gun drawn in Jesse James fashion. The red taillights of the car glared off the slick concrete floor as the driver braked hard and let out yet another high-pitched squeal of the rubber, and just as the bright back-up lights came on, Frank came up lame with a pulled hamstring. He was halfway home.

Frank went to the ground in agony and rolled a few times to get out of the path of the car speeding his way in reverse. Frank took aim and cursed. "Come on, motherfucker…you gonna do it…then do it!" Then the blue and gold Pennsylvania license plates came into view, the inspection sticker current, and instinctively he knew as he said aloud, "If it's him, I'm gonna' kill him." Frank heard an almost recognizable and familiar laughing voice then saw the upside-down head peeking at him from across and under the Lincoln's chassis. "Frank…what the fuck are you doin' on the ground…was that you diving under cars?" Frank yelled again, "And I still should shoot ya', for scarin' the shit out of me." The kid was standing over him now. "Ohhh, Frank…you're workin' too hard." He helped up his comrade and even began to brush him off; then both men began to laugh hysterically. When their teary eyes dried, they gave each other hugs of long overdue friendship.

Tony followed the direction of Batista and parked his car in the appropriate spot then grabbed his valise. He explained to Frank the address his mother gave was for his mother's apartment. "She gave me another address for a Moscola, I go there and knock and knock and ring the bell. What the fuck?" Batista just raised his brow and said, "Yeah, I know…it's confusing." Tony waited for the elevator door to open for the twentieth floor and said, "I just figured this is where you'd be, and bingo…I found the Caddie." Frank let out a short laugh. "Real good timing, kid…real good timing.

Frank gave the kid a quick tour of the place that really met with the approval of Tony. "This joint is aces, Frank, a real nice place… great bachelor's pad." Frank laughed and said, "Yeah, like in the movie *The Tender Trap*, huh? You can bunk on the couch for tonight, and tomorrow I'll show you the other place." Tony made himself comfortable. He took a seat in the middle of the couch and folded his hands behind his head. He sat for just a while then caught a glimpse of the beckoning city lights from Frank's balcony. He got up and slid open the patio door and stepped out. A gentle breeze ruffled his shirt as he gazed at the mesmeric New York skyline in the distance. His eyes closed and he sensed how eerily silent the city streets below were.

Frank was in the kitchen grabbing a couple of glasses. "So what are you drinkin', my friend?" he shouted. Tony shouted back, "Whatever you're havin is okay with me." "Scotch, I'm havin' a Scotch on the rocks." "That's fine with me," Tony answered then said, "Don't get too comfortable with that drink. I thought we would go out to eat." Frank found him on the balcony and handed him the glass of Scotch. "What tonight...I thought you'd be too tired from your trip," Frank stated. The kid turned away from the balcony railing and said, "I been asleep all day at my mother's. I'm itching to go over there...plus, I'm starvin'" His head turned to the city across the river. "Let's go to Little Italy and feast." Frank jiggled the Scotch on the rocks a little and handed him his drink. "Cheers." He took a look at his wristwatch and said, "It's only eight-twenty. Fuck it, let's go. I'm hungry myself."

32

Joan Jankowski thought of herself simply as a career girl, not a career woman, as perhaps that professional term of endearment would evince an older person and not the young, jubilant twenty-two-year-old that she actually is. This fact was evident in her highly successful designs, the latest of which she had on, a handsome yet sexy warm rose-colored cambric woven miniskirt and jacket showing just the right amount of cleavage and nude leg. She had an uncanny way of designing clothing that truly embellished the natural curves of a woman. And any woman who donned her styles wore them with pride. She relished her executive position as she peered out her window high atop the office building that housed her opulent corner office, the corner of Broadway and Thirty-Eighth in the heart of the New York City Fashion District. She proved beyond anyone's shadow of a doubt that she earned that banner and the title of vice president of design and sales to the owner of the multimillion ladies' wear manufacturing firm of Jonah Laurel Inc. At first the ever-so-skeptical Arnold Lewis, Arnie to his closest friends only, shunned her bold and daring designs. That would soon change as would the fashion industry itself.

Joanie was only a month into her first semester at the Fashion Institute when she and a classmate Laurel Lewis became the best of friends. Both were astonished that they came from communities in New Jersey and separated by only one tiny town. "Oh my god we must have passed each other in the mall a thousand times," exclaimed Joanie. Laurel lived with her family—mother, father, and brother—in the nearby town of Bernardsville. Halfway through their first semester, the girls quick decided to share a tiny bare-boned apartment on Twenty-Fifth Street, much to the chagrin of both sets of parents; however, the girls' persuasiveness convinced all—the adventure would build character.

Both girls studied hard and gave little thought to personal pleasures. Perhaps that became evident to Laurel's father who so forcefully found good reason as to why, on many occasions, he would take the short drive from his downtown Manhattan office and take to lunch and dinner and entertain his two favorite girls with nights out at chic restaurants, nightclubs, and Broadway shows. And as a courtesy, he would summon his seasoned design staff to complete homework assignments and critique the girls for the sole purpose of maintaining a high grade average.

Arnold Lewis was a self-made millionaire, in his forties, of Russian and Jewish heritage. He stood quite tall, with a noticeable paunch and a good amount of stylish curly gray hair still growing atop his ever conniving head. He himself the son of a lower Manhattan ragman salesman, he vowed never to schlep as his father did and, by his own determination, created a monumental clothing empire distributing fashionable merchandise to just about every leading department store and specialty shops and boutiques across the free world.

Arnold would tease the two young students, telling them both he intended on using their designs in his next run—but only if their grades were up to snuff . That promise held true for Joanie. That said in spite of the fact his only daughter was also a gifted designer of clothing. It was Joanie's designs and creation that would blow him and his staff away. And it was Joanie who prompted him to actually hand over to his design team and recreate one or two of her current homework assignments. Arnold recognized the unusually gifted mind she had, and by the time her second semester ended, she caught the attention of other leading design houses that all began to actively recruit her for their employ. Arnold encouraged her with obnoxiously insane promises of riches in the industry, his industry—and at his company, exclusively. Promises and statements never made to his own daughter, and as he and Joanie would dine discriminately alone in fine restaurants, her eyes would grow larger and larger with fetching anticipation. She was a diligent student who up to this point had not ever been with a boy of her age sexually, nevertheless a mature gray-haired man. She did not recognize the hidden agenda or the intoxicating nature of Arnold's words of majestic augur pertaining to her future as he gave personal after-hour tours of his offices, both on Broadway and in Secaucus, New Jersey. And ultimately, it was on one of those imposing tours she kept her chaste promise to her mother. Her virginity was not taken by that crude jock from Watchung she once dated but by the father of her close friend, her future boss.

A summer had passed. Joanie was working part-time in the design department of Arnold's corporation, and it was there she became friends with the only son of her boss. His name was of course Jonah, and he was not a complete stranger to her. He was six years older and would on occasion find himself in the company of his sister and the young Miss Jankowski. Jonah did try to hide his feminism, but Joanie quickly picked up on his homosexuality. This did give her some hope of relief and solace though; she was not going to have to sleep with the boss's son as well.

The modest but augmenting affair that the young Joan and Arnie were having was starting to get some press. Arnold Lewis was beginning to realize that fact by the occasional privy and trite remarks both his wife and others around the fashion world were nonchalantly leaking. He considered it not a bribe or a conciliation prize but a solid investment in both of their futures when he informed her, "Go pack your bags." She would be finishing her degree in Europe at the prestigious Istituto Marangoni in Milan, Italy, and then return and begin her apprenticeship at Jonah Laurel.

In the beginning, Arnold flinched at the design changes she brought before him of the already "on the table" pieces ready for production. He said, "Absolutely not," at first then seceded to the costly imported material she selected to be transformed onto a new line of Jonah Laurel sports and casual wear, business wear, and elegant evening wear that will, as she so adamantly put it, "set them apart from and challenge the latest fashions from Italy and France." And this head butting over costs would persist with each change of season, each and every time the two conferred, and as usual Joanie would always get her way. Be that as it may, Arnold's confidence in her was becoming evident, and now, present day, her decisions are etched in stone. She sat on the edge of his desk beaming. He pondered the enormous amount of beautifully sketched figures of thin young models with flowing gowns and drawings of fashion statements of every kind. He chewed hard on his Cuban cigar and read over and over the columns of dollar estimates; his eyes always fell to the bottom line. Joanie looked away, ignoring his disdaining grunts. Her eyes studied the wall of trophies and pictures that filled the wall behind him. He caught her attention by clearing his throat and said, "Go ahead, my dear, I have way too much time, effort, and money invested in you to say no anymore."

Joan Jankowski made some last-minute entries into her leather-bound day timer and also on her calendar. She straightened the portfolio of the design sketches and laid them in a careful pile. She did the same with the many swatches of colorful material that were strewn about her desk. Her final approvals were stamped and signed for the upcoming winter line of 1965 to go into production. The professional voice of her personal secretary came over the multi-featured desk phone. "Joan, I have Mark Cohen on line 1 for you." "Thanks, Cindy," she said. Mark was a cute young salesman with the firm, and he had caught her fancy at one of the road shows they were on, and she thought to herself, *Persistence does pay off.* Joanie rested her right buttocks on the end of her desk and crossed her legs beneath her skirt in a sexy way as if the caller could actually see the pose. She readied herself for the personal call with a flit of her shoulder-length hair as she answered, "Hello, Mark." The conversation from this point on could only be interpreted as completely one-sided, her side of course. "No...no...no...I will meet you there at seven-thirty...well, because if you pick me up at my apartment, you'll want to take me back there with intentions of sexual favors for wining and dining me...I know this is not our first date, but if you do not want it to be our last, then you'll do it my way...okay...I will see you at seven-thirty, my love... no...don't let that go to your head."

Joanie left her office and walked briskly through the showroom lobby. She knocked on Arnold Lewis's door simultaneously as she twisted the knob and entered, without warning or announcement. And immediately he found her directly in at the front edge of his desk, boldly waving a wad of printed papers. "Have you had a chance to take a look at my projections of the orders? I expect a 40 percent increase in the junior's division of sportswear and dresses alone." His voice was subdued as he said, "Yes, my concern is the material, we may be short." Joanie answered with a decisive, "Not going to happen. I've already contacted our people in China, and they're loading a cargo plane as we speak of exactly what I need—yards and yards and yards of the best material your money can buy—and way below market value, I might add. Boss, I'm not going to stop until I get the gross revenue over one hundred million. You may have to add more salesmen, and more factories." "I can't keep track of how many

I have now," he said with a chuckle. She confidently replied, "Sixty, you have sixty salesmen on the road." Then with a curt smile she blurted, "Well, good night, Mr. Lewis." He returned a sincere "Good night, my dear." The door shut and he gave it a long stare with raised eyebrows. His face bore a superficial, almost apparent look of defeat. He was so relieved to have her as an employee now and not a lover anymore, but he still reminisced.

Joanie called ahead to the parking garage below that serviced her building and had her Mercedes 230Sl convertible brought up front for her, "with the top up please." She earned enough now to afford a luxury sports car and the company perk of parking it at her office. She had no real qualms or fears of driving with the intimidating traffic of New York City and actually knew the city streets and avenues quite well. What she hated was trying to find a space to park in either Greenwich Village, Chinatown, or where she was now, cruising up Mulberry and down Mott Street in the section of the city known as Little Italy, looking for the impossible parking space. She settled for a spot on Canal Street next to a pile of empty produce boxes. The silk-screened painted sign attached to the angle iron poles indicated that by all means, it was safe to park here.

Frank convinced the kid to take his car and drive into the city, and Tony obligingly agreed with gusto even though he had never done so. The previous trips there saw a much younger Tony as a passenger only. He was confident enough maneuvering the busy arteries and the Pulaski Skyway that separated both Newark and Jersey City then led into the city itself. His driving skills were honed, and the kid showed no fear racing the eighteen-wheelers and transit buses to the finish line. "It comes from driving all those trucks all over Pennsylvania, Frank. I got a good sense of the road and a feel for the wheel," he said with a short laugh. Frank just rolled his eyes and laughed. "Okay if I smoke?" Tony nodded yes. Frank Batista was in his glory having the kid back and riding shotgun on the way to Little Italy. He felt as safe as a baby.

Frank did most of the talking as he laid it all out for Tony to hear. The drug business he was involved with, the disappearance of his cousin, and his complete lack of trust and disparity with the organization and everyone in it. "I told you before, kid, I got a target on my back." Tony reacted to his bellyaching and agreed. Then he reiterated the reason he came back to Jersey. "For my own revenge and own satisfaction that I will get…in my own way." He continued bellyaching and told of his displeasure of the ruling Ruggeri evoked. "That was to be expected. I found that out from the Montesero gang," Tony said. "That puts a lot of pressure on all of us, kid. A hundred Gs is a lot of money," Frank said. He then told him of Albert and how he offered nothing to help out his old friend. "I got a little we can kick in to get the ball rolling," Frank said. Tony paid the toll and sped up to pass another as he entered the Holland Tunnel.

The tunnel floodlights overhead zipped by as he pushed hard on the accelerator. "I got all the money, Frank, the whole hundred Gs." A silence came over the car, and all you could hear was the roar of the tunnel. Frank rolled the window down and blew some cigarette smoke out. "But I'm not gonna' give the Pope a single dime, not now, not after what you told me. As a matter of fact, I got a whole new strategy," Tony said. The tunnel ended. "This is the part I need a little help with," Tony said. "Follow the road around and head for Canal Street. See the sign?" Frank asked. Tony maneuvered the Lincoln easily over the cobblestone and asphalt streets until the images of Chinese dragons and Italian colored flags and banners told them they arrived. Frank directed more with his pointing fingers then his mouth. "Turn left, and then just drive up past Umberto's." Tony listened and drove. Frank pointed and said, "Right there, on the left, see that kid sitting in front of the fence? That's where we park. It's our own private parking lot for wise guys only. Their club is just across the street." "Should we drop in and say hello?" Tony asked in jest. "That wouldn't be a bad idea," Frank said.

Joanie didn't mind the couple of short streets she walked. She thought it a very colorful neighborhood, half of it was indeed her heritage, and Mulberry Street is *quite safe*, she thought to herself. Her date was waiting patiently, sitting alone at a small, perfectively situated outside sidewalk table with a bottle of wine and two glasses. The place was a renowned Italian eatery, of which there was so, so many in Little Italy. She studied his profile as she approached and identified his big nose as a toss-up between Italian or Jewish. He had a slender nape of his neckline that rose to a neatly parted and well-pomaded full head of auburn hair. She usually saw him only in suits or dress shirts and ties and thought him to be more muscular. Tonight he was casually dressed in a short-sleeve plaid shirt and beige linen pants. The collegiate look, she thought; still he is a good-looking man of twenty-six, even with his immanent baby fat. Joanie appeared, and he quickly rose and greeted her with an affectionate kiss on the cheek. And the so attentive waiter politely pulled out her chair. Her eyes thanked both admirers. She smirked and said, "Ohhh, dining al fresco tonight, are we—well, it's a nice night, and hopefully it will stay that way for the next two hours." He raised his eyebrows inquisitively. She just laughed and blurted an austere "Of course, it will."

And both dinner and drink were as expected—perfect. The conversation and evening went as she anticipated, with her fighting off a young man's affectionate advances, casually, with her hands, elbows, knees, and feet. But she still was flattered.

"I'm almost ashamed to say…in all the years living in New Jersey and New York, I've only been to this part of the city once or twice," Joanie commented. Mark looked a little baffled and said, "Really… never? Why not? You don't like Italian food?" "It's not that…it's, well,

I guess I had so much of this growing up." Joanie twirled her hands and pointed at the Italian inference decor. "My old neighborhood in Newark was like this, all this Mafia-type stuff oozing out of everywhere." With that said the shadiest of characters, with a tilted fedora hat and all, appeared in a doorway next to the restaurant they were at. Both Joanie and Mark gulped and let out a subdued laugh. "Did he hear me? And how does a nice Jewish boy like you know of this underworld?" she said amusingly. "My mother is Italian, and like you I'm half a Guinea." Joanie barked a disciplining "Italian American." Mark pointed and said, "See that store on the corner, the one with all the Italian memorabilia, her family owns it, along with a few other buildings in this neighborhood. You could say I got a little juice." Joanie laughed and said, "Where did you park your car? Probably a mile away like I did." He laughed and nodded his head yes. "Okay, so I don't have that kind of juice. But enough to get me in as a salesmen with Jonah Laurel." Joanie smirked and said, "Yeah, and that too. You're not even related, are you?" "No. My father was a union rep and a friend of a friend...if you know what I mean. Now if I could only get a decent territory or even one closer to home. I spend two or three nights a week in seedy motels."

Joanie expressed an interest in Mark. She liked his semi-tough guy personality and the fact that he had a little dirt under his fingernails. She held on to his arm almost in a caring way as they strolled together just for the one short block. Perhaps she did not want him to get anywhere near her car as he so obligingly offered to walk her to. "Then you'll want me to drive you to your car and the next thing you know is we're making out in a tiny sports car. That is not at all sexy."

She did, however, let him give her a lingering kiss on the corner of Mulberry and Grand that she liked and returned somewhat passionately. The aura of the moment was abruptly interrupted by the shiny Lincoln coupé whose driver impatiently laid on the horn to hurry along some pedestrians walking on the sidewalk up ahead. The nestling couple walked side by side and watched as a young attendant appeared from nowhere and opened a chain-link fence. The waiting Lincoln coupé bounced over the curb and in a flash disappeared from Joanie and Mark's view. The evening ended as both agreed that if they were not going home in each other's arms, they might as well call it a night now and get a good night's rest. "It's only Monday, my love, we have all week to think about doing this again." Joanie gave him another peck on the cheek and proceeded down to Canal Street. She passed the opening of the private parking lot on her right and looked up at the rows of cars until her eyes stopped at the three people standing in the dark, next to the Lincoln coupé. Why do they look so familiar? "Hmmm…" she said out loud, "I guess they have juice."

Frank peeled a ten-dollar bill from his money roll and gave it to the kid that somewhat resembled a valet. He threw his arm around the hefty shoulders of his *paison* and said, "Now we eat. And we eat *good*." Tony laughed as they walked across the street, and as fate would have it, he had no real way of knowing, not a warning shot had been fired, but had he been just a couple of seconds faster he would have run right into the girl who was once the love of his life. He turned his head to the right as he made the opposite curb and watched the cute wiggle of a girl's hips and ass as she disappeared down Mulberry Street. She seemed so familiar? "It a lot quieter here than the last time I came down, but that was years ago during the San Gennaro Feast," Tony said. "It is slow this time of night. The pain-in-the-ass tourists are here either dinnertime or after midnight," Frank said.

They were greeted at the door of Angelo' Restaurant and immediately were led to the back section reserved for organized crime figures only. The owners figured if anyone were to get whacked, let it be away from the regular crowd. The wise guys knew this seating arrangement for a fact and accepted it. For their compliance, an occasional appetizer or complimentary bottle of wine would be sent over.

Soon, more wine, appetizers of all types, imported arugula and fennel salad and cheeses arrived at the table. Next two types of pasta and finally two-inch-thick veal chops. And all delivered within minutes of each other, just as requested. Not many tourists eat this well. But how many tourists would peg these two for gangsters? What would give it away, the fact that they were two men at a table for six and enough food spread around to feed eight? Or it could have been their lack of socks. Tony had on his Italian mesh loafers, but Frank wore Emilio Gucci's. The other patrons at their own tables all took turns guessing.

Frank wiped his jowls and quickly lit a cigarette. "You don't smoke no more, do you?" He noticed of his boy. "Nahhh…I really never did start. I tried, just didn't like it," Tony said. A demitasse cup filled with espresso sat within Tony's reach. He lifted the thin glass of Sambuca and took a small sip then poured the rest into his coffee, being cautious not to spill the three roasted coffee beans that swam at the bottom of the glass. "You know, kid, I bet not one of those assholes over there know what these beans represent," Frank said as he did the same. "It's for luck," the kid chimed. "Yeah, we know that, but…watch this." With that said Frank got up and brought the two empty glasses to a table of four *medigans* who did nothing but stare at him and Tony since they arrived. "Excuse me, folks, but we're not gonna' eat these, and I thought since you had your eyes on them, you must want 'em, so here." Frank left the glasses on the table and turned away. He sat back with Tony and asked, "Are they eating the beans yet?" Tony just laughed and nodded yes.

He looked at Tony with conviction and said, "Let's get down to business." Tony gave him a long look then asked, "How serious are you in getting outta' the life?" Frank took off his glasses and wiped his eyes with a clean napkin and said, "As serious as a heart attack, kid."

"Tell me more about that secret doorway Accardi got in his house." Frank put a worried look on his face and said, "We got to watch him closely. He's evil, he's a real snake." Tony made a cocksure face and said, "I remember him from when my father got it, me and my uncle are sure Albie set up the old man, and that prick Accardi did him in." "Well, baby, here makes three." Frank teased; then he continued. "That's why you got to watch out for him." Tony disagreed. "He's a cop at heart. He thinks like a cop. If he does anything that seems shrewd, you can bet it was Ruggeri's idea. Accardi is a puppet, and one thing I learned from Pittsburgh is sometimes the puppets like to pull the strings themselves...alone." Tony watched as Batista's face broke into a serene smile, and he said, "I trust you, kid, like a father trusts a son. Just tell me what we have to do." Tony reached for the check and said with a smirk, "First, I forgot my money, you pay, and second, set up a meet with the Pope." As they left, a man from the group of four thanked Frank for the espresso beans, and his wife said, "Finally, we know what to do with them." Frank bore a sinister smile and said, "Next time I'll tell ya' what to do with that little sliver of lemon peel."

Both men were tired. The meal they had just consumed seemed to have zapped all the energy and digestive juices from them. The ride back to Newark would be a short one, and hardly a word was spoken. Tony suggested they stop somewhere closer to the apartment for a couple of drinks "to take the edge off." And Frank sanctioned the idea. As they drank the subject of drugs came up again, and Frank took the initiative to put the kid to the test, the test of irresistibly large sums of money to be had for the taking. He told Tony about the two kilos of pure uncut heroine that in the right hands could be worth a small fortune. Batista became animated as he spoke of the empire his cousin created and that "how hard could it be to find guys like Jake Trebbiano or Al Coleman to peddle the junk." Then reality set in.

Tony flat out refused his offer and reminded him that it would mean sticking your neck out even further than it already is. Ruggeri is already making plans with New York for that vacant spot in organized crime. "And besides, Frank, I thought you wanted out of all of this shit because of this exact same problem you want me to get involved in." Frank spoke from his heart, "I do, kid. Forget I said anything about it. I'll tell Dominick to try to get it back to the boys in Brooklyn without creating a scene." Tony's eyes got wide and he said, "No, hold on to it for a while. I just got an idea, and it will work in with my plan. It makes it easier." "So when do I get to hear about it?" Frank mused. Tony stared at his drink for a few seconds and said, "Soon, Frank. Soon. Just set up that meet. This thing is gonna go down real fast. It must go down real fast. " Frank prodded the kid for answers. "You gotta' let me in on it now." Tony stayed firm. "You have to trust me, Tic. I'll tell you everything after the meet…'cause then I'll know really which way to go."

Both men woke up early the next morning fully refreshed with not a trace of hangover. The prior evening and its perfect combination of wine, whiskey, and veal chops induced a much-welcomed sleep. Frank sat alone out on the balcony sipping coffee, reading the paper, and chain-smoking. He found tobacco insatiable in the morning and did the most damage to a pack of Lucky's with his coffee than any other time of the day. His stereo was playing a Sinatra tune. He heard the toilet flush a few times and watched as Tony walked toward the balcony. He joined Frank and gently laid the sports section on the metal meshed patio table. Frank spoke over the top edge of the *Star Ledger*, "You feel better now? You didn't get any on the sports page, did ya'?" They both laughed and commented on how well they did feel in spite of all the food and booze; then again their systems were used to that type of indulgence.

"C'mon, grab your things. I'll show you the apartment. It's right next door where my mother is. Only you're on the eighth floor, you still got a good view," Frank said. "I thought I would grab a shower first," Tony said. "You already christened my toilet bowl, go christen the shower over there. Everything you need is waiting for you. I flip back and forth between this place and over there," Frank said. And so it was agreed. The men would meet in an hour to make some plans and get reacquainted with some old friends. Frank Batista walked tall next to Tony through the underground parking lot. Tony took a turn around and began to walk backward as he took in the full scope of the place. "I like this idea. Our cars are parked out of the elements, it's very classy." "I know, and it would be hard for anyone to sneak up on you, you got a lot of places to duck under," Frank said. "Yeah, like you ducked…or rolled last night," Tony said as he laughed. "The place is filled with doctors and nurses and a lot of professional people….and lots of stewardesses," Frank exclaimed with a wrinkled brow. "Professional people, like us, right?" Tony said jokingly as he climbed into his car. Frank announced that he had just a few errands to run and then his mission was to arrange the meeting hopefully for tonight. "The sooner the better," according to his boy. "Just call my mother's place and leave a message," Tony said from behind the wheel. His arm waved and fell down over the driver side door of the Lincoln coupé as he drove away.

Tony Marino was feeling melancholy and longed for a bit of nostalgia. He drove the length of the avenue up and under the Garden State Parkway viaduct, through the Montclairs, then back down to the lower section of the avenue. He forced himself not to look to his left as he passed the car lot and property that once was his father's. He noticed that the location and awning that stood, the one that read Phillie's Social Club, was gone, and in its place was a Spanish bodega. He cruised the ghetto section as he remembered it, the beginning of the downtown Newark area.

He turned left then another new and quick left as he drove on Route 21 North. To his left he saw the rear of his mother's house along with the rest of the block. This was the first time ever he had experienced this view.

On his way back he detoured through the neighboring town of Belleville and then through Branch Brook Park. Tony took a long slow ride on Lincoln Avenue. He twice drove the entire length of the block at a snail's pace, looking intently at each and every parked car both on the street and in driveways. He parked his car and scaled the front stoop of the familiar brownstone in two long strides. Suddenly he felt chills come over him as he passed through the phantasm of the young and beautiful Joanie who leaped up with opened arms to greet him. A little girl peeked through the slit of the opening she had just made in the eight-foot section of carved mahogany and arched beveled glass double doors then opened it. Tony stood with his hands folded behind his back. "Do you live here?" he asked with a tender smile. A voice shouted from the upstairs, a woman's voice speaking in Portuguese. The little girl answered her back using the same language. "Just a minute please," the voiced echoed down the stairway this time in broken English. "O que ele quer?" The young woman asked the child as she descended the staircase in a bathrobe and her long black hair just toweled dry from an obvious shampooing. The child just shrugged her tiny shoulders and ran back inside the house. Perhaps these people were relatives of the Jankowski family? Tony spoke with an inquisitive look on his face. "Sorry to bother you, ma'am, but I was hoping you could tell me where the people that used to live here moved to?"

The obscure conversation left Tony clueless about his Joanie. As far as he could make out from the young woman in the housecoat, her name is Flavia and she and her husband just rent here, and that it is Mr. Palma, her landlord, that actually owns the brownstone, and that her husband drives a truck. He gave her a thankful nod and raised his palm, indicating that he had heard enough; then he took a long look at her dressed in a bathrobe alone and said with a frown,

"What if I was the Boston strangler?" The girl had not a clue as to the inference. She just smiled.

Tony pulled into the driveway and bolted up the steps to his mother's apartment. The door was locked, so he knocked. No answer. He did half of a jog-step back down and knocked lightly on his grandmother's door. This would be the first time in years since he saw her. A fragile voice asked "Who is it?" in broken English and then a quick "Chi 'e?" "It's me Jack the Ripper," Tony said. The door quickly unlocked and his grandmother began her honorific welcome homes. He stepped inside the apartment and followed her into the kitchen, and no sooner did he sit, his mother came in tow right behind him neatly dressed in a summer dress with her hair pinned up and hardly a trace of makeup on her glowing face.

All three exchanged looks of happiness and concern. Ceil had a large rolled-up brown paper shopping bag from the Grand Union as the wrinkled print indicated. "Whaddya' got in there, Ma?" Tony asked his mother. His grandmother spoke in disgust, "Your mother carries around her sins in that garbage bag." It was the clothes she had on the night before. Ceil gave her a smirk and said, "Ohhh, you shut up too."

The three had coffee and a light lunch of a leftover frittata. Tony explained that he would be living on his own from now on, which was answered by a silent "Thank God" from his mother as her eyes did not spare him and her the relief she felt over that decision. He put her on the spot and said, "Just take some messages for me, and write them down exactly as you hear 'em, no matter how silly they sound." Her eyes rolled as she agreed. And well did she know the drill. "I know…I know…" He knew the encrypted code the crew would speak combined with her horrible interpretation of the English language and penmanship would fool even the most intelligent federal agent. Tony smirked and said, "Oh, and one more thing, Ma, how about dinner on Sunday? And invite Sid over.

I would like to meet him. I'll get Tic to join us. It will be like old times." Amazingly enough she agreed again.

Tony ventured out to the nearest pay phone. He spent just a few minutes on the phone letting his old crew leader back in Greensburg know that he arrived safely and to "take my mother's number down in case you need anything, and don't be strangers. I'll call you again when I get settled in." He quick dialed his uncle Joe and apologized for not being able to spend time with him as of yet, but "Ma is going to plan a Sunday dinner and we will make plans then. I do have something very important to talk with you about." Hs uncle was in complete understanding. He put the phone receiver in its cradle then slid the phone book out and spread open the pages to the beginning As. He scanned the column of names and found the few Accardis that were listed. A fragile smile appeared and he whispered, "Bingo."

The rest of the day wore down in Mobville and went pretty much as expected. Tick Tock Batista gave orders to his stumble bum of a crew to meet a guy in Bayway Elizabeth and drive a truckload of Italian suits to an address in Jersey City. "Finally a good payday," he chimed. Frank then contacted Accardi and planned the much-anticipated reunion. The meeting was set for 9:00 p.m. at the Pope's club. It was billed as a welcoming home and a reintroduction of the son of an old friend. Only a few handpicked capos and soldiers would be invited into the sealed and guarded back room, a room reserved for only the top-notched high rollers that ever sat at a poker table.

Frank did the honors and drove himself and his boy to the prestigious club. "Remember this place, kid?" Frank asked as they walked toward the rear entrance. "I sure do," Tony said. "Tonight you walk in tall, proud, it's your night tonight," Frank said. Tony put his hand up to silence Frank's next words. They were steps away from entering the joint. "Remember, if they ask you anything about what I'm to do in your crew, it's business as usual. Collections, hijacking…that sort of stuff, you got to let me do the talking, and no matter what, say nothing." He felt a surge of energy walking next to the kid, now the man, that just a few short years ago was almost physically tossed out of here on his ear.

The place was packed as usual with the usual mobsters, politicians, and a few of the upper crust from Livingston, Roseland, and Essex Fells, all waiting to bask in the evils of the night. The crowd opened like the Red Sea and made way for the two who were led to the entrance of the prominent room by Vito Tutolo, who also apologized as he patted them both down. Frank was recognized, but only rumors could be said beneath the breath of onlookers as to who was the other guy.

Tony was introduced and greeted with kudos by the societal group of cigar-smoking mobsters from New Jersey and New York, all hovered next to a small portable bar. Immediately after the traditional applause, one New York captain blurted, "We heard you guys had a real good time last night at Angelo's." The story of the espresso beans circulated throughout the gathered group, and all gave up belly laughs. After a few rounds of drinks, and then as if on cue, the mobsters got up and made their way to a large felted card table that was set up at the far end of the room, away from any earshot or chance of being overheard. Albert Marrone was in attendance in just the physical sense of the word. He opted out of the card game that was to begin with a trying "too rich for my blood." All that remained was the four: Ruggeri, Accardi, Batista, and the kid. Batista excused himself and said, "Let me help Albert to his car. Look at 'em. He could just about walk." Ruggeri gave him a wink and said, "Hurry back." The real underling reason Frank got up was to whisper a few words in Albert's ear. He could care less if the old bastard fell to pieces in the parking lot. "Keep it under your hat for now. I'll call you tomorrow," Frank said. Then he hopped back inside and took his place at the table.

Ruggeri looked at the kid through compassionate eyes, and Tony read it right away. He remembered only the look of evil the last time they met. "I know Eddie here explained what my expectations are of you, and it's my understanding you will be under the supervision of your old pal here." Ruggeri pointed at Batista with a bona fide smile. Batista returned the grin and nodded without speaking a word. It was Accardi's turn to speak, and the few words he began with were immediately recognized by Frank and Tony as a replay of the speech at the Belmont Tavern. Tony asked sincerely as he looked directly in the Pope's eyes, "Don Ruggeri, I came here tonight with a speech I been practicing and rehearsing for the last six years, and now I can't remember it." All at the table laughed. "But I want to tell you of my plan to clear my father's name and give you the tribute you deserve. You know of the work that I've been doing with Pittsburgh, and I just want to give you a preliminary taste of what's to come." In his mind, Tony rehearsed this scene over and over, just come out shooting and kill as many as you possibly can.

Accardi's body stiffened and Ruggeri's eyes bugged a little as the kid carefully reached under his lapel and into his inside suit pocket. He gingerly lifted a small plastic laboratory bag out and let six brilliant coins fall on the table with a little bit of a muffed jingle. A couple of them spun some and all fell helter-skelter...some heads and some tails. They were four solid gold and two solid silver coins, commemorative coins minted not as currency but as a novelty collectable with striking images of presidents. One was of the dearly departed John F. Kennedy. Tony watched as Ruggeri's interest increased a hundredfold. "You'll notice that they have no dollar denomination but rather a troy ounce weight." Ruggeri asked, "What are they worth?" Tony answered, "In today's market, about a hundred bucks." The kid read the anticipation on Ruggeri's face. "I have access to truckloads of these coins and an inside man that can tell me within a week of when the large shipments move, the ones worth hundreds of thousands of dollars."

Now Ruggeri was all ears. Tony was well aware that Ruggeri knew of MDS hijacking the minted coins. He even knew the net take of the Pittsburgh score and watched closely as Ruggeri feigned a look of surprise when the story was told again. "The next time we take it down, the score will be big—huge." Tony explained further how the company that mints these coins does it only periodically usually around holidays or special political calendar events. "This next presidential election is gonna be big. My guy says they're expecting orders of the millions of these little JFK mementos," Tony said with wide eyes.

Ruggeri reached deep into his criminal mind and posed well thought out and shrewd questions, but Tony had the element of surprise and all the right answers. He was he holding the cards. "This inside man, he's in the mint or the trucking outfit?" Ruggeri asked. It was the right question to ask, one that a true professional would want the answer to. Tony answered, "He's inside the terminal, full access to spare keys to all the trucks, manifest logs, records, you name it. We've already taken this outfit down for millions, ask the Monteseros if you don't believe me." That was out of line to say, and Tony quickly atoned. "My apologies, Don Ruggeri. I just get excited about these types of scores," Tony said sincerely. "This trucking outfit, they don't get the Feds involved about all of this theft?" Ruggeri asked. "That's the beauty of it all. They let their own security try to nail the thieves, and they do, believe me they do—but they ain't ready for us."

A plan was formulated at the table of which Ruggeri agreed and sanctioned. Tony stressed the fact his guy would not do business with anyone but Tony himself. That shot down the next question or request that Ruggeri threw on the table. "He will only talk or meet with me and me alone. Besides, isn't it better that way, the less we let Pittsburgh know, the better. Otherwise, they want tribute." That statement made all the sense in the world especially to the greedy Ruggeri. "Now all we have to do is sit tight and wait until my guy gives me the word of the increased shipments and we go to work. We only need a day's notice." Tony knew now that Ruggeri would make no inquiries or open any cans of worms about the MDS scam.

It was agreed, however, that Vito be part of the conversation and be involved with the heist itself, kind of an emissary from the Pope's crew. He would assist Tony. "It's a five-hour drive to the terminal, and a five-hour trip back, only stopping for gas. Is Vito up for it?" was the well-placed question Tony threw out there. "I'll make sure he goes into training right now," Ruggeri said. His job would be driver of the crash car that would escort the load back east and handle the expediting of the load when it crosses the state line. Now it is business as usual in Mobville. Everyone shook hands, and not a word was said about tax or tribute. Ruggeri would wait for his money patiently.

Frank Batista was amazed at the amount of information the kid had about this score. They left the club and headed back to the Belmont Tavern for a late-night dinner. It was there that Frank Batista found out just how shrewd his new partner was. "It's all bullshit, Frank. We did make a little score with those coins, but the whole story I just fed the Pope...is all bullshit." Frank wrinkled his brow and asked, "What if the Pope makes a call out there?" "So he hears what he's been hearin' all the other times he's called, and believe me, he says nothing to no one about this mystery score, the million dollar scam."

33

Vito Tutolo was intensely anxious and hot to trot over his role as second leading man of the boasted heist. He picked up Tony in front of the Hindsdale Avenue house early the next day and was nonstop with questions, scenarios, and bullshit in connection with the up-and-coming score. His mouth was nonstop during the entire trip to Jersey City. Tony just patronized his dumb ass with a lot of rhetoric and "You can't say a word to no one." One of the warehouses Vito and his father operated and used for their covert shipments of swag was on Garfield Avenue. It was a big fully enclosed building tucked neatly between an auto salvage yard and a huge scrap metal yard and across the street from some other nondescript buildings or storage sheds that were all covered in rusted galvanized siding.

Vito gave Tony the tour of the place and told him not to get too close to the two Dobermans he had chained to cinder blocks in his office. If they really wanted, they had the power to drag the concrete blocks some before their windpipes gave out and forced them to stop. Tony put his head inside only and said, "What's the sense havin' those both chained up like that in the office, they should be back there with the merchandise." "I let them out at night and leave this door open. It's a cesspool down these parts. No one comes around anyway. That's why we keep the place. The petty thief Moulinyans all know to stay clear. It's okay come on in," Vito said. Tony reluctantly came in and sat down very slowly. The dogs were calm now and lying just about on top of one another. "They're good mutts. I got a male and a female. They don't fight that much," Vito said. "So we bring the load here, it takes how long to unload it?" Vito asked. "Not long. It's a lot of small boxes," Tony said. He decided to just keep the nonsense going. "My concern is getting rid of the truck. When we did the scores in Greensburg, we would actually drive the empty trucks back into the yard." Vito's face indicated "not a bad idea," and he said, "No big deal. Weinstein next door is probably going to melt down the coins for us. I'll just have him scrap the truck too." Tony gave a wink of approval and said, "Good idea." His eyes then focused on the polished stock of what seemed to be a rifle peeking out of the back closet. He pointed his finger and said, "Is it a good idea to keep guns so out in the open like that?" Vito's huge frame turned around. "My old man loves shotguns," he said as he got out of his chair and invited Tony over to look up close. The dogs rose to their feet along with Tony and gnarled their mouths. Tony gave a look of concern and said, "Easy now, you two." He looked inside the storage room and eyeballed the dozen or so shotguns just lying around. Vito looked at Tony with rancorous eyes and said, "My old man, he loves to have this shit all around, he's got fuckin' dynamite and this new C-4 explosive shit from the army, probably a few grenades in there if you look hard enough. He don't care, says if the place gets busted, it's not his worry. His name ain't on the lease. It's in some hobo's name that lives in Secaucus." The tour was over, and Vito drove back over the Pulaski Skyway and into Newark. Tony declined his generous offer of lunch at the Sicilian Café and used Frank Batista as the excuse. "I got to meet with him in an hour at a little deli. I'll just grab a sandwich there." Tony was glad to be rid of the pest. This was the longest he had ever spent with Vito and hoped it would be the last time he ever would have to.

Tony went back to his mother's house and waited for the phone to ring. He sat with her and watched as she scorned the cast of *Search for Tomorrow*. During the commercials was the only time he was allowed to speak. "You like that new recliner, huh?" He took inventory of all the new things about the place and said flippantly, "I'm glad to see you at least spent the money I sent selfishly on yourself, Ma, and not on Sidney—and I hope you got a nice bank account?" She snapped and said, "He's not a rich man, but he's comfortable—he does not ask for a penny from me." Ceil leaned forward in the recliner. Her voice became subtly animated as she continued. "He never lets me spend a penny when we go out. He had a good insurance policy on his wife. The most I do is grocery shop and cook some dinner for him. He enjoys the Kosher Delicatessen food, but now he loves Italian food and he even eats pork." The phone rang and saved Tony from any more sordid details of her love affair. "Good... good...tell him I'm on my way...I'll be there in five minutes," Tony said then hung up the phone. He gave his mother a kiss goodbye to which she shushed and said, "My show is on."

The plan the kid conceived was coming together perfectly. Now another test of greed and conspiracy of a well-known wise guy. Albert Marrone never left his house during the heat of the summer. He lolled and hobbled in chilled air of his brownstone and cursed his arthritic bones that will someday make him a cripple. His opinion was to do as the Pope suggested and go into retirement—just poke your head out when absolutely needed; enjoy your senior years. Tick Tock Batista wanted to flat out whack him, make him just disappear as he knew the Pope ordered for his cousin. The thought of Ruggeri's goons torturing Breeze as Frank thought he did sickened him. Deep inside he wondered if his cousin was a stand-up, or did he rat? Tony declined and made it crystal clear he did not want to harm Albie.

"Not after the stories my uncle told me about him and my father… as kids. I can't do it. I made a promise on my father's grave I would not harm him. He was a traitor, yes, but…Ruggeri was pulling the strings," Tony said. "If this little scam I cooked up doesn't end his career, then…that's that."

Tony pulled his Lincoln in a no parking zone that was directly in front of Corrado's Market. He saw the hunched but still intimidating frame of Albert Marrone. Tony ran up to him with an honest smile and said, "You had a nickname when you were a kid. My uncle Tomasino told me, but I forgot. What was it?" Albert said yes to the question of roasted peppers on his sandwich and "Husky" to Tony. "They used to call me Husky, and I beat the shit outta' anyone that did, even your old man a coupla' times, but then he outgrew me. This teacher we had could never remember my name. She would always say 'Heah you, the husky one,' and of course it stuck." Tony gave the counter man a nod and said, "The usual for me. Albie, you want a soda? They got imported Italian soda here, excellent stuff."

"I could sit and talk about the old days with you like an expert, and I wish I could, but I don't have much time," Tony said. Dominick walked the sandwiches down in their customary skin of butcher's paper and both sliced in half. Tony looked up at Dominic and said, "Thank you. Please…have a seat." Dominick obliged and took a load off. He knew his part in all of this. Tony looked at Dominick and asked concernedly, "Any new news from Naples?" Dominick shook his head no. "And the old man's family, they still bustin' balls about this place?" Tony asked. Dominick shook his head yes. "And the prozhoot, they still won't ship it?" Dominick shook his head no and said, "I m gonna call 'em right now." He got up and walked away, and Albie, not missing a bite of his sandwich, mumbled, "What the fuck was that all about?" Tony peeled open the wrapper on his sandwich and took a healthy bite. He chewed some and said, "This prozhoot we're eating is the best in Italy, just as good if not better than Parma.

Matter of fact they're related, and it's what Tic wanted me to talk to you about." And that began the ball rolling; as the two men ate Tony did most of the talking. "This place here is a gold mine. Problem is the real owner died a month ago, in Naples, that's where he's from. The import license everything is in his name." Albie asked, "So who is he? He's from Naples, and how did he get established here?" Tony looked around in secrecy and said, "Those guys up front, they're all cousins to the owner. His name was Cundari, Giuseppe Cundari. The problem they got is the family back in Naples wants out of this operation. They want these guys to buy out the now deceased brother to the tune of twenty-five Gs." Albert looked surprised and said, "Well, that ain't a lot of money, let 'em come up with it." Tony said, "They can't. They're flat broke." Albert again said emphatically, "So let Batista make the loan." Tony grinned and shook his head in dismay. "The fat guy we just spoke with, he hates Batista. Batista tried to use this place years ago as a laundry. They rejected him hard, and the people in Naples know the Pope…Ruggeri, and it turned ugly." Albert asked, "So how do I fit in, what the fuck you want from me?" Tony looked seriously at Albie and said, "Look, you know I'm back, and I'm gonna be with Tic on some things and with my guys back in Pittsburgh on others. My father always liked you, and so did the old-timers in Greensburg. Now I can go to them for the dough, but guess what, now I get double taxed, triple taxed. Them, Tic, and the Pope. I go to anyone else the Pope eats me alive. I'm figuring for old time's sake and the sake of my father, me and you go in heads first. I already squared it with these guys. They loved my father and would do anything for him, and they trust me. They will do whatever I say to keep them alive."

Albert had swallowed the bait a long, long time ago, but he is like a Moby Dick. He needs to be harpooned deep through his heart. Albert looked around at the entire place as a layman would see it, an Italian deli and market. "So how does the place do as a legit market?"

Albert asked. "Takes in a bundle. They'll show you the books, and speaking of legit, that prozhoot is ready to be shipped to this place exclusively 50 percent less than anything else on the market. We'll clean up on that alone. You get your money back in two months tops then a steady 25 percent," Tony said. He had Albert on the edge of his seat. "How soon you need the money?" he asked. Tony came back slowly but to the point. He raised his brow and said, "Tonight... we put the deal together tonight. I'll have some papers drawn up." Albert stopped the kid's forward progress and asked, "What papers?" Tony quickly replied, "The import agreement papers and the legal shit for the clan in Naples. You know, the bullshit semi-legit stuff so we don't get fucked out of the legit business. And I already got people lined up we launder money for and ten points, plus the bookmaking action that this place never had. Albert, we'll be rich men, and then you can really retire in style."

Tony sat quietly for a bit and just watched the life return to Albert's wrinkled, convoluted face. This was the best he's looked in years. He even seemed to move his arms a little better and the aching complaints and that self-induced physical therapy of rubbing his shoulder disappeared. He was both anxious and antsy. "I'll be right back. I gotta' take a piss. Where's the bathroom?" he asked Tony who just pointed toward the back. When he returned, Tony gave him not a chance for remorse. He chimed right in. "This is a deal you would never get from the Pope. And it's my chance to do good myself. I hear the Pope has all but left you homeless? You got my word...on my father...the Pope will never hear about this deal we make here today." Albert Marrone passed the test of greed and gluttony. His once sworn allegiance and oath that he swore to the Don of New Jersey now was forsaken by the strong grip of his handshake.

Frank thought perhaps the dupe of the old man was for the money, but he realized it was Tony's cunning way of revenge. If the Feds would ever connect this place with heroin distribution, it will undoubtedly frame the doting Marrone. That was indeed the con-cocted plan the kid had hoped for; let the old man live out his years in a federal prison—yes, that would be his penance. But what would Ruggeri say, or do? Tony often lay in bed wondering about the spec-tral force that compelled him to put Albert together with this simple plan, and his answer was to his father, "I'm keeping my promise, Daddy. I'm not the one gonna lay a hand on him."

Tony slid into the red vinyl booth at the Lyndhurst Diner with a distinguished smirk on his face. He took a long, hard look at the empty plate and dirtied fork that sat on the table just a few inches away from Frank Batista's fingers. It had remnants of a New York cheesecake written all over it. He first gave Batista a healthy wink then spoke politely to the waitress who tailed him closely to the table. "Bring me what he just had and a coffee please." Sitting across from him was Batista with a huge devilish grin on his face, holding a lit cig-arette between his fingers. "I can't believe you sold the old cocksucker on the idea. You're a helluva salesman, kid." Tony reached under his Italian knit shirt and pulled out an envelope that was tucked in his waistband. "Here, take this over to that shyster Caruso and have him put together what we need to get Albie's name on the ownership papers." Frank pulled the paperwork out and took a look at it. A lot of it was written in Italian. "What's all this shit?" he asked. "I don't know, but Dominick said it's the original lease and the other legal bullshit connected with the shop. I had the old man sign in a few places for a sample of his handwriting, but just tell Caruso to get to work on the transfer. He'll know what to do. He forges signatures all day long," Tony said incidentally.

Frank talked with the lit cigarette dangling between his lips. "What about the money…is he game for that?" he asked. "The twen-ty-five G number was perfect. Not too much, very believable, and I know he's got ten times that stashed all over his house. That's why the prick hardly ever comes out," Tony said casually. "So when do we get it?" Frank asked. Tony cracked a sinister grin and said, "I already got it. It's under my front seat right now. We left Corrado's and went straight to his house." Frank blew a puff of blue smoke in the air and said, "Kid, you are one hell of a salesman."

It seemed that Frank never wanted to go home alone anymore. He sat with his boy at the diner until the dinner crowd began to pile in and the aroma of meatloaf and gravy permeated the air over the entire community of Lyndhurst. "You hungry, why don't we eat before we head back to the apartment?" Frank asked. Tony said, "Yeah, I am a little hungry, but not for this shit. Let's go up the street to that Chink restaurant."

The boys allowed the tuxedo-clad Asian girl to escort them to a table they both agreed was situated in the room perfectly, to their liking, as if she knew the far back corner booth had their name written all over it. Tony took a sip of some hot Chinese jasmine tea and looked at his wristwatch. He waited as Frank lit up cigarette, and then he said, "We got a job to do later. It's only eight o'clock now, and I got to get back to the apartment to change and pick up a few things. All I need you for is to drive and wait. It's about a two-hour job—all-inclusive—ride and all." Frank subtly asked, "What kind of job, and what time later?" Tony sat back and folded his arms. "One o'clock, one in the morning, that's what I figure. We got a load of dynamite and a few shotguns to steal." Frank said with a little emotion, "From where?" Tony answered with a wink, "Tutolo's warehouse in Jersey City, place is loaded with weapons and this special-type dynamite." "You crazy kid, he's got those vicious dogs—" Tony cut him short and gave him a look of genius as he reached in his pocket and pulled out a small bottle of pills. "Phenobarbital, my man." Frank rolled his eyes in bewilderment. Tony smirked. "You stick in a coupla' inside some Tootsie Rolls." Now Frank's jaw was on the table—Tony busted a huge grin and said, "You heard me right.

Tootsie Rolls. Laced with Phenobarbital. It's an old trick I learned from the hillbillies in Greensburg. The soft candy sticks to their teeth and the roof of their mouths. They can't spit it out. It keeps 'em chomping for a while until they swallow, and then the drugs gets into their system, puts them to sleep in about fifteen minutes. I'll go with you to the apartment and we'll leave together—in the Oldsmobile." Frank still looked flustered. Tony snapped his fingers in haste. "Frank—you with me here?" Frank responded but as if in a daze, "Yeah, of course, Tootsie Rolls, huh?"

The area they were in is a desolate patch of low-lying real estate deep in the bowels of a Jersey City industrial slum. Seasoned thieves knew there was absolutely nothing of substantial value inside any of these obscure warehouses, so for the most part, they stayed away. Even the police recognized this track of murky oil-and-diesel-fuel-infused mud and gravel as a low-crime area and would not soil the tires on their cruiser in this shit. They patrolled and concentrated on the more obvious and essential parts of the city; as a result, the duo had little to worry about except for the mongrel dogs. And it was always better to be safe than sorry.

Both men looked like weary longshoremen, both dressed completely on black, and both seemed to vanish into thin air as they walked to the warehouse gate. Frank was flabbergasted, and both he and Tony fought back roaring laughter at the simplicity of the job. Tony was masterful with picking locks, but a strong wing would have opened both the chained gate and the office door. Tony whispered over the top of the barking animals on the other side of the door, "When I throw the bolt, put your shoulder to the door. I only want it to open about an inch. We don't want those mongrels out." Frank was a nervous Nellie but gave a nod of compliance. The bolt threw. Tony cracked the door, and Frank's eyes showed terror at the pair of snapping fangs that appeared through the crack. The dogs became quiet and unconcerned about the intruders once the candy was tossed inside. "So how long we wait?" Frank asked nervously. Tony gave a cocksure "Fifteen minutes they're out like lights."

The Tutolos relied so heavily on their bloodthirsty mongrels to ward off any intruder, and by all rights they should have. But now both dogs were sound asleep out back in the warehouse. Tony knew exactly where the shotguns were and they only took one. Frank scanned the shelves of the storage room with the tiny penlight and found it hard to refrain from screaming. "Holy shit…these fuckin' nuts got live grenades here, government issue. Dynamite too. They're getting ready for a war. Ah-haaaa…here we go." The faint light could only illuminate a few letters at a time, but when combined, it spelled out "Block demolition, M4 (composition C-4) lot # 32998 – 9811 – 3 mfg date 7/28/61." The boys filled two gym bags with enough explosive to start another war. Frank could not resist the temptation and pocketed two hand grenades. "I wonder if they count this stuff?" he said. Tony replied with a laugh, "Maybe, put one back." He handed Frank his bag and the shotgun and said, "Here, go bring the car around while I lock the place back up."

Frank looked at his watch as they drove down Communipaw Avenue and said, "I gotta' hand it to ya', kid, easy as pie." Both men exploded with laughter as Tony said, "I told ya', Frank, in and out less than two hours—and speaking of pie, let's go get some." The waitress was immediately at their service as Tony and Frank sat at the counter of the busy all-night diner. "It's a workingman's place." Tony joked. Frank leaned into his friend and whispered in his ear, "What if they OD, then the Tutolo's know something's up?" Tony backed away and said, "Trust me, Frank, those mutts are having sweet dreams about humping French poodles. They'll be fine come morning, maybe a little groggy, but okay. I knocked out thousands of dogs all across Pennsylvania. "

The eighth-floor apartment at the Mt. Prospect Street high-rise that Tony so obligingly subleased from his partner had everything in it but a telephone. But as soon as he moved all of his worldly possessions in, he contacted a reliable friend at Ma Bell and had one installed. Anonymity was crucial in the underworld, but the simple luxury of being able to pick up a phone and get a message to someone was essential. Or he could continue to use pay phones and rely on his mother taking messages.

It would be Thursday afternoon at approximately three in the afternoon before Tony would finally wake up and answer the phone that had been ringing off the wall. Yes, Ma Bell did a fine job in the installation, but it was by choice that it would be only in the kitchen. Thank God it wasn't Tick Tock asking for an escort to his car. It was his mother informing him or inviting him over for Sunday dinner, and it would be as fine a feast as he could ever hope to expect. It would be the extravaganza she'd been planning for so many years ago for his long-forgotten birthdays over the years, and no sooner he hung up the phone from his mother another burst of rings shook his world. The quintessential "Whaddya doin'?" of Batista blared from the receiver and brought a smile. Tony agreed to meet him after five and help with some of his way overdue collections; then he said, "Keep your calendar open for Sunday. We're goin' to my mother's for dinner." Batista chimed right in, "So lemme' ask, is old Sidney gonna' be there? I'll bring some bagels instead of Italian bread."

34

Ceil Marino would spend each and every Saturday night with Sidney, and by now it was more than habit; it was becoming tradition. They savored their special time together on what was most certainly considered the height of their week. He had an older car, a 1946 Chevrolet sedan, that was in immaculate shape. It was his pride and joy and cherished it almost as much as Ceil. He kept it garaged at the duplex he rented and would only take it out on special occasions and on certain dates with Ceil. Tonight would be one of those nights. Usually he would be the gentlemanly caller and pick her up at her place for the evening out, but overnight would be spent at his apartment. She would forgo church on Sunday mornings to sit with Sid, in his kitchenette, smiling shyly over light conversation and noshing, as he would call it, on good coffee, loxs, bagels and cream cheese, an inconceivable event not of her past life with Anthony as she could remember.

However, this Saturday, the routine would change, and for the very first time since they started to keep company, Sidney Margolis would stay in Ceil's bed, the one with the new mattress and box spring and the new bedding. She could not afford to waste one minute's time preparing Sunday dinner. She had Sidney drive her to the markets on Saturday afternoon for her needed groceries; then that evening would be a movie and deli sandwiches. Sidney woke up Sunday morning to the unique aroma and sound of meatballs frying and garlic and olive oil simmering in a pot large enough to be called a vat. He commented, "Ceil, it smells wonderful in here. Like heaven." And that was certainly the right thing to say.

Sidney poured a cup of coffee and asked nervously where he should sit. He reluctantly put his hand on the chair at the head of the table and waited for her approval. It came in the form of a sublime smile from Ceil. After a little nosh of Italian pastries purchased the day before, she chased him into the living room with the paper and said, "Go inside and watch TV and let me cook." He was no stranger to her cooking; on many occasions she brought over freshly prepared Italian foods and pasta dishes to his place and even threw together a few things using his measly few pans. But this would be the first time he saw her in real action.

The first to arrive was Joe. He was smart dressed in his best Dickies blue work pants and short-sleeve white cotton shirt, carrying two large boxes of Italian pastries and a brown bag with six loaves of fresh-baked Italian bread inside. Behind him, his son lugging baby apparatus with his young wife and their seven-month-old baby girl snuggled against her breasts. Commotions were made over the baby and the gravy on the stove. Sid heard the group amass and leaped out of the recliner. He walked into the kitchen enthusiastically and, in spite of all of his waving, was completely ignored.

Nicky's wife handed off the baby to her husband and watched in amazement as Ceil rolled the dough on the flour-covered pasta board forming long ropes. Nicky said, "Aunt Ceil, you remember my wife Donna, right?" Ceil said with a warm smile, "Of course I do, but I haven't seen her or baby..." She tried to recall the baby's name but couldn't. Donna chimed in and said, "Lisa, this is baby Lisa." Ceil finished her words. "In such a long time...not since the christening.

Let me see…how adorable she is." Ceil wiped her hands on a kitchen towel and said, "Oh, for God sakes." She walked to Sidney's side and said, "Everyone say hello to Sidney." Introductions and warm welcomes went all around. Joe gave Ceil a wink and walked out of the room. Ceil led the young parents into Tony's old room and said, "You can put all of her things here."

The men congregated around the television set. Joe, acting as if he owned the TV, quickly changed the channel to the Yankee game broadcast and sat in the chair originally occupied by Sid. Nick commandeered the center of the couch. Sidney was about to say, "What happened to the movie I was watching?" but decided not to. Instead, he sat uncomfortably in the open armchair and made believe he liked baseball.

Mama Corollo entered the kitchen and greeted all with a beautiful antipasto tray of assorted meats, olives and cheese, and fresh roasted red peppers. She placed the tray at the end of the table along with a saucer filled with pure green olive oil and some freshly sliced crusty Italian bread. Without missing a beat she took a place next to her daughter and began creating handmade gnocchi and other delicacies cooked and placed at the end of the table. Ceil looked up at the clock that read two forty-five and said to herself, "Everything will be ready by four."

Tony pulled his Lincoln into the narrow driveway and popped the remote trunk release. "Heah, now that's a handy device," Tic said. Tony reached inside and lifted the case of Amarone '*della* Valpolicella. "What no Manischewitz…I thought this guy was Jewish?" Tic asked. "He is, and the more I think about it, we should be nice. He's a diamond setter for a big outfit downtown Newark, ya' never know?" Tony said tongue-in-cheek.

Sidney thought a crowd had just arrived as Tony and Frank entered. The smug little man tried to be funny. "Is it a raid?" he asked Joe, and then he winced in his seat over the cold look Joe gave him in return. All were curious about the commotion that was going on in the kitchen, so all got up to greet the celebrities. It has been years since Ceil had last seen Frank Batista, and she soon made a spectacle of herself about that fact. All of a sudden the clamor ended and Ceil walked about the room with her son's hand in hers. "Sidney. I want you to meet my son Tony. Tony. This is my dear friend, Sidney." She let go his hands and looked at both her men with a wishful "play nice, boys" look on her face. Sidney stood and looked up at her son who was a solid foot taller than he. He offered his handshake, a firm handshake. "Nice to meet you, young man," he said without a bit of hesitation or dread.

Tony liked the guy immediately. Perhaps he recognized a true sincerity in his voice or saw a good man behind those thin-framed gold eyeglasses? Whatever was the vibe Tony felt, he liked. Sidney was smart dressed and had his wavy silver-gray hair slicked back as mobsters do. Tony let out a beaming grin and said, "Same here, ahhh, Sidney." They shook hands as Frank Batista started right in with the humor. "I'm Frank Batista, Sidney...Sidney?" He was prying with snapping fingers, trying openly to fish out a sir name. "Margolis, Margolis is my last name," Sidney interjected. Frank shook his hand and said, "Margolis, that's Jewish, isn't it? You don't sound Jewish. Your voice, I mean." Sidney rolled his eyes and said in his best Yiddish, "*Oy vey...a shmendrick* like me should know better when I talk to goyim such as you all are." A little silence fell over the room then laughter. "And I understand you take my friend's mother out. I hope you treat her good," Batista said. Sidney changed his accent to his normal almost Brooklyn street slang and said, "I do...I do...I take Ceil out and I take her everywhere. But she always comes home." That puzzled everyone until Frank picked up on it and laughed aloud with a pointed finger. "Georgie Jessel?" Sidney returned a wrinkled frown and said, "Henny Youngman, you schmuck!" That was it for Frank Batista and for Tony. They were hooked on this old comedian, and he was ever so shrewd to have played it that way, make no doubt about it. And before long he would have had them eating out of his hands. Frank pulled him to the couch and immediately began talking about the comedic greats that emerged from Vaudeville and the Catskills.

Soon the house was alive with the ado and clamor of a full-blown holiday. The wine was flowing, and everyone darted from room to room with plates and mouths full of antipasto and hunks of olive-oil-drenched Italian bread. Tony spent some time getting reacquainted with his cousin and his new bride. Frank and Sidney exchanged stories of the Jewish mobsters. "No one knows this except for Ceil, but my father's cousin was none other than Jacob Shapiro," Sidney said. "No…not Murder Inc himself?" Frank asked. "The *Gurrah* himself," Sidney said. Score a few more points for the little Jew in the corner.

Tony wandered into the kitchen to pick. His mother gave him a gleeful look and took his hand again. "Look at what we're having in your honor." He glanced at the table full of homemade pasta ready to get plunged into pots of boiling water. "I can't wait, Ma," he said. Ceil pulled him to her side and said, "I haven't made gnocchi since you went away…all those years ago." "You mean old Sid in there never had?" Tony asked. "Nope, this will be the first time he eats them, at least mine anyway," Ceil said. Tony laughed and said, "Well, yours are the best. He eats those and we'll never get rid of him." Ceil put on a devilish grin and asked, "So how do you like him?" Tony gave her a sincere smile and said, "Seems like a real nice guy, so you better make him understand that now he has to stay that way." "Ohhh, you shut up," his mother hissed.

And dinner was served. Tony took the seat at the head of the table where his father would normally sit. Subconsciously, he looked up above his head. His eyes almost seemed to be asking permission. It would be the first time in that seat. He was going to leave it open but decided that his father would have insisted he, and not Sid. To his right was his uncle Joe and Frank Batista sat to his left.

And for a good solid hour the family feasted and told stories both old and new, many of them embarrassing, but told without worry or consequence and all hysterically funny. As a matter of fact, any conversation that had a hint of seriousness was shot out of the sky. Today there were no evils of sickness or disease, no condemnations of enemies or past wrongdoings or rueful wishes undone, just joyous laughter and genuine love.

Tony looked down the table at his cousin and said, "So, Nicky, your father says you went to a special school to learn auto mechanics. He says you're getting real good with those tools." Before Nick could answer, Tic and old Sid were all over him. "Take a look at that baby over there. Looks like the kid knows what he's doing with those tools," Frank said as he laughed. "Frank, are we talking about his *schmeckle*?" Sidney said, bemusing. And thus began another half hour of one-liners between the two of them until finally dessert was served and shut them up.

Sidney used every form of the word *delicious* that his vocabulary of English, Yiddish, and slang Italian could muster as he ate far more than his quota of sfogliatelle and sipped the Marie Brizzard till *she* gave no more. He took the opportunity to speak with Tony and said, "So I hear you and your friend enjoy that high-rise living, like the *mensches* from Hollywood and Manhattan?" Tony gave him a just look and said, "Sid, I would much rather prefer a country home with a big porch or a home down the shore with a big porch over that 'looking down at the world' view of a concrete and glass high-rise." Sidney looked around the table and leaned toward Tony and said, "You'll do okay in life. I can feel it, and take it from a man who has no children. I've been judging other children all my life."

The afternoon began to wind down, and a decision would have to be made if everyone stayed and watched *Ed Sullivan* or went home and watched *Ed Sullivan*. Frank was the first to tire and began the commencement of accolades to the chef. "Everything was so delicious, I am stuffed like a pig. Oh, by the way, Sid, did you know you ate some pork?" Sid smiled and said, "I'm allowed. I know Ceil will make it up to me and cook a nice kosher chicken for me." Frank was too tired for any more. He just wanted to go home and grab some shut-eye. "It was great meeting you, Sid, hope to see you again," Frank said. "Please, give me a warning first," Sid cracked.

Donna gave her husband a nudge and said, "I think we should go too, it's getting late. Go find your father." Nick agreed and started to stand up. Tony said, "You sit, Nick. I'll go tell your father you're ready to leave." Joe was sitting on a piece of worn wicker on the front porch smoking a cigarette and daydreaming about his missing brother. Tony appeared and his uncle said, "That was a meal. I am stuffed. Just like the old days, hah, kid?" Tony laughed and agreed. His uncle blew smoke rings and said, "It's quiet out here. It used to be so much noisier years ago as I remember. But then again all you kids were little Indians then running around and screaming, you remember?" Tony looked at his uncle seriously and said, "Uncle Joe, you remember that day at my father's?" Joe knew all too well the day he was referring. "How could I ever forget…I still have nightmares."

"Did you think my father was serious when he said all that stuff about wanting to get out of the rackets, go legit, go into business with you?" Tony asked in earnest. "I believed him. I was ready," Joe said. Tony pulled the other wicker chair close to his uncle and sat. His voice turned emotional and he said, "Uncle Joe, I got a nice piece of change put aside, and I was wonderin' if you would throw in with me and do that thing with the car lot?" Joe's eyes got wide and he said, "What about…Batista and the life with that crew?" Tony took a deep breath then exhaled. "That is going to be history for me real soon. I honestly can say that I've had my fill and now is the time for me to walk away while I still can." Both men stood and Joe said,

"Look. If you're sincere, you come up with a plan and you can count me in."

The dinner was over, and Ceil Marino found herself in a very familiar place. It wasn't that long ago this type of a soiree had taken place on a weekly basis or sometimes twice a week? A sink full of dirty dishes and an empty kitchen that is bare of any living soul who would offer help. Never in all the years with her Anthony, or anyone from his crowd, did someone come forward and offer help with the dishes. She could count on her toes not even a sister or a sister-in-law that did or did not. And here comes this small-framed man but not small in stature to find it beneath himself to put his arms around her waist and hold tight and say, "Let me help you with the dishes." Tony offered a night of cabareting, but Frank declined. He threw his legs out of the Lincoln and grumbled, "I'm too old for your type party, kid. The dinner we ate was enough for me, go have some fun." Tony sped off and watched as Batista waved from his rearview mirror.

Angelo Ruggeri considered prostitution to be one of his oldest and dearest vices, not to mention the cash cow that it had always been for the family. It was a great source of recreation for the more notable and rakish associates of his, especially the sinful politicians. They had the most difficulty turning down an amoral beauty, especially if she was young or exotic and especially if the pleasure was treated them by the boss of New Jersey himself. The ironic thing about his noted women is that they were not allowed in his club. On rare occasions he would have an emissary from one of his brothels bring one for him personally; she would be indiscreetly ushered upstairs to his private suite and covertly escorted out.

His guests would either be driven by the hired help of the club or given a cab ride to a finest establishment money could buy. Out of the seven that were positioned and located throughout the city, his personal favorite was the eight-room brick colonial in the Forest Hill section of Newark right on Lake Street and not far from where Eddie Accardi lives. It even had two guesthouses in the rear of the property for weekend high rollers.

His brothels were known for their discretion and their safety and for their choice women that embellished the parlor and bar area. And they were not cheap at all as far as the fee went. Ruggeri had his little scam—yes, his guests would arrive under the pretense of a "comped" visit, and that held true for some alcohol, but when it came time for the real action, the girls knew how to pick the pockets of their lustful johns. And even corporate magnates or innocent politicians that honestly left their wallets at home rushed to borrow cash from the bartenders/loan sharks downstairs. The amounts just added to their already running markers.

Tony Marino knew the madam from his younger days when he was the new kid on the block. Gerda Fares was her name. She is an exotic and beautiful woman in her fifties, from Sweden living completely illegal in her private room of the house and enough a beauty still to be requested to sit on a lap or two. It was well known that of course her price was through the slate roof of the house.

The reason for her existence is the fact that she not only runs and keeps her house on the up and up, no drugs allowed, no rowdy behavior, and no college kids, but she oversees the other six.

Many a night the young Tony sat waiting for his friend Tick Tock while he visited and would bust balls when he would return, "Gee that was fast," and Batista would give him a love tap. And every once in a while, his friend Tic would send a little cute messenger to sit in the car with him as he so patiently waited.

So when it came time to pay back a favor or two, Tony took the initiative after dinner at Mom's to pull his Lincoln into the private drive, ring the front doorbell, and to be greeted by Gerda herself. The girls he selected spoke a cute Haitian Creole, and they loved American rock and roll music. They shimmed nicely together in the front seat of the Lincoln as Tony drove them away, both just laughing and bebopping their little asses off. Their scent was intoxicating and married well with the natural moisture of their skin. Tony's choice sat tightly against his side and massaged his genitalia to the rhythm and beat of Mary Wells singing "My Guy."

Frank Batista dozed off in front of his television set with a cigarette burning in the ashtray and a drink about to slip out of his hand. The horrible buzzer of his front door startled him enough to put the finishing touch on that Scotch on the rocks he was totting. The glass made a dull thud and the ice tinkled a bit as it hit the carpet. Panic set in. *No one ever rings the door bell/buzzer except Casa di Pizza and ...of course.* "Thought you might need a little company after all the family influence you had today," Tony said as he barged through the door. Frank was not at all embarrassed about being caught in his blue striped boxers, white Guinea tee, and black ribbed silk socks, one up and one down.

He let out a rueful sigh then stared at the cocoa-brown skin of the rather young women standing in his parlor. "I was sleepin', Tone... who are they?"he asked. "This one is mine. Her name is Honey. And Miss Haiti here of 1963 is your little island cutie. They're all bought and paid for from Gerdas. All you gotta' do is give her cab fare back to the house." Tony bowed his head and watched as Frank's eyes got wide; then he said, "See ya' tomorrow, Frankie mon" in a horrible island accent.

Tony entered his apartment and flipped on the light switch. "My place is a little smaller than my friend's, but it's cozy. Make yourself at home," he said to his guest. She just smiled and said, "I gotta' find dee' batroom' boy." Tony pointed and said, "Use the master bath in the bedroom. Why don't you run us a nice warm bubble bath while I fix some drinks. Whatta ya' havin?" Her voice faded as she squirmed to the bathroom. "Ana-ting dats fiery down dee' trowt."

35

J oan Jankowski held back her taut drapery and peered astutely out the living room window of her second floor apartment. She watched with a jealous frown as Mark Cohen eased his Sedan deVille into a tailor-made parking space, one she could have never hoped to find on the street if she lived to be a hundred years old. He got out of his car and stood in front of the European Renaissance Period building with the terra-cotta stone and the high gables and balustrade in front of the windowed portico. "The only building of its kind on E Eleventh between First and Second Avenue," as described to him by the resident herself. She cranked open the newly installed double-paned window and shouted, "You got the right place, mister, now all you got to do is climb a flight of stairs. I'm the apartment on the right." He just waved and blew her a kiss.

Joanie just absolutely hated dates on a Sunday no matter who it was with. Perhaps Sunday in her mind was usually reserved and promised to her parents, and more than ever now since she moved to Manhattan. But since her parents were attending a company picnic, she opted for an alternative plan. Mark Cohen flashed two tickets for *Funny Girl* in her face as he dropped off his orders Friday past and invited her for either the famed brunch at the Waldorf before the 7:00 p.m. show or a dinner at the Russian Tea Room after. "I shrewdly reserved both and all for you." Joanie smirked and gave him a casual hug and said smugly, "This is not, by no means, what I would call a cheap date. I guess you'll expect to get in my pants later on, huh?" He just blushed. Joanie had a haphazard way when it came to sex, either doing it or talking about it, and she reddened many a face as Mark's was now. She made the determination that if he wanted her this time, and he should, she would let him seduce the hell out of her, which is why she agreed to the Sunday in the park and at her place.

Joanie was by no means an expert on the subject of sex, and she was definitely not a slut, having made the most love with her boss up to a year ago and just three times after that affair with an old flame from her hometown. Both trysts not that impressive as far as she could tell from the X-rated porn she viewed. She was curiously excited to see what the braggart Mark had in store for her.

Her dry sense of humor intimidated most men, and certainly did Mark no matter how much he tried to hide behind his male ego. But after the first ten minutes alone in her apartment, he realized he was very close to victory. "I can see why you're a successful salesman, Mark, you're so punctual," Joanie said as she handed him a glass of wine. "I'm going to select the Waldorf before and drinks only at the Russian Tea Room, that is if they'll have us, and I will guarantee you I'll be feeling extremely sexy later. That Streisand really does it to me," she said with a devilish laugh. Joanie was dressed in one of her own creations, and she looked fabulous. The style and cut of the dress tapered her waist to almost nothing and let her breasts naturally fill out the fabric. And her exquisite legs, they would make anyone of the Radio City Rockettes jealous.

The two exited the cool corridor of the brownstone and felt the midday August heat on their shoulders. Joanie already called ahead to the parking garage to have her car pulled up, a service provided for a couple of bucks to the attendant. She convinced Mark to just leave his car parked where it is because "you'll never find another like it when you take me back here," she said. He registered another yes on his getting laid tonight survey. It was agreed after a brief discussion about hailing cabs on a hot Sunday afternoon that they would take her car, and as slick as he tried to be, Mark still needed directions around the city.

The Waldorf was indeed a place for the hungry beau monde of which both Joanie and her date Mark were, but they thought best to nibble on just a few things as to avoid any gastric or digestive problems later.

Mark cursed himself at the theater for not getting his money's worth at the grand brunch while Joanie became captivated by the stars, the set, and the music of the show. And the more she watched the character of Nick Arnstein, the more seductively sinful he made her feel. His middle-aged physical presence reminded her of Arnold Lewis and their tryst, but his actions on stage for some odd and unexplainable reason drove the image of a young Tony Marino in her head, and it stayed there for the rest of the musical. On the way out she hummed the theme song "Maria" from *West Side Story* and thought, *Oh God, why?* At any time men were going to come and take her to the home for the criminally insane.

She laughed to herself as Mark bitched about the parking rate saying, "You should only know?" As they left the garage she leaned into him and gave a moist kiss to his cheek. "Thank you, that was a fabulous show, and I have a favor to ask." He waited to come to a stop, and he leaned and kissed her back. "What, honey?" "Honey… oh boy…let's go to that little outdoor café where we were last week," Joanie said. "In Little Italy?" Mark asked with a confused look on his face. "Yeah…do you mind…honey…I can't tell how really horny that's going to make me feel," she purred.

Mark let Joanie do most of the talking as he concentrated and weaved his way slowly through Lower Manhattan until he was in an area he was familiar with. He took no fool chances with her car. There was a pedestrian pileup causing traffic jam that slowed the left hand turn onto Mulberry Street from Canal. Joanie voiced her anger at Mark for being too wishy-washy behind the wheel. "Just fucking drive, Mark, don't worry, I have insurance. These people are not going to stop and let you pass, run them the fuck over!" she blared. Mark was somewhat shocked by her vulgarity, yet he obeyed and got cursed out from both sides of the street. "Pull into that parking lot on the left. See it?" She instructed Mark. "I think it's private parking," Mark said. Joanie gave him a pathetic look and said, "Just try." And he did. The fence was closed. A young hipster sat on a wooden bar stool puffing away on a cigarette and ignoring the Mercedes.

After what seemed to be an hour the young punk acknowledged Mark with a snide "Can I help ya', pal?" Mark spoke from the car window, "Can we park here?" The kid looked a Mark closely and frowned. "No, it's private parking." Mark turned to Joanie and said, "See, I told you so." She immediately snapped, "You have to get out and offer him money. Give him ten dollars. It's worth it." He looked at her like she was crazy and said, "Ten dollars, you want me to give ten dollars to park?" "Mark"—she began to reach in her pocketbook—"I'll give you the money." Mark hopped out of the car, and the kid stood and took a defensive stance. "Here I got ten dollars," Mark said as he waved the bill in the air. The kid sat back on his perch and said, "Sorry, pal, it's reserved."

Mark was visibly annoyed by now—his masculinity was at stake. If he could not close this kid, he could only imagine what Joanie would think. He wasn't quick enough though. She opened the door to the Benz and got out. She leaned on the soft material of the ragtop and got indignant. "Listen, you little prick, I want to know why we can't park in that lot." Her voice escalated. "I see a lot of other fucking cars in that lot, and none of them are as nice as mine—" Before Joanie could get the next words out of her mouth a brute of a man emerged from across the street and shouted in a rude crude slang, "Who the fuck are yous' two...do we know you?" Mark felt really in over his head but said with some authority, "Look...the girl wants to know why we can't park in the lot." The goon grit his teeth then pulled a switchblade from his rear pocket. His face became threatening, and he plunged the knife into the soft roof with a fast arc movement and viciously tore a footlong gash in the material as he said, "'Cause your fuckin' car can get damaged...now get the fuck outta here." Joanie screamed, "You big ugly son-of-a-bitch." Mark was in total shock. The goon steamed and spat, "You want more?" And he moved toward the car again. She threw her hands up in disgust and climbed back into the car. Joanie slammed the door behind her and saw that Mark was already sitting and cowering. She said, "This was a bad idea now, wasn't it? Please, take me home."

Mark prayed that he would be able to find his way back to Joanie's apartment without asking her. "Where do I turn?" She was steaming. After a bout of silence between them Joanie leaned into Mark with a sense of affection in her touch. She rubbed his bare arm and asked, "I thought your family had a presence in that neighborhood, why didn't you say something?" Mark looked at her for a second and said, "I guess I panicked, I couldn't speak. That is such a Mafia neighborhood, and I guess I don't look or fit the part. And besides, my family had only a very small presence in that neighborhood and none of them connected."

Mark passed her building and drove the front wheels of the Mercedes over the curb and slowly pulled up to the stop sign inside the parking garage. "Just leave it, they know what to do," she said. Joanie waved at the familiar attendant and said, "Hi, Walter, I'm in for the night."

The couple slowly walked up to Joanie's building; she was cling-ing to his arm with a good degree of affection intended. The bravado mark felt earlier was turned down to a whimper, and he thought this was just a patronizing cue from her. He looked at his Cadillac and thought for a split second to bail out, but Joanie thought differently. She squeezed his hand and gave his arm a childish tug and a reas-suring wink that said "You're going to get lucky tonight." Now his manhood was reinstated, and Mark soon felt a surge in his loins. He embraced Joanie as soon as they entered the building, and they kissed each other hard and passionately. He was a little awkward and almost clumsy with his hands as he fondled her body with a sort of savage grace as they climbed the stairs in stages.

Both were breathing extremely heavy with the height of passion building, and she sensed his desire to take her on the cold mosaic tile of the hallway floor. His hands were under her dress and in a split second down her panties as he forcefully put her against the wall. Her libido was on fire, and she tried to swallow his fingers with her vagina, but the insanity of this act going any further forced her to push him away with a fervent "WAIT." She turned her back to him and fumbled with her house key. Suddenly she felt his hard penis protrude from his unzipped pants.

That excited her a bit as she slammed the door open then slammed it shut behind them. She thought to slow the pace down, but the act of sex ran vividly through her mind. He let his trousers fall while he spun her around and bent her over the Italian sectional. Suddenly she felt his penetrating manhood thrust deep inside her and begin intense almost savagelike movements; then as fast and furi-ous the act began, that's how fast it ended. He hunched over her in a convoluted mess, herself with her head deep in cushion to the point of asphyxiation with her dress flung over her back. He pulled his limp penis out of her and collapsed in a heap on the floor.

She would allow him to regain some composure and thought to herself this can't be the way he enjoys sex; he probably just hasn't had it for a while. She made her way to her bathroom and got undressed. She rinsed her face with soap and water then freshened between her legs with a warm washcloth. As she gargled with mouthwash, she felt so unprepared for this night, and the thought of Mark again didn't interest her at all. Joanie quickly slipped into a terry cloth bathrobe and walked back to the couch; he still was on his back, pants down below his ankles, and his, what she guessed to be an average-sized limp penis, was still dripping on her handmade Moroccan Berber rug.

The next morning reinforced the negativity of Sunday dates with men forever. He lay on her satin sheets fast asleep and snoring while she was already up, completely dressed and ready for work at 6:30 a.m. She agreed with herself to wake him only when she was on her way out the door. Joanie had poured herself a cup of coffee and recapped her previous night of mad, passionate sex and rewrote it in her mental diary as just mad sex:

It was just after 11:00 p.m. and the *Late Show* was just going on. Mark picked himself up off the floor and pulled up his trousers. He gave her a sort of apologetic look as he made his way toward her bathroom. She lay in bed naked with half of the satin bedsheet wrapped around her like a Roman toga, starting between her legs and loosely draped across her bare breasts. It was truly the sensual feel of a fabric that her boss had gotten her used to.

Her eyes rolled with the thought of getting pregnant by this guy, and it was as horrible a thought as years ago with her jock boyfriend whose name she now couldn't remember. But that idea repelled with yet another teaching and endorsement of her first tender and mature lover. She had started the pill on the order of Arnold and had never stopped. He refused to wear condoms noting their high rate of failure and the sheer inconvenience.

The worry of a sexually transmitted disease was slim based on what he said, and she heard from Arnold that "Jewish men did not contract VD."

As she waited for Mark to come out of the bathroom, her sexuality trembled inside her, and she wanted to make love as she interpreted it. He aroused her anguish with a tease, and now her body ached for intercourse and hoped for foreplay. In this session she wanted it all: the intimacy and the erotic petting she shared with Arnold that yet he too often concentrated on hugging and kissing and loving her more orally than the actual basic fucking.

Mark anxiously clamored back into bed naked and again began his savage attack of the human body. She made an attempt to kiss his lips and he let her, but as soon as she began caressing his back and shoulders lovingly and then touching his penis, he began his guttural tenor and rose to his knees.

He turned her over and began a feverish session again, doggy style. Not satisfied with the traction he was getting from the satin sheets he pulled at her waist and positioned her on the edge of the bed then stood on the carpet. She felt his fingers probe both of her orifices feverishly and she thought the worst. He began his thrusting. She felt as if she was being accosted by a professional wrestler. A vile thought of Jim Breuer entered her confused head. Her inner self screamed and said, *Did he just sodomize me?* And once again a violent quickie left him writhed with ecstasy and dripping on her carpet.

The morning sun was bright outside her front room window, and it reflected lucidly off the chrome bumper of Mark;s Cadillac. Joanie Jankowski downed another cup of coffee and shouted, "All right, big boy, rise and shine. No, you don't have time for a shower, and you can get breakfast at the corner luncheonette. I have to run."

36

Tony Marino had a well-thought conspiratorial plan and a retaliatory agenda in place. He acknowledged wholeheartedly the forthcoming act or acts of murder were truly likened to the hunting and killing of dangerous animals. At first he thought to seek the help of his uncle but quickly dismissed that idea. His uncle survived once already and did not need to risk anything else. Tony did concede his plan would work *only* if it were revealed and carried out in specific steps, and this next step would be the most crucial of all. If he failed at this, all would be lost. His life would be worthless if in fact he was allowed to live. Tony had wholeheartedly concurred with Batista that as of now, both their lives and the life of his uncle Joe were in imminent danger. Once the Pope and Accardi succeeded to regain the tribute owed by the decimation of Joe's business and whatever monies he would scurry from the hands of Batista, they were all to be executed.

Tony had to act first. It would be easy to whack the likes of Accardi; he sat pat without a care in the world, his balls still as brazen as when he was on the force. But to get to the likes of Ruggeri, that would be almost impossible. He was heavily surrounded by bodyguards at all times, and no one ever got close enough since the attempt on his life years ago. Still Tony had to go on with his original plan and strike at Ruggeri when the plan fell into place. He was confident with his decision and with his ally Frank Batista and the element of surprise—and he hoped for the karma associated with the idea history repeats itself.

A light rain had been falling since early morning, and it remained just that as Tony backed the 1960 Ford Fairlane out from its spot in the parking garage. The car was purchased just two days prior from the Damato brothers who obligingly wrote the temporary tag out in the name of Anthony Moscola. Frank put his hands on the door and talked to the kid through the open window. "Listen…I want to wish you good luck with this, kiddo. I really hope it works," he said. Tony just bit his bottom lip and said, "Yeah, me too." Tic watched as his trusted friend drove away. He watched the taillights disappear onto Mt. Prospect Street and stood frozen, repeating over and over in his mind the last thing Tony said to him, "I gotta' rat you out today, Frank." He tried hard to digest the insanity of the plan Tony was about to propose. Frank understood it all, and he ran the scenario over and over in his mind. And it sounded damn good and looked even better on paper, but if one thing goes wrong, it could prove disastrous.

One slight hiccup, one miniscule X factor, oversight might just force a war between the two of them alone, against the entire underworld, or it could just be Frank's end solely or his boy. One thing certain, the kid had the confidence and the balls to try to pull it off, and if he was successful, it would alter the course of (history) many things to come.

Tony positioned his car just up the street from Accardi's driveway. If all holds true, Accardi's wife will be the first to leave for work in about ten minutes and she will drive the Chrysler. It was 7:00 a.m. If her husband was a gentleman, he would walk to the ornamental wrought iron gate and slide it open for her so she needn't get wet.

And if that being the case, Tony would make his move as soon she drives away. And if he doesn't, he will just sit and wait for Accardi to leave, and that would be no later than 8:00 a.m.

He was confident the rain and gray skies would put a damper on any early morning joggers who might just happen by, and surely anyone looking out a window will not be able to make a positive ID of who is sitting behind fogged and rain-soaked windows of the older model Ford that hadn't any plates.

Tony sat patiently and felt at ease. He twiddled a bit with the steering wheel then took a condensed inventory of the neighborhood with admiration. His eyes drifted from his objective at hand and became engrossed with the beauty of the stately Georgian manors with their lush green manicured lawns and mature trees and shrubbery of all sorts neatly tucked in with smaller but still prestigious homes. He especially liked Accardi's his semi-private little mansion with the huge Victorian porch and the exquisite brick and wrought iron fence that ran perpetually around his entire boundary and his New England–style garden. *Nice house and all that on a cop's salary!* Tony thought to himself. If Newark's finest were up and about this early, they would surely be at the diner or a coffee shop of some sort. Tony replayed the entire plan in his head and kept his fingers crossed. This had to work.

The steady rain distorted Tony's vision, but from the angle he sat, he managed to see the white gate slide open. The Chrysler backed out and stopped at halfway in the drive and the street. A milk truck passed and kicked up a mist from the road then stopped up ahead next to Accardi's driveway and for a brief moment closed the curtain on the stakeout. Tony caught a glimpse of the professionally dressed Phyllis Accardi struggling to close the gate, and the rain, doing its job, kept her head in a downward position as she scrambled back to her car. She is not married to a thoughtful or considerate man.

Tony watched until the Chrysler was out of sight then made a hasty decision to start the Ford and roll it past the Accardis' corner. He focused his eyes on the side door and the driveway all the way up to the garage as he hoped to catch Accardi piddling about. No such luck. He would return to another vantage point and wait.

Accardi's routine throughout his day is methodical. A retired cop, now *consigliere* for a powerful Don of a notorious mafia family, is systematic and precise. He does not dawdle with his time or waste his physical energy. Perhaps he considers it much too valuable now. The one consistent thing about Accardi's routine, Tony observed over the last week, was that he always left his house at precisely 8:00 a.m., and he crossed his fingers and prayed it did not change this rainy Thursday morning.

Accardi left his bathroom showered, clean-shaven; his pencil-thin moustache was now gone per the boss's orders. He dressed in casual clothing, a dark blue police insignia windbreaker and ball cap, tan khaki slacks, and sneakers. He was at his gate at precisely five minutes past the hour of 8:00 a.m. Tony felt a little tremble but forged ahead. Accardi was always prepared for danger, and at the exact second the unfamiliar Ford pulled parallel with his gate, out of habit he dropped down in a crouched position with his .38 caliber drawn and aimed. Tony had to take the caution away from Accardi immediately in a way that only Frank Batista could get away with. "Heah…what if I was the paper boy?" Tony said with a forced laugh. Accardi looked behind the car then up and down the street. "What the fuck are you doing here?" Accardi said with ire. Tony remained calm and pointed at the pistol. "Your neighbors are watching." Accardi holstered his weapon in the small of his back and walked to the open car window. "So what, kid, they all know I'm a cop." His keenness showed as he asked, "Whose car?" "It belongs to Frank's uncle. My car wouldn't start this morning. Listen, you're getting wet. I got to talk to you, life and death type of shit that you and only you can hear. Hop in and I'll tell 'ya about it," Tony said very calmly and convincingly. Finally something Tony said that got half of a smile from Accardi: "You can even bring your gun." "I can't now," Accardi said. "Now c'mon and move your car, I'm runnin' late," Accardi said as he turned and walked away.

Tony felt a weakness in his stomach, butterflies. He sensed he's losing the deal. "Well, when then…unless you're not interested in Batista and half a million in heroin." Tony snapped with the authority that he had to show. That stopped the consigliere dead in his tracks. The rain was now just a drizzle, and the sun was breaking through a cloud. Accardi studied the kid and read him as telling a true story. "I'm interested. Let's hook up later somewhere."

Tony was not concerned with the when; it was the where that was crucial. The two could not be seen in public. Tony looked at his wristwatch and said, "Where you gonna be in let's say an hour?" Accardi hemmed a little and said, "I could meet you here." "Tony shook his head no and said, "Too many neighbors. I don't want to be seen with you, too risky. I shouldn't even be here now." Accardi's curiosity was beyond intense; now his eyes were like owl's eyes. Tony squinted and said, "Meet me in an hour in the park. I'll be in the parking area just past the Ballantine Gates, deal?" Accardi frowned and let his eyes go to slits. "In an hour. I'll see you in an hour." Tony went out on a limb, but it had to be said, "And don't tell no one, especially the Pope."

Although Tony had never seen Ruggeri's castle, he heard the entrance to the Roseland fortress was indeed very much like the sentry gates that led into Branch Brook Park at this particular entrance, evidence of the Roman Empire influence in Scotland thousands of years ago. Tony entered the park from Ballantine Parkway and drove to the meeting spot. He sat alone and waited. His mind was racing with the miniscule details and fears of having left something out. Everything was analyzed with the precision of a true criminal mind and acted out on both sides of the fence. How would Ruggeri play this? How would his crew in Greenburg play it? How would it be scripted for *True Crime Magazine*? An hour had passed and cars were now cruising Christopher Columbus Drive at a steady rate.

Accardi's converted police cruiser was now painted a solid black. Not a trace of police memorabilia was showing. It looked somewhat civilian. He wanted it solely for its mighty V-8 engine. The commissioner did complain some, but he was allowed to keep it and the side spotlight. He made his way through the gates and drove to the exact spot where Tony was parked and waiting. He backed into a spot at the other end, which was actually the better choice spot to be; it was well shaded and concealed by a closely planted group of cherry trees. Tony immediately recognized the power play; it was up to him to meet this villainous person on his terms, so he carefully exited his car and began to walk, smiling a sign of peace and hands in plain view. Accardi eased himself out of his car and stood leaning against the cruiser with his legs crossed at his ankle. His windbreaker was open, and another weapon was made visible.

The rain had all but stopped now, and just some residual drops fell as an occasional wind shook the tree branches. Tony spoke aloud exactly what he was thinking, "I remember the last time we were here in the park…" Tony then seemed to be at a loss for words as his facial features indicated. "Ya know, I don't know what to call you… is it Detective or Sir or Consigliere?" Eddie let out a laugh and said, "Call me Eddie." Tony gave half a smile then extended both arms out away from his side. It was a sign that read "Go ahead and frisk me." Accardi just gave a nod of compliance. He knew the kid wasn't packing. Again, just out of habit, he squinted with eagle eyes, in all directions. When he felt comfortable with the situation, he said, "Get in the car." Eddie watched as Tony walked around the car and sat flush and square in the seat. Accardi was confident now the boy had a legitimate piece of information to divulge.

Eddie's face was impassive. He could only stare at the cool Tony Marino and wait for him to talk. "Eddie, like I said before, do you remember the time you picked me up off the avenue and brought me here to the park?" Tony asked. That vision replayed in Accardi's mind, vividly. Eddie took a cautious breath and said, "Yeah…I remember. What's on your mind, kid? I don't think you brought me here to reminisce, did you?" "In a way, I did. I gotta' refresh your memory. That day you were fishing for information, drug information. Ohhh, not about me, about Tic…am I right?" Tony said. Accardi squirmed in his seat a little and threw his right arm over the seat back. He made a grimacing facial expression and thought hard to contrive that day years ago. "Go ahead," Accardi said. It was request to tell him more. "I told Tic about it. He picked up on it right away. Me, I only had a slight idea that he was dealing heavy-duty drugs and not that penny ante shit he did with Trebbiano, but you knew that, or Ruggeri knew something more was going on, and now I know for sure." Tony spoke with coolness that Accardi could not draw a bead on. He was right on the money so far though. Accardi sat poker-faced and asked, "So, kid, you still haven't made your point. Are you ratting to me the ex-cop, or to me personally? I don't get it." "I don't feel that I'm ratting at all. To me this is a business proposition between two men," Tony said. "My point is this, that afternoon as soon as you dropped me off, I went to meet Tic. When I told him about the whole ordeal, it spooked him real bad. We drove to the market." "What market?" Accardi asked. "Corrado's. I heard him on the phone with his cousin. When we left, he was white as a ghost. He was carrying a gym bag full of H. We went to the Pope's club right after that. I was supposed to work the game that night. You weren't there, and that's when more shit hit the fan, about my old man and the money he owed, anyway the Pope got real pissed at Batista and made him throw me out of the club." Accardi was mesmerized by the story and said, "Keep going, this is getting interesting." Tony put on a wry face and said, "I'm walkin' home in the pouring rain and here comes Tic beeping his horn and flashing his lights. I jump in the car and he's real jumpy." Tony took a deep breath and paused for a second then said, "Okay, here's the deal. Frank thought he was next on the hit list or he was in for a shakedown—either way, he panicked. He dropped me off at my house and asked me to hold on to the bag." Accardi just blurted, "The dope, he gave you a bag of dope, didn't he?" Tony raised his brow and said, "Six kilos of *pure* heroin." Accardi was eager to hear more of this complicated tale, and he himself was ahead of the boy and formulating his own theory. "So let me guess, you went on the lam after your father died and took the junk with you, didn't that just make your friend a little mad?" Tony quickly came back with "Oh, he was mad all right, but way before I went to Greensburg, that night when we got the news about my father, Tic was on his way over to get his stuff. Problem was, I found out later, that he saw you at the front door and he headed for the hills, didn't see or hear from him until the funeral." "So when I came to your house that night, the shit was …" Tony spoke over Accardi' s words "Under my bed…right under your nose. Ohhh, I hated you that day." Accardi smirked and asked, "And that note…what was that all about?" "That was the key to the whole operation. It was correspondence from their people in Naples. It was a list of all the shipment dates and drop locations for the next two months, written in Italian code. It still goes on at Corrado's, but now Tic has to find another crew to set up shop." Accardi felt the tension at the base of his neck. His alter ego was about to show. "Let me guess, he wants you to throw in with him." "Bingo, that's why I'm here, but like I said, not to rat him to the law or even to Ruggeri," Tony said with certainty.

Accardi was both cynical and shrewd, a reason he survived so long on both sides of the law. He would probe in his sly way until he was satisfied with what he was hearing as if questioning a suspect. He had absolutely no reason to believe what he was hearing was anything but the infallible truth. "Kid, you beat *me* outta' six kilos of H and I don't throw you a welcome home party…I kill you. How come Batista is such a nice guy?" Tony let out a laugh and said, "Oh, he was pissed all right… at you. He thinks you grabbed the bag. I convinced him of that, and to this day he thinks that." Accardi was now fidgeting with his hands waiting for the ending to come. He started to flinch as Tony became animated with his tall tale. "My old man came home that afternoon right after I did. I guess it was about two o'clock. He said he forgot something, and don't you think as I'm pulling my wet shirt off my back, he's on me like a bull, his hands buried in that gym bag and up to his elbows in heroin. What could I do. I told him the truth. It was Tic's stuff, I said. He wanted me to hold it for a while. My old man went ape shit. He said 'Who the fuck is Tic to give you this, do you know what could happen?' He wanted to beat the shit out of him and me. I thought he was going to. He grabbed the bag and said he was gonna ram it down Batista's throat. He made it as far as the back door, then he calmed down. He dropped the bag back on my bed and said make sure I get rid of it, and that's the last time I saw of my father alive. " Accardi had a blank stare on his face and said, "Kid, you got me really confused, is that what happened or is—?" "That's what happened, but that's not what I told Batista. The very next day, when he came over and asked for it back, not a word of sorrow about my old man, just 'where's my dope?' And that's when I decided to fuck him. I told *him* my old man took it to his office at the lot, and that was the last I seen of my old man and the H. That shit traveled all the way to Greensburg and back. I even unload one kilo there, now I got five more and I can't sell it back to Batista. Eddie, I need a partner, someone I could trust not to rat me out. That deal I told Ruggeri about, you know the coins from Greensburg. I got a feeling that may not go down for a while, a long while. I need to turn this H into cash to satisfy Ruggeri now, pay my-my father's debt, understand?"

Accardi began to rub his jowls. His stare was intense. You could see his wheels in his head turning a mile a minute trying to visualize the story at hand. "Why not turn it over to him?" Accardi said abruptly. Tony took offense to that. He had to keep up the charade. "Who, the Pope? Yeah right… and watch him get rich and I'm still left with a high tax bill. You know that ain't gonna fly. Batista knows Ruggeri is trying to muscle his way in on his operation. I can't go that way." Accardi became austere and said, "You know you took a chance coming to me with this, don't you?"

"Why…are you gonna rat me out? You gonna whack me? Then we all lose. I could just as easy head back to Greensburg and make camp with Montesero family, right now, give them a treat with this shit. They'd welcome me with open arms, and I'd be sure to get a pass for anything they might or might not believe about all of this. Who knows? Ruggeri may even think you did glom the H, or you could do the right thing…unload it for top dollar, right here, split the take with me, and then take credit for the rest of the information I can give you about Batista's operation on the QT. Then I leave here, peacefully. I'll move my mother down the Shore and you'll never see or hear from me again." Accardi smirked and began to nod his head with an almost acquiescent manner.

Accardi was smiling to himself now, convinced that the elaborate plan would work in his favor. He was holding the cards, so he thought, and the power to both count the kid in or double-cross him as well. "How do I know you got what you say you do, and how good is it really?" Tony put his finger up and winked. He lifted his shirt and exposed an envelope tucked down his waistband. "Here, it's a sample ounce, have it tested at your police lab, see what they say. If we have a deal, call me at this number nine o'clock Saturday morning. If I don't hear from you, I got to figure the worst and I go on the lam. Deal?" Accardi took the package and sealed everyone's fate with his handshake.

Accardi made a casual visit to his old headquarters and did exactly what the kid had suggested, and the answer back from his old friend in the crime lab was, "Ninety-nine percent, Chief, I had never seen anything this pure." Accardi just said, "Keep it under your hat for now." It was agreed, and Accardi would show his gratitude at a later date with a comped meal at the Sicilian Café or maybe some Yankees tickets.

Eddie Accardi was hot on the tail of both Batista and the boys in Brooklyn. It would only be a matter of time before he could bring hard evidence to Ruggeri. This newly discovered evidence would certainly score major points if handed to Ruggeri and turn suspicion to fact. A war was surely to follow and a costly one at that. Everyone would suffer financially. Then pieces of the empire would be hand carved and divvied up amongst the surviving heads of the five families, and ironically, Accardi thought, the most powerful of capos and consiglieris would see only a pauper's share even after they risk their lives, including himself. And as usual, Angelo Ruggeri and his politicians and judges would walk away with the fattest of envelopes. Accardi took a hearty swig of scotch and his greedy mind thought, *The fucking kid is right.*

Accardi sat in his easy chair of his Upper Montclair basement office, his ever favorite jazz blaring from the stereo speakers that were mounted in two corners of the large square room. The house now belonged solely to his wife who hardly visits since settling the estate papers. She turned a blind eye and conceded full occupancy and privacy to her husband. Eddie sat with drink in hand and pondered his fate as to what road to take. He had all afternoon to do so. His arrangement with the Pope was "on call" much as a surgeon would be, always at his beck and call, but he was allowed unadulterated freedom. And he had already prepared Ruggeri for the upcoming schedule in advance of the days off and the weekends at the lake house. Ruggeri always refused his open invitation to come and stay; he wanted no part of it.

Tony traveled with exact precaution as he moved about the city. The imminent threat of a tail or ambush played heavily on his mind. A lot of the stops and errands made were unnecessary but done so with careful regard, a way of reconnoitering. He knew Accardi was watching, and in some respects he wanted him to be, to watch and see, business as usual between him and Batista. He wanted Accardi's guard to be down and never utter the word *double-cross*. He arrived at Frank's place with fresh hot bagels and cream cheese and a pound of Nova lox. As they ate they pondered over Frank's options regarding his exit of the States. Frank poured them both hot espressos. The list Frank had on the table was beginning to show telltale signs of completion as he double-checked a written chore then put a line through it with a pencil. Tony asked an almost rhetorical question, "You got all of your IDs in order, your passport, and travel visas?" Frank winked and nodded yes. His mouth was filled with food. He swallowed hard and asked, "How should we handle Corrado's?"

The original plan was to have it burnt to the ground, meats and all, to send a message to both Dons and the Naples gang, causing everyone to point fingers at one another. Of course the Feds might get involved since the place was already on their radar, but that would be welcomed by the plotting duo. The story might also surface about Marrone and his blind interest in the market, but that was dismissed by Tony, who said, "He would never confess his going behind the Pope's back." That conspiracy would surely go to the grave with Albert Marrone. Tony shaped his hand in the style of a pistol and held it to his head. "As a matter of fact he just might think the Pope burned the joint down to spite him. Who knows, Marrone may blow his own brains out."

The second plan was to leave it alone. Simply let it rot and become the problem child of Albert. After all he was now the legal owner of the business. He would be left to contend and deal with the suppliers and the city utilities and the landlord of the property. They even discussed letting him find a kilo of heroine in the walk-in refrigerator. Perhaps that would give the old man more reason to kill himself or give reason for the Pope to do so? It would certainly send him to jail for a bit. The idea of murder in the kid's eye could only be justified as his father once put it to him, "They're only animals, wild animals." He did not want the blood of Albert on his conscience, a conscience that as of now is crystal clear. The two tossed ideas back and forth to one another. They acted out scenarios and weighed in a lot of what-if's.

Next on the list was the star of the show; the six kilos of pure Middle Eastern heroine. Batista had been in contact with the Bruno brothers, Joseph and Carlo, the crazed hatchet men of Red Hook, Brooklyn, ever since his cousin had mysteriously disappeared, asking their opinion of what happened. The Brunos had no doubt about who did the hit, nor did they have any qualms whatsoever in saying his name, Ruggeri. It was rumored to be a fact all over the streets of Brooklyn.

The Brunos were made men of the Profaci family, but their ruthless acts of murder and their insane ways instilled fear into all the New York heads of family, labeling them renegade. The standing orders were to just let them be for now. And for the most part the Brunos were let alone to dabble in what they do best, murder for hire, and to act as a negotiator when and if the situation required. For some strange and devilish reason, the Brunos admired Bobby Breeze and helped with his rise to independence with his drug business. Perhaps he threw them a bone every now and then, treated them with their due respect, respect not given by the other family members.

Joseph Bruno agreed to purchase the six keys at a below wholesale price and to carry out the deed that both he and Tony decided
the fate of Corrado's. "Fuck it, kid, let it burn to the ground. What
an aroma it's gonna be in the neighborhood." Agreed also was the
fact that the fire *had* to look like *arson*. There was to be no mistake
about it. It had to be a sloppy job, and it had to happen as soon as
possible. Tomorrow will be too late. The two men drove home from
Red Hook with a sense of satisfaction. The Brunos would check into
a motel in Secaucus on Saturday and wait for the shipment of heroine that Frank had guaranteed. Then Corrado's would be torched.

The next couple of days left would be trying and troublesome
days, and they had an auspicating feel of getting worse and worse,
a normal feeling of stage fright. Tony and Frank were, in their own
minds, already underground. The older car that Tony drove was
parked on Mt. Prospect Avenue a block away from the high-rise.
He more than Frank felt endangered. It was a critical move he was
up to, deadly and dangerous. He was confident Marrone said nothing about the secret pact they had made; evidence of that would be
gathered firsthand from Batista whose diligent ear was always to the
ground at the Pope's club listening for a murmur of scuttlebutt. But
he was only 90 percent sure about Accardi. Tony had to be prepared
to defend himself until the day of acquittal if in fact his archenemy
was thinking anything but the deal on the table.

Ceil was all alone enjoying a bowlful of oatmeal and a piping
hot cup of strong black coffee when she heard the metallic rustling
of her doorknob. *Who the hell is this*, she thought, *coming so early and
how rude not to knock?* "Just a minute," she said, her words garbled by
a mouthful of Quaker Oats. "Oh, it's you," she said surprised. Tony
would usually just barge right into his mother's house but not necessarily this early. It was 7:00 a.m., and he did not want the chance of
missing Accardi's expected call. He leaned over and gave his mother

a little peck on the cheek. "Mornin', Mom." She frowned over his whiskered face. He was dressed in a pair of stained chino work pants, remnants from his hijacking days, and just a stale white crew neck T-shirt that seemed small on him, his arms and chest bulging at the seams, and on his head he wore a tan and tattered Flying A ball cap. His mother had never seen him look or dress so shabby. "Just expecting a phone call, Ma, I'll get dressed later."

Tony was more at ease now after he hung up the phone with Accardi. It was an eerie calm that reminded him he could never trust a cop. The entire conversation was coded, but the gist was to get the heroine to Accardi fast and with complete secrecy, not in view of any bystanders, so that ruled out restaurants' parking lots or any public place for that matter. The simplest of detail was now creating an annoyance, this by design, and so much for any coded words now. Tony knew Accardi would not trust or risk coming to either the Mt. Prospect apartment or the Hindsdale Avenue house as he suggested but would agree only to, and as Tony had hoped for, "meet at the Upper Mountain Road house." Tony played it coy and spoke apprehensively, "I don't know about that place." As Tony hemmed and hawed, Accardi exploded. "Well, where the fuck is a safe place, kid? You're beginning to aggravate me now." Tony had him to the point of spitting. He knew Accardi was a man of little patience and now would be adamant about the meet as Tony said in complete agreement, "All right—it's your place, but I need directions."

The bounty on the heroine was set at seventy-five thousand dollars, a tidy sum but far below the street value. It would be a one-time payment in cash from Accardi. Tony wanted to let Accardi win with that negotiation to further accentuate his dire need for money, to unload the shit quickly, so it was settled and agreed and confirmed that the two would meet the next day, Sunday, September 19, at 8:00 a.m., at the well-hidden house that sat down in the valley. Accardi spoke ever so calmly, "Take Bellevue Avenue to the end, and make a left. I'm the third house on the left. The one with the circular drive-way—my car will be the only one there, I guarantee it, and if you don't like what you see, keep driving till you hit Pittsburgh."

Unbeknown to Accardi, his Upper Mountain residence, his alter ego of a household, was well anticipated as the only safe bet for the meet and was already cased days prior. During those clandestine visits, Tony would dress incognito in a hooded sweatshirt and sweat-pants. On three separate occasions he jogged the neighborhood in the morning and in the afternoon and finally at dusk, well into the blackness of night, as Batista drove close by in a getaway car, just in case. Tony was actually able to wriggle his way through the dense shrubbery until he was able to hide in the shadows of the house and take physical inventory and to memorize, with eyes closed, a path to be used that led to safety if an emergency exit was needed. No one occupied the place as far as he could tell. It was left completely empty except for the times Accardi would make his pilgrimages to his base-ment retreat, a fortress room, much like Ruggeri's design but more livable, more family friendly—and of course, this coming Sunday. Tony guessed it was waterproofed, soundproofed, and bug proofed. The house itself had visible signs of a cheap ADT alarm system with contacts on the doors and windows that could easily be de-armed. And if all goes well with the plan, this would not be necessary. If Accardi had a contracted cleaning service or a landscaper, neither would interfere with the Sunday morning siege that was going to take place. The fact that the home was part of a snotty, blue-blooded neighborhood made it that much more advantages. There would not be a worry of neighbors dropping by before or after Sunday service at the local parishes. The boys found an isolated pay phone on nearby Valley Road and tested it for service both in- and outbound calls. Frank Batista would be waiting for the call at this point, who was only a three-minute drive to Accardi's house exactly.

Frank Batista was unshaven and still showed signs of just getting out of bed. He had on the clothes a mobster would wear on his day off, a rust-colored polyester sports leisure suit and a pair of Keds with no socks worn. Both coffeepots on the stove, regular perked, and a bialetti moka bubbling-hot espresso. On his kitchen table was a list of address he would need to stop at before he left the city and a few letters written that only needed postage. Suitcases and cardboard boxes were laid out on his bed and the floor of his bedroom. His closet was in sections with clothing tightly bunched together. The possessions he seemed necessary to take. In his mind he wished he was packing for a European vacation. If the phone call came and was anything but positive news about the conspiracy, Frank estimated that by the time Tony returned to the apartment he would be packed and ready to run. Frank sat hypnotized holding a cup of piping hot coffee inches away from his lips. The rising steam was fogging his glasses. The kitchen wall phone was on its third ring then forth then fifth; finally he leaped up and answered. The expression on his face was twofold—first, a mimed display of victory, then a sullen look, a reality check of the high-profile murder he was about to carry out.

Franco "Tick Tock" Batista was planning to do a lot more than just go into exile for a bit. Relocate to another part of the country? Go on the lam? Not according to his agenda. He was to disappear completely as a magician performs the "vanish into thin air" illusion—step behind a garish curtain and then now you see him now you don't. Tony understood this all too well, and he gave his word to assist any way he possibly could. And his role in this undertaking would never be discovered if all went according to plan. Batista was not at all worried anymore. He would survive the fallout of all the upcoming events, hopefully. But it was a cold, hard fact: Frank Batista was going to cease to exist, one way or another.

Dozens and dozens of pictures were being sorted out, some he wanted and needed, and others, the bulk of the accumulated photos, had to go. He lamented aloud as he tossed them into the fireplace and watched as all were destroyed, parts of his past life along with all the other memorabilia that could connect him as a former member of the crime family La Cosa Nostra. The dozens and dozens of matchbooks from the nightclubs he frequented burst into a sizzling flame as they were flicked, one by one, into the already burning fire contained within the glass-enclosed fireplace.

It was just days ago he talked at length with his co-patriarch as to where he would like to live out his golden years. Cuba was his first choice. "Maybe I could get a deal on Ruggeri's old place? And you know, I like those little chiquitas." His fondness of the Latino island was realized years prior the political turmoil of his good friend but no relation General Fulgecio Batista, and has encompassed the current government of Fidel Castro; this, another principle reason he had to change his name. Frank Batista was always the die-hard comic as he spoke to Tony, "Ask Sidney, maybe he has a connection down in Miami Beach could hook me up?"

The Corrado brothers had already fled the country. The last thing they did before they put a sign on the door that read Closed Until After Labor Day was tell the *caporegime* in Naples an elaborate story of treason and collusion regarding the Ruggeri family, how they are plotting to take over the drug empire that was once theirs and how they are suspect to the assassinations of Bobby and his two operators, and most certainly will send henchmen to carry out the much-anticipated execution of Frank Batista. They feared for their own lives as well. The brothers sailed out of New York Harbor aboard the SS Cristoforo Colombo under the guise of galley help. Upon arriving in their home country they got a message to Frank that the drug capos in Naples simply shrugged their shoulders when they got news of the missing six kilos of heroine. They raised their eyebrows when the Corrados told of how they barely escaped with their lives. The theft of the dope was written off to the cost of doing business.

The mafioso of Naples realized to try retaliation against the New York/ New Jersey families would be a costly and a futile effort. They knew that sooner or later their product would be needed, and then they would seek retribution for the spoils of war.

37

Tony and Frank both took late separate naps Saturday afternoon. When they awoke, they showered and dressed in clothes that wise guys are supposed to wear then met back at Frank's place. The complex to-do list was down to its final agenda. Tony gave Frank a pensive stare and watched as he drew two lines through the last sentence written on the flash paper. A match was lit, and both watched in a ceremonious way as the paper burst into flames then curled into black ash in the sink. They left systematically, a few minutes apart and in different directions. Eventually they'd meet by Tony's car in a few minutes. It was acknowledged by both men as they sped off in the Lincoln, no tails.

"Should we?" Frank asked. Tony killed the engine to his Lincoln and said, "Why not, it's the only way we're gonna' know for sure now, ain't it?" Frank cocked his head to the right and said, "Let's go—business as usual, right?" Ruggeri's club was abuzz. Wall-to-wall wise guys, drinks in hand along with cigarettes and expensive Romeo and Juliets, cigars dandling from between sneering teeth or animated fingers. Jokes and tall tales floated around the room, grabbing hold of the blue smoke being exhaled from their mouths. A bunch of lawyers and a few politicians congregated around a card table watching the mayor of Newark hold his own in a high-stakes poker game.

Frank nudged the kid and said, "Let's go pay our respects." Tony looked at the familiar section of the room that Ruggeri called his own, exclusively. You sat there only by appointment. The only thing missing from the ten-by-ten area of the room were the velvet ropes that swung from brass posts. Tony felt his blood chill as the sight of Eduardo Accardi came into view, his belly wedged in tightly against the table. He turned away from Ruggeri and looked the kid straight in his eyes then at Batista. He stayed silent. "Looks like a busy night, Pope?" Frank said.

Ruggeri acknowledged the two men with an imperious nod. Frank and Tony both stood tableside. The invitation to sit had not been given. Ruggeri's eyes became glint, and just a slight smile rose from the left corner of his mouth as he began to speak, "So... how's the deal comin' along, kid?" he asked Tony. The kid could only try to tell a partial truth. His mannerism would be read by Ruggeri. "It's takin' a little more time than I figured, but soon, Don Ruggeri, soon." Tony hoped his apprehension was not showing. His fear was Accardi came clean to the Pope about the proposed scam. Ruggeri leaned his weight slightly to his left and reached into his pocket. He produced a glimmering gold coin and flicked it high into the air with his thumb and trigger finger. Ruggeri caught the coin in midair and slammed it on the table. He had a sly look on his face, a raised eyebrow and a childlike smirk. "Call it." He demanded of Tony. "Heads" was his confident answer. Ruggeri slid his hand and the detailed profile image of President John F. Kennedy was boldly staring them all in the eye. Ruggeri smiled candidly and said, "Does it look familiar? I got that from your old boss, a gift. I got faith in you, kid. Don't rush the job...do it right." Tony caught a glimpse of Accardi looking up at him. He quickly darted his eyes in return then back at the Pope and said, "Thank you." Accardi kept his part of the bargain. He did not say a word to Ruggeri. Tony was absolutely sure about that.

Eddie Accardi made it a point to be up and about early, 5:00 a.m. He was brewing coffee in the kitchen of his Upper Mountain home annoyed at the fact there was no Sunday paper to read. He wore his service revolver proudly. It clutched his left side from the shoulder holster apparatus that now was fitting a little too snugly over his V-neck T-shirt. The second weapon he always carried, in the small of his back, was disregarded this morning.

He took two mugs out of the cupboard and placed them on the table. In a very churlish and gruff voice he said, "You drink it black, right?" He was talking to the man sitting still half asleep at the end of the table. Anthony "Hoss" DeSanti groaned some and rubbed his eyes lightly with the palms of his burly hands. "Yeah, black is fine, boss." Accardi snapped back at the oafish thug, "I told ya' we had to do this early, didn't I? You had to be a tough guy and stay out all night long. Fuck this up, my friend, and I will be burying two bodies tomorrow."

Accardi weighed all of his options about the decision to get involved with this plot days prior. He wanted to believe the kid was on the up and up with the proposition, and he had a strong hunch that he was. But Accardi was a distrusting cop for far too long to go it alone, without any backup. His soldier DeSanti was there for insurance, and while not fully aware of the true reason as of yet, sequentially he will also take part in the classic double-cross.

It took Tony Marino years and years of soul-searching and reasoning and then to actually formulate, and now finalize an actual plan of revenge, a simple one—basic, forthright, and to the point. It was a plan that could very easily be executed by two men trained well in the field of crime, kidnapping, and murder. This was their way of life. It was accepted by all as a dutiful act of war, eliminating the life-threatening enemies of oneself and one's most valued possessions, their family. There would be no need for dramatics or elaborate scheming. Simplicity would be the key along with the most valuable element of surprise.

Both men worked in complete silence. Tony turned the tattered gym bag upside down and rapped his knuckles on the hard vinyl-covered bottom. The army green duct tape held the .32 Browning automatic securely to the bottom. He proceeded to place the kilos of heroin into the bag; then he zipped it shut. Batista slid the pump shotgun into a hunter's bag and zipped it shut then placed a wired and taped device of some sort into a provision-type box containing three whole separate and sealed prosciuttos. How odd?

It was a chilly September morning, and both Frank and Tony wore loosely fitted dark gray athletic sweatpants and shirts and sneakers and NY Yankees ball caps on their heads. They looked like commandos as they took synchronized steps from the apartment down the stairwell and into the parking garage. The sneakers they wore made an eerie squeak that echoed off the concrete walls. Frank hopped into the Olds 88 and Tony the Chevrolet.

Frank drove to the designated spot on Valley Road and pulled into the empty parking lot next to the pay phone. His only risk was a passing patrol car on routine rounds would notice his presence in which he would be forced to look like he was actually using the phone booth; the other bothersome would be an innocent citizen walking by in the next ten minutes and actually need to use the phone. The odds on either occurring were extremely rare. Tony faced the real risk. He rolled his window down and spoke with his arm dangling down the side of the car door, "Thirteen minutes...no, make it fifteen minutes from now. If that phone doesn't ring, that means something is wrong. You either make a run for it or come in like gangbusters, your choice." Frank smirked. "That's some choice, kid."

There was no turning back now. No matter how seasoned the criminal or how numb his conscience to warrant the moniker "nerves of steel," no true human, mobster or otherwise, is immune to the angst of a planned crime, especially one like this, one so dreadfully malevolent. Tony was shit scared of what type of man he was going to have to face on the other side of the doorway. Perhaps the evil, cynical cop would be waiting, gun in hand, and ever doubting, or the culpable mobster eager to line his pockets as all mobsters pine for. The fact remained: Edward Accardi was to be assassinated this morning, within the next fifteen minutes, in the secluded privacy of his Upper Montclair neighborhood, come hell or high water.

He slowly and cautiously pulled into the large circular drive and eased up to the already parked car of Accardi. He saw a curtain move. He was tense and alert now, thinking through each detail. Was he being watched as he popped the trunk and reached for the gym bag? Suddenly he remembered the story he told the cop. He sold a key already. The cop would surely pick up that blunder if he indeed counted six keys in the bag. He hoped Accardi would not notice as he nervously eased one key from the bag and shoved it to the far front of the trunk. The kid surveyed the area then lifted the gym bag from the trunk. He thought a second curtain moved. Of course Accardi was at the door peering out of the windows, he thought to himself. Again a bout of nervousness began to set in. Now was not the time for panic, and Tony had to remind himself he had been in much tighter and riskier places, but not in his lifetime. He thought, *Take that worried look off your face, right now. It's a dead giveaway.* Where was his father's reassuring voice? Why did he not speak? Tony committed murder before, and he would do it again on his father's command. He knew this was the absolute right and necessary thing to do. It was Accardi's due justice. He was truly just another threatening wild animal.

The door would open before Tony had a chance to ring the stately doorbell or knock on the carved oak door. He was right. Both sides of the curtain moved. DeSanti stood off to the side with his revolver in hand and ready to fire. Accardi shot a demon look at him and said in a whisper, "Whatever happens, do not shoot him."

Accardi took a step back and allowed the kid to cross the threshold. Accardi was in control now as he pulled his revolver from its holster. Now two guns were pointing at the kid. Tony's heart stopped for a brief second, and his brain turned his world silent as if he was plunged head first under an ocean wave. His legs became numb, his strength all but gone. He offered no resistance as Accardi relieved him of the gym bag and slammed the front door shut. The ex-cop instinctively said, "Get against the wall, hands up," as he gave him a pat down, his service revolver poked hard in Tony's ribs.

"I thought we had a deal, Accardi?" Tony said meekly. Accardi swung the kid around and gave him firm jab in the back with the snub nose .38. "Go ahead, walk." Another harder jab made him flinch his eyes as he took a hesitant stumble step to his right. Tony asked, "Where we goin'?" He knew, but he had to engage conversation to try and get an edge. "Walk down to the doorway on the right," Accardi said then signaled DeSanti with a waving hand to cover the kid as he went ahead and opened the heavy door.

The door swung on precision hinges. They made not a sound as Accardi turned the doorknob and pulled it completely open. Tony heard a faint sound of what seemed to be jazz music and saw a dimly lit room below his feet. He glanced over his left shoulder and saw the huge head of DeSanti behind him almost bounce with every step down he took. Pulling up the rear of the pact was Accardi who closed the door behind him.

Tony could only think it was locked. All three men descended the stairs sideways, never once taking their eyes off one another. Tony's breathing was normal now; he inhaled deeply through his nostrils and exhaled out his mouth, the way trainers instruct their prizefighters to do. It keeps your brain supplied with fresh oxygen so you can think crisply. As soon as his foot hit the floor after the final step, he quick spun and faced both men.

The maneuver startled DeSanti who was moving a little slow trying to carry out Accardi's orders. His position was to be behind the kid. Accardi grunted at him for not moving fast enough. Tony raised his hands slowly in a surrender pose. He looked at his wristwatch and saw that only five minutes had elapsed, if he could only get a message to Batista who was waiting calmly without any inclination of the doom that was waiting.

"So what do we call this, the classic double-cross, huh, ACCARDI?" Accardi did not like the way his last name sounded coming from the kid. It seemed threatening. "I see you're not wondering what to call me now, huh, kid?" Accardi said. "I could think of worse," Tony answered and then said, "So really what happened to the deal we had, how did this guy get involved? I came here in good faith. Alone as we agreed and I walk into a trap." Tony spread his legs to secure balance. "You're both lucky I don't get real mad about this." The two jailers took dead aim at Tony's midsection, "Whoa, pal…don't make any slick moves. It'll get you killed before your time. As a matter of fact, take a seat," Accardi said. He nodded his head to DeSanti, and in turn, DeSanti gave a hard forearm to the back of Tony who stumbled into an armchair.

Tony's eyes evaluated the room and the double threat that was standing before him. Seven minutes had gone by. Accardi took a seat on the couch and dropped the gym bag on the floor next to his feet. He unzipped the bag and looked inside for the first time since the three descended the stairs. He holstered his weapon and made a security check on DeSanti and his captured man with glaring eyes. He carefully pulled the top kilo out and laid it on coffee table, then another. He shuffled the remaining three at the bottom of the sack and searched for contraband. He found nothing.

Tony's eyes were wide as he watched. He hoped the small caliber weapon would not be discovered. And it wasn't. But what good would it do him now? He was at a severe disadvantage. His clear thoughts acted out a charge, but the positioning wasn't right. First of all, he was seated, and was too close to DeSanti and too far away from Accardi—he would surely get shot.

Accardi threw the two kilos back in the gym bag. He made no attempt to open the wall vault Batista had talked about. Tony was sure of its location as he stared at volumes of the "Book of the Month Club" selections on the top two tiers. The third tier down had only a small cluster of three green-covered books with gold trim held together by cast-iron bookends forged in the shape of Civil War cannons.

Accardi lit a cigarette and began to speak in a no-nonsense tone of voice, "You see, kid, we still have a deal here. I'm just changing the rules of the game some, and the players." Tony listened with intent all the while keeping his focus on DeSanti. Eddie continued his talk. "What if I were to go to the Pope with all this? How long do you think you or your uncle would last? Batista, he's already good as gone. I just got to figure out what position you're gonna play?"

Accardi stood and said to DeSanti, "Let's go." Then he pulled his revolver out again. DeSanti took a few steps back then motioned with his gun for Tony to stand as he mumbled, "Get up real slow, champ." He gave Tony a wink and said, "I heard how you can hit." Tony stalled for a brief moment as he desperately searched for a plan. He needed only two more minutes to find out if Batista is a stand-up guy or another rat bastard. Tony ignored the order. Instead he began to speak in true wise guy fashion, "You know what this reminds me of Accardi…that rainy afternoon at my old man's place, the night you killed him."

Accardi raised his eyebrow and listened with intensity as the kid rattled on some more. "Only the players were different there too, but you never knew that, did you?" His question directed at the heart of the ex-cop. "It was Joey Lotta, and ahhh…help me out here?" he asked Accardi, who said "Alteri." "That's right…how could I forget Gaetano Alteri. You know who else was there, Accardi?" Tony said indignantly as he now rose to his feet. DeSanti reacted and was prepared to shoot. Accardi intervened and shouted, "Let him talk, let him talk. Go ahead, kid, I want to hear this." "The main player that day was me." Accardi's eyes bugged as the kid spoke, "And my uncle Joe. But you already knew that. He sat on the ground while Alteri held a gun to his head. They watched as that gorilla Lotta beat my old man with a blackjack. Pope's orders, right?" Accardi nodded and listened. Tony became more animated and took small daring steps around the room. His personal fear had left him even though he still had two guns pointed at him. Tony's face broke out in a proud grin. "They didn't expect me that day, not there, and certainly not with the gun I had….the .45 automatic. You saw how tight the group of slugs was in Lotta's chest, didn't ya? And you had no idea? I put 'em there…then my uncle and my old man pummeled the other asshole." Tony paused and the room became silent. Accardi knew not what to say. He was speechless. The memory of that day had been jogged to the point of him smelling the spent gunpowder and the foul smell of human death. He pictured in his mind the corpses and the fact of the well-placed slugs in Lotta's chest. The kid was the mystery shooter. All theories were correct about more than just Big Anthony acting alone. Accardi now had even a more inexorable and cruel reason to punish Tony. And he could not wait to inform the Pope and hand his catch over on a silver platter. He listened intensely to Tony's words and confession and took it all personally, as if it were a vindication plus an insult to his own soul and intelligence. The kid was jeering at him, rubbing it in about how everyone laughed all these years; the masterful sleuth could not solve the crime. He was duped by a ragtag bunch of amateurs. This made Accardi feel emasculated.

Frank Batista sat in the Oldsmobile and prayed for the phone call. "C' mon ring…ring." His fingers nervously tapped out a cadence on the steering wheel, and his legs crammed together to ease the cessation to urinate. He knew the kid was precise in his actions and was hell-bent and determined with doing this job. If Tony said fifteen minutes, it was fifteen minutes. But Batista let the fifteen turn to twenty before he leaped from the driver's seat and stood squarely in front of the elongated black phone box. He fiddled with the Ma Bell logo and screamed to himself, "Ring, you dirty cocksucker, ring!" He conscientiously lifted the receiver and gave it a gentle tug as he followed the thick black cord to where it was connected. He reached in his pocket for a coin. He heard the familiar ring tone from the box as he dropped a nickel in the slot then listened for a dial tone. It sounded loud and clear. Frank laid the receiver down and heard a faint echo of shotgun fire in the distance, two rapid bursts then two more. His face became drawn, and his eyes drew to slits behind his thick frames. He walked to the trunk and flung it open. He felt and let his hands touch the outline of the shotgun that sat in the canvas bag then looked at the box of prosciuttos.

Early Sunday was by far the most popular time of the week for practicing sharpshooters and avid hunters who belonged to the Upper Montclair Trap and Skeet Club, especially during the fall and winter hunting seasons. Wives and children went to church while men loaded their expensive Beretta shotguns and took aim. The facility was well hid in the deep woods far away from the posh and very private golf club, the non-NRA members and gun control activists, and depending on how the wind was blowing determined what community in Essex County heard the reverberations and echoing of the target shooters. Today it refreshed the ears of the citizens of the Montclairs. Just about all ignored the stifled blasts. Most of the upper crust community was immune to the dull cannonade. They read their Sunday newspapers and sipped their coffee and would not even bat an eye. Even churchgoers gave no heed to the distant sounds of gunfire that mixed with the chiming church bells.

The gunfire of the trap and skeet shooters was not recognizable at all to the three men in the well-insulated basement den. Their ears heard only Tony's continuous chastising words. "You know what the mystery has been for my family all these years?" His question was directed to Accardi in a loud chaste manner. "When me and my uncle left the car lot, Joey Lotta was dead as a door nail and Alteri was on his way out, but my father was alive as could be, wasn't he, Accardi? You should know, you found him, didn't you? Alive…waiting for help. He called Albie for help and the Pope sent you, you motherfucker, you killed my old man, didn't ya? I knew it all along—all these years." Accardi turned red. His body trembled, forcing him to grip his weapon with both hands. The room fell silent. No one heard the two dull thuds and the cracking of wood and metal of the front door that echoed in the upstairs foyer. Nor did anyone hear the doorknob to the basement rattle in its locked position.

Tony had Accardi to the point of breaking; his thick Sicilian blood and ex-cop mentality was boiling. Tony breathed in and out through his nose heavily. He sized up his quarry for one last time before he attacked. He knew this would be his final hurrah before bullets rained down on him out of retaliation, and if luck would be in his favor, the idiot DeSanti would shoot the wrong guy. There was nothing wrong with his psyche; the fight-or-flee gene deep inside of his soul was prepared for a fifteen rounder if the fates allowed.

He began to speak loudly as if he had all the aces in his hand. "And of all the dumb fuckin' things I heard about you, Accardi"— Tony covertly put himself in a defensive stance much as a gladiator of Ancient Rome would do; then he laughed out loud—"recruiting this fuckin idiot has to be the dumbest thing you ever did. Sure, he's the only dumb fuck of the entire crew that would buy into your bull-shit." Tony shot a fast glance at the now visibly red DeSanti. "Ain't that right, stupid? What does Ruggeri really think about you, ass-hole?" What happened next was done with such speed no one actually would ever to be able to recant it. What little reasoning DeSanti did have had left him. The absence of logic showed in his face. He was at the point of completely losing his temper. He made the fatal mistake of looking away, looking at Accardi for direction.

Tony connected solidly with a vicious left hook that landed right on DeSanti's jaw, sending him into Accardi. Tony looked for a way to keep him down and grab his pistol. Just at that moment, two mighty shotgun blasts from the top of the stairs ripped through the sturdy hinges of the basement door. The sound and repercussion caused everyone to take heed. Splintered wood and debris flew down the stairs and settled on the carpeted floor of the den. A forceful kick dislodged the security door as it slammed open against the wall and handrail before it too sailed down the flight of stairs. A confident and commanding voice echoed into the basement: "FBI. THIS IS A RAID. THROW DOWN YOUR WEAPONS AND COME OUT WITH YOUR HANDS IN THE AIR." In a split second later a hand grenade bounced down the stairs and rolled almost to the center of the room where it just spun like a top. DeSanti stared in amazement while Accardi braced himself for the explosion. It was only Tony who recognized the pin had not been removed and realized exactly what was going on. It was a scam.

Hoss DeSanti still dazed from the punch would be the first distracted. He was foolish enough to say, "Oh shit," before he took aim at the stairway just long enough to have his gun hand and wrist violently twisted by the now attacking Tony. The snap of his wrist bone and trigger finger was audible to all as was the single shell fired. Accardi had his eye on the grenade then fired his weapon. Tony used his opponent to block the aim of Accardi and the now airborne DeSanti slammed into the cop as all collapsed on the coach. Out of nowhere, a powerful jab from the wooden stock of the shotgun wielded by Frank Batista caught DeSanti on the base of the skull and numbed him while another quick shot opened a gushing wound across the bridge of Accardi's nose. Tony pushed away from the pile and said to his amigo, "Thank God for the calvary."

Tony rolled over the lumbering body of Anthony DeSanti and eyed the dampened hole in the mobster's pant leg. A stray bullet from Accardi's revolver caught his meaty thigh. He was semi-unconscious and breathing in heavy pants. "Well, he ain't dead, Frank. You're slipping," Tony said. "Give him some time," Frank replied, gasping for air. Tony calmed a bit and gave Batista a nod. Batista caught his breath then quickly held Accardi at bay with the barrel of the pump shotgun. "Drop the gun, Eddie." Frank put some force behind the shotgun and leaned it hard into the chest of Accardi until he released the weapon and watched as it hit the floor. Frank motioned to Tony with his head. "Frisk him." Accardi stayed slumped in the thick cushion of the leather couch. He found some reserved courage and said, "Now what, boys? How you gonna explain this mess?"

Tony's face was stone. He grabbed Accardi forcefully by the front of his shirt with both hands. They made a loud clapping sound against his chest as he was roughly readjusted in his seat and then began to pat him down searching for a concealed weapon. Tony ran his hands inside and underneath the seat cushions of the couch searching for any other hidden weapons. The burgundy leather bleated under the weight and friction of Accardi's body and Tony's knees as he again readjusted the ex-cop facedown into the couch. "He's clean," Tony said. "He ain't been clean a day in his miserable life," Frank retorted.

Tony kicked the gym bag full of heroin away from the couch then picked it up. He laid it on the coffee table and placed the loose hand grenade inside then zipped it shut. He flipped it over on its side and, with a few tears and tugs, freed the .32 automatic from the bottom, wrapping his hand around the small grip and putting his finger on the trigger. He used it as an extension of his arm as he said, "Ya know, Accardi, I knew you would pull something like this, and as much as I prepared or tried to predict this setup, I couldn't." Then he dropped his knee heavy in the back of Accardi and put the slide barrel of the gun to his eye socket. "But you, my friend, had no idea it would turn out like this, did you?" Tony's words were calculating. "I'm gonna give you the choice, or I should say your family the choice, to have an open casket or a close one at your wake. I only wish my father was alive so he could piss on your grave. I'm also gonna leave it up to you if your family and your widow receive your policeman's pension after you're gone." Accardi spoke with misery in his voice, "Marino, you and this prick friend of yours got no chance in hell getting away with this." "I would love to blow the top of your head off right now," Batista said with gritting teeth as he poked the barrel of the shotgun to Accardi's head. Anthony DeSanti opened his eyes some and let out a moan of agony. He instinctively reached for the area of his leg that was the source of some of his pain; then he reached around and massaged the back of his neck.

Tony Marino could not afford to let one iota of sympathy or empathy cloud up his spiteful thoughts or the evil task at hand. This was accomplished by his reconstructing in his mind the murder of his father. Who empathized for him? Who cared of his widow or the loved ones he left behind? This is the life they all chose. He must stay apathetic toward the animals now at his feet. A code of conduct must be respected, and a system of checks and balances has been in place for years and years with this thing of theirs. And never allow your true enemy a second chance.

Tony got off Accardi and pulled him to a seated position. The facial skin around his eyes was now black and blue, and red clots of blood formed inside the one-inch gash between his eyes. "That's how my father looked when I saw him lying on the floor. Lotta stood over him and was gonna hit 'im again if I didn't step in." Tony squinted and shook his head at Batista. On cue he slammed the gun stock to the cheekbone of Accardi, who let out an uncontrollable sigh of pain. "Your choice, Eddie? Open or closed coffin?" Tony said. "Tell me how you shot my father...cold-blooded, right?" Tony took a side-step around the centered coffee table and turned the reel-to-reel tape player off, ending a trumpet solo prematurely. He looked the ailing DeSanti in the eye for a couple of seconds and studied in detail the deformity and size of his horse head. "What was the plan he told you? Where were you gonna take me? To the Pope, right? 'Cause nei-ther one of yous' has the balls to think for yourselves." Tony ranted. DeSanti kept silent. Accardi waited for a reaction as his head writhed with pain. Tony pulled the slide of the gun back and loaded a round into the chamber. He fired a single low grain bullet into the fat man's good thigh then another into his left kneecap. Tony spoke through an evil grin, "Just in case you were thinking about running away." DeSanti screamed like a baby. "Or were you were gonna whack me? That was the plan, wasn't it? After Accardi got the information he wanted about him." Tony cocked his thumb at Batista. DeSanti couldn't answer. "You know what, don't tell me, who gives a fuck?" Tony said.

Frank Batista chimed in with a rage of anger directed at Accardi, "And how 'bout me, ya' prick...all these years of lookin' over my shoulder, you guys got pretty close this time." Frank jammed the barrel of the shotgun into Accardi's heaving chest then brought it under his chin and said, "Let's just blow his fuckin' head off." Accardi winced then closed his eyes tightly when he heard the familiar deadly clicking sound a pump shotgun makes as a round enters the chamber.

Tony walked over to the bookcase and ran his hands all around the perimeter of the polished wood. Then he perused the third shelf. He found an indentation on the left side of the shelf just next to the cast-iron bookend. With a little force applied to the button the case sprang open with a metallic ping. He swung it completely open and stood in amazement. Behind the bookshelf was an elaborate and well-constructed series of cubbyholes, drawers, and shelves, all custom built with boxes of files and notebooks, ledgers, photographs all stacked, and their meaning quite apparent. The star attraction was a six-foot high wall safe built into the concrete foundation.

Frank repositioned himself and let his jaw drop as he rifled through the cache. Then he said in amazement, "Will ya' get a load of this—a blackmailer's paradise." Both looked at the stereophonic equipment that now was exposed. It was running but silent. Not a sound coming from any speaker. It had a different look than the one visible in the den. Frank and Tony watched the two reels of magnetic sound tape connected to the face of the silver box that was built into the hidden shelving of the bookcase, the tape slowly unwinding from one reel and rewinding onto another. But where was the sound? Both men studied the electronic and so sophisticated apparatus in silence; then Batista exclaimed, "It's a fuckin' tape recorder. Like the ones the Feds have." He looked dead at Accardi and said, "This prick has us on tape!" He fumbled with some switches until he found the one that reversed the reel then played back. The descriptive audio of what had just transpired bled into the air through tiny speakers built into the obviously sophisticated recording device. Frank put the machine on rewind and let tape run back to the beginning.

Anthony DeSanti began to curse the entire situation. He was delusional with pain, panting like a wounded bear and foaming from his crazed mouth. He desperately tried to raise his crippled body and render some form of primal retaliation. Batista silenced him with a single blast of the twelve-gauge shotgun fired point blank. The mobster died instantly, and what was once his massive torso was splattered all over the walls around him and the easy chair he was in. A gaping and still smoking hole in his chest oozed blood and organs. Everyone was deafened by the blast, and all felt the fluids of DeSanti splash them. A foul smell of gunpowder and stale excrement suddenly circulated the room. This made Accardi turn a ghostly white. He knew he would be next. These men were here to commit murder. He felt all of his adrenaline and his mortal strength and energy leave his body. His eyes grudgingly closed. Gone was his brazen courage and intrepidity he once brandished on the streets of Newark. He wished only to be able to close his eyes now and slip into a deep sleep.

"Open it," Frank barked. Accardi's crusted eyelids snapped open, and he took a deep breath. Batista yanked him hard by his collar and threw him to the floor in front of the safe. Accardi wept inside about his mournful situation then aloud. He would have no time to say goodbye to Phyllis or his sons. What would become of them? How would they perceive his life and his untimely death? He wished he had been killed years ago in the line of duty, a more honorable death. Would Phyllis be able to still receive his pension? His daydream of chronic questions was abruptly ended. "Open it, ya' cocksucker, or I'll open your fuckin' skull, just like your stooge over there. See this?" Batista was loud. He pulled something from his pocket and waved it in Accardi's face. "You know what it is? C-4 explosive. We'll blow this fuckin' safe to the moon with you tied to it. Now open it goddammit." Tony knelt down to Accardi and whispered, "Your choice… open or closed casket. Give it up, you never were a real hero, but we'll make it look like you were."

Accardi began to groan aloud and openly sob. Frank held the barrel of the shotgun to his head and said, "Open casket, right?" Accardi's fingers turned the tumbler right, left, right, and he pulled the lever that released the lock. The safe opened with an audible click. Frank whistled in amazement, and he and Tony stared inside with wide and astounded eyes at more paraphernalia—and the cash—piles of neatly wrapped bills, stacked wall to wall and to the top. Accardi spoke with desperation in his voice, "Let's make a deal, boys. It's not too late." Frank turned to the kid and said, "I'll go get the body bags—you okay alone with this rat bastard?" Tony squinted and said in a serious tone, "I'm okay."

Frank straightened himself up a bit and went outside the front door. The door lock was shattered clear through the inside jamb, the force of a solid kick, but Batista was still able to keep it close and in place. He lit a cigarette and listened as the faulty exhaust of a sports car zoomed by on Upper Mountain Avenue. The front and side landscape design of tall trees and mature shrubs made it impossible to see anything around the front of the circular drive or the bricked veranda that Batista was standing. The neighbors on both sides were sheltered and out of view. The echoing of rapid shotgun fire from the gun range, sometimes loud and crisp and other times faint, could still be heard in the distance.

Frank opened the trunk of the Oldsmobile and pulled out two large folded green duffel bags, a few newly purchased kitchen towels, and two pairs of rubber dishwashing gloves. He stood silent and accessed both sides of the circular drive then looked up at the swaying branches of the trees overhead, his head turned toward the continued barrage from the rifle range in the distance. *No, I don't have any regrets*, he thought as he gently let the trunk lid drop and lock close. When he reentered the basement, the scene was almost chivalrous. Frank listened intently to the last bit of a dark conversation that had been going on. And he watched the almost macabre face of Accardi as his mouth formed the baneful words spoken.

Accardi was sitting painfully on his executive leather couch, his body leaning forward and his elbows resting on the tops of his bent knees. A bar towel had been filled with ice and gave comfort as he held it to his swollen face. He was taking deep drags from a cigarette. Tony sat opposite him in the armchair with the shotgun tucked under his left arm and the small automatic pistol in the firm grasp of his right hand, reminiscent of a Wild West lawman. The bloodied body and face of DeSanti was half covered with a Newark Police

Department sweatshirt. It was Accardi's voice Frank heard. It was a sorrowful voice. "So they sent me over. Albie told the Pope your old man wanted to come in, give himself up. Ruggeri gave the order to… well, you know how it ended. Ruggeri gave the order. What could I do? What would any of yous' have done in my shoes?" Everyone in the room began exchanging looks of contempt and sorrow amongst each other.

Eddie Accardi was the first to turn away and become fixated with a framed picture that hung on the wall. It was larger than the others that formed a collage around it. The black-and-white photograph was of him as a young police officer shaking hands with the police commissioner. Alongside him were his parents, smartly dressed and looking on so proudly, and in the background was a group of political people—dead center, Angelo Ruggeri, hands frozen in an applauding position. Accardi blew some blue smoke out of the side of his mouth then snubbed his cigarette out in the crystal ashtray. It would be his last.

38

I t was mid–Monday morning, the twentieth of September. A young pimply-faced kid of twenty-one walked into the bustling lobby of the Federal Building, Newark, New Jersey. His rubber-soled dress shoes chirped on the high polish of the terrazzo floors that he tread on. He was extremely careful not to step on the United States insignia outlined in brass as he traveled across the bustling lobby. His uniform, credentials, and hall pass gave him permission to ride the elevator and roam the halls in search of the offices of the men identified on the labels of the four wrapped and sealed packages he carried. His first point of contact was Field Agent Keith Murray. Each package contained a sample of the cache of evidence that was to be found in a small abandoned unit somewhere on Watsessing Avenue in the town of Belleville. All of it the findings of what was contained in the wall safe and the locked secret compartments in Accardi's basement retreat. One of the packages was specifically addressed to Field Agent Robert Ritacco—among its exclusive documents was a written note of where to find the nameless murdered corpses and a reel-to-reel tape. The messenger was immediately detained, and the owners of the Action Messenger Service was summoned to the FBI Headquarters ASAP, both grilled as to who ordered the delivery.

Their answers were honest and congruent: "Some old man came in off the street and paid for the service in cash." That's all they knew.

Agent Ritacco pondered why he was singled out and chosen to receive such a bounty, and immediately his supervisor placed him in charge, the lead man of what was soon to be a top organized crime investigation. *Why am I so blessed?* was his silent thought, but the satisfaction that soon came from the investigation and the notoriety fanfare made him proud to be an Italian American? Or would it make him a better agent?

The other three packages were addressed to other top supervisors of the FBI and the United States Attorney General Office. Inquiries were immediately made to other law enforcement agencies throughout New Jersey asking if anyone of their respective departmental heads received any unusual or anonymous information regarding the alleged crime. This was handled in a hush-hush manner. All chiefs answered no.

It was on or about the same time the Feds were receiving their packages that Frank Batista stealthily parked the Olds in an inconspicuous spot behind the Pope's club on Bloomfield Avenue. It would prove to be the closest route to the side door, the one used mostly for deliveries. If his forecast was correct about the head count, this would be the perfect time to walk in the joint. Mondays in general were as quiet and dead as dead could possibly be. Hardly any suspicion would arise about what is in the armful of corrugated grocery box that had the words *Tomatoes* printed in red on its sides.

And just as anticipated, one of the regular suspects would be found at his usual place; Albert Marrone would be alone, slurping coffee and playing a friendly game of gin with a local citizen. There was a disenchanted bartender, sitting down, leaning on the bar with head rested in hand and his eyes half closed. And that was it, no one else in the place. Marrone was all eagle eyes as Batista carried the box past him and placed it on the bar. The familiar leg section of the prosciutto ham stuck out of the top and was as apparent as the aroma of the meat itself. All total, there were three cured and sealed hams in the box. "Whoa…where they come from?" Marrone yelled. He did not bother to move; his arthritis was acting up. Batista gave him a casual look and said, "Corrado's…where else." Marrone screamed, "That place been closed for almost a month, what gives?" Frank answered with a glib statement, "Since when you so interested in that dump." *Dump?* Marrone was beginning to act worried. He realized no one at this stage of the game knew of his supposedly silent partnership with the deli. "Bullshit, Albie, I just came from there." Albert moaned as he slid his hulking frame from the booth, his eyes wide as could be. He walked over to join Batista at the bar. Batista shoed away the sleeping bartender, lifted the hinged section of the hardwood bar, stepped in, and grabbed a glass. He looked into the empty shot glass then blew away any evidence of dust before he helped himself to Scotch. Albie commented, "You look like shit." "I had a rough night last night—it's why I'm drinking so early. By the way, what's new?" Marrone answered in his usual gruff voice, "New, what the fuck could be new?" Batista replied, "Just asking, Albert, just askin'."

Albie poked his nose in the box and savored the distinct aroma of the cured pork, but his sense of smell missed the four pounds of C-4 explosive wrapped in newspaper and buried under the meat. "You want me to leave one up here under the bar? There's a small Frigidaire to keep it in." Frank asked. Albie asked in return, "What were you gonna do with them?" Frank pulled the cured piece of meat from the grocery box and slammed it down on the bar. Then he said, "I was gonna put it downstairs, in the ice box where they keep the beer kegs. Here put this behind the bar for the guys, I'll stow the rest."

Batista knew the way exactly. He would walk down the staircase, and then left to the end of the short hall, beyond the next door, a dry storage room and then a few more steps to the fridge. He breathed heavily and looked over his shoulder. No one was watching. He pulled up the heavy handle and entered the Fridge, carefully stepping around the chilled and sweating beer kegs; they seemed almost as intricate as his device attached to their "on tap" apparatus. He pulled the hams out and laid them on the top tier of a stainless steel baker's rack. His eyes scanned the ten-by-ten room, and his brows lifted in attainment as he saw the ideal spot. Frank Batista pulled the intricate-looking device out and slid it overhead, between the room's roof rafters. After just a few adjustments the device was wrapped tightly in bar towels and out of sight. He held his breath to silence his heartbeat and listened. He took a couple of steps back and positioned himself in front of the Fridge door and inspected his work. The distant and faint *tick tock…tick tock* of the device could not be heard, overshadowed by the refrigeration unit itself. His eyes stared at the inside thermometer. The consistent temperature of 38 degrees Fahrenheit would have no effect on the chemical compound or the intricate wiring of the bomb. Within minutes Frank reentered the main parlor of the Ruggeri's posh club and caught Albert rewrapping the hunk of ham in the sports section of the leftover Sunday newspaper. "What the fuck are ya' doin'?" Frank asked. He refrained himself from roaring with laughter. "I'm takin' it home. No one here would appreciate such a nice piece of pork."

Frank gave him a wink along with a smile of approval. He also slammed a key on the bar under the cover of the palm of his hand, and with a look of befuddlement he said, "Oh, by the way, one of the guys at Corrado's said here's the key." Marrone gave a look of exasperation. Batista grabbed hold of the mobster's arms and whispered in his ear, "I hear our boss wants me to take a long vacation. If you see him before I do, tell him 'Arrivederci' for me." Batista was off to meet the Bruno brothers.

Field Agents Ritacco and Murray assembled his team and chose the hour of 3:00 p.m. of the aforementioned morning to investigate the tip about the Upper Mountain home. There were six agents in total and arrived at the posh residential area in two unmarked cars. They were shocked by what they saw. The area DeSanti's corpse was in was covered in dried blood that was splattered in formidable patterns. The unmistakable smell of death and excrement filled the room and caused the men to gasp even as the air-conditioning unit ran full tilt. No visible windows could be opened to relieve the rank odor. The place was a tomb.

Ritacco ordered photographs taken. Hundreds of snapshots were fired off the crime scene. He carefully lifted a wrinkled kitchen towel off the head of the body that was posed on the couch as if he were in a casket: head propped up on a makeshift pillow, hands folded atop his diaphragm, feet crossed at the ankles. The wounds about his cold face had been cleaned and the death mask of the corpse would bear an expression of peace. Agent Ritacco instructed the photographer to get close-up shots. "They're small caliber holes, one behind each ear. He was assassinated." Within moments the murder weapon was found. "This must be it. It's a .32 automatic." Then the orders went in for the FBI crime lab to be dispatched along with the medical examiner and coroner. Murray held up a wallet. "I couldn't tell you who this guy is, but the one with the bullets in the head, he's a cop." The now discovered dead bodies were positively identified as ex-NPD detective Edward Accardi and a known associate of organized crime Anthony DeSanti. This resounding news would surely force the city of Newark to explode.

The neighboring residents of the Upper Montclair address were interviewed that same night. And all the following week, federal agents knocked on every door within a square mile of the crime scene, including the posh country club, desperately seeking a suspect or a single clue of the murderer(s)? Nothing transpired of it; no one saw or heard anything out of the ordinary, and they were all the *waspy* type, true American blue bloods. They wore their cashmere sweaters over their shoulders with the sleeves neatly folded in a tidy knot atop their chests, as if it were an ascot. They kept their distance and did not get at all close to the agents, but all were eager to talk if they truly had something to offer. They wanted to be helpful citizens.

The enormous amount of hard-core physical evidence the federal agents found when they forced open the steel rolling garage door of the storage unit opened their eyes to the real and centrifugal enterprise of illegal activity. Special Agent Murray was overheard whispering under his breath, "Holy mother of Jesus…will you look at this shit," as they examined the contents of the green duffel bags. He leafed and read notebooks containing detailed acts of heinous crimes along with names and dates, small reels of recording tapes, hundreds of them all neatly packaged and dated; some had clear initials, and others had coded events written in ink. Handwriting experts would later come forth and corroborate the fact it was Accardi's penmanship on hundreds of documents and ledgers dating back some twenty-five years or so. And court-qualified voice experts would identify just about each and every person recorded. It would soon cause an avalanche of woe to fall upon the residents of Mobville, especially the little dictator known as the Pope. Shovels full of shit would reign upon his head.

That Monday evening, while agents were sorting through all the evidence regarding the Upper Montclair bloodbath, and the rest of the mob's activity, reports resounded from the teletype machines, red alerts informing FBI headquarters of the possibility of a mob war or some kind of a retaliatory action taking place. "Right fucking now—as we speak" was the refrain echoing from everyone's lips as they all scrambled. The first report over the wire was at 10:00 p.m. It came from the office of the New Jersey State Police, Bloomfield barracks. It was a detailed report about an explosion and a bright fireball that blew through the roof and front windows of an Italian market on Bloomfield Avenue. Another report came soon after of an explosion or multiple explosions that rocked the underground parking lots of a high-rise building on Mt. Prospect Street. They were believed to have originated inside of automobiles. The blasts sent chunks of concrete and sheared black pipe of the plumbing system flying like shrapnel. The repercussion caused alarms to sound and fire sprinkler systems to rain down on the parked cars of the residents who were sound asleep but soon were awakened and now being evacuated. That second series of blasts were within minutes of another massive detonation. It was described as a high-caliber-type explosive that literally blew away half of a building, a mansion located on the corners of Bloomfield and Watsessing Avenues; included with that transmission was a captioned report of possible critical injuries to occupants and pedestrians. Bloomfield Avenue was immediately sealed off from the rest of Essex County as was Mt. Prospect Street. Both areas were to be considered and treated as war zones. Every engine company dispatched its firefighting and rescue equipment to the scenes with a constant carillon warning. The state police and every able-bodied uniformed officer, including both departments' special operations teams, converged to the area. The only regimented and uniformed persons not visible or present were the National Guard. The commotion awakened each and every mortal soul in North Newark. Panic was surely about to set in.

Tony Marino had just laid down his head on the pillow as the fireworks went off. He heard the sirens blaring in the distance. He was not at all surprised, nor was he worried. His just washed and polished Lincoln was safely parked in his mother's driveway. The Chevrolet and the Ford he was driving along with Frank Batista's Cadillac were just transformed into a smoldering pile of twisted steel and manufactured pieces of charred automobile parts that once were complete and drivable machines. The Oldsmobile 88 abandoned at the Newark airport would have to wait. It was finally towed away after a late January's snowstorm forced the ground crew to "get it the hell out of there." It hindered the snow removal process. The owner of the car was never heard of or found.

Angelo Ruggeri was woken by a dire messenger and told of the destruction of his pompous club. No one has been identified as of yet, but the body count of dead mobsters was up to three that lay already in the morgue of Clara Mass Hospital. Four more anonymous characters sat in the emergency room moaning and groaning about their wounds; none at all would be cooperative to the inquisitive police and federal agents that filled the room. The word on the street that got relayed back to the Pope was New York, more specifically the Brooklyn-based family seeking retaliation over the Breeze drug situation, but no one was 100 percent sure.

All of the Pope's capos were accounted for with the exception of two. Only a couple of low-ranking soldiers were killed in the blast that rocked his club, and two citizens and a bartender that were caught napping also suffered mortal wounds. Ruggeri was saddened as was he more puzzled by the news of Albert Marrone. The coroner positively identified the charred remains that were found inside the torched Corrado's Market as his. And some experts even considered him the arsonist. Perhaps he had a reason to torch the place? It was later found out that his name is on record, listing him as the sole owner of the failing establishment. Marrone must have gotten careless with the detonation? The true fact was he unlocked the front door just past 10:00 p.m. as the Gallo brothers were hard at work. And God is the only witness to say why he ventured into the place. And God would be the only one who could have saved him. The rogue Gallo brothers took a break only to waylay the intruder that unbeknownst to them was the mobster Marrone. He took two hard blows to the head from a ball and claw hammer that sent him to the ground. He was never to wake up again.

There was now only one man from the Pope's organization officially missing, and that was Frank Batista, his whereabout unknown. Tony Marino was found by two of Ruggeri's button men at the Belmont Tavern after the funeral service for Albert Marrone. He was escorted to Ruggeri's Roseville Avenue club. He could only speak the truth when he said, "I have no idea where the fuck Batista is. He screwed up all of my future plans. But I'm still working and ready for the score we all talked about—any day now." Ruggeri dismissed the young Marino boy from any further investigation labeling him a "jinx," a *sfortuna presagio*. The Pope cried, "Every time he's around, something bad happens. Keep him away from me, and I do not want him hurt just yet. His father still curses me." Everyone understood the black magic reasoning of the Pope.

In time, storied threats from the other families forced the crime boss to seek the shelter of his castle keep deep in the bowels of his Roseland castle. He cowered and listened behind the sturdy steel doors. He would not be seen again on Bloomfield Avenue until all the smoke cleared literally, and then it would be in handcuffs. Only emissaries of select wise guys would relay information from the street then up the long driveway to the castle. Every phone was disconnected except Ruggeri's private line. Unfortunately, he would have not the sufficient time needed to react or recover from this initiative of war; he would not be able to properly sort out this chaos. His attackers and true enemies would never be discovered. The only imminent ones would be the agents of the federal government.

Eddie Accardi was promised an open-casket wake and funeral service, and that he had for just one afternoon and one evening at Megaro's funeral parlor. The Belleville, New Jersey, establishment was chosen by Phyllis over Zarrillo's funeral parlor, probably for the same reasons the Marino family had done so, years prior. She knew of her husband and his business with the mob. Mr. Megaro applied his trade as a cosmetician ever so gingerly to the face of Eduardo. He would look majestic lying atop a satin pillow inside the bronze coffin. He spoke softly to his assistant, "Someone went to great lengths to keep the swelling down." "I remember thinking that the night the corpse was brought into the embalming room," replied the assistant.

Phyllis could not stop the ceremonious fanfare and service that went with a law officer's demise. And the rumors of how he died were manufactured fables of heroism invented to subside and appease the Medias. It was a proud moment for the Accardi family that day and for just a few short weeks to follow before it all came crashing down. The highest-ranking city and government officials from all over New Jersey paid their respects to Phyllis and her husband's family. High-powered attorneys and important business people filled the room

of mourners. Other policemen and detectives offered sincere condolences as they passed by the coffin and the grieving family. His
old partner Patsy Covella got on his knees and wept with Phyllis's
hand in his. Ironically, it would be his damaging testimony at the
federal grand jury that would tarnish the name and badge of Edward
Accardi and bring to their knees just about everyone in attendance
of Accardi's funeral. Even Tony Marino and his bereaved mother
attended. His uncle Joe could not find it in his heart to be there.

Tony stared over the corpse of Eddie Accardi but offered no
prayer. Accardi was laid out in the ornate coffin wearing his best dress
uniform, his chest covered with the medals he had been awarded
during his career, and his gold shield still intact. Where was your Boy
Scout merit badge? Tony snarled to himself. He stared coldly and
without remorse or sorrow; his soul was empty and the words of his
uncle rang in his ear about how good he slept after the murder of the
Russian animal pimp. He overheard his mother thanking Phyllis for
the job her husband did in helping to raise her own son and keeping
him out of jail.

One man was noticeably absent from the heavily perfumed
room filled with all the close associates of record. Some would choose
to visit in private to pay their respects to the widow but not the blood
cousin of the Accardi family, Angelo Ruggeri himself. He stayed far
away, fearing for his own life. But during that early time period of
mourning that was sure to be the beginning of the end, he did manage to send flowers, his usual garish display with an embroidered
banner of fine silk that read "Rest in Peace."

The funeral of the fallen mobster Albert Marrone was held at
Megaro's as well, just two days after Accardi's. His life or death was
not as celebrated. No one understood the reason behind his visit
that night to Corrado's Market. No one bothered to put a logical
explanation behind it, not even the police. No one now cared. It was
obviously an omen that sent shivers down the spines of the neighbor-

hood mobsters, a disembodied reason that kept Albert's cronies away from the funeral parlor.

Heads dropped to a familiar pose of mourning as the attendant placed the urn in the small grave site at Mt. Pleasant Cemetery. Tony Marino commented to Albert's oldest son on how the two dear friends would now be literally raising hell with the other members of their dead society. This statement drew a glib look from Tony's mother. Tony Marino had sincere tears in his eyes at the gravesite as did his uncle Joe. Tony did not make good on his promise to his father but quickly dismissed the entire situation on "That's how the fates wanted it, Daddy." Albert was to burn up in a fire.

The small party of mourners, friends, and family attended a catered memorial lunch at Albert's Lake Avenue home. This is where the subject of selling the property was brought up, by Tony Marino. Both of Albert's sons were living on their own, and they were both establishing careers on Wall Street and kept an apartment there. They agreed they had no use for the antiquated property. The money would be better off invested in a Manhattan property. Both of Albert's sons had ample time to gather their late father's belongings and personal effects and decide a suitable fate for the memorabilia. And both the Marrone brothers agreed to the selling price of twenty-five thousand dollars, and it would be executed as a private seller, no realtor type transaction. The papers necessary to complete the December 1 closing of escrow and transfer of title would be handled ever so promptly and meticulously by none other than the Law Office of William Caruso.

Tony Marino walked silently throughout the handsome brownstone of the late Albert Marrone that he now owned. He used all of his keen sense to rationally figure out if in fact there was a cache of cash hidden, as rumored. Albert Marrone's sons were not raised as mobster's kids. They were sheltered from the reality of it all. They lacked the street savvy only a true heir of a wise guy possessed when it came time to pack up all the bequeathed possessions their late father once owned. Louis and Albert Junior were raised and educated under the guise their father was an honest businessman, a union delegate. Perhaps that was the story their mother told them as children as she tucked them into bed each night, alone. She passed at a young age and never confessed to her sons of the type man their father really was. He would never take a dollar of illegal graft from anyone? His estate went through probate without a hitch, and the twenty thousand dollars cash that sat in a savings account at the Investor Savings and Loan was doled out in a timely and proper manner to both his heirs. That was uncontested.

The shrewd Tony Marino knew differently. He had a sneaking suspicion that something was overlooked by the sons of the late Albert Marrone and the building inspector who cleared the dwelling for sale. He immediately began remodeling. He chose the basement as his place to start. He was on a mission. No one found it odd that the late mobster had never finished the job he started? Albert Marrone just hinted at a slipshod job of an attempt to remodel his basement by the placement of a few odd lots partitioned walls. The ceilings were certainly high enough, eight feet? The room was left dark and dreary, almost tomblike. Only the walls were freshly painted? Cheap handiwork the old man threw up to dupe lookers? He noticed another wall that was separated by an open doorway. On one side the furnace area and stairwell, on the other a large utility room where the washing machine sat next to a commercial clothes dryer. There was another partitioned wall that held separate another complete kitchen, a common sight found in the basements of most Italian homes. Tony stood dead center of that doorway and noticed the longer wall was slightly thicker than the shorter one the other side of the doorway, and a sturdier type crown and base molding ran the length top and bottom. It was certainly not a load-bearing wall, a partitioned wall at best. A couple of swings of the sledge and a few rips from the contractor grade pry bar and down came the heavy sheetrock, even thicker than the building code required for a partitioned wall. His hunch was right on the money literally; over one hundred and fifty thousand dollars cash, all neatly wrapped in plastic and arranged like proverbial bricks in the wall.

40

The federal indictments marked Organized Crime had been culminated, sealed, and distributed. Also carefully sealed were the many cardboard storage boxes of accumulated evidence that had been labeled and alphabetically categorized by heads of crime families, their subordinates and their titles, criminal and code violations, dates and individual achievement of violent crimes. Then came the thousands of notations of miscellaneous offenses of general racketeering; all were painstakingly deciphered and written in layman's terms compiled and stored using the same identification process, much like a card catalogue in a library. This made the separation of the key elements and facts from hearsay fiction and anecdotal mafia lore far simpler for a grand jury of ordinary citizens to physically see and analyze. The selected grand jury panel would be able to identify and place real men, mobsters, and corrupt politicians alike alongside the crimes that had been committed in a more understandable light.

US Attorney Katzenbach dreaded the workload associated with bringing down the top leading mob associates in New York and New Jersey and their patriarchal bosses. This task had to be done in confidentiality. The secrecy of it all could actually work against him, and he must silence and quell the buzz about his office and its personnel of the anticipated arrest indictments sealed as well. He did not want anyone under his watch to sell out. He called the one person whom he could trust for sound advice, his predecessor, Senator Robert F. Kennedy. RFK creamed his pants knowing some of the most unsavory people holding government office in New Jersey were about to topple over and land in shit. There was a reason everything to do with this federal organized crime crackdown was sealed: to alert a single suspect in the group would prove to be disastrous for the operation. This is why the resolute message was sent to the federal government exclusively. The informants knew of the widespread corruption within the system. This prompted Senator Kennedy to tell his brother Ted in confidence, "Of course this neat package of information came from someone in their organization. They knew handing it over to anyone short of the federal would tip the mob off. We should thank him. Whoever he or they are. When the names of the departed or missing come forth, we will have a better idea of the stoolie—and why for God's sake did this not happen during my years at the helm?"

The entire legal process took a total of only three short months; by mid-December the federal judge tapped his gavel and gave the go-ahead to round up and start to arrest the bunch in one clean swoop. Every available law enforcement agency was summoned for the task at hand. Dozens and dozens of single named federal indictments would fly as would search warrants forcing the rats and the weasels to surface. A new federal commission had to be formed with an amendment to the Constitution called the Organized Crime Control Act. This would give birth to the now existing Federal Witness Protection Agency. It would be a governmental Christmas gift; the timing was arrogant, instead of envelopes fat with graft, *sorprendere*. Warrants for their arrest would be doled out. How ironic.

Special Agents Robert Ritacco and Keith Murray were chosen by FBI Headquarters to head up the task force, much to the chagrin of its director. The first choice selected by J. Edgar was the churlish George Lindsay. Katzenbach dismissed that idea based upon the rumored reputation of his "being too wild in the field" and that he was a native New Jerseyan; RFK advised Katzenbach and thought personally everyone from the Garden State was corrupt, and the proof would be brought forth as soon as the indictments were opened. Lindsay's integrity was not challenged whatsoever, but the newer, younger breed of untouchables seemed to have the energy and fortitude to see the job through to its dissolution. And fortitude plus stamina was what it was going to take to move the operation's progress from that explicit morning nearly three months prior.

In the wee hours of a brisk December morning in 1965, over one hundred federal agents, special agents from the US District Attorney, Essex County Prosecutor's Office, New Jersey and New York State Police, and of course local city and county police embarked on a massive sweep, or RAID as the newspaper headlines described it. Over sixty known and named members of organized crime were rousted, handcuffed, and dragged to state and federal lockups with signed indictments between their teeth. Among the top echelon of the group, and arriving last, was the ever notorious Angelo Ruggeri.

A convoy of twelve marked and unmarked police cars and one large van from the Essex County Jail stormed his castle gates. Armed uniformed and plainclothed officers sprang from the vehicles with weapons drawn and cocked. They immediately and with extreme prejudice began to physically throw the assortment of Ruggeri's soldiers against their cars, the stoned retaining walls, and to the ground. With their weapons drawn and ready to fire, the law enforcement brigade began a loud verbal announcement of who they were and just what it was they were there for. Anyone of the Pope's crew that hinted at the slightest bit of resistance was brutally reprimanded by a gun barrel, rendered incapacitated, and then handcuffed tightly behind their backs.

The convoy poured through the top gate in the same fashion. The chained guard dogs began snarling at the occupants, their drooling teeth snapping and clanging first on the windows then biting at the rolling tires of the cars as the unmarked cruisers slowly passed by. A Ruggeri goon took it upon himself to release the most vicious of the black shepherds that answered to the name of Lady into the crowd of congregating agents. She was shot dead and he was pistol whipped. It was made apparent to all on the team of Angelo Ruggeri that this was not going to be a social call and that any type of filibuster would not be tolerated.

Angelo Ruggeri sat tense behind the thick steel door of his war room. He heard and well understood the muffled tirade of legalities being read to him from the other side of his temporary shelter. His eyes scoured the four walls, and he conceded to his soul there was no way out. All the money spent on this safe haven? The hard vibrations of the battering ram smashing into the reinforced door shook the small-framed mobster as he cowered in his leather swivel chair. Dust and debris rained from the ceiling and began to turn everything in the room a drab gray. This went on for some time until finally the hinges of the door gave way and four special task force officers surrounded Ruggeri with automatic pistols aimed dead center of his torso.

Agents Ritacco and Murray emerged amidst the dust of broken concrete and said, "Angelo Ruggeri, we have a warrant for your arrest…" Ruggeri heard nothing but a loud buzzing that clouded his brain and deadened his sense of hearing. The brigade of legal authorities began to exercise their right of search and seizure. They produced search warrants for every square inch of the Roseland property including up to eight feet deep in the surrounding grounds and garden itself. Ritacco turned to Murray and boasted. "There—I told you we did not need helicopters."

Phyllis Accardi would not have any Christmas decorations adorn her house as it had been in the past. Her husband was not there to put up the Noel of ornaments and lights, nor would she bother to put up a traditional Christmas tree. The holiday of Christmas would not be celebrated in her home. Phyllis Accardi would hold the Yuletide heavy in her heart. Every bit of remembrance of this past year she would try to erase from her memory. But it would be impossible to do so. The horror of the ordeal scarred her and her children for life. Luckily for her sons, they would soon be graduating Newark Academy, and both opted for colleges far away from New Jersey. Not a single finger would dare be pointed at them condemning their father.

She opened and read the letter from New Jersey governor Hughes explaining his ruling about her late husband's pension. She was to receive a cash settlement that would reflect only the estimated 8.5 percent of his income contributed toward the fund. Nothing else would be paid. His words were kind and spared her the hurt and humiliation of being married to a corrupt cop. This was indubitably proved posthumously through resurrected taped and live witness testimony conceded during the trial.

Now nearly three months after she laid her dead husband to rest inside the Gates of Heaven cemetery she felt it time to move on. She placed her Forest Hills home on the market. It was decided that the family home should be sold before the neighborhood began to change, something that was ever so prominent throughout North Newark. It was a subject of everyday conversation she had with her late husband only just a few days before he was killed.

Christmas morning on Hindsdale Place came ever so peaceful just as God had promised. The small colored lights of red and green and white, mostly white, sparkled and gave life to the evergreen tree.

The seraph angel Ceil Marino had proudly put on top was displayed with the hopes of converting Sidney to Catholicism. To that he said no, but he always liked the gift giving and the commercialism behind the birth of Baby Jesus. Sidney had spent the night, something he was now perhaps more brazen about. He nestled next to Ceil with coffee cup in hand and gently tore open the little pile of gifts that all bore his name—written boldly on colorful tags that also read from Santa. The small box found was from Tony addressed to "MOM AND SID." Sid lifted it nimbly with raised brows as he removed the contents of the neatly wrapped box. "A ring, a chain, nothing in the way of jewelry, and I'm a jeweler for God sakes?" Ceil's eyes opened wide. "It's a key. A house key?" Ceil boasted. The enclosed note said, "Not a Christmas gift, but a WEDDING gift." Sidney took a backseat to the connotation and smiled, and handed her an almost identical tiny package. "This is a ring, an engagement ring." Ceil opened the modest one-carat perfect stone surrounded by another two carats of baguettes. It took her breath away. "I had nothing to do with the real estate investment, Sidney, you got to believe me," Ceil said as she leaped from the couch. "I'll call my son, this is his doing."

Tony Marino sat alone Christmas morning, his apartment barren of anything Noel. He sipped black coffee and pondered a melancholy thought that continually ate away at his very soul. Oh, how he wished with all his heart that his dear friend was here by his side. He first wished most of all and hoped his old friend was all right, alive and well wherever the hell he was held up. He missed his irrepressible mobster friend as much as his own father. But he had not even an old photograph of the slick mobster. There wasn't one picture to be found anywhere in the entire state of New Jersey. The few group shots of Frank Batista that adorned the walls of the Sicilian Café were confiscated as was the others. The place itself was silent and shuttered with a bold NO TRESSPASSING GOVERNMENT PROPERTY sign attached to the ornate doors, they themselves chained and padlocked.

Frank Batista had a neat bundle of almost three hundred and sixty grand when he vanished. It was just about one hundred thousand more than Tony had, but it was agreed by both partners Batista keep more from the cache they found in Accardi's safe since it would be used to finance his getaway and help establish a new life somewhere far away, someplace that never heard of the Mafia or organized crime. Is there such a place? Besides, that sneaking suspicion Tony had of buried treasure at Marrone's brownstone had paid off in spades.

Still he wanted to give Frank Batista a gregarious hug, a victory hug, and a solid handshake to go with it. He wished they could toast with the finest of Napoleon brandy. He wanted to yell from the top of his lungs, "I knew we would get even. I knew we could beat 'em." It was all over now, the entire ordeal. Big Anthony's murder was avenged. But Tony Marino must stay silent. There would never be a right time to ever talk about it. Not even amongst his uncles, but they would know?

The following summer saw the completion of one of the most infamous and intense criminal trials ever to be heard in federal court. The guilty as charged mobsters and corrupt politicians who did not cooperate as government witnesses would be going away for a long, long time—to carry out harsh prison sentences, life sentences in many cases, all reminded of the fact there is no statute of limitations on the capital crime of murder. Most would wither and die in the confines of cold concrete and steel cells. And for the living, all housed at state and federal penitentiaries in the worst parts of the country. Ones that house other vile criminals like the young boys on death row and due to be hanged in Lansing, Kansas, for their roles in a cold-blooded murder case. And the leader of the troop of Boy Scouts that ran on Bloomfield Avenue, the Pope, Angelo Ruggeri would be leading the way. His life would eventually end comfortably, but behind bars at the ripe old age of ninety-three. Only one unanswered indictment remained. It was served posthumously and went on file listed as a missing person, a fugitive under the name of Franco Batista, alias Frank "Tick-Tock."

Not one single high-priced glib attorney could weasel a pardon or an acquittal or a suspended sentence or even perhaps forbearance for any of their client's wrongdoings. No better truism was ever spoken: "You can beat the law every day and line your pockets, but they only have to beat you just one time to empty your wallet." Most went completely broke funding their defense. All the indicted mobsters would be swept away like the remnants of a Wall Street ticker tape parade.

And it seemed that everything that was deemed either good or bad happened in the month of August, so close to Tony Marino's birthday and the anniversary of his father's death, so be it as it may, in the light of exceptionally good news, Tony still pined heavily and wished his dear friend and father were both here with him and his uncle Joe as they stood on the corners of Bloomfield Avenue and Orange Street. He wished that they could all watch, arms hung over one another's shoulder, as a team, the new illuminated sign being lifted high atop its sturdy pole that proudly read MARINO MOTORS— QUALITY USED CARS. It sat out in front, next to the entrance of the newly remolded auto showroom and expanded paved lot. The partners and owners of the business were allowed to have the lighted sign erected two feet higher than code, a granted favor in return for a set of car keys, so it might be seen by motorists riding the Garden State Parkway both north and south.

The centerpiece of the poured terrazzo showroom floor was the ebony black 1959 Cadillac Coupe de Ville in all of its grandeur. It sat dead center of the place and could be seen by all through the glass partitioned walls of the building. Its thick layer of carnuba wax reflected like sparkling diamonds, every ounce of glimmer the ceiling floodlights had to offer in splendid glory and was not for sale at any price. It represented the preserved and final wish of his late father to "turn this place into a legit car lot."

The summer thunderstorms had passed, and all the "like new" luxury automobiles were polished to an eye-striking gleam and sat poised and positioned like toy soldiers, not one Cadillac bumper out farther than its neighboring Lincoln or Mercedes Benz and not one tire a slight askew. And finally the last bit of celebratory news rang out on Bloomfield Avenue. It chimed from Hindsdale Place. Sidney Margolis and Ceil Marino were to be married by the justice of the peace, city hall, Newark, and have a very small but "grand celebration at Nanina's in the Park," as the select invitation read. The date set was the last Sunday in September the year of our Lord 1966, and Sidney could not wait; perhaps it was cheaper now than next June? Sidney insisted he pay for it. The newlywed couple honeymooned in, of all places, Miami Beach for two glorious weeks then returned to their new residence on Lake Street. The brownstone was certainly big enough for Ceil and her new husband and her mother who had her own basement apartment, after a slight renovation by Ceil's brother, Lefty. Sidney always wanted to have Italian in-laws. And it was decided that the Hindsdale Place home would stay in the family; perhaps Sidney wanted to be a landlord as well.

41

Tony Marino occupied a small tidy office next to the appointed sales manager's office at the used car lot that both he and his uncle Joe co-owned. The title on his etched brass nameplate that was proudly displayed read general manager. And as strongly expected his office seemed barely lived in while the other was something comparable to a war zone. They had been open only a short time and already realized the huge earning potential of the place aptly named Marino Motors, if it was operated properly. Perhaps that was the reason the Marino team sought out the most vicious of manager the auto industry had ever seen who also was currently unemployed and available. His name was Humberto Giancola. He soon became known as Uncle Bert to the humbled sales staff under his rule. The dapper-dressed boss previously ran a Cadillac dealership in Morristown for years and very successfully until the son of the actual owners decided Mr. Giancola was getting too old for the job. The elderly Giancola knew every angle and facet of the industry and took an oath of allegiance with Joe and Tony Marino. They gave him full reign of the place and reminded him of his anticipated ingeniousness. Tony also remembered Bert's mobster brother Gerardo and conveyed his personal distress of the fact that he just took a fall in the recent neighborhood sting. Tony also appreciated the fact Bert spoke nothing but praise for the late Big Anthony; after all they were in his old office.

Connections were made with the various auction houses that deal in wholesale inventory: good, clean late-model luxury and exotic imported and foreign machines that were in a high demand and sought after by the fortuitously rich and famous. The Marino boys were able to corner the market in that area. All in all everyone was satisfied so far. People traveled from all over New Jersey and New York and as far away as Florida and New England to buy a quality "Used Luxury" or "Imported" sports car from Marino Motors, and for once the kid himself was earning an honest income—his first ever?

Tony lounged comfortably on his sofa, daydreaming and acting the kid again as the TV blared with Saturday morning cartoons. He savored the fact that he did not have to go into work, a feeling a child would have on a school snow day. Ample bodies are in place to run the operation. This is the benefit of being a true boss. Stay home. Stay away from the shop. Just sit back and relax and daydream. But as bosses go he would eventually venture in just to make his presence known. He would show up unannounced, right after a healthy workout at the health club, and dressed in his best sweats.

He had little to no regrets with his decision to walk away from the effusive life that once was a prodigal part of his own being. He was a young man with money, lots of money, honestly earned money and not the blood money once described by his grandfather. This made him feel holy. He moved to a penthouse apartment in the same building he and Frank had shared. He had a few chums he could call his friends and still ventured into the elusive clubs in New York City and on Bloomfield Avenue and mingled well with the new breed of wise guy that was surfacing, many of whom were his customers. He continued his casual style of dating woman and kept his membership current at the Lake Street brothel. But alas, there was still something missing from his life.

Every once in a while he would receive a colorful picture post-card from a resort far away, and its arrival would always bring an exuberance throughout his soul and command a broad smile. The postcards would always be inscribed in a sort of scribble, "Wish you were here," signed "Uncle Louie." And all were of different hand-writing. Surprisingly one day a small color photo arrived showing Frank Batista in all his well-earned freedom. Oddly enough it was a tropical beach scene that bore a Canadian postmark. Frank hated the Canadians but loved the beach. He knew it was Frank letting him know things were going well. But there was never a mention of him ever returning to New Jersey if only for just a stealthy overnight's stay. Frank must know the threat he once feared of being whacked was over, but the threat of never seeing freedom again was always present. And as much as Tony knew he could keep his *paisan* from harm's way if only he had the chance, a chance could not be taken. After all, he still was considered a fugitive from justice. No one knew better of the tentacles of the mob or the FBI than both Tony and Tick Tock Batista.

And on occasion, and as portended by his uncle Tomasino, Tony would still hear his father's voice echo loudly then be carried off in the faint distance—his way of letting him know things were okay in his world also. It would ring from nowhere, and then be everywhere, without rhyme or reason, sometimes in broad daylight and sometimes in the dead of night, while he slept: "Everything's all right, son." His uncle Tomasino would always say, "I hear it myself… all the time." However, not Joe Marino. Perhaps he was the lucky one.

Joanie Jankowski considered Saturday morning a high and holy day not because the majority of leaders in her industry observed it as a Sabbath but because she would be dead tired by the time it eventually rolled around. Her circle of friends and relatives knew never to ring her phone before 10:00 a.m. Even the doorman of her building was not to disturb her for anything less than a three alarm fire. She enjoyed a simple cup of coffee along with toast or a single soft-boiled egg prepared in her own kitchen at her leisure, not a rushed buffet-style breakfast served daily in her office building by the inhouse caterers. She welcomed the fact that even her cultured and fashionable wardrobe could remain on velvet hangers in her closet and she was allowed to prance around her apartment in her underwear and a comfortable and tattered T-shirt.

She sat comfy in her breakfast nook and scanned the cover of *Woman's Wear Daily Magazine* that was sitting atop of other industry publications. She picked up the magazine and turned to the page she had previously marked. She took a bite of buttered toast and jotted some notes down on a yellow legal pad. These were not designing changes but ideas for an article she was commissioned to pen for the sexy June Bride edition of *WWD*.

The phone rang. Joanie gave it a look of approval after checking the time of ten forty-five. But still who the hell could this be? The excited voice of her cousin Barbara was on the other end. Joanie had saved her cousin from the dregs of the Secaucus office steno pool and had her move to a large mahogany desk with the title of personal assistant to the vice president of marketing for Jonah Lewis Fashions. Her only conscience-bearing attribute was the full disclosure of any and all company gossip. "So get this," Barbara began, "Mark not only gets drugged by a couple of hookers, so he says, but they took all of his money, his jewelry, and his sample rack from the room." "No… well, it couldn't have happened to a nicer asshole if you ask me, and believe me, I know," Joanie said in sanctified jest.

The incident took place at the Chelsea Hotel in Atlantic City. He was showing the line at a convention of buyers and got caught in the oldest scam in the book. "You think he'll get fired?" Joanie asked. "He just might. I heard a rumor to that effect, but don't say anything, especially to him. The police are trying to hush it up because of the Democratic Convention or something or other," Barbara said. Joanie rolled her eyes and said loud enough for even Barbara to hear, "I haven't seen or talked to that little prick since…that night at my place, what a degenerate."

Barbara's eyes got wide as she asked, "So speaking of degenerates, have you heard about that gang from Newark? It was billed as the "trial of the century. All found guilty…mobsters and politicians walk hand in handcuffs…" Barbara read quotes from the *Star Ledger*. "Didn't you know them? Weren't they from your neck of the woods when you lived in Newark?" Joanie leafed through yesterdays *Daily News* and found a huge article reading the same similar headlines and containing the story. Familiar names were noticed as she read. "Yeah, but not personally," Joanie retorted. Barbara laughed and said, "What about that young handsome guy you were nuts about, remember the kid we almost kidnapped when we went down the shore years ago?" "Oh, him," Joanie recalled fondly. "He's another I haven't seen or heard of in years. I heard that he moved to Pennsylvania right after that summer." Barbara jeered. "You must have scared him away, girl. He knew of your reputation with the male gender." The two spent a little more time on the phone; then Joanie rushed her cousin to hang up. They came to the conclusion they needed a night out just themselves, no men friends; neither were lucky enough to have found Mr. Right as of yet. Perhaps there was a reason for that?

So they decided to rendezvous at Joanie's parents' home in Warren Township. "My mother would love to have us down for the weekend. We can take a ride down the shore and have some lobster. I'll see you there in a couple of hours," Joanie said as she bounced off the chair. Suddenly the thought of New Jersey and mobsters and

Newark gave her an indiscernible thrill. She couldn't quite put her finger on it, but nevertheless it felt real.

The girls were dressed to the nines and off to dinner and a night of swank cabareting. Barbara drove as Joanie fiddled with the radio. "You're making enough money now to be able to buy at a car with at least a better radio," she said amusingly. "I know...I know," Barbara said with a shrug of her shoulders. "I'm just cheap." They were on the Garden State Parkway heading north en route to a swank dinner club in Clifton when Joanie caught glimpse of the sign that read Bloomfield Avenue 1 mile. She felt a strong urge to grab hold of the steering wheel as they were about to pass the familiar modern high-rise apartments that came before the next exit. Instead she just commanded her cousin. "Hurry. Get off here—Bloomfield Avenue. I want to see something." Barbara made a hard turn into the right lane that led to the off ramp and the toll booth. She just wrinkled her nose in a bemusing way as she handed the toll attendant a dime. "You want to visit the old neighborhood, drive past your old house?" Joanie sat up on the edge of the car seat and stared at the immense, illuminated sign that was now clearly visible, MARINO MOTORS, her eyes fixated on it. She smirked and let her head and neck contort and twist as she watched it disappear as they exited the Parkway ramp then drove up the avenue. Joanie looked curiously at her cousin and said, "How did you know that, that's exactly what I want to do...at least I think I do." Barbara laughed back. "I thought I heard you say that, was I wrong?" Joanie's eyes were glued to the window. She was mesmerized by the old sights of the avenue. She whispered an answer that was much more evident of her talking to herself, "No...I didn't say a word."

It was not the old neighborhood of Lincoln Avenue or Hindsdale Place or Bloomfield Avenue that compelled her. It was the feast of Saint Anthony being held at the church on Broadway, and within minutes they were right at the entrance gates. Barbara kept the crux of being subconsciously led to Saint Michael's Church to herself, and Joanie never questioned as to why either. A young boy with jet black hair and a familiar gait waved a hand and led them to a parking space no more than a car's length away from the front steps of the church. Barbara commented, "Now that was a miracle." She turned to thank the kid, but he just vanished into thin air. She always found it difficult to parallel park, but now the wheels seemed to turn by themselves. The 1960 Chevy Malibu seemed to have parked itself. Barbara's eyebrows lifted high as she commented again on "another miracle."

The rule in place was that Marino Motors closed at 6:00 p.m. on Friday and Saturday nights, a wise guy tradition. Card games and *goomattas* were far more important than the legal business of selling cars. Of course the salesmen liked the idea of an early Saturday night out with wives or girlfriends. The other rule of thumb was that Uncle Bert left only after the boss did. Tony grabbed hold of the framework of Bert's office door and said, "I'm outta' here." Bert looked up from his ledger and said, "I'll be here a little while longer. We had a good day today. That new hire, the kid from the neighborhood, sold two cars today." Tony replied a short but sweet "Good for him" as he turned away. The words heard by Tony were loud and clear, "Meet me at the feast tonight…the feast." It sounded like his father? Tony stopped dead in his tracks and popped his head back into Bert's office. "Whaddya' say?" Bert looked up with a baffled and bemused look on his face. "What I say…I said nothin'…you hearing things?" "I must be" were the only words that came to mind. Suddenly Tony's night was outlined and ordained. He would bolt from his office, run back home, and take a long, soothing shower then dress in his best clothes and attend the feast of Saint Anthony, the Italian saint of whom he was so inappropriately named after. It was the last weekend of the feast, and he felt compelled to attend the neighborhood gala that he had neglected for so many years.

He walked to the church parking lot behind Saint Michael's with the hope and expectation the sounds and smells of the venders would carry him back to his childhood. He retraced the same steps he once traveled as a child and thought that if he imagined with all of his heart and soul he would be able to feel the tug of his father's hand in his or the playful slap on the back of his head or the rough rustle of his hair. He would hear his old man yell at the con artists that stood behind the wooden barriers that separated fact from fiction; all would taunt him to play a carnival game, and the young Tony would watch as dozens of the attending underworld would come and say hello to their old friend Cheese. He would hear his mother's voice asking her husband for more money to buy this and that or play one more game of chance.

Joanie's eyes sparkled at the sight of the fair. She was dead silent and in absolute awe of the feeling of high anticipation, a child's Christmas morning type of flush that entered her soul and made her shiver some. She leaped from the car without waiting for Barbara; her high heels scraped the curb as her ankle buckled. She sliced through the macho male crowd that were all turning heads and shouting wolf calls because of the darling miniskirt she was wearing. The men ogled at her shapely legs, and some whistled as Barbara gave chase behind her cousin, and she would occasionally turn and smile at the admiring young Italian Americans; some were right off the boat. Joanie saw the broad shoulders of the guy centered among the thick crowd from afar. He was oblivious to her presence. Then suddenly a distant and familiar voice carried his name "Tony" above the crowd. It was a female voice. He heard it clearly, but it was too far away to pinpoint—he turned his head nevertheless. His black hair was being brushed and teased by an overhead vinyl flag of the Italian colors that snapped in the breeze. He ignored the voice for the second time as he went about his business and conversation. His arms were flailing about as he spoke, and the fellow behind the counter was laughing hysterically. Tony's profile became strikingly authentic as Joanie stood in the distance. Now on tippy-toes she called his name while she waved a frantic arm with the hopes of getting his attention.

Tony glanced over his shoulder but only saw the almost familiar everyday faces of the neighborhood and nothing else. Perhaps someone in the crowd shouted out for another? He was certainly not the only Tony at the feast? Without a second thought, he began to chomp on a couple of fresh Zeppoles from his cousin's popular stand and throw down a few shots of anisette. The decorated Zeppoles booth was always at the same location during feast time, all the way to the rear of the parking lot. And always it was the carnival stand with the largest crowd of people gathered around it and of course the priests of the church. Perhaps it was the anisette served, illegally of course?

Joanie raced through the crowd but was forced to stop in her tracks just a few short feet away as a young couple in front of her knelt down to adjust their one-year-old in her baby stroller. Joanie refused to shout his name anymore; instead she just approached with determination. She muscled and shoved her way through the last of the crowd of the young and old until she managed to get right behind the guy. Then she signaled a barefaced "Shhhh" with her forefinger held to her pouting ruby red lips, this directed to the young man facing her from behind the concession stand who watched in jest. He said not another word. Joanie looked again with wide eyes to make absolutely sure she had the right guy. Her heart was racing. She did. He had his back to her, oblivious. She began to teasingly poke the big guy's shoulder blade, and she did so a few times and with the most beaming smile one could muster as she said tongue-in-cheek, "You know something, mister, I had a date with you...right here...

at this exact spot, and you had the nerve to stand me up. How many years has it been?"

Tony froze momentarily; he knew this voice. His eyes became lidded and his ears became deaf to the outside world and its fanfare. He hoped and prayed it was her. Then he spun around. His eyes opened as wide as they could possibly get until they began to tear. He was shaking in his boots. Never before had such an excitement swept his soul and he let out a cheering "JOANIE" that turned heads in all directions. The only thing he had enough sense and ability to say was "Is it you? Is it really you? I can't believe it…I can't believe it?" Now he was breathless.

Joanie gave him such a little girl look, her large oval eyes enticingly innocent. It was the look he always commandeered from her when she saw him. Her laugh was impassioned. She just jumped up and pressed her lips to his as her mouth opened, wanting and wishing for a sensual kiss. Her reverent wish was granted. She held him as tightly as she possibly could. They embraced and held that wistful kiss until both almost turned blue. They untangled for only a moment before just to look into each other's eyes. Joanie studied his features. "You're taller now…and your hair is shorter. I like the style." She did realize he was a little older now; that made him seem just a little different, sexier in her mind. He smiled softly, showing her his still boyish side. His eyes swallowed her whole as he said, "And you're more beautiful than ever." Then he reached for another passionate embrace and found one. They kissed again deeply, passionately. This time he held her with a feeling that let her know she was not going to get away.

It was not hard at all for Tony to convince his newfound love to leave the feast alone with him. It took only a slight tug and a commanding "Let's get outta' here and go be alone somewhere." Her cousin Barbara understood completely, and she made a conscious decision to join Tony's cousin Joey for a drink after he closed down the stand. Joanie gave her a kiss on the cheek and danced away with her hand held tightly by her knight in shining armor. Her face took on a mirthful expression as he led her to the special parking space his new Lincoln Continental and held the door for her ever so chivalrously. It prompted her to ask, "Was that your name on the sign I saw before? The big lit up one that you could see from the George Washington Bridge?" in a reserved manner. Tony beamed and said, "Yeah, me and my uncle reopened my father's old car lot. We own the place now. It's legit." Joanie laughed and said, "All the kids in school knew how you always liked tinkering with cars, but that's because we all thought you were stealing them, not selling them." Joanie suggested a drive to the city—what a perfect place to get reacquainted. Tony crooned, "Ahhh-haaaa..." and immediately got the wrong intentions when she said, "I have an apartment there." She sensed his desire and laughed devilishly as she said, "You just reminded me as if déjà vu that time we met in the summer, on my front porch." It was going to be a good night.

Joanie listened curiously as Tony brought her up to date with the happenings in his life as they drove. He cried some about the death of his father, and both acknowledged that was the last time they saw one another. That was years ago. "I knew I was nuts about you way back when," he said. She snuggled tightly against his arm and chest. "I always thought about you...always. I wondered what had happened. And I always knew one day we would be together." She had a million questions and tried to ask them all on the short trip to Manhattan. He stretched just some of the truth and completely lied about the others. But the loving arm he embraced her with was sincere.

Joanie noticed the familiar concrete and cobblestone artery that led to Canal Street and New York's Little Italy section. Apprehension set in as soon as Tony turned left onto Mulberry Street. Perhaps it was the ugly thought of the last time there. Now she noticed that sleazy parking lot that they were headed for as he turned in off the street. Tony had the long body of the Lincoln half on the sidewalk and just waited nonchalantly. Joanie held her disgust as she recognized the street punk that was always in attendance. And she felt like telling off the bruiser accomplice sitting on his stool in the doorway of the tenement house across the narrow street the place that had MEMBERS ONLY written on the glass window in gold leif paint. He was the thug that knifed her convertible roof.

She was so nail-biting tempted to tell Tony of the incident but thought it better to just stay quiet. The kid pushed open the gate and Tony drove in. He turned off the car ignition and said to the impromptu valet, "Whaddya say, Sal?" The kid gave him a smile back and a nod of thank you as he reached for the ten-dollar bill Tony extended. Joanie rescinded her hatred of the kid and asked Tony slowly, "Who do you have to know to be able to park here?" Tony smiled as he opened the car door for her. "All you have to know is these two guys. Heah, fellas." He waved over the watchdog. "Say hello to Joanie." Joanie said hello to Sal and Gino. "You guys take a good look at her 'cause if she ever tries to park here without me, I wanna' hear about it." Everyone laughed, and the parking lot guards watched the two cross the street. He explained the story. The lot was property of the mob and only associates can park there. "Not that I am or anything. They were friends of my father."

Tony let his girl talk for the rest of the night. He encouraged it as they ate and drank a Pinot Grigio that the gracious waiter of Angelo's brought especially to the table, compliments of the house. Joanie asked what was so funny about the comment everyone laughed at about the coffee beans, and asked where his friend was that they never see anymore. "He was an old, dear friend of my father's" was his solemn answer. "So your father had a lot of these type friends, huh…I knew that…we were neighbors." Joanie hesitated between her doubting words. "And you're not one of these guys…like your father was?" she asked gingerly. He smiled over the wineglass and shook his head no. "And you have nothing at all to do with this mobster stuff I hear all about at my office and read in the papers?" He shook his head no again. "And I don't have to worry about guns and things like that?" He continued shaking his head no, no, no. Then he laughed aloud and said sincerely, "Baby, you don't have to worry about anything ever again." They sat and ordered another bottle of wine, and they reminisced with open hearts about their adolescence, past loves, and their careers. He commended her on her success and laughed about how he just got lucky; education had absolutely nothing to do with it. He kept his dark past off the table.

Hands were held and shoulders were caressed. Joanie thought of it not as a seduction; it felt completely normal to her as she let her childhood sweetheart rub and caress just about every piece of exposed flesh on her tight body. The night was still early, and both had gads of energy. While they walked to a nearby pastry shop and Tony asked, "Do you feel like something sweet?" Joanie felt a sparkle and said daringly, "I really feel like going to my place." The doubts Joan Jankowski had about her own sexuality since the debacle with Mark Cohen was all put to rest. He was not her last date but he was the last time she had experienced sex. Tonight she would again give herself to a young man that she envisioned the act of lovemaking with time and time again. The lascivious and almost carnal type of love the two made throughout the night was monumental. Never before had either one experienced such heights of passion. It flowed so naturally for the both of them almost as if directed by the Roman god Eros himself. And truly the night's activity would be entered in someone's Ripley's book of orgasmic records.

Joanie woke at exactly noon, her eyes still closed a bit as she stretched out her body and noticed herself alone between the satin sheets. The sun was high and filtered softly into her bedroom, just grazing her smiling face. The scene was not at all as tense as the usual mornings after. Today was a serene and satisfied feeling that she embraced. She had to urinate in a bad way and could not wait for Tony to exit the bathroom. The sound of running water from the sink she heard made the feeling worse. She knocked and she heard him say through a gargling voice, "It's open." Joanie was completely naked. He stood against the sink modestly, in just his boxers. "Is that my toothbrush you're using?" she asked as she squatted on the toilet seat. His foaming mouth along with the hissing of the warm flow of pee emptying into the bowl forced them both to laugh. He said, "It's the only one I could find. What's the matter, you never have guests over?" She made an oops face as a tiny peep of flatulence exited her. "That's it," Tony said as he gargled and spit into the sink. "The honeymoon is over." She wiped herself and jumped to her feet. Her perfect breasts jiggled as she embraced his body and said, "Uh-uh…it's just beginning." And that it was. And they never again separated from that moment on. Only for that brief afternoon when he drove Joanie to her parents' home to retrieve her car, and he still was apprehensive of her dad. He declined Joanie's invitation to come in the house. Tony sneered bit and said, "That's okay. I'll meet them another time. You father probably still hates me, the crazy Pollack that he is."

EPILOGUE

The young, adoring couple divided all of their cherished time together between Joanie's brownstone apartment in the city and Tony's high-rise penthouse on Mt. Prospect Street. Joanie couldn't argue the fact that his place was immaculate—beautifully decorated and well furnished. He was allowed to keep his custom-made round bed; however, the apartment was never to be called or referred to as a bachelor's pad ever again. So just as an added precaution, Joanie imposed some of her expert critique and of course her charming woman's touch all over the place, especially in the closets. And one would think such a young couple who literally fell back in timeless love at first sight would require a lavish and ostentatious wedding, but they did not. As if to make up for all lost time the couple hastily drove off to the nearby state of Maryland the following month of June, on Father's Day, and received their wedding vows sacredly by a resident preacher also justice of the peace. On the drive back home Tony detoured and drove to Greensburg. And every grand story he could conjure up of the place was told to his Joanie on the way.

He wanted his country farm family of Uncle Tomasino and dearest Aunt Josephina and Grandma Rosa to be the first to meet his young bride. Joanie enchanted them. She herself told stories of her childhood romance with Tony Marino in an "ever since I could remember fashion." She commented to all on how much the farm-house looked so much like her parents' home buried back in the woods of Warren Township and sharply reminded her husband that he never asked permission for their daughter's hand in marriage. They were sure to hear it when they got home. Mr. and Mrs. Henri Jankowski were sure to cringe at the news. The bride's parents did no such thing. After all they were young and in love once, but they did want the couple to think about a proper Catholic wedding ceremony in a proper Roman Catholic Church. Both newlyweds agreed to consider the thought. The idea of confession made Tony hesitant.

It would take almost two years, after their second child was born, before Tony Marino could find the courage to kneel and speak to a live parish priest from the other side of the mesh screened confessional about his past, and he did so in a whisper. He spoke to a young priest from the new age diocese of the Roman Catholic Church. Tony found it easier to confess all to him. In his heart it was not murder but coerced acts of self-defense, and this was depicted by the priest of record as being just that.

The young priest soothed and chastised in the same breath. It was a gift he possessed. Tony asked if he was without a soul for his lack of conscience about his committed sins to which the priest said, "One's soul is much like one's destiny. You will know when yours is found. Our God works in mysterious ways. If he has not already touched your face softly or tapped you on the shoulder, or kicked you in your behind? Give him time…he will. For your penance say…" Tony accepted that and his blessed and chosen destiny. He and his uncle had continued success with Marino Motors. They were actually contacted by a funny-named Japanese auto manufacturer and offered a new automobile franchise of some sort. And it would be one of the first one ever in the States.

Tony and his bride would eventually raise three beautiful children. His daughter Dolores Marie Angelica was going on five. She was known by all and called DeeDee, and his son Anthony Thomas Jr. was approaching two and a half and was appropriately called Anthony Jr. Joanie Marino was in the family way for just about six months now with number three. It would be a baby girl they would simply name Joan.

Joanie Marino's career also continued to soar to the heights of unbelievable success. She now headed up her own line of fashion and aptly named the new company JJ Unlimited. She ran the company with grace and oversaw the production. Her original designs were for both the contessa and the office girl as well and soon became the trendsetter in the fashion world. When not in her office in Manhattan, she worked leisurely from her home office loft that sat overlooking the entire first floor of the new house they lived. Both she and her husband gave up their penthouse apartments and settled into a life in suburbia. Her husband was content with his designated space in the basement. It was ample enough and retained a level of raw unfinished, and that's just how he wanted it, with just enough of life's comforts without going overboard. Tony had his billiards table and card table, even makeshift wet bar. Hanging from a thick chain was a professional boxer's heavy bag named Everlast. A few free weights scattered about a makeshift gym area. Black-and-white photos of the past and present were strategically nailed to just about all the walls. Next to his favorite "night at the opera" photo was the one of the man he addressed to those that asked as his uncle Louie; only a rare few actually recognized his true identity.

This photo was in color and enlarged from its original size. It sat in a special frame. It was a tropical scene, an unknown white sandy beach with soft blue water in the background. The small, gentle waves just about breaking gave you a feeling of serenity. Dead center of the picture was an almost black tanned man clad in a patterned swimsuit. He was lying comfortably on his side in a hammock. The roped hammock was centered between two arced palm trees of course. His face hid behind large jet black Ray-Ban sunglasses. The silver hair on his head and chest glistened brightly from moisture in the sunlight. There was a drink in his right hand and a pack of Lucky Strike cigarettes lying next to an ashtray in the sand, and two bikini-clad island women with shimmering cocoa brown skin sat at his feet, young of course. And of course the grin he wore was magnificent.

It was a grand Indian summer's day in late September. It was two weeks past Labor Day weekend and very close to Sidney and Ceil's wedding anniversary. The total years married and exact date were already a mystery to the couple who still held hands everywhere they went. Sidney would often quote a famous Catskill comedian and say, "I hold my wife's hand all the time. If I let go, she shops."

The screen doors and windows were opened throughout the country house, allowing the fragrant smell of the outside gardens of late blooming flowers to circulate throughout the kitchen and mingle with the fragrant smell of savory meatballs and sausage frying in hot olive oil. The grand balustrade open-air veranda that surrounded the perimeter of the mini-mansion was alive with children running endlessly from one end to the other, then into the back and front yards, pausing some to ride swings that dropped from the limbs of the mighty trees.

The women were all inside preparing the Sunday family dinner that was always the tradition at Tony Marino's house at least once a month. And it would be painstakingly prepared for no more or no less than twelve people, not including children. The aroma of red gravy and braciole sweetened the air. Overcooked green vegetables swam in shimmering olive oil alongside portions of roasted garlic, and baskets of fresh Italian bread sat next to plates of rich antipasto at both ends of the table. His uncle Joe and his uncle Lefty and Pop Pop Sidney, as he was now officially called, were in the great room slurping beers and intelligently arguing the game of baseball as they watched it on the television.

Tony was outside in his niche corner of the grand porch. He sat comfortably with beer in hand on the cane-weaved wicker chair that adorned soft cushioned pillows with colorful flowery print. The woven slats of the furniture would moan their own individual sigh as the weight of his lumbering body shifted now and then. He was talking with his first cousins and his father-in-law Henri who also sat and watched as the children played all around them together, the games young people play. Tony could sit and listen for hours to the sounds of innocent feet stomping on the treated wood floor of the veranda—kids chasing after one another, their individual laughs and shrill screams of delight that accompanied, as they run up one stairway and down another, and all chasing one another in their proper pecking order. And if a child should fall and scrape a knee or an elbow, the tears would be wiped away gently, and they would be encouraged to get back in the game. He made sure his son Anthony had just enough dirt on his face and clothes to distinguish him as true Marino blood and to warrant a snappy "Go wash up" from his mother.

This was the home he and his Joanie had designed and built for their children and with future childhood and adult memories in mind. A grandiose farmhouse, a stately Victorian-style farmhouse that was custom-built to go along with and sit in the center of a majestic veranda deep in the suburban forest of Livingston, New Jersey. Perhaps it's a place that will always keep from harm's way and garner the innocence of all that stayed on and within the confines and the balustrade boundaries of this magical porch. Until of course dinner was ready to be served. Tony swore it was his own father's voice that echoed, but today Sidney had the honors of opening the screen door and yelling, "Okay, kids, let's eat."

The End

ABOUT THE AUTHOR

Anthony Angelo Nardone was born in Newark, New Jersey, to working-class Italian American parents. He was raised during the same period, the 1950s, in the rough and tough neighborhoods and on the same felonious streets he writes about.

He worked with the Teamsters Union in both the trucking and automobile industry and spent almost twenty years in Las Vegas, Nevada, reliving the days of the rat pack.

He now spends his leisure days with his five young grandchildren either fishing down the Jersey Shore or babysitting.